EAG   Eagle, Kathleen.

Ride a painted pony.

$31.95

DATE			

LVG

Ride a
Painted Pony

**Center Point
Large Print**

**This Large Print Book carries the
Seal of Approval of N.A.V.H.**

Ride a Painted Pony

KATHLEEN EAGLE

CENTER POINT PUBLISHING
THORNDIKE, MAINE

This Center Point Large Print edition
is published in the year 2007 by arrangement with
Harlequin Enterprises Ltd.

The text of this Large Print edition is unabridged. In other
aspects, this book may vary from the original edition.
Printed in the United States of America.
Set in 16-point Times New Roman type.

ISBN-10: 1-58547-902-0
ISBN-13: 978-1-58547-902-3

Library of Congress Cataloging-in-Publication Data

Eagle, Kathleen.
    Ride a painted pony / Kathleen Eagle.--Center Point large print ed.
        p. cm.
    ISBN-13: 978-1-58547-902-3 (lib. bdg. : alk. paper)
    1. Large type books. I. Title.

PS3555.A385R53 2007
813'.54--dc22

2006025711

For the Prairie Writers Guild—
Pam, Sandy, Mary, Judy and Kathy. *Vive* PWG!
And
to honor the memory of
Little Ted

ACKNOWLEDGMENTS

Finding the key to a plot problem isn't always a *Eureka!* moment. Keys must be ground to fit the lock, and that can be a grueling part of the writing process. But those keys are invaluable. Two important sources of inspiration for this book were the wonderful group who attended Midwest Fiction Writers' "Big Retreat to Little Falls" at Linden Hill in Little Falls, Minnesota, and a series of articles concerning Indian gaming and casino race books in one of my favorite sources for real news, *Indian Country Today*—both the newspaper and its wonderful Web site.

1

Twenty-seven miles of dark road and driving rain were all that stood between Nick and the bed he'd reserved for what was left of the night. He might have pulled over and waited for the downpour to pass, but he was set on having himself some pleasure this night. Real, rock-solid pleasure. He was *this close* to laying himself down flat, stretching out his whole long, bone-tired body over fresh white sheets and soft pillows. If he had just pulled over, he might have spared himself the one thing he always took care to avoid. Nicholas Red Shield hated surprises.

But more than the surprise of a pair of wild eyes staring back at him in his high beams, he hated making roadkill.

Eyes left. Wheel right.

It was a tricky maneuver. His empty horse trailer fishtailed as he shifted into Neutral, kicked the brake and arced the steering wheel to the left. Getting the trailer in line was only half the battle now that the rubber no longer met the road. Every scrape against the pickup's precious chassis felt like a bloody gouge in Nick's own leathery hide. His beautiful blue two-ton dually—as near to new as any vehicle he'd ever had—mowed down a mile-marker post, jolted, shuddered and went still.

Rain pelted the roof of the cab.

Nick took a deep breath and slowly loosened his grip on the steering wheel. He glanced in the rearview mirror, searching for familiar eyes.

"You okay back there, Alice?"

His passenger popped her head up to assure him that she was only slightly less bored with him than usual.

Nick was okay, too, *thanks for asking.* A little shook up, but he wasn't going to let it show, even when nobody but the cat was looking. Bad form was bad form.

And stuck was stuck. He couldn't tell whether the main cause was mud or the mile marker, but his efforts to get loose soon had six tires spinning in all gears.

Nick was not a man to curse his luck. He wasted nothing, including breath. Ever equipped to handle his own problems, he practiced taking care of business to perfection. If the mile marker was the hang-up, he hoped the business of jacking his baby off the damn thing wouldn't take all night. He chuckled and started humming as he reached under his seat for the flashlight. "Jackin' my sweet baby off," he sang softly. Times like this, a little humor couldn't hurt. He exchanged cowboy hat for yellow rubberized poncho and climbed out of the truck with an unconscious smile. He could really be funny when nobody was listening.

But the sight of his truck's skewered underbelly was nothing to laugh at. It would take more than a flashlight beam to assess the damage, especially with the cold spring rain rolling off the hood of his poncho. He could have sworn he heard her groaning softly, just like a real woman.

"What do you expect me to do in this rain, girl? Beam you up?"

Something behind him snapped. Nick pivoted and swept the light over the roadside slope until it hit on a clump of bushes and a clutch of bobbing branches. Damn, had he clipped that deer after all? He grabbed his pistol and a loaded clip from the glove box and then sidled down the steep, wet slope. He'd been lucky. Better his precious pickup had impaled herself on a post than gone tumbling trailer over teakettle down the hill.

The bushes weren't much taller than he was, but they were dense and filled out with new foliage. And they weren't moving on their own. There was definitely something in there. Nick parted the branches with his gun hand, flashed the light into the tangled thicket and found two more of the night's thousand eyes.

They weren't doe eyes, but they were almost as big.

"Don't," a soft voice pleaded as the eyes took refuge from the light behind a small, colorless, quivering palm. "Please don't."

A woman? A child? Nick's heart wedged itself in his throat. He flashed the light away from her face.

"It's okay. I won't . . ." He shouldered branches aside and dropped down on one knee to discover a woman who wasn't much bigger than a child. "That wasn't . . ." He could barely get the words out. She

11

was curled up, soggy and shaking to beat hell. "Jesus, that couldn't have been *you* in the road. Could it?"

"Wh-who are you? Who sent you?"

"No one sent me. Listen, did I . . . did I hit you?"

"Who are you?" she demanded, pumping up the volume.

"Name's Nick Red Shield. I could've sworn I missed the, uh . . ." He gestured toward the scene of the crime with the barrel of his pistol. "Sorry. I was expecting a deer." He tucked the gun in his belt and then pulled the poncho over his head. She needed it worse than he did. "How bad are you hurt?"

"I don't know."

"Anything broken? Can you move your . . ."

Move what? The arms she'd knotted around her knees? He felt like some idiot hunter who'd awkwardly wedged himself into a rabbit's hole. They were nearly nose to nose, but he didn't dare touch her, and she didn't dare move. She couldn't draw back any farther without becoming part of the undergrowth. Her violent quivering made his bones vibrate.

"Let me help you." He offered his hand, palm up, as though she might want to sniff it first. "I'll be real careful."

"What kind of a name is Red Shield?"

It seemed like a crazy question, under the circumstances. *Check out my hand, sure, but my name?*

"I'm an Indian." He couldn't help bristling. Squaring up, he braced the rebuffed hand on his upraised knee. "Sioux. South Dakota. Look, I didn't

12

see you until you were right in front of me, and I did everything I could to avoid hitting you. If you want me to try to flag someone else down, I will, but there isn't much traffic tonight, and I don't have any way to call anyone. Do you?"

"C-call who?"

"A cop or an ambulance."

"You . . . you'd call the police?"

"I would, but I don't have a phone. And if I leave you here and go for help, I'll damn sure get charged with hit and run. So make up your mind. What'll it be?"

"What are my choices?"

"Trust me or don't. Can you walk?"

She stared at him, sizing him up while she drew several breaths, miserably shaky on the uptake. Finally she loosened her grip on her folded legs and felt around for something besides him to hang on to. She didn't seem to care what the bushes were doing to her hands, and he could barely hear her answer.

"I think so."

But it was tricky. She was such a little thing, he could have carried her like a baby if the rain hadn't made the hill slicker than a cat's ass. He put the flashlight in her hand, covered her with his poncho and hauled her up against his side, which left him one hand for grabbing whatever solid ground he could find. And, like a cat, she hung on. He could feel her trembling, feel her fighting for control against chills, pain, fear—probably all three—and he gave her credit for holding back on the noise she could have been making, tears she should have been crying, curses she must have been saving up for a time when the man who'd done this to her wasn't the only help around.

He put her on the back seat of his crew cab, took the wet poncho and started backing out the door.

She grabbed his arm. Shivering and scared, she was little more than the huge pair of eyes that questioned his every move.

"I've got blankets in the trailer, and maybe something to . . ." What he could see of her face now gave him pause. Mean dark patches spattered over frail and pale skin added up to battered flesh and flowing blood. "Listen, lady, I've gotta get you some help."

"Can you . . . please . . . get me away from here?" She had him by both arms now, had him with her eyes and surprisingly strong hands. "Can you, Nick?"

"Yeah." He nodded, swallowed hard, tried to ignore the goose bumps crawling over his shoulders and down the back of his neck. He slid into the seat beside her and felt her relax her grip. "Sure. I can do that." He reached over the front seat and felt around for his denim jacket. Locating the jacket also meant he found the cat, but he was able to claim the jacket without trading a strip of skin. Alice wasn't totally pitiless after all.

"What's your name?" He didn't mean to pry, but he'd told her who he was, and he needed to say something while he was wrapping her in his jacket.

But the question set her off on a sobbing jag.

14

Damn. Now what? He drew the jacket tight around her, his fists coming together beneath her chin, whispering, "Try to keep it together. You've been doing so good. Do you live around here?"

"No. Oh no." Head bowed, she slumped toward him, shuddering and sobbing and saying, "Oh no, oh no, oh no."

"Shh. Just tell me your name."

"Ohh . . ." She was like a wet rag, starch draining away, drooping, dripping, sagging against his chest. "Joe-eeey, Joey, Joey . . ."

"Joey what?"

But she was all out of answers. And he'd never been one to ask too many questions. Part of a name was enough for now. She could give the rest of it at the next stop, where somebody with a form and a uniform would be writing it all down.

"You want some dry clothes?"

Still leaning on him, she shook her head against his chest, forming his chilled nipple into a glass bead.

"You'll have pneumonia on top of—"

She shook her head again and whispered blubbery words that made no sense but sounded as desperate as he was beginning to feel.

"Okay, Joey." He patted her hair clumsily. "Okay, we'll get movin'."

With a hydraulic jack and a heavy dose of cowboy ingenuity, he was able to lift the pickup off the hook he'd accidentally made of the steel post, then twist the thing out of the way without ripping the guts from his sweet ride. He'd unhooked the gooseneck trailer in the hope of getting the truck back on the road. But nobody ever expected great traction from a dually, and his four back tires were only spinning themselves deeper into the Missouri mud. Without a push, his baby would soon be up to her axles in moonshit. He threw her into Neutral, braced his chin on his left arm and glowered at the road untraveled.

"Joey?"

A glance in the rearview mirror revealed nothing. He hadn't heard a peep out of her since he'd turned the heater on full blast and she'd thanked him before he'd gone back out into the rain. He turned now and found her huddled up in the corner with the cat. The two pair of eyes peered expectantly toward the front seat.

"Joey, I need you to help me. Do you think you can take the wheel? I need a driver."

"Drive . . . the truck?"

"I need a hand to rock the cradle, so to speak. You know how to do that?"

She made a funny sound, like laughing through tears. "Rock the baby?"

"Yeah. Rock my baby. With a little rockin', a little pushin', I know she can get us out of here. You rock; I'll push. Can you help me?"

"I think so."

"Only you gotta be careful not to run me over," he said as he opened the back door. Hovering over her with his back catching the rain, he helped her out of the back seat and around the door toward the front.

"Not run you over," she repeated as she mounted the running board and pulled herself up by the door handle.

"Yeah, 'cause then we'd be in big trouble." He lifted a lever and pulled the front seat from one extreme adjustment to the other. "Can you reach the pedals?"

"Of course." She demonstrated. Brake was good, gas was only just.

"You drive a stick?"

She nodded.

"Can you see over the dash? I'm gonna be right there." He pointed to the front corner on the right. "As long as you can see me, we're fine. If I disappear, then you stop the music. Okay?"

"Stop the music." She almost smiled. "Like hold the presses?"

"Yeah, like that. How many fingers?"

"One," she answered. He doubled his digits. "Two."

"Good. You pass. One back, two forward. One finger, you put it in reverse and I push. Two, you put it in low, and I get out of the way. Timing is everything. You think you can handle it?"

"If you can push this thing, I can steer."

Nick's brawn harmonized with Joey's timing on the gear changes. Soon the pickup was free from the mud and Nick was covered with it. He threw his tools into the box, used the water in the portable tank to wash off some of the mud, and grabbed a blanket from the trailer.

He found her slumped over the steering wheel.

"You okay?"

She responded simply by sitting up.

"Can you slide over?"

She did, but not easily. She was hurting.

He took her place, making every effort to reassure her while he tucked the blanket around her. "We're in business now, Joey. I'm gonna find you some help." He reached across her. "Here, let's buckle you in."

"I feel sick. I need to lie down." She leaned toward him as she pushed the seat belt away. "No, no, this thing hurts. If I don't lie down, I'll probably . . . get . . ."

"Please don't." He gave up on the seat belt and took charge of the wheel while she toppled over beside him, head at his hip. "But try not to fall asleep, okay?"

"How about if I just pass out?"

"Don't do that, either."

"Talk to me, then," she muttered as they finally hit the highway.

"It's better if you talk," he told her. He felt a little sick himself, watching his precious gooseneck trailer shrink in the side mirror. He hoped to hell it would be there when he came back for it. "Where do you hurt?"

"Inside. I'm aching in ways you can't understand, Nick. You're a man."

"Oh, Jesus," he groaned. Females and their mysterious inside parts. It was a wonder there wasn't blood everywhere. "You're not, like, pregnant or anything, are you?"

"No."

"That's good." At least the hit wasn't a twofer. "I'm not from around here. Maybe you could tell me—"

"I'm not, either."

"Oh, yeah," he said, remembering. He glanced at the mop of wet hair that had become a fixture on his wet hip. "I'll find you a hospital just as quick as I can. I'm having trouble makin' out the road signs in this damn rain, but don't worry. I'll find you some help."

"All I need is a bed. I need to be still for a while, so my head stops spinning."

"Lady, what were you doing on the road like that?" he demanded, more heated than he'd intended. "In the night," he added softly. "In the rain."

"Fell out of a car."

"Fell?"

"No more questions, Nick. Please."

"I'm sorry. I swear to God, I didn't—"

"It was my fault. My own fault."

"Like hell," he muttered, craning his neck, squinting. Like squinting would do any good. "Is that a hospital sign?"

"No, please. No hospital." Her hand found his thigh. "No more trouble, Nick, please."

"Shit. 'Falling Rocks.'" He sniggered. "Hell, how about one for 'Falling Women'?"

"*Fallen* woman." She gave a sad, soft groan as her hand slid away. "What a joke. Here's your sign. Wear it in good health."

"Sorry. This is no time for smart-ass remarks."

"No, it was funny, Nick. And true. I just can't laugh

19

right now." She paused, then added quietly, "Keep talking to me, Nick."

"'Deer crossing,'" he read aloud as they passed another sign. It wasn't much, but it was what he could do to keep himself talking. If she wanted a talker, she'd thrown herself in front of the wrong truck. He chuckled. "Now they tell me. I thought you were a deer, Joey. I thought I'd swerved to miss a deer. Are you a Deer Woman?"

"I'm dear to somebody," she said. "I hope so, anyway."

"Somebody who drove off and . . ." *Shut up, Red Shield.* She didn't need him rubbing it in. "Forget I said that."

"No. Someone else. I have someone else."

"Somebody we can call when we get to a phone?"

"No. He can't help me." She raised her head, pushed herself up for better effect. "But you can, Nick. You seem like a good man."

He spared her a glance. The wounds on her face made the wounded look in her eyes that much harder for him to bear, knowing he'd caused it all. "I'm not about to put you out on the road, if that's the measure of a good man."

"It's a start."

"And I'm workin' on the next step, which is to find you some medical attention."

"Please don't, Nick." She lowered her head, but this time she laid it on his thigh. "I really don't need a doctor."

20

Flummoxed, flustered and suddenly way too hot, he whacked at the heater control and cleared his throat. "How do you know?"

"I just know. I don't need one. I don't. Not now." She moved her head just enough to get a rise out of him. "Nick? You're making me a pillow, Nick."

He said nothing. He didn't dare. All she knew about him was that he'd nearly killed her. Either she didn't know what she was saying, or she really was Deer Woman. The supreme seducer in Lakota lore, that was Deer Woman. Nick focused every ounce of attention he could muster on the road ahead. Between windshield wiper whaps, a swelling of light served as a welcome distraction from the unwelcome swelling between his legs.

What the hell was this woman trying to do?

"Nick?"

"Okay, we're coming to a town. We're just outside of Mexico. Mexico, Missouri. But all I know about it is the motel where I was gonna stay tonight, which is coming up on the right."

"Go there."

"You're sure?" He was blinking. His blinker was blinking. The neon was flickering, and none of the signs were good. "No vacancy. No more rooms. I've got a reservation, but just the one room."

"I don't take up a lot of space, Nick."

Jeez Louise.

"I'll sleep in the truck if you want me to," she said softly. "I just need to be still for a while."

21

"Yeah, you're right. And there'll be a phone. I won't be driving up and down the street in the damn rain looking for hospital signs."

"No more signs, Nick. I've seen enough signs."

"Look, I'm not . . ." Not stupid? Not sure? Not horny, after she'd made herself known to his good-man-be-damned parts?

"Not what?" she chimed in.

He sighed. "You're safe with me, Joey."

"Thank you. You have no idea how good that sounds."

"But you're hurt, and I want to get you some help. I *have to* get you some help, Joey."

"You're all the help I need."

He parked in front of the motel office, shut the engine off and tried to shut himself down by staring straight ahead while she gathered herself over one arm and pushed herself up, sitting up, sitting close but no longer touching him. Thank God.

Curse God. Or Deer Woman. Or female parts and man parts and absurd accidents that planted the party of the first part smack in the path of the party of the second part. He did not need this shit.

"Nick, you didn't hit me. You *found* me."

He turned to her, scowled at her, tried to make sense of her claim. "There was something in the road."

"It wasn't me."

"I didn't knock you off the road?"

She shook her head.

For some reason, he didn't feel convinced. It made

22

sense, but it didn't feel right. The woman had jumped over the fence and back again, playing him for what? Champion or fool?

"You coulda told me."

"I'm a little discombobulated right now."

"You and me both." He jerked on the door handle. "I'm going to check us in, and then—"

"Don't tell anyone *anything,* Nick. Please. You didn't pick anyone up on the road. Nobody's hurt." She grabbed his arm. "It's just you checking in here, okay?"

"Who the hell cares whether . . . ?" He made the mistake of looking into those sad, badly bruised eyes again. He hadn't hit her. Whatever happened, he'd had no part in it, and he owed her nothing. He had to get that through his head. Right now would be the perfect time.

He shook his head, but the wrong words came out of his mouth. "Okay. Just me."

"You told me to make up my mind, and I have. I trust you."

"Yeah, well, now you've got more choices. You've got—" his gesture took in the lights of a town that was nothing to him but a handy stop and a catchy name "—all of Mexico."

"I trust you, Nick."

2

Nick returned to his pickup carrying a key and a promise kept. No one had asked, but if they had, he would have kept the woman on the other side of the rain-streaked glass a secret. *His* secret. He couldn't remember having one before. Not that he couldn't keep one, but he simply had little cause in his life for secrets.

Now he had one. Lying there on the front seat of his crew cab was one sweet little secret. Banged-up, dressed in tatters, stripped of everything but her instinct for self-preservation, she had become a major hitch in an otherwise routine trip. As a rule, he wasn't real big on sweets, but her sweetness was growing on him.

Nicholas Red Shield had his own instincts, too. The urge to protect the helpless ones had been bred into him from way back, or so he'd been told by people who were interested in the history of his breeding. He could go way back when the subject was horse breeding. As for what his partner called his "warrior instincts," he would take Dillon's word for it. So he hadn't hit the woman with his pickup. He could still help her out. It wasn't like he was going out of his way.

"The room's around back." He tried not to get her wet as he slid behind the wheel, but she wasn't giving him much margin for dripping. "You awake?"

"Sort of."

"When is this damn rain gonna quit, huh?"

Taking her silence for lack of interest, he checked the number on the key again as the pickup crawled past the bumpers of vehicles belonging to boarders presumably tucked in for the night. He was surprised to find a wide-open and empty parking space in front of the door with his number on it. He smiled, thinking the signs, they were a-changin'.

If Joey was at least "sort of" awake, then her claim that nobody was hurt was bullshit. When he hauled her off the front seat, she made sadly little effort to add her own steam to the task.

"I've got you," he told her, cradling her in his arms. "Just relax and pretend you're not somebody I picked up on the road."

"I'm your dry cleaning."

"Oh, yeah. I'm real big on dry cleaning."

"You're a good man. A big man. A man who isn't afraid to do the right—" He'd shouldered the door to the room shut and was about to lay her down, but she dug her fingers into his shoulder and told him no. "Keep the bed dry. I'm soaked to the bone."

He put her in a chair, turned on a lamp and sat on the corner of the bed across from her, waiting for his next cue. He still felt guilty. Responsible. It was rude, looking at her this way, like he had a butterfly trapped in a jar and didn't know what to do with her.

First off, man, get her some clothes.

25

She was wearing what had probably once been a nice dress. Like everything else—he was just noticing the blood on her legs—it was in bad shape.

"It's really not as bad as it looks," she insisted. She hadn't gotten close to a mirror yet, but she didn't need one as long as she could read him.

He glanced away.

"How bad does it look?"

He gave her half a smile. "Sure you weren't hit by a truck?"

"I should have kept quiet." Gingerly she touched her fingers to her swollen eyelid, bruised cheek, gashed chin. "I could've used it for blackmail."

"And asked for what?" He braced his hands on his knees. "What is it you need, Joey?"

"Joey," she echoed wistfully. "Funny name for a girl, isn't it?"

"People go by all kinds of names these days. I know a girl named George." He leaned closer. "Are you in some kind of trouble?"

"Yes."

"How bad?"

"As bad as it gets."

He nodded toward the nightstand that stood between the two beds. "Listen, there's a phone here. How 'bout making a call?"

She shook her head.

"Nobody?"

"Do you have someone, Nick? A wife? A girl-friend?"

"No, not right now, not . . ." He arched an eyebrow. "You're really good at turning the tables. You're the one who needs somebody. Some family, some—"

"Right now I have no one except for one very good Samaritan." She closed her eyes, drew a deep breath and made a valiant attempt to smile for him. "Are you from Samaria, Nick? Did you walk straight out of the Bible?"

"I drove straight off the damn road," he reminded her. "I don't know what the maps call Samaria these days, but currently they're calling my country South Dakota. How 'bout you?"

"I've been to South Dakota," she said.

"I'd say just lately you've been to hell and back."

"And hell hath no phone number for a woman scorned."

"If you say so." With a sigh, Nick pushed to his feet. "Besides dry clothes, just tell me what else you need so I don't have to ask any more damn questions."

"I'd love a hot bath. But it's your room, so I'll wait my turn."

"Right." Three strides took him to the bathroom. "I'll come out and find you passed out in that chair."

"What are you going to do?"

"What any *good man* would do," he grumbled.

He glanced in the mirror above the sink on his way to the tub and toilet, which were tucked separately behind a door. Mud, matted hair, homely mug—not a pretty picture. It was a wonder the injured bird hadn't chosen to stay in the bush. He adjusted the bathtub faucets until he had a warm flow going. Then he treated his face to a sink full of hot water and plenty of soap.

She opened her eyes as he lifted her from the chair. "How do you wanna handle this?" he asked.

"Just put me in the water, clothes and all."

"Good idea." She was shivering like crazy. Maybe the water would clear her head enough so she could start figuring out what the hell she wanted to do. "I'll be right outside. Here's soap and . . . Joey?"

Her eyes were closed; her small chin skimmed the water. Her torn green dress drifted around her like seaweed, and her yellow hair billowed about her shoulders.

"Are you alive?"

"Barely."

"Can you . . . ?"

"I don't think so."

He would start with the hair. His knee cracked as he knelt beside the tub, and he knew that if he stayed in this position very long it would fill with fluid. The concern passed quickly as he filled his long brown hands with shampoo and water and mud-clotted hair. It occurred to him that he hadn't washed anyone else's hair since he was a kid. Being the oldest, he'd often been given charge of the little ones. But he was the first to grow up and move on, and he'd passed the job on to Louise, the next one in line. Louise had been followed by Bernadette, who had still been sitter-in-residence when Nick had joined the army.

Johnny had never had to take his turn.

As quickly as his brother's name popped into his head, Nick pushed it back into mental storage. He had enough misery on his hands.

Namely, her face. He hated to touch it. He'd tended tender flesh in his time, but he'd never seen wounds such as these on anything so fair and fine. He took it slow, irrigating each abrasion with soapy water squeezed from a clean cloth, while she kindly kept still and quiet. She had to know he was feeling none too easy with any of this. He was no medic. Most of the supplies he carried with him were for the horses, but he was pretty sure he had a few medicines for people in his duffel bag. Probably been there for *tona* years, but maybe they were still good. There was one bad place on her scalp that he thought could do with a couple of stitches, but it wasn't bleeding much. Maybe it would be okay.

Or maybe not. But he wouldn't be the one to decide. It was no good pushing people unless they were pushing you.

Motel management had provided a small bottle of mouthwash—good ol' piss-color purge—that made her flinch when he applied it to the cut high on her nose. He flinched sympathetically.

"I know it stings, but that's supposed to show it's working."

"Don't use it all on my face." She pulled up her sleeves and exposed scrapes on both arms. "From hitting the road."

29

"Hell of a way to bail out of a car."

"And I forgot to yell *Geronimo*."

"Just as well. No yelling, and you got yourself a live Indian instead of a dead one." His glance skated across her face. "You got any more you want to show me?"

"Not until I know you a little better."

Her wan smile abruptly had him tongue-tied. The only wonder was that it hadn't happened to him sooner. Well aware of his limitations, he shut the lid on the throne, took himself a seat and jerked the shower curtain far enough across the side of the tub so he couldn't see anything above her knees.

"Give me those wet clothes and I'll hang 'em up."

The tattered dress came first, followed by a slip, bra, panties. He didn't know much about quality in women's underwear, but hers was a matched set, and it wasn't cheesy. He started to wring the water out, but on second thought he turned the sink into a man's laundry tub—clothes, bar soap and tepid water. He wagged his head at his reflection in the mirror. Nick Red Shield washing a woman's underwear. Hell of a sight.

Feeling edgy, he turned the TV on, flipped through the channels and turned it off again. A glance at the clothes rack inspired a search through his duffel bag. One of his T-shirts would cover her nearly to her knees. There were jeans, socks, a couple of Western shirts. Besides his favorite fixes for junk food cravings, he had an extra toothbrush, some aspirin, Band-

Aids and topical ointment, some pink stuff for stomach trouble and a prescription drug for his weak knee.

Uninspired, he called out to her. "Take your time in there. I'll go out and get us something to eat."

"No, please." Real fear had insinuated itself into the voice beyond the door. "Don't leave me here alone. I might . . . I'm really sort of . . . unsteady."

"I'll wait, then. If you need anything, sing out."

She did. Screeched, more like. He'd gone to the outside door and barely touched the knob, which told him she had the ears of an owl to go along with the voice.

"Hey, I'm not going anywhere," he reported. "Just goin' out to the pickup to explain the lack of food to the cat."

Silence.

"Hey! I said—"

Disaster struck in the bathtub to the tune of slosh, clang, thud and splash.

"Shit." Nick strode from one door to the other. "Joey? I'm comin' in!"

"I got dizzy," said a voice beneath the fallen shower curtain.

"You okay?" He tossed the tangle of rod, rings and curtain onto the floor behind him while she splashed around, scrambling to clutch her knees to her chest. Then they were both still, staring eye to eye. Reflexively he reached, closed his hand tight and drew back, firmly persisting, "Are you all right?"

"No worse than I was."

A little better, he thought. At least she had some color.

She nodded. "More embarrassed is all."

"We're long past that." He snatched a towel off the rack above the toilet and then bent over her, flipping open the drain.

"Since I'm the one without clothes on, I think . . ." He'd already handed her the towel, but still she claimed, "I get to decide."

"Suit yourself. I've got a T-shirt for you."

"Thank you."

"One more dizzy spell and you're outta here, lady. I'll be callin' a doctor."

"Don't."

"One more." His index finger signaled *final word*. He turned away, going after the promised shirt and muttering, "One minute she's dizzy, the next, who knows?"

"I'm not going to die. I know that much." She was on her feet now, one hand taking support from the toilet tank, the other clutching towel to breast. "Not tonight, anyway," she promised him softly as he slipped his T-shirt over her head. She gave a shy smile. "I'm past that, thank you very much."

She made slow work of getting her arms through the sleeves and letting the soft white shirt fall over her torso, as though she'd released the cord on a window shade. Whether she was putting on a show or truly struggling was the kind of question that could only lead to trouble. A smart man would back off, let it ride.

32

And a slow one would get himself caught by the arm before backing out of her reach.

"Thank you, Nick. I'm past that tonight because of you."

"Hey." He shrugged. "It wasn't a good day to die. So you live to fight another day."

"You've helped me more than you know. I owe you—" she glanced away blushing, disconcerted by whatever she imagined "—so much more than thanks."

"Truth is, you're indebted to some unidentified flying animal that also lived to fight another day. So it's all good." He pulled her away from the wall. In her eyes he saw her imagination running just as crazy as any wild animal that had ever crossed his path. "All I want right now is a shower," he assured her as he moved her toward the door. "Help yourself to the phone. You gotta know *some*body. Whatever arrangements you can make, I'll try to help you find a way to get there."

Once he'd lathered himself head to toe, he hung his head, letting the hot water run over the back of his neck and claim his spine for a riverbed. It felt like God's tears. One by one the muscles in his shoulders gave in, and he permitted his scarred body a rare indulgence in pity and pleasure. But it was an unholy image his mind's eye conjured for his pleasure. The only player in it besides himself was close at hand and dependent upon the mercy of that hand. She owed him. She'd said so herself. *So much* more than thanks.

For his continued good grace, she'd hinted that she would favor him in return. Maybe the hint was more like a promise.

And the favor would be more like a payment, which he didn't need. He had to wonder how hard the woman had hit her head.

He *really* had to wonder what kind of demon she had dogging her.

She lay still beneath the blankets. He moved quietly, hoping she'd somehow managed to fall asleep. Silently he cursed his noisy knee as he pulled on his boots, but the chinking of his keys was the killer.

"Are you leaving?"

"I need to get my trailer off the road."

"Trailer?"

"Horse trailer."

"I didn't see any horses."

"Just an empty trailer. I'm picking up some horses tomorrow."

"But tonight . . ."

"I'll be back with some food." He moved a step closer. "You think you could eat something?"

"How long will you be gone?"

"An hour, maybe. Did you get hold of anyone?"

"I've told you, Nick, there's no one I can call." She jacked herself up on her elbows. "Maybe I could go with you."

"Maybe you could get some rest. Look, I'm leaving my gear." With a nod, he tried to direct her attention to his duffel bag and all the stuff he'd left around the sink, but he could see she wasn't buying. He removed a small red-and-white charm from his key ring. "Hold on to this for me. I'll be back soon."

Her fingers curled around the scrap of leather and beads. "This is important to you?"

"As important as keeping my word. I'm not gonna run off on you."

"And you're not . . . going to tell anyone."

"Joey?" He hated to wake her, but he had to be sure she was all right. There was always the chance of a concussion, which was nothing to mess with. He'd had a bad one himself once, so he knew from experience that you were supposed to keep waking a person up to make sure they could still cuss you out for not letting them sleep.

But all this woman did was open those big sad eyes of hers, which gave him an unwelcome hard-on. A guy had to be pretty hard up to get juiced by such a pitiful sight, even if she was wearing his own well-worn shirt and nothing else.

"You want something to eat?"

"I can't."

"I want you to try."

Jesus, talk about pitiful. When had he started wanting somebody else to do anything but suit herself?

The brown paper sack hit the small table with a solid *whomp.* "What I mean is, I think you should give it a try. It's just soup. If you can't hold anything down . . ."

"I can. If I show you, will you leave me alone about doctors and hospitals?"

"For now."

But he wasn't sure how long he would stay this stupid. If she went unconscious on him, who would back him up when he tried to tell some cop that not getting checked out right away was her idea?

They spoke little while they shared the meal he'd brought. He figured he'd probably traded in his cowboy boots for combat boots by the time she'd reached the age she looked to be right now, drowning in his T-shirt. Her small shoulders quivered with the breath she drew as she presented the cup to show him she'd finished more than half the soup.

He nodded. He needed to remember his own father's example. Kid shows you his small accomplishment, you hold back everything but that nod. *Yeah, kid, I see. It's no more than what's expected, and you damn sure don't want to come up with any less.*

She set the foam cup on the bedside table and closed her eyes. "Thank you. That was good."

He finished her soup. He'd paid for it.

And he went on paying.

Once the lights were out, Nick was doomed to lie still in his separate bed and pretend that her crying into her pillow wasn't keeping him awake. She was trying to stifle them, but those quivering, watery breaths of hers were deafening. Sputtering, stuttering, tearful little noises. He tried not to imagine himself crawling into her bed and finding ways to comfort her.

36

A man asleep would have shifted and settled again, but Nick was afraid to move. *Afraid,* for crissake.

He was no good with women. He had no moves, no words, no charm.

You should have taken her to see a doctor, you jackass.

She wouldn't go.

Who was driving?

Absolutely. Take her to an emergency room and leave her there—that was exactly what he should have done. Leave the rest up to her. It was the only way to deal with people, the only way that made any sense. Own up to your own part and leave them to do theirs. Don't get stuck with anybody else's shit.

Now you're talkin', man. Nick Red Shield is back in the saddle, back in his own ugly skin.

Absolutely.

Anyway, what was one night?

3

It was oddly comforting to be called by her baby's name. Lauren Davis had been left for dead, but Joey was alive and well. The sound of his name, spoken to her by another human being, made everything else bearable. She had a connection. The physical cord had been severed, but her baby was still part of her. If Lauren was Joey, surely Joey still belonged to Lauren.

From the day he was born, little more than a year

ago, until the day he was taken from her, she had not let him out of her sight for more than a few hours. Her father used to say that she was born to ride. She now knew that she was born to be her baby's mother. Every time she closed her eyes, she saw his little face. Birthing pain was nothing compared to a mother's pain for the child who had been ripped from her arms.

Her whole life, Lauren had shed tears maybe one night in a thousand, but tonight she couldn't stop. Lying in a cheap motel bed next to a second one occupied by a man she hardly knew, she worked a cold, shaky hand against hot tears and tried to stem her sniffling. The man knew too much about her already. Too much for her own good, and not enough for his. But she had run out of choices. She needed time and a safe haven, and this man was all she had. He seemed to be the kind who couldn't walk away from trouble without carrying a piece of it with him.

And she was trouble. She was a human train wreck. She couldn't think straight, nor could she shut her brain down and make it rest. Start with something simple, she told herself. Just lie still. Simply breathe. She steadied herself in her own embrace and rubbed the soft sleeves of the shirt that smelled faintly of horse tack. The taste of chicken broth lingered on her tongue. Joey loved chicken with noodles. Lauren had packed several jars of the stuff in the bag she'd prepared to take with them when they'd left.

But Raymond Vargas had other ideas. . . .

. . .

Pulse pounding in her ears, Lauren glanced toward the top of the stairs. Everything she'd planned to take with her was packed and ready to be loaded in the car. All she needed was Joey. Vargas caught her between the garage and the stairs to the room where her baby slept.

"What do you think you're doing?" Anger reshaped a face once handsome, now a daily horror. Before she even saw it coming, his punch had landed. He drew his fist back, opened his hand and flexed his fingers. "I think I made myself perfectly clear. You're not taking my son. End of discussion."

Lauren's left eye was tearing, but only because his ring had connected with that side of her nose. She refused to cry. She would not even touch her face in a way that acknowledged the blow. As long as she had breath in her body, she would not relinquish the strength of her will.

She stood her full five feet, two inches tall and maintained strict control over her voice, her stance and her wits. "Raymond, you have no more interest in Joey than you have in me anymore. Just let us go."

"Where?"

"I'm not sure yet. As soon as we're settled, I'll give you all the—"

"We're settled, you and me." His cold gray eyes challenged her to doubt him. "Like this discussion, which I settled days ago. Women come and go, but this is my only kid. He stays."

"You didn't want me to have him, Raymond. Remember? You told me to have an abortion."

"Yeah, with good reason. You haven't ridden since you found out you were pregnant."

"I haven't *raced*."

"And you were hard to replace. You get up on a horse, you're like some kind of Roman goddess— waist-up woman, waist-down horse." A quick laugh brightened his eyes, but not with warmth, for which they had no capacity. "I half expected you to give birth to a little creature with four legs."

"He's a baby, Raymond, and he needs his mother. Being his mother . . ." It was useless to try to explain to this man how motherhood had turned the order of things on its head. All she knew was that her child was always on her mind, and his needs came first. He had gone from nonexistent to top of all lists.

She shook her head. "I'm not getting back into it, Raymond. I'm not immortal, and I'm not a dumb beast. If I'm trampled, I know what happens. I've seen it."

"You started thinking instead of riding. That's your problem."

"It doesn't have to be a problem for anyone, Raymond. Certainly not for you. I know that I'm human, and I understand the rules. If somebody puts a gun to my head and pulls the trigger, I'm dead. Exactly like George Kobe."

"He put the gun to his own head."

"He was riding for the wrong people, and he was winning."

40

"You're safe riding for me."

"I'm safer not riding for anyone." Without thinking, she touched her smarting cheek. "I'm finished, Raymond. *We're* finished. We've been finished for a long time."

"Finished fucking," he acknowledged with an easy shrug. "That's fine. No shortage of replacements there. But I never thought about having a kid. Blood of my blood, flesh of my flesh and all that. Every time I look at him, I see more of myself."

"You'll always know where we are," she promised quietly.

"Damn right."

"Just let us go."

"Not on your life." Cold eyes, cold smile. "Not *with* your life."

Lauren knew all too well that it was a mistake not to take a Raymond Vargas threat seriously, but in the long run, staying with him would be more dangerous than leaving. Life with Vargas could never be good for her son, with or without her presence as a buffer.

Letting him make decisions for her had been surprisingly easy at first. She had become the breadwinner for herself and her father long before she was old enough to hold a job almost anywhere except a racetrack, where age didn't matter if you knew your way around horses and any chore that came with them. But her earnings increased when she became an apprentice jockey at the age of fifteen. During her apprenticeship, she was widely considered to be more than gifted. By the time she was eighteen, she enjoyed media as well as social attention. Her introduction to Raymond Vargas was inevitable. He found her attractive. She found him fascinating. For a time he gave her everything she wanted, including the chance to ride some of the most remarkable horses she'd ever met.

She'd never asked about Vargas's business dealings. After he'd taken her off the open market and mounted her handsomely on his horses and in his bed, she'd determined to stick with him exclusively in both respects. She'd thrilled to the notion that she could run with a dangerous crowd in the company of a daring man. She didn't concern herself with where his money came from. She suspected, in fact, that too much information in that regard might be bad for her health. She relished the newfound means to run and ride and spend and play. Within the course of a single day she was free to be womanly and childish, accomplished and dependent, careful and crazy. No more worrying about consequences. As long as Raymond was pleased with her, she was golden.

And as long as ever-serious, ever-silent strong man Jumbo Jack was around, Lauren was safe. She indulged herself in a short, sweet, overdue adolescence.

But she'd gotten pregnant, and again life had changed. Her insights and her outlook had steadily broadened, while her relationship with Vargas had withered quickly. Any affection they'd shared was gone, and with no legal ties to him, she was ready to go her own way. She'd told him as much. Since he had shown little interest in the baby during his first year, she hadn't foreseen his objection to her plan or the obstacle he would become. It was impossible to reason with him and dangerous to defy him. She'd tried both.

Now, having failed in her first attempt to take her baby and run, Lauren hardly expected a second chance to materialize the same day. But after the confrontation on the stairs, Raymond's power trip had taken him down the road, presumably for his regular weekend overnight with his latest girlfriend. He'd clearly figured he'd made his point. And he'd certainly made *a* point. Lauren's head pounded with it. She'd taken some nasty spills in her time, but getting punched in the face was a new experience. It was one she didn't intend to repeat. Her bags were still packed, and her car was in the garage.

Surely the man hadn't thought he could stop her from running the most important race of her life simply by punching her in the face.

He had not, as Jumbo Jack Reed's appearance attested. She had started up the stairs, and suddenly there was Jack, on his way down the steps in all his burly substance.

"You might want a raincoat."

There was no way she could get past him. "Where am I going?"

"This weather won't be lettin' up anytime soon."

43

His response to her ricocheting glance was more direct. "Don't worry about Little Joe. He'll be taken care of."

"He's asleep in his . . ."

The big man's demeanor was imbued with a vague sadness as he slowly wagged his head. Any display of emotion was rare for Jumbo Jack. His dark eyes, droopy jowls, stiff slit of a mouth and hulking frame were the parts of a wholly unexpressive man who never wasted a move or a word. But he'd always shown as much concern for Lauren as he did for anyone, and his sadness gave her a spiky chill.

She turned away, forced her way past him up the stairs and peered into an empty crib. Even his favorite blanket—his "binky"—was gone. Lauren dug her nails into her palms as she gripped the crib rail and drew deep breaths of baby-scented air. *He was just here!*

"Where's my baby, Jack?"

"We're taking your car."

"Is . . . is that where Joey is? In the car?"

"Yeah. He's in the car."

But not in Lauren's car. It wasn't a good fit for the big man, but he took her keys and wedged himself behind the wheel. Lauren had gone with him without objection, but she couldn't give up trying to coax him to tell her what was going on. True to form, he said almost nothing until she hit a nerve—something she was surprised to find he had.

"Are you taking me to my baby?"

His attention to the road visibly wavered.

"Jack? Who took him?" Getting punched in the face had left her a little pixilated. Somebody had slipped in and out of the nursery while she was loading the car. "Was it Raymond?"

The windshield wipers whacked steadily, barely staying ahead of the deluge. She glimpsed a sign— *Leaving Illinois*—whap, whap. Bigger sign—*Welcome to Missouri*—whap, whap. Her face ached all the way down to her teeth. Raymond had shoved her around a few times in recent months, and he'd let her know there was more where that came from, although not in so many words. No words at all, really, but attitude. Plenty of attitude. She'd been playing around with the wrong big gun, and now she was in Missouri, and her little boy was . . .

"Just tell me he's safe."

"He's safe."

"He needs me, Jack. He's only a baby." Taking her cue from the windshield wipers, Lauren whacked steadily at her rising emotions, barely keeping her own waterworks at bay. "Why is he doing this?"

"I don't ask questions. It's better that way."

"Better than what? Better than what's going to happen to me?" She swallowed hard. The fact that she was no stranger to the big man was her only potential advantage. She sought an effective tone. Not fearful. Not angry. Not accusatory. "Are you going to kill me, Jack?"

Her simple, straightforward curiosity was met with

silence. But he blinked. She was sure he blinked.

"What's the point?" she asked quietly. "I'm nobody."

"When did you get to be such a talker? We're goin' for a quiet ride here."

"I'm not a talker, Jack. I'm really not. No matter where I go, I will see no evil, hear no evil, speak no evil. So what are we doing in Missouri?"

"Ray makes the decisions."

"And he decided on Missouri. So don't cry for me, Illinois."

"You always had spunk."

"Not so much anymore. Once upon a time I wore spunk like designer spandex. Things change when you have a child. I've always wondered and never asked, Jack, do you have a wife or any—"

"Listen, I got one rule, and tonight is the first time I let it slide."

"We shouldn't be talking," she acknowledged quietly. But he had just extended her single advantage.

"Say what you want, but don't ask me nothin'. I'm just drivin' the car."

"I'm glad to hear that, because . . ." She shifted in her seat, willing him to see her, notice her face. "Because I've always believed that nothing bad could happen to me as long as you were around. You were there for Raymond, but you made me feel safe, too. I always knew—"

It all flew from her head the instant he pulled the car off the road. She knew nothing. She imagined nothing.

The rain, the engine and the wipers blended into a high-pitched humming in her ears, and she felt cold, hollow, slightly sick.

"Get out of the car."

She stared at the big man, dumbfounded.

"Get out of the car and disappear while I'm not lookin'." He turned toward the side window and muttered, "I won't take after you or nothin'."

It made no sense. "I can't go anywhere without my baby."

"You're already without your baby. Get used to it." He turned to her again. His eyes had gone cold. "Get out of the car."

"It's my car," she said thickly. "If you're going to kill me, do it here."

"I'll make you a deal." He glanced away quickly, as though the very suggestion embarrassed him. "Lauren Davis is a dead woman, all right? This is your chance to run. Get as far away as you can. It's the best deal you're ever gonna get." He stared ahead, muttering, "Jumbo Jack's gettin' old. Gettin' soft."

She imagined the huntsman giving Snow White the famous fairy tale reprieve. Despite the royal decree, he couldn't bring himself to kill her.

"Please, Jack, couldn't you help me get my baby back?"

"Not *that* damn soft." He nodded toward the roadside. "Go on now. Somebody'll pick you up. You gotta forget everything and start over."

"What are you going to do?"

"Make it look good. They'll find your car, but as long as there's no body, your disappearance is a mystery. The news'll go ape-shit for a while, so you might wanna dye your hair and try to ugly yourself up some."

"You don't understand, Jack. Joey's my life now. I can't—"

A ham-fisted blow to the side of her face literally made Lauren bite her tongue. She gagged on the taste of her own blood. Ear-ringing shock numbed all other sensation.

But not for long. He jerked the car door open, dragged her out of the seat and dropped her on the steep slope at the side of the road. Up became down, dryness got wet, light turned to dark, and chaos was all bound up with pain. She slid over bruising gravel and prickling grass, words of warning tumbling over her, spiny bushes tearing at her clothing and flesh. It was a relief to give in to the fall and finally be still with her pain.

So much for gentle protectors and fairy tales.

4

Nick rolled out at the same time every morning, no matter where he was or how long he'd slept. When his customary time finally came, he was sure of only one thing: he'd heard enough crying.

He headed directly for the shower. He started with

hot water for untangling the knots in his gut, followed by an icy blast to get his head straight. Tempted by the last fresh, folded towel, he made do with a damp one, all the while silently kicking himself for a fool on at least a dozen counts. He had a fuel-efficient route all planned out. He had business to attend to, meet-up times and places all arranged. What was he thinking, throwing an open-ended promise into the mix? He could only hope she had people somewhere close by.

Not that Nick put any stock in hope. Hope belonged in a holiday storage box, along with promises and polite manners. Whatever she could arrange, he'd said he would help her get there. But he hadn't offered door-to-door.

He found her dressed in her own clothes and perched on the edge of the bed as though take-off might be imminent.

"You got time for a shower. There's a dry towel left."

"I'm fine, thanks."

She was a sad excuse for fine, and the shower was the only remedy he had to offer. That and another promise.

"I won't leave you."

"I'll only be a minute, then."

She sprang to her feet before he had time or sense to back away, bringing her face closer. "It looks a lot worse this morning."

Jesus, since when had his tongue cut off all ties with his brain?

49

"It does?" Her small voice betrayed the added injury.

"I'll get you some more ice," he offered, for want of any way to take back the truth. Red-and-black eyes, puffy lips, one side of her face double the size of the other—what could he say? He'd seen bull riders headed for the hospital looking way better than she did. To boot, she grabbed his arm before he'd finished reaching for the ice bucket. He wasn't used to being grabbed, and he had all he could do to tamp down the impulse to jerk away.

"I'll be right back," he promised, falling back on his old proof. "See? My gear's still here. The cat's here, too. I brought her in last night."

"I don't want to hold you up."

"There's time." Man, those little hands were like a vise grip. "The ice machine is only a few doors down, Joey."

"It probably won't help. Let's just—"

"Humor me." He turned the act of pulling her hand off his arm into twirling her toward the bathroom—a move he didn't know he had in him. "Dance on into that shower. We'll never know until you try."

By the time she emerged, he'd made the ice run and turned his attention to the road map he had opened up and laid across the foot of his bed. Without looking up, he directed her to the pillowcase he'd transformed into an ice pack. "It should cover your whole face."

"Are we borrowing or stealing?"

"Neither. We're paid up until checkout time. We

50

have the use of the bed linens until then. It's called renting." He pointed to the yellow highlighter trail he'd applied to the map weeks earlier. "Any friends or relatives anywhere along here?"

"I doubt it." She lay there with her head beside the map and the folded pillowcase over her face. "But it's hard to tell with a bag over my head."

"You didn't look. Mind you, I don't mind going off track some."

"Is Canada on your track?"

"Hell, no." He glanced at the pillowcase. "You got relations in Canada?"

"I haven't had relations in ages and ages."

"I could put you on a bus to Canada. You got any ID?"

She gave a small chuckle as she peeked out from behind the pillowcase. "You are the sweetest man, Nick. Do you know how—"

"Cover your face, woman. That thing won't do any good unless you keep it on."

"I don't know anyone in Canada. I was just asking."

"I'm on my way to Des Moines, picking up five horses, then two more in Lincoln. I'm driving all the way across Nebraska, so anywhere along I-80, if there's someplace you wanna go, no problem. Right here, we take 76 into Colorado." He knew she couldn't see the map, but he said it just to give her an idea. "I wouldn't mind taking you to Denver. Wouldn't be too far out of the way. One more stop in Wyoming, and then—"

"Where's home, exactly? You mentioned South Dakota."

"No place you've heard of, but we'll clip past the Black Hills. Ever been there?"

"I've been everywhere, which is why geography is my best subject."

"Then pick a place where I can drop you off. You got your airports, your bus stations along the way. But I haul livestock for a living, and it's my business to connect these dots. And I'll be taking a horse home with me this time around, so I'll need to—"

"You're picking up a horse for yourself?" She was peeking at him again. Something he'd said had put a little spark in her eye.

"Yeah, that's . . . I bought a Paint stud, and I'm picking him up at the breeder's in Colorado."

"I can tell you're excited about him."

Wait a minute, that was *her* spark. He was only telling her where he was heading. Deadpan, as always.

"I've been lookin' for the right stud for a long time."

"And you're sure you've finally found him. I know that look. My father was horse-crazy, too."

"I'm in the business of raising horses. If that makes me crazy . . ."

"It does. You're a gambler. You can never be sure with horses, and you've got a lot riding on this one. Am I right?" The ice pack slid to the bed as she propped her head up to take a look at the map. "That's a long haul. I could be useful."

"Your face looks a little better. The ice helped."

"I can help you with the horses." She glanced up, working on him with her bloodshot eyes. "Seriously, Nick."

"Seriously, Joey, where can I drop you off?"

"Anywhere. Nowhere. Nowhere would be better than somewhere."

"That's where I picked you up." He pointed to that very nowhere spot on the map. "Right there. Maybe you want to put up a marker."

"A memorial to my near demise?"

"The place where the turnip fell off the truck. Look this over and come up with a plan for yourself while I load up. We'll take some ice along." Another quick appraisal of the bumps and bruises on her face satisfied him that she would live. "But it's not too late to change your mind about seeing a doctor."

"I don't believe in doctors." She swung her legs over the side of the bed and sat up. "Against my religion."

"Yeah, and picking up hitchhikers is against mine, but I make an exception whenever I hit one."

"You didn't." She turned her head, giving him a pointed glance, along with a glimpse of her wounded profile. "And I never make exceptions."

Nick didn't mind helping his customers load their horses into his trailer, but he didn't expect to handle the whole job himself, especially when the animals were barely halterbroke. He wasn't much of a fan of Arabians, and the five he'd agreed to haul out of Des

Moines made him feel even less friendly toward the breed. They were flighty as hell. When the fourth knothead balked halfway up the ramp and jerked the lead rope through his hands, Nick was about to say the hell with it. He would be doing the buyer a favor if he unloaded the first three and left the whole bunch in Iowa. Save himself and his trailer considerable wear and tear.

And then Joey appeared.

"Thought I told you to stay in the pickup."

"May I?" Her nod signified the lead rope as she quietly approached the horse.

"He'd just as soon knock you over as look at you, but, hell, why not?"

"What's a few more scrapes, huh? Settle down, boy," she murmured. Remarkably, her whole body and bearing connected with the horse. Muscle by muscle, the animal relaxed, and the woman spared Nick a pointed glance. "Both of you."

She'd spent some time around horses, all right. A moment ago the gray gelding's ears were laid back, every hair on his body aquiver. Suddenly he was all happy ears and willing hooves, following the little woman in the flimsy shoes and tattered dress up the ramp as though she'd washed her hair in alfalfa juice.

"Watch your feet," he called out to her as he headed back to the corral for the last horse. Hell, all he needed to top off a trailer full of high-headed Arabians was a hitchhiker with a broken toe.

But the last horse was loaded without incident. Nick

54

was back on schedule, and Joey was buckling herself into his passenger seat.

"I hope the buyer isn't a friend of yours," she said.

"Nope."

"Does he know what he's getting?"

"I know what I'm hauling. I know what he owes me on delivery." He turned the pickup onto the highway, putting the gravel farm road behind him with a signature dusty wake. "What would *you* say he's getting?"

"Nothing my father would have gone crazy for. I know that much."

"And that much makes sound horse sense," he observed. "I'd like to meet your dad. Any chance you could arrange that, say, today or tomorrow?"

"Not unless you're adding the Happy Hunting Grounds to your itinerary."

"Sorry."

She stared at him for a moment and finally shrugged. "Me, too."

From mutually sorry to blissfully silent would have been fine with Nick. What did it matter why she was sorry? The number of times he'd ever asked why could be ticked off on one hand. "Why has two ears and a long tail," he used to tell his brother, who would then punch him and try to rephrase the question somehow. *Quit runnin' your mouth, Johnny boy. Watch and learn.* But his little brother had never mastered the art of watch-and-learn. He'd been an oddball Indian, that one.

"You're smiling," she said.

"Am I?"

"Sort of." She gave a bruised-lip version of returning the favor. "I was about to promise no more clichés."

"Water off a duck's back," he said with a chuckle. "Here's another one—nothing personal."

"Right. Agreed. So tell me about these horses you're raising."

"I'm just gettin' into it." Which meant there wasn't much to tell, and she ought to take a rest. "You can lay that seat way back. The lever's on the side. There's a blanket and pillow on the back seat."

"Thanks." She ignored every aspect of his suggestion. "You're into Paints?"

You want me to talk you to sleep? So be it.

"Like I said, I finally found the stud I've been looking for. He's homozygous, so he'll throw color every time. And he's built like you read about. Leggy, nice head on him, solid hip, powerful chest—everything my mares want."

"Everything they're lacking, or everything they desire?"

"We'll see. He's young, so I don't know how desirable they'll find him. It takes more than good looks to impress a mare."

"Looks can surely deceive."

"Yeah." With a glance he acknowledged the truth of that. "You take my broodmares. Or not. At first glance you probably wouldn't take them, you or your dad. But if he's really got horses in his blood—if he did, I mean—he'd give them a second look. He'd say, wait a minute, there's something different about these girls. Something special."

"Are they mustangs?"

"Good guess, but they're much more than that."

"I'm not guessing. I hear it in your voice. You're out to save them."

"I've already done that. They belong to me."

"Were they feral horses?" On the tail of his nod, she added, "True mustangs, or just wild horses?"

"Wild horses can be anything. They can be descended from draft horses turned loose by farmers who didn't need them anymore. They can be from animals that escaped or from stolen horses, or—"

"Indian horses," she concluded. "That's it, isn't it? That's what's so special about them. But how would you know? There's no way to tell a horse descended from Indian stock from any other wild horse." On second thought, "Is there?"

"What kind of horses did your father favor?"

"The kind that run fast."

"Was he a breeder? Trainer?" He cut her a quick glance. "Player?"

"Some of each," she said with a dismissive shrug. "Tell me about your mares. Are they registered American Indian Horses?"

"I'm a registered American Indian, and they're my horses. Does that work for you?"

"I know there's a registry for the American Indian Horse, but you did say that your mares were feral horses that you rescued from—"

"Did I say that?" Relentless, this woman. "We'll be halfway to Lincoln pretty soon, and I still won't know where I'm supposed to drop you off."

She let the ball drop. For a moment it lay still and quiet.

Then, in a tone so humble it stung him, she asked, "How bad would it be if I rode with you all the way to the end of the line?"

"You know somebody there?"

"Not well, but give me the extra mile. When we get to the next stop, and I'm still riding with you, not taking up much space or anything, just—"

Relentless.

"Just looking like somebody rolled a pickup tire over your face."

"I told you, Nick, you didn't hit me. I don't know what you saw in the road. It probably *was* a deer. But I know it wasn't me."

"What were you doing on the road like that?"

"In the night," she echoed. "In the rain."

Familiar refrain.

She'd offered no clues the first time he'd asked, and he wasn't getting any this time around. Did he really want any? He did all his traveling in his own territory without taking side trips into other people's business. He didn't ask for directions, never gave any, worked hard for what he got and didn't expect bonuses. He didn't go around looking to help people, but a guy sees a bad need rising, what else can he do? Here he was, and here *she* was, and the need for information he didn't really want was becoming a pain in the ass.

He glanced at her with the words *answer me* poised to jump off his tongue.

Her blue eyes brimmed with apology, and he swallowed hard. What was a little pain in the ass compared to the depth of despair in those eyes? He hated pressing her, but he had wandered into unfamiliar territory and had no idea how to proceed.

"What kind of trouble are you carrying around with you, Joey?" When she didn't answer right away, he pressed with, "How bad?"

She stared off at nothing, biting her lip in defense of her secrets.

"Look, you asked how bad it would be, and I don't know how to answer that. I don't know you. I don't know what's behind you. I take you to my place, what are you gonna do there?"

"Have the tire tracks removed," she said with a smile in her voice. "Maybe you have some kind of rubber eraser at your place. Remove the tracks, replace with new skin, give it a few days to heal."

If she was looking to amuse him, she'd missed the mark. With a sharp glance he told her as much. Too far afield.

Too close to home.

"How 'bout you give me a straight answer?"

"I'm pretty sure this is as bad as it gets." She turned her face from him and spoke softly to the side window. "I was left there. In the night, in the rain, I was left there after . . . a difference of opinion."

The breath he drew too quickly pinched him deep in his chest. He scowled. "Your man did this to you?"

"My man?" She gave a derisive snort. "A man, yes, and thank you for not saying *your husband*. I was dumb enough to be with him, but not dumb enough to be married to him. I'll say this for you, Nick Red Shield, you're quite intuitive for a man, but you presume nothing." She turned to him again. "Except responsibility."

"You took your sweet time setting the record straight about my responsibility."

"I was scared."

"Can't the police—"

"No, please. That would only make it worse."

"If I gotta be lookin' over my shoulder, it would help if I knew what to look for."

"No one's looking for me right now. You picked up some roadkill is all." She gave him a chance to laugh, and when he didn't, she offered him that sad excuse for a smile. "I need some time, Nick. A few days to get my head straight. It feels as bad as it looks."

"Truth is, you cleaned up pretty good."

"I can do even better. You wait and see." She laid her head back on the headrest. "Tell me about your horses, Nick. Where did they come from?"

"You've heard of Sitting Bull?"

"You mean the Indian chief? Of course."

"Of course. Most famous Indian in the world. Geronimo is a distant second, even with all the fools who go around yelling his name."

"Before jumping out of some moving frying pan into . . . Why do they do that, anyway?"

"Who knows what makes white people tick, huh?" He winked at her—a pretty amazing gesture for Nick Red Shield, but there it was. "I'm from Sitting Bull's band. Everybody knows Sitting Bull because he kicked Custer's prissy ass at Little Big Horn. Actually it was Crazy Horse and Gall who did the ass-kicking, but Sitting Bull had the dream and made the medicine.

"The rest was a matter of doing what warriors do— what needed to be done. But Sitting Bull, he was the man. After it was all over but paying the price for defending ourselves, Sitting Bull took most of his people into Canada. But it was a hard time, and the people were so homesick after a few years that they came back and surrendered. The army took all the horses, and imprisoned Sitting Bull and his followers at Fort Randall for two more years.

"So what happened to Sitting Bull's horses?" he put to her finally.

"I was just about to ask."

"He comes back from Canada, early 1880s, surrenders at Fort Buford in Dakota Territory. The army takes the horses, keeps what they want, sells the rest. You heard of the Marquis de Mores?"

She shook her head, but he seemed to be holding her interest.

From amazing gesture to amazing speechifying. What had gotten into him?

"Just some guy who bought a bunch of the mares because, like your dad and me, he had good horse sense. But no business sense, apparently, because his cattle business went bust." He glanced at her and smiled. Her eyes were closed. "Long story short, the horses got loose. You want me to stop?"

"Please don't. I'm interested." And suddenly all eyes. "I want the long story with all the details."

"I was thinking more like a rest stop."

"I'm not resting; I'm listening."

He gave a skeptical chuckle.

"Really, I'm fine. I know how men hate to make too many stops when they're truckin' down the highway."

"You do, huh?" He took the turn he'd decided on a few miles back when he'd noticed a sign. By his standards, it was way too soon for a stop, but it would take more than a simple gas station to get the woman fixed up properly. "That's why we have truckers' malls. One stop fits all."

After gassing up and parking his outfit a safe distance from curious eyes and bumping vehicles, Nick pried the woman out of the passenger's seat. He knew she was embarrassed about the way she looked, but nature being what it was, he finally had to warn her straight out that if she didn't go now, he wasn't stopping again no matter how desperate her situation. Then he left her to think that one over, which didn't take her long. The sound of her quickstep coming up behind might have made him smile if he hadn't been angry with her for making him say the obvious. Bad enough he had to take on a passenger, but he'd be damned if he was going to travel cross-country with her acting like a kid.

Once inside, she took off from him immediately. No chance to suggest a bite to eat in the restaurant or a little shopping for personal items, nothing. He felt funny about hovering around the women's restroom, so he staked out the aisles he thought might be points of her interest until he started feeling funny about his stakeout. A guy knew when he was being watched. He grabbed some of the items he'd been looking at, took them up front and gave the cashier the legendary Red Shield evil eye.

Yeah, lady, I've got cash.

The transaction was completed without a word from either side. Not a please, thank you, or have a nice day. And still no Joey.

But he was blowing this unfriendly joint, with or without her.

Maybe she'd skipped out on him. He was really going to look like an ass, carrying this particular sack full of stuff back to an empty pickup.

How're you gonna look like anything with nobody there to see?

Nobody besides that know-it-all cat. One word out of her, and she was going back in the trailer with the crazy Arabs.

But the cat had made herself comfortable with the woman, who was staring straight ahead, fighting to beat hell to keep her bruised eyes open. No reason to get a mad on, Nick told himself, as he opened the passenger door. Presumably she'd done no more and no less than what he'd told her to do. And she made a sweet picture, cuddling the big orange, never-before-cuddly tabby.

"I see you didn't lock the door behind you. But here, drink this," he ordered, handing her a bottle of orange juice, followed by a chicken sandwich wrapped in plastic, which changed the cat's mind about springing into the back seat. "And eat as much of it as you can. I paid six bucks for it."

The cat took bumblebee sniffs at the edge of the sandwich.

"Will one make me grow and the other shrink me? Because I think small would be better. Small head, small headache."

He took the bottle of ibuprofen out of his pocket and held it up for display. "But you gotta eat at least half that sandwich first."

"Do you always act like a mother hen?"

"You're my first chick."

She laughed. "I'll bet you have children, though."

"Not a one." He tossed a large package into the back seat, and then he handed her a small one.

"What's this?"

"Ice pack. That's for later, after you eat. You break up whatever's inside, and it gets cold." He glanced back at the store. "The woman in there looked at me like I was Jack the Ripper."

Joey nodded as she unwrapped the sandwich. "She asked if I needed help, and I asked where the bathroom was. She leaned closer and whispered, 'I mean real help. Do you want me to call the police?'"

"Jesus." He gave the store a second glance and made a mental note to watch the speed until he was safely past giving the locals any probable cause to stop that Indian driving down the road in a fine rig.

"Yeah. Scary. I told her I'd been in an accident. I know you were trying to be helpful, getting me in there, but I really need to stay out of sight for a while, Nick. I'll just stay in the pickup with this bag over my head."

"I'll have to get you a bigger one." He pushed the lever on the side of the seat and told her, "Lean back. You wanna ride with me, you gotta eat, drink and then rest."

"What happened to *be merry?*" she asked when he got back behind the wheel.

"You missed the party truck."

He kept an eye on her progress, especially with the sandwich. She kept trying to feed bits of pricey chicken to the cat, but the Red Shield evil eye kept the activity to a minimum.

"What's your cat's name?"

"She's not my cat." He curtailed another food-slipping attempt, his critical glance meeting her wide-eyed claim to no blame. "She doesn't belong to me."

"Who does she belong to?"

"Herself. She wanted a ride. Never said where she

was going. Guess we haven't come to *her* stop yet, either."

She gave a lopsided smile. "You're a very nice man, Nick Red Shield."

"Don't you believe it," he warned against that injured smile. "And if you can't help yourself, at least don't tell anyone."

Later, just when he thought she'd gone to sleep, she proved him wrong again.

"Nick?"

Man, she was fighting it. He said nothing.

"Who was the Marquis de Mores?"

Who the hell cares? "He was just some rich French guy."

"What was he doing in—"

"Listen, there's nothing wrong with peace and quiet. You took some ibuprofen. I don't mind if you rest now."

"Do you mind talking to me?"

"I don't have much to say."

"Yes, you do. You have stories."

"Are you afraid to sleep?"

"Kind of."

He sighed. He knew the feeling. At least she'd picked a subject he didn't mind talking about. His sturdy, resilient girls.

"Okay, well, this de Mores married an American and built a big ranch in Dakota Territory, near the North Dakota Badlands. Have you heard of Medora?"

"Was that his ranch?"

"It's a town in North Dakota named after his

ranch. He named it for his wife."

"Romantic," she muttered softly.

"Yeah, well, he was French. Built the woman a big house where they could have parties and entertain people by hunting big game, playing cowboy and like that. So he bought around two hundred fifty head of the horses the army had confiscated from Sitting Bull's people. Mares, all of them. De Mores was suitably impressed, claimed Indian ponies to be better than any other type of horse. Said he was gonna raise them. But the horses had other ideas."

"They ran away?"

"De Mores wasn't much of a rancher. He built a plant for processing the beef right there on the place, but his grand plan went to hell in short order. When he sold out, he only had about sixty horses left, and that was after only two years."

"And the rest of them . . . ?"

"Took to the hills. The Badlands, where they roam to this day. And they've got the typical coloring, square build, fused backbone of the mustang or the Indian horse. They've got that heavy muscle and that big—" he glanced at her "—that big, heavy heart of the ones who were taken away."

She was looking at him, big, sad, blackened eyes eating him up as though his attention might feed her somehow. The heaviness in her heart was more than private, beyond ancestral memory. It was present. It was pressing.

It was killing her.

5

The second pickup of the day was no easier than the first. By the time they'd reached Lincoln, Nick had already made a liar of himself by making another stop. Any excuse other than puking, he would have played the smart-ass, but when the woman said she felt sick, his pickup changed course faster than a hummingbird. Not so much for her sake, but a guy had to preserve his dignity, and there was one smell that did him in every time, especially on the road. Before the vehicle had come to a complete stop, the door flew open, the woman bolted and Nick turned up the radio. He'd managed to head off a downturn in his own stomach, but by the time she took her seat again, she'd lost what color she'd gained.

She'd blamed the sandwich.

Rather than discuss the matter any further, he'd apologized for the meal.

On the road again, he'd given up on the idea of making up time in favor of a steady-as-she-goes plan. She goes to sleep; we keep a steady pace. No stops. No flying low. No cops. We won't make quittin' time, but we'll get there before closing time.

A safe six-horse delivery was bird-in-the-hand kind of money. He liked that. As long as she slept, there would be no more stops. Six hundred miles was an easy, average, normal horse-hauling day. And Nick liked normal. He thrived on normal. He would have dearly loved getting back to normal. But normal had flown out the window the night he'd plucked a certain mysterious bird from a Missouri bush.

Okay, so maybe he wasn't doing normal quite as well as he normally did, even if he didn't have a rider. But what did he expect when his own private Christmas morning was only a few hours away? Extra complications had added an extra wake-up to his plan, but no more. He was almost there. It was officially okay to anticipate, enjoy the gooseflesh, allow himself to do some secret smiling. Hadn't seen it yet, but he was close enough for the believing part to start kicking in.

He was finally getting his horse.

It hadn't been easy to come up with the final payment on Nick's dream. His name was True Colors, and he was a black-and-white tobiano with a family tree full of equine royalty, a face to make the angels cry and a body that would surely have old Sitting Bull standing up to make a song. He had a lot of running blood in him for a Paint. To boot, he was flashy. Color was what was selling these days, and True Colors would give his offspring the kind of color guaranteed to catch a buyer's eye. Once his babies' color had separated them out from the rest and they'd made the gate cut, their other attributes would make the sale.

Nick would have to stop buying and start selling really soon, and True Colors was going to help him by making a name for himself. The horse had earned some halter points, but Nick had no use for leading a horse around the show ring to be judged on conformation. Neither he nor his horses had time for politics. Performance, yes, as long as performance meant allowing his horses to be horses. Why would anyone ask such amazing animals to be anything else? Carefully coached and patiently coaxed, they would permit a man to mount, meld and experience every magnificent move they made. And they could do it without sacrificing their own God-given grace.

It was a fine balance, made more wondrous by its very delicacy. Big, brawny, sleek and shy meets brainy, bold, dicey and dangerous. How two such different creatures could come together in the incredible alliance called horseman was beyond reason. It was beyond natural. It was mysterious and holy, and it was pure magic.

It was the one trust Nick Red Shield indulged himself, and he held it sacred.

With True Colors, Nick would begin to fulfill his commitment to that trust. His sturdy horses and his worthy heritage—the best bones in the business—repackaged in twenty-first-century Paint skin. Heads would turn. Anyone who had any interest in horses would hear the story. And Nick would combine business with mission.

So the final payment had been hard to put together, but it would be easy to part with. The money order was burning a hole in his pocket. He was feeling it in his fanny. His gluteus maximus was pouring on the molten lead, draining it right down his right leg and into his gas-pedal foot. A highway sign told him he would make Ogallala in plenty of time to unload his trailer, hit I-76, and breeze across the state line into Colorado with daylight to spare.

But a siren told him otherwise. The no-stop promise he'd made to himself was about to bite the dust.

As he eased the rig off to the side of the road, his sleepy passenger stirred. "What's going on?"

"I got ahead of myself, I guess."

"Police?" She turned to the side mirror.

"I couldn't have been speeding. Not with this load." He reached across her, aiming for the glove box. "What's the matter, Joey? I didn't think you could turn any whiter."

She said nothing.

Nick wasn't sure how to go about reassuring her, seeing as he didn't know what he'd done. In his case, being "off the reservation" really meant something. And he didn't enjoy seeing his reflection in some white guy's sunglasses as he handed over license and registration—the signed, sealed and certified combination of his personal and prized documentation. It was especially nerve-racking when those papers left his sight in the hands of "the law." Nick tried to keep an eye on them in the side mirror, unconsciously tapping the steering wheel with his fingertips while the cop put his information through the legal strainer.

"I don't know about where you come from, Mr. . . . . Red Shield, is it? But here in Nebraska we use lights

71

on the back of both the pickup and the trailer. You don't have any trailer lights."

"Yeah, I do." Of all the accusations Nick had considered in his mental run-through, this one hadn't made the list. "This is practically a new trailer."

"It's a nice one," the cop said. "But no lights. You do the wiring yourself, Mr. Red Shield?"

"No. I had—"

"Who's this you've got with you?" Young, eager, feeling the weight of the uniform, the officer angled his fresh little face to get a better look past Nick's hawk beak. "Ma'am? Are you all right?"

"She's fine, except for feeling a little sick."

"I'm asking the lady. Do you need any help, ma'am? You look like you had a run-in with a tomahawk."

Nick tried to resist, but his pride wouldn't have it. He shot the man a glare worthy of war paint.

"Thank you for your concern, Officer, but . . ." She gave a little titter. "Tomahawk, I get it. He's joking, Nick. And it flew right past me. Oh! Flew past me. Get it?" She punched his arm. "Oh, it hurts to laugh. But it helps, too, after the day we've had. No, sir, everything's all taken care of."

"Did something happen today? It looks like it just happened."

"She had an—"

"I spooked the horses when Nick was trying to get them loaded. Sooo stupid. I've been around horses all my life, and nothing like this has ever happened to me before. I don't know what I was thinking."

72

"You're taking her to a doctor, right?"

"I'm—"

"He already did. Turns out, it looks a whole lot worse than it really is." She touched his arm, easy this time. "I'll bet that's what happened to the trailer lights, Nick. When those two geldings . . . Officer, you can't believe what a ruckus I caused. The wonder is that we even have a trailer, after the way they kicked—"

"Is this your wife, Mr. Red Shield?"

"This is—"

"Oh, no, I'm just . . . Nick's hauling my horses for me. I'm so sorry about the lights. We had no idea, did we?"

"They were working," Nick said doggedly, begrudging her not so much her quick thinking as the play itself, the role she'd carved out for herself and the one she'd left for him.

"They were working just fine. I'll pay for the repairs, Nick, I promise. And the ticket, if you feel you have to cite us, Officer. What's one more headache after all the trouble we've had today?" She gave an over-the-top sigh. "My own fault, I know."

"I didn't—"

"I know you didn't, Nick, but I can say it. It really was all my fault. You didn't bargain for some ditz getting all panicky over . . ." She turned in her seat. "Officer, I would be so grateful if you could let us be on our way. We don't have far to go, and I really don't feel well. The doctor said I might have a slight concussion."

"It could be a short in the wiring," said the shiny young fellow, copping a whole new tune. "You'll have to get this fixed, but get her home first. Ma'am, you let Mr. Red Shield take care of unloading the horses for you, all right?"

"I will. I promise."

"You're sure you'll be all right?"

"I'm fine, Officer. Thank you so much."

"She's not fine," said the officer, just between us men.

"No shit," Nick grumbled.

"You were going a few miles over the limit, but under the circumstances, I'm gonna look the other way on that one, too."

Nick watched in the side mirror as the patrol car pulled a U-ie across the median and headed east.

"Are you always that quick with the bullshit?" he asked as he maneuvered the rig back onto the road. He still occupied at least one driver's seat.

"It worked, didn't it?"

"Didn't even make any sense."

"Of course it did. If I didn't come up with something, he was going to think I was afraid to talk."

"You look like you've seen a doctor like I look Irish. If he really fell for it, he needs to get himself a different job."

"He did his job. He's not a detective. All he needed was a reasonable explanation."

"Why didn't you tell him the truth?"

"Because the worms must be kept in the can. At

least for a while." She turned her attention to the side window, where the view of plowed fields hadn't changed much throughout the day. It was springtime in Nebraska. "Where are we, anyway?"

"Like you said, we don't have far to go." Hell, he could match her for questions dismissed.

"We'll be stopping soon?"

"The Arabs are gettin' off the bus at Ogallala. We're almost to the state line."

"I must have slept quite a while."

"What about you, Joey? Where's your stop?"

"You passed it."

"Right."

"But I'm not complaining. I'll catch it next time around."

It was almost funny, the woman acting like she'd done him some big favor. He didn't mind seeing her get a little wind back into her sails, even if she'd done it at his expense. Anything was better than standing by while she'd puked up what little she'd eaten.

He'd planned to pick up the stud and finish his run without another stop, but he was fast learning that plans were made to be broken with Joey tagging along. His customer in Ogallala seemed happy with his new horses, which only proved to Nick that one man's herd of knotheads was another's dream team. But he kept his opinions to himself, pocketed the man's payment and accepted his help with fixing the trailer lights while Joey listened to him for once and stayed in the pickup. In return, he decided that she deserved a comfortable night's rest. They were back on the road with enough daylight left to allow him to see his stud, pay off his debt and maybe hit Joy and Gwendolyn up for a night's lodging for the two fillies he'd picked up in Lincoln.

Comfortable with his new plan, he took the turnoff to the Painted Ladies Ranch.

"Well, okay." Joey stared as they passed the sign. "So I'm definitely staying in the truck this time."

"It won't take long to do my business and pay my bill. These ladies are a lot of fun. Friendly, real hospitable. I'll leave the fillies, and we can go get a room . . . or two."

"Which road did we take when it forked back there? Are we in Nevada?"

"What happened to geography being your best subject?"

"Wyoming, then? Are places like this legal in Wyoming?" He questioned her with a look. "The sign says 'The Painted Ladies Ranch,' for Pete's sake. You think I don't know what this is?"

"You can't see my stud if you don't get out of the pickup." He raised an eyebrow. "Who's hackin' on who here?"

"If one of us were teasing, it wouldn't be me. I did my show for Mr. Policeman. Even if I had the heart right now, it would hurt my face too much. And it's impossible to tell about you, Mr. Red Shield, since you hardly ever crack a smile."

76

"I've got my face to consider, too."

"I'm considering it as we speak. Solid. Stiff. Quite studly, yes, but you might get a reduced rate from your friendly, fun-loving ladies if you could soften that serious—" Her eyes brightened. "There you go. I'll see your stud now that you raised me a smile."

"How you talk, woman." Eyes on the road, he shook his head. His mouth would not stay straight. "How you talk."

But once again she hid her face in the pickup while he took care of his business. The Painted Ladies' owners, Joy and Gwendolyn, were expecting him. Joy ignored the hand he extended, forcing a wet kiss on his neck, while Gwendolyn appraised the new trailer and asked him straight out how much he'd had to give for it. The fillies were granted a pen and hay on the house, payment and papers were exchanged, and Nick turned down the offer of a night's lodging for himself on the excuse that he had someone with him.

"You go out there and get him, bring him on in," Joy suggested with an expansive gesture. "We've got plenty of room."

"He didn't say if it was man or mare," Gwendolyn scolded.

The ladies peered at him, waiting for clarification.

"She's asleep."

Still they peered.

He lifted a single shoulder. "She's had a rough time lately. That's all I know."

And it was more than he felt like telling, but there it

77

was, just in case Joey stepped out of the pickup either looking like a woman on her way to losing her cookies or acting like one determined to win an Oscar.

Truth was, Nick didn't know too much about anybody, including Joy and Gwendolyn. No more than he needed to. The ladies ran a nice little operation, raised good horses and knew how to treat a customer. Collecting unnecessary information about people had always struck him as a rude enterprise.

"She doesn't want to stay?" Joy asked.

"She's asleep." That was all they would get out of him. He glanced out the dusty office window toward the barn. "Is he around?"

"Of course he's around. You think we'd let him out of our sight with you on your way to close the deal?"

"The man hasn't seen his horse in months, Joy. Can't you see he's dying here?" Gwendolyn slapped him on the back. "Come have a look. You're leaving him overnight, too, right?"

"If it's no trouble. Just wanted to stop in and take care of all the details. I'm planning on getting an early start," he said as he followed the pair across the sage-dotted yard.

Typical of serious breeders who lived with their horses, the best facilities on the place were built for the animals. The small ranch-style house had an office and a comfortable front room, with slip-covered furniture where the ladies had served him strong coffee and white bread sandwiches a time or two. But, man, they had a nice setup outside. They wasted no time growing anything just for show. The only grass that wasn't native was a half section of alfalfa. There was a fence around their vegetable garden, which hadn't been planted yet, a henhouse and a pretty little pond. The rest was maybe half a million dollars worth of housing for horses.

"It doesn't look to me like your friend is sleeping," Gwendolyn said as they passed his pickup on the way to the paddock on the west side of the barn. "She's sure welcome to come in and make herself—"

"I told her all that." He noticed some movement in the cab. Looked like lazy ol' Alice had taken on a new life as a playful kitten, boxing with some toy Joey had rigged up for her. "Like I said, we're not really friends. She's just hitchin' a ride."

"Maybe I should go say—"

Gwendolyn grabbed Joy's arm. "Maybe you should help me mind our business and reassure our buyer that you won't be stickin' your nose into his."

Nick was past caring what any woman was up to at the moment. He had only one thing on his mind, and that was the horse he'd gladly traded the equivalent of the skin off his back to get. He knew exactly what that meant; he'd done it before. Hell, for the papers in his hand and the dream-come-true standing in front of him, no question, he would do it again.

The lithe and leggy boy had filled out, slicked off and turned himself into a prince among horses. In Nick's eyes the two-tone beauty wore the plush black tail and silky mane as royal attire and carried his head

79

as though he'd been born to rule. Nick's involuntary chuckle was part appreciation, part pure wonder that an image of anything as foreign to him as royalty would spring to mind, that Nick Red Shield would actually feel giddy, and that he could barely resist the urge to tip his head back and unleash some weird, wild and winning howl.

The stallion turned his glossy head and pricked his ears in a show of mutual interest.

"Are you going to run him?" Gwendolyn asked.

"Race?" It wasn't the question so much as the sound of an ordinary voice that surprised him, and he spared it only marginal attention. "Haven't decided."

"I almost named him Roll Your Own. He's got all the makins'. Of course, you know that. I've been impressed from the first with all you know about bloodlines."

"As far as horse sense goes, you're almost as impressive as Gwennie," Joy said. "I'm not a particular fan of horseracing myself, but it would be fun to see what this one could do."

"Main thing for him to do is make babies."

Gwendolyn laughed. "Most males would kill for that job."

"Some would. Some have." He couldn't stop smiling as he waited for the horse to complete his majestic, if shifting, approach, weighing curiosity against caution. He spared Gwendolyn a glance, and his chuckle could have passed for a nicker. "How's that for awareness?"

"Student of history, are you?"

"My partner's the history man." He could almost hear Dillon having himself one hell of a laugh over Nick offering even the slightest comment on the nature of man. Like he cared. "I'm all about the horses, and this is as good as it gets. Get him home, get to know him, then we'll see." He offered his palm for the horse's inspection. "No rush, huh, boy?"

"We'll leave you two alone," Joy said. "If I miss you tomorrow, stay in touch with us, Nick. Let us know how this big boy's doing."

Distantly aware of their departure, he credited the Painted Ladies for delivering perfection—the perfect horse and the perfect private moment. It was sunset at the edge of the prairie. In the cool coming of evening, warm breath filled the space between the mouth that would take a bit and the fingers that would ply the reins. But this was a moment to be savored in its purity, before the testing of strength, wit or trust. It was like a mother finally face-to-face with her newborn after all the waiting and the work. All things were equal now. There were no names, ranks or numbers. Velvet muzzle nuzzled veteran hand.

Hello, you.

His next action came as instinctively as the last. *Get Joey over here.* He turned and found her standing near the pickup, watching and waiting. She'd draped his denim jacket over her shoulders, and the sleeves dangled nearly to her knees. With a nod, he beckoned her to join him at the fence.

The horse took as much interest in Joey's hand as he had in Nick's. Maybe more. Envious, Nick imagined walking his own lips over the same small hand.

Looking for what, for God's sake?

Indulgence, maybe a little petting. No more than any stud would enjoy.

Nick felt a smile coming on.

"This big boy's going to have plenty to say for himself," Joey was telling him. "You won't have to send out announcements, Nick. You've got yourself something quite special."

"I do, don't I?" He didn't need assurances, but he liked the warm way her words struck him, like the sun's last rays spiking a puffy cloud. "I wanted you to meet Joy and Gwendolyn, but they can be kinda nosy."

"I'm not feeling especially presentable."

"All banged up, you still look twice as good as any woman I've ever brought along for the ride."

"I knew it." She punched his chest with her fingertips. "That business about me being the first, that's such a line."

"Let's say, any I've ever *imagined* comin' along with me."

"Thank you," she said quietly. "I don't need any more questions about my face."

He knew the feeling. "The fillies are on their way up to Casper. Ever been there?"

"Oh, yes. Many times." She caught him before he

could ask. "But I don't know a soul there."

"You're pitiful, you know that? You've been lots of places, but you don't know anybody. No family . . ."

"No friends," she finished for him. "Pathetic, I know. And shameless. Quite ready to take advantage of your willingness to pity me."

"You've got a way of looking up at me with those big black-and-blue eyes that's hard to resist."

"If you've got it, flaunt it. That's my motto."

"You hear that, True?" *True.* The name had a strong feel. Nick was suddenly all smiles and sharp wit. "When a female starts in with the flaunting, just you remember—what you want, they've all got it."

"You're onto us, huh? And you said I was the first woman you'd taken for a ride."

"Ain't exactly what I said."

"Close enough. I can't wait to see True's harem," she enthused, and Nick questioned her with a look. "You know, the mares you've got lined up at home, just waiting for him. Painted ladies in waiting."

"If you're ever in the neighborhood, stop in and we'll show you around."

"I'll do that."

He nodded. "Be sure to call first. I'm on the road a lot, and my partner's the kinda person you wouldn't wanna be dropping in on unexpected."

"Man or woman?"

"Don't matter."

"Your partner," she insisted. "Man or woman?"

"Depends," he said, feeling playful. "Sometimes it's

hard to tell. It's just the two of us out there, so we're not too picky."

"About what?"

"I'm just sayin', be sure to call first."

She tossed her hair, catching a glint of sunlight. "You're a very mysterious man, Nick Red Shield."

"Yeah, real mystery man." He chortled. "I still don't even know your full name."

"Don't matter," she muttered. A poor mimicry of his deep voice, it nevertheless won her an unintended smile. The instant she tried to return the favor with a look she probably imagined as cute and saucy, he wished he'd held back. She reminded him of a black velvet painting of a mock-happy clown.

He was glad she was nowhere near a mirror.

"So you're inviting yourself for a visit to the Wolf Trail," he surmised as he walked her back to the pickup and opened the door for her. Figured it wouldn't hurt to practice some white man's gallantry now that he owned a prince of a horse.

"Is that your ranch?" she asked, and he dipped his head to confirm. "I'm pretty sure you invited me. *If you're ever in the neighborhood, stop in.* Wasn't that an invitation? Not the most enthusiastic or heartfelt one I've ever received, but in your case, I'll take what I can get." She gave a coy smile. "Especially since I'm planning to be in the neighborhood."

"And when will that be?"

"Depends."

"On . . . ?"

"Weather. Road conditions. The good working order of this vehicle and the good humor of its driver."

"Sadly, lady, you've got me pegged all wrong. No humor. Don't even try tellin' me a joke." With Joey settled in, he closed the door and thumped the open window frame. "But the vehicle seems to be working just fine. Nothin' short of a miracle, with all she's been through. So you've got your vehicle. Don't be lookin' for humor on top of it."

Circling the front of the pickup, he sensed that he had a tail. Sure enough, the cat jumped in ahead of him as soon as he opened the door.

"Hello, kitty, what's that you've— Yikes!" The cat bounded onto the front seat, up to the top of the back-rest, pausing long enough to display her find, and then leapt down into the back. "Nick, I think she's got a mouse."

"She's a cat."

"But she just brought a mouse in here."

"Supper's pot luck tonight," he told her as he busied himself with his keys, ignition and seat belt. "But don't worry. I'll get you something else. Wanna try some more chicken?"

"You know what's missing from your humor? You're so funny, you forget to laugh."

"So does everyone else, which is why I don't tell jokes. I've been warned." He chuckled as he pulled out onto the road, remembering one of Dillon's empty offers. "Hell, I can get paid not to tell jokes."

"By somebody who has nothing better to do with his

money? Who would that be?"

"My partner loves to throw money around. Crazy pastime, if you ask me, stuffing your money in other people's pockets."

"For not trying to be funny?"

"He says it's worth it."

"Settling the earlier question of gender," she pointed out. "What's his name?"

"Dillon. After the cowboy, not the singer."

"And it's just the two of you out there together," she concluded. "You don't have a family?"

"I've got a partner," he repeated with exaggerated patience. "And he's family."

"That's all you've got?"

"Hey, I'm one up on you." He glanced askance. "All right, yeah, I've got some younger sisters and the usual relatives. But I'm on the road a lot. They see me when they see me."

"Lucky them."

"If there's a need, they know they can call me. Like when somebody gets left out in the rain and needs a place to stay."

"Yes," she said softly. "Lucky them."

"Lucky us." He set his turn signal toward a vacancy sign. "Room at the inn, or so it appears. Wanna go in with me and see which face gets the most stares?"

Joey declined Nick's invitation, as well as his offer to get her a separate room. Both passes pleased him. Staring eyes made his skin crawl, and the two of them together—a small, beat-up white woman in the com-

86

pany of a big, mean-looking Indian—they'd already drawn their share. So much for being presumed innocent.

Not that he had any illusions left about the way most of the world viewed his face. He stood out in a crowd, which was plenty of excuse for not being anywhere two or three were gathered, no matter what the purpose. He wasn't like Dillon. Wherever there was a fight so Indians could be heard, Dillon would be there, speaking up like the mighty wind. Nick would be keeping mightily to himself. It hadn't always been by choice. Thanks to endless days and nights in a hospital bed, he'd read all the books, he'd seen all the movies, and he knew all the lines. But he rarely spoke them. He'd done way more prattling in Joey's presence than he was used to.

Even before doing his "big empty" time in the hospital, he'd been inclined to keep his thoughts to himself. Going all the way back to junior high school, he'd been tagged "big Indian." Not only because he was big, which he was, and dark-skinned—great for scar cammo—but mainly because he wasn't one to run at the mouth. He wasn't out to prove anything. Figured as long as he wasn't bothering anybody, he shouldn't have to.

And neither should the tiny woman with the big fresh hurt. With nothing of her own to haul into the room, she'd settled on the cat. Walking tall and feeling like he'd won the lottery, the Nick he never knew followed along chanting some lame verse about the woman taking the cat and the cat taking the mouse. But he got no laughs, no credit for being the only show in town. Didn't matter. He was on a roll. He unloaded his baggage, shooed the cat away from the bag of take-out food they'd detoured to buy, glanced up and realized the problem.

Joey had discovered someone in the mirror above the sink. She leaned closer, peered for a moment as though she wasn't sure who the woman was, and then closed her eyes. *Oh, yeah, it's me. I remember now.*

He tried to imagine her with the kind of a man who would do this to her. He'd known a few. There wasn't much to them. A big temper, but nothing much otherwise. One of his sisters had been with a guy like that. Hard to understand how a woman could be too unhappy over losing something so worthless.

But Joey was feeling bad over something more important to her than her face, and that something was probably a man. He would be some sharp-dressed, sharp-looking, sharp-tongued white dude, and right now the woman was looking at her face in the mirror and worrying whether it would sicken this guy, the spineless wonder who'd left her beside the road. He'd be sorry, she was thinking. By now she was probably hoping for a knock on the door. That would be *her* miracle.

But when she opened her eyes, she looked not at her own reflection but at Nick's. She gave a small smile, squared her shoulders and tried to fix up—rearranging her hair, wetting her puffy lip with a careful tongue.

"Does it still hurt?" he asked quietly.

"Kind of a dull ache. Not throbbing as much as it was this morning. But it almost looks scarier now than it did." She turned to him. "It scares you, doesn't it? My face scares you."

"Hardly." He stepped back, away from the mirror and the light, unwilling to lend his own face to such close examination. "It did at first, but knowing I wasn't the cause of it makes it easier. Not for you, of course, but for me."

"It looks worse than it feels."

"You're talkin' to a guy who knows better." His hand itched to touch her, but he didn't know where or how. "You'll be okay."

She nodded.

"Even better if you stay away from him." He turned to the jumble of paper bags he'd just set beside the TV, which was bolted to the dresser, which was nailed to the wall. "It's none of my business," he muttered into his shirtfront as he leaned over to pull some of his purchases from one of the bags. "Just a suggestion."

"A good one. Getting away and staying away was exactly what I had in mind. But my plan didn't work out quite the way I wanted it to."

He turned to her, a pair of small jeans and a long-sleeved cotton T-shirt in one hand, and a pair of clunky shoes that probably wouldn't fit her in the other. The stuff he'd bought earlier was nothing compared to the challenge he had no right to make.

How about a plan for putting the bastard behind bars?

She glanced away quickly, as though she could see the question in his eyes and it embarrassed her. Like she was to blame for something.

Rarely did he feel like asking for the details of anyone's life. Anything most people volunteered was more than he wanted to know, and he knew damn well this should be no exception. Asking personal questions was a way of implying that you had a free shoulder and you didn't care if it got wet. Damned if he would ask. She could tell him what she wanted him to know. He didn't need to be saying shit like . . .

"You wanna tell me about it?"

She shook her head.

Good. He'd made a once-in-a-lifetime offer, and she'd rejected it. He should have been relieved, but he stood there hanging his head like a kid ready to say please.

"I don't know if this stuff will fit." Thank God for the small favor of something even less appealing to talk about. "I wanted you to pick something out at the truck stop, but you disappeared on me. They didn't have much in the clothing department."

"Oh, Nick." She took his gifts without any inspection. "You are the sweetest man. Thank you."

"Yeah, well, wait till you try them. Don't be offended if they're too big. I was way off my turf."

"But I . . ."

"You can't get around the horses dressed in what

you've got on. I don't want that whopper you told the cop to come true," he said as he released what had begun to feel like hot potatoes into her hands. "You want first crack at the shower?"

"You go first." She looked up at him, all teary. "I'd love a long, hot soak."

His throat went prickly on him. *Damn her eyes.*

He took the bed closer to the outside door to give her proximity to the bathroom. She'd eaten only part of a hamburger—he knew what part because she'd asked him to finish it for her—but if that didn't agree with her, he wanted to let her think she could sneak off to the bathroom any time without bothering him. The fact that she was bothering him more all the time was his problem, not hers. He did what he could to make things easier. He wore jeans and a T-shirt to bed, faced the outside wall, sheltered his head with the extra pillow in an attempt, however futile, to cover the second base of bother. At least he would see none and hear none, and he promised himself that if he spoke none, he would have all three bases under control.

But she crossed him up completely. At the touch of her hand on his shoulder, he stiffened like a deer headed home on the roof of his ol' man's Chevy.

"Do you mind if I sleep with you tonight, Nick?"

He pulled the worthless pillow down and rolled onto his back. "You mean . . ."

She sat down on the bed. "I'll be very quiet and very, *very* still. I promise."

By way of invitation he tossed the pillow past his head to the empty space next to it, staring all the while at the ceiling. The mattress gave so little beneath her weight that he couldn't be sure exactly what she was doing unless he looked, which he wouldn't. He could feel the length of her beside him. Head-to-toe warmth. Head-to-toe itch. Head-to-toe bother.

Toes, he didn't worry about.

"Joey? I'm not gay."

"Okay."

One small word in the dark. One giant statement to hold up to the light.

"When I told you about my partner, that's what you thought, wasn't it?"

"Isn't that what you wanted me to think?"

"I was putting you on. Kidding."

No comment.

"I just want to make to make sure you understand that I'm . . . not gay."

"Whatever you say, Nick."

"It's not only what I say," he explained patiently. "It's the way it is."

"What I don't understand is why it matters." She gave a soft laugh. "Your partner's right. You shouldn't try to be funny."

He hadn't been trying to be funny; he'd been trying to have fun. He was pretty sure he knew the difference.

And he was damn sure it mattered.

6

Even with his glasses on, Dillon Black could not believe the sight unfolding on the ground below him, right in front of his sore eyes. The big blue dually had just rolled to a stop, the doors had opened, and what to Dillon's wondering eyes should alight but a tiny woman. Nick had brought a woman home.

A little bit of a thing wearing somebody else's clothes, but she sure walked like a woman. Dillon couldn't hear much from where he stood atop his makeshift painter's scaffold, but he could see the way she was talking, just like a woman. Nick wasn't doing much talking back, but that was just Nick acting bucky. Once a big Indian, always a big Indian. He was the last of the great Indian hand talkers, that guy, sparing the woman a slight nod and a heavy-handed gesture, something about the barn and the hills out back.

But since his partner was supposed to be coming home with an essential piece of their business plan, there damn sure better be a horse in that trailer, Dillon told himself as he set aside his paint scraper. Not that Nick was the kind of guy who would trade the cow for magic beans—a move like that would be more like Dillon's own style—but there was a first time for everything. As far as Dillon knew, this was the first time Nick had ever picked up a passenger on one of his stock-hauling runs. Not only picked one up, but brought one home. And a woman to boot.

Dillon couldn't wait to have a closer look. Bracing a hand on the platform, he took the five-foot hop and made a solid two-foot landing next to the big front door of his transplanted church. Good landing, good score, good first impression. Embarrassing Nick in front of a female guest, whatever their connection, would not do. It was one of many considerations Dillon took upon himself out of respect for the man he loved like a brother. Not that Nick would ever see Dillon as a brother—anybody claiming that particular chair at Nick's table risked losing more than his seat—but Nick's tunnel vision was no harder to deal with than Dillon's myopia. Except for the part about the ugly glasses, which he furtively tucked into his shirt pocket.

He approached the couple with his usual swagger, but nobody seemed to notice. Beyond any topic of conversation, they had a considerable togetherness going on between them. Dillon had a nose for such things. But he also had eyes, and the closer he got, the clearer his focus, and the queasier he was feeling about the look of Nick's woman. She'd been worked over, and the damage was fresh.

"Joey, Dillon Black," Nick said. "My partner."

"Pleasure, ma'am." Dillon gave the lady a handshake and his partner a theatrical aside. "Tell me you didn't do this."

"She says she doesn't have anyplace to go," Nick explained.

Dillon could have predicted his comment's flight path. Straight up and over his partner's head.

"I had an accident," the woman recalled in a voice whose echo came across as its own astonishment. "It was crazy, really. Nick stopped to help me, and then, when he couldn't figure out what else to do with me, he let me ride along with him."

Dillon appraised the cuts and bruises with a deep whistle. He could feel Nick's disapproval, but knowing Nick . . . "You figured out she needed a doctor, though, right?"

"Right."

Dillon got the point. Nick was ready to step between prying eyes and pitiful injured party. But this was no time for Nick to be taking a person at her word, not a female-type person. Half the time they didn't even want to be taken at their word, as anyone who'd ever been married to one could verify.

"It's really not as bad as it looks. Really," the woman insisted, making it two *really*s, which canceled each other out, according to Dillon's math. But she smiled and flashed her rescuer a look so appreciative that Dillon had to wonder whether the ol' boy might have permitted her to thank him properly somewhere along the road. "I was just lucky Nick found me," she enthused. "It was dark and desolate, and it was raining cats and dogs."

"That explains it." Dillon slapped Nick's chest with the back of his hand. "You took her for a stray."

"I took her for a deer," Nick said.

"Are we talkin' the sweet kind of dear, or the kind with hooves?"

"Hooves."

"Ah, Deer Woman." Dillon slipped the woman a subtle wink while he made a pretense of counseling his partner. "You realize we'll both be dead by morning, cuz, but what a way to go."

"You go away with your damn mythology," Nick said, holding firm against the threat of a smile. "Unless you're interested in having a look at a real stud."

"He's a beautiful animal," the woman confided, giving Dillon a tentative glance to let him know she didn't quite know what to make of him but was willing to give him a temporary pass. "Excellent choice."

"Thanks. You, too." He chuckled. She was still half a beat behind, but catching up. "No kidding, you've got good instincts. Most people would wait for another ride rather than get in with this guy. He's got a helluva bark on him, but he don't hardly ever bite."

"She knows that," Nick said over the rattling of trailer latches. "Better than you, looks like, for all your talk about good instincts." He shot Dillon an unmistakable warning glance before he disappeared into the trailer. *Keep your mouth shut until I come out.*

But Nick had to build a little suspense, leaving Dillon to stand at attention in the rutted hardpan drive-way. Man and horse shifted around inside the trailer, where small talk was permitted—easy boy, ho, easy—

while the man fussed over the horse's appearance with a degree of attention he would never afford himself. Nick was probably the one person Dillon knew who never made an entrance. Ah, but give the man a horse . . . Not until the travel kinks were combed out and the dust brushed off the animal's sleek hide did Nick make his presentation.

"Now, that's what I'm talkin' about," Dillon crooned as Nick led the Paint in a circle around his audience of two. "That picture of him you've got hangin' in the kitchen? I thought sure it was airbrushed. But he's even better lookin' in person." With an easy approach, Dillon invited the horse to check him out before offering to pet him. "You sure know your horses, Nick."

"That I do." Nick turned to his new friend. "It'll only take a minute to make this boy comfortable, and then I'll figure out something for you."

"You need help?" Dillon asked.

"I'll help," the woman said quickly.

Nick almost smiled. "That's two more offers than I know what to do with."

But the woman knew. Without a word, she claimed the lead rope and looked to Nick to show her where to go. She wasn't letting the man out of her sight. What was the old womanly wisdom? When you go to a dance, stick with the man that brung you. This one was sticking, all right, following that man straight to the barn. Maybe for a little Lakota two-step?

Dillon hung back and took in the strange show. It

pleased him on the one hand; on the other, maybe it rankled a bit. People usually took to Dillon right away. It was Nick they were never too sure about, and Dillon had made a habit of preparing the way. *He won't seem too friendly at first, but once you get to know him . . .*

Be damned if Nick hadn't gotten something going on his own this time.

Maybe Dillon should have bitten his tongue on his usual *helluva bark* remark.

Nick was fond of Dillon's cooking. Of course, he preferred almost anyone's cooking to his own, and he never offered a hand when better hands were available. But Joey-on-the-spot was a different story. She pitched right in with the potato salad, looking for alien components like a rubber spatula and celery. This was the Wolf Trail, for crissake. But Nick didn't have to say anything. As long as Dillon had all the answers, Nick was free to sit at the kitchen table with a book and wait for his supper.

It was good to be back. His trailer home was no palace, but it met his needs. It was a warm, comfortable place to come home to. He had his bed, his books, all the necessary facilities and then some. A little company once in a while didn't bother him, either. The picture would have been perfect, except that with all the chatter going on in the galley, a guy couldn't possibly keep track of what he was reading.

Dillon had his ways of doing things with whatever was on hand, but could he just shut up and get the job done? Hell, no. He had to try her way. Don't cut the root end of the onion off first? How clever. Man, he'd have to put this knife to the whetstone, but be damned if her trick wasn't working just slick. No tears!

Just chop the goddamn onion, Dillon. It's the knife that's working.

More precisely, it was Dillon's hand working the knife while he jacked his jaw and kept Joey entertained. No glasses, Nick noticed. Dillon was always pretty vain when it came to the glasses. Joey had pulled her hair back and tied a towel around her waist—no vanity there, but she only had the one shirt—and the two of them were standing hip to hip, or close to it, merrily making supper for the real man, who didn't hang out in the kitchen. Not in how many years?

Plenty.

"That's plenty," Nick barked. He wasn't sure when he'd left the table and stationed himself behind the island divider where he could see what was so damned exciting about this onion. The two faces turned, questioning his judgment. Hell, he knew what he liked.

But he rarely felt the need to tell anyone. Committed, he lifted one shoulder. "Too much onion spoils the potato salad."

"You're kidding," said Dillon, eyeballing Nick as though he'd just shaved his head or something.

"No, he's right," Joey said. "Let me finish the potato salad. We'll wrap up the extra onion, and you'll have it already chopped for something else. I did find some pickles. What about the eggs, Nick?"

"Lots of eggs."

"How about a touch of mustard?"

"I never use mustard." Dillon interjected.

"Mustard sounds great." One by one the muscles in Nick's shoulders unraveled. *When had he tensed up?* "But you make it your way. I'm not picky."

"Never used to be, anyway," Dillon muttered. "I supposed I should ask you how you want your burgers. Knock off the horns and wipe the ass?"

"You don't want to get E. coli from rare beef," Joey warned.

"You hear that, partner? You go poisoning me, you'll never be able to live with yourself or my share of the business. Cook 'em up healthy." He turned to Joey. "Do they have to be burnt?"

"Cooked through," she instructed. "Brown is better than pink."

"Hear that, partner? Brown over pink."

"Have you tried it yet?" Dillon spared him a pointed glance as he tossed a red patty into the iron skillet. It hissed at him like a snake in the garden, and Dillon chuckled. "Brown over pink? Once you get started, you'll be coming back for more."

"As long as it's healthy," Nick said. "No time to be gettin' sick. I've got plans."

"Oh, it's healthy, cuz. And it's about time you got picky about what you eat. Time you got some new cooking stuff, too, like maybe one of them rubber things Joey was lookin' for."

"You make a meal in the kitchen you have." Nick slipped Joey a deadpan glance. "Not the kitchen you wish you had."

"Like he's some TV show cook," Dillon said. "Not that he ever watches TV."

"I watch the news."

"Not anymore," Joey put in. "Now that True Colors has come into your life, I can't see you wasting even a minute in front of a television set."

He shook off the impulse to ask how she *could* see him wasting his time.

"When do I get to see True Colors' harem?" she asked. "Or should I say brood? They're broodmares, right? But a brood would be like chicks or something, wouldn't it?"

"This is a ranch, not a farm." Nick reached across the counter and plucked a hard-boiled egg from the small pan in the sink. "We don't do chicks."

"Speak for yourself, partner," the burger-flipper advised.

"I like *harem*," Joey said. "True Colors definitely deserves a harem."

"What you're tellin' us is, you're not a country girl."

"Not at all." Joey exchanged glances with Nick. He was rolling his egg between the counter and his palm, while she was a whacker-cracker. She smiled, amending, "I mean, that's not what I'm telling you. I'm saying a glorious specimen like True Colors has every right to expect them to be lining up at the barn door."

Dillon laughed. "Better yet, he has every right to herd his mares around and take his pleasure the way God intended. Can I get an amen, brother?"

"Amen." Nick slipped the shell off in one piece and laid the egg in Joey's hand. "Let's just hope they don't kick the hell out of him."

"If they did, then he wouldn't be much of a stud, now, would he?" Dillon judged. "There's a couple of 'em out there he'll have to show who's boss, but he looks like he can manage. Pretty soon he'll have 'em backin' up to him like a parade of tankers taking on liquid gold."

With a glance, Nick warned Dillon not to go there. Anything to do with trucking oil was not to be mentioned under Nick's roof. "He's young," he said aloud.

Dillon shrugged. "So were we, once upon a time."

Bowl cradled in her left arm and spoon in hand, Joey turned to Dillon. "Maybe you'll clear something up for me. What's your relationship to each other? Partners, cousins, brothers, what?"

"All I know is, he gets all pissed when I call him Uncle Nicky."

"Uncle Nicky?"

"Or Grandpa. He's such an old man. You try to show him how to have a little fun, you're wasting your time. Believe me, we tried back when we were kids, but this guy—"

"You need to remember we're business partners and make sure you're takin' care of business," Nick said. "Did you fix that stock tank?"

"To me, he's like my older brother." Dillon caught Nick's glance as he moved the skillet off the hot burner. "Okay, *bigger* brother. You're bigger than I am. Hell, she can see that." He turned back to Joey. "And, no, I'm not his real brother." Loading up a platter, he gave a wave of the spatula between burgers. "I don't claim to *be* him," he said firmly, turning back to Nick. "I said *like*.

"And, yes, I got the parts for the stock tank. I haven't quite gotten around to fixing it yet, but in case you haven't noticed, it's spring, and every streambed in the country is filled with runoff." He switched tones for more delicate ears. "He forgets he's not the only one who has a real job."

"What do you do?" Joey asked as they carried supper to the table.

"I'm a dealer."

"A dealer?"

"Drugs. Name your poison, dear lady."

Nick groaned.

Dillon chuckled. "See? I've got the best poker face in the state."

"I knew you meant card dealer."

"I had you goin' for a second. Admit it. I know that look." Dillon gave a self-possessed look of his own. "Haven't seen it for a few years, but I know it well."

Joey set out a mixture of plates and utensils that had clearly served long and well, but she arranged everything on the table in a homey way. Nick gave Dillon credit for cleaning off the table somewhere along the

103

line—it didn't get eaten off much—and decided to return the favor by fixing the stock tank.

"I'm sure I don't know what you're talking about," Joey was saying as she chose the chair across the table from Dillon.

"She even sounds a little bit like Monica, doesn't she? *I'm sure I don't know what you could be talking about.*"

"Your wife?"

"My ex-wife. Had a wife, but couldn't keep her. She wasn't much of a country girl, either. Hey!" A spoonful of potato salad had somehow inspired Dillon. "Here's one for you: What's a cowboy without a girlfriend?"

"I'm sure I don't know," Joey said, already smiling.

"Homeless," said Dillon.

"But you're not homeless."

"Ain't no cowboy, either," Nick informed her as he thumped the bottom of the ketchup bottle, unloading half the contents on his hamburger.

"Used to be," Dillon insisted. "I hung up my spurs for that woman, but she left me, anyway. Didn't want her babies growin' up to be cowboys. She got real nervous when our boy said he wanted to be a cowboy when he grew up. 'You have to choose,' she said to him. 'You can't do both.'"

Nick filled his mouth with overcooked hamburger and cold, runny ketchup while the two of them laughed.

"How old are your children?" she asked.

"Emily's almost eighteen and Dylan is thirteen.

104

Fourteen. They sure don't stay babies very long. The growin' up part happens real fast."

"So I've heard."

"It's like one of those little sponge toys they get at a carnival. You put it in a glass of water, and the next morning it's full grown. You turn your back for a second, and those babies disappear. Little people turn into big people. When Emily was born, she was so small, she fit—"

"We get the point, Dillon." Nick wiped his fingers on the paper towel Joey had thought to put next to his plate. For all the red stuff dripping off them, he might have been the one who'd gone at the onions with a dull knife. "Aren't you working tonight?"

"Yeah. Late shift." Dillon was still staring at the empty cradle his hands formed.

"How far away are they?" Joey asked.

"Minneapolis. Less than a day's drive, but the days pass, and you get to makin' the drive less and less."

"How long has it been since you've seen them?"

"Emily came through here last fall on her way to start college. She's at U of M Western." He grinned. "Dillon, Montana."

"Also named for Matt Dillon?"

"I don't know if I'm named for . . ." He chuckled. "Yeah, I guess I am. I think my parents ran out of apostles."

"But your son is named for you."

"Actually, he spells it with a *Y* in the middle. Or his mother did."

"Like the singer," Joey said.

"Like the poet. And she named Emily for a poet, too. Monica likes poetry. You gotta be named for something, right? Ol' Nicholas here was aptly named for a saint."

"First Nicky, now Nicholas," Joey said, with a smile.

"And a man's name is his bond, right, partner?"

"Word," Nick grumbled. "It's his word, not his name."

"Aw, hell, words are a dime a dozen, but a name says who you are and where you came from. My daughter found out about Montana Western because she saw her dad's name on the map and found out there was a college there. So she got to checking it out and found out they had this horse program, and her mind was made up. I mean, there was no more discussion."

"A woman after my own heart," Nick said as he pushed back from the table. They'd hardly touched their food, and he was finished. "I'm going out to the barn."

Pausing only to grab his hat, he made a direct but unhurried exit, gently closing the back door behind him. A deep breath of the South Dakota evening cleared his head. Standing there on the wooden step, ostensibly surveying his spread, he could hear their voices through the open window. He wasn't listening, but he had ears.

"He likes you."

"I don't think so. I'm afraid I'm a bit of bother."

"Oh, you're a big bother. A major bother. And nobody ever needed bothering more than good ol' Saint Nick."

It was just Dillon being Dillon, Nick thought. He was damn lucky Nick was immune.

Nick tossed his hat over the nearest saddle horn and plowed his fingers through his hair, one palm skimming over the scar he'd dubbed Dragon Lady. In its early days, it had looked like a brutal lover's long red fingers crawling up the side of his neck. It was one of many souvenirs of the day his waking memory all but denied. If it hadn't left its marks, he might have been able to strike that day—hell, strike the whole twenty-ninth year of his life—right off the books. But he had his indelible reminders. Each to his own form of body art, he reminded himself as he rubbed the crinkled skin.

He felt better now that he'd made a firm pact with himself. Every part of him, body and soul, was on notice. Other than keeping the one promise he'd made—and he wasn't sure anymore just how far he'd said he would go—but other than that, Nick Red Shield was not available. His mama hadn't raised no fool, and only a fool would offer himself up to be strung along by a woman with no last name. If Dillon wanted to take over where Nick had left off, so be it. If she expected Nick to help her get to a safe place, she needed to pick a dot on the map pretty damn quick. He had work to do.

He'd parked the trailer, unloaded some gear—not a pressing chore, but something to do—and set about stowing it in the stall he'd dubbed his tack room. Every halter had its hook, every saddle its rack. Before he knew it, he was singing, "Every cow . . . boy . . ."

A funny feeling stopped that noise cold. He had company. Smug, smiling and prettier by the hour.

A guy couldn't even warble in private.

"True Colors seems a bit disgruntled," she reported, stepping out of the soft evening shadows into the cone of light cast by the bare bulb affixed to a rafter. "He's running the fence."

"He knows they're out there." Funny feelings ran true to his gender.

"His harem." She moved in on him, pushing her interest in his horses ahead of her. "When will you take me out to see them?"

"When I get time."

"The chores never quite get done, do they? Is there something I can do?" Skirting the rack of bins he'd built to create a divider for his sanctum, she affected a telephone voice. "How may I help you, sir?"

"You got the wrong number, lady. I didn't call for any help."

"So. You can dish it out, but you can't take it."

"Don't need it. Thanks, anyway."

Sooner or later he had to clear horseshit out of the trailer. If he'd done it sooner, she might have been quicker to get out of his way. As it was, he couldn't even get to the shelf behind her without nudging her over to one side, then back the other way. The woman's determination to take over his space had rankled since day one.

What day were they on now?

"Dillon's quite a guy," she said.

Sounded like a song to go along with the dance. Nick felt no obligation to join in.

"Your partner. Dillon."

Ignore her, and she'll go away.

"Partner and some sort of blood relative other than—"

"I know who you're talkin' about," he said patiently. "Yeah, he's a guy. I'm pretty sure I told you that."

Patiently? What happened to the good ol' Red Shield bark?

His better instincts—the ones that kept people at a distance—seemed to have deserted him.

"I was going to say, you're quite a pair, but I was afraid you'd . . ."

"That's two brilliant observations. Can't think of a thing I could add either way." He reached over her head and slipped the rings of two cotton cinches over one of the coat hooks he'd inherited from Dillon's church. "I mean, the word *quite* kinda says it all."

"You don't make it easy, that's for sure." She was peeking up at him from under his arm, her little nose inches from his beak.

Man, he could kiss her so easy right now. . . .

He rubbed his chin on his denim jacket sleeve, staring into those disquieting blue eyes, letting her know she shouldn't expect any change. But since he had her cornered, he had to be the one to back off this time.

"So how does this work?" she asked artlessly. "Do you share everything fifty-fifty? Property, labor, expenses . . ."

"Women?" He challenged her innocence with a passing glance as he lifted the lid on the footlocker he'd taken with him along with his army discharge. "Sure way to kill a partnership."

"I should think so."

"Everything but True Colors. I bought him on my own."

"He's a gorgeous animal. I don't know much about breeding in Paints, but I do know something about syndicating horses, and a good stud—"

"That horse is mine." *Thwap* went the trunk lid under his hand. "One partner is more than my limit."

"You remind me of my father," she said, unfazed. Her attempt to get a look inside the trunk—on purpose or not—had been purposefully cut short. "He loved the horse business, and love was his reward."

"I've heard that love is its own reward. Personally, I wouldn't mind turning a profit." Nick planted one booted foot on the old G.I. chest and braced a hand on his troublesome knee. "Dillon's the romantic. He'll do anything for love. He's been workin' on that crazy old church building over there God knows how long, God knows why."

"For the love of God, maybe?"

He gave a dry chuckle. "Maybe. A little white town north of here wanted it moved, so he got it for practically nothing."

"A *white* town?"

"A town that belongs to white people. No offense. You got a better term?"

"I never thought of a town . . ." She laughed. "I had this image of a whole town painted white to match the church. Sorry. I'd never heard of a white town."

"Yeah, well, you're on the rez now. You're the minority. We gotta call you something." He squeezed the flesh around his stiffening knee. "So, Dillon, he can't resist a deal on something he calls 'a piece of history'—God knows whose history—and he buys himself a church. Movin' the damn thing, now that was another story, but he did it."

"With a little help from his partner?" she asked, and he lifted a shoulder. "That sounds like love."

"Real funny."

"Like a brother," she pressed. "Not a *real* brother because we seem to be touchy about that distinction, but helping him move a whole building, and a crazy one at that, well . . ." She gave him one of her benevolent smiles. "With some people, the love goes without saying."

"Guess you've got it all figured out."

"Not quite. I think Dillon misses Monica quite a bit, even though she broke his heart when she left and took the kids."

"He told you that?" *What a bullshitter, that guy.*

"Not in so many words, but like you said, he's a romantic. And he doesn't seem the type to swear off women and become a priest or a monk."

"You got that right."

"So I think he's building a house. He's making a house out of that church because he wants Monica back. It's like one big ongoing prayer. Am I on the right track?"

Nick lifted a shoulder. "You'd have to ask him."

"But he still cares for her, doesn't he?"

"You know what?" He didn't realize he'd been kneading his knee until he caught her glancing at his hand, which froze instantly. "I wasn't around him much when they were together. Their place was across the road, and he burned it down after she left."

"Burned it—"

"And if you want any more details, you'll have to ask him."

"I was only . . ." She stared at the hand on his knee. "What about you, Nick?"

"What *about* me?" He straightened his back, drawing his hand up to the middle of his thigh. "Are you gonna get personal with me now?"

"Not if you don't want me to." But she was closing in on him, thinking like any small creature sensing weakness in a bigger one. "When you lose someone you've been with . . . someone really close, like a wife or . . . someone like that, you know, it makes you a little crazy."

"So you're looking for a little company for your misery because you lost somebody on the road back there in bum-fuck Missouri?"

"No." She looked surprised, even wounded. "Not Missouri."

"Yeah, it was." It was his turn to press. "I found you in Missouri."

"That's not where it happened."

"Where *what* happened?" He leaned down, nose to nose, daring her to own up or back off. "I'd like to know, because I must've taken the wrong turn somewhere. I'm going down the road one minute, next thing I know I'm flyin' off course and then blowin' off my best-laid plan, all because I ran into you."

"And you didn't even run into me."

"Which means it makes even less sense." The look in her eyes was a serious source of irritation. Did she think she had some big dumb lug all set to roll over and play best friends? "I don't know who you are, and I have no idea why you're here."

"I'm here because you're a very sweet—"

He grabbed her by the shoulders.

"Stop it with that shit. I'm not sweet. Okay? I'm not—"

He had to kiss her. He had to put his lips against hers and taste that sassy mouth, tease that sharp tongue, give her the kiss they both needed. She met his mouth, caress for caress, stroke for stroke, measure for measure, and, God, how he wanted to hold every part of her against every part of him, pull out all the stops and grow this thing.

The sound of her protest was so small, he nearly missed it, but there was no mistaking the tears in her eyes. Touching her tongue to her bruised lip, she hung on to his jacket like a cat climbing a curtain.

"I'm sorry."

"No," she whispered. "Don't be."

He released his grip on her arm and touched the corner of her mouth with a blunt fingertip. "I wasn't thinking."

She held his apologetic gaze with the force of her own. Somehow she knew how hard it was for him to stand for this kind of exchange, how unnatural it felt for him to look her in the eye, the way he was feeling. It was an act that took his power away, but not his strength. She knew it, and still she played her hand. She released half her hold on his jacket, trailed her fingers along the path of his thigh, took his knee in hand and rubbed his deep-tissue ache like toothpaste from one part of the tube to another.

God help her when the cap came unscrewed.

"It's okay." She slid her other hand around his neck and drew him down, whispering against his lips, "Let's try gentle."

Nick loved morning light and spring chill mixed together. The world was golden, every old familiar thing renewed by the rising sun—chirpy sparrows and whistling hawks, thirsty dogs and curious cats, steam off his dream horse's fresh droppings and his own laughter as True Colors sprinted from pen to paddock like a kid distancing himself from the mess he'd just made. Never let it be said his majesty's shit didn't stink.

He noticed a light on in the kitchen as he headed back to the trailer. Something else was on the rise, and the absence of Dillon's car perked up even more promise. The aroma that blasted through the back door put Nick into a holiday frame of mind. If it was spring, this must be Easter.

"I hope you like pancakes."

Joey stood watch over the same cast-iron skillet Nick's mother had used, the one she'd given him the first time he'd set up housekeeping on his own. Joey smiled at him as she tucked a strand of butter-colored hair behind her ear. She'd clipped most of it high on the back of her head, but there were jaunty bits brushing her cheeks and the back of her neck. She had the look of a doll, made for play.

"Every red-blooded American boy likes pancakes." He set his cowboy hat on its crown on the shelf above the two coat hooks beside the back door and finger-raked his own shaggy hair. He kept it long enough to shield the back of his neck from cold air and colder eyes, but it was probably time to get it shaped up some.

"I believe it," she said, her tone turned wistful.

"Did you sleep all right?"

"I did, thanks." Busy pouring batter into the skillet from a glass bowl, she lifted one shoulder. "Well, I took a bunch of your ibuprofen."

"A bunch?"

"Three. Or so. Whatever, it was just enough and no more." The report was directed at the front of her shirt, and he wasn't sure whether she was uncomfortable with the fact that she was using the stuff or that she'd taken it from him. Before he could let her know that it was fine either way, she looked up and smiled. "How's True Colors this morning? I'll bet you were up at the crack of dawn."

He nodded, surprisingly pleased with her awareness of him.

"Did you try him out?" she persisted.

"He's green."

"And?"

"And it's the prettiest green you've ever seen," he confirmed, slipping her a smile on his way to the coffeepot.

"I'd love to take a turn around the track on him. I'm a pretty good rider."

"Soon as I get the track built, I'll give you a call."

"A turn around the pasture?" She flipped a pancake and tried again. "Maybe just one teeny circle around the barn, then."

She wasn't getting what *green* meant. "I've got a couple of nice saddle horses out there. We can take a ride after breakfast."

"Thank you for . . . last night."

"Did I miss something?" He figured she was playing some kind of trump card from a woman's personal deck. A couple of kisses were supposed to add up to gratitude on somebody's part.

"I don't think so. My guess is you rarely miss a beat. You gave me a bed last night. I'm not sure whose it was, but I'll try not to wear out my welcome."

"This is my house. The beds and everything else belong to me. I'll let you know when you're not welcome."

"Where's Dillon?"

Ah, there it was. The new attraction.

"I expect the boy's in church by now."

"Is it finished inside?" she asked offhandedly as she shoveled a big golden pancake onto a blue enamel tin plate.

"How do you mean, *finished?* There's electricity, but so far I only know of one junction box. The water's there whenever he settles on a place to run the pipes."

"Did I push him out of *his* bed?"

He raised his brow over a slurp of hot coffee. "Now, that I wouldn't know."

"You're the one who told me to take that room, but I didn't know—"

"Did you see him around here when we came back inside last night?"

"No."

"Well, there you go." He sipped again, giving her a moment to figure out where *there* was. "He went to work, remember?"

"That's right. The late shift." She gave a self-conscious laugh. "I wasn't sure what to expect, and the part about him working completely . . ." She tapped her temple with her index finger.

"You were afraid we'd be lookin' to go two on one?"

Her shoulders stiffened as she flashed him an icy look. "Where I come from, it's called *ménage à trois*. And it's not my sport."

"I agree. I got enough trouble with English." His smile was as tight as his gut. "I gave you the room I cleaned up before I left."

"Your room," she finally concluded. "You gave up your bed."

"Like I said . . ." He shook off the notion of repeating himself. Either they dropped the subject, no matter what the language, or get it on and get it over with. The welcome and its wearing out worried her, and the game with all its nuances wearied him. He stepped closer and peered into the skillet. "These are some interesting pancakes."

"You like those?"

"What's this?" A face with ears covered the bottom of the pan. "A bear?"

"Or a mouse. I guess it's pot luck."

"This one looks like a train engine." He pointed to the variety of shapes that had already been off-loaded onto a plate. "And a horseshoe."

"Made especially for red-blooded American boys. Oh, and I almost forgot." She shoved her hand into her jeans pocket and came up with his beaded key chain. "Thank you for humoring me. I was a little nervous about getting dumped again." She pressed the trinket into his palm and gave him a blue-eyed heartbreaker of a look. "I was actually pretty scared."

"You're not anymore?"

"Not like I was. I don't think I've ever met anyone quite like you before, Nick. I wish my father could have met you."

"Am I *quite like* him?" A little mocking, a little teasing—best way for a guy to keep his head on straight.

"Not *quite*." She flopped the mouse on top of the train. "You're more sensible. You have your dream, but you're going about fulfilling it in a practical way. My dad trained and raced his own horses on small tracks for small purses. Lots of claims races. He'd have a good horse one day, and the next day it would get claimed."

"Isn't that the name of the game? I haul all kinds of horses, so I hear lots of stories. Running horses through claims races is a gamble, just like anything else in the horse business. It's all about picking the right one."

"That's true. But my dad never got a chance to develop anything. When you're small-time and it's your whole livelihood, you tend to turn the horses over pretty quickly. You can only go so long without a paycheck.

"Dad would put a price on a horse in a claims race, and you'd have to keep a poker face around the paddocks before the start. You never knew who was betting, who was buying, and who was a tourist coming out to admire all the pretty horses. Dad was good at it. He could be friendly, easygoing, just as open and honest as you please without ever giving anything away."

"Like what?" He braced his butt against the sink and sipped his coffee. "What would he hold back?"

"Whether he was desperate for a win or a sale. The one thing you can't afford to be carrying around with you at the race track is desperation. And if you are, you can't let it show."

"A guy shouldn't get himself cornered like that."

"Really?" She raised an eyebrow, connecting with his hard-line stare. "I'm here to tell you, it happens to the best of us."

"Is *that* why you're here?"

"Yep. Your own personal messenger, sent by the Fates. Stay away from corners, Nick. Don't let anyone box you in," she instructed, punctuating with a wag of the spatula. "Room to maneuver—that's the key."

"You wanna see *room to maneuver,* you've come to the right place. Look it up in the encyclopedia, you'll find the Wolf Trail."

"I'd rather look at it from the back of a horse."

"You say you're a pretty good rider?"

"The truth is, I haven't been on a horse in quite a while. But I used to ride a lot. My parents split up when I was pretty young, but I spent a good deal of time with my father. I learned a lot from him."

"Like how to converse with somebody without giving anything away?"

"I don't think you need any lessons in that department," she said as she turned off the gas burner.

"Yeah, but my way, you just don't converse."

"That's hard to pull off in most circumstances."

"It was workin' pretty good for me until I ran into you." He reached over her to claim plates from the cupboard, so close that the edge of his jacket brushed her hair.

"You didn't—"

"Didn't run into you, I know. But somebody sure did."

"But I look better today, don't you agree?" She reached past him for the plate of pancakes, noticed her image in the shiny toaster, paused for closer scrutiny. "The swelling's gone. Cuts are scabbing over." She tilted her head, and the image ballooned. "Huge nose, tiny eyes, rubber-band lips."

"Right. This is a fun house, and you're the lead clown."

"The bruises are turning some pretty colors." Her quick turn surprised him, and he stepped back, little realizing that he was in for another surprise. "I have some doozies underneath my clown jeans. Wanna see?" She filled his free hand with the plate of pancakes, turned and pulled her shirt up and her waistband down, exposing her black-and-blue hip. "This one looks like a map of Florida tattooed on my butt."

Nick caught his breath. The soft curve of her hip, the narrow waist, the slope to her spine, so smooth, so tender, so terribly discolored.

The back door swung open.

"Morning, buckaroos! Do I smell . . . uh . . ." The end of the narrow counter was all that separated Dillon from the examination going on in the kitchen. "Am I interrupting something besides breakfast?"

"The answer is yes." Nick shouldered past his snickering partner. "You're buttin' in, and you stink like—"

"I thought so. Because I've seen that look before. I'm the father of two teenagers. Quick release is what that move is called." Dillon lifted the front of his white dress shirt to his nose. "I stink like what?"

"Fish bait. What are you angling for this morning?"

"I stink like smoke. In the casino biz, that's the smell of money." Leading with his nose, Dillon followed the plate in Nick's hand. "Mmm, pancakes are just about the best breakfast there is. Did you find the grape jelly? There's a new jar in the cupboard." The plate clattered to the table. "Hey, cool. This one has ears."

"Purely decorative. Kinda like those fry breads you're wearing." Nick said, indicating Dillon's ears with a jerk of his chin.

"Looks like there's plenty. I'll fill up a plate, take it to church with me, let you guys get back to what you were doing." He glanced over his shoulder as he reached for a fork. "Hey, can I have this Volkswagen? I've always wanted my own little bug."

Joey laughed. "Another red-blooded American boy."

"Yeah, great mileage on those suckers. I've heard a tank of gas and a good tailwind will get you halfway to Florida in one . . ."

Nick shoved the edge of an empty plate into Dillon's gut.

"What? What'd I say?"

"Did you just get off work, Dillon?" Joey asked sweetly. "You don't have to—"

Making a production of straightening his shirt as though he'd just been accosted, Dillon grinned at Nick. "Yeah, I think I do."

"Let me make some more coffee," Joey said.

"Not now, thanks. It's bedtime. Breakfast, then bed."

"I was just asking Nick whether your church is finished inside," she said, taking Dillon at his word and a seat at the table. Nick followed suit. "You're turning it into a house?"

"Haven't decided exactly what it's going to be yet, but I've got some rooms framed out. When I'm working nights, I like to bunk in over there where it's quiet during the day. Kinda like when we were kids, we'd sleep outside all summer. Remember, Nick?" He pummeled Nick's shoulder, jogging his syrup-pouring arm. "As soon as the trees leafed out in the spring, we'd cut some branches and thatch the shade. Some people call it a 'squaw cooler,' but Nick's sister, Louise, she'd kill us if she heard us use that word. Remember how Louise was all politically correct after she started getting involved in stuff at school? But she was right. It's an insult. You know what *squaw* means, Joey?"

"I know what a white town is," Joey said.

"It is what it is, right? It's not a slur. It's just a town on the rez that belongs to white people. And white women, like you, we don't call you anything. Is she white? Is she Indian? Either way, it's the same word for woman. But *squaw* is what the old fur traders and mountain men used to call Indian women, referring to their, you know . . . private parts. It's like calling someone a—"

"Jeez, Dillon. Who wound you up?" Nick sliced a butter curl off a stick and tucked it between two smiley faces. "I'd like to eat these while they're still warm. Nothin' worse than cold mice."

"Engine in these things is in the rear," Dillon said as he rolled his VW into a cigar. He dipped the end of his creation into the syrup on Nick's plate, chomped it off and smiled. "Still warm."

"Just sit down and eat," Nick said. "You're like a bird on a wire."

"It's from working the graveyard. You're just gettin' started, and I gotta decompress."

"Getting started? I've been up since—"

"Yeah, I know, around here we don't waste daylight. Let's build us a shade this year, huh? Breezy spot to kick back and swat flies. This trailer house gets to be a bitch by about July the fourth." Dillon polished off the pancake roll and eyed the shrinking stack on the table. "One more, and then I'm outta here. What's this? A train? Monica used to do this for the kids. You got any—"

"Oh!" As she reached to pass Dillon the pancakes, Joey bumped her cup and sent a river of coffee streaming across the fake wood tabletop. "I'm sorry. How did I do that? I was just reaching for the . . ."

"I've got it." Nick tipped his chair back and snatched the upended roll of paper towels off the counter.

"The pancakes," Joey said quietly. "I must have been feeling nostalgic this morning. My dad was into pancake art. He'd make a contest of it. We used to eat a lot of pancakes."

"I knew this wasn't Uncle Nicky's recipe."

"How about my breakfast recipe for the man on the go?" Nick offered as he made a paper dam for the coffee river.

"Bring it on, man."

"Put an egg in your boot and—"

"—beat it," all three said in unison. But only Joey laughed.

Dillon slid off with a groan. "There's a reason why the straight man doesn't get to tell the jokes." He gave a parting salute on his way to shutting the back door. "You need any more Indian humor, Joey, you come to me. I'll be sleeping in church."

The ensuing silence was shared awkwardly by two people eating cold pancakes. Nick almost wished Dillon would come back. His yapping had served to keep some of the uncertainty at bay. He couldn't shake the image of that beautiful black-and-blue hip from his head, couldn't stop wondering how much it hurt and why she thought so little of showing it to him. He tried to concentrate on the chore at hand, soaking up syrup to help choke the pancakes down. He looked up from his plate as he finished. On cue, she did likewise. Like prisoners handcuffed to each other, they had become inescapably connected. He gathered dishes and got up from the table, obliging her to make the same move.

"You're not smiling," Nick said. "Dillon usually leaves 'em smiling."

"I'm lookin' at you, kid." She slipped her plates beneath his, and they stood with the plates between them, fingers brushing fingers, neither taking nor relinquishing. Handcuffed.

She applied a bit of pressure and won the plates.

And smiled. "You won't take off without me while I'm cleaning up the kitchen, will you?"

"Who's a kid? Lady, this old face don't belong to no kid." He touched her cheek with a wind-chapped hand. "But this one might. I thought about it last night after you went to bed. Pretty risky for a guy to be kissin' a girl who looks like you without carding her first."

"You knew I was cardless. I thought that was why you were checking my teeth."

"Busted." He chuckled, his eyes tracking her every move between stove and sink as though she were performing a task he might have to replicate.

"Dillon might well be the silver-tongued devil in your family, but I'd venture to say yours is golden. Not that one kiss earns you any medals, but so far you've scored very high." She turned her back on the running faucet and bubbles building in the sink, presenting him with a warning finger. "And I know what you're thinking. *She hasn't got her wisdom teeth yet.* Rest assured, they've already come and gone."

"That explains a lot."

"So," she said, slapping the faucet down in a behind-the-back play, "turnabout being fair play and all, it must be my turn."

"I'm forty-three, and I still have all my teeth."

"Dillon's right. You are a killjoy."

"Maybe, but there's a lot of things I'm not, and one of them is easy." He closed in, one slow step at a time. "'Course, that don't mean I can't be had. It's happened before."

"Had by a woman?"

"Oh, yeah. You're a hard-hearted bunch. I know that much." He cupped his hand around her face, dark skin over light. "Now it's your turn."

"Twenty-nine. Almost. Missing only . . . those . . . four . . ."

He kissed her softly, exchanging his essence of Karo for hers. She slid her hand over his shoulder, tucked it underneath his collar against his neck and measured his hair between her fingers.

"What happened here?" she whispered when given scant space.

"I just told you." Such word games were not his way, but neither was explaining the scar that lay beneath her hand. "I got burned."

"Burned . . . by a woman?"

"Left a handprint." He actually tipped his head to one side to improve her view. "See the fingers?"

"How?"

He took her hand in his and took a step back, assessing the look in her eyes. It was an ugly scar, and it wasn't the half of it. She was looking to him for a story that would profit no one in the telling.

"A woman really did that to you?"

"I really got burned." He squeezed her hand. "Let's leave the dishes to soak. You ready to ride?"

She laid her hand on her chest and the long-sleeved blue T-shirt he'd picked out for her. "This is as good as it gets. My whole wardrobe."

"You might need a jacket. Man, I've got nothing that small." He drew her by the hand to the tiny closet that formed a room divider for the dining area. "Let's see what Dillon has hangin' in here. How's this?" He pulled a green plaid shirt jacket off a hanger and gave it the sniff test. "Prairie hay and fry bread."

She grabbed the shirt, sniffed, shrugged. "It's fine. Your nose is way too sensitive."

"Thought about goin' to work for the DEA, but I don't do well on a short leash."

He found her a cap, and she used the adjustable strap as a ponytail holder. Once they were outside, she took the lead, a newfound vigor pumping some bounce into her step. Could have been the hat, he thought. Big honkin' tractor above the bill. His sister had pressed it on him with the claim that it had brought her luck at the slots one night and she wanted to share. He'd suggested a share of her winnings, but Bernadette had told him to take the hat and get his own. He never had. He wasn't a gambler.

A blue roan pup bounded across the bone-dry yard as they approached the barn. Joey spun on her heel and greeted her with outstretched arms.

"Hello, puppy. What's your name?" She scratched the dog's head and patted her ruff, encouraging vigorous dog-style dancing and prancing. "What's that? Wags? Oh, Paw-Paw." The two shook on it. "He's trying to introduce himself, Nick. Can you help us out?"

"I've been callin' her Mama."

"Oh. He's a she. How did I miss that?"

"There's another one around here somewhere. We call him Buzz, short for Buzzard Bait. He's real shy when strangers come around. There he is." Nick tucked his tongue against his teeth and whistled louder than necessary, he-man enough to impress. The black shepherd hung his head and approached warily. "He was skin and bones when he moved in."

"Moved in?"

"People don't want a dog anymore, they drive out in the country and drop it off. I guess they figure if there's a house anywhere in sight, they've found the animal a new home."

The dog took a slow turn, closing in guardedly before taking a seat right next to Nick's boot. Nick rewarded him with an affectionate head scratching.

"Somebody found one for Buzz."

"Nobody did him any favors. Buzz found his own way." He liked to give credit where it was due. Survival deserved big points, the fancy two-door doghouse she was noticing on the south side of the machine shed notwithstanding. "Yeah, Dillon built that. Made it into a duplex when Mama came along."

"She was Mama before she met Buzz?"

"She whelped within a couple of days after she moved in. Somebody got rid of five dogs in one. The pups all went to relatives—mine and Dillon's—and Mama got fixed. Nobody gets to reproduce around here without my say-so." He slid the big white barn door along its overhead track, making a mental note to get up there with a can of WD-40 and lubricate the damn thing. "Wild horses are one thing. Wild dogs, that's something else."

"Is it a big problem?"

"Sometimes."

During last spring's foaling there had been a bloody "for instance," but he'd taken care of both newborn kill and vicious killers, keeping all but the simple statistics to himself. *Shit happens. Bury it and move on.*

"Hey, kitty." Joey seated herself on a small stack of square bales inside the barn door, where the mouse-bearing tabby dropped in from a higher vantage. "Another successful hunt, I see."

"We've had breakfast already, but thanks for the thought, Alice."

"Alice?"

Nick gave a diffident smile. "You know you've been on the road too long when you're having two-way conversations with a cat, callin' each other by name. But she's still not my cat."

"You just feed each other."

"What're friends for?" He headed for the racks in the first stall. "You see a saddle you like? This fourteen-inch is the smallest seat I've got."

Joey joined him in the search, soon settling on the oddball in the bunch. "This one suits me better."

"Dillon picked that up at an auction. Says it's Australian. I tried it out, but it's too damn flimsy for my taste." With his long reach, he easily hauled the hornless lightweight down from the top rack. "I suppose it's a little closer to what your dad used."

"A little."

They brushed the two saddle horses he'd penned earlier. By tacit agreement, she bridled and he saddled. The docile sorrel was his choice for her.

"Rusty's no plug, mind you, but I trust him out in the hills with my five-year-old nephew, who thinks he can . . ." He caught her disapproving glance. "Well, you said it's been a while."

"I'm sure Rusty and I will get along famously. A leg-up?"

The request was a little foreign to Nick, but she was small, the horse was tall and the stirrup was well beyond her reach. He took her bent-knee cue and managed the hoist without popping his own knee out of place.

"What's your horse's name?" she asked as they put the last of the corral gates behind them.

"Nothin'." He patted the buckskin's withers and greeted Joey's frown with a smile. "That's his name. One of my nieces hung it on him when she was about two. Which is probably why he won't let her near him."

"Sounds like you're everyone's favorite uncle."

"Don't have much competition." He adjusted his hat against the sun as they headed down the well-worn trail that led to his favorite place to ride. Nothing but sage and buffalo grass as far as the eye could see, easy draws and hills rolling out to the bases of buttes that rose to support the overriding sky.

"It's so beautiful here, Nick," she marveled. "Such enormous peacefulness."

"A little livelier where you're from?"

"Sometimes." She shrugged. "Okay, most of the time."

"I have another run scheduled for next week. Think you can stand this much peace for that long? Then I can maybe take you—"

"Is that an invitation?"

"To what?"

"Stay?"

"It's bad enough, people putting dogs out on the roadside," he said. "No choice, I guess. I have to let you stay until you tell me where you belong."

"I promise not to move in." She turned to him, squinting into the sun, her ponytail fluttering like a yellow flag. "Unless Dillon wants to add on to the duplex."

It was a pleasure to watch Joey merge her mental and physical motion with that of the horse. She was a natural. Clearly, no amount of time away from riding had weakened her gift. Nick gave himself over to simply enjoying the ride. No checking on the thirty head of stock cows he and Dillon had bought one at a time whenever they had cash to spare simply because they needed a practical reason to lease range land. No riding fence or fussing over the windmill pump that mostly never worked on the stock tank that had sprung another leak. Today was all about saddling up and taking a girl for a ride—something Nick hadn't done in years, unless the girl was missing at least one tooth and sported blinking lights on her tennis shoes. As hard as he worked, he figured he had a real joyride coming to him, and today was the day.

They were both pleased to discover his much-discussed mares enjoying the mid-morning sun atop a breezy ridge. She loved the picture they made against the blue sky, and he was surprised to see the first foal of the season—a frisky buttermilk filly. He challenged Joey to help him chase the herd into a pasture closer to the home site, where men and dogs would more easily deter predators. With everything working for her but the whistle, she took to the task like a seasoned hand.

Back at the barn, she found fault with her own dismount, complaining of "jelly legs," which surely didn't show. She promised Rusty a rubdown, but she climbed between the rails to pay True Colors a visit while Nick pulled the saddle.

"Come, let me tell you about the beautiful girls I saw waiting out there for you," Nick heard her say as he approached. She turned, eyeing the saddle he had pulled off the sorrel and was still carrying. "What are you doing?"

"You got enough left in your legs to try him out?"

"I've been found worthy?"

He said nothing. The notion had just hit him, and hit him hard—the handsome sight they would make, one on top of the other. He couldn't wait to make it happen. The way he was dancing around, True Colors had to be pretty keen on the prospect, too, and Joey could barely contain herself. Before he gave her a leg-up, he took off the baseball cap and buttoned every button on the shirt jacket. Nothing would be flapping or flying off.

He was not disappointed. He stepped back to admire the way the pair fit together, both visually and physically. It was perfection. He opened the gate to give them space to stretch, remounted the buckskin and followed them into the field. It took a few strides to catch up.

And he caught her smiling.

"Would you say he's a Cadillac compared to Rusty?"

"At a walk?"

"All right, kick it up a notch, but let's not—"

A trot.

"Ah, yes, definitely more action," she said. "Not a Caddie, though. More of a high-performance vehicle, say a Ferrari or a Porsche."

"How about a Mustang?"

"I don't know cars, but I know this boy wants to go."

The easy canter lasted a few strides before Nick lost touch with *easy* in his futile attempt to coax the buckskin to keep pace. If she didn't watch out, the stallion was going to take off on her.

"Hold him, Joey," Nick said calmly, even as his pulse began to race against accelerating hoofbeats. "Shit."

He couldn't tell whether the horse had run away with her or she was trying to give him a heart attack on purpose. If he gave chase the stallion would only run harder. The buckskin could be hotheaded, but ol' Nothin' had *nothing* on the Paint. He followed, but made a wide circle, hoping to direct the stallion and avoid disaster. He knew the ground. No holes to speak of—the flat had been worked with a plow. If the horse tripped . . . if Joey lost her seat . . .

But the speed began to diminish, the direction gradually changed, and Nick released his breath. They weren't going to hit the fence. The rider was in charge.

Damn her purple hide.

Nick rode in close and ponied the stallion to help Joey settle him down. She gave a thoroughly exhilarated laugh, as though she did this every day, taking off across an open flat on a galloping stud, and wasn't it fun?

"That wasn't cute," he told her as he steered her through the gate he'd left open.

"My dad was in the racehorse business, for heaven's sake. Nick, do you—"

"Your dad wasn't riding my horse. What business are *you* in, lady?"

"I knew what I was doing. And Nick, he's—"

"You say it's been a long time since you've been on a horse. What the hell . . . ?"

"I warmed him up first, Nick. A little bit. Do you realize what you have here? The spirit, the spark, the motion, all channeled in—"

"Crazy woman," he snapped as he swung down from his saddle. "I thought he was running away with you."

She dismounted with the ease of a gymnast, handed

him the reins and peered up at him, amazed. "We scared you?"

"Damn right you scared me." And confused him. He glanced back and forth between horse and rider, both of whom, if he wasn't mistaken, were feeling pretty cocky at his expense. *"What I have here* is the *spark plug* I need to ignite the engine to drive my dream. And what you have here is . . . is a hell of a nerve."

"Were you scared for me or scared for him?" she asked softly.

He couldn't say. *Shouldn't have to say.*

"You're right, Nick. I had no right to breeze him like that. But look at him." She gestured eagerly. "Such quick recovery, you could put him in an endurance trial, Nick. He didn't even break a sweat. This boy is golden!"

"Not with a broken leg, he won't be golden."

"We rode this ground earlier. I knew there weren't any holes."

"Worked it last fall," he admitted. "We're putting it into oats."

"Is there a track around here? We should clock him."

"*We?* You got Alice's mouse in your pocket?"

"I'd almost forgotten what it was like," she enthused as she patted the stallion's muscled neck. "Discovering that promise for the first time. Owners and trainers might see it in the breeding or the anatomy or whatever, but for a rider, it's less reason and more rhyme. You know?"

Disgusted, he shook his head. "Tell me."

"You do know. You just want to hear it from someone else. Confirmation, right? Do you know what I know?" She delivered the last part in a little singsong.

"Tell me," he insisted, his brain juggling the new pieces of the far-from-complete puzzle that was Joey.

"You know what it's like when you're perched up here on top of the world with everything in place, and you know there's nothing missing in this one, that it's all right here between your legs, every essential element tuned to perfection. You know what it's like to be right there, on the verge of ignition. There's no holding back. Takeoff is inevitable, and when it happens, you get to share in the flash and the flow." She grabbed his hand. "You've been there. I know you have."

He couldn't say. All his juices were rushing southward.

"The reason I know is because you own this horse. You chose him." She eyed the horse. "Maybe he chose you."

"Were you a jockey? Is that what you're telling me? Did you ride your dad's horses?"

She turned to busy herself with the saddle, undoing, unfastening, unburdening. "I rode a few times for my dad," she said offhandedly, "but by that time he was getting out of it. He couldn't afford it anymore, and his health was deteriorating. He was working at the track, living on the backstretch. When I was with him, I took whatever jobs I could to help out. Horses are a lot of work, but it's a good life for a kid, being around them every day."

"You gave it up for something better?"

She turned her face away from him, letting the wind brush her hair out of her eyes. He'd brought up that sore subject again. Not something but some*one*. It was written all over her face. He wasn't one to pick at scabs, and he didn't know why he persisted in worrying hers.

"All right, look, I have to go into town today and pick up some supplies," he said. "What do you say we look for some clothes that fit you better?"

She looked down, pinched at her jeans. "You did very well. Nothing's too tight. Nothing's falling off."

"I'll do better when nobody's runnin' off on me."

"I don't want you to . . ." She touched his hand. "You don't have to buy me any more clothes, Nick."

"Should we steal them?" He laughed at her expression of mock horror. "No? Then we'll buy you what you need, and you can work off the bill. Like you say, horses are a lot of work. You can't be wearing the same clothes every day." He glanced down at her as he lifted the headstall over True Colors' ears. "I've got a sensitive nose, remember?"

8

Lauren had lost count of the fine horses she'd ridden over the years, but True Colors could certainly prove to be among them, given the chance. His power and speed hadn't surprised her. What she hadn't expected was the surge of excitement she'd felt the instant she'd sighted a stretch of flat ground through the notch of an eager horse's ears.

And now she was excited for Nick. He'd picked himself a winner. She didn't know what he'd paid, but she was sure he'd gotten the kind of bargain her father had chased after most of his life. For the average player, the trick was getting the right horse at the right time and having the resources to make the right moves. Not that Nick was a player—and this was probably no time for him to try to become one, given his agenda—but, damn, he had the horse.

A horse like this doesn't come along every day, Laurie-girl.

After a two-year respite, one morning's ride had her thinking like her father's daughter. Or, worse, Raymond Vargas's—

Don't go there, she told herself as she gazed out the pickup window at an endless sea of grass that was still more winter brown than spring green. One rainy night and a couple more days of sun would bring the prairie to life. Before her time with Vargas, she had watched

140

a lot of countryside fly past the window of many a pickup. Just about the time it had become unbearably boring, she'd gotten old enough to help with the driving. She, too, had been a partner once, before she'd allowed herself to become a piece of Raymond Vargas's property. His piece; and his property. *How disgusting.*

She stole a furtive glance at her new driver. It seemed a crime to entertain any thought of Raymond Vargas in Nick's presence. Nick was a good man. He was a *real* man. He was nothing like Vargas, and if it weren't for Joey, she wouldn't even crowd the two names into her head at the same time. But she had to find a way to get Joey back without getting herself killed, which would do her son no good. She wasn't much—she'd done enough of Vargas's bidding to compromise any self-respect she'd once had—but she was Joey's mother. One worthwhile role in life—not a piece, not a property, but a mother. She had been racking her brain for options, and Nick's good will was all she had going for her.

He was a man of rough-hewn features, obviously forged by hard knocks. His hair covered his jacket collar but didn't hide the scar on his neck. He said he'd been burned. Probably an understatement. Tall and lean, with strength earned on the job instead of a weight bench, and she'd noticed that he favored his knee at the end of a long day. He didn't complain or demand, embellish or boast, and she found him more attractive with each passing hour.

God help her, she had no business bringing the man her kind of trouble.

He glanced at her, his eyes seeking clues to her thoughts. He seldom asked, rarely challenged. Played his hand close to the chest, earning him a smile.

"Are we going to a white town or an Indian town?"

"We're crossing the bridge." They'd topped a rise, and he nodded toward the road and the river basin below. "This side is Indian country. On the other side, you've got your stores, your restaurants, your banks and ATMs. That's where we're going."

Welcome to Mobridge, South Dakota, home of the Sitting Bull Stampede.

Lauren had tried to tell him that all she really needed was a change of clothes and a few personal items, but once inside what he termed "the closest thing we've got to a general store," Nick behaved like a man who only saw his kid on holidays, offering to buy every little thing that caught her eye. The boots were the biggest extravagance, but he told her she wasn't getting on his horses again without them. And he shouldn't be giving her Dillon's jacket, couldn't take her up on her offer to help with chores unless she had a decent pair of gloves, wouldn't mind seeing her in another dress if she wanted one. He declined to give an opinion on underwear, and when she held up a box of tampons and asked—*shouted,* he later insisted— "Can I get some of these?" . . . well, she succeeded in shifting the balance of power.

"You said you had sisters," she teased.

Taking refuge at the paperback book rack, he gave his signature chin jerk toward the cashier. "Let her ring up whatever you want and call me when it's time to pay."

"How about—"

"If you need it, get it."

She spotted a display of telephone cards. A pay phone, she thought. A way to place an anonymous call. Yes!

And then what?

She wasn't sure, but she slipped one of the cards between the antiperspirant and the tampons. Even as the scanner beeped it onto the bill, she felt like a thief. It was a need she didn't want to explain, mainly because it was more gut than reason. She knew what she had to get done, but she hadn't figured out how to go about doing it.

But she knew the telephone card was safe from his notice as long as it went into the bag with the tampons. He would undoubtedly consider examining the receipt to be an invasion of her privacy. Or an embarrassment. Either way, for whatever it might be worth, she had her phone card.

Following Nick's suggestion, she left the store wearing all new clothes, and she felt like a new woman. She availed herself of the sun-visor mirror, dabbed some cover-up on her cuts and bruises, applied a couple of licks of mascara and a swipe of drugstore lipstick, toss-fluffed her hundred-dollar haircut, and turned to find him watching her, bemused.

"Better?"

"Is that *you?*"

"Of course it's me."

He chuckled. "How about the new you and the old me go get some supper?"

"Anything but chicken." One more glance in the mirror and she folded the visor, satisfied with her minute's worth of handiwork.

"You got your drive-in, your phone-your-order-in and your walk-in-and-have-a-seat."

"The last one sounds good."

"That would be the Dew Drop Inn," he said as he hit the turn signal. "Best beef anywhere."

"You're sure I look okay?"

"Good enough to get me arrested." He surprised her with a smile.

The restaurant's dark interior was a relief to any eyes coming in from the unremitting brilliance of Dakota daylight. Decor that had not been touched since the place was built—Lauren was guessing 1970s—seemed straight-street clean and flat-town practical. It was early, the place was quiet and the booth was cozy.

And the *Restrooms* sign in the far corner also read *Telephone*.

"Will you excuse me while I . . . ?" She gestured in the direction of the sign and then pointed to the menu. "Order me this salad."

"What else?"

"Skim milk and a glass of water."

"What about some meat and potatoes? Around here nobody orders a salad for a meal, so you're probably in for a disappointment."

She tapped the menu with a persistent finger. "It says 'chef salad.' That's a meal."

"Maybe when it's made by a chef, but this is . . ." He turned a plastic-coated menu page. "Be adventurous. Ever tried chicken-fried steak? It's got nothing to do with chicken."

"All right."

"With fries, or mashed potatoes and—"

"All right, I'll have a cup of soup with the salad. Soup of the day, whatever it is. How's that for adventurous?"

She followed the sign behind a room divider and found the phone on the wall next to the door to the ladies' room. Just a quick call, she told herself. A woman's voice answered, and Lauren hung up, her hand shaking. She'd charged ahead and broken her own ice.

It would be easier next time. She would keep trying until she heard the right voice, she promised herself as she pushed through the next two doors on a tear. Inside the toilet stall she wrapped her arms around her middle and held on until she stopped shaking. She could only think of one possible inroad, and it was the one who had put her out on the road. It was a long shot. But what other shot did she have?

She returned to the table and drank most of her water before she noticed the way Nick was watching her. She had stopped trembling. Hadn't she? She drew a deep breath and slid the glass across the table, feigning disgust.

"I know beggars can't be choosers, Nick, but I've gotta say, the water around here sure tastes funny."

"Good well water is hard to find. Around here it's mostly artesian. This tastes better than the stuff at my place." He sipped, smiled. "And you . . . I gotta say, you ride better than I do."

"Oh, no, I'm really rusty." She gave a smile for a smile. "Like the horse. Rusty is as Rusty does."

"Rusty *is* reliable, and he *does* well by me as long as I do the same in return."

"I should not have done what I did." The admission applied to several impulsive moves she'd made, and the day wasn't over yet. "But, oh, Nick, that horse is something else, and I wish you'd let me do it again."

"I'll see if I can locate a grandstand for you."

"It wasn't like that." She leaned forward, peering, pondering. "You have no interest in racing him? You strike me as someone who might value performance, and your boy is a runner."

"That's what Gwendolyn said, too. I could tell she didn't want to sell him to me at first, because I'm not into that part of it. I know she'd like to see him get some points for something. But she likes my mares. She warmed up to the idea of crossing a gorgeous Paint with a piece of history.

"Some people just don't see it, you know?" He leaned closer, as though some of those people might be listening. "Those horses still know what it really means to be a horse. Even now . . . Hell, I don't have that much land, but what I do have is right for them. It isn't a habitat that somebody created for them. They're natural horses."

"They can't be natural if they're broke to ride?"

"Sure they can. Indian ponies were broke to ride, but it was more like a partnership. Horses aren't like dogs. They're a lot happier hangin' with their own kind, and that's what mine are doing most of the time. But there isn't much freedom left in this world, not for any of us. If you don't serve a purpose, you don't get to take up space, except maybe as a specimen."

"But your stud has been carefully bred for color and performance. I wouldn't call him a natural horse by any stretch."

"Carefully chosen, too. If we can breed the best of both worlds into his offspring, we'll get respect. We'll have value."

"Space permitted," she said. No matter what else was on her mind, she could always talk horses. *Whither goes the horse, so goes the rider.* Or so went Daddy's horseshit philosophy.

"Yeah, when you're as common as dirt, there's no value, so you get squeezed out, start dyin'. You finally get to be a rare specimen, people take notice. Plus, you can't take up much space anymore, being a rare breed." He shrugged. "It's a crazy world you've got here, Joey."

147

"Look again." She spread her hands. "I've got nothing."

"Hell, you've got new boots and a change of under-wear." He leaned back to accommodate the waitress. "And the soup of the day. What more do you need?"

"I could help you, Nick."

"With what?"

"I know a little something about horse racing. We could try him out locally and see what happens."

"Locally?" Hungry for blood, he tested his ribeye with the stab of a fork. "We're gonna have to do some driving just to find you that grandstand."

"We'll get your map out, and we'll check your next itinerary against the racing circuit. Paint horse races are a little harder to find, but Paints are permitted in lots of Quarter Horse races. We'll find out which ones." She tasted her soup. Bean du jour. "I'm telling you, Nick, this horse will make the kind of a splash your plan needs."

"Are you a trainer now?" He eyed her.

"I learned a lot from my father. It was valuable experience, and it, um . . ." She picked at her salad. "It's not as complicated as you might think. You're already halfway there, and it can be fun, which is something I think both of us could use."

"According to my partner, *fun* is mostly a state of mind." He chuckled. "Kinda like, rusty is as rusty does. Jeez, one shithouse philosopher in my ear is bad enough."

"Well, just think about it." She choked down two

more forkfuls of iceberg lettuce. "You're right about the salad. It's obviously not the specialty of this particular house. Will you excuse me again for just a few minutes?"

Studiously avoiding his eyes, she slid across the vinyl seat and tore away. The series of numbers kept repeating itself in her head, and she had to try it again while she had the chance.

This time the numbers yielded pay dirt.

"Jack? Jack, is that you?" Silence scared her. "Don't hang up! Please, Jack. I need to know what's going on with my baby." More silence. "Jack? You're the only one I can trust."

"Whatever gave you that idea?" came the deep, hushed response.

"The fact that I'm still alive."

"You won't be if he finds out."

"Or . . . maybe you won't be. Don't hang up, Jack. I don't want you dead. You're much more . . . *valuable* to me alive."

"Don't be a fool, girl. Don't be trying to twist on the tiger's tail. You won't get anywhere with that."

"Where's Joey?"

"He's with his father. They hired a woman to look after him. He's okay."

"I miss him. I know he misses me."

"Probably."

"You been seeing him much, Jack? Does he get to go to the park and the duck pond and all his other favorite—"

"Little Joe doesn't go anywhere without me." Jumbo Jack gave a very un-Jack sigh. "It's not the best job I've ever had, I'll tell you that much."

"You're a bodyguard. What difference does it make?" *Wrong thing to say. Try again.* "He should be with me, Jack. I'm his mother. He's hardly . . ." Hardly weaned from her breast. She'd known little more about breast-feeding than what she'd read, arbitrarily planned to nurse him for the first few months and then, possibly for the first time in her life, actually enjoyed letting nature take its course.

"Look . . . you shouldn't call here," her former protector was saying. Even hushed, his voice evoked the image of a human tank. She imagined gaining control of the turret and turning the gun. But the fantasy faded with the words "You wanna stay alive, you shouldn't call here. It doesn't matter about me."

"Let me call your cell phone, Jack. Just so I can find out about my baby. Give me the number."

"It changes."

"I know, but what is it right now? Please, Jack, give me this much. Some connection, some peace of mind." *He was still there. He was listening.* "Without that, it doesn't matter about me, either."

He gave in. She flagged a waitress down, borrowed a pen and wrote the number on her palm. When she looked up to return the pen, the waitress was gone. Nick Red Shield stood in her place.

"Thanks, anyway," she said. "I'll try again in a day or two."

Nick said nothing after she hung up the phone. He watched her pocket the phone card, must have known he'd paid for it, but he made no comment, posed no question. Not even with his eyes.

"I'm sorry to keep you waiting. I just thought of someone who might be able to help, but . . ."

"Didn't know if you'd fallen into the john or flown out the window," he said flatly. "I've paid the check, and I'm going out to the pickup."

"I'm coming."

She had to redouble her pace to keep up with him after the waitress got between them carrying their plates. He'd barely touched his steak. She wouldn't blame him if he slammed the door and spun out, leaving her standing on the sidewalk in front of the Dew Drop Inn with her precious phone card in her pocket and her boots too stiff for walking.

But she knew he wasn't like that. She was depending on it.

"I don't mind if you use my phone," he said quietly after a silence that nearly brought her to tears.

"I'll pay you back," she whispered, too embarrassed to do anything but hang her head.

"I'm not worried about that."

More silence. She tried to think of something else she could offer, but nothing came close.

"Is Jack the guy who—"

"Please, Nick, don't go there. It could mean trouble for you, worse than I've already caused. I mean, right now I'm a nuisance, which is bad enough. If they knew . . ." She closed her eyes, mentally rephrasing. *Keep them separate.* "It's better for both of us if I don't make calls from phone numbers that can easily lead to me."

"I'm not afraid of some weasel who beats up on women."

"That's the problem, Nick. You have no idea."

"Try givin' me one," he suggested without taking his eyes off the road.

"It's very complicated and very . . . painful. Inside and out."

"What's that supposed to mean, Joey? You wanna call him, go ahead and call him. If he shows up at the door, you can go or stay. I'll back you either way." He spared her a glance. "Just be straight with me."

"I've never met anyone like you." She meant it. She felt it so deeply, she had to turn away. "The last thing I want to do is cause trouble for you, Nick. What was . . . done to me was . . . could . . ." She shook off the notion of playing the for-your-own-good card. It would be the ultimate lie. If she cared enough to spare him, she would not be asking, "If you could just give me a couple more days . . ."

"Take your time. You're no trouble." He gave a wry chuckle. "Not much, anyway."

It was as plain as the damage on her face. True Colors was born to run.

By the time Nick had parked the pickup in the gravel driveway at Wolf Trail, Lauren had secured his blessing to try the stallion out on a lunge line. She wasted no time attaching a generous length of nylon to his halter and putting him though his paces. The horse was green, but he'd clearly been handled and was no stranger to working the circle. He seemed to enjoy showing her his stuff as much as she appreciated the view. He was a stretchy, stylish, two-toned eyeful and he moved like a wish with wings.

Lauren's best mounts had been Raymond's Thoroughbreds, but she had also ridden her father's Quarter Horses, which were a step down only because her father had never acquired the horse among horses. Even though Paints were not major players in racing, they were gaining recognition, and more and more race tracks were making room for them, either in a class of their own or running against Quarter Horses. Nearly half a century of selective breeding had produced a registry of horses that many in the business considered to be the source for the next crown jewel in the horse world.

Lately, even Raymond had shown some interest in the growing popularity of the breed. A few months past he'd mentioned seeing one he liked at a track. Lauren had paid little attention to the remark at the time, but watching True Colors switching directions and changing leads like an old show horse brought the comment to mind in a new light. A Paint racehorse had caught the eye of Raymond Vargas, but he had yet to possess one.

Raymond was no horseman. He wasn't even comfortable around horses, but they were among the effects he had taken to collecting. He considered himself to be a major player, and he was obsessed with owning the best of whatever was in play. Gambling with what he owned excited him, particularly when it moved him a step up on the ladder of ownership. Any kind of ownership. He relished long shots, took special pleasure in getting in on the ground floor or discovering an unknown, be it a dark horse or a nameless jockey. If the horse became a winner or the jockey made a name for herself, he was on to the next venture. But always on his terms.

Lauren's decision to take herself out of the game before he was finished with her had been her first mistake, but by the time she understood the gravity of that first one, she had compounded it several times over. She had misjudged the man at every turn. She should have known better. He owned a stable, but from day one she had known that he had no love for horses. He owned lush property, myriad toys, and maybe as many people, but he showed no contentment with any of it. There was only his obsession with owning more, securing control, spreading his power. He'd extended his obsession to include the child he hadn't wanted. Immersed in her newfound joy, she hadn't seen it coming.

And she called herself a mother. What kind of a mother would allow such a thing to happen to her baby?

"One in a million."

Lauren turned to discover a spectator. Dillon swung

his leg over the top fence rail and settled in.

"You just don't see that kind of action every day," he said.

"No, you don't," she called out over her shoulder as she continued her turn, following the line that connected her to the cantering horse. "He's very special."

"Nick says you rode him."

"I did."

He dropped down from the fence and ambled closer, joining her at the center of the horse's circular course. "You got to ride him before I did."

She laughed. "Sorry."

He moved to stand directly behind her. "No, I'm just sayin' . . ." It took him a moment to decide. "I never could get the hang of this. Not that I ever saw much point in it."

"Lunging?"

"You might as well take 'em for a spin."

"Lunging has its uses. Here." She handed him the line and the long, supple willow branch Nick had cut for her to use as a whip. "It's just a matter of getting him to keep the line taut."

"I get the idea, I just don't . . ." He kissed at the horse to keep him moving, but he didn't seem to know what to do with the willow.

She took it back from him, gave it a quick flick and made it whistle. The horse drew the line tight again. She glanced up, offering Nick's handsome partner an equally tight smile. "I thought you were in the horse business."

155

"I'm a rider, not a trainer." He chuckled. "Kinda like, I'm a lover, not a fighter."

"I get it," she assured him. She worked the willow, but left him the line. This way, he wouldn't be standing right behind her making her nervous. "Somebody has to do the training."

"Just like somebody has to do the fighting. That would be Nick." They exchanged glances—hers doubtful, his knowing. "Again, not something you'll see every day, but he'll fight if he has to."

"And you?"

"Me? I'll call Nick." Without taking his eyes off the horse, he grinned. "Tell you what else you don't see every day. Nick's sittin' in there workin' on his books. That part isn't unusual—he's just as particular about his business records as everything else, including who gets to ride what horse. He comes back from a run haulin' stock, usually does his books the same day. But this time he's sittin' in there by the window."

"Let him trot now," she instructed. "He doesn't like to sit by the window?"

"His desk is in the bedroom. He's a creature of habit, is our Nick. He does bookwork at his desk. Always." He glanced toward the trailer house as he turned the lead over to Lauren. "Tell you something else. Those expenses ain't gettin' entered in that ledger with him watchin' out the window."

"I'm surprised he isn't out here keeping close tabs on my every move," she said as she reeled the horse in, greeting him with pats and praise.

"Then you don't really know the man," Dillon said. "He's got no time for anyone he has to keep tabs on. If he didn't trust you with this horse, you wouldn't be out here."

"But you say he's keeping an eye on me."

"No, I didn't. I said *he's watching*. What I'm tellin' you is, he's enjoying the show."

"Why doesn't he come out here and enjoy it up close and personal?"

"Because he's generally distant and private. I don't know where you came from or how you've gotten this far with him, but my hat's off to you."

"It's not like I have any designs on him."

"Then what are you up to?"

She answered with a scowl.

"Hey, I'm not Nick. I don't mind askin' the tough questions point-blank."

"I'm not up to any . . ." True Colors nudged her shoulder, as impatient with Dillon's interrogation as she was. Time to walk. "You're trying to protect Nick? *From me?*"

"I'm glad somebody found a crack in the ol' shell," he said, following along, one of a pair of human bookends bracketing the prancing horse's head. "Just be careful how you poke around in there."

"I don't intend to . . ." She peered past True Colors' long face. "Aren't you the one who's poking around at the moment?"

"Sure, but you're the one who's trespassing here.

It's only right I should be asking you what you're up to."

"What I'm up to with Nick," she clarified. "Not quite the same as asking what I'm doing here."

"Yeah, it is. Unless you're researching a book or playing the slots, Indian country is flyover territory. *He's* the reason you're here."

"Because he brought me here. Because this is where he lives. *Because . . .*" She glared at him for emphasis. "I had no place else to go."

"Like I said, Nick allows very few people into his life beyond a certain point. If you've passed that point—I'm not askin' for any details, mind you, but I'm just sayin', whatever it is you're looking for . . ."

"A safe place," she assured him. "And only for a little while. And if I can, I want to find some way to be useful while I'm here."

"He'd kill me if he knew I was talking to you like this. I'm probably way out of line, but it wouldn't be the first time." A blessed moment of silence passed as they reached the fence. "You could tell him, you know," Nick suggested. "Whatever it is you're running from, you can trust Nick with it."

"It doesn't matter." She turned her back to the fence and began winding the lunge line carefully around her gloved palm in measured loops. "It really isn't . . . that important."

"See, now you're lying, and that's what I'm gettin' at. Whatever happened, whatever you've done, he's not gonna throw you out."

"I haven't done anything, and look at my face." She looked at him, giving him the total eyeful. "I don't want this happening to anyone else."

"Are you married?"

"No. And that's all I'm going to—"

"Wouldn't matter. Nick wouldn't care if it was a husband or boyfriend. I saw what he did to his sister's husband—now ex-husband—even when she begged him not to. You wanna beat up on women, you make sure they're not related to Nick Red Shield. Do you have any kids?" Dillon braced his back against the rail fence. "I asked you before, and you never answered. See, I've got kids. My kids were taken away from me. I know what it's like."

"You're guessing, and you have exactly zero to go on."

"I'm a blackjack dealer, Joey." He reached out to rub the Paint's cheek. "He's been good to you, hasn't he?"

"He's been very good to me."

"I'm askin' you to return the favor. He ain't half as tough as he makes out to be." Dillon shoved his hands into the front pockets of his jeans. "What happened to your kids? *Kid.* Which is it?"

"I take it you're the tough half of the partnership. Funny. Nick said you were the romantic."

"Romantic?" He gaped at her. "He really said that?"

"Said you'd do anything for love, including turning an old church building into a place for your family to come home to."

"He wouldn't say that. I haven't said what it's gonna be. Haven't decided yet. Too big for a house." Sun in his eyes, he squinted in the general direction of his white elephant. "Too hard to heat, too open. Too damn churchy."

She smiled, pleased with herself. She had his number. "Why did you buy it?"

"It was cheap." He shrugged. "Seemed a shame to tear it down. It was an Indian mission at one time, before the farmers moved in and built a town around it. There was a schoolhouse, too, but somebody else bought that. There were stories about one of the missionaries and how she tried to speak up for us Indians. Gotta love that. She was friends with Sitting Bull. She built the first YMCA in the Dakota Territory right here on Standing Rock."

"What's Standing Rock?"

"Standing Rock Indian Reservation. That's where we are." He laughed. "You don't even know where you are."

"I've been to South Dakota many times, but not this part."

"See? Flyover territory."

"All right, you got me there. But you did buy an old church building just because you fell in love with the history of it. You're definitely a romantic."

"It's not just the history. Hell, that ol' church is built to withstand a buffalo stampede."

"But you don't know what you're going to use it for."

"I've got some ideas. I don't like to tell anyone about my plans while they're still formulating."

"Cautious and coy," she teased. "Typical of the true romantic."

"No way. Charming, sure, but romantic? I don't believe Nick would say I was—"

"A hopeless romantic," Nick confirmed from behind the fence. Lauren and Dillon turned toward each other like a pair of interlocking gears and peered over the rails. "I said it. It's true."

"How does somebody as big as you manage to sneak up on a person like that?" Dillon asked as Nick scaled the fence.

"It's easy when the person loves the sound of his own voice as much as you do." Nick dropped to the ground. "This woman is tryin' hard to make herself useful, and you're out here bending her ear."

"Lemme see." Dillon made a pretense of examining Lauren's ear. "Don't look bent to me."

"We lunged twenty minutes," Lauren reported, handing Nick the coiled nylon line. "Somebody's obviously been working with him, Nick. He's ready and willing. If you'll give me the go-ahead, I'll set up a conditioning regimen for him."

"Conditioning for what?" Dillon asked.

"Takin' a run at those mares." Nick slid Lauren a pointed glance as he raked his fingers through the Paint's mane. "You got a harem to satisfy, you get yourself in top form before you show up at the gate."

161

"Well, sure." Dillon folded his arms and scowled at the horse. "But it sure wouldn't take me no twenty minutes."

9

The three of them had shared a moment, but Lauren had no idea where she'd stood with either of the men when it ended. Dillon made his suspicions abundantly clear, but at least he was friendly, while Nick did his best not to be. In the end, he'd walked away again, and she knew exactly which of her remarks had been the stinger. They'd all been smiling when Lauren offered to make Dillon something to eat before he went to work, tossing off easy regret that he'd missed out on the early supper at the Dew Drop Inn. Dillon shrugged it off, saying he never went hungry at the casino. And the smiles evaporated as Nick walked away with his horse.

He had work to do, he'd said, and he'd left her to squirm in the presence of Dillon's glib charm and perceptive misgivings. For all his efforts to keep to himself, Nick was easy to read, and unlike any man from her previous life, he had a giving nature. He couldn't help himself. He'd found her with nothing, and he had to provide. Even more imperative, he had to protect. All he asked was honesty. *Be straight with me.*

He asked too much.

At the very least, she could give him some space.

Over at the barn right about now, True Colors was probably getting an earful about female treachery. Lauren imagined herself as a fly on the wall. She would happily flit from the man's shoulder to the tip of the horse's ear and back again. Or become the mouse in his pocket or the cat in his hayloft—anything but the woman he'd left alone in the house.

The sun had set, but darkness had yet to set in. Spring daylight was wondrously stubborn on the high plains. But so was solitude. She turned on the TV for company, cutting into the middle of a news broadcast. "Missing is three-time Breeders' Cup-winning jockey Lauren Davis, whose car was found in the river after—"

She turned the volume down and huddled close to the speaker. Her picture appeared on the screen. It was an old one. She was wearing silks, and sported short blond hair and no bruises on her face. The old Lauren. The one who had taken time off "for personal reasons."

"—Vargas, owner of those horses and others ridden by Davis, said in a statement that Davis had been suffering from depression since the birth of their child, who is now in his father's custody."

Depression?

"—called off temporarily due to heavy rain."

Lauren snapped the TV off, turned and stared at the phone.

Don't call from here.

But she didn't know when she would get to a pay phone again.

And you don't know who's going to answer.

Jack was her only chance, and how much chance was that? How much leverage did she have with him?

There was a job not done, for one thing. She wasn't dead.

Blackmail?

How would a person go about blackmailing a henchman? She had to understand what was in his head, why he'd let her live. And she had to be right on the money. If he was capable of feeling anything, she had to know what it was. Sympathy? She needed more. Guilt? He needed more. Affection? In his dotage, maybe, and he was probably getting there. Old enough to be her father, and no family or friends to speak of. Loyalty to Vargas was all Jack knew. That and the two innocent lives assigned to his portfolio. She had to know whether she and Joey counted for anything with Jumbo Jack.

Which meant talking to him.

The first ring sent Lauren flying off the floor. She snatched the receiver on the next ring.

It was Dillon with a message for Nick. Irrational guilt prompted her to handle the call with extreme care, even going so far as to take notes. Dillon laughed when she asked him to repeat the highway number. He reminded her that there was only one.

She had just hung up when Nick walked in the door. New guilt. Or maybe just guilt hangover. Whatever it was, it showed. Nick looked at her expectantly, but he wasn't going to ask.

"Dillon called," she said quickly. Even the truth felt like a lie. "He said that some of the horses got out on the highway."

"Where?"

"He said he ran them back into the pasture, but he says the fence is down."

"Did he happen to say where?" he asked with exaggerated patience.

"Exactly three-quarters of a mile north of the bridge. He said it's hard to see from the road because it's in a low spot. There's a post rotted out, but the wire is still strung." She handed him her silly notes, jotted on the back of an envelope. "Wanted to make sure I had all the details."

"And Dillon gets points for running them in," he allowed, turning to go back out the door.

"So where are you going?"

"If they try it again, they could get hung up in barbed wire. Might as well take care of it now."

"In the dark?"

"Nope." He jacked his eyebrows, mocking her. "I've got headlights."

"How long will you be gone?"

"An hour, maybe." He nodded toward the TV, as though he'd decided to play host. "That thing only gets two channels, but it'll keep you company. And you can use the phone." On second thought, he flipped on the TV himself and handed her the remote. "There. Catch up on the world—"

She pressed the power button, quickly cutting off

the news. "I'd rather go with you."

"In the dark?" he mocked.

"With you." She grabbed her new jacket off the back of a kitchen chair. "If you don't mind my company."

"Guess I'm gettin' used to it," he allowed as he followed her out the door.

He was getting soft. He knew better, but he didn't seem to be doing much about it. Getting used to her company was just too damn easy, and there would surely be a price to pay down the road. For now, he had a fence to fix, had himself some company, and it was all good. He caught her watching his every move, caught himself feeling good about being the object of her attention, spotlighted by the headlight beams.

She stood close to him while he pounded a new post into the ground with the steel post driver. Almost in his way, but not so much that he couldn't deal with it. She could stay and ask her questions, oblige him to speak the answers, self-evident as they might be. He liked the sound of her voice. Maybe she liked his. Maybe it was no different from the racket the crickets were making in the darkness beyond their pool of light. It might be the same sound every night, one someone else wouldn't think bore repeating, but it wasn't a racket if you were a cricket.

The mares stood watch on the ridge above them. Hard to see them in the dark, but Nick knew they were there. He wondered how they compared notes as they watched him plug the hole they'd discovered. *Can we go now, Mama? Can we go now?* They were geared up for overdue spring grass, and the lead mare had to be planning her next move. *Just as soon as the man gets out of the way.*

"The days seem longer here," Joey was saying. "Even at night, it doesn't seem so dark. I like that." She dodged his elbow as he switched tools, trading the post driver for the wire stretcher she'd been tending for him. "I think I've turned into a big chicken."

"No surprise after what you've been through. Hell, we don't mind having a chicken on the place, long as it's just one. Otherwise, we don't—"

"—don't do chickens, I know. This is not a farm." She gave a nervous giggle. "Why did the chicken cross the road?"

"What chicken?"

"The one who's always crossing the road."

"It's the horses I don't want crossing the road. The chicken can build a nest in the passing lane and lay eggs for all I care."

"Work with me, Nick. I'm the big chicken."

"Then tell me." He cranked the handle on the wire stretcher. "Straight from the chicken's mouth."

"To find a place to hide."

"From . . . ?"

"From what was on the other side, which was—" she smiled when he looked up from his wire stretching "—the guy who does do chickens."

"I gotta meet this guy."

"What would you do?"

167

"Well, any guy mean enough to do a chicken—" he stepped back, eyeing the newly planted post and tightened wire for a moment before he slid her a sly glance "—guess I'd have to challenge his little cock to a pissing contest, huh?"

Pleased with himself for getting a real laugh out of her, he laid his gloved hand high on her back and guided her up the slope to the pickup, which would not be crossing the road just yet. Reluctant to put an end to the night's outing, he turned toward the ridge rather than the highway.

"Where are we going?"

"A place I didn't show you this morning."

The mares took the hint. They fled the headlights, following the fence line for several yards before turning suddenly like a school of fish and darting off into the darkness. The horses would take the short way, while the pickup would ply the long way. But all ways led to the river.

He had a favorite place. It was a piece of riverbank lined with scrub oaks and carpeted with tall grass. It wasn't a secret any more than anything else on the place was a secret, but it was a place he sought these days only in solitude. Pretty much the way he lived his life.

But not tonight. Tonight he was walking through his grass, underneath his trees, along the banks of his cresting river, with a woman. The sky was velvety and thickly dotted with stars, and the crescent moon lent the river a silvery cool sheen.

Like children rushing for choice seats, the horses had beaten them there and were already calmly grazing, as though there had been no escape, no chase. But their quick breaths made telltale steam. Nick had given Joey a flannel throw, which she carried at her waist over folded arms as she walked close to his side. When he asked, she said she wasn't cold and nothing more.

He stopped, laid his hand at the base of her neck and pointed across the water. "My great-grandfather's cabin stood over there."

"On the other side of the water?"

"Before they dammed up all the rivers out here, this water was much narrower. It's a tributary of the Missouri. The dam they put in south of here created all this backwater, mostly on Indian land. Drowned the trees that provided the firewood, the best home sites, the sweetest garden plots." Reaching over the water and into the night, he was mapping it out with his hand, like the Indian in the pictures, showing Lewis and Clark the way. "But it's been like this since I can remember, all fat and full, especially in the spring. We used to come here to swim when we were kids. It's not the best for fishing, but sometimes we'd catch bullheads and crappies."

"You and Dillon?"

"Whenever we could get away from the girls, this is where we'd come."

"The girls wouldn't leave you alone, huh?" She sidled in close, and he gathered her closer as she tipped her face up to him and smiled. "Must have been tough."

"Sisters. My two and Dillon's whole gaggle. We pretty much scared them off from swimming with stories of snapping turtles and water moccasins."

"Water moccasins don't live this far north. Do they?"

"Johnny swore he found a nest of them right down . . ." He caught himself and the curiosity in her eyes. "My little brother, John, he got to tag along. We'd come out here on horseback, meet up with some other friends sometimes. We built a raft one year. Good times."

"Good times," she echoed softly. "Would you go back?"

"And be a kid again? If I could pick one of those days I would."

"Just one day?"

"The days were longer then. The bad ones were endless, but on the days when everybody's cool and things are goin' right, man, when you're a kid you can turn bread into cake and water into honey."

"It sounds like you had a pretty glorious childhood. You and Dillon and all those sisters. And Johnny? Where's your brother now?"

"John's dead," he told her. He squeezed her shoulder, hoping she would get the message. *Not right now.* "How 'bout you? What was little Joey like?"

"Little." She shrugged. "I was a little girl when I stayed with my mother and a little tomboy around my

170

father. But I've always been little."

He wondered whether she'd always offered so little, or was it just him? And while he was wondering, she claimed his hand, placing hers against his, palm to palm. He slipped his fingers between hers and considered the weaving they made—dark alternating with light, rough with smooth, strong with slight. Slowly he bent his fingers and clamped them firmly over the back of her hand.

"Little Joey meets Big Indian. People stare." Oddly, the idea made him smile. "Strange pair."

"And how."

"I can make poetry, and you can talk Indian. *Hau.*" He chuckled as he lifted the blanket from her arm. "Hello, Joey. Who would name their girl Joey?"

"You would."

"You're not my girl. He shook the blanket open with one hand and draped it around her shoulders, bringing the ends together beneath her chin. "Did I name you?"

"Sort of." She rose on tiptoe. "Kiss me, and I'll be your girl."

He looked her in the eye. "For how long?"

"How long can you make a kiss last?"

Long enough to make her quit teasing. But he held back.

"Not long enough?" She stepped back, giving her head a little shake. "Then how about one of those perfect, endless days you were talking about? For that long. I don't think I ever had a day like that."

"We used to have them. Must have been before you

171

were born. I'm a lot older than you."

"In some ways, maybe. At least you got to be a kid for a while. I've had a very long adulthood."

"Can't tell by lookin' at you."

"What can you tell by looking at me?" She closed in again. "Look at me, Nick. Please, look at me and tell me what you really see."

"I see you. You're a beautiful woman." He touched her cheek. "Scared, hurt, feeling lost, don't know whether you're comin' or goin'. The one thing you must know for sure is that my eyes see a beautiful woman."

"I'm afraid to look in the mirror," she whispered. "It's not about the cuts and bruises. It's about . . . being all undone, you know? Coming apart in so many places. I'm scared I'll find big chunks of myself missing." She grabbed his hand. "How much is left, Nick?"

"More than you think."

"How do you know?"

"I know because I've been there. What's left is a body caught in a trap and a big pair of eyes lookin' for a way out." He drew her hand to his chest, tucked it against his shirt. "But your body is still beautiful. That's the only part I can tell by lookin' at you."

"And yours?"

"Mine never was."

"Are you willing to let me be the judge?"

"If this keeps up, you *will* judge. It won't matter whether I'm willing or not."

"You're the sweetest man I've ever known." She lifted her chin. "If I'm so beautiful, why won't you kiss me?"

He took his time, first pressing her hand to his lips before drawing it over his shoulder and taking her in his arms, all the while locking in on her eyes, searching for clues. He didn't care who she was right now, but he cared what she felt. He touched his lips to hers without pressing, and she opened them, willing to receive him. But still he took his time, tasting without consuming, nipping and sipping and helping himself to bits of her lips without betraying his hunger, until she lifted herself to him and gave herself through her lips. No longer did his time or his mouth or his breath exist. Everything was *theirs*.

Arms pulled; knees and tall grass cracked with their bending. They sank to the ground together, exchanging kisses on the way down. He lifted her onto his lap, thinking to cradle her, but she swung her leg over his hips and straddled him, taking his breath away. He wanted to do the same to her—kiss her too hard, hold her too tight, press her too close to allow for breath or thought or doubt to seep between them—but even as she took his hat and tossed it aside, he kept his head.

As long as she's giving, let her have her way. Let her back off when she's had enough. Don't scare her. Don't do anything to scare her.

Gently he caressed her strong back and her small bottom, moving her clothes without taking them away, reveling in the feel of his mouth against her perfect skin—her velvet earlobe, satin neck, the silk stretched over her collarbone. She tried to sneak her hand past his shirt collar and down the back of his neck, but he caught it, kissed it, slyly drew her hands to his sides. She leaned into him, her thighs cleaving to his hips like a rider preparing for a jump. A little elevation on his part and he would take her up and over.

If she would take him in.

He lifted his head, glimpsed the wet gleam of her parted lips and caught them with a kiss that drove every part of him and drew against her secrets. She countered with her tongue in his mouth and her hands at his back tugging at his shirt. He groaned and pulled them away, but the kissing went on as she reversed his hold, laced her fingers with his and pressed him. He gave in, allowed her to push him over. By the time he lay all the way back in the grass, she was laughing.

"Ride me, then. Where do you wanna go?" He rolled his hips, knocked his aching cock on the door between her legs. "Wanna go home? I'll take you home if you—"

She stopped laughing.

"I . . . don't . . . have . . . a home." She drummed each word into the ground with their clasped hands. "I don't," she whispered hotly. "I don't."

"Okay." He drew her down into his arms, and she stretched out her legs and slid down next to him. "Okay, Joey, okay."

"You said I could be your girl."

"Okay."

"You did say it, didn't you?"

"Probably." He pulled the forgotten blanket around her shoulders and tucked his free arm behind his head. "You've got me saying all kinds of crazy things."

"I know you don't trust me, Nick, and I don't blame you, but give me a chance to show you . . . that . . ."

"That what?"

"That having me here isn't such a bad thing."

If he spoke, he would say something foolish. It would be about having her, about the fact that he would like nothing more. Trusting her was another matter, but why bring it up? They were just two people hankering for a good fuck, which really didn't require too much . . .

"What happened to your brother, Nick?" she asked quietly. "Tell me what happened to Johnny."

Too much in the way of trust.

"It was an accident." He didn't know why he answered. It wasn't like him. It was even less like him to elaborate. "A fire."

"A fire," she whispered. "Oh, Nick, I'm so sorry."

"It was a long time ago."

"What kind of—"

"The bad kind. We were workin' in the oil fields, Dillon and my brother and me. Explosion on a rig."

"Were you there when it happened?"

"I was there."

"Was it—"

"It was a long time ago." He placed two fingers over

175

her lips. "You lost your home in a bad way. I lost my brother."

She slid her arm underneath his jacket and around his middle, and they held each other. For a long moment Nick lost himself in the stars overhead. Johnny wasn't lost. He had traveled the Wolf Trail—the Milky Way—the road to heaven. On nights like this Nick imagined reaching for the sky and finding John's hand in that river of stars. They didn't look like balls of fire from here. He'd survived a ball of fire, and it looked nothing like a star. Had he lived, John would surely be telling about it. Hell of a storyteller, that guy. He would have been thirty-five. Unbelievable. He would have had his own family by now. He would be tribal chairman or manager of one of the casinos. An artist, maybe, or a musician.

Joey would have liked him.

They might have been a pair of grouse cozying up in the grass for the night. Unconcerned with the nesting pair's presence, the horses went about the night's pleasant business, snatching mouthfuls of tall grass, spanking themselves with their tails, swishing and sliding, shadow through shadow. The new foal suckled, loud and sweet.

"I've been thinkin' about letting you earn your keep," Nick confided. "I was planning on putting True Colors with a trainer for a month or so. I had a guy in mind, but—"

She pushed herself up and hovered over him. "I can do it, Nick."

"I usually train my own horses, but I've never had one like this before. You seem to know—"

"*I do.* I know a lot about training and conditioning horses. Seriously, this is something I really can do."

"I figured you could be good for something." He pulled a piece of grass from her hair. "Besides making goofy pancakes."

"And following you everywhere you go."

"You start gettin' in the way, you can be sure I'll let you know."

Nick lay nude on his stomach, kitty-corner across bed sheets that smelled of smoke. Cigarettes and sage. Dillon's job and his romance with the past. Nick liked sleeping in his own bed—looked forward to it after being on the road for days and nights on end—but he'd given his bed away out of pure-D mortification. He knew the spare bed would smell like Dillon. He should have added in a stop at the Laundromat on the trip into town.

He liked his own bed, but the nude part felt strange. No one ever had his back. He kept it covered all by himself. He'd spent so damn many days and nights lying in a hospital bed on his stomach, just like this, with nothing touching his back except the Dragon Lady's evil fingers. They had put up a tent to protect his raw flesh from the outside world, but there was no keeping her away.

He'd made his peace with her, let her melt into him, agreed to carry her on his back for the rest of his life.

In return, she'd agreed to let up on him enough so that he could bear to go on living. With time, walking around in his fried hide had become less of a chore. Time and the family he'd driven back time and again. Family and the few friends his lifelong preference for solitude had permitted. Friends and the splendid four-legged creatures who didn't care what a man looked like as long as he wasn't bent on harming them.

But there would always be the Dragon Lady. He could feel her with his hands, but he never had to look at her, and he hardly ever did. He kept her covered. Nudity was reserved for the kind of Dakota summer heat that settled in and stayed heavy, even after the sun went down. Times like that, the Dragon Lady didn't want anything touching her. Other times, he kept her covered. It was part of their truce. Once the fire had gone out of her, she'd shriveled into a homely old thing that couldn't stand to let anyone stare at her. Privacy was a condition for any peace in his life.

But there in the dark he lay, back exposed, door ajar, brain abuzz.

What kind of person tempted fate this way? A masochist? An idiot? Maybe a character in one of Dillon's eternal fables or infernal history lessons. Whoever, whatever, Nick didn't know what he thought he was doing.

The hell he didn't.

Joey was still prowling around out there. They'd done the you-go-ahead, no, you-go-first, routine with the shower, but now that all that was done, she ought to be in bed. Nick's bed. Where he dearly wanted to be.

But first, maybe she would stop and tell him good-night. And if she did, she would push the door open. She would peek in and think he was sleeping, but she would come to him, anyway. She would see the way he was, *but she would come to him, anyway.* He would tell her to go away, but she wouldn't listen. He would warn her not to mess with the Dragon Lady, but nothing would scare her away.

Damn you, Red Shield, you're so funny, you forget to laugh.

She probably thought there was something wrong with him. The night was clear, the stars were perfectly aligned, and she'd given him all the right signals. He should have done what they'd both been dying for and then some. The hell with tricks, trust or Trojans, sometimes good judgment was nothing but a pain in the ass. And it was bound to hang on for days.

She had to be thinking there was something wrong with him.

And there was. But it had nothing to do with performance. Underneath his scarred hide, Nick was the real thing—not much for show, but he could sure perform when he got the chance.

Or took advantage of an opportunity.

Next time.

10

Nick could hear his sisters coming from *tona* miles away. Once upon a time, it had been their little-girl voices. Nowadays, the noise was always motorized. Both of them went through used cars like most people changed socks. At any given time there was usually only one functioning vehicle between them, and today Louise was driving.

"For a quiet woman, you sure have one loud tailpipe," Nick teased his sister as she emerged from next month's trade-in. She'd parked it dead center in the gravel driveway, letting him know that he could put anything he was thinking of doing on hold for now. The girls would have their due.

"Too much beans in her Indian tacos," their younger sister Bernadette said. She was the little one with the big mouth and the parade of kids. "And you, my brother, have a funny way of keeping your promises to your nephews," Bernadette scolded while she unloaded the two ambulatory kids from the car. "You told Tony he'd be the first to see this super horse you were getting, and he marked it on the calendar when you'd be coming back. You've been back how many days?"

"It took me a little longer—" He greeted his nephew with the handshake due every visitor. "Hey, cowboy, what's up?"

"Is he here yet, Uncle?"

"He sure is."

"When is Dillon gonna stop scraping that church and get to painting?" Bernadette planted fists on ample hips and gave Dillon's eternal project a disdainful once-over. "He's been scraping on that thing for, what, two years? Pretty soon he'll be scraping through to the studs."

"It keeps him out of trouble," Nick said. "You kids want some pop?"

"We came to see your new horse. Can we ride him?" the one they called Bubbles wanted to know.

Another child's voice in the back seat of the car drew Nick's attention, but all he could see was an ample butt on toothpick legs in stretch pants. "Louise! What are you doing to my namesake?"

"It's the buckle on that old car seat," Bernadette explained. "I need a new one. They say those things go bad after a while. Even if you haven't wrecked, which I haven't. Only barely bumped that one farmer's truck that time backing out of the post office."

"So that car seat's been through one run-in with a farmer and how many kids?"

"Four. Five? But they weren't all mine. To boot, my car died, but I'm getting a bigger vehicle pretty soon."

"Bigger?" The childless sister backed out of the car with her arms full of fussy baby. "Are you pregnant again?"

"No, but I've gotta be able to fit two car seats plus

181

all the rest. Tony was fussing to come out here, and Bubbles had to go to the clinic, so I had to leave Bernie and John with Tina because I couldn't fit them all in."

"You think you've got enough brothers and sisters, Nicky?" Nick took the baby from his sister and settled him on his hip. "You wanna see what your uncle brought back from Colorado?"

They were on their way to the barn, Nick leading the way with Tony at his side, keeping pace like a jumping bean. "I can ride him, can't I, Uncle?"

"No, but you can take turns on Rusty."

"But I wanna ride the super horse."

"We have to get to know him a lot better before we can trust him that much." Who'd come up with *super horse?* Had he said that? "We know Rusty, and we know he'll take care of you."

"I can take care of myself," Tony grumbled.

"Who's the woman?"

Bernadette couldn't have caught more than half a second's glance at Joey through the open barn door, but she had an eagle eye, that girl.

"She's . . ." The sisters gaped at him, hungry for a shocker. "She's my new trainer."

Both faces fell.

"You've got a trainer?" Louise was quietly amazed.

Bernadette wasn't buying. "So who was your *old* trainer?"

"Eddie Arcaro," Nick deadpanned.

"He was a jockey."

182

"It was the only name I could come up with. Hey, Joey, can you name me a famous trainer?" She appeared again, pausing in the doorway, and he gave an invitational nod. "Actually, Joey's father was a famous trainer, but the name escapes me. Joey, meet my sisters, Louise and Bernadette," he said, indicating each one with the customary jerk of his chin. "And Tony, who came to see his uncle's new horse. And the cheeky one over there, we call her Bubbles. I can't remember if that's her real name or—"

"It's Barbara Ann," the little girl said.

Bernadette snorted. "If you wasn't gone so much, you'd be able to—"

"Every time I see her, she's added another one to the brood." Nick shifted the baby for Joey's inspection. "This handsome fellow is Nicholas."

Joey greeted each one in turn, but the baby quickly claimed her full attention. She pulled the leg of his miniature blue jeans down, smoothed and patted. "How old are you, little one?"

"Nicky's one year and one month," Bubbles reported as the baby, taking equal interest, reached for Joey. Her eyes lit up as though she'd been asked to dance. She offered open hands, nodding eagerly, and little Nicky went to her as if they'd been friends for life.

"He likes everybody," Bubbles said. "But watch out. He leaks. And he pulls hair."

"And he's almost as big as she is, brother. Bubbles, you take—"

"Oh, no, please." Joey bounced the big boy on her hip while he angled for the bill of her cap. "Yes, he likes my hat. Don't you, Nicky? I borrowed your uncle Nick's hat. Let's see how it looks on you. Oops." Nicky's mop of black hair and half his face disappeared beneath the cap. Laughing, Joey adjusted it. "There. It's big for me, too. I have it on the tightest notch."

"He just wants to get at your hair."

"And once he gets hold of a handful . . ."

"Hair's too much fun, isn't it, Nicky? Such a big boy," she cooed. "Are you walking yet?"

"Trying, but he's too fat," Bubbles said.

"Tony!" Bernadette aimed her command toward the corral fence, which her five-year-old had decided to scale. "That's a stud horse. You don't go in there without Uncle."

Stripped of one charge and duly reminded of the other, Nick headed for the corral as the Paint poked his nose between the rails to see what the boy might be offering besides fingers.

"Joey's the one who can really show him off," he told the group. "He's broke better than I thought, and, man, can he run. E'en it, Joey?"

"True Colors is amazing. He really is." Making baby talk with his namesake, Joey hardly spared Nick a glance. "You wanna ride the horsey, big boy? Or walk first? We have to learn to walk first, huh?"

"Where're you from, Joey?" Bernadette asked.

"Nick brought me up here from Missouri."

184

"Sort of a package deal," Nick supplied. "Brought them back together, horse and trainer."

"She staying in town?" Bernadette persisted.

"We were listening to Bobby Big Eagle's radio show on the way over." Louise flashed a shy smile. "He wants people to call in with news tips."

"You girls're killin' me," Nick said, chuckling as he slid the bolt on the corral gate. "You wanna throw a saddle on him, Joey? Give my sisters their news flash."

"You go ahead, Nick," she said. "I just worked him out, rubbed him down, the whole bit. It's your turn."

Bernadette offered to take the baby.

"No, please go ahead. I'll watch Nicky for you."

Nick rested his chin on his arm, casting a furtive backward glance while he held the narrow corral gate open for the family parade. Bent over with a baby hand fastened to each of her thumbs, Joey was already testing little Nicky's progress on two legs. Nick didn't want to move. He wanted to hang on the gate and watch her, the better to learn her. But he had family to attend to.

They all trooped into the corral behind him. Nick put Louise in charge of the box of horse treats after he gave Tony and Bubbles two apiece, the better to make friends with the stallion. The sisters acknowledged his beauty—*eeez,* said one, and *ahhh* said the other—but neither of them had ridden a horse since she was in grade school, and then rarely. Once every Indian kid's birthright, horses were disappearing from reservation life. Nick meant to do his part to keep his sister's children interested, but he'd been busy lately.

Hell, he'd been putting them off. Old habits were hard to break. His sisters knew about his plans, and they never called him crazy when he said he was going to bring the Indian pony back. And not just any Indian pony. Lakota stock. The children would hear the stories and know that not only were the Red Shields Sitting Bull's descendants, but their horses came from his horses. These were the details that lived in growing minds, along with size and beauty and speed.

They should see how this horse could run.

But a quick peek past the corral rails gained him no glimpse of his horse trainer. He shook his head. Women and babies. *Put a baby in a woman's hands and she forgets everything else she signed on for.*

"Your sister and me, we agree," Bernadette buzzed in his ear as he took a seat beside her on a homemade feed bunk. He questioned her with a look. "It's good to see you taking an interest in a woman."

"You think I don't have any interest in women?"

"Not since that Kay Mart woman."

"Her name was Kay Martin, and I barely saw her a few times before you two drove her off with all your snooping around, checkin' up with your friends at Turtle Mountain."

"And we found out about her steppin' out on you," his sister reminded him. Keeping an eye on the children and an ear on the adults, Louise nodded surreptitiously. She stood three feet away and didn't say much, but neither did she miss a word.

"She was just a friend," Nick said. "I didn't have that much time for her. Hell, I'm a busy man, and women are a lot of work."

"This one you brought here looks pretty young."

"And white," Louise said quietly.

"She's *really* white. Way young, and too skinny. More like Dillon's type," Bernadette said. "Looks like the wind blew her into a wall or something. Did she get into a fight?"

Nick leaned forward, braced his arms over his knees and shook his head.

"She's really a horse trainer?"

"See why I don't come around that much? You two girls, you're one big wind." He lifted his chin, squinting into the sun. "Lou, I'm counting on you to put a sock in this one so none of this discussion or your speculation gets back to Joey. She's having a rough time, and I'm helping her out. End of story."

"I'll ride Rusty. Uncle?" Nick turned to connect with Tony, who was standing at his elbow. "I said *okay*. I'll ride Rusty."

"Me, too," Bubbles said.

"You'll have to ride double, then."

"I get the saddle," Tony said. "You gotta ride behind me."

"Quit your bossing. You can each have a turn in front." Nick pushed to his feet. "It's all about keeping the peace between brothers and sisters."

"Uncle's right. No bossing," Bernadette ordered.

"Or meddling," Nick added, eyeing the children's mother.

"Don't worry. We've given up looking for a woman for you. As long as she's nice and you like her, we're not gonna mess anything up for you, brother."

"Besides," Louise added coyly, "we don't have any informants in Missouri."

Dillon woke up slowly from a peaceful day's sleep in the rudimentary loft he'd created in his church, the beginning of an ever-changing plan for a place to live and dream. He dreamed big, and because he also dreamed often, he didn't object to an awakening, as long as it wasn't overly rude. And this one wasn't, not really. After all, he was the one who had left the front door open. But he'd only meant to invite the spring breeze inside.

He rolled to his side and braced himself on one arm. It was Joey, wandering into what she no doubt took for an empty building and a source of entertainment for her charge. He gathered her latest assignment must be baby-sitting. The baby had to be one of Bernadette's kids. At that age, they all looked alike to everyone but the parents.

He opened his mouth to speak, but then closed it in deference to the winning sound of woman conversing with a baby as though she were having a two-way exchange. Perched on his mattress and still half asleep, Dillon fancied himself a bit of bric-a-brac on a shelf. Better yet, the casino's security camera, the "eye in the sky." He would keep quiet—no evil could be found in this sweet little scene—enjoy the view and leave them to their play. They'd already discovered the workbench stool with the swivel seat and caster feet.

"I won't let it get away from you, sweetie. Oh, big boy, look at you, walking it across the floor. Oops!" She tucked the stool between her legs and pulled the boy onto her lap. "Here, let's take a ride. Isn't this a fun car?"

Not too fast, Joey, that thing can get away from you.

But she spun and rolled into the wall, pushed on the wall and spun around again, filling the rafters with the kind of baby giggles Dillon couldn't think of cutting short. Finding a spy on the wall—now that would be a rude awakening.

"Your uncle Dillon has some really cool stuff here, huh? What's that?" Back on the floor, the baby had discovered a block of wood. "Another car? Oh, look, Joey, here's a whole bunch of blocks. We could build a house."

Joey?

"I mean Nicky. I'm sorry. Watch, here's one for you, and one for . . ."

Dillon tuned in with new interest in the woman sitting cross-legged next to a box of scrap wood. She chattered away as she and the baby took turns stacking discarded end pieces like play blocks—two-by-fours and four-by-fours that Dillon had indeed cut up and saved with just such a thought in mind. Had he heard her right? He listened closely for another slip, but it was only "sweetie" this and "big boy" that.

Suddenly the baby grabbed the woman's blouse and gave a mighty tug.

"Uh-oh. You're hungry, huh? You're still nursing? I'm sorry, honey, but I'm not . . ." Head down, watching, she did nothing to stop the tugging, nothing to back up her feeble protests. "I can't. I wish I could, but it's not . . . my faucet doesn't work anymore."

No surprise, Dillon thought. He'd had her pegged all along for a young mother. He didn't want to think about what might have happened to her child. She'd had some trouble, no doubt about that. Again he started to declare his presence, but the baby's actions tied a quick knot in his tongue. It was little Nicky, all right—the one who saw his mother's blouse as a refrigerator door. He'd drawn a bead on a tit and wasn't taking no for an answer.

"I hate to disappoint you," she whispered, but she wasn't resisting. Her shoulders, arms, hands, molded into a soft shell around the baby, cradling him against her as though they did this together every day. She tipped her head back, eyes closed, and chanted, "I really, really hate to . . . I'm sorry, Joey. I'm so sorry . . . so sorry . . . so . . ."

The baby didn't seem sorry.

But Dillon was. He couldn't take his eyes off the amazing sight, couldn't speak, couldn't forgive himself for not speaking. If he had any manners, he would duck. Now.

Too late. He was looking straight into a tearful pair of blue eyes, and all he could think was, *Nick would kill me if he walked in right now.*

He couldn't tell what the woman was thinking. At first she only stared; nothing moving but the tears silently slipping down her cheeks. But then her shoulders began to tremble, and she shook her head slowly, methodically, a strange spark igniting her eyes.

"You're not taking him."

"Okay," Dillon said quietly. He'd seen that look. He'd heard those words. He knew that state of mind. More like chaos of mind. Without losing eye contact, he found the top of the ladder and quickly made his way from sleeping platform to main floor on stockinged feet.

"You can't take him away," she said, voice on the rise, arms clutching for dear life. But it wasn't this baby's dear life. It was someone else, somewhere else.

This woman was someone else. And Dillon, for just a moment, was somewhere else, trying to talk another wretched soul into letting go. He closed his eyes and shook off the memory as he knelt beside her.

"He needs me" came the raspy claim, and from the sound of enthusiastic sucking, on that count she wasn't too far off.

"Joey, it's okay. Nobody's taking anybody." A juicy smack signaled the release of suction. Dillon glanced down at two big brown eyes and one distended pink

191

tit. He wasn't asking, and the baby wasn't telling. He averted his own crazy-curious eyes, but he managed to sound pretty calm. "Look. He's all finished. Looks like he enjoyed himself, too." *The little scrounger.* "Didn't you, Nicky? His mom named him after Nick. Kinda looks like his uncle Nick, doesn't he?"

"Nick?"

"Yeah, Nick." The name seemed to bring the woman to her senses, her eyes into focus. Dillon craned his neck and scanned window to window. "You don't want him to see you like this, do you?"

"Nicky?"

"Baby Nicky. Nick's little nephew. He's a cutie, huh?"

"He is." Still clutching the boy close, she took a swipe at her tears with her free hand. "He really is. We were just playing."

"I know. I didn't mean to . . ." He pointed to the loft. "I was up there sleeping. That's where I sleep whenever . . ."

"Because it's quiet here." She gave a tight-lipped nod. The baby was beginning to squirm. "I'm sorry. I didn't think there was anyone . . ."

The sound of voices outside startled them both.

"It's Nick. Please don't—"

"It's okay." Dillon gave her a pointed look. "Better button up."

"Joey?"

Dillon stood quickly and stepped between the woman on the floor and the search party. He knew damn well he was wearing guilt on his face like tomato paste, and for what? Being out of his . . . boots?

Nobody moved while Nick took visual account of every detail before assuming the jealous lover's tone.

"What's going on?"

"Nothing," Dillon said calmly. "They just came in here to play. Joey thought the place was empty."

"I'm sorry I woke you up," said the woman on the floor behind him.

Wordlessly, Bernadette stepped in and reached for her baby. For a moment, Dillon wasn't sure the woman who called herself Joey would give him up. Her breasts were covered, but her tears were unmistakable.

"Now look what you did," Bernadette crooned to her boy, who was vacating a dark wet patch of denim in Joey's lap. "This lady's a trainer, and you are sooo not trained, little Nicky. I'm sorry about that."

"I should have seen it coming," Joey whispered. Dillon turned to offer her a hand, but Nick was there first. She looked up at him, all sad-eyed and wounded, and Dillon didn't know what to think.

Bubbles broke the silence. "I told you he was leaky."

"We'll be getting along now," Bernadette said. "It was nice meeting you. You want me to take those jeans and throw them in the wash? I know these guys don't have a washing machine on the place."

"I still have chores to do today. A little diaper leakage only adds spice to the mix." Joey drew a deep breath, now studiously avoiding both men's eyes. "And since I'm on my way back to the barn, I'll walk out with you. We hardly got a chance to talk. Did you kids have a good ride? What did you think of True Colors?"

She had pulled herself together with amazing ease. In his stockinged feet, Dillon was unable to do the thing he most wanted, which was follow the crowd. And he knew Nick wasn't going anywhere. When the women and children were gone, Dillon was going to have to face up to the Man. And he hadn't even done anything.

"What happened?"

Dillon stared at the door, shaking his head. "I'm not sure."

"What do you mean, you're not sure? Why was she crying?"

"Nick, I'm tellin' you, that woman's got . . ." Dillon gestured—door, Nick, door again. "You don't wanna get yourself . . . she's seriously . . ."

Nick was still waiting.

"I didn't do nothin' to her, if that's what you're thinkin'." Dillon sighed. What was he supposed to say? "She came in here with the baby, didn't know I was . . ." *Draw him a diagram.* "I was up there sleeping. She was down here playing with the baby. That's it. That's . . . I swear to God."

"I'm not accusing you of anything." But Nick stared long enough to extract a confession if there was one to be made. Finally he lifted one shoulder. "I figured you must've said something to her."

"Like what?"

"Like maybe you don't like the idea of her staying here. Maybe you accused her of something, made her feel bad."

"I don't know anything about her, Nick." The roar of a car engine drew their notice, and they exchanged glances. *Women.* Dillon raised his brow as the tell-tailpipe beat its raucous retreat. "Except her name sure ain't Joey."

"I don't care what her name is."

"Me, neither," Dillon said quickly. "Names don't mean much. Especially white people's names. Smith, Anderson, Jones—you run into a hundred of 'em, same name, none of 'em related."

"You forgot about *Black.*"

Dillon chuckled. "My great-grandfather's name was Black Bear Runs Him. I'm thinking of claimin' the whole thing back again. Maybe in Lakota."

Nick wandered over to the window nearest the driveway, halting several feet away with a scrape of his boot heel. She couldn't see him, but they could both see her headed for the trailer house and not the barn.

"Why won't she tell me her name?"

"In the old days, everyone had a secret name. It was between you and *Tunkasila.* If you told it around, the name lost its power." Although Dillon didn't think this was true for women, it sounded good. He was reaching, but what was a partner for? "She came to

195

you with little to show for herself except a big fear and a big loss."

"She knows I won't hurt her."

"She needs to keep some kind of power to herself right now. They say knowledge is power. Maybe just knowing who she is might be too much power for her to give away. It might be all she's got."

Nick turned away from the window, maybe taking some kind of comfort from Dillon's words, or at least his presence. He gave half a smile. "You scare me sometimes."

"When?"

"Times when you talk like that and it starts to make sense." He shook his head. "I don't have a secret name. How 'bout you?

"Hell, all my best secrets became scandals a long time ago."

"They did? Where was I?"

"You had my back, just like always." Dillon nodded toward the trailer house. "Now you've got hers."

Nick folded his arms and stared out the window again, this time at the barn. "How would you feel about racing True Colors?"

"Me?"

"Us."

Horse racing? *Nick?*

"He's your horse."

"You're my partner. It's not gonna happen unless we both agree."

Dillon grinned. "What's the one thing that sets a

196

man apart from a dumb beast? It's the courage—"

"—to take a chance," Nick recited. It was a maxim they'd used on each other more times than either could count.

But horse racing? Dillon had thought *he* was supposed to be the dreamer in this outfit.

He clapped a hand on Nick's broad shoulder. "Welcome to the dark side, man."

11

Nick found his mysterious guest sitting on the floor beneath the wall phone, hugging her knees, the John Deere cap dangling from her fingers. Like a big-eyed child wary of a scolding, she watched him every step of the way as he crossed the warped brown linoleum from back door to boxy kitchen. He washed his hands, drank some water from a coffee mug, peered through the unadorned window at an unclouded sky, all the while trying to come up with something to say. It was no good asking. That much he knew.

He'd begun to worry that at some point she might decide to give him the answers he no longer really wanted. All too often, truth was a bitch. Whatever it was in this case, sooner or later truth would take her away—which would have been fine just a few days ago. How long had she been with him now? Less than a week, and he'd let himself get all tied up inside over something that made no sense. But the reason it made no sense was because he was tied up over it. The truth about Joey was none of his business.

Believe it, he told himself, *and keep it simple on your end. The only truth is what you see for yourself, what you do and the way you do it. That's it. The rest is only talk.*

When he turned to her again, she stood slowly, as though he'd summoned her. "I was just about to . . ." She made a futile gesture toward the phone.

"Go ahead. I'll leave you alone if you want."

"I don't. It's the stupidest thing I could do right now." She took a step closer. "I don't know what happened to me, Nick. You must think I'm crazy. Dillon must think—"

"He's okay with racing True Colors," he said quickly. He noticed the change in her expression right away, the vacancy beginning to fill. "I mean, trying him out. Says he'll go with my decision, but if he's got real *cante*—you know, heart—seems like we oughta give it a shot with you here." He lifted one shoulder. "As long as you're gonna be here, anyway."

"Give me a few days with him. That plowed field is a pretty good place to work him, but if there's a track close by, I'd like to run him against a stopwatch." Her passion swelling as the plan grew, she touched his arm. "I won't waste your money."

"What do you charge?"

"Not me, but all the other fees that have to be considered. You can easily afford me, Nick. I don't eat much."

198

He wasn't worried so much about his bank account as about the fact that sooner or later she would make that call, and he wasn't sure what he would do when the sonuvabitch showed up at his door, looking to take her back. He'd seen it before, good women like his sister letting love get the best of them, suck them dry, then leave them feeling ugly and ashamed. Louise was doing fine on her own, but there had been a time when she'd needed more convincing than Nick could stomach. She'd gone to the phone, gone to the door, offered the friggin' parasite more chances.

Okay, so he *did* know what he would do. He'd done it before. *The only truth is what you see, what you do and the way you do it.* And he would do it again.

"Did Nicky tear out a chunk of your hair or something?" He wanted to brush a stray lock back from her face, just for an excuse to touch her. He tried a smile instead. "Last time they brought that little rascal over, I gave him a ride on my shoulders, and he got two little handfuls off me. I didn't cry, but I came damn close." She glanced away. He knew he'd hit a nerve. "You okay?"

She shook her head in a way that said it hurt to move. "Could you just hold me for a minute?"

He drew her into his arms, held her against his chest and imagined her being his to keep. Anybody came for her right now, he knew exactly what he would do. When the door opened, he turned his head and gave his unsuspecting partner a look that left no doubt.

Dillon nodded, backed out and closed the door without saying a word.

Far be it from him to interfere unless he wanted to sacrifice a few body parts, Dillon thought. Which he did not. Better to get a cold drink from the garden hose than try ribbing or ragging his way into the kitchen past *that* thoroughly astounding little scene. It had been too long since Nick had let a woman into his life, and he was guarding this one like a pit bull. It was no use warning him about the boatload of baggage she was carrying. As far as Nick was concerned, all she had to her fictitious name were the clothes on her back.

She also had a kid somewhere, a detail Dillon would happily file under *none of my concern* if he didn't foresee this thing biting his partner squarely in the ass very soon. Any other detail but a matter of the heart. Any other heart but Nick's. He wished he didn't have to know so damn much, but everybody had their gifts. Dillon knew women, and the look on that woman's face had been unmistakable. She was no wet nurse. She'd had a baby, and she'd lost it somehow. Death was the obvious guess, but Dillon wasn't ready to place any bets.

He headed for the barn, where the water from the pump would be cold, if nothing else. He still had time to ride out to the south pasture and fix the leak on that stock tank before he got ready for work. Leave Nick alone with the woman for a while, he thought. Maybe he was getting something out of her.

She would have Dillon's full sympathy along with Nick's—if it was just her. But suddenly Nick was doing the unthinkable, dropping vital bits of his hard-earned body armor at her feet. What would stop her from reaching into his chest and tearing the man's heart out? Once exposed, Nick wasn't much of a defensive player. Dillon knew Nick, and the signs were clear. His partner was one lovesick puppy.

Yup, Dillon wished he didn't have to know so damn much.

He wished he didn't have to remember any of what all his damn knowledge had cost him. And the people he loved . . .

The army had prepared Nick for the kind of work that was left to be had in the Western oil fields. The boom in the late seventies and early eighties had long been busted. The drop in foreign oil prices had put the cap on countless wells, but with enough activity left and a few new friends, Nick had found work with a drilling contractor when his hitch was up. And because jobs at home were tight, Dillon had laid claim to Nick's shirttail. But when Nick's little brother, Johnny, decided that his time had come, Dillon had his doubts. Not that he didn't think of John as a brother, too, but Nick hadn't been around for a while, and Dillon had.

Johnny Red Shield was twenty going on twelve. He was the kid who would perform an Olympic-caliber swan dive off a tree branch without checking the depth of the water first. On one occasion Dillon had fished him out of the river and later teased him about the gallons of water and the number of minnows he'd coughed up. Nobody ever faulted Johnny for the way any escapade turned out. He was too damn lovable. Johnny was the kid you never left behind when you went on a party, even though you knew you would have to carry him home. He was the one who got the girls. He was the one who had the bottle rockets or the weed or the keys to somebody's car.

But Nick hardly knew the twenty-year-old Johnny. He remembered the kid brother who was everybody's pet, back when calling John a roughneck was all in fun. The three of them had shared some good times when Nick was home on leave, but those times were like holidays. To really appreciate the day-to-day Johnny . . . well, you had to be there. Nick had been there until he wasn't. His parents were still around back then, and they'd expected Nick back in the fold. Time in the military was for going, doing and bringing home the tales. Nick had kept order in the household before, and he would surely return to restore it.

But Nick had other ideas. He couldn't help his family without making a life for himself—a job that required, well, a job. Starting out as a roughneck, he soon picked up more specialized rig-crew skills, a truck driver's license, considerable respect and connections with operators and contractors throughout the area. He'd saved Dillon's newlywed bacon by setting him up with the contractor, but he hadn't known what he was in for when he'd said, *Come on out, Johnny-boy. I'll train you myself.*

If John was the family favorite, Nick was the hero. If anyone could provide, decide, protect, redeem or rescue, it was Nick. Roughnecking was hard and often dangerous work, but jobs of any kind were tough to find on the reservation. You get one shot on my say-so, he'd told Dillon. Learn your job, do it well, and you can support a family. He'd given John the same advice. One shot, he'd said. No screwing around.

What Nick didn't understand was that screwing around was Johnny's stock in trade. Dillon's misgivings about John strained his relationship with Nick. Give the kid a break, Nick would say, even though he never took any breaks for himself. He brought his sister out to Montana close on John's heels, put her in school, then enrolled in a class on his day off. But John was allowed to "work into a routine." One shot became three and then five. The slack was never cut; it was stretched thin and made light. Too easy, Dillon had said, and he'd been wrong about that. Dead wrong. He would never forget his last quarrel with John.

Nick will always be the brother you want and the one I've got.

Maybe he was right. God knew Dillon had enough problems of his own without worrying about what was going on next door. His strong-minded wife was threatening to "move back to civilization," where she could deliver what would have been their second child "by a doctor who knew the difference between a woman and a ewe." Nick was trying to drive a truck part-time, attend college part-time, work in the field full-time and keep two female housemates—his sister and his girlfriend—from killing each other at any given time. Johnny was barely hanging on to his job, sleeping on Nick's sofa and enjoying life when he wasn't hungover.

Nobody ever talked about John's condition the night of the fire. According to Bernadette, John had claimed to be sick, said he wasn't going to work. He wasn't staying home, Nick had told him. He was getting in the truck. John's sofa time was over. Nick would take him to work or the bus station.

John was in no mood to go Greyhound.

Monica was due any day, and she was miserable. Dillon was trying to get home early when John showed up for his shift on the same rig. Nick wasn't scheduled to work that night, but he'd offered to finish out Dillon's shift. Or at least Dillon chose to recall it as an offer, but maybe he'd asked. Or hinted, or complained about what was going on at home. He remembered feeling slightly queasy when Nick had clocked in. Johnny was hanging back looking sulky and green around the gills. Nick was pissed. The vibes were bad all around. It was no time for Dillon to press his momentary edge over Johnny to squeeze out a favor, but he'd done it. No question now. John would pull his shift because Nick would see to it.

And Dillon was outta there.

He'd tried to breathe easy after leaving the field. Hell, Nick was the one who'd brought the kids out there. Dillon was a family man. He was making his own way. He was highway- and homeward-bound when he heard the explosion. John's face flashed in his mind like a slide projected on a screen. Something told him Johnny was a dead man.

Fire and smoke filled the night sky. The stench of oil aflame seared Dillon's nose and sickened his stomach. His pulse skated on the screams of a dozen different sirens, and there was no real thought given to what he would find or what he could do. It was all Nick, Johnny, drive and run.

Heat, smoke and flame consumed the night. Soot-covered men dashed around like ants. Directions meant little in all the noise and confusion. Questions meant less.

"Which rig is it?" Dillon shouted into one face. "Have you seen Nick Red Shield?" he spat into another. He grabbed an arm. "John? Johnny Red Shield?"

He found them at the core of a knot of paramedics who were trying to pry John's body from his brother's intractable embrace. Both men were tattered and charred. John flopped like a rag doll draped in the arms of a would-be animator, while there was monster life in Nick's eyes and ungodly voice in his throat. With the whole world on fire, Nick's rage ruled. His own pain was unthinkable, his injuries so hideous even trained eyes betrayed their shock. But he stood tall and kept them all at bay in that horrible splinter of eternity that eventually became, simply, the night Johnny died.

Dillon doubted Nick remembered much of it. But he had no way of knowing for sure beyond his personal belief in a merciful God.

It was hard enough for Dillon to live with the memory. Monica had lost the baby. Nick had lost a big chunk of his life. Years later, Dillon had lost Monica and everything that went with her, including the two children—their daughter and the son they'd made while they were trying to hang on to their life together. Some people tried too hard; some didn't try hard enough. Either way, *trying* didn't seem to count for much in the final tally. The only way to get by was to adopt a life-goes-on philosophy and maybe convince the kids to get an education. "Nobody loves a roughneck," Dillon would say to them. He was pretty sure they had no idea what he was talking about, but they always humored him. "Yeah, Dad, we know."

But Nick had gone too quiet. He had spent too much time alone. He never turned family away, but he seldom sought anyone out. He had been the only sur-vivor from the five-man rig crew, and he never talked about it. Never mentioned luck, bad or good, his or Dillon's. Never said he regretted surviving, but Dillon wondered sometimes, the way he kept it all in. He was present, but he was untouchable.

Nick will always be the brother you want and the one I've got.

So what? Dillon wanted the answer now as much as he had then. They treated each other like brothers. Always had, according to Dillon's way of thinking. The doing mattered more than the being, but since John no longer *was* and could, therefore, no longer do, Dillon often wondered which brother the boy had carried to his grave—the one Dillon wanted or the one John had?

And how much of Nick had survived *the night John died*?

"You're playin' in the water again."

Dillon turned to find Nick peering at him through the barn door, halter and lead looped in his gloved hand. Always doing something, that guy.

"Tank was low."

"I just filled it this morning," Nick said.

"*My* tank."

With a quick slice of his hand, Dillon sent a sheet of water toward a crow dropping in for a landing on the tank rim. The bird flapped, squawked and sent him away from his stock-tank reflections with a wistful smile. "We should get one of those automatic horse waterers. Kinda like a drinking fountain."

"We can work with what we've got." Good ol' straight-answer Nick. "I was thinkin' we'd take the stud out to the rodeo grounds and let Joey try him out on the track. You wanna go?" He offered the invitation quietly, without looking up from the project he was

207

making of reversing a twist in the nylon lead. "If you have some time."

What? Dillon was about to be included? Sure, they'd had a little talk. Not exactly a heart-to-heart, and no indication that Nick believed he hadn't done something to make her cry or act crazy. The new limitations on Dillon's welcome were pretty clear, especially around the woman.

"When were you thinking?" More touched by the gesture than he wanted to be, Dillon opted for sarcasm. "I can't make any promises until I check my calendar, but I can sure pencil you guys in." He scribbled a couple of loops in the air and added a punctuation mark. "You gave this Missouri woman full access, and haven't even let me touch him yet, man."

"The stud? Hell, I just barely got him home. Nobody's stopping you from trying him out, especially now that Joey's already started—"

"See, that's what I'm talkin' about. You're all about *Joey* all of sudden. Take it easy, man." Dillon laid a hand on Nick's shoulder. "It isn't like you to go stickin' your neck out like this."

"I've been saying all along, if we're going to make it in this business, we need a stud that's a proven winner."

"I'm not talking about taking a chance on the horse." Dillon took a step back, and his hand fell away. "Okay, what do I know? I know what you're thinkin', man. I married a woman who came from another planet, and look what happened. She hopped the next space shuttle, back to where she came from. But she never tried to pass herself off as anything but an alien. This one you're mixed up with, Nick, I'm just sayin' . . ."

Nick snorted. "Man, you're worse than my sisters."

"I'm just sayin', it's one thing to pick up a stray cat, but this ain't no animal somebody left on the road. This is a pretty mysterious woman. Pretty and mysterious. You're thinkin', kinda makes her interesting. I'm thinkin', kinda makes her dangerous. Because you don't know who she is, and you don't know where she's been or who her people are. I'm just sayin' . . ."

"Say it and get it over with." Head down, hat brim tipped low, Nick thought he was hiding his amusement. But the corners of his damn mouth were twitching.

Dillon sighed. What could he say? His whole life, Nick had been out of control exactly once. Who else did he know who could say that? Not that it was something Nick would say, but Dillon was the talker.

"Hell, I'm just talkin'. Figured I was on a roll." Dillon grinned. Getting Nick to smile had that effect on him. "Louise never misses *America's Most Wanted*, so if Missouri Woman turns up on the show, you're covered. Otherwise, I suggest you keep the family jewels in a safe place."

"I'm covered there, too, D. Any more advice before we see what kind of a quarter-mile True Colors has in him?"

Dillon shrugged, feeling more than a little foolish

for preaching safety to Nick, who handed him the halter. Wordless instructions. Nick would hook up the two-horse trailer while Dillon collected the horse.

"Hey," Nick called out to him before he reached the door at the far end of the barn. Dillon swung around. "Her name's still Joey."

It wasn't much of a track by any horseman's standards, but Joey pronounced it fit for her purpose. Situated at the edge of town, the track circumscribed an arena that played host to outdoor events in the summer, including the Fourth of July rodeo, various forms of entertainment involving monster trucks and crashing cars, and the occasional western-style horse race. Mobridge was a cowboy and Indian town—owned by cowboys and frequented by Indians.

With a feed store and a veterinary clinic conveniently located nearby, Nick was able to fill Joey's initial shopping order for hot feed, supplements, wraps, Absorbine and, most important, a stopwatch. In the process of talking the vet out of a load of sympathy over her "crazy freak accident" and into loaning her a stethoscope for gauging stamina, Joey piqued the young man's curiosity and soon had him examining True Colors and fairly swooning over the horse's excellent physical condition. No charge.

Nick wasn't sure what to expect at the track, and he felt funny about taking Joey's instructions, considering what a messed-up little mouse she'd been until the moment he'd lifted her into True Colors' saddle.

Instant authority. Now she had him and Dillon both stepping off yardage and swinging gates for her. Dillon got his chance to try the horse during the warm-up, but he was clearly not the same horse under Dillon's adept but merely human hand as he was for Joey. How many hours had she spent with the stallion? Judging by the fit the two of them already had going for them, those hours defined the cliché *quality time.*

What Nick had seen the first time she'd ridden the flashy stud had been a pale prelude to the display they put on for their audience of two in the early evening shadows behind the crow's nest of the Sitting Bull Stampede arena. Even without a proper racing saddle, she somehow adjusted herself and her gear into a sleek, seamless package, a natural fifth appendage. There was no starting gate, whistle or gun, only some imperceptible signal that ignited an explosion of equine energy and jolted human heart rates. Bent low over the horse's outstretched neck, Joey fairly floated in the saddle, her arms pumping like pistons precisely tuned to push the horse's nose through time and space.

It was over in little more than half a minute. Nick glanced at Dillon, who shook his head in disbelief even before he managed to uncurl his fingers to reveal the face of the stopwatch. Speechless, they turned to watch horse and rider take a pace-easing turn at the far end of the track. Joey had risen taller, knees still bent, weight in her calves, yellow-gold hair fluttering like a major-league pennant.

"Was that as fast as I think it was?"

"I don't know," Dillon said, dazed. "My thumb might have been slow on the uptake. But I'm thinkin' that is one fast Paint horse."

"That's not a horse, man, that's a cheetah. Told you I could pick 'em." Nick punched his partner's shoulder, a parting shot before he scaled the fence. He hadn't felt this giddy in . . .

He had *never* felt this giddy.

Dillon scrambled up beside him and grabbed him by the arm. "She really knows what she's doing."

It sounded oddly like a warning. Nick chuckled. "No shit."

"That's no lady, Nick. That's a jock." Dillon's pointed look was vaguely disturbing. Accusatory.

Nick shook off his partner's hand. "She helped her father out when she was growing up. I told you about that, didn't I? Or she told you."

"I'll bet you any money, that woman's a professional jockey."

Any other time, Nick would have won the staredown, but the sound of trotting hoofbeats and the feel of Joey's approach pressed him for attention. "You got it," he said as he dropped to the ground on the track side.

"How much?"

"You name it," Nick called over his shoulder as Joey rode up to him, her mount prancing like a stakes winner.

Joey dismounted with catlike grace before Nick had

a chance to offer her a hand. Her fireball mount lowered his head like a docile pup to enjoy the reward of a vigorous neck scratching. She flipped the reins over his ears and favored Nick with a new kind of smile—one that said *yes!*

"Name what?" she asked.

"The first baby," Dillon said, catching up. "If it's a girl, I vote for Joey. If it's a boy, I still vote for Joey. You're a hell of a jockey."

"He means True Colors' first baby." Nick patted the horse's mottled shoulder, impressed with the animal's relative calm on the heels of delivering his burst of speed. "We're already making bets."

"What did you get for a time?" she asked, exhilarated, her face flushed and glowing. She spared Dillon's proudly proffered stopwatch a glance as she loosened the cinch.

But the arch of her brow wasn't the response the men expected. *Hell, she could have won a race with that time, easy.*

"Like I said, I probably added a second on either end," Dillon said. "If I'd'a blinked, I coulda missed the whole thing. You wanna go again?"

"That was a good run," she said as they fell into step with her, heading for the horse trailer. "Let's not push it. He's in fine fettle, as my dad would say. And look at him, so cool and collected. He's such a sweetie. But what's really sweet is the way he moves," she enthused as she parked the horse for loading.

Nick pulled the saddle, while the stallion, in

response to some private signal, lowered his big head into Joey's small hands to be relieved of the bridle. Her tone mellowed. "So steady and smooth, every joint oiled," she murmured, as though she were pouring a lover's praise into the horse's long black velvet ear. "Every muscle tuned perfectly to the bone, and all that momentum flowing from his body . . ."

Saddle in hand, Nick stared, waiting breathlessly on the finish.

She glanced at him, looking startled, as though she'd caught him standing outside a window eavesdropping on her.

"We've got ourselves the makings of a racehorse here," Joey said, going immediately back to her chirping. "It's all there. All he needs is careful feeding and the right workout regimen."

"They start racing this month in Pierre, next month in Aberdeen," Dillon said, and Nick reminded himself that his partner had a talent for going from skeptic to believer in no time flat. "You got one track in Iowa, one in Minnesota, a bunch in Nebraska. I don't know how many allow Paints to race against Quarter Horses, but I can find out."

Nick handed Joey a halter in exchange for the bridle. "You sure you wanna do this?"

"For you? Yes. Absolutely."

"How much racing have you done?" Dillon asked. "You can't tell me you're not a jockey."

"Not now, but I was." She offered Nick an apologetic glance. "I started out with my father, but it was more than that. I had a good run myself."

Dillon persisted. "How long ago did you quit?"

"I've been out of it for a couple of years. I was ready for something else."

Ask her, Dillon. You're doing fine so far.

But whatever she was ready for and the choice she'd made were only pieces of history that didn't interest Nick's partner. And Nick decided he didn't need to know. The woman was here for now, staying at his place, eating his groceries. She might as well be useful.

"Hank Two Dog still has that bay gelding he raced last year," Dillon said. "Did pretty good his first time out but didn't bring much *toniga* to the table after that. I bet we could run this one against him, kinda like a tryout."

"Let's see where we are with him in a week," Joey said. "What's *toniga?*"

"Guts," Dillon said. He grinned. "The edible kind."

"That's not the right kind of saddle." Nick eyed the two saddles on the trailer racks—the heavy western style he was comfortable with and the one he'd just stored that struck him as a hybrid, neither fish nor fowl, Western nor eastern. He shut the curved door on the front of his old two-horse and snapped the padlock. Damned if he wasn't thinking about hunting her up a saddle.

"It'll do for now," she said as True Colors loaded readily for her.

They stopped at the last gas station east of the river,

which gave Nick's passengers an excuse to disappear. Dillon had to run across the street to Gibson's to "check the magazine rack" for God knew what. Whenever a new interest came crashing down on him, Dillon loaded up on papers and magazines. Nick filled both the pickup's gas tanks, paid the bill and asked for change for the pop machine. Then he stood there, feeling like a jackass. Dillon was just doing his usual, but Joey . . .

It'll do for now.

If she was playing with him, at least she had the decency to make do with what he had. He was pretty sure she wouldn't be around much longer. Nick knew where the pay phone was in this place. He didn't need to walk around the corner to the side of the building to know who was using it.

Getting her shit together while you wait.

And wasn't that exactly the way he wanted it?

12

Over the next few days, Nick tried to pay attention to the work he had to do, while Joey threw herself into the work she'd made for herself. What he wanted to do was go his own way, meet up with her in the kitchen for supper and then go off to bed without too much talk. When she was ready to leave, he wanted to be ready to take her to the airport without asking any questions.

But nothing was working the way he wanted it to.

For one thing, he wanted to get the dirty jobs done around the place before he had to take off on his next hauling run. He prided himself on well-maintained pens and a barn that smelled more or less clean. More saddle soap and horse hide, less hay dust and horse manure. To that end, he was forever pushing the front end loader on his faded blue 2N Ford tractor around the yard or shoveling, forking and hosing the crap out of the barn, especially after a long winter. He didn't keep any wrecks around unless he could keep them running, no cast-offs except the few four-leggeds he couldn't exactly turn away and no ramshackle buildings except for the one Dillon had been inspired to drag home because God had let it go for a song. He'd never had a trainer working for him—likely never would again—and he wanted her to look back on her time at Wolf Trail Ranch and remember him as the big Indian who ran that neat little horse operation.

Okay, he wanted to make an impression, but it wasn't like he was going out of his way. His way was to walk the walk, do the work, spend his free time wheeling barrows full of manure out to the compost pile. Watching was also his way, and the training of True Colors gave him something well worth watching while he worked. The painted beauty of considerable stature willingly danced for the pale beauty whose size was immaterial. Separately each had turned Nick's head, but when they worked as a team, he was hard-pressed to look away.

217

But getting blinded, hooked or outright had was not his way, either.

One more thing Nick wanted was for the vision of his flashy Paint horse galloping ahead of the pack toward the finish line to die on the vine. He'd been hanging around Dillon too long. The smoke from his partner's damn pipe dreams was finally getting to him. He couldn't seem to keep his mind on building up the manure pile when his first and undoubtedly last female house guest was tearing down his mental resistance to anything involving smoke, dreams or her kind of woman.

In case anyone asked, Nick was no expert, but he had a few ideas about what *her kind* was. A guy had to be careful around the kind of woman who made canned soup taste like homemade simply by putting it into two bowls—one for him, and one for her. Or the kind that disappeared behind the bathroom door smelling like horse sweat and came out distinctly damp and drifting on a scent that had definitely fallen from the night sky rather than his showerhead. Or the kind who kept on going throughout the day, tending to the task she'd assigned herself, staying a step ahead of her steadfast melancholy until it finally caught up with her when she took it to bed at night. She was the kind who could break a man's heart without trying.

On the other hand, there was always *his* kind—the kind he carried on his back. He hadn't met a woman yet who could stand up to the Dragon Lady, who was itching to take on the newcomer. After hours of shoveling and considerable sweating, he'd used up what was left of the hot water trying to settle the Lady down. The shower soothed her some, but her kind had no sweet scent. He sometimes wished she'd been grafted onto some other part of his body, where he could easily reach her with some of that cream they'd used on him in rehab. He'd dreaded being touched, but after a while he'd learned to enjoy his massage therapy. Nowadays he tried to tell himself the itching was all in his head, but in her younger days, the Dragon Lady had been a great one for plastic surgery, and to this day she couldn't stand a chill. His body was literally too thin-skinned in some places to handle any direct cold.

He slid into a clean pair of jeans and reached for the long-sleeved shirt he'd hung on the hook on the back of the door. But getting dressed to walk across the hall in the dark suddenly seemed pretty stupid. Why bother? Joey had retired to his room, his bed. He was headed for the other room, the spare. Hell, he acted like an old boarding school nun sometimes. He left the shirt on the hook, left the bathroom light on, left his door open to remind his guest that she wasn't alone in the dark. She was a big chicken, she'd said.

And he was chickenshit.

He stood at the window and watched his beautiful Paint pace the fence in the blue-white moonlight. The stallion knew that his females were out there somewhere, and he didn't care that it was too early in the season for him to breed them. Another month, Nick wanted to assure him. But what consolation would a man's assurance be for a hungry, healthy stud? Especially coming from a man feeling the hunger but missing out on the health.

Yeah, he knew it was all in his head. Ugliness had a way of messing with a man's mind. True Colors wouldn't know anything about that. The mottled pattern on his hide only added to his beauty. His colors didn't repulse the females. It would probably even draw them to him.

The moment his mind showed him female drawn to male, he felt a hand touch his back. It took the form of a small shape, a cool contact, and the only thing that kept him from flinching was the knowledge that he'd developed a powerful imagination. When he thought about something hard enough, he could almost make it happen. He could banish physical pain, and with it he could set a whole host of feelings aside—loneliness, guilt, anger, desire. He could put all of it on the run.

He waited, but the feel of the hand would not go away. On a deep breath he caught her scent, and he thought Dillon might have been right. He had gone over to the dark side, where people lived in dreams. The hand stirred slightly, lightly, moving over his taut and terrible skin.

An unholy hand, or that of an angel?

"It's your turn," he ventured. "Tell me what you see."

Her hand nearly left him, all but the tips of her fingers tracing a long, hard, puckered ridge of tissue that could not be called skin. More like the "proud flesh" on a horse with a poorly healed wire cut. Some of his own raised scars had been removed, but there was dense testimony still scribbled on his skin, and she seemed intent on reading him with her fingers. He lacked the will to stop her.

Finally she said, "You left the door open."

"I thought you were asleep."

"That's the first lie you've told me since we met, Nick." She pressed her hands flat, fingers splayed over his shoulder blades. "Tell me what you wanted me to see."

"That I'd left the door open," he confessed quietly, tempted to warn her about leaving permanent prints. "That you could come in if you wanted to. Or have a look and then walk away."

"This is a test?"

"A setup, maybe. If I'd wanted you to see the whole truth, I would have turned more lights on."

"What I saw through the door you left open was a sexy, sexy man. Tall, broad shoulders, strong back tapering into a pair of—" shivers trickled down his back, chasing the slide of her hands, pooling at the base of his spine "—soft jeans that fit him just right."

He sucked in his breath as her fingertips slipped beneath the waistband. He told himself to turn around, but *himself* shot back, *Don't spoil this.* He braced his hands on either side of the small window as she laid her cool forehead against the middle of his back.

"I see the truth," she said, her breath a delicate caress. "I can't imagine what you must have gone through. Is it tender at all?"

"I feel cold a lot. Your hands . . ."

"Hurt?"

The word had no meaning in the company of wet lips and tongue tip skating in and out of live-nerve territory, tracing tiny circles on his back. No sound, he told himself. No movement, no scaring her away. *Any noise you could make now would sound pitiful, anyway*, himself warned.

"Tell me if I hurt you," she whispered. "Tell me if I do something I shouldn't."

"I'm not . . ." He started to turn to her, but she pressed her thinly clad body against his back and slid her arms around him. Her hands, tucked in his waistband, came together on his belly.

"Not so fast, mister. This is what you get for turning your back on me." She unbuttoned his jeans. "Is this okay?" she whispered as her unholy hand went for the zipper, intent on lowering it tooth by saw-blade tooth.

He sucked it up, said a quick prayer, told himself there was no going back now. Himself said *amen*. And the free-wheeling hand of an angel slipped nimbly between biting zipper and tender flesh, barely touching him. *Barely* bearable. Nick drew a quick breath. Losing his precious control was not an option. Mentally he jammed his cock into the zipper.

"It would seem so," she said, sliding her hands over his hips and peeling the jeans off his cowboy ass.

"Yes, ma'am." He kicked them away as he turned and took hold of her waist. "That works fine."

"How fine?"

He chuckled. "I'm willing to let you be the judge."

Her hands went to his shoulders, and he lifted her, met cotton-covered breasts with nose and lips and tongue as she wrapped arms and legs around him, doing her damnedest to impale herself even though her panties and his resistance stood in the way.

Mount him and crack the whip on him, would she? There was no way in hell he would cross the line before she'd been there and back a time or three. Convinced she was riding high, she had placed her butt in his sling and given his hand easy access—over, under, around and through—ah, so slick and easy the way she'd spread her legs around him and left herself wide open for a stealthy finger foray, barely touching, tenderly obliging her physical pleas for more.

It was her turn to catch her breath in surprise as he laid her on the bed, stripping her, kissing her, touching her, tasting her. With measured patience, he coaxed her to come fully and safely and with complete impunity, making it too good to be anything but a leg-up. And up. And up.

But the full ride would require one more bit of tack. Closer to crazy than he realized, he tore into a packet and tore a hole in the damn condom.

"Smooth move," he grumbled, and she moaned. "Hold that thought, honey."

"No, it's okay." She dug her nails into his buttocks.

"I want . . . I *want* you to."

"Don't worry. Got a whole damn . . ." He fumbled for the box, leaving him only one hand for her, while her two for him were going for the goal without a fumble.

"I'm not worried, Nick," she whispered as she took him inside her. "I'm not worried, I'm not worried, I'm not . . . not worried."

Worry was nothing. The finish line was all.

He held her close, cherishing the weight of her head on his arm and the feel of her heartbeat mixing with his. She wasn't asleep. She was tucked against him like a contented cat, one moment still, the next stretching and stirring one limb or another, exploring him with foot or fingers. No discovery had thus far turned her away. Maybe his body was more distinctive than it was disfigured.

And maybe a little pipe smoke floating around the mirrors in a guy's head wasn't such a bad thing, as long as he didn't get hooked.

"I'm leaving day after tomorrow for a four-day run," he told her. He'd mentioned it earlier, but that was *before*. "I'll be heading east this time, south and east. Making a circle through Minnesota, Wisconsin, Illinois, Iowa, back to Minnesota and then home again." *And?* "I could make a swing into Missouri if need be."

For a moment she said nothing. Finally, "What need would there be?"

"Whatever need it is you can't tell me about."

"Are you thinking of putting me back where you found me?"

"Not anymore." He was thinking about keeping her as long as he could. Right now, that was all he was thinking. "Are you on the pill?"

The breath from her small laugh prickled his skin.

Of course she was.

"Dumb question, huh? I don't mind using a condom. I mean, I use 'em. Always have."

"I got a little carried away. I wanted . . ."

"I did, too." He leaned away, seeking her eyes in the shadows. "I don't want you to go, Joey, but I know the time's gonna come. Okay? I'm not a fool."

"I don't want you to go, either. Four days is a long time." She smiled, her hand absently traveling over the highs and lows of his hip. "You're going to be surprised how much I can do with True Colors in four days."

"You've been long on surprises, but tonight you outdid yourself."

"That explosion on the oil rig," she began tentatively. "The one that killed your brother. It almost killed you, too, didn't it?"

"Damn near."

"What caused it?"

"Drill stem hit a pocket of natural gas while we were making a connection. Gas came rushing through the stem, covered the rig floor. All it took was a spark and it was great balls of fire, baby." He glanced down at her. "That's what they told me, anyway. Truth is, I don't remember too many details. Don't much want to." He touched her hair, tucked a bit of it behind her ear. "So don't ask, okay?"

"Okay." She kissed his shoulder, touched the image of fingers that had once clawed his neck. "It's like a tattoo."

"Battle scars. It's always seemed easier to keep the bad times to myself." He caressed her hip. Pale moonlight revealed the dappled bruise, but no colors. And no story behind the colors. "How about your map of Florida? I tried to be careful."

"It doesn't hurt anymore, but you'd never know from the way it looks."

"It'll be gone soon, and it'll stop hurting inside, too. You won't forget, but you'll put it away somewhere safe. You'll go on to something else."

"Like you?"

"Like a different state, maybe. A different town, different friends, a different kind of—"

"No, I mean, like you putting the hurt away and going on to something else. I don't think you've done that." She rubbed his cheek with the backs of her fingers. "You'd be a wonderful father, Nick."

He snorted. "And you can tell that just by looking at me?"

"I could tell by watching you with your sister's children, by listening to you talk about them. I can tell by the way you treat me."

"If I've been treatin' you like a kid, I guess that phase of whatever we've got goin' is officially over.

Even though . . ." He gave a humorless chuckle. "I'm way too old and too beat up for a girl like you."

"I have news for you. Between the ages of fifteen and fifty, a woman doesn't appreciate being called a girl."

"I hear them calling one another *girl* all the time."

"That's different. I think. I've never really had any women friends. Or girlfriends, either. Well, one. Amy. She worked on the backstretch for a summer job when I was apprenticing. She said she was coming back to her job the next year, but she worked for a veterinarian instead. Which was a good plan, you know? She was in college, getting all kinds of good experience. We lost touch, but I'm sure she stayed in school and became a vet. She knew what she wanted."

"And what did you want back then?"

"I wanted to ride."

"Among other things," he said, echoing her tone from an earlier remark. "You said you quit because you were ready for something else."

"Clearly I was wrong. The first time I rode him, True Colors showed me just how wrong." She propped herself on one arm, her confidence in the moment displacing memories. "Everyone dreams of finding a horse like that, Nick. A Seabiscuit or a Seattle Slew. When a horse from a big-name farm becomes a winner, big deal. No surprise. He belongs to some oil-rich sheik or Texan or some, you know, *business*man. Who cares?

"But when a real horse lover discovers that one-in-a-million horse, and you know it's heart-to-heart, one heart finding the other in the dark—" she touched his chest, pointing out the place of discovery or punctuating her point, he wasn't sure which "—that's a dream come true. From the jockey to the trainer to the little old lady in line with her two-dollar bet, who wouldn't want to be a part of something like that?"

"I don't know. Maybe the big Indian who just wanted a great stud for his mares?"

He liked the part about one heart finding another in the dark, but the image it brought to mind wasn't so much about horses' hearts or human hearts as it was about one tender piece of a clueless whole casting around in some big, empty space on the off chance of bumping into its destiny.

And if he had any sense, he would be worrying about all this image-conjuring he'd been doing.

"Well, you got him," she said.

"But we're not talkin' Seattle Slew here," he reminded her. And himself. "If you get him in shape, we're just talking about trying him out on a couple of South Dakota tracks."

"I can almost guarantee you won't want to stop there."

"Dillon's the one you won't be able to stop. Me, I'm the cautious kind. One step at a time."

"Does it scare you?" She tilted her head. "Taking chances?"

"What have I got to lose? Like you said, I've got the stud. If this thing doesn't work out, hell, I wasn't

228

looking for a racehorse."

"How about taking a chance on me? Does that scare you?"

"I think you know what you're doing." He laughed. "Kinda wish *I* knew what you were doing, though. Yeah, that part scares me a little bit." He touched her chin. "Tell you what I'm not afraid of, and that's your boyfriend."

"My boyfriend?"

"Whoever left you the way he did. I've been through fire, Joey. A lot of guys claim they're tough, but I wear proof. Whatever it is I don't know about him, it don't mean shit. I know all I need to know."

"Good," she firmly pronounced as she laid her head back down in the pocket of his shoulder.

"Except his name and where he lives."

"And what he does."

"I see what he does. He beats up on women."

"He rarely does that kind of dirty work himself." She popped up again. "No, Nick, listen to me. The kind of man who does something like that himself is bad enough. But someone who pays other people to do it for him . . . we're talking a whole different league."

"Sounds like something out of a gangster movie." He looped his arm around her tense shoulders and drew her back down. *You're safe if you stick with me.* He chuckled. "I like westerns, myself. One on one."

"What a myth that is. If it had been one on one—one cowboy, one Indian—I have a feeling we'd be looking

229

at some different faces on Mount Rushmore."

"You sure as hell wouldn't be lookin' at human faces. You'd be lookin' at Paha Sapa the way it was when Iktomi brought the first man through a cave to the upper world."

"It was a *man,* was it?"

"So they say. A Lakota man. You never hear about women falling for Iktomi's tricks. It's always men. They say it was warm and safe inside the earth, but Iktomi, the old spider, he talked the first people into being born through the mouth of that cave—Wind Cave in the Black Hills. Once they got out, they couldn't get back in." He slid her a glance. "Not for lack of tryin'."

"Back to the womb, where it's warm and safe," she reflected. "Is that what getting inside a woman is all about?"

"It is if it works for you. Sounds better than the truth. Something like, *You want me to act like a man? I'll stop being a baby if you'll let me get in there and make one.*"

"And if I don't?"

"I'll howl at the moon."

"We can't have that." After a pause, she asked seriously, "Why don't you have children, Nick?"

"I'm gettin' too old to have kids."

"No, you're not."

"I'm not married, for starters. I know some people don't think that's important, but I do. I'm gone a lot. When I'm home, I don't go out much. I live in a trailer

230

house on a post-Custer, pre-casino Indian reservation, which means you gotta drive half the day to get to a shopping mall." He gave her something close to a smile. "These are not preferences you're gonna find listed in the lookin'-for-love ads."

"They're not deal-breakers, either."

He tucked chin to chest for closer scrutiny. "You lookin' for another job?"

"Maybe I'm looking for a place that's warm and safe, and a man who isn't afraid to take a chance on me." The kiss she planted on his chest instantly hardened his nipples. "Somebody who doesn't care what my name is and doesn't scare easily."

He didn't scare easily, but none of whatever this was came easily. And she scared him more with every minute they shared.

A clap of thunder rattled the trailer from skirting to shingles, rousing Lauren from secure sleep to abrupt panic. Nick stirred, shifted, and settled quietly. She wanted to crawl inside him and hide, but a lightning flash sent her stealing from the bed. She had groomed and fed and cleaned and restored, but she couldn't remember whether she had left Nick's clever system of gates in overnight order. A glance out the window told her that she'd already fallen down on the job. True Colors could only be standing in the rain because he couldn't get into the barn. Off the floor and over her head went the nightgown that had once been Nick's T-shirt.

Quiet. Quiet as a mouse in Alice's mouth.

Near darkness, rumbling night. Within the small front closet no slicker came to her fumbling hand, but she felt flannel. Shirt jacket over T-shirt, bare feet in new boots—*don't think, just dash, do it, dash back.*

Where was a flashlight when you needed one?

Never mind. Do what needs doing and be done, lickety-split.

The wind ripped the trailer door from her hand. She fought to recover the handle, and *bam*! Another gust smashed the door shut with Lauren pasted on the outside like a postage stamp. She was soaked to the skin by the time she made the halfway point—the leeward side of Nick's truck. She slid her back along the driver's side door until her butt hit the rubberized running board.

Another bolt of lightning shattered the night sky. A dash back to the trailer would have been her next move but for a distress call from True Colors. Tamping down her fear in response to his, she pushed off from the running board and ran headlong until she tripped, landing on hands and knees on muddy gravel.

Thunder danced circles around her.

She was facedown in the road again. Bare legs, bare hands, bedeviled by gravel and mud beneath and death overhead. A sob tore at her throat, but she didn't let it out until the steel cable of an arm looped around her waist, plucked her out of the mud and hauled her to the barn like a sack of feed. With a one-handed shove, her blessed rescuer opened the barn door just wide enough to roll them both inside.

She huddled against his bare chest, struggling for breath. Finally he moved away from the door.

"You okay?"

"I left True Colors . . . locked out."

Wordlessly he sat her down on a feed box and tended to her oversight. All it took was the release of a bolt on the bottom of a Dutch door, and the agitated horse was admitted to shelter. Nick's words of comfort reached Lauren's terrorized head and soon stayed her trembling.

She found the switch for the tack-area light, gathered some of the paraphernalia she'd put away earlier, and made her amends to the horse with a soothing rubdown. Nick took up the cause on the opposite flank, and the three of them recovered in tandem.

"I'm sorry," Lauren said finally, wiping her liniment-drenched hands on a horse-hide-treated towel.

"I must be gettin' old." Nick clapped his hand over the left side of his smooth chest. "You gotta stop scarin' me six ways from Sunday, woman."

"I'm sorry. When I heard that thunder, it hit me right away. You showed me how to secure those gates so he could go in and out at night, and I woke up—"

"Why didn't you wake me up?"

"You needed your sleep. You have a long day ahead of you tomorrow. And I didn't expect that wind."

"Out here, you expect wind and you respect lightning. Look at you."

She followed his orders from the ground up. Boots,

bare legs, skinned knees, wet T-shirt that would win her no contests, droopy flannel shirt, all of them smeared with South Dakota clay. Her eyes finally met his, caught them smiling.

Rain hammered the metal roofing. More thunder brought a pitiable complaint from the mighty stallion on the other side of the wall. Two whining, wet dogs slunk through the narrow opening he'd left in the barn door, and Alice the cat's glowing eyes peered down from a stack of square bales.

"What a crew." Nick shook his head, chuckling. "We should all say good night and go back to our corners."

"Our separate corners?"

"Tomorrow the sun'll rise and give us back our self-respect."

Two claps of thunder collided just beyond the walls. Lauren ducked under Nick's arm.

"Well, all right, tomorrow's still a ways off."

"You'll be gone tomorrow."

"Back in four days," he promised, rubbing her back. "You're quivering like you're plugged into a live socket. We need to get you dry."

"I'm the live socket." She looked up and smiled. Strands of wet black hair framed his angular face like a boyish mop. "You're the plug-in."

Ka-boom!

It was his turn to tighten his hold. "Damn, that was close."

"Too close. What have you got out here for blankets?"

"Out here? They're mostly covered with horsehair." He raised his brow. "Wait."

The small single light bulb over the tack stall cast garish shadows on his back as he walked away, affording her a view of the spiderwebbing and Rorschach-like blotches that covered his skin. The taste of ash and tears burned in her throat.

"Got a couple stored up in my footlocker," he was saying as he opened the box and began rifling through its contents. "Gifts, too nice to use." He pulled out two thick horse blankets. "Louise made these. And this." It was a star quilt, carefully wrapped in plastic. "We're big on blankets. I put some cedar in here, and some sage." With the plastic peeled back, he took a sniff. "Not too bad." He started to hand them to her.

And froze in the act. The look in his eyes reflected the tears standing in hers. She hadn't felt them coming. He challenged her without saying a word. But he didn't have to. He had already predicted that she would judge, and he was ready for judgment. But not pity.

"Have I told you that . . . you're the kindest, gentlest man I've ever . . ."

He nodded once.

"And that's what I see. That's really all I see, Nick."

"Bullshit," he said softly as he laid the blankets in her hands. "And I mean that in the kindest, gentlest way."

"I mean, I . . . I see what happened. I can almost see you on . . . on fire, almost. And I want to . . ."

"Feel my pain?"

Throat burning, she stared until she blinked, unintentionally shaking a tear loose.

Damn his eyes. *They were smiling.*

She dropped the blankets and stumbled over them getting to him, getting her arms around him, scolding him. "Yes. Yes, but don't you dare laugh at me, don't you dare, because I really just want to . . ."

"Want to what?"

"Take you inside me where nothing bad can touch you."

He kissed the damp streak on her cheek, smoothed her wet hair and made a soft claim on her lips. "You should've held that thought until I finished making your bed."

"Don't worry," she promised. "It's not going anywhere."

He lifted her hay-bale seat by its twine bindings, heaved it into the corner next to True Colors' stall and fished a jackknife from his pocket.

"We'll be like camping out." Clutching their bedding, she watched him cut the twine and then took the hint to break up several straw bales and make their nest. "Is it dangerous being in a metal building during a thunderstorm?"

"In case you didn't notice, I live in a metal building." He broke open another bale near the barn door. "This is for you two. Here." He whistled, pointed, called the dogs by name. "Lie down."

He turned off the light. "Now you," he said as he

took Lauren's hand and led her to their two-bale pallet topped with horse blankets. "Come here."

"Don't I get a whistle?"

"No, but you get to lose the boots." He pushed the flannel shirt off her shoulders. "And this thing smells like Dillon."

"The one underneath smells like you."

"No, it doesn't, 'cause I wash mine."

"To me it smells wonderful, like you. And it feels soft, like you've worn it a hundred times, and last night when I put it on, I . . ." She laid her hands on her chest and rubbed the loose shirt over her nipples. "And it made me dream about you."

"What did you dream?"

"That I'd gotten under your skin."

"That was no dream," he whispered as he whisked the wet T-shirt over her head. "But I wasn't gonna tell you."

She asked, "Why not?" Not because she didn't know or need to know, but because a naked woman crawling into a haystack had to keep up conversational appearances.

And because he understood, he kept up his end, putting them on par appearance-wise by shucking his jeans and conversation-wise by confessing, "I was afraid you wouldn't like it there."

He shook the folds from the quilt, swung it around his shoulders and gave her his body for her blanket. Storm-chilled and rainwater soft, skin welcomed the feel of skin, warmed to the task of warming and burned with the freedom for loving. She tried to keep up with him, kiss for kiss and caress for caress, but she fell behind about the time gentle hands gave over to sucking lips and teasing tongue traveling over and down and deep inside, giving her fits and preparing easy entrance to the place where nothing bad could happen to him.

Dillon loved the morning-after smell of a prairie thunderstorm. It was the smell of cool water and quick greening and life teeming in the grass. He parked his pickup near his bargain sanctuary, got out and had himself a full body stretch, making a lazy grab for one of the morning sky's scarlet streaks. It had been a long night, with enough gamblers trapped by the storm and enough cash in the ATM to make it interesting.

Almost as interesting as Nick's barn door left standing open. Dillon chuckled as he struck out across the yard. Later he would have to razz ol' Nick about leaving his barn door open, see if he could trick him into checking his fly. It was only a matter of inches, but anything Nick left out of place begged notice. Handle in hand, Dillon started to tug.

Then he stopped, his jaw gone slack.

Curled together in a pile of hay near the door, the two dogs lifted noses in his direction. But they'd clearly been ordered to stay, and stay they did. In a darker corner far from the door lay a bigger pile of hay, a longer bed, but this one had blankets. The mop of black hair at one end explained half the mystery.

Could be trouble, Dillon thought. A sick horse. An orphan calf.

Or . . . could be a guy in the doghouse. Could be funnier'n hell.

Dillon's gaze traveled to the other end of the blanket roll, where a helix of legs and the sweet embrace of an unmatched pair of feet had escaped the covers. He backed away, grinning, as the sun popped up between two buttes like a golden bubble. He would have to make the man he considered his brother a victory song, but a pesky nursery rhyme threatened to spoil his composition.

Big bad Nick, never blows his horn,
But the dogs in the doghouse were all forlorn.
Where's the big man who found Little Bo Peep?
Shackin' in the haystack, fast asleep.

Full of himself and jazzed for his partner, Dillon sprinted around the corner of the old church, punched his fist in the air and leaped for an imaginary lay-up in the hoop he would put up over the door someday.

13

Lauren's arm was cocked and set to throw a stick for Mama and Buzz when the porch light came on and Dillon appeared on the trailer steps. He called her name and made the universal hand sign for telephone call.

Her pulse rate's giddyup told her it couldn't be

anyone but Nick. She pitched the stick and jogged across the driveway.

"Is it Nick?"

"Deep voice, man of two words. 'Joey there?'" Dillon reported as she sidled past him at the door. "That would be—"

She grabbed the phone. "Nick?"

"Hi."

She grinned like a teenager with a severe crush. "Hi."

"She wasn't, but she is now," Dillon teased, loudly enough for Nick to hear.

"Tell him to go outside for a while," Nick said. "Yours is the only voice I wanna hear right now."

Still smiling, she glanced at Dillon.

"Stop talkin' dirty to her, Nick," Dillon shouted. "She's blushing."

"Isn't he late for work?" Nick grumbled in her ear.

"He has the night off. He made the best chicken and dumplings for supper, and he even cleaned up while I went back outside and fed the horses. I was just . . ." She turned her back on Dillon, leaned her shoulder against the wall and imagined Nick's face. "How was your drive today?"

"Long. Lonesome."

How could two words hit home so hard from so far away?

"I notice Alice is gone." She also noticed the quiet click of the trailer door closing behind her.

"The cat was the only rider I had waiting for me this

morning. I was kinda surprised. Half expected you to come running out the door at the last minute."

"Will you be half surprised if I'm still here when you get back? Don't answer that," she said quickly. "Because then I'll have to wonder whether you'll take me for granted if I don't keep you guessing, and you'll have to figure out which half of the surprise you really prefer, and I don't think we want to go there right now, do you?"

"Right now, let's keep it real simple."

"Perfect," she said, thinking only of Nick, and fixing on *simple* and *perfect* and *right now*. "True Colors had a good workout today."

"That doesn't surprise me. You're good for each other."

"You sound tired."

"Thought I'd fall asleep soon as my head hit the pillow."

"You're in bed?"

"With the lights out, fresh air coming through the window, trucks out on the highway whooshing past in the night. Usually all I need after a long drive. Didn't do it for me this time." He sounded unusually edgy. "Talk to me, Joey."

"Buzz isn't shy around me anymore. I was playing with him and Mama when you called. He likes to fetch. She doesn't. She'll let him get the stick, and then she'll try to take it away."

He gave a deep chuckle. "That bitch."

"Do you mind if I let them in the house?"

"I don't keep animals in the house." Pause. "But, uh, you can if you want."

"I wish you had a phone beside the bed. We could be like teenagers and talk until we fall asleep."

"I didn't have a phone when I was a teenager. I don't even like talking on the phone. Usually."

"You have the nicest telephone voice, Nick. I wish I could take it to bed with me. The phone, I mean, with your voice coming through it, into my ear." She closed her eyes and rested her head against the wall. "But Alice has you all to herself now."

"Like she gives a rat's ass."

She smiled. "In her case, a rat's ass would be a lot to ask. I'm sure she'd give a fig."

He would have laughed, she thought, but he was tired. She would have laughed, at least a little, but being utterly alone for the first night in a very long time was no laughing matter.

"You gonna be all right tonight?"

"I wish you were here. Right now. I'd make it perfect for you. I'd keep it simple."

"I'm as close as the phone, Joey. I'll give you the number here, so you can just pick up the phone. And don't worry about waking me up. Is Dillon around?"

"He went out."

"Tell him to stay—"

"I'm not going to tell anyone to do anything. I'm fine. I'll be fine. It's just so good to hear your voice. Could we talk a little more?"

"As much as you want."

"Could *you* talk a little more?"

He laughed.

"That's good, too. Laughing. You have a nice telephone laugh. Voice, laugh—what else can you do over the phone? Breathe?" She listened, but there was nothing. "Can you sigh for me, Nick? Can you make me believe you've just kissed me and you hated to pull away?"

"How about I just made love to you and hated to pull out? Would you like to hear that one?"

"Not now," she whispered. "I don't want to hear that one except for up close and in person."

"And I don't wanna play guessing games," he said. "Will you be there when I get back?"

"I should be there with you now," she said. "So much can happen when someone goes away."

Nick had clearly been drifting off when Lauren finally let him off the hook—or laid him down gently on the hook. She would have to be content that one of them could sleep and hope that canine companionship would turn off her worries for the night. She peered out the window into the twilight, where a man wearing a cowboy hat, a denim jacket and jeans bent to tousle an attentive shepherd's ruff. Clothes didn't make the man, but they were a reminder.

She glanced over her shoulder. Plenty of quiet books. She could turn a switch for sound. TV or radio—she could have her pick. Or she could turn to Dillon, who pulled no punches. She went to the front closet and reached for a windbreaker with sleeves so long it had to be Nick's. She pressed it to her nose and smiled. Sweet leather and spicy Nick. He hadn't washed himself out of everything.

Dillon dropped a glowing cigarette underfoot and crunched it in the gravel as she approached. He shoved his hands into his jacket pockets. "How's the man?"

"The man is tired." Lauren chuckled as she boosted herself onto the open tailgate of Dillon's pickup truck. "He said I could take the dogs in the house overnight."

"After you told him I had the night off?"

"Of course not. I mean, it's not about you. It's about me being scared at night. It's about me and my paranoia, which is crazy. Of course. Paranoia. Crazy. Right? But nobody's going to find me here." She scooted to one side, making room for him to join her. "Do you think?"

"I try, but it helps if I have something to go on." The tailgate rattled as he levered himself up. "Like, who's looking?"

"Nobody." She lowered her voice. "I'm supposed to be dead."

"Dead?" He was genuinely surprised. "Hit and run?"

"Something like that. It's complicated."

"More complicated than your boyfriend being an asshole," he surmised.

"Isn't that what an asshole does? Complicate things? Speaking of which, do you know whether . . ."

She paused. She wasn't sure she should ask. But one of the things she was learning to appreciate about the two men she'd been imposing on was their generosity with the benefit of the enormous doubt she must have stirred up for them. "When you use one of those pre-paid telephone cards at a pay phone, do you know whether the calls can be traced? It's too late—I've already done it—but what would it take to trace a call like that? I mean, I'm sure they can find the phone, but can they find out who bought the card?"

"Who's *they?*"

"Say, the police. Or the FBI."

"You got me there. The FBI hasn't solved a case on this reservation since Columbus, but nowadays, I think they can find out anything they want to. Especially about people who aren't out to break any laws." He eyed her. "You're not, are you?"

"Not at the moment."

He gave a fair-enough nod. "Breakin' that man's heart, that would be a crime."

"He won't let that happen."

"He won't let it show." Dillon adjusted his cowboy hat as though he were using the sweatband to scratch his head. "I guess there's no point in me asking who you're talkin' about calling."

"It isn't a boyfriend or an ex-boyfriend, but it is someone who was involved with . . . the incident."

"The one that left you stranded on the road," he assumed.

"Mainly I'm just trying to make sure I'm not putting

anyone else at risk. I'm not a criminal, but . . ."

"You have criminal friends?"

"Acquaintances," she acknowledged. "Associations."

"An association of criminals? You mean, like *real* dealers?"

"I don't know exactly what they deal in. I've generally chosen not to ask too many questions. Even what I knew, I chose not to know."

"And it caught up to you."

"It caught up to me." It was a relief to admit it, especially to this man. It was almost like talking to Nick, but safer. Dillon willingly served as the buffer Nick wouldn't want to know he had.

"What about . . . ? Did they do something to your—"

"Please don't ask me to talk about that part of it, Dillon. It's like that oil rig fire Nick doesn't want to talk about. Or the time you burned your house down."

"He told you about that?"

"That's all he said. After your family left, you burned your house down."

"Aw, Nick." Dillon gave a wry chuckle. "I don't mind talkin' about it. I was a nutcase. What do you wanna know? What kind of fuel? Gas, siphoned out of Nick's pickup, because mine was empty. In those days it was always empty. Everything was empty. Was I drunk? Very." He made a presentational gesture. "Your turn."

"How long ago?"

"Six—seven years ago. Lucky seven. Statute of limitations on guilt is officially up. And it was your turn for tellin' me something, not asking."

"Give me seven years."

"If I quit askin', that doesn't mean I'm gonna step aside for anybody who tries to ride roughshod over my partner." He grinned. "If you're gonna ride him, you do it barefoot."

"Is that Indian humor?"

"We're talkin' humor with some teeth to it." He leaned closer, confiding, "Like, 'If Dillon has the night off while I'm gone, you might wanna keep the dogs in the house overnight.'"

"It wasn't like that. In fact, he said . . ." He was laughing at her, silent but sure. "You're kidding, right? Between the two of you, I never know who's putting me on. But I do know that there's absolutely no problem with you staying wherever you want to."

"If he comes home and smells dog in the house, you won't be able to quit cleaning until he can't smell it anymore."

"He's *so* sensitive to the way things smell."

"Yes, he is." He went quiet for a moment. "Have you ever smelled burning flesh, Joey? I'm talkin' living human flesh that's actually on fire." She hadn't, but he wasn't really asking. "I can't say I have, either. I got there too late. They were already burned and blackened, like roasted meat. John was . . ." He shook his head. "The only way I could tell it was him was by Nick holding on to him the way he did. Nick was the one brought him out. Nick was the one. He smelled flesh on fire—his own and his brother's."

"It must have been horrible," she said softly.

"Words don't cut it sometimes. There's no way to know what he lived through that night, no way to describe what he went through afterward, month after month. You've seen the scars?"

She nodded. "Battle scars, he said."

"It was a long, hard battle. It helped him, being with people who know what that means. His military service qualified him for treatment in a VA hospital. He battled the pain, and then he battled the pain medication." He sighed. "Damn, I know I'm talkin' too much."

"I won't tell him."

"He's a private man. But just so you know, he's already done his time in hell. Just so you know."

She gave a nod. As Dillon had already pointed out, words were inadequate. Nick trusted her. Clearly Dillon didn't, but he credited her with having a conscience, which was more than she probably deserved. She wasn't sure she trusted herself *or* her conscience anymore. The rhyme from a children's game echoed in her mind: *Heavy, heavy hangs over her head . . .*

"I made some calls today," Dillon was saying. "Got the scoop on racing True Colors down in Pierre and then after that in Aberdeen. If you want to take a break sometime tomorrow, maybe we could take a ride down to the casino where I work. Some people I want you to meet."

"I'm really not—"

"We could even, like my ex-wife says, *do lunch*. The next time you get to the Cities, we'll *do lunch*, she says. Like a grilled cheese sandwich is some big event."

"No thanks, Dillon, really. I'm steering clear of introductions and social events at the moment."

"One of them is Hank Two Dog. He still has that racehorse I told you about. He thinks he's gonna make a ropin' horse out of him, but that's another story. He's willing to let us use him if you need a training partner for True Colors. Plus, Hank's seriously into this stuff. He knows a lot about the races they run around here. Only two tracks in the state, but he's ventured out-of-state some, too. He's got his doubts about racing Paints, of course. He's a Quarter Horse man."

"He can keep his doubts," she said. And then, against her better judgment on the one hand, but in the interest of her best judgment on the other, she submitted. "But I guess I wouldn't mind borrowing his horse."

"It's a date, then."

Lunch was done on Hank Two Dog's lunch break. Hank was someone Lauren had known in many guises. His job at the casino paid the bills, while his be-all and his end-all were tied up in horseflesh and steeped in horse lore. He let Dillon carry the conversation while he consumed a pile of food that had started out on the buffet table as separate dishes. He

249

nodded, put in a word or two between forkloads, nodded some more.

When the last of the meat-cheese-mayonnaise gravy had been wiped from the plate and consumed with half a dinner roll, Hank turn to Lauren. "Dillon says your father trains racehorses."

Lauren stared, her brain slow to shift gears. She'd almost forgotten where she was and what she was supposed to be doing there. When had her father been mentioned?

"I've been around the tracks for a long time," Hank went on. "Maybe I know him."

"My father's been out of it for a long time. He died eight years ago."

"Ohan," Hank said. "Where you from?"

"Nebraska, originally, but I've lived a lot of places," she recited by rote. But she added the rare tidbit, "A lot of trailers, a lot of backstretches."

"Feels like I've seen you somewhere." Oddly, he wasn't looking at her, and she didn't think he really had been.

"I was around the tracks for a long time, too. Who knows?" *Besides CNN?* she thought. This meeting was a mistake. Or a wake-up call. Her face had been banged up but not rearranged. If she started hanging around horse racing people, eventually someone would recognize her.

"You wanna use my horse for a workout, you'll need another rider," Hank said. "My son Ben's your man for that. We built a stretch of railed track we use for practice, nice and wide. You can bring your Paint over to my place. I wouldn't mind getting in on it myself."

"Early morning is best," she said, turning to Dillon. "Whenever you have the time."

"Ben goes out and messes with the horses a little bit before he catches the bus most mornings," Hank said.

"Tomorrow?" Dillon suggested. "Or do you wanna wait for Nick?"

"Tomorrow. The maiden race is always a crapshoot. But we'll be ahead of the game if we give him some practice against experienced competition."

"Nick showed me the breeding on that colt he picked out, and I told him the papers looked impressive. I'm surprised he didn't say nothin' to me about racing him." Hank turned to Dillon. "Have you read the stories they've been runnin' in *Indian Country Today* about this offtrack rebate business some of the Indian casinos are getting into?"

"Heard some guys talkin' about that on the floor the other night. What's the deal? We're cutting into the bookie trade?"

"Times are changing. You got your Internet betting, your simulcasting sites in places like North Dakota, where they don't have a track but they have a racing commission. We're living in times of virtual reality, man."

"And I was just getting adjusted to *real* reality," Dillon said with a smile. "Sounds like a rebate is some kind of a kickback to people betting big money on the ponies through these offtrack sites. Are we getting into that here?"

"Not so far. But it's big money, and a couple of the tribes that are into it, sounds like they might be rubbin' shoulders with the bad guys. That's what the Indian casino critics always want to see coming. You'll be getting yourselves mixed up with the Mafia, they like to say. 'You'll have to start packin', and you know what happens then.'"

"You'll shoot your eye out, kid," Dillon aped, and the two men harmonized in a belly laugh.

"Which mafia?"

The men looked as if they've just remembered her presence.

"Aren't there a bunch of them now?" Lauren asked innocently. "The old godfathers seem pretty tame next to the Colombians and the Russian—" She glanced from one attentive face to the other and shrugged. "I don't know. Are they all called mafias, or is that reserved for the Italian brand? Maybe not all of them are into gambling."

"The horse racing industry has been trying to clean up its image, but lately it's been one thing after another," Hank said. "Mostly it's stuff they say goes on all the time with Thoroughbreds. You know, doping, fixing races. I always say you just can't go wrong with Quarter Horses."

"Paints are racing alongside Quarter Horses," Dillon pointed out. "Paints are squeaky clean."

"And too pretty to win a race," Hank argued. "We

don't care about color. You start worryin' about color, you lose track of what counts. You take that kind of thinking to the track and you lose. I mean, that's—" Hank checked his watch. "Shit, I'm late. Let me know when you're coming out to the place," he said as he pushed his round belly away from the edge of the table. "I'll have my horse and my boy ready to show you the difference between a Quarter Horse and a Paint."

Dillon turned to Lauren. "Ready?"

"Oh, yeah." She smiled at Hank Two Dog's retreating back. This would be fun. "I'll be with you in a minute, Dillon. After I make a quick pit stop."

"Wrong racetrack, Joey. What should we call a pit stop in our sport?"

"I'll let you figure that one out. Shall I meet you back here?"

Dillon decided to check his work schedule and suggested meeting at his truck. Lauren's trip to the restroom took a detour as soon as they parted ways. She called Jack's cell phone.

"Can you talk?"

"Yeah, but make it quick. I'm sitting out here in the car, waitin' on this damn woman."

"I thought you were looking after Joey."

"The woman they got taking care of him, she had to bring him over here to play with her sister's kid. Hell, it's not like Little Joe plays with kids yet. She just wanted to see her sister."

"You don't like the nanny?"

253

"I don't like being her chauffeur. But she'll be gone pretty soon. He wants a real professional, he says. Not somebody who looks like Robin Williams in drag. What's up?"

"My baby's okay?"

"Looks fine to me. I don't think you have to worry. I mean, about him getting everything a kid needs."

"I want to see for myself, Jack." Lauren closed her eyes, fighting the nausea that consumed her every time she thought about the prospect of someone else caring for her son. "I don't know how I'm going to do it, but I have to find a way to see my baby. Just to hold him for a few minutes and watch him eat his food, change his diaper, teach him to say a new word. Just one more word, Jack. Does he still say *mama?*"

"He's doin' okay. You gotta believe that," Jack said quietly. She heard the sympathy in his gruff voice, recognized it for the real deal. Rare, but real. "How about you?" he asked. "You found someplace to stay?"

"I'm with the man who found me."

"Nice guy, is he?"

"Yes." She covered her eyes with an unsteady hand. "He's a lifesaver."

"That's all I wanna know about him," Jack said. "You get on with your life, okay? This life you had, you put that out of your mind."

"You know me better than that, Jack. I'm not a loser."

"You're not a corpse, put it that way."

"No. I'm not a loser, and I haven't lost my son. Jack, what do you know about using Indian casinos as rebate shops for—"

"People do it. It's legal."

"Is Raymond involved with any of that?"

"I wouldn't know, and I wouldn't be askin'. You were always pretty smart like that. What do you wanna—"

"I'm going to ride again, Jack. I'm working for someone who has a horse that could really go places, and I could take him there. I think Raymond might be interested. Can I tell you why?"

"Hell no. You're fuckin' crazy."

"Maybe. And I used to be smart like *what?* Like what I didn't know wouldn't hurt me? That didn't pan out, Jack. So now maybe I'm crazy like I've got nothing to lose. Can't be a loser if I don't have anything to lose."

"Little Joe," he reminded her.

"You're saying he's still mine to lose?"

"I'm sayin' you could get us all killed. You, me, the man who saved your life—all of us."

"Aren't you the one who's supposed to do the killing? What if you weren't his man anymore? What if they gave a war and nobody came?"

Jack snorted. "This ain't the sixties, little girl, and you ain't no Hanoi Jane. You need to get real."

"I guess Hanoi Jane took a pretty big chance, didn't she?"

"Damn straight. I'd'a shot her myself when she

255

pulled that publicity stunt, except I was sittin' in some mud hole south of the DMZ while she was sittin' on an antiaircraft gun havin' her shits and giggles with an NVA gun crew up north. Take my word for it, little girl. When they have a war, people always show up. One way or another, the guys in charge get other guys to carry the guns. It never pays very well, but what're you gonna do?"

"I didn't know you were in Vietnam."

"I was supposed to do the killing there, too. And I did. You get them before they get you. That's just how it works in this life, little girl." He sighed. "But I'm getting old, and I'm getting real tired. So, yeah, you play with fire, you could get a few people killed. Maybe not much of a loss. Guess it depends on how you look at it." Then, urgently, "I gotta go. The woman just came out of the house. Man, her sister's uglier'n she is."

"Joey?"

"He's wearin' that little baseball cap with the chin strap. He's gonna be a Cubs fan. Good man." Finally, solemnly, he repeated, "He's gonna be a good man."

Lauren eased the telephone receiver into its cradle and rested her forehead against the top of the phone. Raymond Vargas would never raise a child to be a good man. It would never happen.

14

Nick's original plan called for him to be home by midnight, but pushing every stop but one put him back in the Wolf Trail driveway by what he hoped was suppertime. He'd been eating fast food in the pickup for four days. The ache in his chest had to be heartburn. But no sooner had he parked near the barn and dragged his stiff body out of the driver's seat than the ache was gone. Chased away by a voice on either side making music in his ears.

"We were trying to decide between frozen pizza and mac and cheese. You're just in time to break the tie," his partner reported loudly.

"You should've called, Nick," his woman said softly. "We would have made you a nice homecoming supper."

He started to close the door, then remembered to reach back inside and let the cat out of the duffel bag he'd left sitting open for her on the passenger side. Rudely awakened, Alice emerged with her cat eyelids at half mast, and took a look and then a leap, knocking Nick's cowboy hat askew on her way over his back, down to the ground and off to her own races. All the while, the two he'd left behind were catching him up.

"We've got True Colors entered for his first race down at Pierre," said Dillon.

"I rode him against Hank Two Dog's gelding, and he

ate it up, Nick. The ground, the competition, the second hand on the stopwatch, the admiration of your friend Hank."

"Yeah, ol' Hank didn't have much to say about his damn foundation Quarter Horse breeding after True Colors smoked his Peppy Two Jacks Three Bars in His One Good Eye, or whatever the hell his name is."

Nick chuckled. Dillon had hit just about every name in the Quarter Horse stud book.

"We didn't *smoke* him," Joey said. "We could've, with all the gas True Colors had left in his tank. But we didn't."

"Seriously smoked," Dillon begged to differ. "Gave Hank's horse a new name. Smoked Pepper Jacks Jerky."

"We did what we needed to do without making a show. I wanted him to come from behind, because he probably won't get a good start the first time out." She finally looked up at Nick, took a breath and smiled. "How was your trip?"

"Who, me?" Nick adjusted his hat. "Not too bad. I'm still back there on choices for supper."

"We could go have supper at the casino, say hello to ol' Hank," Dillon suggested. "I have to work later tonight, but—"

Nick clapped a hand on Dillon's shoulder. "I am not goin' anywhere, partner. You guys go on ahead. Just curious—how long has that pizza been gathering frost?"

"I can do better than that if you can wait a little

longer," Joey said. "What time do you have to go to work, Dillon?"

"Tell you what, the more I think about my suggestion, the more I like it." Dillon slipped Nick what he probably thought was a subtle wink. "It's prime rib night. If I leave now, I can beat the crowd."

"Before you go, let's see what you think of this," Nick said, leading the way to the tack room in the front of the big horse trailer. "Hauled some Thoroughbred colts to a guy in Wisconsin, and we got to talkin' about saddles. Ended up hangin' out a little longer than I should have." He pulled his surprise off the bottom peg on the saddle rack. "He sold me this one. Says it's top-of-the-line, and it's almost new. He said his jockey was too heavy for it. I told him mine was a featherweight." He turned to Dillon. "Makes that Aussie saddle look like it was made for a knight in full-dress armor, doesn't it?"

Joey laid her hands on the poorest excuse for a saddle Nick had ever run across. The thing didn't weigh more than five pounds and looked like a leather Band-Aid. Black with a white seat, the colors matching his horse, it had caught Nick's fancy when he first saw it, but now that he'd brought it out for Joey, he was seeing less True Colors and more *two* colors, one more than he should have dared.

It probably didn't show, but when her eyes met his, he felt like he was blushing.

"Did I do okay?"

"It's perfect, Nick, but you didn't have to buy a

saddle. Hank offered to loan me one."

"You're riding my horse, you won't be sittin' in Hank Two Dog's saddle. This guy threw in a bunch of other stuff, including an old jockey shirt that my sister Louise will be using for a pattern. Don't worry. You're not wearing anybody else's sweat-stained silks."

"Why can't I make my own? You don't think I can sew?" She laughed. "Okay, you're right. I can't. And you're the sweetest man."

Dillon groaned. "Gettin' a little deep around the ankles here. Time for these boots to be walkin'." He tapped Nick's arm. "Nice touch, man."

Dillon earned major points for knowing exactly how and when to walk off into the sunset. He was getting so good at making himself scarce that Nick made a silent vow to start contributing to his church.

They checked in with True Colors, and then Nick helped Joey turn macaroni and cheese into a meal fit for a traveling man's homecoming. But he was less interested in the food sitting on the table than he was in the woman sitting on the other side. Intent on reporting every bit of progress she'd made with his horse, she supplied most of the table talk. And he was grateful. It was good to be home, good to be able to hear her voice and watch her lips move at the same time. But the few times he glanced at her eyes in time to catch her gaze, she rejected the contact in favor of a change of direction, subject, tone, whatever it took to escape him. Something was going on behind those blue eyes that she didn't want him to see.

Fair enough, he said to himself. You're the same way. You've got plenty of private problems. It doesn't mean you're hiding anything that makes a damn bit of difference to anyone else. Bitter tastes, bad odors, hard feelings—some things a person didn't need to be spreading around. He could plainly see that she was healing on the outside. On the inside, that was her business. Hers to suffer, hers to share. He could go either way.

But her problem had nothing to do with the fact that he was back and dying to take up where they'd left off. She quietly made that clear when she joined him in the shower stall that he would never again curse for being too small. She made it even clearer when she rubbed lotion into his road-weary back, from his nape to his knees. Clearer still when she lay with him, thrilled to his touch, took him to the only place where a man dared to tap the source of a woman's primal power. He loved that she became monstrous and insatiable, that she held him and demanded of him, claimed all he had, and when he was spent, she held him still. But now she was back to being a small, soft thing, quiet and content in his embrace. She made him part of something beautiful, something he had never been, and it humbled him.

Moving carefully, he reached for the covers they'd kicked aside. She stirred to help bring the sheet to their shoulders, letting him know she was still awake.

"You like the saddle?" he asked. "You'd tell me if it was a bad idea, right?"

"It's beautiful." She caressed his chest, applying the word there, too.

"It won't hurt my feelings or anything if you don't use it. Is Hank's better? I mean, better for you or the horse or . . ." He sighed. "I probably came off sounding like some bigheaded . . ."

"Not at all." She scooted like a caterpillar, using his body as support until they were face-to-face on his pillow. "I was looking for some way to take care of some of the extra stuff myself. When we win a purse, I won't feel so bad about the expenses, but until then, this whole thing was my idea."

"You're just trying to cop all the credit in advance." He smiled into her big looking-glass eyes. In the space of no space and the time of no time, she had gone from hot mama to eager-to-please girl. "I like to drag my feet until I've got no heels left on my boots, but once I'm in, I'm in all the way."

"I noticed."

"Yeah." He kissed her forehead, for better or worse, blessing or curse. "I want you to have all you need, but you have to clue me in."

She smiled and messed with his hair. "You did fine."

"I got an earful from the guy who sold me the saddle. He says if we do well, it can really add to the value of the horses we raise. I told him about you, and he says a good trainer and the right jockey can make—"

She went still. "Told him what about me?"

"That you've had a lot of experience."

"Is that all?"

"Joey." He took hold of her hand and pressed her fingertips to his lips. "That's about all I know."

"I guess it's a good thing. It's more than I want anyone else to know."

"All they have to do is watch you ride." He braced himself, head in hand. "Joey, I want to know why you quit."

"I was ready to move on. It's a sport, Nick. A game. After a while, you move on."

"Did something happen that I should know about?" No response. Against his strongest nature, he persisted. "Joey, if you had an accident, if you got hurt in any way, that's something I should know about."

"You can't be a jockey and not get hurt. It's more dangerous than . . ." She tried to reassure him with an upswing in her voice. "I took my spills over the years, but nothing serious. If you were a more discerning lover, you might have noticed that I have one or two little souvenirs from the racetrack."

"This finger." Of the four he had just kissed, he singled out the center finger, center knuckle, rubbing it between his own thumb and fingers. "Broken?"

"Three times. Once by a horse and twice by doctors trying to fix it."

"This leg," he said, feeling for the surgical scar he'd noticed below her knee. "Broken?"

"A three-horse pileup when I was eighteen. You can't see the other breaks very well. Here." She drew his hand to her collarbone. "Feel that little bump? And a chipped tailbone. That was the one that hurt the worst."

"All at once?"

"Oh, no. The finger and the tailbone were part of the same incident. I didn't notice the finger at first because of the other." She pulled his arm around her back. "If you've ever *really* fallen on your ass, you don't joke about it."

"And what's this?" He kissed the scar at the base of her neck.

"Okay, so you *are* discerning. That's from a trach tube. Little windpipe dysfunction. Part of the collarbone accident."

"You've had enough," he said gruffly. "No wonder you quit. I'm not letting you do this."

"This stuff happened early on, Nick, before I had all that experience you were bragging about."

"Finish that statement you made a minute ago. More dangerous than what?"

"I don't know. What's not dangerous these days? I only told you because you asked, and I have to be honest. Right? You wanted an honest answer. Yes, I've had a few hard knocks. But I'd almost forgotten the flip side, which is the part you live for, and that's finding a horse like True Colors. Finding him and having the chance to develop him and ride him. I've never really done that before. Not on my own."

"I don't want you getting hurt."

"I don't, either, which is why I'm going to be

careful. True Colors is in good condition. I'm in good condition. We're going to be fine." She hooked her leg over his. "But there's one more thing I need."

"What's that?"

"A new identity." Her moonlit eyes sought his. "I need a name."

"Joey's pretty new for you, isn't it? I don't know where it came from, but I'm pretty sure it's a new handle."

She acknowledged the truth of his presumption with a tip of her head. "But I don't have a last name." She was struggling to get where she was going, and taking the long way around didn't help. "I was thinking maybe Red Shield."

"You don't look much like a Red Shield." He wasn't going to make it any easier. Sooner or later she was going to have him turned fully inside out, but she was going to have to work for it.

"What about a *Mrs.* Red Shield?" she said.

"You want to pose as my wife?"

"If posing is my only option."

"You're . . . proposing?" He couldn't believe she would go that far. "Marriage." He said it only because somebody had to. Somebody had to stop the dance and say the word so that somebody else could back off. "Is that what you're suggesting?"

"Yes."

"For how long? You're thinkin', one of those perfect days we talked about would be easy enough. As long as everybody's cool and things are goin' right."

"And you've thought, one of these days, maybe I'll get married. Haven't you? I'm suggesting we make it a perfect day for me, one of these days for you."

"Why?"

"I can't be who I was anymore. I need to be somebody else, and I want to be Mrs. Nicholas Red Shield."

Are you satisfied? You've pushed for it, and now you have it. A desperate woman's desperate lie.

He drew a deep breath. "What's your name? Really?"

"It's Lauren."

"Who's Joey? Your boyfriend?"

"No. Joey is not and never has been my boyfriend, and that's another honest answer." She tucked her face against his neck, her nose taunting Dragon Lady's claws. "It was just a thought. Maybe one of these days, hmm? You think about it."

Think about it?

Thanks a lot, woman. Like I have a choice.

"That's not the way it's done, Joey. Or Lauren, or—" Exasperated, he slid his hand over the side of his neck—protection for or from Dragon Lady, he couldn't say which.

"Joey," she said. "It's better if you call me Joey. It's the name you know me by."

"Hell, it's not done that way no matter who you are. I get to propose, and *you* get to think about it." He slid his hand into her hair. "You're killin' me, Joey."

"That's the last thing I want to do. I promise you,

Nick. No matter what, I won't see you harmed by my crazy . . . by getting involved with me."

Running his own horse in a legitimate horse race was almost exciting enough to overturn the woman's latest attempt to mess with his mind. Nick had done some bronc riding as a kid, but he was out of his element at Fort Pierre Racetrack. It had to be small potatoes for Joey, but he felt like a boy pulling in for his first day of school. Even Dillon, for all his usual cool, was noticeably wide-eyed.

It was Joey's time to shine. Pierre was only a hundred miles away, but they stayed overnight so that horse and rider would be fresh on race day. Joey was up at the crack of dawn for a light workout on the track. She pronounced True Colors to be the perfect racehorse—eager, energetic, sharp and sound. There was, she said, no match for him anywhere on the premises. Nick wasn't going to say anything, but it wasn't True Colors who gave him concern. Just like driving down the road, it was the crazy drivers with their bald tires and bad brakes that a guy had to watch out for.

Nick played owner, trainer and groom, while Dillon claimed the scout's role. He wasn't a big gambler, but he'd been to the races. No matter what the occasion, event or attraction, Dillon was always curious about its flip-, back- or underside. He had no qualms about snooping around until somebody chased him off. The practice, he claimed, was called *getting the lay of the land,* and for once Nick was willing to call it *good work.* Dillon's scouting report was replete with rumors about which jockeys were likely to ride dirty, or herd, box in or bully the competition. The horses in True Colors' maiden race were all inexperienced, but there were fears that this one might drift or that one might sag, and fears were often muttered on the backstretch.

To boot, Dillon returned with the day's track program. He opened the folded paper underneath Nick's nose, pointed to the fourth race and ran his forefinger beneath a line of print starting with True Colors' name. *Owner, Wolf Trail Ranch, Trainer Nick Red Shield, Jockey Joey Red Shield.*

"How did this come about?" Nick asked.

"I just did what I was told. She said it wouldn't look good for the jockey and trainer to be the same person." Dillon cocked an eyebrow. "Real disappointed I missed the wedding."

"You and me both."

"Congratulate me, fellas. I made weight without tossing my cookies," Joey announced as she approached her team—two men and a horse. "Just kidding. Not having to worry about my weight is one of two major advantages I have over the guys. The other is that horses just naturally like me better. I'm convinced they prefer women."

This was not the time to quibble over names or roles or preferences of any kind. It was post time. The black-and-white stallion was the standout in a field of two sorrels, three bays—one with flashy white socks—a brown-and-white Paint, and True Colors himself.

Nick wasn't holding his breath. From the flipping gates to the flailing hooves to the rocketing finish, he simply didn't need to breathe. It looked more like sailing than running, and the running took less time than registering the win.

It hit Dillon first, and Dillon hit Nick with a solid backslap that further curtailed his next breath. He had to gasp for air as he grabbed his partner's shoulder with one hand and the fence rail with the other.

Dillon was pointing to the scoreboard, but Nick's gaze followed horse and rider. His magnificent prancing horse, *his* gloriously elevated rider.

"They did it," he marveled quietly, wary of believing and broadcasting the claim too soon.

"Come on," Dillon enthused. "We're her entourage."

And because he was familiar with "the lay of the land," Dillon took charge of leading True Colors, rider still aboard, and parting the small gathering at the winners' circle to take center stage. Long-odds bettors wanted to show their appreciation. Joey fumbled with her goggles, while some anonymous camera digitized her smile, minus her distinctive blue eyes. It was a brief moment, but not brief enough for Nick, who couldn't wait to put himself between his jockey and the handful of people representing *the public*. She was flushed with the victory, uneasy with the attention.

Dillon actually had to remind Nick that the winning owner had a purse coming.

The drive home took a little over two hours. Piping up from the back seat, Dillon said he wanted to treat everyone—especially Hank Two Dog—to a celebratory supper. But Nick was having none of it.

"It was a helluva lot of fun, and we sure proved our point, but it's been a long day. Taking first takes a lot out of a guy." Nick glanced toward the passenger seat. "You wanna back me up on that, *Mrs. Red Shield*?"

"Yeah, what's that about?" Dillon asked. "I was countin' on being Nick's best man someday."

"I decided *wife* might not be credible," Joey said, flashing him a coy smile. "I went for *daughter*."

"Waahn," Dillon teased in typical Lakota fashion. "Credible to who?"

"Anyone who might be asking, which is nobody," she said, adding, *"Yet."*

"Like I said, we proved our point. If we don't want anybody askin', maybe we oughta quit while we're at the top of our game."

"The Fort Pierre Racetrack is hardly the top of my game."

"This is really gettin' good," Dillon said with a chuckle.

"It'll be a while before anyone notices us, Nick. Today we ran a maiden horse, first time out, and we had beginners' luck."

"We did? But you keep saying—"

"That's what *they're* saying—anyone who's talking

about the fourth race at Fort Pierre, all maiden horses, all small-time owners and unknown jockeys. We're a little backyard, family operation. Hobbyists. We're mentioned at the bottom of the sports page in a newspaper too small to have sections."

"Indians with backyards and hobbies?" Nick chuckled. "Now, that's news. Careful with the details if you don't want anyone making a story of it. We might all look alike, but there aren't many of us left, remember. And you still don't look like a Red Shield."

"But, hell, Indians with a first-place finish, that's—"

"That's what you want," Joey insisted, cutting across Dillon. "You're on your way to making a name for your stud. His own name, not just the names a generation or two back. You'll have something you can take to the bank."

"Not to mention the prize money that covers—"

"That covers expenses for this race and one, maybe two, more," Nick said. "Beginners' luck ends when?"

"Since he won, he can't run against maidens anymore. But the next win will still be considered a fluke. The third . . ." Joey slid her hand across the seat in his direction. "We might not win every time. Are you going to quit if we only place?"

"How soon before my horse risks getting claimed?" He'd entered True Colors in an allowance race as a horse that was not available for purchase, but unless or until he reached the level of stakes racing, the claims races that were available to him would eventually require him to set a price on his horse.

"We'll cross that bridge when we come to it. It's not an issue at this level."

"You're sure?"

"I'm sure. I know what I'm doing. My father made his living at this." She gave a perfunctory smile. "It wasn't a great living, but it kept pancakes on the table."

"It isn't how I want to make my living."

"You're not feelin' the fever yet, partner?" Dillon chuckled. "You got a fever, all right, but it ain't horse fever." He started whistling the tune to "Jackson."

"Look what you've done," Nick grumbled, slipping Joey a sideways glance.

"You *could* make an honest woman of me."

"I doubt it."

"What's the special tonight at the casino, Dillon?" Joey asked, turning to the back-seat troublemaker. "Mrs. Red Shield would love to celebrate *taking first* with something besides glorified macaroni and cheese."

The very last thing Lauren wanted to do was hurt Nick in any way. In her whole life she'd only perfected one salable skill, and that was riding a fast horse to finish ahead of the pack. If he wanted nothing else from her, he could at least accept this much without misgiving. Not that he had any way of knowing how much this was, since he didn't know who she was, but surely he could see that she was no bug jockey, no amateur, certainly no hack. If she put his horse in a position to be claimed, it would not be without doubling, *tripling,* his investment. And only if such a move turned out to be the one that would save Joey.

But Nick was hurt. From where she stood outside the glass confines of the casino restaurant waiting to take another stab at calling Jack, she could see Nick's lack of interest in the conversation he and Dillon were supposed to be having with Hank Two Dog and the manager of the casino, for whom she had vacated her seat at the table. Nick had agreed to the dinner suggestion after they took True Colors home. He would have preferred to stay with the horse, but she and Dillon had tag-teamed him. And so there he was, looking impatient, even angry. The truth was, he had good reason. More than he could imagine.

The idea of marriage had popped into her head one minute and rolled off her tongue the next. Her impulses had a way of showing up half baked, half dressed, and already half realized. *I love you. Let's do it.* Of course, she'd wisely left out the *I love you* part. Talk about total exposure . . . Put those three words together and you had full lunacy. But saying them might have made all the difference. Had she told Nick she loved him, the name she'd signed at the racetrack might not have been a lie.

And then what?

And then another half-baked idea she was trying to cook up could be moving closer to fully baked and possibly accomplished without turning her into a thief. If she could use Nick's horse to get Vargas to expose himself somehow, there was no question. She would do it. She would do anything to get her baby back.

And so, from where she stood outside the restaurant, she could clearly see that Nick's struggle mirrored her own. They had nothing going for them—no trust, no truth, no time—and yet, for her part at least, she could say the words right now and mean them. *I love you, Nick.* But he would never know.

Her third try finally yielded pay dirt.

"Jack, I've been calling—"

"You gotta stop this. I'm tellin' you, the boy's fine."

"Does he have a new nanny or the same one you don't like?"

"No changes yet. Look, I know where you're calling from."

"How do you know? You can't—"

"Some Indian reservation in South Dakota. Am I right?" She swallowed hard. "You see? I *can*. And so can he. There's only one secret that's keeping you alive, and that's a secret I'd like to keep between us. But you're makin' it real tough."

"Jack, I was thinking. Why couldn't you *disappear* Joey the same way you disappeared me? You could disappear, too, Jack. We could all—"

"It doesn't work that way. That baby is his son, and he's the one who calls the shots. I'm the doer, and *I did not do her*. You get what I'm sayin'? That's . . .

274

that's the kiss of death. And you're nothing, little girl. You've gotta get it through your head. *You. Are. Dead.*"

He cleared his throat. "Listen to me now. I don't know why you asked about betting rebate shops, but take my advice and keep your nose out. I don't know what you think you're gettin' into, but it's no game. You hear me? No horseracing, no casinos and no cops. Because nobody's gonna connect him with any of that. He's real careful that way. But if you or anyone who looks like you starts showing up at the tracks, he'll know. And he'll connect you with a bullet. You and me both. You get what I'm tellin' you?"

"Yes," she said softly.

"What's that?

"Yes, Jack, I understand."

"You're nobody now, but you used to be somebody. A little somebody, but a somebody. You were all over the news, right? You know that."

"I only saw one—"

"Yeah, well, pretty face, mob connections, horseracing and all like that, it's news. You get back into race riding, you don't think somebody's gonna recognize you?"

"I'm not exactly hanging around the backstretch at Santa Anita. This isn't even a Thoroughbred."

"What isn't a Thoroughbred? You gotta stay away from any kind of horseracing. I'm tellin' you, little girl, you've had your reprieve. You're smart, you'll make a whole new life. Hook up with a nice guy, have yourself a couple kids. I'll look after Little Joe. I swear to you, that boy—"

"Now *you're* the one who doesn't understand." She pressed her back against the wall in the telephone alcove, closed her eyes and remembered her baby wearing the baseball cap she'd bought for him a few short weeks ago. It was an image she had to hold fast in her mind. She had nothing, not even a picture of him. "You can't cut me off, Jack. You have to let me call. At least give me that much."

"The night I let you off, that's the only time I ever done anything like that. The only time I went soft. Fuckin' stupid. I don't know what I was thinkin'." Silence came cold and hard. But then, in a voice too small for Jumbo Jack, "I'll take your calls when I can. Just . . . just you be careful, little girl."

"Thank you, Jack."

But the line had gone dead.

15

Nick had taken a far-corner seat in Louise's living room and buried his nose in a newspaper, feigning a lack of interest in the "costume" fitting that was going on a few feet away. He was an old-fashioned Lakota male, which meant he had his standards. As a rule, he couldn't be hanging around when the girls had their hands busy with their creations and their mouths going with the stories females everywhere traded among themselves.

But no self-respecting Lakota male permitted somebody in his charge to participate in a public doings without the best garb he could provide. Joey had worn used silks in her first race, and he would not have her wear the shirt a second time. It was probably pretty obvious that anything to do with Joey interested him, but beyond that, there were certain appearances people tacitly agreed to keep up and respect. A good event costume was important.

Louise was the seamstress in the Red Shield clan, but Bernadette was on hand to offer her opinion. With most of the children in school, she had at least one hand free to fetch and pin and iron, while Louise made use of the sewing machine that occupied its usual place at the kitchen table. A master quilter, Louise had pieced Nick's selection of fabrics into a tapered red blouse with an inset V-shaped black bib, the canvas for the appliqué she had fashioned incorporating the initials Joey had requested—RS. On the sleeves Nick had suggested a smattering of stars.

"I like these colors." Bernadette held out an open pin for Louise, who was fussing around Joey, eyeballing and setting pins where the final seams would be.

"Red for Nick and black for Dillon." Arms outstretched like a scarecrow, Joey caught his eye from across the room and smiled. "We should make a logo for the Wolf Trail."

"We have a brand. What would we do with a logo?"

"We'd put it on a sign, put it up where you turn off the highway. On the Web site, too." She glanced down at the front of the shirt and risked getting pricked as she touched the red letters with an admiring hand while Louise worked under the opposite arm. "You could incorporate the colors and letters, maybe. What are the stars for?"

"The Wolf Trail is the Milky Way. It's a bridge between this world and the spirit world," he told her as he leaned over to give little Nicky a hand in getting a rubber ball out from under his chair. "There you go, baby."

"Do the spirits wander back and forth?"

"I hope not," he said. "I see them winging, not wandering. I see them racing one another on beautiful spirit ponies, gliding from star to star. A freewheeling ride on a good horse must be about as close as we can get to touching heaven. What do you think, Bernadette?"

"I think our brother Nick went away so this Romeo could come. E'en it, Lou?"

The girls were giggling as Joey smiled innocently. "It certainly works for me," she said. "We won't need heavy boots or helmets, but we'll wear silks like this. This is beautiful, Louise."

"I don't see why they call them silks when they're made of nylon," Bernadette said.

"They can't call them *nylons*. Those are stockings." Louise reached for a bit of black cloth strewn with appliquéd red stars. "Is this the way you wanted the helmet cover? I made it to match. You'll wear stars on your head."

"I love everything about it, Louise. You do such beautiful work."

"Nick says he has to be hauling horses the next time you race," Louise said.

"Dillon's going to take me. It's in Aberdeen."

"Would it be all right if I go and watch?"

"Of course. We'll be coming back the same day, so lots of driving for a very brief show, but it would be fun to have another woman along."

"I don't mind the drive. I just want to see how this shirt looks in the horse race. They have a printed program, don't they? With all the names? I want one of those."

Joey exchanged glances with Nick. "I'm riding under the name Joey Red Shield," she confided.

"Ee'n it?" Louise stretched out the all-purpose idiom in amazement as she turned on Nick. "Did you get married without telling us?"

"'Splain your way out of this one, Lucy," he muttered as he went down for the lost ball again and rolled it across the floor to the baby.

"The truth is, I asked him, but he turned me down." She flashed him a so-there smile. "It's just that I don't want to use my real name. There was this man who . . ." She made a self-conscious gesture toward her face and the injuries that were hardly noticeable anymore. "He might try to find me, and he could be dangerous. He's totally psycho."

"I know what you mean, but don't worry. My brother enjoys kickin' that particular brand of psycho ass."

"You know what, girls? Kickin' ass is one thing. Takin' names is something else." He heaved himself out of the saggy-bottomed chair, much to the relief of its whiny springs. "I'll be waiting in the pickup."

Nick was headed for a pickup in Sioux Falls. He'd left home on a head of steam hot enough to fuel his whole trip, but a few hours on the road had a way of settling a guy down. He felt bad about taking off the way he had, a day early. He couldn't believe Joey had brought up the bit about asking him to marry her. Busting his balls was bad enough, but getting a guy's sisters in on it was downright indecent. What people said about him was probably true: he couldn't tell a joke, and he couldn't take one. He was too damn touchy.

This was a typical run, covering a lot of his usual territory. Melting snow and greening grass were good for his business. People bought and sold a lot of horses in the spring. It was a time to ride and rope and race, and soon it would be time to breed. He was looking forward to putting his new horse to work on the job he'd been chosen for in the first place. June 1 was the target date. By then his life would surely be back to normal. Publicly he would be talking up the plans for the crop of fillies and colts in the making. Privately he would be counting the advantages of the lone-wolf lifestyle. If he was down to counting them on one hand, he would never tell.

And the Wolf Trail partners would already be reminiscing about their days as racehorse owners. Dillon would make it out to be a brush with racetrack immortality. *This close* to the record books, Dillon would say, and Nick wouldn't counter with any reality checks. He wouldn't want to become a character in one of Dillon's updated Indian myths. *Romancing the Jockey*. A twenty-first century Iktomi tale. Haunted by the image of a lonely wolf succumbing to the wiles of the trickster, Nick held out against calling home. He tried to get Alice to pretend she enjoyed his company, but she didn't seem to like his attitude. After a good thirty-six hour sulk, he didn't, either. So he called home, got no answer, left a curt message and went back to sulking. He sulked from Nebraska to Colorado to Wyoming and back to South Dakota, where his mood finally started to improve.

There was no way he could make it back in time to attend the race, but as the drive time wore on, he realized he was actually thinking about it. He'd lost all touch with reality. He was coming in from the southwest, marking the familiar sights that usually signified *almost there, almost home,* but his heart and mind were skipping past the end of the trail and tagging another hundred miles on to his journey. Didn't seem to matter that this race would be starting right about the time he pulled in at the Wolf Trail. He was one pure-D pathetic cowboy. He would saddle up old

Rusty, take a ride down to the river and clear his head just as soon as he parked his outfit and unloaded his gear. Maybe he would call the track at the Brown County Fairgrounds, too, just to make sure his horse had made it through the race without any mishaps.

And his jockey.

He'd barely gotten in the house and shut the door behind him when he had to change his plans. He had company. He didn't recognize the car or the two men who emerged wearing white shirts and pants with ironed-in creases. They were either missionaries or cops, both equally unwelcome at the moment. Since they weren't smiling like car salesmen, he was betting against anyone proposing to show him the light today.

Which left him looking at another encounter with the dark side.

The guy with the receding hairline and the bushy red mustache led the way. He would be the talker. The sidekick was probably Indian, at least part. Presumably he was the token. But Nick never discounted the deceptive nature of looks. Best reason a guy ever had for getting a handle on the situation by employing the senses over the tongue. He met the men outside, choosing the shade of a small cottonwood, the only tree in the trailer house yard.

The talker pulled out FBI identification and introduced himself as a special agent. "And this is Michael Dacotah, with the NIGC. We're looking for—"

"Where are you from?" Nick's question was for Dacotah.

"He's with the National Indian Gaming Commission," the talker supplied. "Our agencies are working together on a broad investigation involving some off-track betting activity and a possible tie-in with—"

"Back up," Nick said quietly. He lifted his chin. "I'm askin' *him*."

"I'm from Cheyenne River."

"Charlie Dacotah?"

"He's my father's brother. I've been gone for a while. Went to school in Kansas and then out East. I'm working out of the field office in Tulsa."

Satisfied with the sidekick, Nick turned to the talker. "What did you say your name was?"

"Special Agent Thomas Bowker."

"I just pulled in from a long haul. Haven't hardly gotten in the house yet." But he gave a nod toward the front steps. The talker was all name, rank and agency, but the sidekick had roots. It wasn't much, but enough to get them through the door. "You guys want some coffee?"

Nick offered coffee and chairs at the kitchen table. Bowker declined the first offer, which left only the chair, and he turned that down, too. It was only after Nick made it clear that there wouldn't be much talk until the coffee was on the table that the agent finally gave up on the idea of a drive-by snooping.

Bowker started off with questions about what kind of traveling Nick had been doing and how long he'd been gone. Nick knew he didn't have to answer—this being billed as a "friendly visit"—but questions seemed to pass for small talk with this guy, so Nick gave small answers. He'd been out west for a few days. On business. Horse business. Other people's horses.

Michael Dacotah didn't speak until he had shown due respect for Nick's coffee by drinking more than half a cup. Then he explained what had led the two men to Nick's door.

"My concern is Indian gaming," Dacotah said. "Tom's focus is organized crime. Lately some of our Indian casinos have added what they call a race book to their business, and it's brought in a whole new crowd of players with a different set of connections. Between Tom's agency and mine, we've got our eye on one individual in particular, and we're trying to track a few leads back to the source, which we think might be our man."

"You're talkin' to the wrong guy," Nick said, feeling strangely relieved. "My partner's the one who works at the casino."

"We know that." Bowker braced an arm on the table and leaned in. "We also know that you own a racehorse, and that you recently ran first in a race at Fort Pierre."

"Bought the horse to use as a stud. He's a Paint, but he's bred for speed. Thought I'd let him prove himself." Nick glanced at Bowker and then turned to Dacotah. "I don't have any kind of connections. That was a maiden race for both of us."

"But not for your jockey," the sidekick said.

"We just had a conversation with some people over here at your casino. Everyone's talking about a woman calling herself Joey who rode your horse against one of the locals. What was his name?" Bowker looked to Dacotah for help in the native department.

"Hank Two Dog. And it's not everybody talking," Dacotah said. "It's mostly Hank Two Dog."

"He says the woman rides like she might be a professional jockey. We're wondering how long you've known her, Mr. Red Shield."

"Awhile," Nick said. Relief had given way to defensiveness at the mention of his jockey. "You accusing me of something?"

"Not at all, no." Bowker leaned back in his chair, eyeing Nick as though he were trying to decide which card to trump him with. "We're looking for a jockey named Lauren Davis."

The talker had thrown down his ace.

"No reason to be mysterious about it," Bowker claimed. "Her disappearance has been reported in the news. Disappeared in Illinois, car turned up in Missouri, no driver, no body, no explanation. It's a long shot, but you got a female jockey disappearing there, one turns up here, you gotta check it out, right? There aren't that many of 'em."

"Did you check the race card?"

"The what?" Bowker sat up straight. "I said *female,* not—"

"He's talking about the *horse*race," Dacotah said,

subtly arching an eyebrow for Nick's benefit. *Trying job, this translating.*

"You mean down in Fort Pierre?" Bowker was asking. "Didn't have to. Your first place win is big news around here."

"Guess Hank must be our big news announcer." Nick chuckled. "Check the race card. My jockey's name is Joey Red Shield. She's my wife."

Bowker glanced at Dacotah. *Did we know this?*

Dacotah shrugged.

"How long have you been married?" Bowker persisted.

"Long enough for me to know she's not the woman you're looking for. What did this woman do?"

"She's likely dead," Dacotah said.

Then let her rest in peace.

Lauren Davis. Nick had been turning the name over in his mind, trying to figure out what to do with it, and now he knew. Bury it. Put it on one of those accident fatality markers, find that fateful spot on the road to Mexico, Missouri, and pound the damn thing deep into the ground.

"Her boyfriend is a man named Raymond Vargas," Dacotah continued. "He's been under investigation in a case that involves some members of one of our better-known crime families in an offtrack betting ring that's used the services of certain tribal casino race books. They're also suspected of money laundering, tax evasion and fixing races. It's a big case, and Ms. Davis might be able to help us if she's still alive."

286

"And we might be able to help her," Bowker put in. "We don't know why Vargas would want her dead. But we do know that people associated with him have been known to disappear, commit suicide . . ."

"Die in horrible accidents and like that."

"The stuff movies are made of," Nick reflected. But he was busy filing away another name. Raymond Vargas. He pictured it carved on a stone marking a real grave and a real corpse. *Here lies the boyfriend. May God damn his soul.*

"Yeah, the next *Scarface*," Bowker predicted. "Only this guy's never been touched. Good friends, good looks, good taste in clothes, which are all made of Teflon. A few years back they almost had him for fixing a race—doping a long shot that beat the favorite by something crazy like a dozen lengths. Vargas owned the favorite. Turned out Vargas and his associates won a shitload of money by losing. They might've nailed him if the jockey hadn't committed suicide."

"He's part of the mafia?"

"Not exactly, but we think he's connected," Bowker said. "He's a gambler who's gotten by with some lucrative racetrack schemes. We think Vargas and his associates are setting something up through some of the rebate shops that your tribal casinos have been opening up lately."

"Which is legal in a lot of states," Dacotah explained. "High rollers get rebates on their action. Kinda like when you buy a car? You get a deal for doing business with the shop. The money comes from fees they would be charged if they were betting at the track."

"What kind of fees?" Nick asked. The more he learned about horseracing, the less, he realized, he really knew. And the less comfortable he was participating.

"The track fees that make pari-mutuel betting possible. You need the fees for purses, taxes, stuff like that. But offtrack betting over the phone or on the Internet is a way to get around those fees. Kinda like bookies, only it's legal. In *some* states."

"For the moment," Bowker hastened to add.

"But it's becoming big business, with plenty of potential for moving large amounts of cash from pocket to pocket," Dacotah said. "Very attractive to the kind of people we're talking about. And our tribal gaming businesses are particularly vulnerable."

"Okay, you've convinced me. Joey and me, we're done with horseracing." Nick pointed a finger skyward and recited dramatically, "From where the sun now stands."

Dacotah laughed. "It's all right, Chief Joseph, nobody's suggesting you surrender your horses. These small racetracks aren't dealing with the kind of money we're talking about. We heard about your jockey, and we thought she might be our boy's missing girlfriend."

"If she's hiding out, what better place than an Indian reservation?" Bowker suggested.

"You kidding?" Nick protested. "Word gets around by moccasin telegraph faster than the Internet."

"Only if you're hooked up." Dacotah finished his coffee, signaling that he would be leaving now.

"Is that the right time?" Bowker was checking his watch against the clock on the wall.

Louise had made the horse-head clock from a kit and given it to Nick for his fortieth birthday. It was the only clock in the house. Good clock, dead batteries, Nick would have said if he'd thought the man was really asking.

But Bowker was giving his kind of signal. He knew the time.

"We won't make it back before five, Mike. May I use your phone, Mr. Red Shield? My cell never wants to work out here."

"Sure." Nick pointed the way.

"He's got the wrong service," Dacotah said. And then, with a smile, "Can't tell *him* that, though."

"Gotta have those moccasins."

"I heard about your broodmares. You got a hold of some of that Badlands bunch, supposed to be descended from Sitting Bull's horses." The man from Cheyenne River glanced out the window, searching the horizon. "You believe it?"

"Why not? They went missing. If they couldn't get to an Indian reservation, what better place than the Badlands?" Nick said, recalling Bowker's earlier comment. "Wilderness is the only safe place for a fragile creature."

"Ohan." Dacotah passed him a card within a handshake. "Good luck with your horses."

His visitors gone, Nick sat staring at the card. National Indian Gaming Commission, working with the FBI. Interesting. Like most Indians, he was pretty skeptical about the FBI. They were supposed to investigate any serious felonies committed on the reservation, but their track record was dubious, at best. Nobody had trusted them since the heyday of the American Indian Movement, back in the seventies. But with all the talk of connections, Nick was beginning to think he might need some of his own.

Pocketing Michael Dacotah's card, he glanced at the horse-head clock and smiled. Louise would never say anything about it, but it would please her if he remembered to replace those batteries. Built into his brain was a reliable timepiece. He didn't need a clock to remind him that a hundred miles away, his horse had already run his race. He could probably get the results with a phone call, but they wouldn't be able to tell him whether Dillon had come up with any dirt on the competition. Or how Louise had felt seeing her red-and-black handiwork come flying out of the starting gate. Or whether Joey had glimpsed heaven through her goggles, even for a split second.

Or whether anyone had gone to the fairgrounds looking for a woman named Lauren Davis.

A call that couldn't yield the important answers wasn't worth making. Let them tell him all the news themselves. They would be home safe soon, and tonight they would either be celebrating or commiserating as they replayed the race. Either way was okay by him, as long as there was no disagreement over the plan he was formulating for tomorrow.

16

Rarely had Nick given as much thought to what he would say as he did while he was keeping watch for Dillon's pickup. It seemed strange enough to be watching for people—he'd stopped minding anyone else's comings and goings long ago—but thanks to a visiting FBI agent and his sidekick, he found himself looking for a different someone in the coming than she had been in the going. It was no laughing matter, but it sure was funny. Whoever the hell she was, he could hardly wait to see her face.

Sighting a dust wake on the approach from the highway, Nick determined his own approach and headed outside to mind his family's comings. *His family.* His sister, his business partner and a woman he'd taken in off the highway. Watching them pile out of the truck looking all drained and defeated, he was beset by the urge to gather them in and tell them how little the loss of a horserace mattered to him. But he resisted. He would show them what was important to him by lightening their load. He headed straight for the back doors of the two-horse trailer.

But he was cornered before he could even start the chore.

There was shy Louise, taking the trailer doors right out of his hands. There was Dillon, suppressing a grin while he pulled out the ramp. And Joey, still dressed in her silks, was wearing all new hair, which was more noticeable but less important than the twinkle in her eye, the twitch at the corners of her mouth and the sassy swagger that could not help undoing any show they had planned for him. His family had brought home another victory. Anything else on his mind would have to wait while he gave their surprise its due.

"Guess what?" Without waiting for the obligatory *what?* Joey jumped him, legs around his waist like a kid on a stick pony. She was lucky his reflexes functioned well and he caught her. "We won."

"Another first place?"

"Your horse so completely outclasses and outperforms all his competition, it is just . . . You won, Nick!"

What could he do but hug her and laugh with her and say fool things like, "You little monkey, you're just full of surprises."

"Which is a surprise in itself, because you thought I was full of shit." Her big smile and bright eyes captured his fancy as she dug her fingers into his shoulders and hung on. "Didn't you? Come on, admit it."

"No way," he said, grinning. "The horse maybe, but not—"

"You should've seen her ride, man," Dillon enthused as he emerged from the trailer at the front end of a backing horse. Joey slid off her mount with a proud smile. "She flies like this little Red Baron, gunnin' it down the track, dive-bombing the finish line."

"I should've been there. We gotta get a movie camera." Feeling strangely discomfited, Nick adjusted his hat. "I like your hair." The truth was, he didn't know what to think of the sorrel color and the mop-chop cut, but he figured he was supposed to say something.

She plunged her fingers in and fluffed. "You do?"

"You almost look like a different person."

"Like a whole new identity?"

"It's a start."

"Here's the real man of the hour." She turned to the big Paint and claimed the lead from Dillon. "Tell your boy what you think of him."

"You kinda like this game, huh, True?" Nick rubbed the horse's black-velvet muzzle and then checked his legs, one white stocking and ivory hoof at a time. "Got you runnin' your socks off? Looks like he threw a shoe."

"It was on when we loaded him, so it must be in the trailer."

"I'll take care of him. You guys go on in the house and get yourselves—" He took the lead rope from Joey's hand, took another long, gratified look at her face. "You look so different."

"Pretty sure I'm still me," she claimed quietly, but she looked down at her hand as if to check and make sure. "I didn't throw a shoe, but I think I broke a—"

He had planted a doubt that needed removal. In spite of all the witnesses, Nick hooked his arm around Joey's neck and kissed her, first hard and quick for her achievement, and then soft and slow, purely for his pleasure. And the witnesses made themselves scarce.

But Dillon found his way to the barn soon enough after Joey had gone inside. With True Colors cross-tied in the aisle, Nick had already bent his back to his horse-shoeing chore, the animal's pastern braced against his knee, hoof upturned to receive Nick's full physical attention while Dillon filled his ear with who was doing what in the house. Showering, making coffee, putting sandwiches together—generally settling in, being back home.

"We'll get something to eat, and then I'll take Louise home," Dillon said. "She really enjoyed herself. I'm glad she went."

"I am, too." Nick tapped in the first nail.

"You know, you've been gone the better part of a week." Considerable pause. "And you didn't call."

"Yeah, I did." Nick lopped off the nail head. "Couldn't seem to catch anyone in."

"Anyone waitin' to talk to you was in every night from dusk to dawn." Dillon squatted, sitting on his boot heels with his arms braced on his knees. "I know, cuz. I've had plenty of doubts about her, and I still do.

But I know one thing—she's not doing any of this for herself."

"She wants to earn her oats while she's here. You gotta respect that." Nick dug into his jacket pocket for another nail. "It's a good way to be."

"You must've made good time today. Didn't expect you to beat us back."

"Got back a couple of hours ago."

"You had visitors, did you?" Nick spared him a glance, and Dillon added, "Two coffee cups."

"I did." Nick lined the nail up with the hole in the shoe. *Tap, tap, tap.*

"I did, too. Last night at the casino."

"Bowker and Dacotah?" Nick sensed his partner's reluctant assent. "What did you tell them?"

"I didn't tell them anything. Dacotah's been around before, checking out who's into what around the casinos. Bowker's FBI out of Minneapolis by way of Aberdeen. I knew the name. They started asking about your new horse and this professional jockey they'd heard about. I just played the big Indian. Told 'em they'd have to talk to you. But I spoke with Hank after they left. He said they asked him about some guys he knows down in Oklahoma, where one of the tribes has some kind of affiliation with a pretty big racetrack. Anyway, he let slip that he was impressed with your new horse, and this woman you had training and riding him."

"Did you tell Joey any of this?"

"Thought I'd tell you first."

"Did you tell them anything about her?"

"Nothing. I told 'em she was your business, and that you were away. Said you might be back today." Dillon's knees cracked as he stood, giving a sigh. "Hell, man, I didn't even refer to her by name."

"I told them she was my wife." Nick set the hoof down. The horseshoe clicked against the cement. His knee ached, and his brain buzzed. "By tomorrow she will be."

Nick waved to his sister as Dillon turned his pickup around and got ready to taxi down the Wolf Trail runway. Joey was still inside the house, but he knew that she would come to find him, and he kept busy while he waited for her. He had things to say, and the trailer was no place for him to say them. The warm spring had dressed the prairie to host his proposal. The soft evening sunlight, the long slant of its shadows, the easy breeze and the tweedling grass-nesters would accent whatever plain words he managed to string together.

He rode his stallion bareback around the corral with only a hackamore, just to see what the horse was like skin to skin, or nearly so. He was impressed. Joey had put such a sweet handle on him, the horse could probably be ridden Indian-style—a length of rawhide looped over the lower jaw and a blanket on his back. Back on the ground, he went over the horse's painted hide with a bristle brush and discussed the secrets of putting females at their ease before you approached them with your studly proposition.

Warm as the air was, Nick shivered inside when Joey walked up behind him in the corral. She said nothing. She simply laid her hand on his back and moved it back and forth. It felt like encouragement.

"Let's take a ride on True Colors," he suggested as he turned to her.

"Both of us?"

"We're not going far."

He put her up first and then mounted behind her. With Joey resting against his chest like the proverbial nesting spoons, he turned his back to the sinking sun and pointed the stallion's nose in the direction of the river. Not for the first time, Joey's slight weight and small frame struck him as an unlikely mate for his body, but the fit was perfect. She could find full refuge from the sun in his shadow, complete protection from the wind under his arm. He gave her the reins and slipped his arms around her.

"Did Dillon tell you how much money we won?" she asked after a long easy silence.

"He gave me the check. I'll take out some gas money for him, and the rest is all yours."

"No way. I'm earning my keep, remember?"

"We're past that. You should have something for yourself." He pointed toward a grassy ridge. "We're going up that hill, but go around. There's an easy approach on the south side."

"Hold on," she said. "Let me show you what True can do."

She urged the horse through a smooth trot and into a rocking-horse canter, signaled and controlled by her seat. "And that's bareback with a hackamore," she said proudly as they reached the top of the ridge.

"And two passengers."

He lowered her to the ground and then followed. Pretty smooth, he thought, even with the hard landing on his weak knee. She was already admiring the scenery, exactly as he'd intended. He took a seat in the grass, and she followed suit. He liked this spot because no buildings or roads were visible, but they could see the river and the rolling hills and the buttes at the edge of the sky.

"It's beautiful out here, Nick. You're so right. It's the perfect place for horses."

"It's the perfect place for anything that eats grass or anything *that eats anything* that eats grass. Some trees cling to the riverbanks and the creeks, but nothing else really wants to grow here." He plucked a stem near the patch of new grass True Colors had quickly set to work on. "This grass—buffalo grass, it's called—the roots go down so far into the earth, you gotta work hard to kill it. And when you take those roots away and plant something with little feet, like corn or wheat, the earth misses those sturdy roots so bad, she just dries up and blows away.

"But you see how she's lovin' up the grass with just that one rain we had? Because ten, twenty feet down, that's where the roots tickle her womb. That's where she's always moist and fertile, even if she's gone without water up here on the surface for season after season. So this is the perfect place if you can thrive on what it has to offer."

"Or you're willing to adapt?"

"Sure. The Lakota people took a long time to get here, but the grass and the grass-eaters suited us, and we suited them, so here we are." He lifted one shoulder. "People don't like Indians and buffalo, you'd think they'd go somewhere else. They don't like the way the river flows and the grass grows, and they're not here to adapt. They want to kill what's here so they can replace it with something else."

"But they failed," she said decidedly. "The grass is coming back for another season, and I saw some buffalo when we went to Louise's house. You've survived, Nick. And thanks to you, so have I."

"You live to fight another day," he said, thinking, yes, they had something in common. "Somebody else would've come along and helped you."

"Or not. Who knows what would have happened to me?"

"The important thing is, what happens now?" He nodded toward the northeast, where the backwater made its fingerling forays into the river channel. "That direction, our land goes all the way to the river. I have a quarter section across the road, and there's almost a section on this side that I own with my sisters. Dillon owns a little land, too, and we lease another section south of the house. I run a few cows, but the horses are my life. I make a pretty good living. I'm not a big talker or spender or dreamer, but I'm nobody's fool." He eyed her speculatively. "I don't make any promises I don't mean to keep. I'll keep you safe for as long as you want to stay with me. I want you to marry me."

From the look in her eyes, she hadn't seen it coming.

He swallowed. Big speeches sure required a lot of spit.

"Will you do that?" he persisted in the softest voice he could find.

"As long as you're willing just to *call* me your wife, that's probably—"

"Not enough. It has to be real. You need an identity, and it has to be real. But you're not stealin' my name. You have to let me give it to you."

She smiled as the breeze carried a lock of her hair across her eye. "You really want to?"

"I really want to." He lifted the hair from her face. "But I need a straight answer."

"Yes," she whispered. Then, in a stronger voice, "My straight answer is yes."

"I can line up a tribal judge tomorrow. Dillon's uncle . . ." He'd surprised her again. "What? Too soon?"

"The sooner the better. Is there time to find me something to wear? A dress would be nice. I could probably . . ." She reached for his left hand, rubbed her small thumb over his knuckles. "Would you wear a ring? Maybe I *will* take some of that money, just this once."

He took a white box from the breast pocket of his

denim jacket, opened it and showed her the two gold bands he'd ordered on his way out of town and picked up after his unexpected visitors had left. He'd thought to get her one, just for show, but the guy at the store had given him a deal on the set, and he'd thought, *What the hell?* "I can always take these back if they're not right, get something else."

"When did you decide?"

"You told me to think about it," he reminded her. "I haven't been able to think about much else. Somewhere along the way, it started making sense."

"Sense?"

"Yeah," he said. "Which means it's what I want, so I thought up a bunch of reasons for doing it. The rings were . . ." He took the small one from the box. "When something makes this much sense, I like to be prepared. You wanna try?"

"You try," she said, offering her hand. "For practice." He slid the ring over her knuckle, and she looked up at him with a smile. "How did you know?"

"My hands remember things. As for the dress—"

"I can use the one I came in. I'll bet Louise can fix it up just fine. This is the important part." She stretched her arm for a long-distance view of the ring on her hand. "How does yours look?"

"Haven't tried it. The guy measured. It should fit. I thought you should be first to put it on. But not for practice."

"No, for real." She snatched her ring off and quickly put it in the slot inside the velvet-lined box. But she took a moment to admire the pair. "Mine looks so small next to yours."

"I bought you a dress, too. I went into the store for . . ." She was looking at him again like he was turning weird before her very eyes. "I don't even know why I went into that store. I was on the road, stopped at a café, and there were these dresses in the window next door. And this one was . . . well, I could see you wearing it." He smiled, glad for the evening breeze cooling his face. "Like I said, I haven't been able to think about much else. If a guy's determined to make a fool of himself, he might as well do it in a big way."

"You said you'd keep me safe as long as we're together."

"Or die tryin'," he said, only half kidding.

"That's not funny." She closed the lid of the ring box and tucked it back into his pocket. "I don't want to bring any trouble here. I really hope I don't. But you have to know that you're taking a risk."

"Like I've never done *that* before." He chuckled and tugged on True Colors, who had reached the end of his tether. "There's a character in Lakota tradition—a god, I guess you'd say, but more like a force of nature. His name is Yum, the Whirlwind, and he's the spirit of chance, risk, games—those are things we've always prized. To hear Dillon tell it, casinos fit right in with Lakota tradition. And horse racing? In the old days, a good Lakota would bet the farm on a fast horse. Or the equivalent of the farm. Everything he had."

"The tipi, maybe?"

302

"Never the tipi. That belonged to his wife. No risk involved. That would be sure calamity, betting the tipi."

"Chance, risk and games," she echoed. "A whirlwind of excitement, all your basic amusement park rides. Tightrope-walking, free-falling, flying around a track on four legs or four wheels . . ."

"Playing with fire," he added ruefully. "Chance, risk, games . . . wasn't there a fourth?" He smiled. "Oh, yeah. Yum was also the source of love. Interesting mix, don't you think?"

"The ultimate gamble," she acknowledged.

"Compared to all that, standing between you and your badass boyfriend seems pretty low on the risk scale."

"Badass *ex*-boyfriend."

It was not an outfit Lauren would have chosen for herself, but the choices she'd made in another life didn't fit anymore. Amazingly, the soft blue dress with its slightly flared skirt and tailored jacket fit her perfectly and didn't look half bad with her new hair. It matched her eyes, Nick said, and she felt prettier than she had in a very long time. Nick wore a blue shirt and a bolo tie with a tan jacket that looked new, even though he said he'd bought it many years ago. He thought he'd worn it maybe twice. Tapered, with a western cut, the jacket enhanced his long, lean torso. So different from her badass ex-boyfriend's *GQ* style.

So blessedly different.

Dillon, Bernadette and Louise met them at the judge's chambers in Fort Yates, home of the Standing Rock tribal offices. The paperwork was completed first, declaring Nicholas Red Shield and Lauren Davis to be husband and wife. Dillon's uncle performed the wedding ceremony, and Dillon played a haunting song on a carved wooden flute. Then he announced that the best man would treat the wedding party and all their kids to dinner at the casino.

"No way am I taking kids," Bernadette said. "I have a babysitter for the rest of the day and a date with a slot machine tonight."

Nick took his share of teasing at dinner. Louise's remarks were gentle and sparing, but Bernadette was merciless. Her brother, the mighty oak, had fallen hard and fast. But watch out when he made up his mind, she warned her new sister. "He doesn't fool around. Much."

A live band played country music. Lauren managed to coax her new husband out on the floor for a wedding dance, which stretched to two and three, as long as the music was slow and easy. The downbeat of a rock song prompted their retreat from the floor. But he promised her a surprise in return for letting him off the dance hook.

Their retreat was stymied at the edge of the parquet floor.

"Hey, Nick." An attractive man with an eager smile offered a handshake. "Mike Dacotah."

"I remember." Handshake accepted, Nick slipped

his free arm around Lauren's shoulders. "You work for the BIA. Or, no, you're Indian gaming . . . something or other."

"Some government acronym. Hard to keep them straight. This must be your wife."

"Joey, this is Michael Dacotah. My wife, Joey."

"Hank Two Dog says you're quite the jockey," the man recounted as he offered his hand. The gesture, she was learning, was typically neither firm grip nor pump-handle, but rather the easy touch of one hand to another.

"Nick bought a fabulous stud, terrific breeding," Lauren said. "When we realized how fast he was, we just had to try him out. I did some race riding when I was a teenager."

"Not that long ago, I'm guessing. How long have you two been—"

"Awhile," Nick said. "But I think we've already had this conversation. Joey and I are celebrating another first-place win, and we don't get the chance to do this very often." Nick made a move to shoulder past the man, asking quietly, "Not tonight, okay?"

"You know how to get in touch with me." Oddly, the man took Lauren's hand again. "Pleasure meeting you. Hope your luck holds." He smiled. "Sounds like you've got yourself quite a horse."

"What was that about?" Lauren asked as Nick hustled her past a row of flashing, ding-dinging slot machines.

"He thinks I know something about some case he's

investigating for whatever department he works for. I've owned a racehorse for all of, what, a month?" He nodded toward a pair of elevators. "Let's go upstairs before somebody else wants an introduction."

"Upstairs?"

"We have the bridal suite tonight." He pushed the call button and grinned. "Yeah, there's really a bridal suite."

There were also spring flowers, a bottle of sparkling wine chilling in a bucket, thick white robes lying at the foot of a king-size bed and an oversize whirlpool bathtub. Nick found some music on the radio. Lauren left him to deal with opening the wine, took one of the robes into the bathroom and filled the tub. When she returned, she found him stretched out on the bed, arms tucked behind his head. He sat up quickly, as though an alarm had gone off.

"Are you done already?"

"With what?"

"Your bath."

"That's *our* bath, silly." She offered a sassy smile as she cinched the belt of her robe. "Have you poured our wine?"

He nodded toward the two glasses he'd poured two-thirds full and carefully arranged beside the bottle in its silver bucket, the vase of tulips and lily-of-the-valley and an array of votive candles on the table next to the window.

"Louise brought the flowers and candles," he said. "I think the champagne came from the hotel." He reached for her hand. "Come look at the sky."

Beyond the window, rose-blue dusk provided a setting for the stars appearing by turns, winking at the newlyweds.

"You've turned out to be quite a wedding planner." She held her wineglass with one hand, flipped open his belt buckle with the other. "But I hope you don't think you're going to be wearing the pants in the family all the time."

"You gonna fight me for them?"

With a flick of her wrist she unthreaded his belt from his pants, dropped it on the floor and began unbuttoning his shirt. "Are *you?*" she asked.

"Not if all I get when I win is my own damn pants."

"*If* you win," she said as she pushed his dress shirt off his broad shoulders, "you get *your* pants *and* mine."

"What would I do with *your* pants?"

"Wear them on your head."

Laughing, he swept her up in his arms and carried her to the bathroom. "Game over. Hey, this tub really is big enough for both of us."

"I'll go get the wine while you test the water. And then I want you to make yourself comfortable."

With the party transferred to the bathroom, Lauren turned out all the lights except for the candles, whose reflections danced in the expansive mirror. She felt incredibly sexy as she peeled back her robe, let it drop to the floor and stepped into the water, all for her husband's viewing pleasure. He made room for her between his long legs, and she lay back in his arms and enjoyed the love of his hands until her need for him drove her to turn and take him for the first night's ride.

In the aftermath, the whirlpool jets mixing with languid satisfaction felt glorious. They added more hot water and determined to become water creatures.

"I could get used to this."

"More wine?" Lauren started to rise, but he stopped her and retrieved his glass from the floor.

"Take mine. I don't drink much, and I'm not ready to let you move." He wrapped his arms around her. "Tell me about the race in Aberdeen."

"We won by three lengths," she said after a long drink. "And he's really only been breezing so far. He's got a lot more in him. We should start thinking about more competitive tracks."

Nick was quiet for a moment. "I'm thinking about retiring him to stud."

"He can get in plenty of sex between races. I mean, I know his jockey's a married woman now, but she's not exactly—"

"Ready to be a broodmare?" Beneath the water, he rubbed her belly. "Don't worry. Your horse and your ol' man are two different kinds of stud. I need him to produce."

"He can do so much more, Nick."

"It's too damn risky. Nobody's looking for Joey Red Shield. That's who you need to be right now. You signed Lauren Davis away this afternoon."

"It was just a name. I'm still . . ." She set the wine down and turned to face him. "I'm still good at it, Nick."

"You said you gave it up long before you met me."

"But now I'm back into it. This horse is such a—"

"Joey, listen to me." He laid his hands on her shoulders. "Like they say in the movies, you gotta lay low for a while."

She giggled. "This is your imitation of—"

"Take your pick. It's been a while since I've seen a movie. You changed your name and your hair. Now you need a new profession. You want excitement? How about—"

"I'm not talking about big tracks, Nick. We could go to Canterbury in Minnesota. We could go to Nebraska, Oklahoma. I would never be recognized there."

"You could be recognized right here." She tried to shake the notion off, but he wasn't buying. "Lauren Davis is missing, and they haven't found her body. If somebody was paid to kill you, either he wasn't very good at it, or he doesn't know the difference. Either way—"

"Either way, he's not a threat. If his little slip-up is discovered, he's dead, and he knows it."

"It's your health I care about, not some hit man's. I said I'd keep you safe, and since I don't know much about your enemies, I don't trust anybody." His hands slid away with a *plunk*. "I can't even trust my friends."

"You mean Hank Two Dog? He said I could ride. So what? A lot of people can ride." She smiled. His hair

309

framed his face in spiky wet tendrils. Her husband was adorable. She offered him the odd assurance of "Lauren Davis is dead."

"*Presumed* dead. The trouble is, she hasn't been buried. I don't know about anyone else, but the feds are looking for her. I know that for a fact."

"They have to, don't they? But that'll be over soon. They say if they don't find a missing person within the first few days . . ." It occurred to her that he wasn't talking about some routine investigation going on in a world outside theirs. "How do you know that?"

"Look, I'm not a particular fan of the FBI. Nobody around here is. But you're, you know . . . white. Yeah, it makes a difference. Maybe it wouldn't be such a bad idea to clue them—"

"You haven't, have you?"

"No, I haven't, but they're asking around, and they're gettin' close."

"How could they be . . . here?"

"Hank told somebody you rode like a pro. The guy downstairs? He's with some federal Indian gaming commission, but he's already paid me one visit in the company of an FBI agent. And they've questioned Dillon, too. I doubt there's more than one female jockey gone missing lately." He sighed. "Like I said, I'll keep you safe or die trying, and I don't know much about your enemies. I'm trying to protect you from anyone who looks at you sideways."

"Oh, God." She stared at him. For all his lovely brawn and all his harrowing experience, his innocence shone like a beacon. "You *would* die trying, wouldn't you?"

"I don't plan on it."

"No, but I know you," she claimed, leaning closer.

"Right."

"I do. Your heroism is legendary."

"Right. You know what, it's our wedding night, and I'd rather . . ."

She smiled, kissed him, slipped her hand between their bellies, found his penis and turned it rock hard with a deft caress.

"Oh, you're talkin' about *that* hero. You might have something there."

"I certainly do have something here." Something more, and now more, and still more.

"You get him on the case, he will definitely—" he groaned and whispered "—die tryin'."

"How do I get him on my case?" She sank into the water until her chin touched the warm surface, scanned her husband's smooth chest, met his eyes and smiled. "I think I'll have a little talk with him."

The underwater tête-à-tête lasted until she had to come up for air. "He's interested in my—"

"—in your case, *inside* your case." He pulled her over him, and she wrapped her legs around him—nightwings enfolding starfire, taking in and holding on and praying that the gods would make it work, just this night, one perfect night. "Inside my wife . . . my wife . . ."

"My sweet, sweet husband."

17

Nick lifted his face from the pillow, grabbed the receiver in advance of a second shrill offense and gruffly responded, "Red Shield."

"How's married life?"

"Damn you, Dillon, what—"

"I wouldn't be asking, but I had a feeling you were either asleep, tied up or dead."

"What are you talking about?" He rolled to his back, reached across the bed and had his answer. He jack-knifed and surveyed the empty room.

"If you hurry, you can catch her," Dillon was saying in his ear. "The airport shuttle leaves in about two minutes, and she's planning to be on it."

"Stop her."

The paunchy security guard was all business. He wanted to know who she was, what room she had stayed in and what she was carrying in her canvas tote bag. She didn't need this. Sneaking away from her bridal bed had been difficult enough, and then she'd had to slip out to the pickup after she'd asked the desk clerk about transportation to the airport. Leaving Nick was not something she could achieve without bearing down, blinkers on, full attention to the road ahead.

"I don't have anything," she insisted as he claimed the bag. "I didn't even—" She glanced toward the front desk, the lobby, the elevators, the alcove with . . . *Oh, God, here comes trouble.* "Dillon, please tell this man I'm not a thief. I'm taking the shuttle to Bismarck so that I can surprise Nick with—"

"You've surprised him, all right, Joey. He's on his way down." Dillon turned to the desk clerk. "Tell Nick Red Shield to meet us at Security."

"Please let me go," Lauren said quietly, grabbing his arm. "It's for his own good."

"What are you gonna do with this, Mrs. Red Shield?" The guard's discovery in her tote bag turned all heads.

"Isn't that Nick's gun?" Dillon demanded. "The one he keeps in—"

"The pickup," Nick said, turning all heads in another direction. "Joey, where do you think you're going with that gun?"

The security guard elbowed Dillon. "Isn't that a song?"

"Close, Artie, but this ain't the time."

"Am I under arrest or something?" Lauren asked, studiously avoiding Nick's eyes.

"You could be," the guard said. "Or your husband could be. Depends on your story."

"There's no story," Nick said. "A misunderstanding, maybe."

"Will she be taking the shuttle?" the desk clerk asked. "They're ready to head out."

"Tell them to go on."

"I've decided to go home, Nick." A fleeting glance

was all she dared spare him. "My flight leaves in—"

"You don't have any ID."

"Yes, I do. Trust me."

"Never trust a woman who says *trust me*." He laid his hand at the base of her neck. "We're going back up to the room."

"You can't make me," she protested, spinning away from the warmth of his hand. "He can't make me go back up there with him, can he?"

"Jesus, Joey . . ."

She turned on him. "I made a terrible, terrible mistake. You're not the man I thought you were, and I'm certainly not the woman you thought—"

"Artie, could we . . ." Nick nodded toward the security office door. "I need to speak with my wife."

"I'll be right outside." Artie hefted the pistol Nick had greeted Lauren with the night they met. "I'll just take this with me."

"It's not loaded. Not unless she found the loaded clip in the console. The one in the gun is empty." He glanced at her pointedly. "I don't know how she thought she was gonna get it on a plane," he said as he ushered her into the office and closed the door.

"I was going to check it. And I was going to pay you back."

"For what?"

"Everything." She folded her arms, making her stand in the middle of the small box of a room. "Including the money I took from your wallet."

"That first night we were together, I didn't get any

sleep for the noise you made with all your cryin'. But you're sure quiet when you're sneakin' off."

"You sure sleep soundly after . . ." She waved her hand, as if she might actually wipe the precious hours away. "Oh, Nick, you could've saved us both a lot of trouble if you'd kept quiet and just let me go."

"You think I wouldn't have gone after you?"

"Where? You don't know where I'm going."

"I'd find you. For a small woman, you have a way of cutting a wide swath."

"I guess it's a good thing you stopped me, then. You knew I wasn't going to be around forever. No promises, you said, and I thought, *this man gets it*. You never said anything about going after me."

"Why did you marry me? What good is the name without—"

"That was just another one of my stupid ideas." He pulled an incredulous frown, and she quickly added, "I'm sorry, but it was. I'm sure you can go back to the tribal court and just have the whole thing erased."

"Erased? It's a legitimate court. You don't just erase . . ." He raised his chin, eyeing her speculatively. "Come to think of it, you can divorce me in tribal court, but I don't think I can divorce you. They have no jurisdiction over you."

"Then how can they marry us?"

"They didn't. We did. The judge is recognized by the state as a justice of the peace, but we're the ones who got married. You took me, and I took you."

"I *took* you, all right," she claimed, turning her

315

shoulder to him. "I had a plan, Nick. I was going to try to use your horse to get to the man who tried to kill me. I might have been able to lure him into doing something that would . . ." She searched the ceiling for help. None found, she sighed. "I was going to let him claim your horse."

"Why?"

"What does it matter? I'm in trouble, and I'll do whatever I have to do."

"I don't see what good it would do to—"

"I didn't say it was a *good* plan. It was just a plan. But if the FBI knows about me, then . . . then that's not going to work." She pointed a finger. "Which means you're no good to me, Nick. And this place isn't exactly out of sight and out of reach anymore, is it?"

"Then what was last night all about?"

"It was all about—" she glanced away and back again "—sex. Good sex. It was good, wasn't it?" He nodded. "I really did try to earn my keep. And I thought . . ." She gestured toward the door. "I just thought this way would be easier. You know? I can't stay now."

"Are you sure you don't want to talk to the authorities?"

"The authorities," she said, and she couldn't help smiling. "That's funny, Nick. Like, the coppers. And the gangsters. Maybe you haven't been to the movies lately, but you've sure seen a lot of old ones."

He lifted one shoulder. "Whatever you want to call them, the police might be able to help you."

"Maybe I'm not quite as white as you think. As in lily white." She gave a humorless laugh. "I really don't want you to know what I've done or where I'm going or who I've been involved with. I want to be Joey for you. Okay? Can we just leave it at that?"

"Sure," he said, his eyes devoid of feeling. "But now that your getaway plan failed, there's no rush, is there? You might as well come home with me and pick up your stuff."

"I really don't have any stuff."

"And then I'll take you to the airport, bus station, friend's house, wherever you wanna go. Just like I've always said I would."

"Nick . . ." She turned away from him. "I have to—"

He grabbed her arm, spun her around and kissed her so suddenly that she had to kiss him back. Without thinking, she rose up on her toes to meet him, to artlessly, fully open herself to him.

He came away from the kiss with eyes alight.

"You're good at a lot of things, but lyin' ain't one of 'em. I know what last night was about. The sad thing is, I'm not the only one you're lyin' to."

She shook her head, desperate to recover her resolve.

But he was relentless. "I don't care what you've done, Joey. I don't care if the devil himself wants you dead. He'd have to get past me."

"I don't want that."

"What, then? I'd walk through hellfire for you, and

you know I'd—" He grabbed her shoulder when she tried to back away. "Look at me, Joey. Tell me you don't love me."

Pressing her lips together to keep them from trembling, she wound up and slapped him as hard as she could. Her hand, heart, eyes ablaze, she stood firm.

"You can't make me stay."

"I could." His hand came away slowly from her shoulder, finger by finger. "But one time, and one time only, I made somebody I cared about do something against his will. I live with the consequences."

She turned quickly, opened the door and strode past the security guard, who sat outside the office door.

"Artie, give me the gun," Nick said.

The guard released the magazine, glanced at the couple and then shoved it back into the butt of the pistol. He handed it to its owner without checking for rounds Nick had already said weren't there.

Nick handed the weapon to his wife. "Take it. I use it for rattlesnakes mostly. I keep the spare clip loaded and handy, but this one's empty. When you get there, first thing you do, you get a box of bullets and you load the damn thing. I hope you don't mind shooting the sonuvabitch the next time he decides you've been around long enough." He paused. "You change your mind, Joey, you know where to find me."

She could not look him in the eye. Nor could she change her mind.

Dillon returned from his errand feeling like the bad-luck best man. Driving the runaway bride to the airport the day after the wedding wasn't supposed to be on the list of his duties. But it was Nick's call. If the situation were reversed—and in some ways it had been—Nick would do the same for him without jawing over the details. It was a long drive up to Bismarck and an even longer drive home, where he found Nick's pickup parked next to the barn. The man would want a report. Maybe even an ear.

He was currying True Colors. Dillon had watched Joey perform the same chore standing on a cinder block, and he'd knocked together a wooden step for her so she could reach the horse's back. She was no slacker. That much he could say for the woman. A cold bitch? Maybe. But Nick had seen fit to do what he did, and he had his reasons. If he'd made a bad call, if there was a price to pay, so be it. They both knew the drill.

"You got her to the airport okay?" Nick asked without looking up. He was generously applying the elbow grease, kicking up puffs of dust and horse hair.

"Yep." Dillon wished he could say what Nick wanted to hear—that she'd changed her mind and was waiting for him back at the house.

"Got her some more cash?"

"Yep."

"Did she say anything?"

"She said thank you. And I didn't say shit. You know how hard that was?"

"Next to impossible." Nick dropped the currycomb

into a rubber bucket and unhooked the cross ties. "I'm thinking I'll put him out with the mares this week."

Dillon patted the horse's flank. "Give 'em our best, big guy."

Nick opened the Dutch door and turned the horse loose in the corral. "Thanks for standing up with me yesterday and helping me out today." He laid a hand on Dillon's shoulder. "You're still workin' graveyard, huh? You must be tired."

Dillon had to ask. "It's none of my business, man, but was it because of her kid?"

Nick scowled. "What kid?"

"*What kid?* Nick, she has a kid somewhere, or *had.* I'm guessin' a real young kid."

Nick's hand slid away. "She told you this?"

"Not in so many words."

"Yeah, well, you're dreamin' again." Nick gave a mirthless chuckle. "Something like that, she would've told me."

His tone said no skeptical commentary invited.

"She's like you, keeping the bad stuff to herself." Dillon tapped his partner's chest with the back of his hand. "Nick, the day she was playing with Bernadette's baby and I was asleep up in the loft? She didn't know I was there, and it was kinda one of those deals, you're caught between hoping they'll go away and coming out to—"

"What happened, Dillon?"

"You know what that baby's like. No ears, that one. She tried to tell him no, but he tore into her blouse and latched onto her tit. Thing is, once he started, she kinda gave him a little help. Plus, she called him *Joey*."

"So, you . . ."

"Well, the choice to stay out of sight was already gone by the wayside. You saw her that day, she was . . . I mean, I can't believe you didn't—"

Nick's patience thinned to the see-through point. "Did she tell you *what happened to her kid, Dillon?*"

"No, but I told her I knew what it was like to lose your kids, and she just looked sad. I figure her baby died, or he got—"

"—taken from her. She wouldn't go back there otherwise. We're talkin' some serious evil where she's headed."

"She's obviously been workin' on *something* for a while."

"Whatever she thinks she's doing now, it isn't what she planned. She got scared." He glanced out the open door. "I'm going after her. They've already tried to kill her once."

"That plane already flew."

"I have to find her, and I'm gonna need some help. There's no time to backtrack and go searching under every rock."

"I'm with you, man. Whatever you need."

"I'm not sure what that'll be. Joey was gonna let this guy Vargas claim True Colors. Why, I don't know. According to those two agents, Vargas is into high-stakes gambling and all kinds of criminal crap, which

. . . Hell, he tried to *kill* her."

Dillon nodded. It all sounded pretty dramatic, but if Nick started painting his face for war, Dillon would take on his share of the charcoal.

"I'm gonna give Michael Dacotah a call. Jesus, I hope I can trust him." Nick shrugged, shook his head. "I got no choice."

Michael Dacotah was more than happy to stop at the Wolf Trail the next morning on his way back to the area office in Aberdeen. Nick had a feeling the man was expecting his call but not necessarily his news.

"My wife took off on me," he told the man soon after he arrived. No coffee offered, no chair. Simply a handshake and the reason for the meeting.

"You think she went back to—"

"I don't know where she went," Nick said. "Where this Vargas holes up. If you can tell me what you know, maybe we can help each other out."

"That's not the way this works, my friend. We trade information, and you're the one who goes first."

"You're gonna be sorely disappointed. I picked her up off the side of the road down in Missouri. She'd been left for dead. I didn't even know her name until—"

"So she's not really your wife."

"We're married. That much is legitimate. She wouldn't say much about what happened to her. Said she needed to disappear, forget the whole mess, because the guy responsible was some badass sonuvabitch. But there was one detail she couldn't leave behind, and I don't know why I didn't see it."

"Her son."

"Joey," Nick said. Dacotah nodded. It had to be true, then. "How old is he?"

"Little guy. A year, maybe." Dacotah shook his head and did Nick the courtesy of staring off toward the highway. "She was hiding out with you, and you had this horse and she's a top-rated jockey, so you decided to get into horse racing? Not the best way to keep her identity a secret."

"I don't know what was up with that." *Are you sure you don't want to talk to the authorities?* he'd said, and she'd laughed at him. He couldn't blame her. He wasn't one to talk, period, and here he was, running off at the mouth. "She wouldn't tell me much at first, which was fine by me. I offered to drop her off some-where, but she said she had no place to go. She told me she'd ridden her dad's racehorses when she was a kid. Other than what you've told me, I don't know anything about this Vargas she was hooked up with."

"Raymond Vargas is slick, and he's deadly. A small businessman and a big gambler, although nobody's been able to pin down just how big. He keeps a legit-imate profile in the horse-racing business. He's owned some winning horses, mostly when he had Lauren Davis riding them, but she's been out of it for at least a couple of years."

"She had a baby."

"Right. By the way, they were never married."

"I know." Certain things, a guy just knew. "What's his connection with Indian gaming?"

"We don't know for sure what they're trying to set up, but Bowker is working a case in New York involving a gambling ring that's handling sports betting all over the world. Offtrack betting. Some of our Indian casinos—especially the ones that are too isolated to get a lot of foot traffic—they're looking for Internet traffic. Frankly, they're getting some shaky advice. Especially when the tribal leaders aren't as involved as maybe they could be and they've got management companies working deals for them."

"Is Standing Rock into this Internet stuff?"

"Not so far, but this kind of stuff can start out looking perfectly legal. They just busted a guy in Fargo for doing illegal wire transfers. But his business was hooked up with UND in an offtrack betting service that was legit. You see the offtrack handle jumping from ten million to more than two hundred million in a single year, you start to wonder."

"Is this guy connected to Vargas?"

"Jigsaw puzzle. That's the name of the game," Dacotah said with a smile. "You pick up a piece here and a piece there, you try to fit them together. We know that Vargas and his associates are interested in doing business through conduits like the kind we're talking about. Charitable gambling, Indian gaming— they must look like the new frontier to these guys. They could launder all kinds of money, not just gambling proceeds. The more cash you run through, the harder it is to account for it. Any criminal activity you can name—and I mean the big stuff, from drugs to terrorism—you follow the money."

"This is getting way too 007," Nick said. "I just want my wife back."

"Bowker thinks we can connect Vargas and his associates to charges big enough to put them away indefinitely. We want to head off any plans they might have for turning Indian casino race books into channels for dirty money. The New York Racing Association has already canceled contracts with some of the casino rebate shops. They want full disclosure, and we're urging casinos to comply voluntarily. We're the ones who noticed this possible connection between the FBI's case and our race books. We want to help them get these guys."

"You get Vargas . . ."

"You get your wife."

"If he doesn't get her first." Nick shook his head. "Why in hell would he be interested in claiming my horse? Joey says . . ."

He gave an apologetic smile. "Lauren. My wife. She says the horse is capable of competing at a much higher level. But surely these guys are into big-stakes races, Thoroughbreds. My horse is a Paint. She was talking about taking him to bigger tracks, but we were talking Minnesota, Nebraska, Oklahoma, not—"

"Oklahoma," Dacotah said, fairly pouncing on the word. "We had some reports out of Oklahoma. There's an Indian casino has a race book with one of the tracks down there, and some contacts . . ." He made the wobble-hand sign for *shaky*. "Could be some movement afoot. I can tell you where Vargas lives, but I'm interested in what he's up to. Which probably has nothing to do with your wife, but maybe it could. How much do you think she knows?"

"Nothing. She went after her baby."

"Do you know where she went?"

"No. She took a plane out of Bismarck. She didn't have anything when I found her, so I don't know where she came up with ID or what name she's using."

"She must have some connections of her own. Nick, this woman could be using you."

He accepted the notion with a shrug. "I'm all she's got."

"You don't know that. You don't know how far she'll go."

"She'll go as far as she has to. And so will I."

"We can track the flight and check phone records, but we don't want Vargas to get wind of this investigation. If we can find Lauren Davis . . ."

"Joey Red Shield. Maybe Lauren Red Shield."

"All of the above," Dacotah decided. "I think she's got something with this idea of using your horse as bait. How much are you willing to risk, Nick?"

"Everything I have."

18

Lauren "Joey" Davis Red Shield was flying the way she rode a good racehorse—by heart, instinct and keeping the saddle just barely in contact with the seat of her pants. She'd never been good at making plans, and this day was no exception. In her last contact with Jack she had arranged the fake driver's license she'd needed to build a new identity, which had come in handy for boarding the plane. She had detected unusual urgency in Jack's voice when he told her to *be* this new person now. No going back, he'd said. Things had changed, and she might not be able to count on him much longer.

Her escape had done a number on two men. Nick deserved better. Maybe Jack did, too. But right now there was only one man, one number—enemy number one. In movie terms, Vargas's number was up. Lauren smiled as she approached a bank of phones at the Springfield airport. She decided against calling Jack in favor of taking a cab all the way to the farm and using the drive time to consider what she might face and how she would deal with it so she could leave Nick to his horses and Jack to his . . . to whatever Jack had in his life besides his boss. It was up to her to get her child back. No matter what identity she assumed, she was, first and foremost, Joey's mother.

She remembered the security code, along with the

general idea of how to use the gun packed in the small bag she'd bought at the Bismarck airport so she could get it onboard in checked luggage. Following Nick's advice, she made one stop on her way west from Springfield. Your basic big-box store—one-stop shopping for bullets, a bagel sandwich and baby toys. She'd grabbed a toy pickup truck on the way to the sporting goods aisle. A big blue one, like Nick's. Her husband, Nick, the man she'd slapped silly because he didn't deserve to die for her sins.

She looked at her right palm—where she could still feel the sting every time she thought about it—and the back of her left hand, where Nick's ring glimmered in the early evening light. He had given his "big Indian" heart, which her heart, for all her little white lies, would not allow her to turn away. He would have given her the ride, the horse, the shirt off his scarred back, and she would have taken it all for Joey's sake.

But not his life. She couldn't go that far.

The life of Raymond Vargas was another matter. She was going to kill a rattlesnake with Nick's rattlesnake gun. If he hadn't changed the security code, and if he went into the library for his usual nightcap after everyone else in the house was in bed, she knew exactly where and how she would do it. She could even take out the new girlfriend if need be. Do the woman a favor. Lauren sat back in the cab, smiled, and thought about Nick and his old movies. She was on her way to carry out a hit, and she was smiling.

Lauren entered the house through a quiet patio

entrance and found the place dark and apparently deserted. She checked the garage and discovered that Raymond's Porsche was gone but the Escalade was there. Raymond was out. Jack must have taken Joey and the nanny somewhere, since they clearly weren't on the premises. She couldn't have planned it better.

Please, God, bring Raymond home first, so I can kill him.

Not the most reverent prayer, but she could ask forgiveness later.

Raymond's "library," where the books were for show and the bar was for real, was a perfect room for a murder. The bar was visible from the foyer, and the double doors, which always stood open, gave her a place for both easy cover and access.

Mrs. Red Shield, in the library, with the gun.

But she would leave no clue.

Approaching headlights shone through the sheers on the library's floor-to-ceiling windows. Lauren's heartbeat tripped into overdrive. She took her place and waited, ears attuned to every sound. The door from the garage admitted him to the house. Footsteps on the wood floor. The clicking of the light in the bar cabinet. Cocktail glass, decanter stopper, glass-on-glass clink. Now was the time. Lauren came out from behind the door, concentrating on the heft of the gun, the need for two hands, straight arms, gun pointed toward the light. She was unsteady, and she rushed her shot, but she took it. It was all noise. Quick thunderclap, shattering glass.

And then she realized that she hadn't shot Raymond Vargas. It was Jumbo Jack, who was still standing, slowly turning, with a pistol in one hand and a glass in the other.

She was a dead woman.

But he drained the glass, set it down on the bar and inspected the new hole in the shoulder of his sport coat. Then he looked up at her and laughed.

Laughed.

"You shot the wrong guy, little girl. The man you really wanna see dead has gone to the races."

"Oh, Jack," she gasped. She looked down at the strange, heavy thing she was holding, suddenly confused about what it was doing in her hand and how to safely separate the two. She looked up. Jack, still standing. Herself, not dead yet. Table. *Phone.* "I'll get you some help."

"What are you doing?"

She traded the gun for the telephone receiver. "I'm calling 911."

"Put the phone down. This is nothing. I've got a friend who'll look after this. Used to be a medic."

He was there beside her. Jumbo Jack, still standing after she'd shot him, taking the phone from her, picking up the gun while she, wide-eyed, watched the dark patch on the shoulder of his sport coat grow like the time-lapse blooming of a blood-red rose.

"I shot you, Jack. I'm sorry." She looked up. Why wasn't he angry? "We have to do something. You're bleeding."

"It smarts, too. But I don't think you hit anything but fat. It went clear through, see?" He turned to show her the matching flower in back. "If you had to shoot me, this was the way to do it."

"I didn't. I wanted to—"

"You got the documents you wanted?"

"The ID, yes. Thank you." She stared, befuddled. "Where's Joey?"

"They're gone. We've had a changing of the guard here. New nanny, new rules." He turned toward the bar, his movement faltering slightly. "Shit, look at that mess. We gotta find that bullet and pick up the—"

"What can I do, Jack? We need towels, we need . . . I think you should let me drive you to a hospital."

"I don't do hospitals, little girl." But he allowed her to tuck herself under his arm on the uninjured side and help him to a chair. He wouldn't sit, but he braced himself on the high back. "I'll bleed to death first."

"No you won't. Tell me what to do, Jack. This wasn't meant for you."

"Since your mark is outta town, no murder will be done tonight. So what I'm gonna do is, I'm gonna take you with me. We'll get me fixed up, and we'll get you—"

"I want to see my baby. Please, Jack."

"I'll arrange for that. I promise. But can we take care of this first?" He waved his hand toward the bar. "I'll let you pick up the glass. We don't want him to see somebody's been here."

She brought ice and towels, cleaned up the debris

and found the bullet lodged in the dark oak cabinetry. By the time she finished, Jack had taken a seat and was looking slightly peaked.

"Do you want me to drive? We can't afford to get stopped."

"I almost forgot to get what I came for." He hauled himself to his feet and took some papers from a desk drawer. "Okay, I'm gonna let you drive, but don't let me pass out, okay?" He chuckled. "It's not that bad. It's just the blood. Makes me light-headed."

"The sight of blood?"

"Only when it's mine. Crazy, huh?"

Lauren had her doubts about Jack making the climb to his friend's apartment. What he'd claimed were "a few steps up" turned out to be three dimly lit flights. The apartment smelled of Pine-Sol and burnt toast, and the square-faced woman who lived there seemed more disgusted with than concerned for Jack's condition.

"Jack Reed, you never come here but you're draggin' ass and spilling blood all over my floor."

"I brought supper and a movie over just last Tuesday."

"Like I said, barbecued pork butt sandwiches and *Rocky*. Get in here before somebody sees you." The woman offered him a hand, but Jack took the offer as an invitation to brace his hand on her shoulder and use her as a crutch after he'd refused Lauren's repeated offers. "Who's the girl, and why should I let her in?"

"Harrie, this is . . . what name are you goin' by now?"

"Joey," Lauren said, following the pair to a kitchen table that reminded her of the one in Nick's trailer. "Harry?" Lauren smiled. "Joey and Harry."

"It's Harriet." She peeled Jack's jacket off before settling him into one of the two chairs flanking the table. "What's he done now?"

"It's what I've done. It was an accident. Mistaken identity."

"Interesting." Harriet padded into the kitchen, sliding pink scuffs across the laminate floor, adjusting the tie belt on her flannel robe. "Hard to mistake Jack for a quail, so it must be moose season."

"I thought he was a—" Lauren winced at the sight of the hole in Jack's shirt, the blood, the damage she'd done "—prowler."

Harriet peeked around the cabinet door she'd just opened. "I know who you are, missy."

"Harrie, don't," Jack warned.

"I've known Jack a long time. Since Vietnam."

"He said you were a medic." And somehow she'd been expecting a man. Harriet's face didn't scream *female,* but the mass of gray-and-black hair that hung past her waist must have been glorious in its day.

"Jack's word for nurse. I've patched him up more than a few times." Harriet was filling a stainless-steel kettle with water. "I saw the story about you on the news. Jack said you got away okay and didn't want to be found."

"She came back for Little Joe," Jack said. "I was afraid she would."

"Where is he, Jack?" Lauren perched at the edge of the sofa. "You said I could see him."

"I said I'd arrange it. It might take me some time." He'd plunked his shoulder holster on the table and set about unbuttoning his shirt. He and Harriet had clearly gone through this routine before. "What was it you wanted me to do about that horse you've been talking about?"

"Raymond loves owning the winning horse that comes out of nowhere. I thought I had one for him. I thought if I rode him, staged Lauren Davis's public resurrection, then we'd all have something on each other, so nobody could afford to cross anyone else. Plus he'd get the horse, I'd get my life and my baby back." She sighed. "Joey's nothing to him, Jack. An ego trip."

"Why didn't you go to the police?" Jack wondered, sucking air through his teeth as Harriet started the process of cleaning the back side of his wound.

"And tell them what? You left me on the highway? I know how Raymond operates. He would have come away smelling like a rose."

"Is that a wedding ring?" he asked.

Her right hand flew to cover the gold band. Protect it, keep it safe from doubts of any kind. If she had nothing else to her name, there was still the ring and the sweet memory of the man who had thought to buy it.

"Part of the act?"

"I took his name," she said quietly. "I took . . ."

"His gun?" Jack's chuckle turned into a *yowch!* He jerked away from Harriet's prodding, but then he was back to reprimanding Lauren. "That was stupid. Slim chance you would have plugged your real mark."

"I plugged you, didn't I?"

"Yeah, but *he* woulda plugged you right back. I picked up some information. Haven't had a chance to look it over, but I'm thinking there's a chance . . ."

"A chance of what?" He was thinking about helping her. While his friend tended the wounds Lauren had inflicted on him, Raymond's personal enforcer was toying with a notion. "Jack?"

"You're gonna have to stay here for a while with Harrie," he told her finally.

"You're not going anywhere for a few days, either," Harriet warned.

"I'll keep my promise, little girl, but I need one from you. No more of this." He brandished the shoulder holster he'd laid on the table. "Can you keep her away from the windows and doors?" he asked Harriet.

"What are you going to do?" she asked.

"I'm going to see a man about a horse."

"You're not talking about Nick, are you?" Lauren panicked. "Because he's totally out of the picture now. He gave me a place to stay, and I came up with this racehorse scheme. He almost went for it, but I think he realized . . . Well, he got cold feet."

"Usually they get cold feet *before* the wedding."

335

Harriet slid a pointed glance in Jack's direction.

"Nick decided gaining a wife and losing a horse might not be such a great deal. I decided my chances would be better with Jack." She hastened to add, "For getting my baby back. You'll help me, won't you, Jack?"

"I said I'd arrange for you to see him. I don't know what it's gonna take yet, but you're staying with Harrie until I say otherwise. You're not equipped to kill anybody, little girl. Get that out of your head. *Fuck!*" Another assault on his torn flesh had the big man turning on his nurse. "What have you got to drink around here, woman?"

With stitching to be done, the patching up of Jack Reed turned ugly. Lauren cried. Jack got a little teary himself, but mostly he got drunk and finally passed out. Harriet, the battlefield nurse, drank a little, cursed a lot and did her job with a steady hand. Jack was removed to the sofa, and Harriet finally accepted Lauren's offer to help out.

"You can clean up the operating room while I make us a nice cup of chamomile tea."

"I'm sorry to impose. Story of my life, I guess." Lauren rolled Jack's ruined clothes in a towel. "You and Jack must be very close."

"What makes you think that?" Harriet deposited a rag and a bottle of Pine-Sol on the table.

"He trusts you. A man in Jack's position can't afford to trust just anyone. In all the time that I was with Raymond—and Jack was always around, you know,

Raymond's right-hand man—I never heard anything about Jack's personal life. He never mentioned friends or family. Of course, I never asked. I knew better. I didn't even know he'd been in Vietnam," she said as she mopped blood off the chair. "It was all about me. My experiences, my acquaintances, who could and couldn't talk to me, never going to the track unless he was along. For my own protection, he would say. And when I got pregnant, when I had Joey, oh! Don't get me started. Jack was like this hulking shadow, always there."

"You resented it?"

Lauren glanced at the big man sleeping—passed out—on the sofa. "I'm sure it seemed that way, but the truth is, for a while I enjoyed being treated like a queen. But I got pregnant, and I was dethroned."

"The only reason he told me as much as he did about that night—about you getting away and calling him and all that—was because the whole thing tore him up pretty bad." Harriet emerged from the kitchen with steaming mugs hung with tea bag strings. She, too, glanced at the man on the sofa.

She lowered her voice. "He doesn't have any family. No friends to speak of. But he had a daughter. Jack tried to get her and her mother out of Vietnam, but they were both killed."

"Oh, no," Lauren whispered in his direction. "Poor guy. No wonder he wasn't too keen on the baby-sitting job."

"Men like Jack live by their reputation," Harriet said

quietly. "They're efficient, obedient and loyal, much like the best soldiers. Any deviation, word gets out. When that happens, they're expendable." She lifted a shoulder, sipped her tea, met Lauren's gaze. "Like soldiers."

"But soldiers are allowed friends and family."

"I said *much* like. Jack never allowed himself any attachments until you came along. You were part of his job. Couldn't be avoided." She sat in the chair Lauren had just cleaned. Too late to warn that it might still be wet. Too late and too trivial.

Harriet set her tea aside. "I know all about how he beat you up and left you. I know it was raining. I know it was cold. I've heard." She pulled her sheaf of hair to one side and began braiding it. "He should've gotten rid of that cell phone, but he couldn't bring himself to cut you off."

"Do you think he'll help me get Joey back?"

"Yeah." She gave a tight smile. "He'll try. He hasn't said, but I have a feeling he's not working for Vargas anymore. Whether Vargas knows it or not." She pulled a rubber band from the pocket of her robe and popped it over the end of her braid. "You ask me, Jack's got some kind of mission in mind. And if you pull any more stunts, you're liable to fuck him up big-time. So you're staying with me until he gets your ducks in a row."

When the call came, Nick snatched the phone off the hook. He'd been expecting to hear from Dacotah for hours. Days, it seemed like. He had been ready to hit the road ever since Dacotah had made the suggestion. The only question was, where were they going?

"Is this Red Shield?"

Wrong voice.

"Who's asking?

"A friend of your wife's. Are you missing a pretty little semi-automatic Ruger .22?"

Shit. "What happened to her?"

"Your wife or the pistol?"

"Is Joey okay? Where is she?"

"She's all right, but you oughta be pistol-whipped for letting her take that gun with her. She didn't know what she was doing."

"She could've taken *me* for protection. She chose the gun."

"She thinks you're safely out of the picture. Safety first. Safe for you, that is." Pause. "Well, are you?"

"Who's asking?"

"The guy who took a bullet meant for Raymond Vargas."

"Jesus." Guns, bullets and Vargas. "What's going on? Where is she?"

"She's in a safe place, but I don't know how long I can keep her there. She's trying to get her kid back. Listen, Red Shield, I don't know what kind of a man would let her come back here after—"

"You listen to me," Nick growled. "I *do* know what kind of a man it takes to beat her up and leave her to die."

"She wasn't left to die. She was left alive. Look, I have her safe now, and I might be able to get the baby. Anything beyond that is out of my hands. If Vargas isn't neutralized, everybody involved is in deep shit."

"Are you a cop?"

The caller laughed.

"Can I talk to her?"

"She doesn't know I'm calling. The two lives she cares about are Little Joe's and yours. Look, she says you've got some kind of a flashy, dashy horse that might interest Vargas. He's pretty sensible about everything but horses. Put the right kind of bug in his ear about some up-and-comer, he'll get him a jones on, and he'll go for it. We can work this from two sides."

"Me and who else, and what two sides are we talkin'?"

"The name's Jack, and I'll be workin' the dark side."

"Everybody claims the dark side lately." Nick smiled. It didn't much matter—light or dark, fire or ice—he was ready for whatever waited for him wherever Joey was. "All right, Jack, my horse has run and won exactly two races, so I don't know if that qualifies him as dashy. I'll go for *flashy*, though. His looks, and the way Joey rode him was definitely flashy."

"Then all you have to do is sign him up and get him down to Oklahoma. You bring the dash, and I'll meet you there with the flash. Don't worry about Vargas getting the line on the horse. I'll set that up.

And the jockey is Joey Red Shield."

"Will she know?"

"All she'll know is she gets to see the kid."

Dacotah was going to love this no matter what, but Nick had to ask. "Why Oklahoma?"

"Lots of horse racing, lots of betting. Vargas went down there to set up some business. It's got nothing to do with the size of the track. It's the simulcasting, off-track betting, the race book." He chuckled. "I'm not into this stuff myself. I'm just a hired gun. You know more than I do about Indian casinos and those rebate shops."

Yeah, right, Nick thought. The Indian's latest "government handout." Casinos and rebate shops.

He wondered whether Jack was Italian.

19

Nick was skeptical, but Michael Dacotah was all over Jack Reed's plan, or what there was of it. Reed would get Joey to the track if Nick would bring the horse. The part that interested Dacotah was that Vargas was already there and he was "doing business." But Nick wasn't letting Dacotah in on part B—hooking Joey up with her kid—mainly because Reed hadn't gone into specifics, and Nick didn't want anyone screwing up that part of the deal. Reed had promised Joey that she would see her baby. "And she'll have him back for good, long as you work with me on this without asking too many questions. Trust me."

Trust me. Damn, but he hated those words.

Dillon all but outfitted himself in cloak and dagger, and Joey's silks were packed in a duffel bag, along with the jeans and boots she'd left behind. Nick admitted that he didn't know much about Reed except that he claimed to be Joey's friend. Nobody was making book on his reliability. But he was all they had. And he had Joey.

Blue Belle Downs in eastern Oklahoma was the biggest racetrack Nick had ever seen up close and personal. Large grandstand, glass-enclosed clubhouse overlooking the track and the paddocks, restaurant, racino for televised action, poker parlor—all the amenities for a day at the races. The barn was huge, and it was almost as clean as Nick's. True Colors occupied a pricey box stall in a prominent location, thanks to some influential friends.

It was prominent enough to attract the attention of a man who stood out in the Oklahoma crowd. His upscale dress with a touch of gold jewelry, shiny shoes, slick hair and slicker demeanor drew attention to his party of four. He was touring the barn in the company of a quiet man, a stylish woman and a baby in a stroller.

Sitting six inches from the floor in his low-rider with nothing to commune with but big people's knees, the little guy looked lost and lonesome. Nick caught his attention with a look and a smile. He waggled his eyebrows, then tossed and caught the shiny apple he was just about to share with True Colors. A wide-eyed stare morphed into a friendly baby grin.

"What's the story on this Paint?"

Every muscle in Nick's body tensed at the sound of the pretty man's voice. No question, this was the enemy. A vision of cold-cocking the bastard made his hand itch. He tucked his right thumb in the pocket of his jeans and waited for a remark worthy of response.

"I'm looking over some of the claimers. Pretty hefty claiming price on this one," the man said.

"I don't really want to sell him. Had to put the price on him to get him into the race."

True Colors stuck his head over the stall door and sniffed Nick's arm, shoulder to elbow. He knew there was an apple around here somewhere.

Talk of this prick claiming his horse brought a bitter taste up from Nick's gullet. But he glanced down at the baby, who had him, the apple and the horse in his sights. Nick winked at the boy.

I'll get you to your mama, little man.

"I figure nobody's gonna claim him at that price," Nick continued. "Hasn't shown in enough races."

"He's a beauty." The man was shuffling through a handful of literature he must have picked up in the track office. "Is this the right pedigree?"

"That's it. Solid top and bottom sides. I'm the owner, Nick Red Shield."

"Ray Vargas. Pleasure." He had the good sense not

to offer his hand. "Who's the jockey? A relative, obviously."

"Yeah. We're new at this, so we're using homegrown. But we think we've got something special here."

"So I've heard. He's about the prettiest Paint I've seen. They're really coming into their own on the track." Vargas reached, but True Colors went high-headed to avoid the hand.

Vargas turned to Nick. "I'm here with a friend who has a horse running against the big fella, here. Pretty stiff competition. There's a lot of interest in this race."

"I didn't know."

Maybe someone else would claim his horse. As Nick understood it, if multiple claims were made, the management would draw lots to determine the new owner. Anybody but Vargas. Unless the deal came down to True Colors for the little boy who was pulling against the stroller restraints, quietly working to free himself.

"Oh, yeah, you put this boy up against some movers," Vargas said. "Should be an interesting race. Marla, get the kid out of there before he gets loose in here."

Nick rammed his thumbs into the stem end of the apple and snapped it in half. Little Joey took pains to watch, leaning away from the woman who threatened to get in his way. As she lifted him, Nick showed him half the apple before offering it to True Colors. Joey laughed as the horse crunched it up.

"This horse loves apples," Nick told the boy with a smile.

"Ap-ple."

"Can he have this?" Nick asked the woman. "It's from the restaurant's buffet. I just—"

"He has his own food." The woman turned to Vargas. "I'll take him outside. Now he's going to want an apple."

"I'm finished here," Vargas said, and to Nick, "Good luck with your claimer."

Over the woman's slender shoulder, the baby's big blue eyes held Nick's gaze until the group turned the corner at the end of the aisle.

"Was that him?" Dillon asked.

Nick turned, surprised to find Dillon and Dacotah coming up behind him. Nodding, he took a bite of the apple. He loved the smell of a juicy apple. Comfort food. Sweet and soothing. He swallowed his consolation and gave the rest to True Colors.

"Why can't I just kill him and get it over with?"

"He's goin' down, Nick," Dacotah said quietly.

No consolation there. Nick imagined having the man's blood on his hands, marking his own face with it. Now, *that* would be cause for a victory dance.

"Have you heard anything about Joey?" Dillon asked.

"I don't know what good this thing is." Nick plunged his hand into his pocket and came up with the mobile phone Dacotah had provided. "It doesn't ring."

"Sure you've got it on?"

Nick handed it to the expert for another equipment check. "I've gotta get out of here. I feel like this place is crawling with unseen eyes and ears." He turned to Dillon. "You mind staying with True? With Pretty Man and his kind skulkin' around . . ."

Dillon gave a subtle thumbs-up. "Keep your powder dry and your phone on."

Dacotah wasn't letting Nick out of his sight or the cell phone out of earshot. But once they'd safely closed the pickup door, he didn't seem to mind clueing Nick into what he'd learned earlier in the day through his local contacts, as though Nick were part of the team.

"Vargas has been down here for more than a week now," Dacotah said. "Supposedly on vacation with his family."

"His family?"

"Oh, yeah, he looks like a real family man, taking the baby and the nanny all over—casino, horse farm, zoo—totally average guy. Last week's nanny apparently became this week's girlfriend. That's the public stuff. But he's had several meetings at the tribal casino I told you about. We think their race book might be vulnerable. They're a small band, and they have a new management company."

"Does Vargas bet on these races?"

"Not at the track, but he does plenty of offtrack business. And he buys and sells horses all over the place. He picked up a claimer last year and won big with him later on in the season. There were rumors of doping, but no solid evidence. *Yet.* These guys are pros, and they do it all, from petty to grand. You pay for their lunch while they're stealing your soul. That's the way they operate."

The cell phone vibrated against Nick's hip. He flipped it open. "They're here."

Another flight, a rented car, another hotel room. Lauren was reduced to tagging along with the man who had done her a favor by putting her out on the highway with nothing but the clothes on her back. Following, trusting, hoping that the flight to a small-town Arkansas airport and the crossing of another state line really would get her closer to her baby. She wouldn't have to deal with Raymond, Jack had promised. He would take care of that. It was necessary that they act quickly, and all Lauren had to do was cooperate.

She was trusting the henchman.

Another racetrack, a room at the Blue Belle Motor Inn. Lauren tried to remember a time in her life when she'd felt like she actually belonged somewhere. Vargas's house had actually been *home* for a time, especially when she'd prepared the nursery, and when her baby had come and filled the space in the house and in her life. And Nick's house. Her time there had been too short. Her time with a good man had taught her heart to hold out for nothing less. If she got through whatever action was to be taken, if she came out on the other side with her baby in her arms, she would find a way to get back to Nicholas Red Shield. Once their gangster-loaded, landlocked coast was clear. And this time, she would tell him everything from day one, right up front. *This is who I am, and this is how I feel about you.*

She checked the room service menu while Jack took a phone call. He left the room, and Lauren knew something was coming. She could feel it, from the phone call to the way he'd told her to wait to the key in the lock a few minutes later. She jumped off the bed, praying he had Joey with him and not, *please, God, not Raymond Vargas.*

But it was the antithesis of Vargas who walked through the door.

"Nick?" Lauren's pulse raced. She wanted to run to him like some pathetic lost lamb, but she managed to hold her whole coming-apart-at-the-seams self in check. "What's going on?"

"Jack called me."

"Why?" She searched the two faces—the beloved brown one under the cowboy hat, the familiar bassett hound one under the receding hairline. "What are you doing, Jack? You said Raymond would be here with Joey."

"He is," Nick said. "I saw him at the track not too long ago. He came into the barn, checkin' out the horses."

"You saw *Raymond Vargas?*"

"I saw your baby, too." He took one step closer, the softness in his eyes giving his heart away. "Cute little guy. Looks like you—big blue eyes, light-colored hair. Not much of it, but it's coming. He saw True Colors, and he was ready to—"

She closed the distance between them, and he was ready for her. She buried her face in the open vee of his shirt and inhaled the tangy scent of his skin. The sting of tears engorged her eyes, but she held. And she held.

"It's gonna be okay, Joey," he whispered.

She nodded against his chest. "You can't be here, Nick. I should have left you alone with your ranch and your horses and your—" she looked up, searched his loving eyes "—your life. Nick, what are you doing here?"

"We're getting your baby back. That's all I know."

She backed away, loving him more and trusting him less. He didn't know what he was doing any more than she did. She turned to the man who damn sure better have a plan.

"Why did you do this, Jack?"

"Because you're gonna need him, little girl. He's your friend, lover, husband, whatever. He's the man."

"No, he's . . . I *left* him."

"So what?" Jack tossed off as he slumped into a chair. "You tried to kill me."

"I was trying to kill—" She turned back to Nick. "I went to the house to get Joey back. It's true that I had every intention of killing Raymond."

"I figured you were going back with him." Nick gave his hat a needless adjustment. "You put me to

349

shame, Joey. I had the same urge myself today. Wanted to break the bastard's chicken neck so bad I could . . ." He shook his head, smiling. "But you actually took a shot."

"You can't be involved with this, Nick. You didn't sign on for this."

"I signed on for you. For us, for whatever chance we have."

"You didn't know what you were getting into," she insisted.

"Who does?"

"This is different. Please let me handle this. I'll come back to you as soon as I get Joey back. It's all I've thought about since I left. You and me and Joey *together*."

"Which would explain why the part about getting past Raymond Vargas wasn't very well thought out," Jack put in from his sideline chair. "I told her I'd arrange for her to see the baby. She thinks she's just gonna take off with him." He hauled himself to his feet again. "That's how you got into this mess, little girl. I don't know anybody who crossed Ray Vargas and lived to tell about it."

"I brought a couple of guys with me," Nick said. "How many do we need?"

Jack laughed as he sauntered across the room. "First off . . ." He unzipped the bag he'd left on the desk, stuck his hand under some clothes and pulled out Nick's pistol. "Don't give it to her," he warned as he laid it in Nick's hand. "She's lucky she got me in the left wing instead of the right. So Ray came lookin' for your horse? Who else was with him?"

"A woman, mostly lookin' after the baby, and some guy. Vargas said his friend's horse was entered in the same race as mine."

"He doesn't have as many friends down here as he does at home, so that's something. The day they left, he told me I wouldn't be going with them, that I was due some time off. I don't know how stupid he thinks I am." Jack rubbed his grizzled chin. "The guy who was with him is probably my replacement. Either him or the guy who took a shot at me the day after they left." He waved off any coming protest. "Not you, little girl. The one the forensics specialists haven't identified yet." He turned back to Nick. "Tell me about the woman."

"Tall and skinny, long dark hair, talks with a Texas accent."

"New girlfriend?" Lauren asked.

"New nanny. He had the hots for her from the day she was hired. Guess I'm not the only one who just got replaced."

"I brought the horse, and he's entered to run in the seventh race," Nick said.

"Am I riding him? Of course I am. If you want to win, I'm riding him."

Nick laughed. "What difference does it make if he comes in dead last? He's set up to be claimed." He turned to Jack. "That's what it's gonna take, right? You told me to get down here with my horse and you'd see to it that Vargas would come after him. I don't know what we're in for tomorrow, but I'm thinkin' I should hire a jockey off the track."

"No, she rides the horse." Absently Jack flexed his left hand and rubbed his sore shoulder. "Her name is Joey Red Shield. She can even pass for a boy. Nobody's gonna recognize her."

Nick hadn't told Jack Reed that he was working with federal agents, nor did he plan to give Jack up to Dacotah. As far as Nick was concerned, the agreement was all about getting Mama Joey and Baby Joey safely out of Vargas's hands. Dacotah was hoping to get an indictment against Vargas out of the deal. The possibilities made him fairly salivate as they stood behind the backstretch fence and watched Dillon work True Colors early on race day.

Whatever happened with Vargas, Nick still risked losing his dream horse. But he couldn't think about that. Not now.

"If Vargas plays this true to form, one of these horses is in for a milkshake after his morning workout." Dacotah squinted, used his hand to block the rising sun. "Sounds like a treat, doesn't it?"

"It sounds like doping." And Nick didn't like the idea of his horse and jockey sharing the track with an animal all hopped up on any of the host of drugs that were banned at all racetracks. But horse racing was no different from every other high-stakes sport. Bans were made to be broken. Joey could handle her own horse, but it was always the other driver who caused the accident. Leaving Nick to wonder, "What are you gonna do about it?"

"We're going to take some pictures. My agency wouldn't be interested except for the connection with the casino. But if we can catch him and his associates in the act, we could be launching the case against Vargas from here, this track, this day. Every big bust starts with one seemingly insignificant—"

"Wait, now, this sounds like some dragged-out affair. I'm banking on you putting the sonuvabitch behind bars *from here*. This track, this day."

"With any luck," Dacotah mused, ostensibly watching the workout field.

"So who's taking pictures? I'm getting ready to put my wife up on a horse in the middle of all this." Nick sighed. He was keeping her off the track as long as he could. He had relayed her workout instructions to Dillon, who, just as she'd predicted, was struggling with a frisky horse invigorated by the morning chill and the company of the "morning glories," the workout showoffs who wouldn't do squat when the time came. He shook his head. "I don't like it."

"If this goes down the way it's supposed to, Vargas won't get close to your wife. We'll have the police take custody of the baby, and she'll have him back where he belongs immediately."

"And if it doesn't go down that way?"

"With any luck he won't get away, and if he does—"

"That's the second time you've mentioned luck," Nick pointed out. Dacotah stayed silent, apparently out of predictions. No answer for *if he does*. It was all a big gamble.

And Jack Reed was Nick's ace in the hole.

Lauren had done everything she could think of to conceal her identity. Joey probably wouldn't even recognize her when she finally got to see him. No sun-worshipper, she had gotten herself a tan in a can and was pleased with the results. She might not look like a Red Shield in Nick's eyes, but she would pass in some circles. With time on her hands the morning of the race, she'd gone shorter and darker with her hair. The generous cut of her silks and unisex breeches gave her a nondescript body. She looked small and boyish, like most jockeys, male or female.

Nick seemed impressed and maybe even relieved when he picked her up. "Quite a transformation," he said.

Every step in the routine leading up to post time seemed like one more hurdle she'd put behind her. She presented herself and her equipment to the clerk of scales. Making weight was not a problem, but she was mindful of every person who came around her at the scales, avoided speaking any more than necessary, remained utterly calm and supremely vigilant. Jack had promised that she would have her baby after the race. *Where?* she'd asked. *Should I look for you? Meet you?*

He'd pointed to a radio speaker built into the hotel room wall. "Listen for an announcement. When the roll is called up yonder, little girl, you be there."

She hadn't seen him since he'd left the hotel, but she knew he was there at the track. Somewhere. The henchman would not let her down.

Nick and Dillon met her in the saddling paddock, where the less-than-expert groom and trainer—it was hard to tell which was supposed to be which—prepared her mount. She was there to speak with True Colors, to assure him that they were in this together, that her eyes and ears, hands and mind, would be looking after him, and all he had to do was run with her. She could feel him collect himself at the sound of her voice and the touch of her hand. It was her best advantage. Horses liked her.

"He's going to do fine," she told the two men.

"You ride safe," Nick insisted. "Take no chances."

"I can scratch him, Nick. If the jock says there's something wrong—"

"There's nothing wrong, is there, big guy?" Nick adjusted the saddle cloth. They were number four. "We're running clean and safe."

"And we're the only ones with Yum on our side," she said as she touched his hand. Their gold bands glinted in the sun.

Jockeys from the earlier races had passed through the jock room grumbling about a heavy track, but Lauren determined during the post parade and her warm-up gallop that it wasn't really heavy, though there was some moisture. She would call it slow, and True Colors would call it good.

It was a full starting gate. They were up against some high-strung horses. Lots of blinkers and shadow rolls to keep them from seeing scary things like their own shadows. Every jock in the gate carried a stick except Lauren. She was a hand rider. When the horse in the stall next to her tried to crawl the gate and True Colors ignored the show, she half wished she could scratch right then. He should never have been a claimer. He was the horse her father had spouted poetry about, straight off the cuff. True Colors was one in a million.

He was on the bit from the minute the gate opened. Every muscle, every sinew, every bone, propelled him forward. Lauren steadied her mount as the pack closed around her, then found a hole and broke free. It was then that the number six horse streaked past and took the race by eight impossible lengths. True Colors was a solid second.

Rocket's Blue Streak was still running flat out as the announcer declared him the winner. The animal had streaked, all right, wild eyes nearly popping out of his blinkers as he'd passed True Colors. If they were going to dope the horse, they should have warned the jockey, Lauren thought. The man had probably broken a finger trying to pull him up.

The results of the race were disputed immediately.

"I've been beaten like that before," Lauren told Nick as they walked True Colors through the restricted paddock area. "That horse was feeling no pain."

"Won't they test him?" Dillon asked. He'd assumed the duty of leading True Colors.

"If he had a milkshake for breakfast, it won't show up in any testing," Lauren said. "Of course, if they injected him with testosterone, that's sometimes detectable."

"Let's hope the pictures turn out," Dillon said.

"What pictures?" She glanced from pillar to post, looking for familiar faces as she unsnapped her chin strap and pulled off her helmet.

Nick gave her flattened hair an affectionate tousle. "You two were beautiful together. I wish I had pictures."

"The stewards must have something, or there wouldn't be a dispute. Have you seen Jack?"

"We've been busy watching you win another race," Nick told her as he pulled the saddle for her second weigh-in. "In my mind, you won."

"*You* won. Wolf Trail Ranch is the owner. And if they disqualify the doper, you'll get first-place money."

"They allow up to ten minutes before the race to drop a claim in this state," Nick said. "I guess I'll find out about that little detail soon enough."

"I'll take care of True," Dillon said. "It's time to see which comes first, the cheater or the cheated. Let's hope our friend didn't lay an egg."

"What friend? Jack?" Lauren tucked her arms under the saddle. "Never mind. I can't have this conversation now. Jack knows where to find me. After I weigh in—"

An announcement came over the public address speakers.

"Would Mrs. Nick Red Shield please report to Security? *Mrs.* Nick Red Shield."

When the roll is called up yonder . . .

"You go with her," Dillon said to Nick. "If they took Rocket's Blue Balls to the test barn, that's probably where all the action is and where I wanna be. Along with the lights, cameras and guys in white coats with horse-size specimen cups."

"I'll catch up," Nick promised. But first he had to catch up to his wife.

She made quick work of her weigh-in and asked for directions to Security. The uniformed guard's escort made her nervous, as did his urgent pace. She glanced over her shoulder more than once to be sure Nick was still with her. The tall young guard ushered them down a narrow hall and through a door, where three more were gathered around a fourth, who was holding . . .

Joey.

"Ma-maaa!"

Yes, yes, *yes!* Her baby knew who she was. No haircut or fake tan could fool her son. His little arms clung so tightly around her neck that she could hardly breathe. His skin smelled like sunshine, his wispy hair like rainwater. Yes! She was awake and breathing, and her arms were full of Joey. She brushed a tear away from her cheek and another from his. He wore the blue bib overalls she'd bought half a size too big. They fit him now. Oh, she'd missed days and days and days.

"Where'd you find him?" Nick asked.

"The guy who brought him in—big fella, said his name was . . ."

"Reed," another guard supplied.

Lauren lifted her chin, opened her eyes and ears to the room beyond her and her baby.

"Jack Reed," the guard with Murphy written on his name tag supplied. "Said his baby-sitter walked off the job during the seventh race. Was that your race, Mrs. Red Shield?"

"There's a diaper bag here," said the portly guard on the far side of the desk where they'd been gathered. He pointed to a manila envelope. "He left some pictures of you and the baby, passport—must be in your maiden name—birth certificate. You carry this stuff with you all the time?"

"Homeland Security," Nick said. "I'm her husband. Did Jack say where—"

The office door flew open, and the tall escort leaned in. "There's been a shooting! We've got gunmen in the horsemen's bookkeeper's office."

There was a flurry of guards finding their legs and their guns. Lost and found, they were used to dealing with. Shooters on the premises, not so much.

"Stay here," Murphy told Lauren.

"That guy who left the baby was one of them," the tall one said.

"Oh, God." Lauren hugged Joey close and looked

for Nick. *He's here. We're safe.*

"Stay with them," Murphy told the big slow guard behind the desk. And then, to Nick, "Don't go anywhere."

They were left with the big man, who had found his gun but not his legs and looked as stunned as Lauren felt.

"What's going on, Nick? Was this . . . you and Jack . . . ?"

"No, not me and Jack. I'm here, and Jack's in the bookkeeper's office. And you've got Joey back. That's what I know." He glanced toward the open door. "But I don't know where Dillon is."

"And Raymond?"

Nick started toward the door.

"Murphy said—"

"Shit. I left the damn gun in the pickup." He snapped his fingers. "Maybe I'll get to break his neck after all." He turned to Lauren.

Michael Dacotah appeared in the hallway. "You hear the sirens? We've got casualties."

"Where's Dillon?" Nick demanded.

"I don't know. But Vargas is dead. His associate took a bullet, but he might pull through. Jack Reed . . ." Dacotah glanced past Nick. His question was for Lauren. "Is he a friend?"

"Yes," she said, following Nick into the hallway. "He's our friend."

"You'd better come now."

The commotion had turned the business end of the

racetrack facility into a transit station, with guards directing the traffic of race-walkers, joggers, foot-draggers and rubber-neckers.

"Everything's under control. Nothing to see."

"Move to the west end of the building, please."

"Stay on this side. Nothing you want to look at here."

Dacotah flashed his security pass as he shouldered past incoming policemen and outgoing spectators, leading the way to the "money rooms." Vargas. Reed. Had Lauren not been summoned, Nick would have made his way to the horsemen's bookkeeper sooner to see whether a claim had been dropped on his horse. He would have been there when the shooting went down, too.

"We had him," Dacotah told Nick as they approached the door marked *Horsemen's Bookkeeper*. "Three other guys actually tubed the horse, but Vargas was present. He calls in his bets, like, seconds before post time, and we had that, too. We could've nailed . . ."

Beyond the door lay a grisly scene. Four men were moving Jumbo Jack from a pool of blood to a lowered gurney. Another man lay on a desk in a spread of more blood, and a third person was sprawled on the floor, the head covered with a bloody towel. Lauren pulled Joey's face to her shoulder as though they'd been assaulted by a cold wind. She turned away, loath to see more, but she couldn't help noticing a shoe, a shiny shoe that no real horse lover would wear to the track.

Jack opened his eyes as Lauren called out his name.

He lifted one bloody hand from the hole in his stomach, grabbed the bottom of Nick's jacket and labored over the words, "Make her go."

"I can't make her do anything. You know that." Nick leaned closer and said, "They covered him."

"Little Joe." Jack's attempt to smile nearly broke Lauren. Paramedics were barking orders. The gurney was moving, and Jack was trying so hard. "Good Dakota . . . cowboy . . . name."

"We'll see to it," Nick promised. He'd grabbed Jack's hand and was holding on, squeezing. "They're both going home with me."

"My . . . little girl." Lauren nodded. He motioned for her to lean closer. "Don't . . . look . . . back."

She nodded, blinking against tears. *Say something. Anything.*

"Thank you, Jack," she croaked.

"Thank you," Joey echoed his mother. "Big Jack, big Jack. Go bye-bye."

"We'll follow the ambulance," Lauren called after the retreating gurney. "We'll be there with you, Jack. It's just another . . ."

But he was gone.

She looked up at Nick. "It was you and Jack. You got Joey back."

"It was him," Nick said. "He made the trade. His life for Vargas's."

20

On the first anniversary of Jack Reed's death, Lauren Red Shield prepared a meal to honor him. Thanks to his wife, Nick had gotten into the habit of celebrating every milestone she could come up with, but this one was different. This one was a mixed bag.

The others had been wonderful, often wacky, always joyous. They had celebrated his adoption of Joey with a traditional Lakota ceremony. The groundbreaking for the new house had called for handprints in cement. Birthdays were celebrated with cakes that generally looked better than they tasted, because making them pretty was her strong suit. And the big birthday—the birth of their daughter, Nicole—had been a day for prayers and promises when his tiny wife had refused to consider anything but natural childbirth. She had done it once, she'd said, and by all that was holy, she would do it again. And Nick, who hadn't set foot in a hospital since the last of his burn surgeries, had silently, desperately, taken a vow of chastity with the unholy upsurge of every contraction.

Days ago, on their first wedding anniversary, his wife had released him from his vow. But he'd meant it when he made it. As beautiful as their children were, he'd told her that if she wanted any more, she'd have to figure out a way to get him pregnant. She dedicated their anniversary celebration to exploring that possibility, theorizing that it was a question of position, muscle control and visualization. And she proceeded to drive him wild.

But now it was time to remember Jack Reed. In the backyard of the work in progress that was their new house, Nick hosted a Wiping of Tears ceremony. He announced to his family—now his wife's family—that it was time to let their friend go.

"This man had no family that we know of, but he treated my wife and my son as his family. Whatever else he did, this man gave his life so that Little Joe could return to his mother and me. He was a warrior and a protector. He spared my wife's life when he was under orders to kill her. For these actions, we honor him, and we sing him across the Wolf Trail."

Dillon gave the equivalent of an amen—*"Hau, hau"*—as he struck a traditional drum four times before lifting his voice in an honor song. Then the guests formed a line to receive the ceremony. A holy man brushed everyone present head to foot with an eagle feather and gave them all water to drink.

Louise and Bernadette had helped Lauren prepare the meal. She had made small gifts, which she and Nick presented to their guests. Before they performed their final duty to Jack, Lauren slipped into the bedroom to nurse the baby. With everyone fed, the cleanup complete, and the children chasing one another around the house, Nick looked in on his girls. He could not get enough of the sight of his daughter's tiny mouth tugging on the nipple he loved so well.

"I'll be with you in a minute," Lauren promised.

"No hurry, as long as we get started while there's still enough light."

"I thought we were looking for stars."

He smiled, thoroughly enchanted. "Got a little surprise for you first."

They left the children in Auntie Louise's charge and met True Colors in the corral. His first racing season had come to an abrupt end when Lauren had discovered her pregnancy, but he'd been a consistent winner. Not only had he made a name for himself and his progeny, but he'd helped to furnish his jockey's new house.

They rode double the way they had done the night he'd proposed, and when they topped the first rise, Lauren gave a squeal of delight. On the first anniversary of Jack's death, a buckskin mare—possibly the many-great-granddaughter of Sitting Bull's favorite horse—had given birth to a black-and white foal. True Colors whinnied, letting his mares know they could look forward to more of the same.

"Horse colt," Nick said. "Looks like his daddy. Lots of color and legs that don't quit. Thought we'd call him Jumbo Jack."

"You think? Sounds more like a moose." She chuckled. "Moose season. That's what his friend Harriet said after I shot him."

"Why did she give his ashes to you? You said you thought she was his woman."

"She said it would please him. He lived his life as a

loner, but that isn't the way he died." She rested her head against Nick's shoulder. "Don't look back, he said. And I'm really not. But I have to believe that he chose us, and once he'd made the choice, he did the only thing he knew how to do. If he hadn't been killed, I suppose he would have gone to prison. Still, he chose us over . . . over his boss."

"Dacotah said the other bodyguard copped a plea as soon as he got out of the hospital. He testified in the case they were working on. But they were pissed about losing Vargas in a gunfight."

"Whatever happened to the nanny? The one Jack locked in the storage room at the track."

"I hear she's looking for a job," Nick deadpanned. "You need some help?"

She jabbed him with her elbow.

"Just a little Indian humor."

Slowly they made their way to the promontory Nick now called "Proposal Point," where they waited for the Wolf Trail to make its appearance. A sudden breeze rustled the grass, and grass-dwellers answered with night music. And finally, unfurled like a white ribbon, the river of stars flowed across the black-velvet sky.

Never one for singing, Nick found himself making a song for the ashes his wife spilled into the wind.

The grass would claim the dust of a life, but the warrior's soul would find the Wolf Trail.

Center Point Publishing
600 Brooks Road ● PO Box 1
Thorndike ME 04986-0001 USA

(207) 568-3717

US & Canada:
1 800 929-9108

The Knight

and
the

Dove

Also by Lori Wick
in Large Print:

The Long Road Home
Who Brings Forth the Wind
A Gathering of Memories
Wings of Morning
As Time Goes By
Donovan's Daughter, The Californians
The Hawk and the Jewel
A Place Called Home
The Princess
Promise Me Tomorrow
Sean Donovan
To Know Her by Name
Whatever Tomorrow Brings
Where the Wild Rose Blooms
Whispers of Moonlight

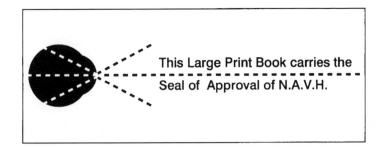

This Large Print Book carries the
Seal of Approval of N.A.V.H.

The Knight

and
the

Dove

Lori Wick

Thorndike Press • Waterville, Maine

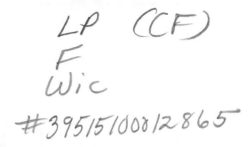
Published in 2001 by arrangement with Harvest House
Publishers.

Thorndike Press Large Print Christian Fiction Series.

The tree indicium is a trademark of Thorndike Press.

The text of this Large Print edition is unabridged.
Other aspects of the book may vary from the original edition.

Set in 16 pt. Plantin by Warren S. Doersam.

Printed in the United States on permanent paper.

Library of Congress Cataloging-in-Publication Data

Wick, Lori.
    The knight and the dove / Lori Wick.
        p.   cm. — (Kensington Chronicles)
    ISBN 0-7862-2955-1 (lg. print : hc : alk. paper)
    1. Great Britain — History — Henry VIII, 1509–1547 —
Fiction. 2. Knights and knighthood — Fiction. 3. Large
type books. I. Title.
PS3573.I237 K58 2001
813'.54—dc21   00-062868

To my pastor and his wife,
Phil and Denise Caminiti.
I praise God for your faithfulness, encourage-
ment, and willingness
to be used by Him. This dedication
comes with my love.

The Kensington Chronicles

During the Nineteenth Century, the palace at Kensington represented the noble heritage of Britain's young queen and the simple elegance of a never-to-be-forgotten era. The Victorian Age was the pinnacle of England's dreams, a time of sweeping adventure and gentle love. It is during this time, when hope was bright with promise, that this series began.

But now travel back 300 years, to an enchanting time when knights and chivalry and heraldry reigned, and King Henry's Tudor England set the stage for all that was to come.

Prologue

"What of Vincent of Stone Lake? He's a loyal lord."

"Yes, my liege, he is," James Nayland, chief adviser to King Henry VIII, spoke in agreement. "Vincent is most devoted. He's one of your dukes."

⸕ "I know my own lords, Nayland!" Henry's voice turned with irritation. "Does Vincent have sons?"

"Only daughters. Two."

Henry scowled at Nayland as though it were the other man's fault and then frowned at nothing in particular, his gaze on some distant spot. He was silent for just moments, however, his powerful mind moving in consideration.

"Tell me of Bracken, Nayland. Bracken of Hawkings Crest."

"Word has come to me that young

7

Bracken has just returned from a trip to see his mother. She lives in the north country."

"He hasn't taken a wife, has he?" Henry's scowl was back in place.

"No, your grace. He's hardworking, engrossed in the running of his keep. I do not believe that such a thing has crossed his mind."

"A viscount, is he?" Henry's mind moved swiftly again, and Nayland knew better than to even smile over Henry's earlier comment that he knew his own lords.

"No, my lord," he said stoically. "He's an earl."

"Vincent's daughter . . ." Henry speared his aide with another glance. "Marigold has been to court, but what of the other? Is she older or younger?"

"Younger. Megan must be 17 by now."

"Vincent would lay down his life for me," Henry said without boast. "I'm sure of this."

"As would Bracken, I believe," Nayland inserted gently.

"Yes," the king agreed. "He has proven himself loyal, but as you said, he is young. I think a union is in order."

Nayland smiled. If Henry felt it would be advantageous to the throne, he would marry an infant to a man gray with age.

"Send word, first to Vincent and then to Bracken," Henry commanded. "The choice of the bride is to be Vincent's, but we won't rush things. I want Bracken content as well. Tell both Vincent and the young earl they have a year. No, make it six months."

"As you wish," Nayland spoke humbly while making notes.

They did not discuss the marriage or Vincent of Stone Lake again. But Bracken of Hawkings Crest was the subject for long minutes to follow.

One

"Who was that, Vincent?"

The lord of Stone Lake Castle turned slowly to see his wife enter the room but did not immediately answer her. Studying her a moment, he thought her beauty timeless; she was as lovely today as she'd been as a bride. But he also knew that her beauty sank no deeper than her skin. His eyes narrowed when he thought of the storm the king's news would induce.

"Vincent!" Annora's voice was no longer softly curious but harsh with irritation. "Is something the matter? Who was that man?"

"A messenger from Henry," Vincent told her.

Annora's eyes widened. "Is the news bad?"

"I fear you will think so."

Annora's eyes narrowed with anger. She had not bothered with a wimple, so she now swung her head, causing her mane of thick, blonde hair to fall from one shoulder.

"What nonsense do you speak?"

"Only that Henry wishes our family to unite with that of Hawkings Crest. He has ordered that our neighbor should marry one of our daughters."

Annora was well and truly horrified. "Surely not Marigold?"

Vincent shrugged. "She is the eldest."

"I don't care!" Annora's voice was turning shrill. "I will never allow her to settle for an earl. We'll keep Marigold hidden. If he never sees her, he can't choose —"

"I am to choose," Vincent cut in.

"Well, it's settled then," Annora said with a laugh that turned from relief to cruelty. "You'll have to send for Megan."

Vincent took a breath. "I will speak to Marigold first."

This time Annora laughed in true amusement. "She'll never agree. I'll fetch her myself and you can ask her."

"You mean she's here?" Vincent's brow lowered. "I thought she'd gone to London."

"No, she's not leaving until tomorrow. I'll go now and send her to you."

"No."

Annora halted in her walk from the great hall and turned slowly back to her spouse. Vincent had to keep from flinching over the hatred he saw in her eyes, but his mind

11

was resolute. He knew that all chance of convincing Marigold to marry would be lost if her mother spoke to her first.

"You will remain here, and we will speak to her together."

Annora took a seat, but Vincent could see that she was furious. He knew she might not speak to him for days or possibly weeks, but he was determined to have his own way this time.

Minutes later a servant was sent to fetch the elder of Vincent's daughters. Her parents settled down to wait in frigid silence.

Marigold never hurried unless it pleased her to do so, and Vincent hated to be kept waiting. Having taken lessons from her mother for the past 19 years, Marigold was an expert at irritating her father. More than 20 minutes passed before she made an appearance, but Vincent was still calm — in truth, he was filled with an amused anticipation. He knew his daughter to be deceitful above all women, and for the first time he rather looked forward to the creative excuse she was sure to give for not coming on time.

Sure enough, Marigold's look when she entered the great hall was one of regret. Her eyes were wide with remorse, her lovely face apologetic, sweet even.

"I was told just this moment that you wanted me," she said softly. Her humbleness was so real that Vincent could only shake his head. To those who did not really know Marigold, she seemed so sweet. Vincent did know her, however, and wasted no time informing her of the situation.

"King Henry has ordered that our household be joined to that of Hawkings Crest," he spoke without preamble. "You will be married to Bracken."

All humility fell away. Marigold's face became a mask of hatred and disgust, turning her normally lovely features into a repulsive sneer.

"Never," she nearly hissed. "I am *not* ready to wed, and when I am, I will *never* settle for an earl."

Her words so echoed those of her mother that Vincent mentally gave up. However, Marigold was not through.

"You may wish to play lackey to the king, but not I. I'd rather die than be married to that oaf at Hawkings Crest, and if you don't have the spine to tell Henry, then I will!"

"It's just as I told you, Vincent," Annora cut in, her voice so like Marigold's. "You'll have to send for Megan."

"Yes!" Marigold caught onto the idea.

"Send for Meg. She'll do anything for you, even sacrifice herself for the king."

Marigold suddenly turned to her mother. "I've changed my mind. I'm leaving for London today." She turned back to her father. "You must think me a fool to even suggest such an arrangement. Well, I'm not. I'm leaving now. I can't stand the thought of one more day in the same castle with you!"

Vincent stood still as both his wife and daughter, so similar in temperament and looks, swept from the room. He should have known that it was useless. Annora had done an admirable job on Marigold's mind all these years, but at least he'd tried.

Send for Meg.

The words still rang in his ears. He could see that he had little choice. At least Henry had given him six months. With a plan forming in his mind, he rang for his scribe. He would reply to his king, as well as send for Megan, but by the time she arrived he would have the situation firmly back in his control.

Sister Agatha, one of the older nuns at the Stone Lake abbey, made her way sedately down the corridor lined with small, sparsely furnished bedrooms. When

14

she was less than halfway along, she stopped outside one wooden door and knocked softly. The door was opened immediately by a short, plump redhead whose wimple was askew and whose face and hands were dusty.

"Yes, Sister Agatha?" The voice was husky and breathless.

"The Reverend Mother wishes to see you, Megan."

"Now? I've only just returned from the village." Megan did nothing to hide the horror she felt, and the older sister had to fight a smile.

"She said 'immediately'."

Megan sighed, but not even the dirt could dim the brightness of her green eyes or hide any part of her adorable, expressive face.

"All right. I have to see to a particular need, and then I'll go."

Again Sister Agatha wanted to laugh. No one else in all the abbey would have dared refer to the need to relieve herself, but then no one else in the abbey was anything like Megan.

"I'll tell the Reverend Mother you'll be along directly."

Megan thanked her, and in her haste nearly slammed the door in the older woman's face. Agatha made her way back to her Superior's office to report on her conversation, which the Reverend Mother accepted calmly.

"I thought Megan was due back from the village just after lunch."

Agatha had taken a seat by the window and answered from there.

"I believe you are right, but Megan hasn't been on time in eight years; I can't think why she would begin now."

The Reverend Mother smiled, but only slightly. Sister Agatha was dying to ask about the message she knew had arrived, but she remained silent, praying for acceptance of whatever was to pass. Her eyes had been on the window, but they now shifted to see the Reverend Mother watching her.

"We're going to lose her," the older nun told her softly.

Sister Agatha's habit lifted with a huge sigh as she tried to deal with this news. They had all known it would happen someday. After all, Megan was the daughter of a duke, something all of them had constantly lost sight of, and it had never been her father's intention that she join the order.

"When?" Agatha now felt free to ask.

"The end of the week."

She nodded and when she spoke again, her voice wobbled only slightly. "Would you mind my not staying, Reverend Mother?"

"No, Sister Agatha. I quite understand."

Such permission was granted not a moment too soon, as Megan knocked on the door just seconds later. Sister Agatha answered it, but exited soundlessly once Megan was inside. The young redhead noticed the older sister's departure, but she was so self-conscious about her appearance that she had eyes only for the Reverend Mother, a woman whom she held in the highest esteem.

"Come and sit down, Megan."

"I'm sorry about my clothes, Reverend Mother. I didn't have time to change."

"You have just come from the village?"

Megan hesitated, knowing that her answer would evoke many more questions.

"Yes. I know I was supposed to return earlier . . ." Megan's rather low-pitched voice was earnest. "But one of the village women had her baby, and, Reverend Mother," Megan's voice turned dreamy, "she's the loveliest thing I've ever seen. She has so much hair, and she's so pink and soft. I just couldn't tear myself away."

Studying Megan's lovely young face, the abbess fought for control of her emotions, thinking things would never be the same after she was gone. She forced herself to remain calm.

"I was under the impression that it was your turn to go to the village and teach the children to read."

"Oh, I did that," Megan told her, her large eyes widening. "But you see, they were doing so well that I let them go early."

"But still you didn't return?"

"No, Reverend Mother. Old Mrs. Murch was working in her garden, and you know how bent her back is. I simply had to help her."

This explained the dirt, but all the Reverend Mother said was, "Then the baby was born?"

"Well, yes, but I didn't see her until after I'd talked with William. He still has it in his head to marry me. I told him how unsuitable I would be, but he won't listen."

Megan's distressed face was comical, but the word *marry* brought the Reverend Mother firmly back to the task at hand.

"It sounds as if you've had a busy day. As much as I appreciate your telling me honestly where you have been, that is not the reason I sent for you."

Megan nodded, having surmised as much.

"Your father wants you home, Meg." The older woman had used her nickname, a rare thing and one that warned her of the Reverend Mother's emotions.

"He has written to me, and you're to gather your belongings and return to Stone Lake Castle by the end of the week." The older woman, by Lord Vincent's request, omitted the news about marriage.

Megan said nothing. She rose and went to the window, her eyes far away. Not one of the nuns would have risen and turned from the Reverend Mother without permission, but Megan was not a nun. She was the daughter of a titled lord, a girl who had lived with them since the day after her ninth birthday. She was now 17, and the Reverend Mother knew that the abbey had truly become her home.

Annora, Lord Vincent's wife, had never wanted Megan. She was happy with her beautiful first daughter and never desired another child. If rumor could be believed, she had tried several purges to rid herself of her unwanted second pregnancy, but all attempts had failed.

Annora might have forgiven Megan had

she been a male heir, but the fact that she was a girl, and redheaded as well, was enough to cause her to shun the child. However, much to Lady Annora's horror, Megan proved to be more than stalwart. The stouthearted little girl did everything in her power to gain her mother's attention, until it became obvious to Vincent that the two must be separated lest Megan come to physical harm at Annora's hand.

When Megan arrived at the abbey, she was insolent beyond description and so active that the nuns thought they would lose their minds. She ran away no less than twice a week and swiftly became a master at hiding and wearing disguises. The Reverend Mother thought they would never survive the first years, but much of that changed as Megan matured. Then near the time of Megan's fourteenth birthday, her heart became sensitive to spiritual matters.

On one occasion, when Father Brent was making his regular visit, Megan sought him out. The kind priest, who had come under the influence of Luther and other reformers, spoke to her about her eternal soul, and she humbly gave herself to Christ. The change from that point was remarkable.

Megan was still a hard worker and compassionate to a fault, but the peace that surrounded her was extraordinary. Her temper was still a struggle, and when it came to defending someone less fortunate than herself, no one would put it past her to take on a giant. Her conversion, however, had been very real.

She had learned to label her sins for what they were and also learned the sweet fellowship of obedience to God that comes from a wholehearted desire to walk with Him.

"Does my father say why I am needed?" Megan finally spoke from her place by the window. "I mean, he's not ill, is he?"

"No, Megan, your father is fine, but as for the reason, I will leave that explanation to him."

Megan nodded. She had a feeling this was something serious, but she could hardly expect the Reverend Mother to be the bearer of the bad news.

"Does he say how I'm to arrive home?"

The Reverend Mother smiled, her first genuine smile since Megan entered the room.

"Transportation has never been a problem for you before, Meg."

The young woman smiled in return. It was true. In her days of escape, she had

21

hidden in hay wagons and cattle carts, dressed as a gypsy and walked with a traveling band, and even gone so far as to dress as a lad and go on horseback. Her generous curves had prevented that disguise in the last few years, but it was true, Megan always knew how to get where she was going.

The Reverend Mother told her that guardsmen from the castle would be arriving on horseback that Friday, just six days away. Megan accepted this news graciously, and when she was ready to leave the Reverend Mother walked her to the door. No words were spoken, but Megan hugged the older woman fiercely before leaving, thinking it felt as though she were already gone.

Two

London was hot and noisy as Bracken turned his horse over to a waiting groom, gave orders to a few of his knights, and made his way to the massive front door of his aunt's home. His long legs, clad in dark hose, ate up the distance with ease. He had not enjoyed the trip from his country estate, but a missive from the king, as well as one from his neighbor, forced him onward.

Bracken found his widowed aunt in an upstairs salon. With barely a word of greeting, he told her what he was about.

"I need you to return to Hawkings Crest."

"Why, Bracken," the older woman spoke in surprise. "I've only just arrived back in London."

"I realize that, Aunt Louisa, but I've just received word that I am to marry, and I need you back at the estate."

Louisa's eyes became huge on this announcement, but she remained silent, waiting for Bracken to explain. He did not disappoint her.

"The king has ordered me to take a bride from Stone Lake, from the household of Vincent Stone to be exact. I have also received word from Vincent himself telling me he has chosen his youngest daughter, Megan, and wishes her to live at Hawkings Crest for a period before we are wed. He wrote to me obviously believing that you were still living with me.

"I think his request a trifle odd, but since I can't refuse the king or my future father-in-law," Bracken's voice hardened slightly, "I feel I have little choice but to ask you to return and act as guardian."

Louisa studied her sister's oldest child in silence. Bracken was usually an amiable man. He was dark in both skin and hair coloring, and the full beard that covered the lower part of his handsome face gave him an almost sinister look. Louisa now studied his mouth and eyes. He was easily given to smiling and typically ready to laugh, but the man before her now was quite serious and clearly disturbed. For Louisa, who knew Bracken well, it wasn't hard to understand why.

Louisa had never known anyone happier in a marriage than her sister, Joyce, widowed now for six years. Louisa knew that

Bracken wanted that same happiness. He was only 24 years old, and his aunt knew well that he was in no hurry to wed. In fact, she believed as much as he desired male heirs, he would stay single all the days of his life rather than live with a woman he didn't love.

"Will you come?" Bracken's voice cut into her musings.

"Certainly, Bracken, but may I ask a few questions?"

The young knight answered her with a slight inclination of his head.

"Is the girl willing?"

Bracken shook his head. "Vincent's letter did not say. He did write that she is just 17 and has been raised at the Stone Lake abbey."

A shudder ran over Louisa's frame. She could think of nothing worse. The girl would either be so austere that she would never warm up to Bracken, or, once released from the confines of the convent, so wild that she would never be faithful to her vows. However, Louisa kept all of these thoughts to herself. She decided then that she would brace up for Bracken, certain it was what her sister would want.

"Well, now," Louisa began. "She could have been much younger, so her age is an asset. And don't forget, Bracken, no matter where she was raised, she is Vincent's daughter. Without a doubt she will be graceful and a true asset to your keep."

Louisa secretly wondered if a girl raised in a convent would have a clue as to how to run a castle, but such thoughts remained unspoken as she watched Bracken visibly relax. Louisa relaxed herself, knowing she'd said the right thing.

"Have you ever met Megan?"

Bracken's eyes narrowed on a spot across the room. "I think I have. It was some years ago, and I must admit that it didn't go well. I made a fool of myself."

"What happened?"

Bracken smiled now, his first since arriving. "It was at court, before Father died. She was just a girl of course, talking with a group of other girls. I remember thinking I had never seen anyone with eyes so blue and hair so light. I gawked at her until she said something quite rude and the others laughed. I was humiliated, of course, but I haven't thought of it in years."

"So she's beautiful?"

"Yes." Bracken's smile became huge. "She is at that."

Louisa's smile matched his own. Her

voice was gentle as she commented, "Beauty is not enough to build a marriage on, Bracken, but it certainly helps when a husband and wife find each other attractive."

Bracken's hand came to his bearded chin, and Louisa chuckled.

"You're asking yourself if she'll find you attractive, Bracken?"

Bracken now laughed at himself. "I am at that."

Louisa's voice became dry. "No such thought should plague you. I feel quite confident that she will think you handsome."

Bracken shook his head in true modesty before the two fell to discussing the dates. Megan was not due to arrive at Hawkings Crest for another two weeks, and the lord of the castle saw no reason for his aunt to have to make the trip sooner.

Bracken stayed on in London until the next morning, and by the time he left he felt somewhat resigned if not thrilled with the idea of marriage to Vincent's beautiful blonde daughter. He would do all that was asked of him.

Bracken did not go directly back to Hawkings Crest, but he and his men rode north on business. With Megan not arriving for two weeks, there was no need for him to hurry home.

The ride on horseback to the castle on Stone Lake was not a lengthy one, but Megan, having to fight anxiety with every mile, would have sworn that she had crossed the country. Her father had been to visit her just six weeks before, but Megan hadn't seen her home or her mother for more than two years. When she had visited that Christmas, she knew she would be returning to the abbey. This time she had no such security. This time it seemed she would be going home for good. But why?

This was the question that had plagued Megan from the moment she had left the Reverend Mother's office. Was her sister going to be wed? Was her mother ill? Had her father given her own hand away? Meg didn't think he would do this without talking to her, but she wasn't sure. Maybe her mother had decided it was time her youngest daughter marry.

"Oh, Father God," Megan prayed. "Help me to trust You and accept this reason Father has sent for me. I am troubled. Please help me to trust."

Megan's mind went to her last nights at

the abbey. She had walked in her sleep each night, something she hadn't done for years. Typically Megan walked in her sleep only when some event of the day upset her.

The first night she had woken alone, shivering in the chapel with no idea how she'd come to be there. The other nights Sister Agatha had found her in the hallway and reported to her in the morning that she'd been on the move.

Megan never did anything dangerous or outrageous when she walked in her sleep, but there was always a very real fear that she would hurt herself. On one occasion she had fallen headfirst down a full length of stone steps. Another time she had wandered outside the abbey and slipped down an embankment into a deep ditch filled with water. Had the water been just inches deeper, Megan might have drowned.

After the first night, Megan had prayed for calm as sleep crowded in, but she had been up anyway. She also knew that she was prone to talk in her sleep if someone spoke. Megan had forgotten to ask Sister Agatha if she'd said anything profound or heinous; she knew she was capable of both.

Vincent paced the confines of his room for more than an hour before Megan arrived. His entire frame shook with emotion when he thought of his youngest daughter marrying against her will, but he saw no other way around the king's edict.

Vincent knew Bracken to be a fine warrior, a man of honor as well as might, and since Marigold would never agree to this match, he only hoped this trial period at Hawkings Crest would help Megan to find herself in a marriage that she at least found tolerable. Vincent had no illusions concerning love, but Megan was tenacious to a fault. Her father believed she would make the best of the situation. She always did.

"My lord?" one of Vincent's vassals said from just inside the door.

"Yes, Giles?"

"Lady Megan has arrived, sir. She awaits you in the great hall."

"Thank you, Giles," Vincent said, but did not move to the door. Once again he visualized himself telling Megan of Henry's letter, and remembered his wife's cruel pleasure in the whole event. Well, at least Annora was away for the day. Still, Vincent couldn't stop the shudder that ran over his frame as he at last moved toward the door.

Megan's eyes ran lovingly over the long tables and benches, the clean rushes on the floor, and the huge stone fireplace that graced the north wall. Megan thought about the rocky relationship she'd always shared with her mother, but she could never fault Annora Stone's ability to run her father's castle.

"Megan."

The young woman turned at the sound of her father's voice and nearly ran into his arms. It had been only weeks, but Megan was always so pleased to see him and now let herself be hugged like a child.

"How was your journey?"

"A bit long. I'd have done better on my own." Megan smiled teasingly at her father, causing him to chuckle, but then her eyes grew serious as did his.

"Are you all right?" she asked.

"Yes, but I have serious news. You are to marry."

Glad that he had told her outright, Megan took a deep breath and followed Vincent as he led the way to the fireplace. The great hall was strangely empty, and both were glad for the privacy.

"Can you tell me all?" Megan asked as soon as they were seated.

"Yes. Henry wants a union between Stone Lake and Hawkings Crest. I told Marigold that she was to marry, but you can well imagine how she responded to the idea of marrying an earl. She left just an hour after I told her, and I haven't seen her since."

"So the duty falls to me?"

Vincent nodded with regret. "Bracken has been the lord at Hawkings Crest for five years now, maybe six, and I know him to be a man of honor. He is young, but I believe he will make you a fine husband."

"So I am to marry soon."

"No. You'll be going to live at Hawkings Crest for a time — a trial period of sorts. It won't stop the marriage, but at least Bracken will not be a stranger to you on your wedding day."

Megan's eyes shifted to the fireplace. When she spoke again her voice was soft, her eyes still studying the cold hearth.

"I have never met Bracken of Hawkings Crest. I am surprised he chose me."

"Henry gave me leave to decide," Vincent admitted, not seeing a need to remind Megan that her sister would have nothing to do with the arrangement.

"And what will Bracken say when he learns he is to have me and not Marigold?" Megan asked, believing that all of England knew of Marigold's beauty.

Vincent caught his daughter's jaw and

gently turned her face to him. "So many years away from your mother and yet you still believe her lies. Your beauty is deep within you, Meg, as well as on the surface. Bracken might find Marigold a beauty, but only until she showed her true self.

"Bracken may well be as dubious of the marriage as you are, but when he gets to know you he will thank me for the wife I have sent."

Megan smiled gently at her father. She loved her father and knowing that he regretted this for her somehow made the act easier. Megan believed that men spent the whole of their lives facing tasks they didn't care for; her father had done so without complaint. Megan told herself she would do no less.

"How long before I go?"

Vincent smiled in the face of her acceptance. "Two weeks. I know things might be a bit strained for you when your mother returns, but I want some time with you. I'll see you to Hawkings Crest myself."

"I assume Bracken's mother lives within the castle walls."

Vincent shook his head. "His aunt. I have not met her, but I trust the two of you will fare well."

Megan nodded, but neither one had

much more to say. They went for a ride a few hours later but did not discuss the trip or wedding.

The day turned out to be so full that Megan took herself off to bed at an early hour, still not having seen her mother.

Having talked with her father and gained awareness of the situation, she slept deeply that night. She would not have slept so soundly had she known he was to be called away early the next morning.

Three

"I have servants for that, Megan." Annora's voice was cold, but Megan stood her ground. They were in the kitchen, and Vincent had been gone all of three days. To Megan it felt like a lifetime.

"Be that as it may, Mother, not one of them knew of this poultice for tooth pain." Megan's voice was respectful but unyielding.

"The servants take care of themselves. Do not disgrace your father's name by acting as a commoner."

Megan's eyes narrowed in anger. "The disgrace is on you, Mother, that you would allow one of your servants to writhe in agony with a sore tooth. Where is your compassion?"

"You will not speak to me in such a way!" Lady Stone nearly spat. "Your return has disrupted my entire life." Annora stopped to let this barb sink in but saw that Megan's face was calm. The older woman was so furious that for a moment she couldn't speak. When she did, it was

35

with the full intention of wounding her daughter the only way she knew how.

"I have decided that you will leave for Hawkings Crest this day."

Megan's eyes widened, giving her mother great pleasure.

"But Father isn't here. He was to take me."

Annora's laugh was heartless. "Your father is more than capable of mounting a horse if he wishes to see you."

"But my clothing, Mother —" Megan tried to reason with her, seeing that she'd pushed too far. "My wardrobe is not complete."

Annora's lip curled with cruel enjoyment. "You seem to be more at home dressed in homespun cloth — look at you! Besides, you have one dress that will suffice, and you won't want to travel in that anyway. I'll send your clothing when it's ready."

Megan stood in mute horror, her whole body trembling with fear over the way she was being sent away. Her heart cried out to God to send her father home early, but it was not to be.

"Now ready yourself," her mother drove home her final thrust. "I will order a guard to escort you. You leave within the hour."

Annora swept away then, but it took a moment for Megan to realize the occupants of the entire room were watching her. Not one of the servants at Stone Lake loved their mistress, so Megan was met with genuine stares of compassion. The young servant girl whose tooth Megan had treated had tears in her eyes.

"I'm sorry, my lady."

Megan gently touched the dark hair on her head. "Don't fret, Merry, all will be well. You take care of that tooth, and I'll see you when I come again."

Megan left with all the dignity she could muster, hoping that no one could see how her legs trembled in shock and terror.

True to her word, her mother sent for her an hour later. Four horses stood in the courtyard of Stone Lake, and Megan fought down every emotion within her to keep her face calm. Hawkings Crest was miles away, and her mother was sending her on horseback with no caravan, which meant no maid, no ladies in waiting, and no entourage of any kind. Just four horses, and three male guards — none of whom she even knew.

One of them helped her mount. Megan kept her face impassive, not wishing to give her mother the satisfaction of knowing how fearful she was of going away to a strange man's castle. She thought of trying to reason with Annora once more, but just a glance allowed her to see the hatred in her eyes, and Megan knew she would be wasting her time.

Megan glanced at the men assigned to accompany her. She did not recognize any of them, but they caused her no fear. Her father would kill them if she came to harm in their hands. Megan thought how sad it was that they had more of a care for her than her mother did. Once on horseback, Megan spoke to her mother.

"Please tell Father that I said goodbye and that I look forward to seeing him when he visits."

Megan gained a small measure of satisfaction in seeing the flicker of uncertainty in her mother's look, but it didn't last. The older woman's chin came up before she bade her daughter goodbye in a cold tone.

Megan, whose throat was suddenly very tight, said nothing. She turned her mount and heeled her forward, tears clogging her throat as she rode.

The sun was dropping low in the sky when one of the men said they would make camp soon. Megan questioned how far they had to go and was told they would arrive at Hawkings Crest before noon the following day.

They came into a copse of trees that would be their shelter for the night. As glad as Megan was to stop, she ached all over as she forced her body to slide from the horse's back.

Not for the first time, Megan was impressed with her escort. There had been little conversation as they traveled, but their care of her could not be criticized. Now they made camp with amazing ease. Just an hour later, Megan was sitting comfortably on a log, eating rabbit that had been cooked over a spit. Within minutes she was feeling greatly refreshed, but when the man in charge, Hubert by name, recommended sleep, Megan was more than happy to comply.

Megan found herself near the fire, the men nearby to protect her, but as she lay down she wondered what her father would say of her situation. She knew that he had planned to leave Stone Lake early in the day with a full band of men and provisions, and have her to Hawkings Crest before nightfall. Megan also realized he would be furious if he could see her now. She

39

debated the wisdom of giving him too many details. Praying that she wouldn't walk in her sleep this night, she drifted off, her blanket literally covering her from head to foot.

The attack on their camp came sometime after midnight. One second Megan was sleeping in her blanket, the next she was being rolled under some nearby bushes where she sat up and looked out in horror at the unfolding scene.

Men, seemingly dozens of them, were in vicious attack against her guard. Megan kept her hand pressed tightly to her mouth to keep from crying out as she watched one, then two, and finally all three of her guards fall dead to the ground. Some of the attackers were dead as well, but at least six men were still standing.

Megan continued to watch as one of them broke open her small trunk and howled in frustration. She watched her belongings fly everywhere.

"*Clothing!* I thought they had gold."

"Let me see," said another.

"*Fool!*" raged yet a third, obviously in charge. "We lost men tonight over a trunk full of homespun rags."

Megan watched the first man lift the

trunk and throw it toward her. She closed her eyes in anticipation of the blow, but the trunk landed beyond the bush.

"What now?" one asked.

"We move on," the third man said. "There's nothing here but some good horse flesh. Let's ride."

There was a flurry of movement as the men departed, taking all four of her father's horses with them.

When the battle had commenced, Megan thought it was going to last forever. Now that it was over, she wondered if only seconds had passed. She was trembling from head to foot, but the night was long spent before she could bring herself to crawl from the bushes to check on the men.

"Oh, Father God," Megan cried pitifully as she knelt beside Hubert and then the others. She asked God to give her strength and wisdom, but she didn't know when anything had so horrified her. They had died protecting her. The thought so overwhelmed her that after just a few minutes she crawled back into the bushes and rewrapped herself in the blanket, still shivering so violently that she had to clamp her jaw shut to keep her teeth from chattering.

Megan didn't know when she slept, but

when slumber claimed her at last she dreamed that her mother was forced to bury these men and explain to their families why they were gone.

Megan heard the voices, but thinking she was still dreaming did not move. Not until a hand grasped her ankle, which protruded from the bush, did she let out a muffled scream and scramble further into the shrubs, twigs, and leaves scratching her face and hands.

"Well, one of 'ems alive, no mistake."

"A man?"

"Don't rightly think it is."

Megan heard more movement. The bushes parted, and a large, bearded face regarded her from without. It was fully light, but Megan held herself stiffly inside the foliage, hoping somehow they wouldn't see her and would leave.

"You can come out, miss. Not a one of us will harm you."

Megan licked her lips, undecided. It was hard to see past the branches and leaves, but she thought she detected a gleam of compassion in the man's eyes. He backed away a moment later, and Megan came slowly out the side, figuring it would put her in a position to run if there were danger.

"Coo," one of the men breathed as soon as she emerged. "Would you look at that 'air."

Megan's eyes searched their faces and immediately recognized them as a group of peddlers. She also saw that there was not a female among them. The men were all staring at her as if they'd never seen a woman before. Even through the dirt on her dress and brambles in her hair, the fact that she was a lady came shouting through.

"Are you hurt?" the bearded man asked, his soft voice seeming loud in the hushed circle.

Megan shook her head with unconscious elegance. She spoke then, and any doubts they might have had concerning her lineage dissolved with the cultured sound of her voice.

"We were attacked. My men fought hard, but they died protecting me." Megan's voice caught. Tears came to her eyes but did not fall.

"We've some bread and cheese here, miss. Would you care to eat?" This came from the bearded man, and although Megan was thankful for his kindness, she couldn't eat a bite.

"Can you tell us where you was headed?" asked a man so taken with the russet red of her hair that he wanted to touch it. Yet his voice and manners were respectful.

"Hawkings Crest," Megan told them. "I don't know how close I am, so I'm not sure if I should try to go home or head on."

"Home?" Again, the bearded man spoke.

"Stone Lake."

He nodded, smiling slightly. "It's a piece back to Stone Lake, and we're going directly to the Crest if you'd care to ride."

Megan was so relieved she could have wept. The men might have been surprised to know she had ridden in many a peddler's cart, but never before had she felt that one had been sent by God.

An hour later they were well down the road, Megan atop the cart sitting comfortably on a pile of rugs. They had pressed food upon her and she had finally eaten, but now the night was catching up with her. Megan couldn't stop the tears that poured down her cheeks. They were partly from exhaustion and partly from the loss of her father's brave men. Within another hundred yards, she was asleep.

Four

Hawkings Crest

"Now get back to work!"

The young woman who had been shouted at did as she was told, but not before she flipped her hair over her shoulder in contempt and glared at her uncle. The older man stood watching her a moment, his head moving in disgust.

"Pen giving you trouble again, Eddie?"

Eddie nearly growled. "My sister has never been able to control her. Has it in her head to work up in the kitchen, she does." His voice was filled with offense. "She's even working on her voice, trying to talk like a lady, no less. I tell you, Mic, that girl's in for trouble if she don't start to recognize 'er betters."

Mic clapped him on the shoulder. "You'll handle her, Eddie." The younger man started to walk away but stopped.

45

"The peddlers are in."

"So I see. At least it's old Elias," Eddie observed, referring to the man with the dark beard. "He's fair."

Mic moved in the direction of the wagon, but Eddie went back toward the creamery. With Pen acting up, he was behind schedule. He decided to brook no more of her high-minded airs or her talk of the kitchens. With a disgruntled frown, he moved inside.

"Thank you, Elias," Megan told him sincerely. She had awakened a half mile outside the walls of the keep and walked in behind the peddler's cart with the men, but now she took the time to thank her rescuers before moving toward the castle. Megan had found them all kind to a fault, and since she didn't know what kind of reception she would receive from the inhabitants at Hawkings Crest, it was a little hard to leave them.

But as usual Megan was made of stern stuff, and with a smile that encompassed them all, she moved rather stiffly toward the main entrance. It was a waste of time. The guards questioned her without listening to her answer, and Megan, knowing she looked even worse than when the peddlers found her, was not in the mood to argue her way inside.

She moved around the keep for a good 20 minutes, impressed with its cleanliness and order before spotting what appeared to be an entrance to the kitchens. A man, looking less austere than the front entrance guards, stood close by. Megan gathered her courage to approach.

"Will you please take me to Lord Bracken?" Megan asked calmly, but felt a fool at the man's look.

"Be away, woman. Return to your work."

He gave Megan the cold shoulder, and in disgust she stomped off around the corner of the building. She hadn't gone ten steps when she collided into something huge, or was it some*one?*

Megan's eyes slowly rose, and she looked up into the face of the largest man she had ever seen. She stumbled back in fear against a stone wall, her mouth opening and closing in panic.

"Lord, B-B-Bracken?" she managed to stutter, but the giant only stared at her, an unreadable expression on his craggy face.

Megan inched her way along, the giant turning with her, his eyes spearing her. When she had a clear shot, she ran. She never looked back to see if she was being followed, but ran behind the creamery and stood asking herself what to do next.

Megan stayed still for a long time, gaining her breath. It was tempting at this moment to join the peddlers. She was willing to do almost anything to escape this foreign keep and the antagonistic stares of its inhabitants, but she wasn't welcome at Stone Lake, so where would she go?

Megan decided to circle the building, thinking to inquire of Bracken with someone inside. Before she could open the door, a person came charging out. He was a good-sized man with a harried look, one that didn't improve upon spotting Megan.

"Why aren't you inside?"

Megan blinked but managed to say, "I need you to take me to Lord Bracken."

"Oh, heaven help me!" the man burst out, startling Megan into speechlessness. "Why must *I* be saddled with uppity female servants?"

Before Megan could draw a breath, she was grasped firmly by the forearm and taken inside.

"You must be new, so I'll give you some time to familiarize yourself. Have you worked the creamery before?"

Rage boiled up inside of Megan, who thought she would not be able to stand one more second of this. She was tempted to stomp on the man's foot and *then* inform him that she had designed the creamery at the Stone Lake abbey. All she said, however, was yes, she had. Megan figured if she worked for a time, she might better determine a way to get inside the castle. So just minutes later, Megan found herself working over a churn. She worked silently and efficiently, not speaking or looking at anyone, but feeling eyes on her. She also listened. If the gossip around her could be believed, the lord of the castle was not even there.

Megan could have howled with frustration, but refraining, simply worked silently until she thought her arms would give way. It was a tremendous relief to have the man who had grabbed her, the one the other women called Eddie, dismiss them for the day. Megan breathed deeply of the fresh air once she was outside.

She noticed the servants queuing up behind a cauldron of food and suddenly realized she was starving. Without a shred of pride left, Megan joined them. Heads turned to stare at her, but she ignored them. At the moment she would have given up her dowry for a bath, but food in her stomach was the next best thing.

The line moved steadily along, but Megan seemed to be the last, for no one stood behind her. She glanced up at one point to find the giant some ten feet away. He appeared to be staring right at Megan, and for a moment she could not look away from his steady gaze. Just then, the man in front of her sneezed loudly, and Megan dropped her eyes.

That the big man was of some importance was obvious, but he terrified Megan. She heard someone call "Arik" and looked up to see the huge man turn. He towered over the person who spoke to him, as he did everyone. Megan dropped her eyes just before the other man left and the giant turned his attention to her once again. It never occurred to her to ask him for help; he was too intimidating for that.

At last it was Megan's turn to eat. She took one of the few remaining bowls, which were carved roughly from wood and a bit greasy, and held it out to the man behind the cauldron. Megan ignored his odd look, so she didn't see the exchange with the giant behind her. Her bowl was suddenly filled to the top, and where the bread pan had been empty, it now held a full loaf. The man broke a huge chunk off for Megan, who thanked him humbly.

She then moved to a place against the wall and sank down to eat. There were no utensils, so Megan soaked her bread with broth for the first time. She ate like a man starved. Her bowl was over half empty and some of the shakes had left her body when she once again looked and found the giant's eyes on her.

Megan's face flamed with the way she'd been eating, and she set her bowl aside. To her surprise, the giant averted his gaze.

Megan's eyes dropped to her bowl, but when she looked up he was still looking away. Still hungry, she reached for the food again, and this time she finished every bite. The giant was still there, but he was not staring directly at her.

The sun was falling fast by the time Megan was through, and since it was mid-summer, she watched many of the castle's inhabitants make their beds along the castle walls. Megan didn't care for the idea of sleeping on the ground without a blanket, so she rose slowly and surreptitiously made her way in the gathering dusk across the inner courtyard to the blacksmith's. The building was empty.

Wishing she could see a little better, Megan entered on nearly silent feet and soon found what appeared to be an empty stall. The hay smelled fresh, and she gingerly stretched out on her side. She was asleep inside of five minutes, and even when the giant of the castle, holding a lantern and ducking his head to enter, came to check on her, she didn't stir. She also didn't stir when he settled down for the night against the wall just outside the door.

By Megan's fifth day at Hawkings Crest, her life had developed something of a pattern. Every night she slept in the smithy's shop and ate with the other servants, but she was no closer to getting inside the castle than she had been the first day. Each day she worked in the creamery, but was never chosen to deliver the butter, cheese, or cream to the kitchens within.

Not that it would have done much good. It seemed that Bracken was still away. Megan struggled with her anger nearly every day over the way her mother had dismissed her. Her intended had obviously been expecting her on a certain day, a day her father surely must have known about. Megan's head told her that her mother, too, had known this all along, but her heart refused to believe it.

The work was just beginning. Eddie came out of the creamery then and found

Megan just staring up at the castle. On the first day and even the second, Eddie would have ordered her back to work, but no longer. No servant had missed the way Arik kept his eye on this woman. The lack of comb for her hair and the simple home-spun cloth of her dress made it clear that she was just a servant, but there was certainly no harm in this knight losing his heart to a servant girl.

In truth, they were all rather pleased for their castle giant, whose odd ways had caused many of them to wonder at times if he was even human. Arik seemed unaffected by the cold and heat, and few had ever seen him eat. He spoke so few words to anyone that the castle folk were not entirely sure what he saw in this red-haired maid, but they were happy for him nonetheless.

Megan finished her inspection of the castle and would have turned to go back to the creamery, but a shout came up from the wall. Although she was in no danger, she stepped back as the gates were opened and a large group of riders came inside. There was quite a stir, and it didn't take long, with the way the castle folk responded, to see that Bracken was among them. He stood out in coloring, height, and breadth, and Megan studied the proud tilt of his head from a distance.

Megan suddenly drew a deep breath. There was now a very real reason to gain entrance to the castle, but how would she do it? With a bit more thought, the inner bailey still in upheaval, Megan returned to the interior of the creamery. The day was early yet; she would find a way.

Bracken scanned the inner courtyard of Hawking Crest with pleasure. It was good to be home. He spotted Arik at a distance, but something in the man's stance told him not to approach. He would like to have questioned him as to the keep's operations in his absence, but Arik could be mule stubborn. Bracken could see, even from across the courtyard, that he didn't care to converse, and he knew from experience that nothing would provoke him to do so against his will. With a shrug, Bracken moved to the castle. In the meantime, he would question Barton, his steward, and deal with Arik later.

Bracken gained the great hall. As always his heart swelled with fulfillment. This had been his childhood home. His parents had run the castle well, and now that it was his, he took great pride in the way he had continued to work at its beauty and efficiency.

Many elaborate tapestries hung from the walls, and Hawkings Crest shields graced the stones over both of the massive fireplaces. The trestle tables and benches were of the finest wood, and Bracken knew that his staff could have a feast on those tables with an hour's notice.

Many knights and servants alike spoke to Bracken, nodding their heads in respect as he made for the wide, main staircase. By the time Bracken entered his bedchamber, a hot bath waited before a freshly laid fire in the hearth. Steam rose from the copper tub, and Bracken spoke to his vassal, Kent, as he undressed.

"Have you been on the field much?"

"Yes, sir," the ten-year-old replied proudly. "Every afternoon you were gone."

Bracken smiled. "Your father will be proud to hear it. I saw your parents while I was in London, and they asked after you."

Kent was bent over, scrubbing Bracken's back with a hard-bristled brush, and did not immediately answer.

"How is my mother?" he said with a slight pant.

"She is well. I would say the baby is due soon."

Kent nodded, his small face serious. "She promised to send word when the time came."

"Would you rather be with her? I'm sure I could arrange it."

The boy thought. He didn't know any man, not even his father, whom he admired more than Bracken. Bracken was huge and black as a bear, but when Kent had overcome his initial fear of Bracken's size, he had found a man with a heart of gold. He then realized his great fortune in his father's sending him to Hawkings Crest to serve as vassal. He cared more deeply about his mother than he could express in words, but even though he had only been there a few months, he couldn't stand the thought of leaving Hawkings Crest and its lord.

"I'll stay here."

"Very well."

The subject was dropped then, but Bracken made a mental note to keep Kent just busy enough to leave him no time to think. Kent was one of many young vassals Bracken had had in the years he had been lord, and as with many of the other boys, he'd come to care deeply for him. He was certain that as soon as the infant was born, all would be well.

Back in the creamery the first churns were ready to be delivered, and for the first time all week, Megan stepped forward and spoke.

"I'll take this for you," she said softly, gesturing to the churn she had been working.

Eddie had not heard her speak since the first day and had forgotten the husky quality of her voice. The quiet authority he heard gave him pause, but he was still going to refuse her. Megan, however, had other ideas. She lifted the churn and held his eyes with her own.

"Thank you, Eddie," she said softly, and before he could utter a word, she moved out the door.

Eddie glanced around, but no one else had heard the exchange, so he lost no face. He went after her then, but only to watch. He was not at all surprised to see Arik following her at some distance.

Bracken, bathed and now well-breakfasted, sat surrounded by his men in what was known as the war room of the castle. They had ridden for days, accomplishing a small job for King Henry without thought of personal comforts, and now that all were clean and well fed, they spoke of all they had seen. Arik was not among them. Bracken had sent for him, but he had not as yet made an appearance.

Hunting trophies of every size and type, as well as archaic weapons of war, lined this large room. It was a place where Bracken felt most comfortable. The men had been talking for the better part of 20 minutes when Megan opened the door, left it open, and took several steps inside the huge room.

Bracken did not recognize this servant and sighed gently. All too often new female servants sought him out, out of sheer curiosity. He was large and dark, and the sooner they saw him, the sooner they could put their minds to rest that he was not half bear as so many claimed.

"We do not need anything at this time," he said kindly to this scruffy-looking maid. "We'll send someone if we do."

"I need to speak with you, Lord Bracken."

Bracken's brow lowered. It was to be one of these; a servant girl who worked on her voice and mannerisms and who had visions of attracting the attention of the lord of the keep.

"Please leave us." Bracken's voice was

hard this time, enough to put anyone off. To his amazement, this impertinent chit moved further into the room. Each one of his men had turned now, and Bracken felt anger kindle within him.

"I'm sorry to disturb you, Lord Bracken," Megan began, her voice humble and soft, her stance respectful. "I have wanted to see you for several days. I am Megan of Stone Lake. My father is Vincent. I did not know that you would be away and I was uncertain what to do, so I stayed on here in your keep.

"While coming to you, my father's men were attacked some miles back. They were killed while protecting me. I came here with a group of peddlers, but I fear that no one was expecting me. I would seek your counsel, my lord, as to what to do next. I will stay on here if that is what you wish. If not, then may it please my lord to provide an escort for me to return to my father's castle."

Bracken sat in stunned silence for a full minute. His men, including Arik, who had suddenly appeared in the doorway behind this girl, had been watching the maid in their midst. Now they turned their gaze to their lord and waited his reaction. It wasn't long in coming.

He stood, his face a stony mask, and pointed a finger at Megan.

"Remove this creature from my presence." Bracken's voice was coldly furious, telling of his insult that she would attempt such duplicity. Bracken refused to believe that this scullery maid could be his future bride.

Unfortunately for Bracken, Megan's anger matched his own. All humility fell away like a cloak, and her eyes shot daggers at the men approaching.

"Do *not* touch me," she commanded with enough authority to stop the men in their tracks. Her eyes raked them before turning like hot coals onto Bracken.

"I am treated like a servant in your keep for five days, and if that isn't bad enough you now treat me like a dog! There is no need for your men to see me out; I shall leave on my own." Megan paused then, but even in her present filthy state she was magnificent. "*You,* Lord Bracken, can explain to King Henry why we will not be wed."

With that Megan swept from a room that was so silent Bracken could hear his men breathing. He had judged her a fake, but now he doubted his own eyes and ears. He glanced up to see Arik still in attendance.

"Has she been here for five days?"

Arik's head barely dipped one time in affirmation.

Bracken drew breath between clenched teeth. "I will check this story myself. We ride in five minutes."

Five

No one at Hawkings Crest could have missed Bracken's departure with his men, but Megan gave it little heed. Not knowing how she would get there, or even if she would be welcome, Megan was going home. For the moment that was all she could think of.

Deep in thought, Megan was standing near the smithery, her mind preoccupied, when she suddenly spotted Arik coming from the castle. Megan started. She had assumed he'd gone with Bracken. She darted around the side of the building, knowing somehow that he must not see her. The area inside the walls of Hawkings Crest was like a small village or Megan would never have gotten away with what she did next.

At the rear of the smithery an old cloak of substantial size had been discarded, and Megan bent to pick it up. Her own stench had been most offensive to her senses for days now, but the oversized cloak made her dress smell like a blossom.

Nevertheless, she was determined. Having to choke down a small gag, she placed the cloak around her, covering her head and letting the garment dangle on the ground. She then moved like an old woman from around the side of the building, walking an irregular path toward the main gate. She had been praying all the while and now sent up a word of thanks when the gate opened for a small group of merchants that included a shoemaker and several women. Megan didn't know what the women did, but she hung behind them and as the door opened, adopted a gait that looked almost painful, and moved forward.

Arik had been standing stock still for many minutes and still hadn't spotted Bracken's lady. He knew well that Bracken didn't see her as his own, but she was. He had known from the moment he laid eyes on her. Now she had managed to disappear. Arik had learned over the years that one found something much faster by thoughtful looking rather than mad dashing-about. On this occasion, however, it was getting him nowhere.

He was turning for the smithery and the creamery when he saw the gate open. No one stood out, in fact he'd have sworn Bracken's lady was not among those leaving, but she had said she was going and something compelled him to follow this assorted group. He reasoned that if she was in the keep, he would lose nothing. If she was a part of this band, she was heading out into unprotected territory where no lady belonged.

With tremendous ground-covering strides, Arik started after the group. It wasn't long before he had to shorten his steps in an effort not to overtake them. A woman in an ancient cloak stood out to him, but he made sure to watch each one. With an occasional glance to the rear, Arik walked on. If Megan was in this group, he would not let her from his sight.

Bracken found that animals had already been at the dead bodies of Vincent's men. He eyed the scene with a combination of remorse and anger. He was sorry for such a brutal loss of life, but his anger stemmed from the fact that Vincent had sent only three men to escort his daughter to Hawkings Crest. From the letter, Bracken had been expecting a most cherished young woman, but this act on Vincent's part would speak otherwise.

At least he knew she had been telling the truth about the attack. Bracken began to wonder whom he'd seen at court so many years ago. Surely the blonde was not now a redhead. Bracken shook his head. Not even with the dirt removed would Megan match the beauty of the other girl. His own eyes told him that.

Bracken suddenly ground his teeth. A redhead! Since talking to his aunt he had been picturing a beautiful blonde, but the woman who had stood before him was most definitely a redhead. Bracken was not pleased. He had not liked red hair since a young vassal had come to Hawkings Crest many years earlier to serve under his father. The boy had had a shock of red hair, almost orange in color, and by the time he'd returned to his family, Bracken was more than relieved to see him go.

Bracken realized that Megan's hair was not orange, but he had never found red-headed women attractive. And why had she been dressed like a beggar and working in his keep like a serf? Bracken's frown was so fierce that one of his men, approaching with Megan's trunk, hesitated in his stride.

"What is it?" Bracken asked calmly, having accurately read the other man's thoughts and quickly schooled his features.

"A small trunk. It's almost empty, but the trunk itself is not damaged."

Bracken lifted the lid and pulled out a garment. It appeared to be much like the one Megan had been wearing when she had come to the war room. Bracken suddenly understood. These were clothes from the abbey. One more dig into the trunk and Bracken found another dress. This was cut from fine cloth, but it was not overly fancy. Again Bracken frowned. He would have thought Vincent could have done better for the girl. Maybe he expected Bracken to dress her. The thought did not please him. Bracken was not a miserly man, but he did not know this girl and seriously doubted at the moment if she truly was Vincent's daughter. That being the case, there would be no wedding, at least not before he had some answers.

Bracken shook his head to dispel his tempestuous thoughts. Right now he needed to return to Hawkings Crest. Men needed to be sent to bury these guards, as well as the dead thieves, and someone must be sent to London for Aunt Louisa. Megan may not be who she claimed to be, but if she *was* the daughter of a duke, things were looking bad, very bad indeed.

From his place behind the travelers, Arik watched the "old woman" drop farther and farther back. She still hobbled along, but when the last of the group turned at a small bend in the road, she suddenly darted into the trees. Arik came to a swift halt before taking his own place in the foliage.

He stood patiently and was not disappointed. That red head poked out after just a few minutes, and with a glance in all directions, Bracken's lady started back down the path, this time with the cloak thrown over her arm, her back straight and feet swift.

Arik moved out to follow her, but it was many yards before she noticed him. She came to such a sudden halt when she did that she nearly fell over.

Megan's heart plummeted at the sight of the giant man, but she was determined to go home and *no one,* not even this Goliath, was going to stop her.

"There is no need to follow me," she spoke from a distance, her voice uncompromising. "I don't know why you pursue me, but I wish to be left alone."

Megan, used to having her orders followed, turned on her heel and walked away. It didn't take long before she realized she had not been heeded. This time she decided to ignore him. It was only minutes after she'd made this resolve that she heard the riders.

There was no place to hide on this section of road, or Megan would have made herself scarce. She was quite sure it would be Bracken and his men, but she continued on her course, refusing to even glance at the horses when they came into view.

She would have learned something of Bracken's men had she looked. The men did not take her presence as calmly as she took theirs. They stared in horror at how far out on the road this young noblewoman had come without an escort. That she did not desire Arik's protection was obvious, and this concerned them as well.

Megan glanced back to see that the men had come abreast of the giant and were speaking to him. Seeing the giant idle, she picked up her pace but still heard Lord Bracken's words.

"Bring her."

Megan waited only a moment before she began to run. Even with the sound of her own feet pounding in her ears and the horses' hooves receding behind her, it became obvious to her that she was not being pursued by a rider, only an enormous man. He caught her in ten yards.

Arik took care not to harm her, but with the ease of snaring a hare he captured her wrist and turned her back to Hawkings Crest.

"Let me go," Megan ordered and found herself ignored. "My father will have your head for this, do you hear me?"

Arik continued to walk.

Megan tried digging her heels in, but it was of no use. Arik only walked on, and Megan was forced to follow or be dragged. She did follow but began to work on the hand holding her wrist. She tried prying his fingers up and, when she couldn't manage that, tried biting him. Nothing worked.

"You're hurting me," Megan said, changing tactics. It didn't work. Arik walked on. Megan was feeling positively violent just then, but thought better of kicking the man or lashing out with her small fists. She opened her mouth to offer the threat of violence, but Arik came to an abrupt halt. Thinking she had gone too far, Megan's heart slammed against her ribs as he turned and looked at her, but a glance behind him showed that they were already back at the castle.

Megan's heart calmed when she understood his intent. He was giving her the option of walking into the inner courtyard on her own. Something in her face must have indicated her willingness, because Arik dropped her wrist and stood back for her to precede him. Megan did just that, Arik falling into a respectful pace behind.

It never occurred to Megan to enter the castle through anything but the main door, but the guards had other ideas. She was stopped like a common serf, humiliation covering her until Arik evidently signaled from his lofty position. Megan wasn't sure what he did, and she was too upset to look, but the eyes watching her changed from aversion to speculation and the way was made clear.

Once inside the great hall, Megan held her head high with an effort. The room seemed to be teeming with people, and in the midst of them was Bracken, his size and look as ferocious as a great beast.

Why, Megan asked herself, *did I not notice how dark and menacing he is?*

"Come here," Bracken ordered before Megan could form an answer. Megan, as much as she wanted to run, felt her feet propel her forward.

Megan of Stone Lake was afraid of no one. At least this had been true up to now, but this man caused her to tremble with dread. She wanted to run home, throw herself into her father's arms, and cry her heart out, something she hadn't wanted to do in years.

Fortunately for Megan, none of her thoughts showed on her face. She stood before her betrothed, back straight and head high, and told Bracken in that instant that she was no commoner. However, this revelation did not soften Bracken's heart. There were too many unanswered questions for him to be at ease.

"I wish to have some answers from you." Bracken turned away then and spoke over his shoulder. "Come here and sit down."

"No."

The word was not spoken loudly or with much force, but it stopped the young lord in his tracks. Megan's trembling increased when he turned slowly and pierced her with his eyes, but she kept her head high when she spoke.

"I have not eaten since last evening, and I wish to bathe."

"And I wish to question you." Bracken's

voice told Megan that this was the end of the argument.

"Is this the hospitality I am to expect from Hawkings Crest? You give no thought to my well-being in your desire for an inquisition."

Megan had unwittingly hit the mark. Hawkings Crest was known for its hospitality, something in which Bracken took great pride. Megan couldn't have chosen more appropriate words.

"Lyndon," Bracken spoke without ever taking his eyes from the scruffy woman in his midst.

"Yes, my lord?"

"Bring one of the women to assist Lady Megan to a bed-chamber and see to her needs.

"You have one hour," Bracken said, turning to Megan, "to be back down here for my *inquisition.*"

Bracken said the last word threateningly and a shiver raced up Megan's spine. She positively hated to be ordered about in this fashion, but when a woman old enough to be her mother appeared at her side, she left with only a glare in the earl's direction.

Nearly one hour later Megan finally rose from her bath. Helga, the servant assigned to her, was there with a piece of toweling, and she had finally stopped goggling. Megan was compassionate. She could almost hear the woman's thoughts.

This is the servant who works in the creamery! The one who came this morning bearing a churn!

Sometime during Megan's meal or bath, Helga must have realized that a mistake had been made. She had addressed Megan as "my lady" at least 15 times.

"I'm sorry, my lady," Helga spoke now. "I have no clothing for you."

" 'Tis all right, Helga. Just fetch me the furs from the bed and then you can do my hair."

"Yes, my lady." The servant was swift to obey, and in just minutes Megan sat wrapped from neck to ankle as Helga stood behind her to brush out the mass of red curls.

The action caused Megan to relax completely. She had always been a survivor, but the last week had been more than even she was accustomed to. The fight with her mother still weighed heavily on her mind, and a quick counting of the days told her that it still wasn't time for her to have left Stone Lake, which meant that her father was probably still away.

Megan let out a deep sigh; she was growing very sleepy. Her stomach was full for the first time in days, and she was finally clean and warm. Her head began to nod. She noticed that Helga had stopped brushing, but she couldn't find the words to tell her to continue. A moment later something soft was laid next to her cheek and Megan stopped trying to think so her body could sleep.

Six

"Did you not hear my words?"

Megan woke to the sound of an angry male voice, but she had no idea where she was.

"I told you to be in the great room in one hour. Is there something wrong with your ears?"

Megan's senses returned to her in a rush, and she looked up to find Bracken towering over her in a conspicuous rage.

"There is nothing wrong with my ears," Megan told him coldly when he continued to glare.

"Then why aren't you downstairs?"

"I have nothing to wear."

"I don't care —" Bracken began, thinking that women could be very tiresome over their wardrobes, but Megan cut him off.

"Yes, I can see that you don't care." She stood now, the furs still wrapped around her, feeling angry as well. "I have known a week of humiliation in your keep, and now you ask me to parade myself in your great hall without a stitch of clothing on. Well, I won't!"

They were toe-to-toe now, but hardly nose to nose. Bracken eventually noticed what she was wearing, and for the first time his normal good humor was restored to him. Here she was, wrapped in furs, hair all around her face, the top of her head stopping somewhere around the middle of his chest, and *she* was giving the orders. Bracken's eyes lit with amusement, and Megan's narrowed with indignation.

"Do you find this amusing, Lord Bracken?" Her voice was low, and he noticed for the first time how husky it was.

"Indeed, I do, Lady Megan," he admitted. "But," he spoke when she opened her mouth to berate him, "I *will* see that clothing is provided for you, and I *will* expect you to join me as soon as you are able. Does this meet with my lady's approval?"

Megan caught the sarcasm in his question, but she nodded just the same. The sooner they could talk, the sooner she might be able to leave.

She stood still while he exited the chamber and was still standing when Helga returned, surprising Megan by bringing both of the dresses that had been left in her trunk.

"What say you, Arik?"

"Concerning your lady?"

"Yes. When did you find her?"

"She arrived with Elias, the peddler. She tried to gain entrance to the castle but was denied." The huge man's voice was rusty from lack of use.

"And she ended up working in the creamery?" Bracken had been pacing the floor of the war room but now stopped for Arik's reply. He answered with a nod.

"Where did she sleep?"

"The smithy's."

Bracken's eyes slid shut. What on earth had possessed the girl to come early?

Watching him, Arik decided that now was not the time to say that the Lady Megan had arisen each night and tried to leave the smithery while still sleeping.

"While here in the keep, did she come to harm in any way?"

Arik didn't bother to answer or so much as lift a brow. It was a foolish question with him as her protector, and Bracken knew it the moment the words left his mouth.

"Bracken."

The young lord turned at the sound of

his name. Lyndon, the knight as close to Bracken as his own brothers, stood just inside the door.

"Lady Megan is in the great hall."

Bracken nodded and shot a glance at Arik. The larger man was studying him, but as usual Bracken could not discern his thoughts. Without another word, he walked from the room, both Arik and Lyndon at his heels.

Megan could feel several eyes on her as she swept down the main stairway and into the great hall, but the hall itself was such a pleasant surprise that she gave the scrutiny little heed.

It was very spacious and could rival her mother's for cleanliness. It sported not one, but two mammoth fireplaces, and Megan thought how practical this was for chasing away the cold on winter days.

Megan stopped before the fireplace on the north wall and studied the family crest above the mantel. Twin hawks, wings up for landing, flew talons-first toward the center, where a shield which sported a huge male lion, his noble head proud, seemed to stare out over the hall. Megan was very impressed with the symmetry and grandeur of the entire crest. She was still looking at it when Bracken approached. Megan heard his footsteps and turned.

She watched him hesitate, and for some reason flushed with embarrassment. She knew she did not look her best. Her dress was not pressed, and she had no combs for her hair. She would have been stunned to know that Bracken's hesitation was over her looks, but not because he found them lacking.

He recalled the other times he had seen her: in the war room, on the road, briefly here in the great room, and then up in a bedchamber. The first three times she had been covered with dirt, her dress a rag, but why when he'd seen her upstairs hadn't he recognized her loveliness?

His eyes now took in skin that looked like fresh cream, lips full and red, and eyes so enormous and green that they seemed to swallow her face. Added to all of this was the most glorious mass of hair he had ever seen. Suddenly it didn't make a bit of difference that it was red. In fact, he rather liked it. Maybe this woman had been to court after all.

It's wonderful when a husband and wife find each other attractive.

Aunt Louisa's words came back to him, and he could testify at the moment that at least part of that statement was true — he found Megan very attractive. But one look also told him that she did not share the sentiment. The eyes regarding him were trying to disguise their fear, but Bracken was not fooled. He knew it was time for business.

"Please, sit down."

Megan complied and watched as Bracken sat across from her. He was a large man, probably taller than her father and definitely broader. She had never seen anyone with such dark skin and so much dark hair. It covered his head in tight curls and even curled down the back of his neck. His forearms were covered and so was the vee of skin at the top of his tunic. The dark color of his full beard made his teeth look very white.

"How is it that you are here ahead of schedule, Megan?"

"My father is away, and my mother sent me. I don't believe she knew of the date."

"Your father was going to accompany you?"

"Yes." Megan was thankful that he didn't seem ready to question her mother's actions. She would have been ashamed to explain her mother's ruthlessness.

"And you lived in the keep?"

"Yes. I arrived Monday, and as no one expected me I stayed on."

"As a servant?" Bracken's voice was harsh, but he was not angry with her, just concerned.

"Yes." Megan's chin went in the air. "I saw no other way. The road home was long, and I'd already watched my men die under attack. I am not afraid of hard work and staying seemed most rational."

"Arik tells me you slept at the smithy's."

Megan's eyes flew to that giant who was standing against one wall across the room. He was looking back at her, and Megan couldn't suppress a shudder. He was so huge and silent.

"There is no reason to fear him. 'Tis true that he's a huge man, nearly seven feet tall, but he would die protecting you." Bracken's voice was soft now, and Megan's eyes went back to his.

"He can talk?"

Bracken smiled. "Yes, but he chooses to do so very rarely."

Megan nodded.

"Because you are early, Megan, there is no attendant here for you."

"I thought your aunt lived with you." Megan's eyes had grown even larger.

"Most often she does. She was coming

early next week to stay until we are wed, but right now she is in London. I have sent a man for her. She will arrive sometime tomorrow."

"Oh." Megan looked flustered, and Bracken went on smoothly.

"It is certainly not ideal that you stay here tonight without my aunt in attendance, but as you slept unaccompanied in my keep for five nights, one more will hardly make a difference. And," Bracken added dryly, "we are scheduled to wed."

"Oh," Megan said again.

The single word caught Bracken's attention. His dark eyes studied her. "What did that mean?" he asked softly.

Megan swallowed. "Only that I wasn't sure if we still would."

Bracken did not want to tell her that he'd had the same doubts, and replied only, "I can't see that we have much choice."

Megan nodded and fell silent. Her father's intent was that she would know this man before they wed, but at this moment that seemed an impossibility. There was something too powerful and dark about him.

"Were you ever a blonde?"

The question, so innocently put, caused

Megan's entire frame to stiffen and her face to grow rigid. Bracken was amazed at the change in her.

"You mistake me with my sister, Marigold."

"Is she older or younger?" Bracken asked, causing Megan to believe he was truly interested.

"She is older." Megan turned her gaze from him now, and her voice became flat. "Marigold's aspirations go far beyond the title of earl, so I fear you are stuck with me."

Megan never did turn her head, or she would have seen the amusement in Bracken's eyes. He didn't want Marigold, not after meeting Megan, but he found a bit of jealousy between sisters to be an entertaining thing. It would be some time before he learned that for Megan, Marigold was no laughing matter.

Bracken lay in bed for nearly an hour that night thinking on the day's events. He knew that Megan had returned to the bedchamber she'd bathed in and wondered if she was comfortable. He mentally shrugged. As soon as Aunt Louisa arrived, she would live in the tower apartments with her. After living in an abbey, Megan would certainly forgive him one night in a stark chamber. Bracken fell asleep then, but it seemed only moments instead of hours before Lyndon spoke his name in the dark.

"Bracken."

"What is it?" A trained warrior, Bracken was instantly awake.

"I think you should come to the hall."

Bracken rose without question, and after he had joined Lyndon on the stairs, both men stood in awe of the scene below.

Megan sat in a chair by the fire looking into the flames. She wore a borrowed night garment, coarse and many sizes too large for her. Beyond her chair, standing and still fully dressed, was Arik. As Bracken and Lyndon watched, Megan stood and started for the door, but Arik was there ahead of her, preventing her from reaching for the handle.

"No, my lady," his deep, gravely voice could be heard.

Megan tried to come around him, but he moved to block her. After a moment she returned to the chair, and Bracken walked down the stairs. He stared at Megan as he passed, but went directly to Arik. Before he could question him, Megan was on her feet again. She came to the door. This time Bracken heard her speak.

"I have to go home."

"No, my lady," Arik said, holding his body between her and the door. Megan's hands came out as if to push Arik off, but no one had moved to touch her.

"Mother sent me away before my clothes were ready. I have to see Father. I have no brush for my hair."

Megan tried to get to the door again, but Arik sidestepped and prevented it. At the same time, Bracken reached gently for her hand, enfolding it in his large one. Megan woke with a start. She stared up at Bracken and then at Arik before reclaiming her hand and tightly folding her arms across her chest.

"Did I say anything?" she asked, her voice so vulnerable that Bracken's heart constricted.

"No," he lied to her without conscience, knowing that if he told her she would feel shamed.

"Let me see you to your room, Megan," Bracken offered. The small redhead nodded and preceded him across the hall and up the stairs. They didn't speak, and Bracken was glad that Lyndon had made himself scarce. At the same time, another thought occurred to him: The tower apartments were not an option. His intended walked in her sleep. He had never known anyone who did, but a fall down the tower steps could mean her death. Bracken would never take that risk.

Seven

Megan had not yet made an appearance downstairs when Bracken cornered Arik in the great room the next morning.

"Whether or not you're in the mood to speak, my great friend, I need to know more about Lady Megan's actions last night. Did she walk while sleeping in the smithy's shop?"

"Every night."

Bracken had not been prepared for that answer. It gave him pause, and he stared at the giant knight without really seeing him. He'd been thinking Megan might walk in her sleep on a rare occasion, but evidently she had done it every night she'd been at Hawkings Crest.

"How did you stop her?"

"I didn't. I blocked her path."

"You never woke her?"

Arik's head moved in denial.

Megan chose that moment to come downstairs, and Bracken moved off after just a few words of instruction to Arik. He met Megan at the bottom of the stairs and noticed immediately that she looked rested but slightly wary.

"Good morning to you, Megan. Come, break the fast with me."

Megan allowed herself to be led to the head table and took a seat at the top of the long bench. Bracken took the large wooden chair that sat at the head of the table and studied Megan for a few silent moments.

"How did you sleep?"

Megan blushed, her eyes on her hands. "I never remember anything if I walk in my sleep, so until you woke me, I knew nothing."

"And when you returned to your chambers?"

She now looked at him. "I slept again right away."

Food was placed before them. For some time they ate in silence. Megan found the fare very appetizing and ate her fill. Bracken was done ahead of her, however, and while she finished, he told her he was working on a change in plans.

"When my Aunt Louisa lives with me, she always occupies the apartments in the tower. I had originally planned for you to live with her. With the long, narrow stairs, that is out of the question. I will have to make other arrangements."

"Do you mean to suggest that you will send me home?" Megan's voice was so hopeful that Bracken had to hide a smile.

"I believe your father wished for us to become better acquainted."

Megan shrugged. "I thought that since we've at least met, it might suffice to see one another a few times before we wed. Would that not serve the same purpose?"

They both knew it would not, but Bracken was amazed over the emotions her words evoked. For a man who would have gladly refused the king's orders, he was certainly working hard to think of ways to keep Megan with him. His pride, however, would not let him admit this to her.

"I'm sorry you do not wish to remain here, Megan, but if you recall, it was not my idea but your father's and the king's."

Megan blushed to the roots of her hair. He must not want this marriage any more than she did. She had no words. She had been adjusting to new situations all of her life, but this was by far the most difficult.

She did not want to be married yet, and having to live with this man who would soon be her husband was the most awkward experience thus far. Every time he looked at her or touched her in any way,

Megan felt utterly defenseless. It was not something she enjoyed. For the most part, Megan was used to being in charge of her own wants. Now she had to answer to this man. He did not strike her as being cruel, but she could tell that he liked to have his own way as often as she did herself.

Megan had not come down early that morning. She had been praying — confessing, actually. She had grown angry many times the day before and had not confessed each occurrence to God on the spot. Her sins hung over her when she had wakened, and she knew she could not start the day with such a heart.

Bracken and Megan were still sitting silently in one another's company when Lyndon joined them. He didn't sit until Bracken gave him leave, but when he did it was on the end of the other bench, directly opposite Megan.

"Megan, this is Lyndon, a loyal knight of Hawkings Crest. Lyndon, this is my intended, Lady Megan of Stone Lake."

"Hello, Sir Lyndon."

"Hello, my lady. May I say that you grace our hall with your beauty."

Megan smiled at the handsome, blond knight, her first real smile, and Bracken stared at her until Lyndon spoke.

"I'm sorry to disturb you, Bracken, but I think you should know of the gossip in the keep."

"All right."

"Lady Megan was not disturbed in any way while working with the servants. I know you will be pleased over this fact, but you will not care for the reason. They did not recognize her as a lady in their midst but believe that Arik had claimed her."

Megan's face paled, and her eyes slid shut. She thought she might actually hate her mother at that moment. She was to live here and become the mistress of this castle, yet they all thought she had some sort of relationship with Arik. For a moment Megan felt beyond despair, but a sudden resolve stiffened her spine. She had risen to countless occasions in her life; would she now allow this one to rule her?

Both men had been watching her. Bracken was on the verge of speaking when Megan opened her eyes and said, "If you'll excuse me, gentlemen." She rose gracefully. "I feel a need for some air."

"Where are you going?" Bracken asked but was roundly ignored.

Both men watched Megan walk toward the main entrance, her head high, her face serene. At the door she spoke to a guard.

Bracken watched the way the man bowed his head in respect as she walked away. She looked in control, but Bracken was not comfortable. With an easy pace that he didn't feel within, he followed, Lyndon by his side. He knew no physical harm would come to her, but at the moment he wasn't certain if she would be attacked verbally or not. Bracken would stand for no such thing.

Megan, no longer in convent dress, her hair shining with cleanliness, drew every eye in the inner bailey. She spoke to several folks as she moved along, to people she recognized and some she didn't. They all seemed to know her, but she didn't linger; her goal was the creamery.

Bracken had also come into the court-yard, Lyndon still with him, and in an effort to keep an eye on her and not be too conspicuous, wandered about much as Megan was doing. Things seemed to be going well for the first several minutes, but then he watched as she moved toward the creamery. Bracken's heart plummeted. Surely she was not going back to work!

"She's headed for the creamery," he commented to the man at his side.

"So I see," was all Lyndon said.

They watched her disappear within, and Bracken debated his next move. A moment later the problem was temporarily taken from his hands. Kent appeared at his side to tell him that his men had need of him on the practice field. He walked away with long-legged strides, leaving Lyndon in the courtyard. As much as he trusted Lyndon, Bracken could not stop himself from looking back at the creamery until it was out of view.

"Hello, Eddie," Megan greeted the man easily as she crossed the threshold. She watched as he removed his cap.

"Hello, my lady."

Megan let her eyes roam the large, clean room and then began to walk slowly around. The women working within slowed some to watch her but continued with their tasks.

"You run this creamery with excellence, Eddie," Megan told him sincerely when she stopped at one point.

"Thank you, my lady. I'm glad you approve."

"Hello, Pen," Megan said as she continued her stroll. "Watch that edge when you pour."

"Yes, my lady." Pen reverently breathed

the words. She did tend to be rather clumsy, but right now all she could see and hear was Megan — her dress, hair, her lovely skin, and the husky sound of her cultured voice.

"I'd like to make a suggestion, Eddie."

"Yes, my lady," the man said. They were back at the entrance now, and Eddie's heart sank with dread. Would she now take revenge for the way he had treated her? Eddie saw himself grabbing her arm the first day and had to stifle a groan. However, he was in for a pleasant surprise.

Megan began to make a most logical suggestion concerning the storage of cheese. Her voice was gracious, and her manner unassuming. Eddie felt as if she'd actually left the final choice up to him. She had also waited until the others couldn't hear. Eddie had not lost face and had gained helpful information in the process. When Megan left the creamery, he wished her a pleasant day with a most sincere heart, his cap still in his beefy hand.

"Oh, Lyndon!" Megan spoke the moment she was outside and spotted the knight; he'd been practically haunting the creamery, listening for raised voices.

"Yes, my lady?"

"Lyndon, where are the cows?"

"The cows, my lady?" Lyndon questioned her with little enthusiasm, thinking he would never forgive Bracken for leaving him there alone.

"Yes. The cows they milk for the creamery," Megan explained kindly.

"In the stables, my lady."

"And the stables are . . . ?"

Lyndon stared into her face. How in the world did one deal with such a woman? She had the face of an angelic five-year-old and a backbone like an iron rod.

"The stables, Lyndon, where are they?" Megan questioned again, her voice not quite so cordial this time.

"Along the north wall of the keep, my lady."

"Thank you," Megan beamed at him and promptly turned and started in the wrong direction.

"Lady Megan," Lyndon called to her. "This way," he said when she turned. "I'll show you."

"Oh, thank you, Lyndon."

And off they set, Megan as pleased as a lass at play and Lyndon feeling that he'd rather be forced to wrestle with Arik than have the charge of Bracken's intended.

"And she insisted on seeing my books!"

95

Barton, Hawkings Crest's steward, nearly shouted.

"She told me that it's my fault that two of me birds have sores on their claws. Wants to reconstruct the whole cage, she does!" the falconer added.

"She actually accused me of stealing!" The steward spouted again. "Said she'd finish reading my accounts later."

Bracken stared at his falconer and steward in disbelief. His stableman and smithy were there also, but they had already had their say. He'd only been gone a few hours, but in that time Megan had evidently turned his castle and keep upside down. He glanced up to see her coming sedately into the hall and dismissed the men around him with a curt nod of his head.

"Megan," he raised his voice only slightly. "I wish to speak with you."

Megan stopped but did not draw close. "I'm busy right now, Bracken."

This was too much.

"*Megan!*" he bellowed, and she redirected her course to stand before him. She did an admirable job of hiding her fear of his anger. Bracken thought she looked utterly serene.

"My steward and smith have both been

to see me, as have others. What have you to say for yourself?"

Megan shrugged innocently. "There are several areas that are in need of change, Bracken. I think your steward might be robbing you blind."

"He's been with me for years," Bracken, now red in the face, retorted.

Again Megan shrugged. "Be that as it may . . ." she let the sentence drop before plunging on, "your birds are not in the best of health. I have a poultice for their feet, but the bars will have to be sanded or the sores will return."

Bracken barely heard her as he began to shout. "I will not have you upsetting every servant in Hawkings Crest! I forbid you to visit the stables, and as for the other areas —"

"That won't work at all, Bracken," she replied, cutting him off in a calm voice. "If I am to be the mistress of this keep, I must stay abreast of its workings. Now, I really must be off, Bracken. I have yet to see the looms."

With that Megan swung away from him in a cloud of long skirts and red hair. Chest heaving, Bracken stood and stared after her until he realized he was being watched. His head moved toward the man who dared, ready to give him the rough edge of his tongue, until he met the amused gaze of his Aunt Louisa.

"She doesn't have blonde hair after all." His aunt's voice was mild.

"How do you know that's Megan?" Bracken shot at her, his mood still dangerous.

"Because you wouldn't let anyone else speak to you in such a manner."

Bracken's shoulders slumped with defeat. It was true.

"Come, my nephew." Louisa became all at once brisk. "Let's go into the war room, and you can tell me all that has transpired."

Eight

Twenty minutes later Louisa asked her first question, her expression one of stark disbelief.

"She actually worked in the creamery?"

"Don't look at me that way, Aunt Lou." Her nephew's look was helpless.

"Bracken," Louisa said patiently, truly wanting to understand, "I heard the girl. There is no way a woman with that voice could be mistaken for a serf."

Bracken shook his head. "Evidently she spoke to no one. She did her work, ate in the courtyard with the other servants, and slept each night at the smithy's."

Louisa just stared at him, and Bracken knew he had to tell all.

"There is more."

Louisa waited.

"She walks in her sleep."

The woman blinked. "You're certain of this?"

"I witnessed it myself. I was going to have her live in the tower apartments with you, but now that is out of the question."

"Yes, I can see that it would be." Louisa replied thoughtfully, and they both fell silent for a time.

"You say she actually slept in your blacksmith's shop?" Louisa seemed unable to let the matter drop.

"I'm afraid so."

"What will her father say?"

Bracken shook his head. "I can't think that he'll be overly pleased, but it was hardly my fault; her mother sent her early."

"Why would she do such a thing?"

"I have not been able to gain more answers. Megan talks in her sleep as well, and mentioned that she'd been sent without her full wardrobe. I would like to know more, but if she knows she spoke to me in her sleep, she will feel shamed."

Louisa's eyes softened. "You care for her, don't you, Bracken."

"Heaven help me, I do!" the young earl burst out. He came to his feet and began to pace. "I've known her 24 hours, and she has interrupted my entire life, but I can't get her from my mind!"

"What of the blonde woman you met at court?"

"Her older sister, Marigold. I spoke of her with Megan, but I do not think them very close."

"But you do find Megan attractive."

A sudden smile parted Bracken's dark beard, and his voice softened. "Ah, yes. She is as lovely a maid as I've ever seen. I do find her most comely."

Louisa was well pleased, but her practical side came to the fore. "Do you think her capable of managing a fortress as large as Hawkings Crest?"

"Yes," Bracken admitted grudgingly, thinking about the way she stood up to him. However, the face of his steward flashed into his mind as well.

"Nevertheless, you heard the men. It's not going to be easy." Bracken had begun to growl, but he worked at calming himself. Knowing his aunt would grasp his meaning beyond the words, he made one last comment.

"I am beginning to think that marriage to Megan might be more trouble than it is worth."

"But as you have reminded me, we have little choice in the matter." Megan's voice came from the doorway, and Bracken spun in surprise. "I will honor my father's wishes and those of my king and become your wife," Megan went on, her tone wooden. "But it is a relief to know, Lord Bracken, just exactly how you feel."

Megan left as quietly as she'd entered, and Bracken stood as though made of granite. Louisa's heart ached at the pain she saw in his face.

"I didn't mean it the way it sounded." Bracken's voice was hushed in the still room, and his eyes never left the closed portal.

"I know you didn't, Bracken. Maybe if you try to explain . . ."

But Bracken was shaking his head. "I think her pride is as great as my own. I will have to give her time."

Even with the little she had seen of Megan, Louisa was forced to agree. They spoke of sleeping arrangements for the next few moments and then went their separate ways, Louisa to settle herself in a suite of rooms down the corridor from Megan, and Bracken to the keep, hoping to get a glimpse of his bride-to-be without actually searching her out.

STONE LAKE CASTLE

"What do you mean she's not here?" Vincent eyed his wife in disbelief, but Annora did not flinch.

"It wasn't going well, so I sent Megan ahead."

"To Hawkings Crest?" Vincent's tone was incredulous.

"Of course to Hawkings Crest!" Annora snapped. "Where did you think?"

"But she wasn't expected."

Annora shrugged. "Surely someone was there. Honestly, Vincent, she was being most impossible. You know what she's like."

"You fool!" Vincent retorted scathingly, widening his wife's eyes with shock and then anger. "Anything could have happened. Has the caravan arrived back?"

"I sent no caravan." Annora kept up a brave front, but in truth she had regretted this action almost immediately.

"What say you?" Vincent's face had flushed with emotion as he tried telling himself that he had heard her wrong.

Annora raised her chin. "I sent Megan on horseback with three guards. I'm certain she fared well."

"So the men have returned?"

"No, but —"

Annora was cut off when Vincent grabbed her forearm with a strength she didn't know he possessed.

"Vincent." Her tone was wounded. For the first time she was a bit afraid. "You are hurting me."

"I'll do more than hurt you if even so much as Megan's reputation is harmed! Now, sit down, woman, and tell me all!"

Annora now knew real fear. Megan had always been such a headstrong survivor. It had truly never occurred to her that her daughter might fall into harm. Annora's voice shook, but she did as Vincent bid and relayed every detail, down to the minute, of Megan's departure. No small thing this, as she had never seen her husband so coldly furious.

Less than 15 minutes later, Vincent and a band of men rode out on horseback for Hawkings Crest. Just behind them rode more men and a large wagon laden with Megan's new clothing and all of her belongings. When they had all left, Annora made her way to the chapel. She didn't pray often, but if Megan was actually lost, she now feared for her daughter's life as well as her own.

Megan stood at the window of her bedchamber, looking into the distance and feeling thoroughly spent with her effort to quell her emotions. Walking into the keep that morning knowing that the servants actually believed her part of a liaison with Arik had been almost unbearable. She had made herself move among them, careful to keep her eyes from lingering too long on any one face, but it had been torture.

Then in the midst of the hurt, Megan had found herself more and more interested in the castle workings. Hawkings Crest was a fine stronghold, but every fortress had areas that needed improvement and Megan could see many at Hawkings Crest. Yet, Bracken had only thought her interfering. His shouting at her had affected her more deeply than she had let on. She hadn't even enjoyed seeing the looms, even though they were run with tremendous efficiency.

Megan suddenly found herself back in the bushes, hiding out of fear for life, listening and looking on in the dim firelight as her three guards were slain. Tears poured down her cheeks, and a sob sounded in her throat. She turned and lay across the bed, burying her face in the thick furs as harsh weeping overcame her. Megan prayed for strength, but at the moment she felt faithless. In the midst of asking God to bring her father soon, she fell into a restless sleep.

"Have you seen Megan?" The question came softly to Louisa's and Lyndon's ears just moments before Bracken spotted her coming down the stairs. She had not taken the midday meal with them, and it was now evening. He had no desire to treat her as a child, but he would not allow her to go hungry. Bracken left Lyndon and his aunt without comment and met Megan at the bottom of the stairs.

Megan came to a stop on the last step and simply stared at Bracken. He returned the gaze, taking in the lovely blush in her cheeks and her bright, serious eyes. Their height difference was lessened in this stance, and for just a moment no one spoke. Bracken turned in profile to her and offered his arm. Megan took it.

"Did you have a pleasant afternoon, Megan?" Bracken asked as they crossed to the tables.

"Yes, Lord Bracken, thank you."

"My aunt has arrived. I would like you to meet her."

"Very well." Megan sounded disinterested, but inside she was tense. She soon learned there was no need.

As soon as they neared, Louisa turned, a warm smile lighting her handsome features. Megan saw in an instant where Bracken inherited his dark coloring. Louisa's hair was as dark as her nephew's, with just a hint of gray at the temples. Her lashes and brows were equally as dark, and the eyes regarding her were a deep brown. The older woman now reached for both of Megan's hands.

"Megan, this is my Aunt Louisa," Bracken spoke. "Aunt Louisa, this is my betrothed, Megan, daughter to Vincent of Stone Lake."

"Hello, Megan," she said still holding Megan's work-rough hands in her own soft ones. "I'm so pleased to meet you."

"Bracken told me you were called away from London ahead of time. I hope my presence has not interfered in any way with your plans."

"Not in the least, my dear. I'm glad to be of service."

"Come," Bracken broke in. "Our food is served."

They all retired to the tables then, Bracken at the head, Megan to his right, and Aunt Louisa to his left. Lyndon sat by Louisa, and another knight, Kendrick by name, took a place on the bench next to Megan.

Bracken and Megan shared a trencher. Bracken was the consummate gentleman, seeing that all the best cuts of meat went to Megan's side of the wooden platter. Conversation flowed freely among Bracken and the others, but Megan had little to say. Bracken's eyes lingered on her for most of the meal, and by the time they finished, he felt he would do anything to see her smile.

As it was, he was about to get his wish. They had just stood when Clive, another of Bracken's vassals, announced Vincent's presence. Megan excused herself and moved with a calm face to the main doors of the castle, Bracken at her heels. She continued to walk sedately until she spotted him coming up the path, whereupon she ran the last six yards and quite literally threw herself into her father's arms.

Vincent hugged her close. When he released her to put one arm around her shoulders, Bracken, who was now upon them, was able to see her smiling face. It took his breath away.

"More wine," Bracken instructed a serving woman and then sat quietly as Vincent and his men ate their fill. In order to give them privacy, Megan and Louisa had retired to the south hearth, but there had been little talk until now. Bracken felt the time had come for him to explain. Vincent had not seemed at all upset, but Bracken knew by the way he greeted his daughter that there must be much on his mind.

"I want to tell you of your men, my lord."

Vincent forestalled him with a hand. "We saw their graves. I thank you for seeing to the burial. Can you tell me what happened?"

Bracken shook his head. "I know little. Megan said they died saving her."

"She was unharmed?" Vincent's gaze grew intense.

"It would seem so."

"And once she arrived here?"

Bracken drew a deep breath. "She was not harmed, but neither was she well taken care of."

Vincent began to scowl as Bracken filled him in about Megan's work in the creamery, and eating and sleeping in the keep.

"I'm sorry, Lord Vincent, I was not here, but I still take full blame since I did not make provisions for the possibility of an early arrival."

To Bracken's amazement, Vincent did not seem distressed. Instead his eyes suddenly lit with good humor.

"You say she slept in a stall?"

"Yes, Lord Vincent."

Vincent chuckled softly. "I think I want you to call me Vincent, and if I told you some of the situations Megan has gotten herself into over the years, you would understand my pleasure. Hear me now," Vincent's voice grew serious, "when I tell you that I would never countenance abuse toward the girl, but Megan is a survivor — always has been. If she had wanted into this castle before you arrived, she would have come."

Bracken's dark brows winged upward. It was true. Megan had been standing before him in the war room little more than an hour after he arrived.

"I'm only glad she was unharmed," Vincent said with quiet conviction.

"Can you tell me why she arrived early?"

Vincent's brow lowered, and all pleasure left his face. "Megan and her mother do not get on. They quarreled, and my wife took it upon herself to send Megan here. Had I been present, I would have stopped her. Unfortunately, I arrived back late last night and knew nothing of this until this morning."

"And now that she is here, Vincent, do you wish her to stay?"

Vincent glanced up at Bracken and then down at his trencher to hide the gleam in his eye. This young lord was trying to conceal his interest, but it was there.

Good! Vincent's heart declared. *He is not a man to be bullied. With his mettle, he will make a fine spouse, worthy of my Megan.*

"Since your aunt is now in attendance," Vincent spoke aloud, "I see no reason for Megan to leave. I had planned on spending some days with her before she left Stone Lake, but I was called away."

"Stay now," Bracken inserted. "Stay at Hawkings Crest for as long as you wish."

"I may do that," Vincent replied slowly, not having thought of it. "I just may, but right now I wish to join Megan. I wish, for the sake of my men, to know what happened the night they were attacked."

Nine

"I'm glad your father arrived, Megan. I think he must have been worried about you."

Megan smiled and nodded. She had not yet seen how well Lady Louisa could read and understand people, but she was comfortable with her. She had experienced little comfort at Hawkings Crest, and she found this a relief.

"I think you must be right. It's so good to see him. We were to have some time together before I left, but then he was called away."

Louisa nodded, accurately guessing more than she was told.

"Do you have many siblings, Megan?" Louisa asked with just the right amount of interest.

"Just one sister, Marigold. I haven't seen her for some years."

"She is older?"

"Yes, by more than two years. We have little in common. Lady Louisa, are you sister to Bracken's father or mother?"

"I hope you will call me Aunt Louisa, and I am sister to Bracken's mother, Joyce. After Bracken's father died, our own father became ill. Taking all of Bracken's siblings, Joyce moved many miles north to our own family's keep, White Hall. Our father is dead now, too, but Joyce and the children have made their home there and are most content. You will meet her at the wedding."

Megan nodded, looking thoughtful. "Has Bracken a large family?"

"Yes. He is the oldest, but after him are Stephen, Danella, Brice, Giles, and Kristine. Danella is married and expecting her first child, but no one else has wed. They live for the most part with my sister. I think you will meet them all at the wedding."

Megan's eyes had grown during this recitation, but she managed one more question.

"And Bracken's father. Has he been long dead?"

"About six years. Greville died in battle, a great warrior he was. He made the king proud. Bracken is very much like him." Louisa added this last bit with gentle pride, while giving Megan a sweet smile.

Megan smiled in return and asked, "And what about you Aunt Louisa, do you have children of your own?"

Louisa did have children, two grown sons whom she adored, but she was not given time to answer before the men strode into their midst.

"I have no want to upset you, Meg," her father began, "but the men who escorted you have families. For their sakes, I wish to know how they died."

Meg nodded, her eyes briefly skimming over Bracken and Louisa before returning to her father. She told her story quietly, her eyes on her father or on the fire in the hearth. She didn't notice how Bracken's jaw became rigid upon hearing the way she sat in the bushes and watched the men die. Nor did she see the pain in his eyes when he heard fear in her voice as she asked her father if he thought she would ever see the attackers again.

"No, Meg," he assured her, taking her hand in his own. "You'll be safe at Hawkings Crest."

"So you're leaving me?" The anxious words were out before she could stop them, and Megan blushed as she dropped her eyes to her lap. An awkward moment passed before Megan spoke, her eyes still downcast.

"I'm rather tired. I think I'll go to my room."

Both Vincent and Bracken stood.

"Will I see you tomorrow?" she asked of her father.

"I'll be here."

With that, Megan briefly met his eyes, wished them all a good night, and walked from the hall. Bracken's eyes stayed on her until she was out of sight. A moment later he was relieved that Lyndon had need of him. He also bid his guests goodnight, leaving Vincent and Louisa alone.

"Would you like to be shown to your chambers, Lord Vincent?" Louisa asked solicitously.

"I believe I'll stay a while longer by the fire."

"May I join you?"

"You do me honor, Lady Louisa."

The two sat again. After a moment Louisa commented, "Megan is a lovely girl."

Vincent smiled. "I know she is not certain about staying, not that I blame her after such a rough initiation, but I truly think it is best."

"Bracken told me that she suggested her going home and his visiting from time to time before they wed." Louisa suddenly thought that such a statement might seem impertinent, but Lord Vincent answered readily enough.

"That's not possible," he said quietly. "Megan and her mother do not get on well. It would be a difficult time for both of them. It would also defeat the purpose of Megan becoming better acquainted with Bracken before they unite their lives."

"This is true," Louisa commented and then fell silent.

"They have not known a good start."

"This is true also."

Vincent speared her with a glance. She was choosing her words very carefully, and there was no need. He told her as much.

"In that case," Louisa said, "I'll tell you that Bracken seems very willing for this trial period. Megan, on the other hand, is not."

Much the way Vincent had surprised Bracken at the table, he now took Louisa unaware by smiling.

"You are pleased, Lord Vincent."

"Yes, I am. If I believed Bracken would shun and hurt Megan I would take her with me, but this situation has promise. Bracken will have to work hard to find Megan's harmonious side, but I know it

116

will be worth his effort."

"She does seem to have a will of her own."

Vincent chuckled. "She's no man's plaything, and if Bracken can get beyond her lovely face and engaging curves, he'll find himself a wife whose worth cannot be measured."

It was one of the most wonderful things Louisa had ever heard anyone say. She stared at Vincent for a long moment, but his eyes were on the flames, a small smile playing around his mouth.

Louisa suddenly remembered the sleepwalking and felt concern. Maybe she should go upstairs. Did Megan's father know of the problem?

"Lord Vincent?"

"I'm sorry, my lady, I was not attending." Indeed, his thoughts had drifted far.

"Bracken tells me that Megan walks in her sleep. Should I check on her now?"

Vincent's frame stiffened. "Megan only walks in her sleep when something is upsetting her."

Louisa did not know what to say to this.

"Bracken asked me to stay on if I so chose. Maybe I shall do so." Again Louisa could not frame a suitable reply.

"I hope you will not find me rude, my

lady, but I feel a sudden need to check on Megan myself."

"Of course, Lord Vincent. I shall escort you to her room."

The problem in the keep concerning the evening guard was swiftly handled by Bracken and Lyndon, so it wasn't long before the lord of Hawkings Crest stood alone atop the wall. The night was swiftly closing in around him; it was one of his favorite times of the day.

Bracken was not a religious man, nor one given to praying, but he did believe in God and that He was in control. He would have given much right then to say that he knew God better, in hopes that he would then know what plans God had for the future. Bracken found himself wanting a life with Megan in a way that he hadn't wanted anything in a long time.

He could easily envision the fine sons they would have and just as easily put Megan's fear of him at the back of his mind so that he could also envision a good marriage between them. It really made no sense. Megan clearly wished to be elsewhere, and he didn't even know the girl. But Bracken felt a sureness deep within him that Megan of Stone Lake was the woman God had planned for him.

Bracken shrugged. He was growing maudlin. It was impossible to know what the future held, and being the logical man he was, Bracken started toward the castle. There was no point in losing sleep over the matter.

Vincent was out of the castle early the next morning, but many of the castle folk were already astir. He walked through the keep and around the grounds and was pleasantly surprised to find Bracken and Lyndon returning from the practice field. Both men were gleaming with sweat, and Vincent saw that directly behind them was the jousting field.

"Good morning to you, Vincent," Bracken greeted him.

"And to you, Bracken. This is one of your knights?"

"Yes. Lord Vincent, meet Lyndon."

"It's a pleasure, sir," Lyndon said with respect and then took himself off to the castle.

"You're up early," Bracken commented as they walked easily in Lyndon's wake.

"Yes. I will accept your offer to stay for a few days, but with so little time, I did not care to lounge in bed."

"Good," Bracken returned sincerely. "I think Megan will be very pleased."

"And mayhap a little more willing to remain here and get to know you better."

Bracken smiled at his perception. "I do not wish to see her pine for you."

"Nor do I. Keep in mind, Bracken," the older man continued, coming to a stop, "Megan lived at the abbey for years. During her time there she learned a great deal, the most important of which is that her life there kept her unspoiled. Always remember that Megan will never yearn for a life of creature comforts. She does not put great stock in her surroundings as much as she does in the people surrounding her."

Bracken nodded. It was a good thing to know. Still, he knew that Hawkings Crest could offer her better.

"I don't know if you've been to see Megan's room, but that chamber is just temporary."

Vincent waved a dismissive hand. "You will find she is most settled. I would ask you, though, to take care with Megan herself. I speak without bias when I say she has many fine qualities, but that is not to say she has no faults. Pray, deal gently with her."

Bracken was impressed with the older man's honesty. "You are telling me she likes to have her own way."

Vincent smiled. "What woman does not?"

Bracken only smiled in reply, but he knew that if he pressed Lord Vincent, the older man would have to admit that Megan was in a class alone.

"I do not wish to stay here, Father God, but I will do as I am asked. Please help me to know control of my actions and emotions. Please help me to deal kindly with all here."

Megan stopped when Bracken came to mind. Did she mean him, too? In truth, she wasn't sure. She had no wish to be mean, but knowing that he felt her troublesome, along with his interest in her sister, made Megan want nothing to do with him.

Megan immediately warned herself not to grow overly emotional. She had no real proof that Bracken was interested in Marigold. After all, he had only asked a few questions, and Megan recognized her own sensitivity where Marigold was concerned.

A knock on her chamber door brought Megan to her feet. She found her father waiting without.

"Come and break the fast with me, Megan."

"Do you leave today?"

"No. I will be here for you."

Megan beamed up at him and took his proffered arm for the journey down the wide stone stairs.

"This flour has been sifted?" Megan asked the baker and let a handful run through her fingers.

"Yes, my lady."

"Please repeat the process."

"Yes, my lady," the man spoke, but Louisa, standing at Megan's side, could see that he was not happy.

The older woman had to keep from shaking her head. Vincent had been gone for two days, and Louisa had steeled herself for Megan's resentment or depression. She got neither. Megan was throwing herself into the workings of the castle with a vengeance.

Megan was the most fascinating woman Louisa had ever encountered. One moment she was tending to a slight wound on the finger of a small child and the next she was telling the milkers, in no uncertain terms, that they would do a better job of rinsing their pottery jars. Louisa knew there were a few who wanted to toss her into the moat, but most of the castle folk were beginning to adore her.

And Bracken was no exception. Louisa could see it in his eyes. Unfortunately Megan did not return his sentiment. She might be talking with Lyndon, smiling at him in true affection, or even laughing at some outrageous remark from Kendrick, but the moment Megan became aware of Bracken's presence she became stiff as a poker. She was even warming up to Arik, but to Bracken she was chillingly civil.

"Aunt Louisa?"

"Yes, dear." The women had made their way from the kitchen and baking quarters and were almost to the great hall.

"Who is Black Francesca?"

Louisa came to such an abrupt halt that Megan started. The older woman took a moment to ask, "Where did you hear her name, Megan?"

"I heard Helga mention her to Lela, but I have met no one at Hawkings Crest with that name."

Louisa licked her lips. "She lives in the village."

Megan nodded serenely, but because she was very curious over Louisa's reaction, she pressed her.

"But who is she?"

Louisa hesitated for only a moment this time; surely Megan was mature enough to understand.

"She is the village prostitute."

Louisa was not prepared for Megan's reaction. Her eyes filled with compassionate tears.

"Is she very young?"

"I'm not sure," Louisa admitted and felt shame for the uncharitable thoughts she'd had toward Black Francesca in the past. On top of these thoughts, however, was one of horror. She couldn't stop herself from voicing it.

"You're not thinking of going to see her, are you, Megan?"

"Well, not right away."

"Megan." Louisa felt panic coming on. "I do not think Bracken would approve." *Disapproval* was too mild a word, but Louisa could think of none better.

Megan stiffened with outrage. "Why? Does Bracken visit her?"

"No!" Louisa's voice squeaked. "No, Megan, never."

Some of Megan's strain left her, but she still looked offended. Louisa sighed. It would seem that Bracken could do no right, not even when he was innocent.

"You judge Bracken too harshly, my dear." Louisa's words were spoken gently, but they had a powerful effect. Megan stared at the older woman and then dropped her eyes. Her fingers came to her lips, and she looked very contrite.

Louisa would have questioned her some, but Clive approached then, announcing, "Lady Louisa, Lord Bracken asked me to tell you that Lord Stephen and Lord Brice have arrived."

"Thank you, Clive."

"Bracken's family?" Megan questioned when Clive moved away.

"Yes, the two brothers closest to him in age. Will you come with me to meet them?"

"They will be hungry. I will join you when I've seen that something is prepared."

Louisa saw it for the excuse that it was and let it go, but she knew that Megan's fears were ungrounded. She was going to love Bracken's brothers.

Ten

"How is my mother?" Bracken asked.

"Well," Stephen told him. "She sends her love, as do Giles and Kris."

"Has Danella's child come?"

"No, but she feels well."

Brice had remained silent during this exchange, and Bracken now transferred his gaze to him.

"What say you, Brice?" Bracken said with a teasing light in his eyes.

"Where is she?"

Bracken smiled. At 18, Brice was preoccupied with the fairer sex. He had been impressed, not dismayed, that the king had taken enough notice of Bracken to order him to marry. He'd thought that was something saved for lords with loftier titles. Now he wanted to know if his brother was to be saddled with an angel or a harridan.

"I believe she's inside. Yonder comes Aunt Lou. She'll know."

Louisa received warm embraces from some of her favorite nephews before she stood back and lovingly studied them.

"You're taller, Brice."

He smiled boyishly before she turned to Stephen and eyed him a moment. His looks so closely resembled Bracken's that it was startling.

"I was certain that Megan would like both you and Brice, but you look enough like Bracken that I can see she may have trouble." Louisa then turned a devilish smile on her oldest nephew, who tried to scowl at her but couldn't quite bring it off.

"What's this, Bracken?" Stephen teased. "Trouble in paradise?"

Bracken chuckled, but Brice cut in seriously.

"Aunt Lou is teasing," he said, believing with all of his heart that no woman in her right mind could find fault with Bracken.

He was soon to learn differently. Not ten minutes later they were inside and meeting Lady Megan, who stared hard at Stephen before transferring her gaze to Bracken. The lord of the keep was clearly amused by her reaction and smiled when he saw her chin go up in the air.

"My brothers are hungry," he said, his tone still light but his eyes watchful.

Megan's raised brows mocked him. "The food awaits, my lord." Megan started to swing away, but Bracken's voice halted her.

"Megan."

She turned back with reluctance.

"I wish you to join us."

It was not what she wanted to hear.

"Very well, my lord." Although clearly not happy, Megan allowed Bracken to take her arm and escort her to her place.

The meal progressed with much talk between Louisa and her younger nephews, but Megan and Bracken were distinctly quiet. The meal was coming to an end when Bracken leaned close and spoke for Megan's ears alone.

"What is it I have done, Megan, to vex you so?"

Megan looked at him for the first time. His face was close, and for an instant she studied his serious, dark eyes. This marriage had not been his idea, nor had it been his plan that she stay at Hawkings Crest. He may not really care for her, but she realized then that he couldn't force feelings onto his heart.

"I'm sorry, Lord Bracken, that my mood has been so poor. I will try my utmost not to brandish it upon you in the future."

"I appreciate your effort, Megan, but I'm sorry you're so unhappy."

Megan sighed. She hated being so obvious.

"I left my home abruptly; I would have wished for a little more time."

It was true, Bracken thought. She had left all that was familiar and had been given little time to adjust.

"Would it help to move you to a more comfortable bedchamber?" he suggested.

Megan shook her head; she was sincerely content. "I shall be fine where I am."

"Playing the martyr, Megan?" Why Bracken quietly baited the girl he didn't know, but it had its effect.

"No." Megan's chin was up, her voice cold. "If there is nothing else," her voice could now be heard by those at the table, "I have duties that need my attention."

Megan stood, nodded to those around her, and walked from the room, her bearing resembling that of a queen. It wasn't long before some of the others left as well, but Stephen found Brice standing alone, a fierce frown on his young face.

"Are you ill, my brother?" Stephen asked.

"What is wrong with her?"

"Her?" Stephen replied, although he knew exactly to whom Brice referred.

"Megan." Brice's voice held strong aversion. "How dare she treat Bracken in such a manner."

"Do not be too hard on her, Brice; she reacts out of fear."

"Fear!" Brice scoffed and finally faced his older sibling. "What has she to fear? Certainly not Bracken."

Stephen wisely held his tongue, but he did believe that Bracken was at the core of Megan's fears and thus her animosity toward him was clearly explained. The brothers did not discuss it again, but Stephen wondered when Brice would find that all men had feet of clay, even their beloved Bracken.

Megan had little contact with Bracken or his brothers in the days to follow, and as much as she tried to fight the emotion, despondency was stealing over her. It seemed to Megan that the castle and keep crawled with people and she could find no solitude of any kind. The only place where she found quiet was her room, but after too many hours within those walls, she had begun to feel vaguely suffocated, a feeling which didn't prove to be very restful.

Megan had not been sleeping well. Several times she had awakened in the chair by the fireplace but not remembered getting there. If she was walking in her sleep, what was keeping her from leaving the room? Not having an answer to her question made Megan even more restless. Feeling almost desperate, she made for the fortress gate and freedom. The guards did nothing to block her path, and to her amazement not even Arik seemed to notice.

Once outside the walls Megan walked on and on, some of the tall grasses coming over her knees. The scape surrounding Hawkings Crest was lovely, and Megan felt her heart calming as she took in the trees and lush landscape.

It really is lovely here, Father God, she prayed in her heart. *I thought nothing could match Stone Lake, but Hawkings Crest is like a rich paradise.*

Megan stopped and watched several squirrels at play, knowing they must have been young with the way they gamboled and chased up the trees. Megan's face broke into a brief smile before she continued to pray.

Please help me to find the same peace in my heart as I see in your creation. Father Brent taught me that contentment is my choice, Father God, and I have not been doing a good job. Please fill my heart and life with You so that my situation or circumstances do not matter.

She hiked on for over an hour, praying and praising God, before sinking down under a tree. The sun sprinkled brightly over her in little patches through the leaves, and it wasn't long before its warmth lulled Megan to sleep.

"Have you seen Lady Megan?"

It was the question on Louisa's lips and then on everyone else's as Megan's absence became apparent. Bracken's face, that of a warrior with a mission, was void of emotional expression, but those who knew him well could detect the concern, the ache to know where she was.

When it became evident that she was not within the castle walls, some of Bracken's knights rode out on horseback, but the rest of the castle folk, including Bracken and his brothers, set off on foot. Megan heard their cries before she regained full consciousness, and when she did waken, she listened in horror to the call of her name.

With a head still muddled with sleep, Megan came to her feet and nearly stumbled out from beneath the trees. She was rushing along the edge of the forest when

Bracken, Stephen, and Kendrick suddenly appeared. The towering rage on Bracken's face stopped her in her tracks. She watched as he spoke to Kendrick and then as he and Stephen covered the distance between them.

"Why are you out here?" Bracken's voice was curt.

"I wanted to be alone."

"So you left the safekeeping of the walls?" Bracken's voice betrayed his astonishment, telling Megan that he would never understand.

"Yes. I felt a need for solitude. I never meant to fall asleep."

"You foolish woman!" The words were spat at her. "I have the entire keep looking for you, thinking you abducted or harmed, and here you sleep! Indeed, you are a fool!"

Bracken seemed to be out of words then, or too angry to say more. He turned on his booted heel and swung away from Megan and his brother. He was ten steps away when Stephen spoke softly.

"You disappoint me, Megan."

She turned hurting eyes to him, wondering from how many she would know rebuke.

"I'd never have guessed you for a woman

who would stand mute while someone called you a fool."

Megan stared at him and then at Bracken, who was swiftly moving away. Her brow lowered menacingly before she raised her voice to be heard.

"I am *not* a fool."

Bracken stopped, turned, and stared back at her.

"Were you speaking to me?" he asked as if she had no right.

"Yes. You will not speak to me in such a fashion."

Bracken began to walk back to her so abruptly that Megan started. As he neared, she was reminded of his ire and began to back away. Bracken came right ahead, backing her into a tree and speaking in an angry growl after she bumped her head on the bark.

"What did you say to me?"

Megan swallowed.

"I'm not a fool." The words were whispered this time as green eyes, wide with fear and pleading, stared up at him.

Seeing that fear, Bracken's heart softened within him. When Megan had disappeared, he had been more frightened than ever in his life. He had handled her and the situation poorly, but flowery words were not in him. When he spoke, his voice was slightly less harsh but it was far from congenial.

"It is as you say, you are not a fool. I would ask, however, that in the future you do not leave the keep without informing someone. It is most troublesome to lay out a search."

Megan didn't sense her own trembling until she was alone once again. She stood against the tree for several moments, fighting down the despair she felt rising within. Would she ever find her place here? Would she ever do that which was expected?

Megan left the tree without any answers and was surprised to find Stephen awaiting her. He did not comment on the scene he had witnessed, but offered to escort her back.

"Thank you," Megan told him softly and began to walk slowly, thoughtfully, toward Hawkings Crest. After several yards, she commented.

"I fear I am nothing but an annoyance to Bracken." Megan didn't normally confide in strangers, but although Stephen looked like Bracken, he was a good deal kinder in Megan's eyes, and she felt desperate for someone to talk with.

"That isn't true," Stephen told her. He'd seen with his own eyes what was happening to his brother's heart.

"I fear that it is. I am a stranger here, and I am troubled that it will always be so."

"You have not given yourself sufficient time, Megan," he spoke familiarly to her, truly seeking to help. "Bracken was stern just now, but he does care. He would not have reacted so, had he not been fearful of your harm."

Megan had not looked at it in such a way. His words made her pause and think. The one time her father had spanked her sprang to mind. She had deserved his hand of punishment far more often, but not until she nearly frightened him to death did he strike her.

"Have I lost you?" Stephen's voice was kind.

"I was thinking of what you said and remembering a time when my father punished me severely. I deserved the punishment, but then I often did. This particular time, however, he did so out of fear."

"Were you very bad?" Stephen found himself captivated.

"I was," Megan admitted. "I bribed his young vassal into letting me dress in his clothing during a tournament. I found myself on the jousting field. I was quite nearly killed by a runaway horse." Megan glanced at her companion then and wanted to laugh at his look of horror.

"It's quite true."

"You say your father beat you?"

Megan nodded. "I couldn't sit down for several days."

"What would possess you to do such a thing?" Stephen was still trying to take it in.

"The usual," Megan said softly. "I was trying to gain my mother's attention."

Neither one felt like talking as they passed through the castle gates. Stephen was still amazed at this new insight, and Megan was completely wrapped up with dread over having to face Bracken at the tables that night.

Eleven

The evening meal was not as bad as Megan had anticipated. Brice and Bracken were very quiet, but Stephen was charming, and Megan, feeling as if someone had rescued her, allowed herself to be coaxed into talking.

"So you lived most of your years at the abbey?" he wanted to know.

"Yes. In truth, the abbey feels more like home than Stone Lake."

"What did you do all day?" This came from Aunt Louisa.

"Well," Megan admitted, "when I first arrived I spent all my time running away or planning to run away, but as I began to grow more settled, I was given responsibilities."

"Doing what?" Stephen asked.

"The abbey is run very much like a keep," Megan explained, "only the nuns give everything away. The abbey has a creamery and small byre. The nuns weave, sew, bake, and cook, but nearly all goods are given to charity. I am proficient in all of these things because I worked right along with them. Then when I turned 15 I was allowed to go into the village several times a week to teach some of the children."

"Your father approved of this?" Bracken, who couldn't help himself, wondered aloud. The abbey did not alarm him but time alone in the village was another matter. Thinking he may have angered her, Bracken held his breath as Megan turned, but for once she was not offended by his line of questioning.

"My father had very definite ideas about my upbringing. He believed I would be a more compassionate mistress to my servants if I spent time in the village. I was never in any danger, you understand. Most of the townspeople knew of my parentage. Since it was common knowledge, they never believed we were trying to deceive them, and in truth, after just a short time, it was not something many even thought of."

Bracken couldn't imagine allowing his own daughter to work in the village, but without asking he somehow knew that Vincent's ideas stemmed from his reaction to his wife's personality. Megan was stern with the servants at Hawkings Crest, but she was never cruel. Bracken now saw that

Megan was the woman she was because she had been separated from her mother's influence. From what little he'd seen and heard, it would at least appear so.

Had they been alone, Bracken might have questioned Megan further. But now was not the time, and he was left to ruminate on what she had said.

Megan was also left with a certain amount of speculation after Bracken made no comment to her story. Through the evening she pondered whether he agreed with her father or thought him a fool.

Two afternoons later Megan was feeling suffocated again. She knew better than to leave on her own, but she could not find Louisa or Bracken. The day had started well, and she did not want to do anything to spoil it, but she *had* to get out. A basket on her arm, she gained the courtyard and with relief spotted Arik.

"Arik," Megan spoke when she stood before him, having lost all fear of his size and stony face. "Bracken bids me to tell someone when I leave the castle walls." She paused and stared at his expressionless countenance, knowing full well that he had heard her. "I'm going into the fields to pick herbs."

Arik didn't blink, nod his head, or acknowledge her in any way, but after Megan held his eyes for just a moment, she turned away, the basket now swinging from her hand, her bright head shining in the sun.

She wasn't 15 steps outside the castle gate when she sensed with certainty that Arik had followed her. She didn't mind. His presence made her feel secure. Megan found the field she sought and happily sank down into the grasses, the morning sun warm on her back. Within minutes she'd forgotten everything around her. Intent on her task, she neither heard nor saw Bracken's brother approaching.

Returning from a hunting party in the woods, Brice had just sent his game ahead to the castle when he spotted Megan in the field. Her hair was a halo of red, a delight to any eye, but Brice frowned. Just days ago the entire castle had searched for her, and now here she sat alone outside the walls. Brice had covered half the distance when he spotted Arik.

He drew up short and felt shamed for his angry thoughts. He knew he was too hard on the girl. They were of the same age and would probably get along well, but Brice loved his brother and Megan's lack of effort in the relationship infuriated him.

He walked on again, but slower, all anger draining from him. He and Stephen would be going home in a few days, and his mother would wish to know how he and Megan got along. Brice was prideful enough to want to report to his mother that he'd done everything within his power to befriend her, not that he believed it would do much good.

"Good morning, Megan," Brice spoke when he was just five yards away.

"Oh," Megan's hand came up. "I didn't hear you, Brice."

He was in front of her now and sank to his knees some six feet away. "I didn't mean to startle you."

Megan shook her head and smiled slightly, her eyes on Brice for just an instant before she turned them back to her hands. She was most aware of his feelings toward her.

" 'Twas not your fault," she said graciously. "I was so focused on my work, I didn't hear a thing."

Brice watched her work a moment. "What is that?"

"Sorrel. It's wonderful in soup."

Brice watched her a moment more.

"Did you not care to send one of the kitchen maids for this work?" It was meant to be a dig, but Megan didn't take it as such. Brice watched her look off into the distance and smile.

"This isn't work, Brice. I love it out here. I love the way the air is perfumed with the aroma of pine and wildflowers, and I love the way the wind moves the trees." Megan let her gaze roam until it landed back on Brice. His look embarrassed her though, and she swiftly dropped her eyes.

"I don't know why I prattle on so, Brice. I'm sorry."

Brice was overcome with shame. She had openly shared with him and he had made her feel a fool. His mind raced for a safe subject.

"My mother uses herbs for healing." Brice blurted the words, but Megan did not seem to notice.

"Oh, how I would love to speak with her. I know of only a few. Most of these are for the kitchen."

"She'll be here for the wedding."

Stark fear covered Megan's face for just an instant, but she quickly schooled her features.

"Yes, the wedding. I look forward to meeting her." Megan's voice told Brice that he had shaken her. Why? What could she possibly fear? Brice was actually on the verge of asking her when he spotted Bracken approaching.

"Bracken comes," Brice casually announced, and then watched in amazement at the change that came over Megan.

"Oh, I'm a mess," she mumbled as she swiftly dusted her hands and came so awkwardly to her feet that she stumbled and fell back down. Brice was reaching to help her, but she regained her balance on her own and managed to put her chin in the air just before Bracken stopped in front of her.

"Aunt Louisa is looking everywhere for you," he said without preamble.

"I could not find her," Megan answered with quiet dignity.

"You could have told me."

"I could not locate you, either."

"So you just came anyway?"

"No. I told Arik."

"But he came with you!"

Megan's hands moved at her side in defeat. All fight was draining from her. Would she ever do what was right? This was as bad as living with her mother; worse, because there was no convent to return to. The thought made Megan tremble all over.

"I did as you asked, Bracken. I did not tell Arik to join me. I never thought —"

"That seems to be your problem," he cut her off. "You don't think of anyone but yourself."

Megan's eyes flashed with fury. That statement had been completely unfair. Megan turned from Bracken and lifted her basket. She left the men without word, her back straight, the basket handle over one arm. Megan had not gone ten yards when Arik moved to follow her. Bracken watched their progress for just an instant before transferring his gaze to the distance.

He was barely aware of his brother, so when he did look at Brice it made the younger man's stunned face even harder to bear.

"She's afraid of you," Brice accused, and the pain in his voice surprised Bracken. "Stephen said as much, but I didn't believe him. 'Tis true. She's terrified of you. She trembled all over."

Bracken had seen the trembling as well, but opened his mouth anyway to try to justify himself. Brice would allow no such thing; he cut him off with a downward slash of his hand.

"Don't speak to me right now, Bracken.

I can't bear it. Mother is going to wish to know of your happiness and that of Megan, and I hate," Brice spat the word, "to tell her what I've observed."

Brice swung away, not toward the keep but back toward the woods. He still had his crossbow with him, and Bracken let him go, knowing he would be safe enough. Bracken took himself back to the keep. The noon meal would be served soon, and when they had eaten he would speak with Megan. He wasn't entirely certain what he would say, but Brice had been correct — he did frighten her.

Bracken contemplated the reason he teased and antagonized her and could only come up with one lame answer. He desired to see some emotion on her face, even a scowl, rather than the cold, expressionless eyes she often turned to him.

Knowing this did not excuse his behavior; nevertheless, it helped him to know what he should do, and that was apologize. If the opportunity presented itself, he would do so over the meal; if not, he would ask Megan to join him in the war room. He was not experienced in court manners or taken to gently wooing ladies, but he *could* tell Megan he was sorry for his actions because he sincerely was.

Bracken, so ready with his plan, fought disappointment when Megan failed to join him at the table. Indeed she did not make an appearance downstairs at all.

Megan, you can't hide in here all day, the small redhead said to herself. But even though her stomach growled, she made no move toward the door. If only she didn't have to face Bracken. She felt as if she must slip into armor every time she met the man, and right now she was too weary to fight.

Megan scowled when her stomach sounded again. She had just decided then and there to head down to the great hall when someone knocked on her door. Thinking it to be Louisa, Megan walked calmly toward the closed portal. She stood in stunned silence when she saw Bracken on the other side.

"May I speak with you, Megan?"

"Yes," she answered, and was about to move into the hall when Bracken's attention suddenly moved beyond her.

Without a word he stepped toward her. Megan was forced to retreat, but Bracken took little notice. He came fully into her bedchamber and just stared. The small room had been transformed. Tapestries and hangings were draped all over the walls. Carpets, thick and richly colored, covered the floor. The counterpane on her bed was a myriad of colors as well.

"You spoke the truth to me. You truly did not wish to leave this room."

"I am more than content in here." Megan's voice was soft.

Bracken came and stood before her now. He looked down into her face and thought her skin looked like that of a child's.

"I regret the way I treated you outside the wall today."

Megan was so surprised and relieved she hardly knew what to say, but she did manage a small "Thank you, Bracken."

He loved it when she left the "Lord" off his name, and for the first time he wished to hold her. She was often so stiff and prickly, but standing before him as she was now, her eyes soft and somehow vulnerable, he longed to take her into his arms.

Of their own volition, his eyes dropped to her lips. He was always amazed at their color. He knew that some women used tint to redden their lips, but looking at Megan's he knew that the dark, dusky red he was seeing was all her own.

Megan noticed his look, but did not understand it. She was even more naive about men than Bracken was about women. And the fact that she did not find herself comely always played a part. After just a few seconds under Bracken's scrutiny, Megan began to assume something was wrong with her appearance. Her mouth would have swung open in surprise had she understood that Bracken found her so lovely he wanted to kiss her.

Fortunately for both of them, Megan's stomach growled and broke the spell. Her manner became all at once brisk as Bracken's presence in her room reminded her of something that had been on her mind. She turned away from him, slightly embarrassed and asked, "Bracken, are you barring my door at night?"

"No," Bracken answered cautiously. "Why do you ask?"

"I think I must be walking in my sleep, because I have awakened occasionally in the chair by the fire. If that is true, I can't think what is keeping me inside — unless the door has been barred from without."

"Arik sleeps outside your door at night," Bracken told her softly.

Megan turned to face him. "Arik knows that I walk in my sleep?"

Bracken nodded, his eyes studying her face, and Megan suddenly remembered the night she woke in the great room.

"How long?" Megan asked, referring to Arik's sleeping arrangement.

"Since the first night after your father left."

Megan took a deep breath. "And what of the time after we are wed? Will Arik continue to lie outside the door and give the castle folk even more reason for gossip?" Megan was not angry, just chagrined.

"I have given great thought to that," Bracken told her. "I think we will bar your door. That way you'll be forced to exit through my room."

"And what good will that do?" Megan genuinely wished to know.

"I am a very light sleeper, Megan, and even if you did get past me, Lyndon would inform me."

Megan nodded. It put a woman in a very vulnerable position to be wandering through a strange castle in her sleep, but try as she might to calm herself before slumber, she was still up and about. Maybe with time her heart would settle in this new place.

"We have no wish to make sport of you, Megan." Bracken thought he needed to explain, and indeed, Megan was comforted by his words, enough to let the matter drop with a simple thank you.

"Have you eaten?" Bracken asked then, and Megan was again warmed by his sudden show of concern. She shook her head.

"Then come, Megan. Come below and eat."

He offered his arm, and Megan took it. She did so praying that this new, kinder relationship would swiftly become the standard.

Twelve

Brice was standing on the wall of the keep, his eyes taking in the countryside, when he realized Bracken's presence beside him. A glance to his side told him Bracken's own eyes were also on the scape, but after a moment, he spoke.

"Stephen and I may look alike, Brice, but make no mistake, it is Stephen who is well practiced with the words ladies love."

Brice nodded, his gaze now back over the land as he answered boldly. "You inherited Hawkings Crest and father's title when you were still a young man. Your responsibility has been heavy; Stephen's not near as much at White Hall. But that is still no excuse.

"Chivalry is dying all over England, but every time I see evidence of this fact, I think with pride, 'Never Bracken. Bracken is a knight of highest honor, never him.'

"But yesterday I was shamed. I have seen with my own eyes that Megan's fear is not of all men, but of you, and for this there is no excuse. As I watched her tremble I thought of how I would feel if a man treated Danella or Kristine in such a way. I would want to run him through with my sword."

Brice finally looked at Bracken and found the older man watching him. Bracken's pride was taking a beating, but Brice was correct. Bracken was supposed to be an example to his brother, and instead he'd incurred his rancor.

There weren't many men from whom Bracken would take such words, but his brothers were beyond value to him, and for this, Bracken took heed.

"You are right, Brice," he told him sincerely. "I have now committed myself to dealing more gently with Megan in the future, but there are times when I know not what to do with the woman."

Bracken's chagrined voice brought a smile to Brice's face. He thumped his older brother on the chest.

"She does have a mind of her own."

"Is that what you call it?" Bracken's tone was now dry.

"She'll surely match you wit for wit." Brice's voice was almost proud, a startling turn about from just days previous, but Bracken's brows rose as though Brice's own words proved his case. Brice accurately read his thoughts.

"Come now, Bracken. You surely want more than a pretty face. Even when you are tempted to lock Megan in her room, you'll have to admit that you do not want it any other way."

Bracken stared at his younger sibling. It was true. He didn't want a decoration for his castle, but a woman who could think and do for herself. Bracken felt a new sort of peace with this realization, a peace that would have been destroyed had he been able to see Megan right then.

"What is this entry?"

Bracken's steward, Barton, whose face was starting to resemble a radish, stared at Megan, whose own countenance was a study in tranquillity.

"It's for wheat."

"Wheat? For what purpose?"

Barton had to bite his tongue to keep from telling Megan to mind her own business. Instead, he said with false humility, "Why, food for the castle folk, my lady."

"It costs this much?"

"Yes, my lady."

Megan studied the small man's face. He wasn't much taller than Megan and very thin, and from Megan's few encounters with him, she had also tagged him a liar. Indeed, Megan would have wagered her life on the fact.

"And how about this?" Megan pointed to another entry, and Barton silently cursed this woman who had been raised in a convent and taught to read.

"Miscellaneous."

Megan's eyes narrowed, but her voice was still serene. "Twenty pounds of miscellaneous?"

Barton's look was that of a child's, but Megan was not taken in.

"Before the sun sets, I wish to see an itemized listing of what you consider to be miscellaneous."

"Yes, my lady," Barton spoke from behind gritted teeth.

Megan turned away from him then, the record book still in her hand.

"But, my lady," Barton called to her, his voice in a panic. "I need the records book."

Megan stopped and stared at the man. "If the items I seek are recorded in the book, then why did you list them under miscellaneous?"

Barton was so angry that he prayed for Megan's death. Megan held his gaze before giving final orders and leaving.

"I am not through with the book, so I

will keep it, and I will expect that list today."

"Bracken, may I speak with you?"

Bracken, so delighted that she had sought him out, rose from his chair in the war room with a smile. The smile faltered when she drew close enough for him to see the records book.

"Bracken," Megan began immediately, "I do not think your steward is being honest with you."

"Megan," Bracken replied, remembering what he'd told Brice and working to keep his voice patient, "you really don't need to disturb yourself with such details. Barton is more than capable —"

"Of stealing you blind," Megan cut him off. "Look at this entry for yard and cloth. My mother couldn't spend that amount in five years."

Bracken sighed, but did not reply. He was always made very comfortable within the walls of his castle and gave little regard as to how that came to be. His greater interest was his training fields and archery range, but he did not think it wise to say this to Megan.

"Can't you see it?" She persisted.

"In truth, Megan, the account books

have never been that important to me. Show me the exact place."

Megan pointed with one small digit and Bracken bent low to inspect the entry. He turned his head after a moment to find Megan staring, their faces very close together.

"Don't you check these books periodically, Bracken?"

"No," he told her, feeling preoccupied with her nearness and the smell of her hair. He was a knight, trained in self-control, so none of his emotions showed on his face.

"What about Aunt Louisa?" Megan brought him back to the matter at hand.

"She can't read."

Megan gazed absentmindedly into his dark eyes and then off into the distance, totally preoccupied with the castle accounts.

"There are too many inconsistencies," Megan muttered, her mind still going over the pages of the book.

"Barton's been with Hawkings Crest for years. He was my father's steward."

"Could your father read?"

"No," Bracken admitted, and Megan's brows rose. She obviously believed she'd made her point.

Bracken held onto his control with an

effort. He knew that she needed to have a hand in the running of this castle, but why must she turn things into utter chaos? Bracken had no desire to fight with her, and so chose to distract himself by studying the loveliness of her face.

Megan saw instantly that she had lost him, but it was beyond her as to what he might be thinking. She found him studying her mouth once again and wondered if she had food on her lips from lunch. A swift lick with her tongue told her nothing was there, and she felt even more confusion when Bracken's eyes narrowed. Megan thought he might be growing angry, but when he spoke his voice was soft.

"Just handle it, Megan," Bracken told her, thinking he had to get away. Megan watched in puzzlement as he turned abruptly and moved toward the door.

"So I may dismiss Barton?"

Bracken turned back at the door and told her simply, "No, you may not."

"Then how am I to —"

Bracken's raised hand forestalled her. He truly did not wish to fight, but neither could he remain.

"Just do your best, Megan."

The small redhead stood still long after the portal closed. What in the world was she to do with the man? He was kinder this time than ever before, but he clearly couldn't wait to be away from her. Megan was still standing in confusion when Aunt Louisa sought her out.

"Megan, there you are. Is everything all right?"

"I don't know," Megan admitted, her eyes now on the older woman.

"You spoke with Bracken?"

"Yes, and he was kind, but he looked at me so oddly."

"Oh?" Louisa's interest was piqued. "How so?"

"He stared at my mouth as though something were amiss. It's not the first time, either. And then he seemed in a great hurry to be away."

Louisa could hardly believe such innocence, but she knew it to be all too real. She debated telling Megan what Bracken's actions meant but changed her mind. He was going to have to win this woman on his own. Louisa had enjoyed a long talk with Brice and quite agreed with him. It was true that court manners came easier to Stephen, but Brice was right in saying Bracken had no excuse; it was his duty to do all he could to win Megan's heart.

"What am I to do?"

"Do not let it worry you, dear. Men can, at times, be complex creatures. I'm sure there was nothing wrong."

Megan nodded. She might have questioned Louisa, but in truth she didn't even know what to ask. Would it be easier when Bracken and she were husband and wife? Megan could only hope so. The reality of their wedding seemed to press in on her with more insistence every day.

Megan walked into the great hall three days later and knew instantly that something was amiss. There had been two groups of servants speaking quietly among themselves as they worked, but after spotting Megan, all seven women closed their mouths and transferred their gazes to the floor.

Megan would normally have given this little thought, but it had been happening all day. By evening she was fed up.

"Helga," she spoke to her personal maid, the first woman to have helped her at Hawkings Crest. "What is going on?"

"Going on, my lady?" Helga's eyes were wide with apprehension, and Megan knew she had come to the right woman.

"Yes," she replied, her voice changing to that of gentle persuasion. "It seems that there is news afoot — news that concerns me. I would only wish to hear of it."

Helga relaxed. She should have known her lady would just desire to understand. *After all*, Helga reminded herself, *it is just gossip. Lady Megan would surely not take heed.*

"Helga?" Megan brought her back to the matter.

"There are rumors, my lady, that Lord Bracken has gone to see Black Francesca." Helga barely kept herself from smiling. She knew her lady would laugh any minute at the joke of it all, and then she would be free to join her.

"Black Francesca?" Megan had gone utterly still.

"Yes, my lady." Helga became concerned for the first time. "All servants gossip, and those at Hawkings Crest are no different."

Megan nodded, her face still serene but her eyes cold. "I won't be turning in just now, Helga. I'll send for you later."

Helga stood and wrung her hands after Megan left. If the look in her eyes had been any indication, Lord Bracken would be gaining a visit, and soon.

"Did you see her?" Megan asked the moment she stepped into the war room, completely ignoring the men surrounding Bracken.

"See who, Megan?" Bracken asked, but he knew the answer.

"Have you been to visit Black Francesca?"

Bracken was very aware of his men. He knew they would have exited, but Megan stood between the group and the door, arms akimbo, her eyes flashing with rage.

Bracken wanted a wife and a lady to keep his home, but he was not going to let anyone monitor his every move. As much as he cared for Megan and truly thought he was coming to love her, he would not let her rule his life.

"Am I to check with you, Megan, before going to the village?" Bracken's voice said that her answer was only of mild interest to him.

"You do not answer my question, so I must assume you are guilty."

"Guilty?" Bracken's chuckle was sincere. "Nay, Megan. I have been to see Francesca, but no guilt rests on my head."

Megan's face flushed with temper. She walked until she stood before Bracken, her eyes so angry and hurt that Bracken had to harden his heart to bear it. When she moved, the men filed out so that when she spoke again they were alone.

"I will not marry you."

Bracken didn't so much as lift a brow. "We will wed, Megan," he spoke with surety.

"Never," she hissed. "I have saved myself for this time, but to you it is no worthy thing. I will not marry a man who would take our vows so lightly."

Bracken shook his head, thinking that if Megan didn't find her place she would be miserable.

"We will wed, Megan," was all he said.

Megan shook her head vehemently, causing red curls to swirl around her shoulders. "I will not stay here, and I will certainly not be joined to you." There was such loathing in her voice that Bracken grew angry.

"Stop this childishness, Megan. I tell you we will be wed."

Megan's laughter was harsh. "I am no child, Bracken, but a woman capable beyond your imagination. It is too bad that you will never understand all that you have lost."

On this cryptic statement Megan spun and headed to the door. Bracken didn't move, but his fist clenched in frustration. It had seemed for a few days that things were softening between them, but right now those days seemed weeks past. As hard as that was to bear, Bracken's greatest hurt was that Megan would think him capable of such an act in the first place.

Thirteen

By midmorning of the following day, Megan was miles away from Hawkings Crest. She had learned through her escapes from the abbey that there was no time like the present, and so she had left less than an hour after her confrontation with Bracken. She had left Helga with the strictest of orders for the night, and even the next few days, but Megan sincerely doubted that anyone would truly miss her, at least not for a time.

It had not been all that difficult to escape the castle walls, but that would not have been the case if she had waited until after dark or until the following morning to leave.

Her night had been a long one. Megan was feeling the effects now, but she trudged on just the same. Sometime before dawn she had lain down and slept, but it was nothing whatsoever like a full night in her own bed. She stopped now and tried to gauge her whereabouts but found she was a bit disoriented.

The night her men were attacked suddenly flashed through her mind, but oddly enough she did not feel fearful. In many ways Megan felt safer on her own than she had with her guard; she was free to hide in caves or climb trees for protection. Over the years she had encountered the occasional boar or other fierce creature, but nothing that ever gave her more trouble than she could handle.

As the sun rose high in the sky, Megan's stomach roared. She found shade at that point and pulled some bread and cheese from the sack on her back. She ate ravenously and then searched for a stream. It took longer than she would have liked and put her somewhat out of the way, but the opportunity to slacken her thirst was worth every step.

Megan was just returning to the road when she spotted the peddlers. It took less than a heartbeat's time to see that it was Elias and his band — the same men who had rescued her weeks before. Megan debated stepping out into the road and asking for help, but before she could decide, they stopped. Megan froze in order to listen and watch from her place in the trees.

"What is it, Elias?" one man asked.

The bearded peddler didn't answer. His gaze swept the trees opposite Megan before he turned and seemed to stare right at her.

"Who's there?" Elias called.

Megan didn't answer.

"Come out," he continued kindly. "We won't harm you."

Megan debated only a moment more before going into action. She drew her ragged cape up over her head, made sure the bag of food on her back was in the proper "hump" position, bent over her walking stick, and moved slowly from the trees.

"It's an old humpback woman," Megan heard one say as she squinted up at them. Her mouth turned back into a snarl that beautifully portrayed the dark beans she'd pushed over two teeth. They gave the impression of teeth missing as well as darkening her saliva, making it look as if her whole mouth were rotted.

"I ain't an old woman," Megan spat, putting on her best cockney tone and glaring at the men. "Whatcha sellin'?"

"Are you hoping to buy?" This came from Elias, and Megan could hear the amusement in his tone.

"I ain't got no coin," she snorted.

"Where are you headed?" another man questioned.

"The abbey at Stone Lake, you nosy scoundrel. Can't a lady have no privacy?" Megan gave a loud cackle at her own joke, and the men joined in.

"We're not going as far as Stone Lake, but we're going to The Crossings. Come," Elias spoke, "ride awhile."

Megan scowled at them. Her feet did hurt.

"I don't care to be badgered with talk for miles," she growled at them, but she was already moving in a painful gait to the wagon. Most of the men made no effort to hide their amusement, but Megan only limped her way to the back and allowed one of them to take her upper arm and help her aboard.

"Well, you're not starved, are ya?" he said, and Megan pulled her arm away.

"Don't be given me none o' your cheek. I'll take myself right back down, and you'll be a missin' the pleasure o' my company."

This brought a round of laughter from the men, but the horse was prodded into motion and they proceeded down the road. Megan told herself to say alert, but it wasn't possible. The ride was hot, dusty, and bumpy, and after very little sleep the night before, she couldn't stay awake. Within the hour her head was draped over a bag of rags while sleep wandered in and out.

They didn't make The Crossings by nightfall, but that was just as well for Megan. She had never intended to go that far. The Crossings was on the way to Stone Lake, but it was faster to go through the woods in order to gain the abbey.

The peddlers had paid her little heed throughout the journey, but when they camped that night, she was made welcome at their fire and to their food. No one was the wiser as to her identity until Megan shuffled off into the woods for privacy. Elias, whose hearing was as keen as that of a fox, heard her shuffling gait turn to easy steps when she found the darkness of the trees.

He waited until she returned and they both had food before he approached. It was the first time he had come close to her. His suspicions were confirmed immediately, but that didn't stop the amazement at his findings.

Megan didn't really mind his sitting near her but simply turned her face into the shadows, the hood still hiding her face, and tried to chew with her back teeth only.

"I must say, my lady," Elias began, his voice almost too soft to hear. "You're one of the best I've ever seen."

Megan froze and then turned to look at him.

"How did you know?" The accent was gone; her voice was hushed.

"Your walk in the woods alerted me, and then if I may say so, my lady, there is no disguising the smell of your hair."

Megan transferred her gaze to the woods, and Elias stared at her profile. It was incredible. He couldn't see it now, but he remembered the gray cast to her skin when she'd come from the woods. That, along with the rotted teeth, rat's nest hair and hump on her back, caused Elias not to give her a second thought, but now, since he knew how she normally looked, this transformation was astonishing to the man.

"Do the others know?" Megan asked suddenly.

"I don't think so."

"And what," Megan went on, her voice still hushed, "will you tell the riders who overtake you? Have you seen the red-haired maid, whose father is lord of Stone Lake Castle and whose betrothed lives within the wall of Hawkings Crest?"

"I have seen no such woman," Elias told her as he transferred his gaze to the fire. "We gave an old humpback woman a ride, nothing more."

He heard Megan's sigh of relief and would have given up half his cart to know why she ran. But this was not his place. A peddler did not ask a lady, no matter how she was dressed, where she was going and why.

"Thank you, Elias," Megan whispered just before one of the men joined them.

Megan turned away, thinking she would have liked to tell him that she hoped he would trade at Hawkings Crest often, but then she reminded herself that she would not be there and wondered over the sadness that filled her on such a thought.

The night was uneventful, and early in the morning Megan thanked the men, made them laugh, and parted from the group. She had a friend in the forest who took her the rest of the way on horseback, and she was at the abbey just hours later.

The food on Bracken's trencher was a delight to the senses, but he gave little notice. His eyes were on the staircase as he anticipated Megan's arrival with every breath, but she did not appear. It had been

48 hours since their quarrel, and he had not seen her once. He felt this pouting was ridiculous, but he was not going to search her out and say so. It was apparent to him that Megan needed to do a little growing up, and he refused to coddle her in this situation.

"Will you go to her, Bracken?"

"No." He turned then to look at his aunt. He picked up a piece of meat and chewed silently.

"What if she really isn't feeling well?"

Bracken snorted. "Is that what she is telling you?"

"Well, Helga is."

Bracken stared at her. "You mean you haven't seen Megan?"

"No," Louisa admitted. "Helga's been taking her food, and when I've gone to the door she says that Megan has asked not to be disturbed."

Bracken shook his head in disgust. It was worse than he feared. This was not brooding, but an out-and-out sulk, and Bracken could think of nothing more aggravating. She was clearly taking her childish tantrum out on the whole castle.

Bracken suddenly dug into his food. Watching him, Louisa knew the reason. She would have put money on the fact that he was going to confront Megan as soon as he'd had his fill.

Not five minutes after Bracken was done with the meal, he nodded to the family members at the table and made for the stairs. Helga, sitting inside Megan's bedchamber and trying not to be nervous, jumped at his knock.

"Lord Bracken," she said respectfully, opening the door just enough to peek out.

"I wish to see Lady Megan," Bracken stated.

Helga nervously cleared her throat. It was one thing to tell Lady Louisa that Lady Megan was ill and wished to see no one, but Lord Bracken was another matter.

"Is there some problem?" Bracken's voice was not loud or even overly stern, but Helga couldn't take it.

"I'm sorry, my lord," she cried. "I was just doing as I was told."

It took a moment for Bracken to comprehend the full import of her words, and Helga scrambled away just in time as he reached to push the door open wide. Angry, disbelieving eyes took in the perfectly made-up bed, the wallhangings and the cold fireplace. All was intact, telling him Megan had traveled light. The room felt as lifeless as a tomb.

Bracken turned to Helga then, who was white-faced with fright, and he saw in an instant that he could not place Megan's foolhardiness on this servant. As she said, she was doing as commanded. Bracken came to this resolve in a split second and now spoke like a calm warrior going into battle.

"How long has she been gone?"

"Two days, my lord."

Bracken nodded, looking preoccupied.

"The morning after we quarreled no doubt." The words were said more to himself than anyone, but Helga answered anyhow.

"No, my lord. She left right away."

Bracken frowned. "You mean that very night?"

"Yes, my lord."

"She's been gone 48 hours then." Bracken was utterly aghast, and fearful for the first time.

"Yes, my lord," Helga said unnecessarily.

"Did she say where she was headed?"

"No, my lord, I swear, she didn't say."

Bracken stayed within the chamber only a moment more before turning and striding out the door and down the main stairs. He was not a man to lose his head, but he was halfway to the stables before he realized it was much too dark to search that night.

"What is it, Bracken?" Brice had followed him without.

Bracken sighed. "Megan has left."

"The castle?"

"Yes."

"Alone?"

"Yes, and it's too dark to search tonight."

"You mean she's left no word of her whereabouts?" Brice was feeling more amazed and frightened by the second.

"No, but I'm certain she headed home. I don't think she ever wanted to leave there — she implied as much — so I'm sure she's made for Stone Lake."

"I'll go with you, Bracken." This came from Louisa, who had just joined the men.

"You knew she was gone?" Bracken frowned.

"No, but when you gained the great hall in such a hurry, I went to Helga myself. I take it we leave in the morning?"

"That is my plan, Aunt Lou, but I must have you remain here."

"But Bracken," the older woman's face was distressed, "when you return she will need an escort."

Bracken couldn't stop his snort of disgust. "She has no doubt traveled all the way to Stone Lake without a single thought for propriety; an escort won't matter now."

Bracken finally looked at Louisa in the gathering dusk. Her hurt face reminded him of his tone. With hands gently on her upper arms, he spoke again.

"In truth, Aunt Lou, we will be riding hard. I would like you to come along, but I do not wish to put you through that."

"But you will bring her back?"

"Have no doubt of it. Megan has not resigned herself to this marriage, but King Henry ordered it and her father did the choosing. Megan is mine, and I will return her to Hawkings Crest."

Nearly an hour later Bracken stood in the war room waiting for his knights to arrive. He had hardly moved from his place by the fire, his thoughts deep on the mistakes he'd made as well as the anger he felt that Megan would pull such a senseless escapade.

If she were in the room at that moment he would be strongly tempted to upend her over his knee. The sight of her, hair ablaze and eyes flashing, standing in that very room while she confronted him over Black Francesca suddenly swam before his mind's eye. What would a group of men do if they found a maid so lovely alone in the forest? Bracken's heart clenched at the thought, even as anger told him she should have known better.

The door opened suddenly, and Bracken turned. It was Stephen and he was alone. He spoke as he came forward, his look serious but his tone light.

"I understand that your dove has flown."

Bracken snorted in offense and turned from the fire, his gaze fierce.

"Do not be deceived, Stephen. Megan is no dove, but a red hawk with talons to gouge a man!"

"Be that as it may, Bracken," Stephen went on smoothly, "you'll not win the girl's heart with such words."

"I'm not the least bit interested in her heart," Bracken stated untruthfully, his voice still harsh.

"Of course you're not," Stephen said patronizingly. "That is why you've already gone to bed without a single worry. You'll sleep late in the morning and ride out when you feel like it to fetch her back."

Bracken let out a great sigh, his anger deserting him in a rush. His hand went to the back of his neck, and he stared at Stephen in torment.

"Why did you not explain to her about Black Francesca, Bracken?" Stephen's voice was gentle.

"It was a mistake," Bracken admitted. "I never dreamed she would flee. When I think of where she could be, I —" Bracken couldn't go on.

"We'll find her," Stephen soothed.

"You'll ride with me?"

"Of course."

"I'll bring her back, Stephen." Bracken repeated himself for the second time that evening, needing to convince himself more than anyone.

"I know you will, but you mustn't plan on dragging her by the hair. Court her, Bracken. Woo her until it would never occur to her to live any other place than Hawkings Crest."

Bracken would have loved to ask Stephen just how he should go about doing that, but they were joined by the other men. As Bracken's men gathered around him, all talk turned to plans for leaving in the morning. He wouldn't think of Stephen's words again for many hours, and when he did, Stephen would not be there to aid him.

Fourteen

The Reverend Mother smoothed Megan's hair from her forehead and wrestled with her own feelings. She could never tell this dear girl that she must not come to them at the abbey, but neither could she sanction Megan's running from circumstances she didn't like or agree with. Bracken's actions were sorrowful, but Megan, from what the Reverend Mother could see, had little choice but to stay and make the best of things.

Megan was such a mixture of woman and little girl. At the moment she sat on the floor, her head resting on the older woman's knee, much the way she'd done as a child. One moment she was a woman capable and strong; the next she was a child, needing to be embraced and comforted. The Reverend Mother knew Bracken to be a man of few years, 20-odd, she was sure. Would he ever understand that at times Megan needed a tender father figure, since so many of her childhood years she'd been without one?

"Reverend Mother," a nun spoke as she came in the door then. She stopped upon seeing Megan. "I'm sorry, Reverend Mother, I forgot to knock."

"It's all right, Sister Blanche. What did you need?"

"Sister Mary Margaret is supposed to go to the village today, but she is not feeling well. Whom would you like me to send?"

"Please, send me." Megan's voice came softly from the Reverend Mother's lap. They had already talked for hours, and although there was more to be said the older woman wondered if maybe it wasn't best to let things lie for the present.

"Please," Megan begged again, seeing the Reverend Mother's indecision. The abbess sighed and looked down into Megan's face.

"All right." The older woman found the words easy to say after seeing the yearning in Megan's eyes.

Megan rose and kissed her. So pleased was she that she could return to the village that she nearly skipped from the room, her heart lighter than it had been in days. Just 20 minutes later she was in comfortable abbey clothes and walking down the main street of Stone Lake village.

She was early for lessons with the children, so she sauntered along until a familiar voice called to her from among the village smiths.

"Well, now, if it isn't little Meggie."

"Hello, Mr. Black," Megan said with a wide smile.

"Where 'o ya been keepin' yourself?"

"Oh, here and there," Megan told him with a grin.

"Going to teach the children today?"

"Yes. Tell Evan and Nigel to be there."

"A'll send 'em on."

Megan continued on her way, stopping to inspect Mrs. Murch's yard and even going so far as to tug a few weeds from her vegetables.

The work was light, and she could hear Mrs. Murch through the window. The old woman was snoring in a chair by the fire. Megan worked as soundlessly as she could, making her way to the rear of the small hut. She straightened when she heard footsteps behind her and turned to find William approaching. His look was one of a man in a trance, and Megan sighed very gently.

"Megan," William breathed, his eyes drinking in the sight of her. "You've come back to me."

"Oh, William," Megan said with a small

shake of her head.

It was enough to draw William from his dreamy state, and he smiled in a way that Megan loved, wide-mouthed and boyish. A few years older, he was the closest thing she'd ever had to a friend. It had never occurred to her to fall in love with him, and even though she never made any bones about the fact that they could never marry, he still persisted.

"Are you married?"

"No."

"Good. Did you run from him?"

"Yes."

"Good," he said again, nodding with satisfaction and not caring for the reason as long as she wasn't hurt.

"Are you well?" he asked now.

"Yes, and you can end this inquisition."

"Ah, Meg, I love those big words you like to use on a simple farmboy like myself."

"Well, don't get too comfortable with them. I'm sure I won't be staying long."

"Oh, Meg." He was genuinely distressed now. "Why must you go away again? I've pined for you till I thought I would die."

"William, William, what am I going to do with you?"

"I'd take a kiss," he replied before he

thought and watched Megan's eyes flash with temper.

"Do not speak to me in such a way, William Clayborne, or I'll slap your handsome face until your ears ring in your head!"

His look was very contrite, and Megan softened.

"How is Rose?"

William hung his head. "She's well. She misses you, although she can't think why. Says she has me for the first time ever."

"And well she should," Megan returned tenderly.

William's head came up.

"I care for her, Meg, you know I do," was all he could say before he simply stood still and gazed at her.

It had long been a thorn between them: Rose loving William and William loving Megan and Megan wishing she never had to marry at all. Amazingly enough, there had never been any hard feelings between Rose and Megan. Rose adored Megan, and it didn't matter in the least that William was in love with her. Rose believed that William would love her someday and make her his wife.

Indeed, Megan had secretly hoped that such a thing would happen after she'd gone. Of course, she hadn't been away all that long, and now here she was again, making William's heart yearn for her. Megan wished she'd thought of that before asking to come and teach.

"I must go, William," she told him now.

"When will I see you?" he asked as he fell into step beside her.

"You won't. I'm sure my father will come for me any day, and I don't know where I'll be after that. I'm almost certain that I won't be at the abbey."

"Ah, Meg —" he began.

"Give Rose my love," Megan interrupted, cutting him off.

"You could give me your love." It was said so softly that Megan almost missed it. She stopped and turned, tears of helplessness pooling in her eyes.

"No, William, I couldn't. I'm sure to be in enough trouble with Father as it is. You have always known how I feel. You would make any maid the finest of mates, but I can't be that girl. I'm not for you, William."

William stared at her with regret. She was the most wonderful woman he'd ever known, full of fun and caring and willing to give of herself without complaint or thought of payback. She was so lovely that he wanted nothing more than to cherish her for the rest of his days. In truth Rose was just as lovely, probably more so in a technical sense with her blue-black hair and tall, shapely body, but it was to Megan that he had lost his heart.

"Will I truly not see you again?" William pushed the words past his tight throat.

"I should think not. I'm glad we had a few minutes, though. Go with God, William."

With that she was gone. William stood, frustration filling him. He had never been able to touch her, not even so much as to hold her hand. It wasn't fair; by all that was righteous, it wasn't fair.

"Bracken!" Vincent spoke with obvious pleasure as he gained the great hall and saw his guests. "Come in; rest yourselves. I'll see that refreshment is brought."

Vincent spoke to a servant, giving Bracken a chance to adjust to this exuberant welcome.

"This must be your brother," Vincent went on, referring to Stephen after he returned his attention to his guests.

"Yes, this is Stephen, and this is my other brother, Brice. You also know my knights, Lyndon and Kendrick."

"Yes, of course. You're all looking well.

What brings you to Stone Lake?"

All the men froze, and Bracken frowned. "Why, to see Megan," he said hesitantly.

"Megan?" Vincent's brows rose with curiosity, but he did not seem alarmed.

"Yes. She is here, isn't she?"

"No." Vincent replied calmly.

"You mean you haven't seen her at all?" Bracken's heart now pounded with fear.

"No, I haven't. Maybe if you tell me why she left Hawkings Crest, I'll be able to tell you where she's gone."

"We argued," Bracken said briefly.

Vincent nodded, not at all surprised. "Then she'll be at the abbey," he said easily.

Bracken stood immediately, and his men followed suit. "Thank you, sir. We'll ride —"

"Sit down, Bracken, sit down," Vincent cut him off. "It's late enough in the day that your appearance at the abbey will not be welcome."

"But what if she's not there? We must leave here at daybreak to continue the search."

Vincent put his hand up. "I'm sure she is there."

Bracken sat back down, as did the

others. His voice belied the way his heart still raced.

"She's been gone from Hawkings Crest for three days. How can you be sure of her whereabouts?"

"Because I know Megan. If you've quarreled, then she will seek the solace of the abbey."

Vincent frowned at Bracken's confused face. "Have you forgotten so soon, Bracken, that Megan and her mother do not get on?"

Bracken's face cleared, but his voice was somewhat harsh. "No, sir, I had not forgotten. Megan does not seem to get on with most people." It was an unfair statement and both knew it, but the older man did not comment.

It was still something that Bracken did not understand. Why would anyone choose to be away from home? Why not live in harmony with others? Was it really so difficult? Bracken felt that this was clearly one more example of Megan's desperate need to grow up.

"I'll send a servant to the abbey now who can report as to whether or not Megan is there. Sup with us now, and you and your men can go to the abbey in the morning."

Bracken looked hesitant.

"I feel it is best, Bracken," Vincent told him, his tone not dictatorial but confident and kind.

"All right," Bracken agreed after a moment. "If we learn that she is safely there, we'll wait."

He'd been so certain that he would see her that very night that his disappointment was keen. Thankfully, Vincent didn't give him long to think about it. Posthaste he dispatched a servant to the abbey, and moments later the men were shown to chambers in order to wash and join the castle folk for dinner.

"Your father sent a messenger, Megan," the Reverend Mother said to the small redhead after supper.

"He has heard of my presence then."

"Yes."

"Am I to leave?"

"No. He only sought information as to your whereabouts. He told Sister Agatha that your betrothed is at the castle."

Megan nodded but did not speak.

"I'm sure Lord Bracken will be here in the morning, Meg."

Megan's face turned to panic. "Oh, please don't make me see him, please, Reverend Mother. Please tell him I've left."

"You know I would never lie for you, Meg." The older woman's voice was stern, and Megan felt shamed because she had asked Helga to do just that.

Her shame didn't last, however. With a note of desperation she said, "Then I'll really leave here. I can go and live with Japheth and Elvina in the forest. She's to have her baby soon and I know they would welcome me."

"What has frightened you, Megan?" the abbess spoke with compassion. "Is it Lord Bracken himself or something else altogether?"

The panic left Megan, and she looked utterly defeated. "I do not know." Her voice was hushed. "Everything began so badly between us, and lately I am not in control of my anger. It's all my mother's fault for sending me on as she did."

"We heard all about it, Meg, and indeed her actions have been wrong, but you must forgive her. You'll never know true peace within yourself or with Lord Bracken unless you do."

The evening was not far spent, and so they talked on for some time, but Megan did not deal with her heart as she should have. She was too busy worrying about the morrow's confrontation.

"It's a pleasure to meet you, Lady Annora."

"We're pleased to have you," Megan's beautiful mother returned, smiling. "How is Megan?"

Bracken flicked a glance at Vincent, who cleared his throat before speaking.

"Megan is at the abbey. Bracken has come thinking she might be here."

It took only a moment for the full meaning to sink in and Annora's face to flush with temper.

"She has run from Hawkings Crest?"

"Yes," Vincent admitted.

Annora threw her hands in the air, unmindful of the way Vincent, Bracken, and all Bracken's men looked on.

"When will that spoiled child ever mature? I tell you, Vincent, she has no care for anyone outside of herself. If she were here right now, I'd slap some sense into her."

The tirade continued for a few moments longer, with Vincent looking uncomfortable and Annora not noticing anyone as she carried on.

Bracken was only half listening. He had not been able to get beyond Annora's statement that Megan thought of no one but herself. He had shared the very same thought, but it now struck him strongly that it simply wasn't so. She was fool-hardy, but nearly everyone at Hawkings Crest had commented at one time or another about the little caring acts she did for others.

"Annora," Vincent spoke and finally got through. "I am hungry, as I'm sure are our guests."

Annora looked affronted at his words, but after tossing her head in the air she invited Bracken and the other men to come to the tables. The meal of quail was excellent and plentiful, and when Annora calmed down, she proved to be a gracious hostess. Bracken studied her from across the table and wondered how Megan could be so different in appearance and temperament. Even when Megan was most upset, she did not rant as this woman had done.

He was still pondering this when he heard Megan's voice behind him. His heart vaulted in his chest as his head snapped back to find her, but instead he encountered a younger version of Annora. He knew in an instant that this was Marigold. He saw that she'd grown older since that day at court, but it was her nonetheless.

"I'm sorry to be so late," Marigold spoke humbly, soaking in the hungry, male eyes that stared at her. "I was sewing by the fire, and the time just got away from me," Marigold, who hated needlework of any kind, lied sweetly and stood still to let each man look his fill.

Vincent, who was not taken in in the slightest, opened his mouth to tell Marigold that she would have to find room at another table, but Annora jumped in.

"No matter, Marigold. Whenever you grace our hall with your beauty, we will gladly welcome you. Come, sit by me."

She too had seen the desirous looks in the men's eyes and felt more than pleased. Not because any of them could have her, but because Annora simply loved having what she considered the most beautiful daughter in all of England.

Vincent was nowhere near as happy to see her. He knew Marigold was home, but she rarely joined them for any meal. Vincent knew that a servant must have told her of the men's presence. Marigold seemed to grow more devious with each passing day, and her presence shamed him. It seemed he could exert no control whatsoever where she was concerned.

The only pleasure Vincent derived from the whole evening was the way Bracken looked at Marigold. The other men at the table were making near fools of themselves, but Bracken's gaze was hooded and cool. It did Vincent's heart good to see it, and it helped remind him to tell Bracken privately not to bring Megan back to the castle with both Marigold and Annora there. He felt it best that Megan be taken directly back to Hawkings Crest.

Fifteen

Bracken had been waiting for over an hour to see Megan when William entered the sunny courtyard of the abbey. He paid the man little heed as he thought about the morning. As anxious as he was to get away, Lord Vincent had been equally anxious to detain him.

He'd toured Bracken and the men around the Stone Lake castle much like a child showing off a toy. And then there had been the journey to the abbey. Bracken saw now that they had come way out of their way by going to the castle first. Megan certainly would have known this and gained the abbey in less time because of it. Still, this did not answer his question of how she had traveled. That, along with a dozen more queries, convinced him that he'd be talking to Megan for the next two days.

Of course, their talk would probably have to wait. If he knew his betrothed like he thought he did, he would have to command her to leave the abbey, and it would be days before she would speak to him about anything.

Bracken mentally shook his head as he pictured himself tossing her over his shoulder, mounting his horse, and riding away with her kicking and screaming all the while. Vincent had sent a mount for her, but Bracken knew this was no guarantee that Megan would use it. As comical as the scene would be to his men, Bracken was serious. If he had to take Megan on his own horse to get her home, he would do it.

"What is it, William? Why have you come?" Bracken heard the sister called Agatha say.

"I must see her, Sister Agatha. Where is Megan?"

Suddenly Bracken was all ears.

"She cannot see you, William." Sister Agatha's voice was compassionate but firm.

"But I must," the young man's voice pleaded desperately. "I just know that if I could see her one more time I could convince her that it's me she needs to marry."

Bracken was like a statue, sitting on a stone bench in the shadows outside the Reverend Mother's office. He watched the earnest face of the younger man and felt something stir within him. How did Megan feel?

"William," Sister Agatha went on gently. "What of Rose?"

"I care for Rose," William told her, "but it's Megan whom I love."

"She is not for you, William. Give your heart to Rose. I have known Rose since she was but a child. She is the woman for you, William."

The younger man's shoulders slumped with defeat. He knew her words were true. He was thankful that it had been Sister Agatha who had confronted him. He'd known her all his life, and she was always the soul of kindness. He could never feel shame with her.

"I can see Rose waiting for you, William," she went on. "Go to her. She will understand and comfort you."

William's sigh was audible, but he did as he was told. Bracken watched with even more questions as the other man turned and walked away.

"He has been here for some time, Megan. You must not keep him any longer."

Megan nodded. She had not deliberately avoided him, but it was almost certain she would be leaving here today, and she had been desperate to see Japheth and Elvina one last time. It had simply taken more of the day than she had anticipated.

"You'll stay with me?"

"Yes," the Reverend Mother said, "for a time."

Megan could do nothing more than agree, and in what seemed like only a second later, Bracken entered the room. The Reverend Mother was seated at her desk, and Megan remained behind the desk as well. She learned nothing from Bracken's expression; in fact, he barely spared her a glance, but his dress surprised her. She had never seen him so formally attired.

His hose and trunks were a rich black, and his tunic was dark gray, but the sleeves had been slashed, laced, and lined with black satin. Beneath this lay an off-white shirt, richly embroidered in black, gray, and pink. Bracken's hair and beard were brushed smooth, but as elegant as he looked, Megan still found his presence too authoritative for her comfort.

"Thank you for seeing me, Reverend Mother," Bracken began as he took a seat.

"It is my pleasure, Lord Bracken. As you can see, Megan is doing well."

Bracken's gaze flicked to her with a

feigned lack of interest and then back to the sister. "I have come some distance, Reverend Mother, and I hope we will be able to come to terms."

"I understand your meaning, Lord Bracken, but I do not stand in the way of Megan's joining you. However, I am not her father and cannot and will not force her to go where she does not wish."

"It is to Megan that I must speak then?"

"Yes."

Bracken still did not look at Megan. She wasn't offended by this treatment; she knew she'd brought it upon herself. Bracken thought she had acted like a child and was treating her as such. However, she was *not* going to return with him. She seriously doubted if even her father could make her do so. She knew it was not right to disobey her father, but she was so desperate right then that she wasn't thinking as she should.

"May I have a private audience with Megan?"

The wise Reverend Mother was not surprised by the question, but neither did she think she should give in too easily. If her guess was right, and it normally was, Bracken had been taking Megan for granted, assuming she would always be there and do as she was told. She would never have said such a thing to Megan, but the older woman thought this running away incident might open Lord Bracken's eyes to a few truths.

"Yes, you may see Megan alone," she stated after a long pause.

Bracken did not miss the way Megan's alarmed eyes swung to the Reverend Mother, but he still did not look at her.

"I will leave you now and return shortly. Megan will be safe in your care?"

Bracken nodded. Under the elderly nun's gaze he felt much like a young vassal rather than a knight of many years. He stood as the nun made her stately way to the door. He waited until the portal closed before turning back to Megan. Again she could read nothing from his face as he took in her attire. She'd had little choice but to don a habit, wimple and all. Bracken thought it made her look like an angel, but he knew better.

"Your clothing does not fool me, Megan," he said calmly. "I know what manner of woman stands beneath."

Her chin rose. "You do not know me at all."

"I know that you are willful and foolish." Angry emotion was now evident in

Bracken's voice; indeed, in his very being.

"You know nothing but your anger," she told him. "And since I am no better with my own ire, I think we would do nothing more than make each other miserable. That, along with your lack of conscience, and I fear to say I want nothing to do with you." The last word was spat. There was such loathing in her voice that Bracken immediately calmed and said what he should have said days ago.

"Since the day I stood over your father's men in the forest and looked upon that useless waste of life, my men have been inquiring."

Megan blinked at this change in subject but did not speak.

"It was reported to me that men, strangers to the area and traveling with extra horses, had visited Black Francesca. In an effort to vindicate the lives lost while making a noble attempt to bring you to Hawkings Crest, I went to her myself to ask whether she had seen such men."

Megan was so crushed she could have cried. All this time she had thought the worst of him.

"Why did you not tell me?" she whispered, pain written all over her face.

Bracken sighed. "It was wrong of me,

Megan, but you were just as wrong to accuse me without knowing the facts. I *do* take this arrangement seriously, and it angered me to think that you see me in such a light."

"I am sorry, Bracken," Megan told him in sincere repentance.

"As am I," he answered.

"But it changes nothing," Megan went on, her voice so reconciled that it caused Bracken's heart to sink with dread, since he was most determined to take her back.

"What do you mean?"

"I mean that my father wanted me at Hawkings Crest to give us time to know each other. I think you would be forced to agree that it was sufficient time to see it would never work between us."

"And what of the king's order?" Whenever he wanted to put all arguments aside, he always fell back on this.

"I will ask my father to speak with Henry and hope that he can be reasoned with. I'm sure you'll agree, Bracken, that both of us would be miserable."

But I wouldn't be miserable, Bracken reasoned to himself, *if only we could continue to talk as we are now.*

Unfortunately, it did not occur to Bracken to share his thoughts. As usual he resorted to force.

"You may ask your father to speak with Henry, but I will ask him not to."

Megan's anger immediately rose to the surface. He hadn't heard a word she said. "He'll never listen to you."

Bracken shook his head, mocking her slightly. "We will be married, Megan. When will you come to accept the inevitable?"

"Never," she nearly hissed. "You can force me to return, but I will fly from you again, make no mistake."

I hear your dove has flown. The conversation with Stephen came so swiftly to Bracken's mind that the air left him in a rush.

She is a red hawk, with talons to gouge a man.

But, Bracken, you won't win her heart with those words.

Bracken suddenly moved around the desk. He approached Megan so abruptly that she jumped and backed into the wall. Bracken would have given much to have Stephen's help right then, but he would have to try this on his own.

"I am most determined to have you as my wife, Megan," the big man admitted, his voice resolute but also very soft.

In her surprise, Megan could only stare at him.

"I am even willing to take you by force, and my men are aware of this. An army of 1000 nuns could not stop me, let alone the few dozen from this abbey."

Anger over his temerity covered Megan's face, but Bracken totally disarmed her with his next words.

"Come back to me, my dove. Come back to Hawkings Crest where you belong."

Bracken found the change in her miraculous. Her eyes softened, and her lovely mouth opened with surprise and pleasure just before her eyes slid shut with the weight of her decision.

Megan's eyes had no more closed when they flew open at the pressure of Bracken's lips on her own. It was a fleeting kiss, but gently given, and it stunned Megan beyond words.

"Come, my little Megan, come back to me," Bracken whispered. Her heart turned over.

"We will quarrel," she tried one last time, but her voice held no conviction.

"Then we will work it out." Bracken's heart pounded as he silently begged her to say yes. When still she hesitated, he was once again tempted to order her but somehow held his tongue. When he thought he could stand it no more and was indeed on the verge of commanding her, she spoke.

"All right. I'll return with you."

Bracken only nodded, afraid to say anything or to let emotion show on his face for fear of destroying her rather hesitant consent. Thankfully, the Reverend Mother arrived just after that.

"Megan will return with me," Bracken told her without preamble, and his opinion of her lifted when she did not look to Megan for confirmation.

"Very well. It is late in the day now. Will you please consider letting Megan stay with us until morning?"

It was clearly not what Bracken wanted to hear. "The ride is long; I would wish to begin now."

"I understand, but you will have Megan for years. We would beg her company for only one more day."

Bracken hesitated, and Megan chimed in.

"I will stay."

Bracken's eyes swung to her and found an angry frown on her face for his even daring to hesitate in agreeing to the nun's request. He knew he was going to have to acquiesce on this, but he was not happy about it. As Megan went off with the Reverend Mother, it occurred to him that he had literally talked Megan into returning with him. His only hope at this point was that she would not make him pay for it for the rest of his life.

"I did not explain myself, Megan," the Reverend Mother spoke as soon as they were in the corridor, "for fear that you would not stay and later be disappointed, but Father Brent is here. I knew you would wish to see him."

Tears sprang to Megan's eyes, and she hugged the elderly nun.

"Thank you, Reverend Mother. In truth, I do not think Bracken would have understood."

The Reverend Mother stopped abruptly on the path to the chapel, her look serious as she eyed this young woman who was like a daughter to her.

"You must not bait him, Megan. It is a mistake to constantly bludgeon a man's pride."

Megan was surprised at the vehemency in the nun's voice. It gave her pause for more reasons than her tone; her words rang true. Megan did pummel Bracken's pride on a regular basis. Not until that very instant did she think how he might feel to have everyone at Hawkings Crest know she had run from him.

And now today, before the Reverend Mother could even reason with him, Megan had spoken up and said she was staying until the morrow no matter what. Megan's conscience pricked her, but only for an instant. Father Brent was here, and she was going to see him.

"What of Megan? You saw her?" Stephen wished to know as he sat across the table from Bracken in the common room of the pub.

"Yes. She is well, but the Reverend Mother has asked that she stay until tomorrow. We will leave at first light."

Stephen nodded. "So it is to be a willing departure."

Bracken shrugged. "In truth, I can answer that only when the time comes. I do not feel the Reverend Mother would deal falsely with me, but I wouldn't put it past Megan to try something."

"So she was not pleased to see you?"

"No," Bracken admitted, and Stephen knew the first stirrings of anger toward Megan. Did she not realize how much

Bracken cared? Didn't she care that he had better things to do than chase her across the countryside, sick with fear for her safety?

When he thought about the way she'd been plunged into this affair, the anger dissolved. It was typical of Henry to use his subjects as political pawns, but it was most unfortunate that Megan had not lost her heart as swiftly as Bracken had. However, Stephen was not pessimistic. He knew that if Megan would only give Bracken a chance, she would find him a man who, although he didn't know flowery words, would indeed cherish her for all his life.

Sixteen

"How are you, my child?"

"Oh, Father Brent," Megan spoke with tears in her eyes, "I've missed you."

The old man gently touched the top of her head, his heart turning over with love for this girl. He remembered her so clearly at 10, angry and rebellious, and then at 14, kneeling to pray for the first time.

"I've missed you too."

"Have you been well?" Megan asked.

"I am as well as an old man can expect to be," he told her with a smile. Megan smiled in return.

"I am only here until the morning."

Father Brent knew all about this and only nodded. "Then I'm glad the Lord saw fit to put us together before you depart."

"Are you ever near Hawkings Crest, Father Brent?" Megan asked anxiously.

"It is far for these old legs, child, but please believe that if ever I am in the area I will stop there."

"I hope to see you."

"The Reverend Mother tells me you are to marry."

"Yes." Megan's eyes clouded.

"What is it, child? What is wrong?"

"It is not what I wish."

Father Brent had figured as much by her reaction. "Through the centuries many have married for love, Megan, but probably just as many married for political gain. How does your betrothed feel?"

Megan's face now flushed with anger, remembering the way he tried to rush her away. "He seems content enough with the arrangement. If only he would protest, Father might try to reason with King Henry on our behalf."

"But you say he seems pleased with the order?"

"Yes." Megan nearly choked on the word.

"If that is the case, can you not give him a chance, child?" Father Brent asked gently, but Megan's face was still set with outrage.

"It's not that easy," she burst out, already sorry she had agreed to return and at the same time confused about the pleasure of Bracken's kiss. In the next few minutes she told the old priest everything. She did not spare herself or Bracken but told all she could recall of that which had transpired in the last weeks.

"And now you're going to tell me," Megan concluded, her voice resigned, "that if I don't make peace with Bracken I'm going to be miserable."

"No," Father Brent said. "I'm not going to say that. This anger you feel — this anger that rides so close beneath the surface that it comes out at a moment's notice, this anger that you say is directed at your mother and Lord Bracken — is not toward them at all."

"Of course it is," Megan argued, but Father Brent would not let her continue.

"Is God sovereign, Megan?"

"Sovereign?" she stumbled over the word.

"The supreme ruler, in absolute, unlimited control of everything at all times," he explained.

"Certainly," Megan answered as soon as she understood. "He is God."

"So whose will is it that King Henry has sent this decree?"

Megan looked at him but didn't answer.

"And whose will was it, hard as it was, that your mother sent you ahead of schedule? God is in control, Megan, and has been all along. The anger that you feel toward all of these people and circumstances is actually directed at your heavenly Father."

Megan's lungs emptied on these words. Her hand came to her lips. What had she done? For weeks now she'd boiled with rage at Bracken, King Henry, her mother, and even her father, but they were not at the source. It was God and God alone. He was in control, and when all the rubble was cleared away Megan could see that she had been lashing out in fury toward *Him*.

"I can see that I've made you think," Father Brent went on compassionately. "And I would be glad to pray with you. But if I remember correctly, you would probably prefer to have some time alone."

"Yes, I would." Megan rose slowly.

"Then before you go, I would like to give you something."

Megan watched the priest bring out a square, thick volume from a bag at his side. It was not overly large, but when he handed it to Megan she found it quite heavy.

"It's the Psalms and Proverbs, Megan, and it's for you."

"The *Bible*?" she whispered incredulously. "In *English*?"

"Just two books, child, but I know God will use them to bless and teach you. I must warn you, Megan, there are some people who would burn such a volume; you must take care with it lest you lose it."

"I will," she said, tears standing in her eyes. "Thank you, Father Brent. Thank you so much."

The elderly man smiled as Megan clasped the book to her and moved toward the door, confident that she would take care of the Scriptures as well as the sin of which she was now aware. He knew that some of the sisters were waiting to see him, but he took time then and there to pray for Megan's heart.

"Delight thyself also in the Lord, and he shall give thee the desires of thine heart. Commit thy way unto the Lord; trust also in him, and he shall bring it to pass. And he shall bring forth thy righteousness as the light, and thy judgment as the noon-day. Rest in the Lord, and wait patiently for him; fret not thyself because of him who prospereth in his way, because of the man who bringeth wicked devices to pass. Cease from anger, and forsake wrath; fret not thyself in any way to do evil."

Megan finished reading out of Psalm 37 and then wept into her pillow.

"I have sinned against you, Father God.

I have been enraged against Your holy plan," Megan cried out quietly. "I do feel like a pawn in the king's game, but You are in control, and I now confess my anger. Please cleanse me, Lord, so that I may know Your peace. I have wanted my way more than Yours, and I confess that as well.

"I know that I'll stumble in this again, Father God, but help me through each trial. I have been so hard on Bracken. I have been so impossible to live with. Help me to care for him and to be the wife I need to be. Help him to deal gently with me and with kindness. Help me to forgive King Henry and my mother and to really see this as Your hand.

"My desire is to do your will, Father God. Please help me to be strong in this pledge. Thank You for sending Father Brent to me. Thank You for his words of rebuke. Help me to heed them from this point on. In Your holy name I pray, Amen."

Megan lay spent now, her body heavy with fatigue but her heart light with her confession. The way she had been acting, the defensive way in which she'd lived, was all so clear. Bracken still intimidated her in many ways, but she could see now

213

that he had been trying.

Megan was not at all hungry, but she wanted to speak with the sisters whom she would not see again. She was weary as she made her way from her room, but the look on Megan's face made it very evident to both the Reverend Mother and Sister Agatha that something had changed.

In the morning Megan made her good-byes swiftly. Leaving the sisters this time was nearly as painful as the first. However, there was a marked difference about her, a serenity, and she caught Bracken staring at her as he helped her onto the back of the horse.

"I'll be leading as we begin," he told her. "You will ride about halfway back. If you have need of me, just send Stephen."

Megan nodded. "Thank you, Bracken."

She watched him stride away, and it wasn't two minutes before they moved out in a double line of about 25 men. Kendrick was beside her, and Stephen was to the front. She didn't know the other men, but they talked as they rode. She soon learned that the man behind her was Owen and the man in front and to the side of Stephen was Stafford. Stafford, along with some of the other men, was not a knight of the realm, but rode in fealty to Bracken's keep.

"What is in your sack, Stafford?" Owen called, a teasing note in his voice.

"You're a busy thing, Owen," Stafford told him in no uncertain terms.

"I'd rather like to know as well," Stephen cut in. Megan could see the smile on his face.

"Stafford is in love with Pen, Lady Megan," Kendrick told her. Megan nodded and smiled as well.

"I know Pen," she stated and watched Stafford's neck go red. "I met her at the creamery."

Stafford couldn't help himself; he turned to look at Megan. Indeed, Pen had told him all about Lady Megan's work out there, and he was still amazed.

While he was still staring at her, Megan said, "She's very pretty."

"I think so," Stafford admitted.

"So what did you buy?" Owen persisted.

"Come now, Owen," Kendrick chided, "do not force the lad to tell."

"Have you asked her to marry you?" Megan asked, feeling a bit nosy herself.

"Of course, Lady Megan," Stafford told her.

"And what did she say?"

The other men laughed because they

had seen the adoring look on Pen's face whenever Stafford was near, but the young knight still only smiled and answered her.

"She said yes."

"So when are you to marry?"

"We're not. I mean, not until I've gained Lord Bracken's permission."

"Why don't you ask him?" It all seemed so elementary to Megan, but Stafford did not answer.

"Bracken takes his job as lord very seriously, Lady Megan," Kendrick gently told her. "Pen is a part of Hawkings Crest and so her well-being, as well as that of the other servants, is of interest to Bracken. He is not a moody lord, but if he says no to Stafford's suit of Pen, the subject is closed. Stafford would rather wait for the correct time."

Megan nodded, her mind busy. "Would you like me to ask him?"

"*No!*" The word was shouted in unison by all four men, and when Megan got over her surprise, her laughter floated high into the air. A moment later Stephen deliberately dropped back to ride beside Megan so he could see her face.

"Stay out of it, Megan," he warned with a playful smile, yet with a significant light in his eyes.

"But Stephen," Megan said with great exaggeration that all the men could hear, "I'm sure I could get him to see reason. Bracken does everything I ask."

Now it was time for the men to laugh. Stephen, having seen that she would not pursue the matter, moved back into position.

Megan had never ridden so far in one morning. By the time they stopped for the noonday meal, she feared that her legs were completely asleep. But another need was pressing in with far more insistency, and the moment Stephen helped her alight from her horse, she made for the woods.

"Megan," he called to her and followed. "You mustn't run off."

Megan turned and stared at him, her voice reasonable. "I assure you, Stephen, I must indeed."

He knew exactly of what she spoke, but he didn't believe the forest was safe for her.

"Just let me check for wild game, Megan, and then you can go."

The redhead's laughter met his ears, and she put a comforting hand on his arm.

"I just walked these woods, Stephen, in

an effort to gain the abbey. I assure you, I will be fine."

Stephen was so surprised by this reminder that he stood still as she walked away and disappeared within the trees.

"She seems in a fine mood," Bracken commented, having come upon them and heard the laughter.

"She does at that," Stephen commented. "And she was certainly determined to get into the woods. I think we came too far without a break."

Bracken grimaced and reminded himself to be more mindful of her needs. "You checked the woods before you let her go?"

"She wouldn't let me," the younger man admitted, knowing what would follow.

"Stephen!" Bracken's voice rose to scold before he began to follow Megan. Stephen grabbed his arm.

"You can't go in there."

Bracken stared at him and then at the forest and sighed heavily. "I tell you, Stephen, I truly do look forward to the day when this betrothal is over and she is mine in earnest."

The men were still standing together when Megan reappeared. Her step was casual until she spotted them. She came to a slow halt a few yards from them.

"Am I interrupting something?"

"No," Bracken assured her swiftly, thinking she looked a bit tired. He came forward and took her arm. "Come, eat and rest awhile. We have many miles yet to go."

Megan learned the real meaning of those words hours later. They had rested for a time after the noonday meal, but with only the exception of a short stop a few hours after that, they had ridden on. Bracken had come back on several occasions to ride with her. Megan had enjoyed his company and explanations of their location. He'd been very solicitous as he'd shown her several points of interest, and Megan had actually been sorry to see him go.

The sun was dropping in the sky and twilight was settling over the land when Megan's eyes grew heavy. She caught herself drifting several times, and twice she nearly fell asleep. When her head eventually nodded and her body went completely limp, she fell to the outside of the line, making it impossible for Kendrick to catch her. One moment she was secure in the saddle, the next she was tumbling toward the ground.

Seventeen

Megan never actually lost consciousness, but the world felt as if it had tipped, righted itself, and then all at once come alive. Horses and dust were all around her. Men were shouting. She shook herself quickly and scrambled to her feet just before Kendrick and Owen reached her.

"Are you all right, my lady?"

"Yes," Megan told them, but she wasn't sure it was true. Her shoulder hurt, and so did the side of her head. Megan shook her head slightly to dispel the image of hurtling through the air, but it didn't work. An involuntary shudder ran over her.

"Are you all right, Megan?" Stephen, who now stood with the other men, asked.

"Yes. Maybe I could just walk for a time."

"There is no need for that. You'll come on Warrior with me," Bracken said reassuringly. He had suddenly appeared and was moving toward her. However, Megan was not so comforted. She retreated, her hands outstretched as if to hold him off.

"Oh, please, Bracken, don't make me. Your destrier is so huge, and if I fall —"

"I'm not going to let you fall, Megan." Bracken's voice was warm, and meant to comfort, but Megan did not attend.

"Please let me walk, Bracken, please. Just for a time."

Bracken heard the tremor in her voice, looked at her for a moment, and then turned and walked back among his men. After a moment they dispersed. It looked as though they were setting up camp.

Megan could not stop the trembling that ran all over her frame, and as fast as the darkness was closing in, Bracken saw it clearly.

"Come rest here, Megan; the men are preparing some food."

"We're camping here?"

"No. Just taking a rest."

A blanket had been laid almost at her feet, and it was a relief for Megan to sink down onto it. Food was brought, and it swiftly became clear that they had stopped for her alone. For this reason she did not allow herself to relax. It would have been heavenly to stretch out and sleep, but Megan made herself sit upright and eat swiftly.

She thanked the men who had served

her and stood up just as soon as she finished. Megan would have stayed on the ground for hours if she'd known what Bracken had in mind to do next.

"Are you feeling better?" He had been close by the whole time. He saw now that the journey had been too much for her and was angry at himself for not sensing it earlier. Nevertheless, all he could do now was try to make the best of it.

"Yes, thank you."

Bracken signaled, and Megan watched as his horse, a huge beast of war named Warrior, was brought forward.

"Where is my horse?" Megan asked as she tried to calm the alarm rising within her.

"One of my men will bring him along," Bracken said as he swung himself astride. Before Megan had time to react, she found herself lifted in Stephen's arms. Their intent was immediately clear to her, and she stiffened with fear.

"Put me down, Stephen."

The fear in her voice wrung his heart, but he knew that Bracken would have it no other way.

Seconds later, Bracken was reaching for her, and Megan found herself sitting across the front of his saddle. Her hands fisted in the fabric of his tunic and her eyes were huge as she pleaded with him.

"Please, put me down."

"No, Megan." Bracken's voice was gentle and as soft as hers had been. "The day has been long, and you are tired. I won't let you fall."

Megan shook her head, and for an instant she buried her face against his chest. She was trembling so violently that her teeth chattered. Bracken's heart turned over, but he knew this was best. Megan's head came back up, and her eyes as well as her voice pleaded with him.

"I'm sorry I ran from you, Bracken," she sobbed. "Please don't punish me this way."

" 'Tis no punishment, Megan," he told her gently, "but a way to keep you safe."

Megan chose that moment to notice they hadn't even moved.

"Why don't we just camp here?" she asked hopefully.

"Because we are only two hours' ride from Hawkings Crest. It is safest to carry on. We shall all be tired, but our beds await us, and that outweighs the risk of sleeping in the forest and going in at dawn."

Megan took a deep breath and made herself loosen her hold on his clothing. She then noticed the large arm at her back. It was like she was leaning against a fallen tree. Bracken's face was disappearing in the darkness, but Megan looked up and saw him watching her.

"I won't let you fall," his deep voice rumbled out from under her shoulder that was against his chest. Megan sat still as Bracken gently plucked a leaf from her hair.

Megan would have spoken, but Brice suddenly appeared.

"All are in readiness, Bracken."

"Good."

"How are you, Megan?" Brice then asked.

"I'm all right," she told him, but her voice said otherwise.

"You didn't hurt yourself in the fall?"

Megan shrugged. "A little on my head and shoulder."

"Which shoulder?" Bracken inquired.

Megan motioned to the one against him, and a moment later she was being lifted like a child and turned. When she was settled once again, Bracken spoke to Brice.

"Let's move."

Brice gave the order, and within minutes they were surrounded by men and moving down the road. Bracken felt Megan tense against him, but knowing that she would soon understand he would never let her fall, he stayed quiet. Megan did eventually relax. Her head fell against his chest, and he could see that her hands now lay limply in her lap.

Megan roused after just 45 minutes of sleep, but she did so easily. All the tension had left her. For an instant she lay still and listened to the thud of Bracken's heart. It was a comforting sound, and the arm and chest around her were warm and safe. After a time she raised her head, rotated her shoulders, and then tried to look up into his face. It was very dark.

"I didn't mean to fall asleep."

"I'm glad you did," he told her easily. "I'm sorry it's been such a long ride."

Megan sighed. "I really have no one to blame but myself."

Bracken didn't comment, but he had smiled slightly in the dark. For a time they rode in silence.

"Can you tell me of William?" Bracken's question had come out of nowhere for Megan, and she took a moment to answer.

"William Clayborne?"

"I am not sure. A man came to the abbey. His name was William, and he was seeking you."

Again Bracken heard her sigh.

"Have you ever been in love, Bracken?"

He could have told her that he was in love right then, but said instead, "Why do you ask?"

"William is enamored with me. There is a wonderful girl — her name is Rose — and she loves William deeply. But he thinks he wants me."

"You do not think him capable of knowing his own mind?"

"I don't know."

"And you, Megan, do you love him?"

"No," she answered softly, but without hesitation. "I care for William. He has been a good friend, but I do not love him. He believes with time that I would have a change of heart. I do not think we could be happy."

"And what of us, Megan?" Bracken questioned while betraying none of the vulnerability he felt within. "Will we ever find happiness together?"

Megan turned to him in the dark but could not make out his features.

"I do not know, Bracken, but I pray so."

He didn't say anything, but after a moment he gently pressed Megan's head back onto his chest. She stiffened for an instant, but it wasn't long before she picked up the beat of Bracken's heart once again. Just seconds later she relaxed. Something was happening within her where this man was concerned, and the swiftness of it astonished her. Megan could only conclude that because she'd surrendered the anger in her heart, God was finally able to work.

Comfortable as she was, Megan began to grow sleepy again, but even in her fuzzy state she was cognizant enough to thank God that Bracken had insisted she ride on his horse.

Megan had apologized sincerely to Helga for asking her to lie, and the faithful servant had been gone from Megan's presence for only five minutes before Louisa came through her door. The moment the older woman saw her, she pulled Megan into a fierce embrace. Then Megan was forced to stand helplessly before Louisa and watch her cry.

Megan did put her arms back around Bracken's aunt, but she was overcome with shame when she realized how little thought she had given her in the last days. In all her selfish running away, it never once occurred to her that she had scared Louisa sick. She confessed this to God as she released Louisa, and then apologized to the woman herself.

"I am so sorry, Aunt Louisa."

"It's all right, Megan," she cried. "As long as you are safe."

Megan hugged the older woman yet again, and Louisa tried to contain herself. Having arrived back late the night before, most of the castle had been quiet and Megan had gone directly to her room. She had not seen Louisa until daybreak, when she nearly burst into Megan's room. The prodigal bride-to-be was up, already reading the Psalms, and so glad to see Louisa that she almost cried herself.

"I am famished," Megan admitted suddenly.

"As am I," Louisa said. "Let us go below and break the fast. How are your mother and father?" she inquired as they started down the stairs.

"I don't know," Megan told her. "I didn't see them."

"Megan," Louisa said in a surprised voice, "why ever not?"

"I did not go home. I went to the abbey."

They had gained the great room now, and Louisa abruptly stopped. "But surely they came to see you."

"No," Megan told her with a shake of the head.

Louisa could only stare at her. Megan had thought nothing of this up to now, but suddenly she felt ashamed. She wasn't sure if the shame was for herself or for her parents, who didn't appear to care for her.

Bracken had spotted the women's descent and now approached. He studied Louisa's face and then Megan's flushed cheeks and frowned. He would have thought that Louisa would be thrilled to see his betrothed.

"Is there some problem?" Bracken asked.

"No, no," Louisa spoke swiftly, glancing first at Bracken and then back at Megan. "I'm sorry I acted so, Megan."

Megan smiled in understanding, but her heart was still troubled. Bracken, reading this, wanted to know more.

"Megan?"

She looked at him. "Aunt Louisa was just surprised that I didn't see Father and Mother."

"I thought they would at least come to the abbey, Bracken," Louisa put in softly.

Bracken read and understood the compassion in his aunt's eyes.

"I saw them," he said.

"You did?" Megan had forgotten this.

"Yes. I did not know you had gone to the abbey until I'd talked with your father. He seemed to think it best to leave things in my hands, so we didn't stop back at the castle on the way here."

Megan nodded, now recalling the messenger who had come to the abbey.

"You did see my mother?" Megan, picturing Bracken at Stone Lake, asked, a sudden thought striking her.

"Yes."

"How was she?"

Bracken glanced at the floor and then at Megan. She saw instantly that he was amused, and for the first time she felt like laughing herself.

"I would say that she was not very happy to learn you had gone to the abbey." Bracken's voice was dry.

He put it so delicately, that for the first time, Megan smiled at Bracken. It quite nearly took his breath away.

"She didn't wish to see me?" Megan asked with huge, innocent eyes that sparkled with impish glee. She knew well what her mother thought of her and ofttimes chose to laugh rather than cry.

Bracken's smile went into full bloom as he offered his arm to Megan. He sent a speaking glance toward Louisa. The older woman took his cue, as well as his other arm, and the three went silently on to the tables to eat.

Eighteen

" 'Tis truly the oddest thing I've ever known," Bracken admitted to Louisa. "Lord Vincent came as swiftly as he could when Megan first came here, but in truth it's as if they don't even care. He never even mentioned seeing Megan at the abbey. He seemed more intent on our touring his keep than anything else."

Louisa looked troubled. It was the end of Megan's first day back, and Bracken had finally sought out his aunt in her chambers.

"And you say that Lady Annora was only angry, not concerned?"

Bracken's look turned fierce. "She was livid, and then when that creature, Marigold, appeared, her manner was so sweet I felt ill."

"It's taken some time, Bracken, but I finally realized I've met Marigold. We, too, were at court at the same time, and I hate to say it, but a more avaricious woman I've yet to encounter."

"She's certainly self-seeking," Bracken

put in. "We never even exchanged words, but I could see from across the room that she thinks of little beyond herself."

"And do Megan and Marigold get on?"

Bracken was suddenly struck by a vivid memory. It was right after Megan arrived. They'd been talking by the hearth, and Marigold's name had been mentioned. Bracken recalled being amused by what he thought to be sibling rivalry.

"I think not," he said now. "We have never actually spoken of it, but I sense that Megan and Marigold have much the same relationship as Megan and her mother."

"And what is that exactly?"

Bracken's face was covered with pain. "Nothing but animosity. Annora does not seem able to stand the thought of Megan, let alone the sight of her. I tell you, Aunt Lou, when I think of my own relationship with my mother, I can hardly reckon with what I see in Megan's family."

Louisa nodded in full understanding.

"You love her, don't you, Bracken?"

"I do, Louisa," he admitted softly. "I will admit that at first it was strictly carnal. I was captivated with her hair and face, but now I've seen things in her that have nothing to do with her looks.

"She fights me, but I so admire her

mettle. She is unendingly kind to the servants, but she brooks no lying from those who would seek to cheat me."

Louisa suddenly chuckled. "She certainly doesn't like Barton."

"Indeed." Bracken now chuckled as well. "I wonder when the next battle will be fought."

"Could she be right, Bracken?"

Something in Louisa's tone made Bracken take his eyes from the fire and look at her. In truth, what proof did he have that Barton would never steal from him? Barton had worked under his parents since before Bracken could remember, but neither his mother nor his father could read. Bracken could read some, but he never bothered to question the man's doings. He was more interested in his training fields and the external functions of the keep.

"I think maybe it would be wise to listen to her," Louisa suggested softly, and for the first time Bracken was open to the idea and not threatened by it.

"I quite agree with you. I'll not seek the matter out, but if she comes again, I'll do my best."

Louisa felt very pleased. She had nothing against Barton, but never had she met a woman of Megan's integrity. Louisa was very certain Megan would never have accused someone whom she did not believe with all her heart was in the wrong.

Bracken did not stay much longer. When he left, his thoughts were on Megan. Louisa too was thinking of Megan, but also of her sister, Joyce, and what she might think of Megan when they at last could meet.

"It's time for us to go," Stephen told Megan, Brice by his side.

"Go where?"

"Home," Brice said, smiling at her look of surprise.

"But I thought —"

"That we lived here?"

Megan hesitated. "No, not that; it's just that I've only been back a week, and I thought you would just be here indefinitely." Megan shrugged helplessly, and Stephen hugged her.

"Does Bracken know?"

"Yes, and Aunt Lou. We don't leave today, but if the weather holds, by the end of the week."

Megan's hands came to her waist now, and she took on a look of teasing. "I was just coming to the point of being able to stand the sight of you, but if you're going to be that way about it, then off with you!"

"You could come with us," Stephen suggested, his voice teasing as well.

"Now why would I do that?"

"To meet Mother." Brice told her simply, jesting also, but not sounding like it.

Megan's face took on such an expression of interest that the two men exchanged a glance of panic.

"Now, Megan —" Stephen began, knowing what Bracken would say, but the little redhead was not listening.

"It's not a poor idea at all, is it? I'm sure Bracken wouldn't mind. I'm always underfoot as it is."

"What is it Bracken wouldn't mind?" the one being talked about wished to know as he came and stood before the group. His heart skipped a beat when he saw his brothers' looks of guilt and Megan's triumphant countenance.

"I'm thinking of seeing your mother."

Bracken frowned. "Well, of course you'll see her . . . when we are wed."

"No, now. Stephen suggested it."

Bracken's eyes swung to that fellow, who was smiling painfully, before returning and pinning Megan to the ground. "You mean

236

go to White Hall with Brice and Stephen now?"

"Yes." Megan's face was filled with delight, but Bracken was scowling.

"I don't care for this idea," Bracken said in a voice he thought would end the subject. He was wrong.

"Why ever not?" Megan wished to know, still congenial.

"Your father wanted you here so we could know each other better."

As usual Bracken had resorted to this excuse, and Megan was sick of hearing it. With a tremendous scowl of her own, she replied, "Well, what else is there to know?" Megan was angry for the first time in many days. "You insist that you want this marriage and that I am to run your castle and keep, but only as long as I don't interfere with your plans and wishes. You are in a good mood until I cross you, and then you're frightening. I am to stay out from underfoot, and the only real place I have any say is in my own bedchamber."

"That isn't true," Bracken told her firmly. Under attack, he had completely forgotten about his plan to listen to her.

"Of course it is. You won't even discuss that thief who keeps your books, and now two of your falcons have died. The others will die also unless you allow me to do something with the falconry. The creamery needs work as well, and so does the byre."

"I have men to see to that." Bracken was angry now himself.

"But they are not following through, and you're too busy with your men to notice," Megan shot back. "If I'm to be nothing more than a figurehead, I might as well go on a journey with your brothers and meet the rest of your family."

"I will hear no more on the subject, Megan," Bracken now said in a voice that left no doubt as to his black mood; indeed, it was as dark as his looks. "You are staying here, and that is the end of it."

Megan's chin came into the air. She glared at Bracken for an instant and then turned and walked toward the castle. She was out of earshot when Brice said, "We're sorry, Bracken. We were but jesting."

Bracken grunted with irritation. "She's obviously quite anxious to be away. One moment I think I know her, and the next I am a man lost."

"What exactly do you mean?" Stephen asked.

"She has seemed so content," Bracken burst out. "We have not had one harsh word since the journey."

"But the more time she spends here, the more discontented she is with the way you run things," Stephen spoke up.

"She told you this?" Bracken's eyes swiftly turned to him.

"No, Bracken." Stephen's voice was matter-of-fact. "She didn't have to. You are right, she has been doing better. But by her own admission she's been looking around the castle, and she's not happy with what she sees. She's even less happy when she knows she can't come to you."

"Of course she can come to me," Bracken argued.

"And hear what?" Stephen shot at him. "That she is to stay in her own place? Or that no matter what she suggests, you will make no changes?"

Bracken opened his mouth and shut it, so Stephen went on, this time very quietly, but with deep fervor.

"Aunt Lou is wonderful, Bracken, we all know that, but she is not true mistress here. She is more than happy to leave the account books to Barton and the running of the keep to you. We eat like kings when Aunt Lou is at work, and our bedding, as well as the rushes on the floor, are always fresh. But Megan clearly wants more.

"You're going to have to ask yourself if

you want to be married to an Aunt Louisa or to a Megan of Stone Lake. If it's Megan, as I strongly expect it will be, you're going to have to free her, Bracken."

"What do you mean?"

"I mean, let her be who and what she is. You're so afraid of losing her that you're holding on too tight. Even her wish to ride with us was innocent. I can imagine her curiosity about Mother and the rest. She understands the workings of a castle — she's already proven that — but if you don't start trusting her, she'll build a wall so high between you that you will never find a way to scale it.

"In the end she'll be your wife, but only because she's been forced. Let the dove go, Bracken, and I truly believe she will fly right back into your arms."

Even Brice was staring at Stephen by the time he finished. The brothers teased Stephen often about his sweet way with women, but neither one of them had ever heard him quite so passionate.

"What say you, Brice? Do you think Stephen right?"

Brice shook his head slightly. "I do not know, Bracken, but even I can see that as things stand it's not working. What harm is there in trying things Stephen's way? You may find Megan more than willing to meet you in the middle."

Bracken nodded and thanked his brothers, and when he turned away, both thought he might seek out Megan immediately. This was not the case. Bracken turned toward the creamery. From there he would go to the falconry and then to the byre. It rubbed him sorely to be doing so, but maybe it was time to make some changes.

The three brothers were very surprised to see Megan at the table for dinner that night, and even more surprised when she was cordial to all, including Bracken. Some of the light of the past week had gone out of her eyes, but it was clear to all that she was trying. Her effort wrung Bracken's heart, but it wasn't until the next day that they had any time together.

"Lady Megan," Noleen, one of the maids, began when she found Megan bending over a loom. "Lord Bracken would like to speak with you."

Megan straightened, glanced at her, and then looked back. "I think it should work now, Elva," she said to the girl at the loom and then turned to Noleen once again.

"He's in the war room, my lady."

"Thank you, Noleen," Megan replied, moving to the door. She was not dreading this confrontation, but neither was she pleased. She knew she'd been out of line the day before, but sometimes it was so hard to apologize. In truth, Megan was sorry only for her tone. She had been meaning to say everything else for weeks, and in many ways it was a relief to have it out. Megan could only wonder why he would wish to see her.

She gained the door of the war room at an easy pace, her composure serene. Inside, however, she was in a royal turmoil. Megan opened the door herself and found Bracken within. He had been sitting, but now rose and held a chair.

"Please be seated, Megan."

Megan did as she was asked and sat uncomfortably for an instant while Bracken stayed behind her chair. Certain her hair must be a mess, she had to force her hands to stay in her lap. When it seemed that an eternity had passed, Bracken came around the chair.

"Your father has sent word to me," he began as soon as he was seated opposite.

"Is he well?"

"Yes, but Henry has been in touch and wishes to know if we have chosen a date."

Megan stared at him. "For the wedding?"

"Yes."

Megan stood abruptly and walked to a window. She took a deep breath and fought down feelings of panic. She lived every day, certain that at any moment Bracken would tell her he had changed his mind about the wedding, but it never happened.

"Is there some problem, Megan?" She could tell from his voice that he had stayed in his seat. She was thankful for this.

"I don't know. I guess I've not truly accepted the fact that you actually wish to wed me."

"What is so difficult to believe?"

Megan turned her head to see him. "Is it really so hard to understand, Bracken?"

"No," he admitted. "But even with our differences, I think we will suit."

Megan stared at him in exasperation and then turned back to the window and muttered, more to herself than Bracken, "You should marry Marigold."

"I do not wish to marry your sister."

Megan didn't even turn to him. "You might feel differently if you could see her."

"On the contrary; I have seen her."

Megan spun so swiftly Bracken thought

she might have injured her neck. "You've met Marigold?"

"Yes."

"When?"

"Well, many years ago at court, and then just last week at Stone Lake Castle."

Megan stared at him.

"What is it, Megan? Did you think I would be struck dumb by her beauty and fall in a heap at her feet?"

At any other time Megan would have laughed at his words, as well as his dry tone, but not now, not about Marigold.

"I don't know what I thought; it's just that —" She stopped and shrugged, her eyes telling Bracken that she was beside herself with pain and confusion. She turned back to the window, and after a moment heard Bracken approach. He did not touch her or say a word, but Megan was very aware of his presence behind her. When she could stand it no longer, she spoke.

"Why do you stand there, Bracken, and not speak?"

He did not immediately reply. Megan turned to confront him, her eyes begging him to answer.

"I am enjoying the smell of your hair."

His answer worked on her just as his

words had at the abbey.

"Oh, Bracken," she said softly. "What am I going to do?"

Her question was not lost on him. "You're going to marry me," he spoke gently. "And the two of us are going to do our best to make a life together."

Megan sighed. "Are you certain about Marigold?"

Bracken's eyes suddenly became very amused. "Yes. My brothers and knights were quite smitten, but she is not the woman for me."

"And you think I am?"

"I do not think; I know."

His words warmed Megan considerably, and Bracken studied her complexion, which always reminded him of the bloom on a peach. Megan saw the answering warmth in his own gaze, but she was unprepared for the way his head lowered. She drew in a sharp breath and stood still in anticipation.

A servant chose that moment to knock on the door. Bracken froze, his lips just a scant inch from Megan's, and stared into her eyes. Megan stared back, unable to identify the emotions surging through her.

"We must set a date, my dove," he said softly when the knock sounded again. He preferred kissing her to discussing the wedding, but she seemed pliant all of a sudden.

"All right."

"September," Bracken said softly, pushing for all he was worth.

Megan nodded, not certain at the moment what year it was, let alone the month.

Whoever was at the door had given up, but Bracken, even though he still wanted to kiss her, now stood to full height, much pleased at how easy it had been. Megan continued to watch him, and Bracken knew it would only be a matter of minutes before the charm dissipated and Megan understood what she had just agreed to.

Indeed it was only seconds. Bracken was at the door when Megan found her voice.

"Did you say September?"

Bracken looked back from the door. "Indeed, I did."

"But this is mid-July."

Bracken's mouth turned up in a very satisfied way.

"Yes, Megan, I know."

When the door had closed in his wake, Megan let her back fall against the window casing. Only one thought came to mind, and she voiced it to the empty room.

"What in the world have I done?"

Nineteen

Two days later Bracken and Megan stood together as Stephen and Brice rode out of Hawkings Crest. Megan was already so lonely for them that she wanted to weep.

"Will you miss them?" Bracken asked her.

"Yes. I miss them now."

"Before you know it the wedding will be upon us, and they will return, bringing with them my whole family."

Megan turned to look at him and saw that he was very pleased with the prospect of seeing his family. His smile increased her wonder over what they must be like, but she didn't question Bracken concerning them. With plans to go back to the castle, Megan was on the verge of excusing herself, but Bracken suddenly said, "What would you do differently in the falconry?"

Megan was surprised, but recovered swiftly and answered in a humble voice, "My father has had several birds for more than 15 years. Your falconer told me that his oldest bird is four years old. I think the main problem is that he is taking too many birds from the wilds. He needs to raise the birds from eggs and keep his pens cleaner and more comfortable."

Bracken believed his birds were important but thought the job sounded huge. And as with his steward, his falconer had been with Hawkings Crest since Bracken was a child. Bracken's hand went to the back of his neck. Did she think that he or any of his servants could do anything well?

"I have upset you," Megan said when he did not reply or look at her.

"No, Megan, but I do wonder if you think I am of any use at all."

Megan didn't know what to say. She had come to love Hawkings Crest and felt he'd done an excellent job of its upkeep.

"Forgive me, Bracken." Megan's voice was now a bit pained. "I have given you the wrong impression. It is true that I feel some things should change, but they are not many at all. Indeed, there is much more that I admire. I have never seen finer horses, and your training fields are beyond compare."

She paused as a look of complete surprise crossed his face, but then kept on.

"But as with most keeps, the lord is more interested in one area than another.

The same goes for the mistress of the castle. I want to see things improve in the account books, the byre, and the creamery because these areas affect my management of the castle and castle folk."

"And what of the falconry?"

Megan's cheeks heated slightly, but she did not drop her eyes. "It has long been an interest to me, and over the years my father has taught me much. I do not wish to interfere, but I can see there are things you can do to improve your falconry. You won't see an immediate benefit, but in time your birds could be very strong."

Bracken nodded. "Tell me what you have in mind."

In just seconds she had laid out a plan of such logic that Bracken was mentally kicking himself for not listening to her earlier.

"So you feel the birds need more air?"

"They need more of everything. Air, sunlight, and whatever else it takes to mimic their natural environment. They are only to be kept in the mews when they are molting. No only will they be healthier, they will hunt better."

Bracken nodded. "And what plans had you for the byre?"

Megan did not need to be asked twice.

The castle was forgotten as the lord and his lady walked in the direction of the cow barn. Megan was not pushy or demanding in her suggestions, and Bracken was once again amazed at her intelligence and instinctive ideas.

It was a godsend that Bracken was able to see Megan at her most competent. It only caused him to love her more. But a new side was soon to reveal itself, one that would cause Bracken's heart to completely melt where Megan was concerned.

"Your mother has sent a messenger, Megan," Louisa told the younger woman the following week.

Megan was not surprised. She knew that Bracken had sent word to Vincent concerning the September 20 wedding date, just ten weeks away. She also knew that her mother would want to come and start working on her wedding dress.

"What did she say?" Megan asked before she remembered that Louisa could not read. The older woman only smiled and handed her the piece of parchment.

Megan saw instantly that she had been only half right. Annora did want to work on Megan's clothes, but not at Hawkings Crest. The letter said in no uncertain terms that Megan should return to Stone Lake immediately. Megan knew there was no real hurry, but Annora liked to have things done very quickly, and where Megan was concerned she was never long on patience.

"Is she coming?"

"No. She wants me at Stone Lake."

"Oh." Louisa thought this sounded fine. She did not notice Megan's lack of enthusiasm. "Shall I go with you?"

"Oh, Aunt Louisa, that would be wonderful," Megan responded, loving the idea. "But I have to go right away." Megan nearly apologized.

"I shouldn't think that would be any problem. Let's find Bracken right now and ask him to arrange a guard." This proved to be easier said than done. No one in the castle knew of his lordship's whereabouts, and not until they tracked down Arik did they learn he was on the practice field.

They found him dripping with sweat. Kendrick had just trounced him soundly on the jousting field, and he was not happy with his own performance. He was a knight, he reminded himself, not some smooth-faced boy, and yet he had fought like young Clive on his first assignment. Thus, he was in a foul mood and not at all happy to see the women. Unfortunately, he didn't bother to mention that his black disposition had nothing to do with them.

"Why have you come?" he asked bluntly.

Megan was instantly put off by his tone, but Louisa, looking forward to going to Megan's home, barged right in and explained.

"She wants you at Stone Lake Castle?" Bracken questioned just minutes later.

"Yes," Louisa meekly answered for Megan, now seeing that they had chosen an inappropriate time.

"Why?"

Megan's chin rose. "It's not my idea, Bracken, so you need not scowl at me so. It would suit me fine to stay right here, but I have no real reason to refuse my mother. If you do not wish me to leave, then *you* may contact Annora and explain why I don't need a wedding dress."

As often happened, her anger amused him. She was so little and feisty, and unless he was angry himself, when her eyes flashed green fire he found her adorable. Megan would have groaned had he shared his thoughts. She did make such a diligent effort when it came to the sin of anger, but right now all she saw was the sparkle in Bracken's eyes, and being laughed at was unbearable to her.

"I am so pleased that I can serve as jester for your keep, my lord, and now that you've had your fun, I will take my leave."

She turned on her heel, but Bracken's arm shot out, and he caught the back of her skirt in one large fist. Megan stiffened with rage and insult but would not turn to look at him.

"Release me!" she commanded, her arms now stiff at her side, her hands balled into fists.

Bracken ignored her and spoke to Louisa.

"When did you wish to leave?"

"As soon as possible."

Bracken nodded before transferring his gaze to Megan. Louisa saw him smile at the back of her. She also watched as he pulled gently on the fabric in his hand until Megan was forced to back up or fall. Not until she was nearly touching him did she suddenly spin and whip the fabric from his grasp. Louisa took her exit on that move.

Megan now stood, her magnificent bosom heaving, and glared at her betrothed. She was ready to give him the sharp side of her tongue, but he disarmed her with one gently put sentence.

"I do not wish you to run from me when you are angry."

Megan stared at him.

"It does no good," he went on. "It only puts walls between us that must be painfully torn down at another time."

Megan's shoulders slumped in defeat. It's so true, she thought, *and once again I have sinned with anger.*

"I'm sorry, Bracken."

"As am I." His voice was sincere. "I was not making sport of you."

"But you did laugh," Megan said, trying to understand.

"Not because I see you as a buffoon, but out of delight."

This made no sense to Megan at all, but Bracken was so new at expressing himself he didn't know how to carry on. Instead he said, "I'll order a guard right now. We'll be ready to leave in less than an hour."

"We?"

"Yes. I'll be going with you."

Megan frowned. "Because you do not trust me to return?"

"No," Bracken answered honestly. Such a thing had never occurred to him. "I would know that you have arrived safely at your father's castle and will return in good health as well. I can't see to this if I'm not with you. That is all."

Megan could only nod. She thanked him quietly and turned away from the field.

How long, Lord, she prayed silently. *How long will I forget myself and sin against Your name? I confess my anger and ask Your strength to resist this sin.*

Megan finished her prayer by asking for forbearance when seeing her mother. It seemed she could never please Annora, but as she could think of little else but seeing her, Megan was feeling very faithless by the time they left for Stone Lake.

The ride was long, and because they hadn't left Hawkings Crest until after the noon meal, they even spent a night camped in the forest. But to Megan's mind, she was standing before her mother before she felt prepared.

Her mother surveyed her with censorious eyes, and for the first time Megan found something over which to be thankful. Her mother was never a hypocrite. It wasn't easy that she never spared Megan's feelings in front of others or put up a false front, but she was honest. She believed that everyone was able to see the deficiencies in her youngest child.

"Go and bathe. I have fabric here, but

you can't possibly get near anything when you reek of horses."

Megan began to move away.

"Don't slouch!" Annora barked at her. Megan, whose shoulders were already straight as a line, put them back unnaturally. She kept on toward the stairs and did not look back, even when she heard her mother say, "Well, at least you seemed to have dropped some weight. I'm sure Lord Bracken does not want a fat bride."

"Annora!" Vincent reprimanded her in a whisper of great heat.

"Do *not* defend her, Vincent," Annora came right back at him, not bothering to lower her own voice. "You know I'm right. Now, please introduce me to Lady Louisa."

The introductions were made, but poor Louisa heard little of them. At one point during the confrontation with Megan and her mother, Louisa had had to put a restraining hand on Bracken's arm, and she was still so shaken by what she had seen and heard that she didn't know if she'd replied well to Lady Annora or not.

A gracious hostess when she chose to be, Annora commented kindly, "You must be weary. Would you like to see your chambers?"

"Yes, please." Louisa's voice was wooden, but Annora did not seem to notice.

"And you, Bracken, would you like to go up also?"

Bracken answered with little more than a nod of his head, but Annora paid little attention. She knew how moody men could be. She saw them both to their rooms, unaware of the way Bracken kept an eye on his hostess. He went to Louisa's room just as soon as the hallway was clear.

"I wish to be alone," Louisa spoke on his knock.

"It's me, Aunt Lou," Bracken said, and the door was opened immediately. He hugged her the moment the door closed.

"Oh, Bracken," she whispered, barely holding tears as she stepped from his embrace. "I had no idea, not a clue."

"I know," he said. "I was certain the situation had to be difficult, but I wasn't aware of the full extent myself. I must admit that I've judged Megan too harshly where the relationship with her mother is concerned."

Louisa went to a chair. She was trembling so badly that she had to sit down.

"I'm angry at Annora," she admitted. "But I'm furious with Vincent. When he was at Hawkings Crest, he made me think his love for Megan was indescribably deep, but as soon as Annora fought with him, he backed down like a man defeated. If he truly loved Megan, how could he do such a thing?"

"I do not know, but I don't think I can take much more."

"What will you do?"

"I am not certain. Were she already my wife, I would not have remained silent, but when the situation is like this, I hesitate to act."

As soon as he had seen that Louisa was going to be all right, Bracken returned to his room and paced for a time. He was most anxious to see Megan, but it had taken more contemplation on what he'd seen to strengthen his resolve in another man's castle and with that man's daughter. In the end he reasoned that although Megan was not yet his wife, he didn't have to stand back and see her abused in any way.

With that thought firmly planted in his mind, he left his bedchamber. A servant was passing, and with the authority that came naturally to him, he said, "I wish to see Lady Megan."

"Yes, my lord," the servant responded,

swiftly changing direction. "I'll show you the way."

Once at the door, Bracken knocked. The door was opened by another servant after just a moment.

"I wish to see Lady Megan," Bracken repeated.

"Of course, my lord. Just one moment."

The door was closed in his face, but the woman was back directly.

"Lady Megan asks if she can meet with you in a few minutes."

"That would be fine."

The servant came out into the hall. "I'll show you to the salon."

Bracken followed without a word and was inside the spacious upstairs salon for less than five minutes before Megan joined him. He could see at a glance that she had bathed, and this reminded him of his own unwashed state. At any rate, the loveliness of her face and form did not distract Bracken from what he considered to be a more important matter — Megan's heart. And Bracken planned to know the state of that vital member before either one of them left the room.

"How are you, Megan?" Bracken wasted no time.

"I'm well," she told him, having understood exactly why he wished to see her. "Bracken, don't mind Mother. She is often like that." Megan smiled to reassure him, but Bracken was not convinced. The young earl refused to believe that Annora's words had no effect. Bracken wanted to know more but wasn't sure how to question her. While he was still weighing his next words, Annora herself interrupted them.

"Megan, I am ready for you."

Does her voice always sound so harsh and impatient when she speaks to Megan? Bracken wondered.

"I trust that I'm not disturbing anything," Annora said belatedly, and in a voice that said it wouldn't have mattered.

"No," Megan answered with a swift look at Bracken. "I'll see you later, Bracken."

"Yes," was all the young knight could manage before both women swept out of the room.

Much to Bracken's surprise, the remainder of the day was not a disaster. He even managed to find some time with Megan in the late afternoon. They were not alone exactly, since the great hall was always occupied, but they had taken two chairs by the hearth and actually talked for an hour without being disturbed.

"How did the dress fitting go?" Bracken had searched his mind for several minutes for something to talk about and was feeling quite proud of his opening.

"Well, there isn't a dress yet, only fabric. I liked one in particular, but Mother wanted another."

Bracken couldn't stop the stiffening in his body. "Which one did you choose?"

Megan's smile was genuine. "Which do you think?"

Bracken reluctantly smiled back. "Do you ever grow weary of her way with you?"

"Oh, yes," Megan admitted, her eyes now far off. "It's easier not to be here, but God has taught me many things through my relationship with my mother."

Bracken frowned. "You make it sound as if it is God's will that she treat you so."

Megan's head tipped to one side. "In a way, it is. It is not a mistake that she is my mother."

"I don't understand."

"I believe God is sovereign, which means He rules over all and has a purpose in each circumstance. If that's the case, Bracken, then He is in control of *everything* — even when it doesn't please Him."

Bracken had never thought of it that way.

He believed in God, but he also believed in himself. He never hesitated to mentally give God the honor for his strong body and wealth, but Bracken believed that if he wanted something, he would have to fight for it. Before this conversation, Bracken would have said that God controlled all, but he wasn't sure what to do with Megan's belief concerning her mother. God had put the heavens and earth into motion — Bracken was certain of this — but right now he was not convinced that God's hand still moved.

"I know that doesn't excuse Mother, but as I said, God has taught me things." Bracken had stayed silent for so long that Megan felt she had to go on. He now nodded in acknowledgement but changed the subject.

"Do you know how long your mother needs you here?"

"No, she doesn't say. Is there a reason we need to be away?"

"No, but I enjoy my own home."

"You could leave me," Megan suggested, although she hated the idea.

Bracken didn't answer verbally, but slowly shook his head. He would never leave her here at Annora's mercy. The subject changed, so Bracken was unaware of what a relief his staying was for Megan.

Not long afterward, the young couple was joined by Louisa and Lyndon. The four visited until it was time for the evening meal. On a whole, the evening ended on a fairly high note, but Bracken was still concerned over Annora's treatment of Megan. Her manner toward her that evening was subtle enough that he felt it would have been inappropriate to comment, but he took himself off to bed hoping they could leave soon and feeling very thankful that Marigold was not present.

Twenty

Bracken woke in the night and knew instantly that someone was in his bedchamber. His breathing never changed, so as not to alert the intruder, but he was fully cognizant and ready to spring into action at the slightest provocation. He was startled upright when he suddenly heard Megan's soft voice.

"I must see if he understands."

"Megan?" Bracken spoke and reached for his robe before moving from the bed.

"I'm sure he'll change his mind."

Bracken heard the words but did not understand. He lit a torch and placed it in a sconce on the wall before turning and finding Megan in a chair by the cold hearth. Bracken could hardly believe his eyes as she sat dressed in a long, heavy night garment. Not looking at him, she still continued to speak. Bracken caught the words as he came nearer.

"I will do my best to make him understand."

"Megan," Bracken said gently. "You may

not be in my room."

"I must find Bracken," she said.

"I'm right here."

Megan shook her head, and it was then that he realized she was asleep. With Arik on guard, the situation at home was so well in hand that Bracken had completely forgotten about the problem.

"Megan, wake up and go back to your room."

"Not until I find Bracken and make him understand."

"Understand what?"

"That I have always looked this way. I have at times been a glutton, but not now, not for many years. I have always looked heavy."

"You look fine."

"My mother is sure to be right; she always is. Bracken will not want a fat wife."

"Bracken does not think you're fat."

It was spoken with such authority that Megan paused. Bracken knew that if he touched her she would awaken, but maybe now was the time to clear this up.

Of course, Bracken now reminded himself. *She never remembers anything in the morning.*

For some reason the thought of waking her bothered Bracken. He remembered so clearly the night he'd touched her and woken her in the great hall at Hawkings Crest. She had seemed vulnerable and shaken, and Bracken hoped it would never happen again. There must be another way. In just a moment, Bracken had a plan.

Megan was talking again, but Bracken ignored her and went to open the door. Lyndon, who had been sleeping in a small chamber to the side of Bracken's room, now heard the noise and joined him. He watched in fascination at what Bracken did next.

The young earl went behind Megan's chair and carefully lifted the back legs from the floor. Why Megan was sitting down, he wasn't certain, but as he expected, the action unsettled her, and she stood. Bracken then moved the chair against her and she took a step forward. It took only a minute for her to notice the open door. Bracken followed her far enough down the hall to see that a maid, having only just discovered her absence, had now come out of Megan's room.

"Come, my lady," Bracken heard the girl say. He stood still until they disappeared behind the closed portal and then turned back to his room. Lyndon stared at him in the dark, thinking how well he'd handled the situation.

"Would you like me to stand guard at her door?"

"Thank you, Lyndon, but I think the maid will take care of things now."

The men stood silently for a moment.

"It is amazing that she can sleep like that," Lyndon commented with wonder in his voice.

"Do you think I should have woken her?" Bracken was suddenly not sure.

"No, you did exactly right. I have never known a woman with such courage and pluck who also needed to be handled so delicately."

"Nor have I," Bracken added.

A moment later they parted, each to try to finish the night's rest in his own bed.

Megan and Louisa broke the fast together, both having slept a little late.

"I haven't stayed in bed that long in years," Louisa admitted.

"Did you not sleep well?"

"Not really," Louisa told her and then fell silent. Megan became alert.

"What is it, Aunt Louisa? Is your chamber uncomfortable?"

"My chamber is fine," she assured the younger woman.

"Then something is bothering you," Megan stated.

Louisa only looked at her, and after a moment Megan dropped her eyes. "I think I would have walked here from Hawkings Crest, as I did before, rather than cause you and Bracken such pain over this household."

"I had no idea, Megan." Louisa's voice was just over a whisper.

Megan smiled ruefully. "It's funny sometimes."

"What is?"

"Me," Megan admitted. "I will stand toe-to-toe with Bracken, even if I'm terrified, but it's not often that I will confront Mother."

"Why do you suppose that is?" Louisa asked. Until that very moment Megan did not know; suddenly it was so clear.

"Because Mother will never back down." Megan's voice showed surprise at her discovery. "She would rather fight around the clock than admit defeat. Bracken does not treat me so. He is in many ways a more mature person than my mother."

It seemed an odd thing for a daughter to say, but Louisa could see it was true.

"You seem to have accepted the situation, Megan."

"I guess I have. I've never lived here for very long; indeed, I have not considered this place to be my own for many years, so I see no reason in trying to alter things.

"And of course now I'm going to wed Bracken, so truly, any home I've known here will be a thing of the past. Aside from all of that, God has shown me that He will never leave me, no matter where I dwell."

Louisa reached for Megan's hand. "I so admire your faith, Megan."

"It is nothing unusual, Aunt Louisa. I would be glad to tell you of it."

"I would like to hear."

Megan smiled, her heart speeding up with anticipation and delight as she tried to think of a place where they would be certain to have privacy. She thought the chapel might be best, but before she could suggest such a thing, Annora entered the room. That she was upset was obvious from across the floor.

"Megan." Annora's voice was penetrating.

Thinking her mother would come closer, Megan stood, but she stayed at a far range.

"I would have an audience with you."

Megan apologized to Louisa with one glance and received a sympathetic look in reply. Megan had no more reached her mother when Annora turned abruptly and led her daughter down a passage and to the room her father used for a den. As with most of the Stone Lake castle, it was immaculate and beautifully furnished, but the coldness of the woman who ruled over it made the room seem chilled.

"You will tell me immediately what you did last night."

"Last night?" Megan asked, her brow drawn in puzzlement. "Before I went to bed?"

"No." Annora's voice was frigid. "I mean when the castle lay sleeping and your father and I *thought* you were asleep as well."

"I don't know what you mean," Megan tried to explain, but her mother's face became so red that she left off what she was saying.

"I know you were in his room, Megan — I know you visited Bracken's room last night."

"Mother, I didn't," Megan began, but got no further.

Annora's open hand seemed to come out of nowhere. She slapped Megan's cheek with such force that her head snapped back.

"Do not lie to me!" Annora was screeching now. "You're sure to be with child; we must move the wedding date."

270

"No, Mother, I swear to you."

Annora struck her again, and while her ears were still ringing, Megan moved, her hands feeling for the furniture as her eyes flooded with tears. The side of her face felt on fire, and for the first time Megan actually feared her mother. Her voice quivering, she spoke from behind a chair.

"I have done nothing wrong, Mother," Megan began, but Annora came after her.

"You lying little strumpet. My maid saw you. Do you think me a fool? And after all your father and I have done for you, you come home and disgrace us while we sleep."

Annora continued to pursue Megan, her intent very clear, but Megan's back was finally at the door. She could see that it was no use trying to reason with her enraged parent, so she dashed the back of her hand across her wet eyes and ran.

"Megan! Come back this instant!"

The small redhead ignored the outburst and continued to flee. Louisa was still in the great hall and took in every detail of Megan's pitiful face, but Megan didn't see her. All she could think of was escaping her mother, and she ran as if her life depended on it.

"Lyndon?" Louisa called to the young knight from across the inner bailey, just ten minutes later.

The handsome young man approached her with a smile on his face that abruptly disappeared when he neared. Louisa's eyes were red and puffy, and the strength in the hand that grasped his arm felt desperate.

"I must find Bracken," she whispered.

"This way," Lyndon said shortly.

A moment later Louisa stood before Bracken, who had been inside one of the turrets mending a halter. The moment she saw him, she began to tremble.

"Bracken, please find Megan. Something awful has happened. Annora was angry, and then Megan ran from the great hall. Oh, please." She could say no more, but nothing more was needed.

Bracken left her in Lyndon's care and began to step away.

"The chapel, Bracken," Lyndon spoke before his lord was out of earshot. "I saw her going toward the chapel. Try there."

The tears had finally stopped, but the trembling remained. Megan knew her mother would never seek her out in the chapel, but the shock and hurt were slow in receding.

"Please help me, Father God," she whispered in the quiet of the chapel. "Please help me to be calm, and please don't let her find me. I have to find a way to explain. If Bracken had been there he could have told her, but if I go and look for him, she's sure to find me."

The tears were starting again, so Megan stopped and tried to calm herself. She wasn't very successful but stayed on her knees until she heard the door open. She bolted into the shadows, but she knew that whoever had entered had heard her gasping sobs.

The footsteps on the cobbled floor halfway up the center aisle were unnerving, but Megan tried not to breathe. She nearly collapsed with relief when Bracken said, "Megan, are you here?"

Megan took a huge breath but stayed in the shadows.

"Is my mother with you?"

"No, it's just I."

Still wary, she emerged from the shadows but did not approach. Bracken came forward as soon as he spotted her and stopped just a foot before her. It was on his lips to make light of the tears, even chide her for overreacting to whatever had occurred, but just enough light from the window streamed onto Megan's face to stop the words in his throat.

With her hands clenched together in front of her, Megan stood still, her eyes on Bracken's face. She remained utterly silent as two of his long fingers came out to rest ever so gently on the underside of her jaw. Very carefully he turned her bruised cheek full into the light from the stained-glass window. The entire cheek was very red and puffy except for a raised cut and a bruise that was forming on the cheekbone.

Megan could not see his face then, or she would have witnessed the movement of his beard, his own jaw bunching, as he regarded Annora's handiwork. He tried to control his emotions before he spoke, but he couldn't quite manage.

"Who did this to you?" he said, knowing already.

Bracken had dropped his hand, but Megan saw it clench at his side. Even if she'd been blind, there was no mistaking the anger in his voice.

"My mother," Megan said, and more tears came. "Please talk to her Bracken, please tell her I didn't visit your room last night."

Bracken's eyes slid momentarily shut. Agony ripped through him. He should have awakened her. When he spoke, his voice was deep with regret.

"You were in my room last night, Megan," he began, and watched her eyes go wide with shock. "But you were sound asleep."

"Oh, no," Megan sobbed. "I never even thought. I mean, it's usually disruptive to me when I visit here, but I just didn't think. And the maid is new. I never thought to warn her."

The tears that had been trickling now came in a torrent as Bracken wrapped his arms around her. Megan sobbed into his shirt for several minutes.

Bracken's hand was gentle beyond description as it smoothed her hair, but his heart was a mass of enraged determination. When Megan calmed some, Bracken's hands went to her upper arms and he held her out in front of him.

"I'm taking you away from here."

Megan blinked at him. Her eyes felt gritty, as though someone had rubbed sand into them.

"Where are we going?"

"Back to Hawkings Crest."

"What will my parents say?"

"It doesn't matter. I won't allow you to stay here a day longer."

Megan opened her mouth to speak but realized she had no words. No one had ever shown her the kind of caring Bracken was now demonstrating. Her mother's word was law, and everyone, including her father, accepted her mother's actions, reprehensible as they were.

Suddenly lighthearted with emotion, she agreed to Bracken's plan with just the smallest nod of her head. A moment later they were moving back outside and toward the castle, where Bracken would leave Megan in Louisa's room and in her keeping until they could be away.

Twenty-One

Bracken found Lord Vincent in his bed-chamber. At any other time Bracken would not have disturbed him in such a place, but at the moment the older man could have been bathing and Bracken would have demanded a hearing.

"We are leaving," he said without preamble.

Vincent nodded. "I have just been informed of Annora's behavior. She did not handle things well; I understand how you must feel."

"Megan will not be back."

It wasn't until that very moment that something in Bracken's tone arrested Vincent's attention. He rose from his place by the window and approached his house-guest. He gazed at the younger man for long moments before deciding he did not like what he saw — repugnance and fury.

"What do you mean she will not be back?" Vincent finally demanded.

"I mean that I'm taking Megan from Stone Lake within the hour, and she will not return here again."

"Her dress is —"

Bracken cut the older man off with a downward slash of his hand.

"I care not for her dress. It is her safety I am thinking of — something she can not find in this castle."

"That is ridiculous! What of the wedding?"

"The wedding will be at Hawkings Crest."

Vincent was now angry himself. "This is my daughter you speak of. You will not tell me —" He stopped on Bracken's short bark of mirthless laughter.

"I will tell you *many* things," Bracken told him ruthlessly. "We speak of Megan not as your daughter but as my betrothed by Henry's order. At one time you told me you would never countenance abuse toward Megan, but the shrew to whom you are married has become violent, and you do nothing. I will remove Megan from her claws before I become violent myself. Dress fittings or meetings of any kind will take place at Hawkings Crest, where I can keep an eye on the woman you seem incapable of controlling."

As far as Bracken was concerned, the meeting was finished, but Vincent's anger now spilled over. His face boiling with rage, Vincent let Bracken get as far as the door before he threw what he believed would be a lethal barb.

"And what of the fact that Megan was spotted coming from your room last night?"

"Aye," Bracken said from the door, his voice still angry but now controlled. "She was there as you say. Asleep on her feet."

Bracken had been the one to throw the final barb, and when the door slammed, Vincent sank into a chair. His dear Megan, so innocent of Annora's charge, haunted his mind. Annora would never see reason. Bracken had been correct, he was incapable of controlling his wife. Vincent suddenly felt old beyond his years.

As when they had journeyed from Hawkings Crest, Bracken's party once again camped in the woods. Stopping well before dark, Bracken was able to take a careful assessment of how his aunt and betrothed were faring.

Louisa looked tired, but her spirits were high. He knew for a fact that she was tremendously relieved to be leaving Annora and the situation at Stone Lake. As they ate, Bracken studied Megan's face, her eyes specifically. He found that she did not seem overly tired, but neither did she appear to be at peace. Louisa ate with them, causing Bracken to hold his comments, but when the older woman rose to see to a private matter, Bracken spoke.

"How fare you, Megan?"

"I'm all right," she told him humbly.

Bracken was not convinced. "Has your mother long made it a habit of striking you?"

Megan nodded. "For as long as I can remember."

"And what would your father do?"

"Remove me, much as you have done."

"But there were no repercussions for your mother? He never tried to change her?"

"No," Megan said with some surprise. "I don't think such a thing ever occurred to him."

They fell silent for a moment, and then Megan asked the question that had been on her heart since they left the inner bailey at Stone Lake.

"My father did not come to bid us goodbye. Did you have words?"

"Yes. I told him I was taking you, and you would not be back."

Megan stared at him. "What of the wedding?"

"It will take place at Hawkings Crest."

Megan now stared into the gathered dusk. Bracken heard her sigh before she softly asked, "What if my parents do not come to the wedding?"

Bracken gently captured her jaw with his hand and spoke after he'd urged her eyes to meet his own.

"I will still make you my wife, and in so doing, I will have the authority to never again allow your mother, or anyone else, to harm you." He steeled himself to hear her protest, but she acquiesced with a small move of her head. Bracken let his hand drop and would have reached for Megan's small one as it lay in her lap, but Louisa was returning.

"I am glad you're still sitting here, Bracken," Louisa spoke with pleasure as she gracefully sank onto the rich counterpane that had been laid out on the forest floor. "I want to ask you a question. What is to be done about Megan's dress?"

"Her dress?" Bracken frowned at his aunt and then turned his attention to Megan's clothing. She looked fine to him in a gown of dark green with rust-colored trim. Indeed, he found her beautiful.

"Yes, Bracken," Louisa continued patiently. "Her wedding dress."

"Oh." It was clearly the last thing on Bracken's mind, and Louisa had to hide a smile. It was on her tongue to jump in with several suggestions, but she sat patiently and let Bracken think. He did not disappoint her.

"Let us give Lady Annora a few weeks to contact Megan and possibly make reparations. If that doesn't happen, then go to the village and do whatever it takes to see that she is properly outfitted."

"As you wish," Louisa stated, feeling well pleased.

Bracken stood then, his eyes sweeping back to Megan's enchanting face, framed by an abundance of dark red curls, before once again resting on Louisa. "Spare no expense," he told his aunt as he moved off toward his men.

Two weeks passed without word from Megan's mother or father. Megan was not surprised that her mother had not been in touch, but her father's lack of communication cut deeply. He had never been a man to lavish great attention upon her, but up until now, Megan had always felt that he cared. Now she was beginning to wonder.

It was only just becoming clear to her that he had never once taken her side, at least not strongly enough to deal with Annora or suggest repercussions as Bracken had mentioned. The thought weighed on Megan's heart. She spent much time in prayer over it, but there were times when she would take her eyes from God's sovereignty and the situation would get her down.

It was at such a time that Bracken spoke with Louisa concerning Megan's dress. The older woman immediately approached Megan, who was a little shocked and very pleased that he had actually remembered. The women decided to leave for the village directly after the noon meal.

The day was warm but not miserable, and Arik, along with a few other men, went with the ladies. Protection was not really needed for the village, but the guard gave Bracken peace of mind as he stood in the inner bailey and watched them ride away.

The trip was fairly routine for Louisa, but Megan, so new to the area, considered it an adventure. She had never been into the town near Hawkings Crest and was more than a little curious. Megan found that it was not a long ride, 20 minutes or less, and the first thing she spotted was a church. It was a simple, squarely built structure, but since not every village sported a place of worship, it was a pleasure for Megan to see. She wondered if they would have time to visit and possibly speak with the local priest.

She was very aware of the attention she and Louisa produced as they rode in on Bracken's finest horses and in clothing of luxurious fabric rich with color. Her face, never haughty, was serene, and her smile melted the hearts of several children and a few old women. They dismounted before a pub, the men assisting them.

"We shall meet you back here in an hour," Louisa informed them, not wanting to be dogged by these men while she shopped.

"Very well, my lady," the shortest of the men answered, but Arik, as they soon learned, took no such notice. He walked slowly, some 20 odd paces behind Megan, but with the clear intention of not letting her out of his sight. Megan didn't really care. Indeed, the thought of shopping had so buoyed her mood that she didn't mind at all.

"I think in here, Meg," Louisa said just ten yards down the street.

The women entered a small shop full of

various dry goods. It was clean and smelled of fresh leather, but Megan could see at a glance that it held nothing suitable. She was surprised when Louisa did not immediately turn to go but instead walked rather noisily through the store, talking loudly to Megan, touching fabrics and commenting on every one.

Megan was still staring at Louisa as if she'd taken leave of her senses when a woman appeared at the rear. Where she had come from Megan was not exactly sure, but when she saw Louisa she smiled a gape-toothed smile and motioned her over with one long, crooked finger.

Louisa followed, and Megan, out of sheer curiosity, was right behind her. They moved behind a high shelf and through a doorway, and Megan immediately saw that this was the woman's living quarters. The bed, washbasin, and kitchen table were all set very close together in the same room. There was also a door, short and not overly wide, and closed tightly. The old woman stopped before it and drew forth a key. When it was unlocked, she pushed the door wide. She stepped inside, Louisa at her heels and Megan just behind.

"New," she proclaimed as she fingered an especially fine bolt. "Just in, it is.

Bought from Elias the peddler."

Stacked on shelves and hanging from pegs in every conceivable nook and cranny, rich accouterments of every type littered the room, but Megan saw none of them. She could not tear her eyes from the fabric in the woman's gnarled hands.

"Megan, what is it?" Louisa asked, having just seen her look.

"The fabric. My mother had chosen this and one other. She preferred the other and that was to be my dress, but this one," she paused, "this was my choice."

Louisa smiled, although Megan still did not notice.

"We'll take it," the older woman spoke softly. The proprietress chuckled softly as she named an exorbitant price.

"That," Louisa stated calmly, "is outrageous." Whereupon she started to dicker with the woman in a way that finally gained Megan's attention. She listened to Louisa in awe and began to wonder if she knew Bracken's aunt at all. She barely gave an inch, and when the bartering session was over, Louisa took the fabric in triumph. It had cost the moon, but she was well pleased. Other notions were purchased, although not haggled over, and within 30 minutes Megan and Louisa were back on the street. Arik was standing nearby, as Megan knew he would be, and fell into step behind them once again.

"Louisa, I've never seen you like that."

Louisa laughed at herself. "I can't begin to tell you how much I enjoy it." She lifted the plainly wrapped package. "And I think you'll agree that it was worth it."

Megan laughed in return, but a moment later Louisa said soberly, "Megan, I'm so sorry your mother sold your dress fabric."

"Thank you, Aunt Louisa, but she didn't want that one for me. I don't know why she bought two and gave me a choice; she had already made up her mind."

"And what of the other fabric? Will you end up with two wedding dresses?"

"No, I'm sure not." Megan shook her head in resignation. "If my mother comes to the wedding, she will no doubt be wearing a dress made from the other cloth."

"But wasn't the color fit for a wedding dress? Surely she will not shame the bride."

"No, there will be no shame. This fabric is most fitting. The other was a light blue velvet."

"Oh, Megan," Louisa said with pleasure. "This cream satin will be so much more beautiful on you. I hope you're pleased."

Megan hugged the other woman. The setting was not the best, but she felt so full of joy that she could think of no other way to express it.

Her joy might have been dimmed somewhat had she looked up to a second-story window above the tavern and seen the woman standing above.

"What are you looking at?" The question came from the man who was lying on the large bed in the sparsely furnished room.

"My sister," the woman at the window answered.

This brought the man from the bed to look out. After a moment, he offered his estimation.

"She's not the beauty you are."

Marigold smiled, her eyes still on Megan. "Few women are."

Roland Kirkpatrick, third son of Lord Kirkpatrick, smiled in return. She was right, of course, but he would never tell her so. She was already so vain she believed herself too good for him. Marigold had never let him touch her, and she wouldn't today, but he didn't care. He told himself that just to be near her was enough.

Marigold had been blackmailing him for weeks. She had found out just days after the incident that he had been behind the killing of her father's men and the stealing of his horses. He had believed them to be carrying gold. Roland cared not one wit if Vincent knew of his actions, but the knowledge had given Marigold a certain form of power, and as long as she kept coming to him for favors — money and whatever small jobs her scheming mind could conjure up to keep her from soiling her own hands — he was content to let her believe she had him at her mercy.

He watched now as she let the curtain fall back over the glass. He knew she was about to leave, so he decided to beat her to the punch.

"I've got to be going," Roland said smoothly, and was well satisfied with the momentary look of surprise in her eyes. "I'll see you later."

"Yes." Just that swiftly, Marigold was back in control. "Who knows when we may need to do business again."

Roland smiled at her, his look amused, but he didn't answer. He would have been pleased to know that she stood thinking about him for a long time afterward.

"Has it been terribly upsetting to you, Megan, that you left your home in such a way?" Louisa wondered that she hadn't asked before, but now the time seemed right. Tired but successful, they were riding home, and because the men were several paces off, Louisa felt free to ask.

"It is hard, Aunt Louisa, but not impossible. At least it hasn't been."

"What do you mean?"

"I mean that the kinder Bracken is to me, the more I see a lack in my family. I had no idea anyone could care like that. It's just another way the Lord is taking care of me."

Suddenly Megan's family was forgotten. "You refer to the Lord so often, Megan. Don't you think He cares for all?" Louisa asked.

"Yes," Megan answered carefully, "but not all embrace Him as I have chosen to do."

A glance told Megan that Louisa had no idea what she spoke of.

"I would venture a guess that most everyone in England believes in God. Would you say that's true?"

"Yes," Louisa agreed readily.

"But I would also guess that not even a fraction of that many believe in His Son, the Lord Jesus Christ. That's where the separation comes. I have confessed to God that I am a sinner and that I need a Savior. People need more than just a belief in God or a Sovereign Ruler. They also must believe in His Son and His lifechanging work on the cross."

"But I believe Jesus died on the cross," Louisa reasoned.

"Yes, Louisa, but do you believe He died to save you from your sins?"

Louisa had no answer to this, and Megan's voice became very tender.

"There is nothing magical here, Louisa. It is a simple act of faith, given by God, to trust in His Son's saving power. In such a state, life here on earth is abundant, and afterward there is the promise of life eternal with Him."

"So you do not believe that all people go to heaven?"

"No, I don't," Megan said, her voice still very kind.

She debated saying more, but the castle was now in view. Megan prayed for an opening, but Louisa was ready, at least for the time, to ponder their conversation on her own.

"I will think on all you've said, Megan."

"I'm glad, Louisa. And if at any point, even in the middle of the night, I can be of help to you, please come to me."

"I will, Megan. Thank you."

The remainder of the ride was made in silence as both women thought and prayed. However, Louisa's prayer was different. For the first time she wondered, since she didn't believe as Megan did, if God actually heard her.

Twenty-Two

"You are a thief and a liar," Megan stated calmly.

"I have been steward here for over 40 years!"

Megan snorted with unladylike contempt. "Is that what you call what you do — acting as steward? As far as I can see, you rob your lord blind and grow fat at his expense."

The little man's face turned puce. Megan knew she had been merciless, but there was simply no getting through to this man.

"I will see Lord Bracken over this," he threatened when he could finally speak.

"Don't bother," Megan told him. "Just pack your things and get out."

Again the man looked as if he were on the verge of collapse.

"Lord Bracken will listen to me."

"He might," Megan's tone was maddeningly moderate, "but you will find I am patient. It may take time, but I will prove your true worth." Megan hesitated as her spirit of fair play came to the fore.

"It's not as if you haven't been warned, Barton. We have talked of this many times. My check on the books just this morning showed more entries which I cannot trace."

"You have been in the books again?" He was clearly outraged. "You had no right!"

"I have every right!" Megan shot back, having taken all she was going to. "And I am also within my rights to repeat myself — pack your bags and leave Hawkings Crest."

Barton trembled with anger, but he was wise enough to see his own defeat. With a head held high in what he would have called righteous indignation, Barton swept from the room. Megan felt no sense of elation or satisfaction. With all of Barton's knowledge of the castle, it would have been wonderful to have him stay, but Megan would never countenance such deceit.

Believing she had done what was necessary, Megan tried to put the incident behind her and move on to another task. She was halfway up the stairs when she remembered Bracken. The thought of him caused her to tuck her lip beneath her teeth. What in the world was he going to say?

"She did *what?*"

"Now, Bracken," Lyndon tried to sound reasonable.

"Yes, Bracken," Louisa put in. "You did say you would listen to her more."

"I can't believe this." Bracken spoke as if he hadn't heard either one. "All this time I think things are going smoothly, and now she does this. Why did she not talk to me?"

"I don't know, Bracken, but she has been unhappy about Barton for many weeks."

"In truth, Bracken," Lyndon added, "she did come to you, just last week, but you put her off."

Bracken opened his mouth and shut it. This was true. Megan had come to him at the archery butts when he was working with Kent. Bracken had sent her away without ever getting back to her. Nevertheless, he did not care for the way she'd handled this.

"She should have talked to me."

"Be that as it may, Bracken, it won't do any good searching her out and blasting her with your temper." Louisa's voice was almost angry, and Bracken turned to look at her. He was slightly amused by her fierce frown and thought how often Louisa had championed Megan since she'd come to live at Hawkings Crest.

"Is that what I do? Blast her with my temper?" He was almost laughing now. Louisa was not.

"You know you do, and if it happens this time, I won't speak to you until the wedding."

All Bracken's amusement fled. "Lou, what is really bothering you?"

Tears welled in the woman's eyes. "She told me that no one has ever shown her the kindness you have. I know you're upset, but I can't stand the thought that you'll hurt her when she's coming to trust and need you so."

The words were very sobering to Bracken, and he tenderly laid a hand on his aunt's shoulder. At the moment he did want to search Megan out and make himself heard, but Louisa was right; he would only frighten and upset her. Yet, every time he thought of Megan going on her own and dismissing Barton, his anger threatened to consume him.

"I will do my best not to fight with Megan, Louisa, but I will talk with her about this."

Louisa could only nod.

"Have you seen her?" Bracken asked of Lyndon.

"Actually I have. I believe she was headed toward the tower."

Bracken nodded, thanked them, and moved toward the door of the war room. Louisa and Lyndon shared a glance. They both hoped that the harmony they had known in the past weeks was not about to be destroyed.

Megan had been on a mission of counting bedrooms, but had long since given up. She'd had no idea how vast Hawkings Crest really was. *Why,* *all of England could come for the wedding,* Megan thought, *and we could make comfortable each and every one.*

She was in the tower salon now, checking on something Helga had told her about and feeling well satisfied that there would be room for all guests.

Megan walked the edge of the carpet until she spotted the trouble: It seemed that the hem was fraying. Kneeling at the edge of the rug that lay before the fireplace, Megan saw that Helga's observation was correct. She would have to order it trimmed. So intent was Megan on her task that she never even heard Bracken enter or noticed as he stood quietly against one wall watching her. She stood, ready to walk directly in front of him, when he spoke.

"Going somewhere, Megan?"

Megan started violently and then grew angry. Her arms akimbo, she faced him squarely.

"*Bracken!* Don't you ever do that again. I never heard a thing."

Bracken only looked at her and asked himself for the tenth time what he was going to do. He had told Brice many weeks ago that he did not want just a pretty face to decorate his castle, but how far was he willing to let her go?

"What brings you to the tower?" he asked at last.

Megan relaxed upon hearing his calm tone. "I was trying to ascertain whether or not we had enough bedrooms for the wedding guests." She now smiled in self-mockery. "I now see that I have wasted my time."

Bracken's own eyes took in the room. Large and airy, it was but one of many just like it, and that did not include the many bedrooms. Megan was right — the castle was a mammoth dwelling.

"I understand our keep is now short a steward."

Bracken was not looking at her or even turned in her direction. The statement had come out so abruptly that Megan was taken completely unaware. She tilted her head slightly to glance at his handsome, bearded profile, but he was still inspecting the room.

"Yes," Megan said.

Bracken then turned to look at her. "That is all? Yes? No explanation?"

"I felt I had no choice," Megan said shortly.

"You could have consulted me."

"You would not listen. I assumed you no longer cared."

"It was never my intent to make light of the situation, Megan; Barton has been with my family for years."

"I am heartily sick to death of hearing that!" Megan burst out so vehemently that it was Bracken's turn to be startled.

"It doesn't seem to make any difference to you that he was *stealing*. Do you hear me, Bracken, he was *stealing* from you! I spoke with him; I gave him a chance; but even knowing that I could read and monitor his actions changed nothing. I was still finding entries that could be nothing short of theft."

They stood, eyes locked, Megan now red in the face and Bracken's face looking as though it was made of stone.

"I still say it wasn't your place."

"You're right!" Megan shot back at him. "It was yours."

She watched his eyes grow hard, and the fight drained out of her. When she continued, her voice was soft.

"If I've learned anything about you while living here, Bracken, it's that you're no fool. This is why I am confused. Only a fool would allow a man to stay in the name of sentiment when that man was stealing from him. I did this for you. I did this for Hawkings Crest. It would seem I've done wrong."

Megan turned for the door, but Bracken's voice stopped her.

"Don't go."

Megan stopped but did not turn.

"Look at me, Megan."

She shook her head no. Tears had come to her eyes, tears she hated herself for. She did not want him to see them, but she heard him move and knew that in a moment he would stand before her. When he did stop, Megan turned her face away in an attempt to hide her eyes.

Bracken did not turn her face to his, but he could clearly see the tear that slid down her cheek. He could also see that she was trying to hold others back.

"Mayhap I am thickheaded," Bracken said reflectively. "You might need to ask me more than once and not give up so easily. Just as you have learned about me, I have also done some learning of my own, and I would say you are not a quitter."

"No, I'm not," Megan agreed, and then realized that quit was exactly what she'd done.

"But you did not pursue the matter with me, and now I wish you had."

Megan nodded; he was quite correct. She chanced a look at him.

"Next time I'll be a shrew."

Bracken took on a look of mock horror. "You mean there's more?"

Megan tried not to smile, but failed. "I'm sure I'll think of something."

Bracken smiled in return, and his voice turned thoughtful. "Just three weeks now, and you will be mistress of this keep."

Megan nodded, feeling more at peace with the prospect than ever before. "Does that have you worried?"

"No," he told her. "I think you will do well."

There wasn't anything that could have given Megan as much pleasure. She smiled at him, and Bracken thought, not for the first time, that they should talk more. They were both so busy and ofttimes going in opposite directions, but whenever they had a chance to speak, he could tell that Megan became a little more comfortable with him.

At that point they walked down to the great hall together. As they moved it came to Bracken without warning: He was swiftly coming to prefer Megan's company over anyone else's. The thought so surprised him that when Megan said she had to see Helga, he barely heard her. It was a thought he pondered on for the remainder of the day.

Stephen rode toward Hawkings Crest in easy companionship with his cousins, Derek and Richard. Brice would bring their mother to the wedding, as well as escort everyone but Danella, whose baby was very young. Stephen had found himself with a need to be in London and so arranged to ride to Hawkings Crest from there with Louisa's sons.

Having not seen each other for weeks, they talked of many things, but the subject of Bracken's betrothed was not raised until they were just a few miles from the castle.

"So, Stephen," Richard asked. "What can you tell us of Megan?"

"Did your mother not write to you?" he questioned evasively, while trying to keep the smile from his face.

"Yes," Derek told him. "She dictated a letter, but other than the red hair, she didn't really describe her at all. What is she like?"

"Maybe your mother was trying to be kind."

The other men were silent for a moment, looking first at each other and then at Stephen.

"Does she have red hair?" Richard, the younger of the two brothers, wished to know.

"Yes, but it's as bright as a fresh carrot and frizzy around her head like a bird's nest." Stephen's tone was cheerless.

Both of the other men now had looks of pity on their faces, and Bracken's brother had to bite the inside of his cheek to keep from shouting with laughter.

"But she's very sweet," Derek now volunteered. "Mother said as much."

"Yes, she is sweet, and as soon as you get past her face and figure you'll probably like her immensely."

"As bad as all that?"

"I'm afraid so," Stephen told them with a sigh that would have worked on any stage.

"What of Bracken? Is he angry over the arrangement?"

"No. I would say he's resigned himself."

Stephen had to change the subject then, or he would have given himself away. As they finally rode through the gates of Hawkings Crest, he had to restrain himself from rubbing his hands together with anticipation.

Twenty-Three

Megan stood over a long, low table in the kitchen and bent her sharp mind as to why the sauce she was working on still tasted bitter. There were not many people in the room at the moment, and Megan's attention was on her work, so it was more of an irritant than anything else when she felt a slight tug on her hair. She glanced down to the side to see if one of the children had come in, but when that place was empty she went back to tasting.

When it happened again, Megan's head came up and her brow lowered. She had not imagined it. She turned slowly at first and then more swiftly when she spotted the man behind her.

"Stephen!" Megan tried to look stern.

"Hello, Meg." Stephen's grin was devilish. "You looked in need of a distraction, so I am here."

"A nuisance is more like it." Megan's eyes sparkled back at him for just an instant.

Her words did not dim his smile in the

least, but it became very tender when Megan continued to watch him. Stephen witnessed the change in her.

"I take it your family is here?" Megan asked very softly and hesitantly.

"No." He shook his head gently.

Megan's eyes widened.

"I came in with Derek and Richard."

"Louisa's sons?"

"Yes."

"Does she know?"

"She's with them now. Come, I'm sure they want to meet you."

All hesitancy was gone as she was swiftly flooded with relief. Megan took the arm Stephen offered, and as they walked toward the great hall she began to question him about his recent travels. She noticed that he seemed inordinately pleased about something, but she shrugged it off, supposing he was glad to be back at Hawkings Crest.

"It's so good to see you both," Louisa beamed at her sons. They were in Louisa's bedchamber, and after she'd hugged them both twice, they settled themselves by the windows.

"How are things in London?"

"Fine," Derek answered her. "Are you missing it?"

"Yes," Louisa admitted. "Although I'm having a great time with Bracken and Megan."

A look suddenly passed over the faces of both men and Louisa became instantly alert. "That's an odd look I'm getting," she commented, attempting to keep her voice light.

Richard shrugged. "Stephen told us of Megan. He said that she was very sweet, just as you had mentioned in your letter, but as for the other," Richard hesitated uncomfortably, "I guess Bracken has rather resigned himself."

Louisa studied her son's face as her mind ran with every possibility. To what could he be referring? She was on the verge of asking when she remembered that they had ridden out with Stephen. Never one to stand in the way of a harmless prank, Louisa forced a giggle back down her throat, knowing a laugh right then would give the whole thing away. She then wondered just how bad Stephen had made Megan out to be.

"Where are my manners?" Louisa said suddenly and with the intent to distract. "You must be hungry. Come below."

They continued to speak companionably as they descended the large staircase, the men completely innocent of Stephen's scheme and Louisa nearly licking her lips in expectation.

"And who is going to order the wheat?"
"Barton did that as well?"
"Yes," Bracken told her shortly. Whereupon Megan bit her lip and stared at her intended.

Lord and lady were standing in the great hall. Bracken's hands were clasped behind his back, and he was slightly bent at the waist, so that he nearly leaned over Megan as he proceeded to quietly destroy her day.

"My mother's cook sees to that," Megan finally commented, and Bracken only continued to spear her with his eyes. She had been under the impression that the matter concerning Barton was settled, but she had been wrong. Clearly Bracken had not fully forgiven her.

"I'm sorry, Bracken," she said when he refused to speak.

"Sorry doesn't see to the feeding of this keep."

Megan looked away from him then. Stephen was standing nearby, but Megan couldn't meet his eyes.

"What would you like me to do?" Megan

asked after a moment, her eyes on the floor.

"First of all, don't act so innocent; it doesn't work on me."

Megan's gaze shot upward, her mouth opening in surprise and hurt.

"Secondly," Bracken went on, "you can find us another steward. Until such a time, you will have to oversee the duties — *all* of them."

The young lord would have gone on then, but Arik entered and approached. Upon Bracken's order he had been to the village, and Bracken, seeing that he was now ready to report, turned to him. Megan saw her chance for escape and took it.

Bracken had turned to Arik, and after just a minute he happened to glance back at Megan. He took a second look when he found her gone. He spun in a fast circle as his eyes took in the whole of the great room, but other than Louisa, Derek, and Richard coming down the stairs, nothing had changed. Helga was by the other hearth, women were working at the tables, someone was shooing one of the dogs outside, and in the midst of it Megan had quite literally vanished.

He looked to Stephen, but his brother would only grin at him without remorse.

Bracken's scowl was fierce, but he eventually looked back to Arik who had waited patiently to finish the report on his findings in the village.

Moments later they were joined by Louisa and her sons. Arik took his leave, and Bracken, after tamping down his irritation with the small redhead who lived in his castle, greeted his cousins warmly.

"Come to the war room, and we'll talk there. I wish to hear of your journey."

"I'll go and order some food," Louisa put in as the men moved forward in a group. Had anyone been looking, they might have noticed the tense line around Stephen's mouth, but he came behind his brother and cousins, and all missed it.

The men were halfway across the floor of the war room when Bracken stopped dead in his tracks. Sitting under a window on the far wall, the account book opened in her lap, was Megan.

"I was not finished talking with you," Bracken spouted without preamble, his family forgotten.

"Well, I was done listening," Megan exclaimed before she thought.

"You," Bracken said, pointing a finger at her, "are the most infuriating woman on the face of the earth."

"And you, sir," Megan shot back, "are rude beyond compare."

"*Rude?*" Bracken was clearly confused. "What are you talking about?"

"I'm talking about letting me believe that the incident with Barton was behind us and then searching me out to throw it up in my face."

"His jobs are not being done." Bracken's voice told her that this reason excused his manners.

"Then you should have spoken to me."

"I did." Bracken's hands were now outstretched in frustration.

"You did not. You waited until you were snorting like a wounded bull and then sought me out to take me apart piece by piece." Tears were evident in Megan's voice now, and Bracken stood quietly. Neither was aware of his audience.

Stephen, standing nearest the door, chanced a look at his cousins and could almost read their minds.

This is the one both Stephen and Mother said was sweet, but to whose looks Bracken has had to resign himself?

Stephen wanted to chortle with glee, but the timing was all wrong. While he stared at them, Derek and Richard looked to him. Both men told him with one glance that they would get even. Stephen's only reply was to grin unrepentantly.

"I did not mean to attack you," Bracken admitted quietly and started toward her. The men took their cue and departed.

"I was not aware of all Barton's responsibilities. It is not the same for the steward at Stone Lake Castle."

Suddenly Bracken took Megan's hand and pulled her to her feet. He stared down into her eyes for a full minute and for the hundredth time asked himself what he was going to do with her. But this time was different; this time he knew the answer. With the words, *just love her,* ringing in his heart, he said, "We will keep at this, Megan, until we get it right."

Megan stared at him in confusion, so he explained gently.

"I come to you too harshly, and you run whenever you are upset. Eventually I will learn to speak to you with kindness, and you will learn to stay still."

Megan calmed in the face of his tender logic. She liked the way he stayed with something. Never before would she have considered herself a quitter, but compared to Bracken, who came back repeatedly in an attempt to do better, she was just that.

"Come and meet my cousins." Bracken,

still holding her hand, turned for the door. Megan stood still and let their arms stretch to the limit.

"The men with Stephen . . . they are Louisa's sons?" She looked and sounded rather aghast.

"Yes," Bracken told her calmly. "I'm sure they wish to meet you."

"Not after what they just witnessed." Megan shook her head with shame. "They probably wish they could leave."

"No, Megan." Bracken was now amused, knowing how his young cousins would view her. "I assure you, they are waiting very close by."

Megan did not know how he could know such a thing, but with a gentle tug on her arm he urged her toward the door. She soon learned he was correct. Stephen, Louisa, and her sons were waiting not three yards away.

"Here they are," Louisa spoke with pleasure. "Come, Megan, and meet my sons."

Megan approached, her cheeks slightly pink, completely unaware of the charming picture she presented. The square-cut neckline of her gown, the nipped-in waist and full skirt, all trimmed in gold braid, only accentuated the loveliness of her figure. Her hair, pulled back in a length of the same braid, was like a mass of red fire around the creamy skin of her face and neck.

Bracken performed the introductions. "Megan, these are my cousins, Richard and Derek."

"Hello," Megan spoke softly and nodded to both men when they bowed politely before her. She had the impression that something was amiss, but didn't become sure of it until the men raised their heads and studied her with unusual intensity.

Megan's gaze flicked to Bracken, whose look was passive, and then to Stephen who looked a little too angelic for her taste. A glance at Louisa told her the older woman was fighting back laughter. Megan knew then that Stephen had been up to tricks.

She didn't mention the matter, but with one look told Stephen she was onto him. He grinned at her in the same unrepentant way, and a few moments of light conversation followed. Knowing they would meet again at the evening meal, all went their separate ways. Richard spoke when he was finally alone with his brother.

"I think some just retribution is due here."

"Toward Stephen? I quite agree. What do you have in mind?"

Richard was quiet for only an instant. "Today would be too soon, but definitely before the wedding. We'll need everyone's help, including Megan's."

Derek loved the look of mischief in his sibling's eye, and his smile widened as Richard mapped out a plan.

At the meal that evening Megan found that Louisa's sons were as kind and gentle as the woman herself, and there were stories and much laughter as they ate a meal of rich soup filled with onions, leeks, cabbage, beans, and pork. There was dark bread on the side and cheese as well. The sweet was cream with a combination of fruits from the trees at Hawkings Crest.

Megan noticed, however, in the midst of all the good food and fellowship, that Louisa did not seem to be having the best of times. This was a great surprise to the younger woman, for she had known how much Louisa was looking forward to Richard's and Derek's arrival. Megan didn't really know Bracken's cousins, but they seemed very kind. Maybe Louisa had quarreled with one of them.

Megan tried to put it from her mind, but at bedtime, when Louisa was still heavy on her heart, Megan decided to seek her out.

Her knock on Louisa's door was answered by Louisa's maid, Kimay, and when the servant told her mistress it was Megan, she was bade to enter. Megan was slightly surprised to find Derek in the room as well. Louisa's features were strained. Megan debated whether or not she should remain, but with one glance at Derek's confused face she came more fully into the room.

"I have no wish to intrude, Aunt Louisa, but is there something I can do?"

Both young people watched as Louisa stood and moved restlessly around the room. She nearly paced before stopping by the bed and facing them.

"Before dinner Derek informed me of a decision he's made, but I am confused."

Megan, desperate to help without intruding, turned to Bracken's cousin. His face was not shuttered, so Megan spoke gently.

"Can you tell me, Derek?"

He nodded. "I have decided to give my life to God — Jesus Christ, actually."

Megan's heart leapt, but she knew that now was not the time to react with outward joy. She turned back to Louisa.

"What is the problem?"

"He says he's giving himself to God. Don't we all belong to God, Megan? What in the world could he mean?" Louisa was near to tears, and Megan did some fast thinking. After just a moment she began to understand. It was one thing for Louisa to have her future niece dedicated to Christ, but when it was her son and she did not understand or share the belief, it somehow said to her that she had failed as a parent.

"I believe Derek feels much as I do, Louisa. I knew a void within my heart, and I understood that Jesus Christ alone could fill that void. A surrendering of oneself to Christ doesn't lessen a person in any way or make it so they have less to give. Indeed, it gives one a greater life to offer.

"Derek's decision should pose no threat to you, Louisa," Megan went on very gently, "unless you feel God is calling you to do the same and you are trying to run."

Megan had shot the arrow straight into the heart of the matter. One moment Louisa was standing defensive and scared, and the next she was sobbing with grief and pain. Derek was the one to approach her, and he led her carefully to a chair by the fire.

"I feel as though I can't find Him," Louisa sobbed. "I have watched you, Meg, and I have tried, but I feel as though I will never have your God. And now Derek has come to know Him, and I am still lost."

Derek slipped his arms around his mother, and Louisa cried into his shoulder. Megan sat across from them and begged God to give her the words. She knew He was just waiting to show Louisa the way.

Megan thought that Derek might want to share, but when he remained quiet for several minutes and Louisa seemed more in control, Megan spoke softly.

"Louisa," Megan called to her and waited until she met her eyes. "In the sixteenth psalm, God says He will show us the path of life, in His presence is fullness of joy, and at His right hand are pleasures forevermore. God is not hiding from you, Louisa. He is waiting very patiently for you to reach out to Him."

"I don't know how."

"It sounds to me like you're well on your way," Megan told her with a smile.

"Really?" Louisa's tear-stained face grew hopeful.

Megan nodded. "The Proverbs say that every word of God is pure, and that He is a shield to those who put their trust in Him. Do you believe God's Word, Louisa?"

"Yes, but I have heard so little."

Megan nodded again, this time in understanding. It had been a true privilege to be raised at the Stone Lake abbey, and now that Megan had been given her copy of the Psalms and Proverbs, she had spent many hours studying what she could of God's Word.

"Then I shall tell you what God says, unless Derek would rather."

"Go ahead, Megan," he told her with an encouraging smile.

"Psalm 22 tells of Christ's death and suffering on the cross; His very thoughts are recorded. And then in Psalm 32 it says, 'Blessed is he whose transgression is forgiven, whose sin is covered. . . . I acknowledged my sin unto thee, and mine iniquity have I not hidden. I said, I will confess my transgressions unto the Lord, and thou forgavest the iniquity of my sin. . . . For this shall every one that is godly pray unto thee in a time when thou mayest be found. . . . Thou art my hiding place; thou shalt preserve me from trouble; thou shalt compass me about with songs of deliverance . . . Many sorrows shall be to the wicked; but he that trusteth in the Lord, mercy shall compass him about.' "

"Oh, Megan," Louisa breathed. "I need only to pray and tell God that I trust Him to deliver me from my sins. He will be merciful to me if only I will ask."

Megan beamed at her and then at Derek, who spoke softly.

"It is just as Megan said, Mother. God is only waiting for you to call on Him."

"I can see that now," Louisa said. "It wasn't clear before."

"Did you want to be left alone, Aunt Louisa?"

"No, dear. I want you both here."

Megan and Derek fell quiet, and after a moment Louisa bowed her head. "I now confess my transgressions to You, dear God, and I trust in You, Lord, to forgive me. Please fill the void in me as you have done for Derek and Megan. Please cover me with Your mercy and let me find a hiding place in You forevermore. Amen."

Louisa's head came up, but Megan could barely see her for the tears. They began to talk all at once. Louisa had dozens of questions and so did Derek. It didn't take long for Megan to see just how new a believer Derek was. Megan did not know the answer to each question, and couldn't really promise to find out, but she told them what she did know. They spent over an hour rejoicing in Louisa's new life in Christ.

The hour was far past midnight before anyone even mentioned bed. Louisa was walking Derek and Megan to the door when she made a comment that brought the younger woman to a standstill.

"I can't wait for Joyce to arrive. I can't wait to tell her."

"Bracken's mother?"

"Yes," Louisa beamed at her. "She told me of her own decision more than two years ago. I can't wait to see her."

Louisa hugged Megan before she stepped out the door and moved on her way. Megan could hardly believe what she had just heard. Not even seeing Arik, outside her door (obviously under the impression that she was in for the night), could disrupt the prayer of her heart.

Bracken's mother believes, Lord; she belongs to You. Oh, Father God, it's such a gift. I don't know if I ever knew just how much You love me.

Twenty-Four

"Bracken?" Megan called to him from her place in the doorway of his bedchamber. She had never come anywhere near this room, but her need to see him had driven her upstairs to where Lyndon had directed.

"Yes, Megan," he spoke as he approached from within the shadowy chamber. Kent had opened the door and now stood back.

"May I speak with you?"

Bracken's eyes roamed her face. She looked tired and upset, and he found his heart burgeoning within him that she would come to him at all. At the moment he thought he would hand her the moon if she asked it of him.

"Why don't I meet you in the salon."

"I believe Louisa is sewing in there."

Bracken opened his mouth to say that he would ask her to leave but changed his mind.

"Give me a moment, and we'll walk to the tower."

Megan waited in the hallway. Just a

minute later, Bracken joined her. They walked silently up the stairs to the tower and when they had gained the first large salon, Megan led the way inside. The room was empty, as Bracken knew it would be, and although he wanted to make himself comfortable in one of the chairs, Megan continued to stand.

She seemed nervous, and it wasn't long before he found out why. She faced him squarely, forced herself to look into his eyes, and said, "My attempts to hire a castle steward have failed miserably. I have let you down as well as all of Hawkings Crest."

Bracken hated her shame. He had never worked at anything the way he had worked at this relationship. He was very pleased at the way she'd come to him, but not at the shame he had caused her to feel.

"The task before you is not easy, but I feel you are doing a fine job. Do not rush yourself. Take your time in finding the right man."

His words were no help. Tears did not come to her eyes, but her voice wobbled horribly.

"But there is so much to do, and the wedding approaches. I do not think I can keep up the pace."

"Then you must delegate the jobs. You take too much on yourself."

Megan's eyes were huge. "You told me I was to see to Barton's duties personally."

Alarm washed over Bracken. That was exactly what he had said. How could he have forgotten? No wonder she retired so early these last nights and looked so tired by the middle of the afternoon.

Without speaking, Bracken took Megan's hand and led her to the double settee. He sat beside her after she'd sat down, but he could see instantly that she was not relaxed. Her back was stiff as a poker, and she did not lean into the upholstered support.

"Megan," Bracken began tenderly.

"I'm not going to cry."

"It's all right if you do," he said kindly.

"No, it isn't," Megan declared. "You are going to think you are marrying a child, not a woman grown and capable. I —"

Megan cut off when Bracken's arms went around her and he swept her over against his chest. Megan looked up into his face, and tears filled her eyes.

"I'm sorry, Bracken."

"Shhh," he hushed her, pressing her head down against his shoulder. "I have asked too much of you. We will find

Lyndon, and he can take over some of your duties. The rest we will delegate as well. I will not have my wife sick with exhaustion on her wedding day."

Megan's look was so comical that Bracken chuckled.

"Now what goes through that fascinating head of yours?"

"The wedding. I have lived here as Megan of Stone Lake for so long that sometimes I find it hard to believe we are really going to wed." Megan looked up into Bracken's eyes. "Do you ever find it hard to believe?"

"Ahh, no," he drew the words out for several heartbeats and shook his head very slowly. The next moment his head lowered, and his lips touched down on Megan's. The kiss might have turned more intimate, but a voice spoke from the door.

"Have I missed the wedding, Bracken?"

Bracken's head came up, and a huge smile split his face.

Megan's response was not so pleasant. Her head spun, and she stared in panic at a small, plump woman with hair so black and curly that Megan couldn't help but wonder how she ever managed a brush through it.

In the wink of an eye, Bracken had them

both off the settee and was turning Megan toward the door.

"Megan, I want you to meet my mother."

Megan's mouth opened in horror. "Your mother?" she squeaked.

Bracken was urging her forward, but Megan's mouth was still moving like that of a fish out of water. Joyce did not seem to notice, and enfolded Megan in her arms as soon as the younger woman was within arm's reach.

"I'm so pleased to meet you, my dear," she said when she was finally holding Megan in front of her. "Louisa said you were lovely, but I had no idea."

Megan had still not made a suitable reply, but again, Joyce did not seem to notice. She turned abruptly to Bracken.

"And what business have you taking advantage of this girl before the vows are spoken?"

Bracken only smiled, his eyes alight with pleasure.

"Now, come and hug me, and I'll think about forgiving you."

Bracken gave his mother a hug that lifted her free of the floor. He dropped a kiss onto her cheek just as he set her back down and spoke with one arm still around her.

"Hello, Mother."

"Hello, dear." Joyce's face was now wreathed in soft smiles. "How are you?"

"I'm doing well. How was your trip?"

"Long, but worth seeing you and Megan."

Joyce now transferred her gaze back to her future daughter-in-law. She reached out and touched the soft skin of Megan's cheek.

"Oh, Megan, Megan, how long I've prayed for you. You must come below right away. The rest of the family is dying to meet you." With that she swept away, and Bracken began to follow. He was out the door by several paces when he realized Megan had not accompanied them.

"Megan," Bracken spoke as he poked his head back in the door.

"I'm so ashamed."

Bracken came back in.

"There is no reason. Mother was but teasing. She does that quite often. I can assure you — we've done nothing to feel shame over."

"But she's right, the vows have not been spoken."

Bracken sighed gently. "It is as I say, Megan; we have done nothing wrong, and in little over a week, we will be free before

God and man to touch each other at will."

Megan's face flamed, and Bracken knew he would have to let the matter drop. He gently took her hand and led the way toward the stairs, thinking as he went that marriage or no, they might not be as free as he hoped.

Megan laughed until she had tears in her eyes. She was in the upstairs salon with both Joyce and Louisa, and the two older women were telling stories from their childhood. Megan didn't know when she'd been more entertained.

After having what Megan considered a poor beginning, she and her future mother-in-law had certainly made up for lost time. Lady Joyce was one of the most delightful women Megan had ever met. Her walk with God was so close that she found joy in nearly everything. In some ways she was a quiet rebuke to Megan, who tended to worry overly much and wanted her way in most matters. Joyce was a true example of the joy Megan read about in the Scriptures.

Megan had not been in attendance when Louisa told Joyce her news, but Louisa reported that it had been a very tearful scene. There were further tears when Joyce then came to Megan to thank her for the part she had played. Megan had been present when Joyce had shared the news with her family, and the look on Bracken's face was still in her mind. He appeared to be skeptical yet yearning at the same time. And Megan was struck by how little conversation they'd had concerning religious matters.

His sweet treatment of Megan had been growing as the days passed, but there was very little time for them to be alone. Nearly every barrier was down between them, and Megan had few reservations over the marriage.

"Now, Megan," Joyce suddenly said to her. "When will your parents arrive?"

"I'm not sure they will," Megan told her matter-of-factly.

Joyce's look became very intense then, and her voice changed as well.

"Can you tell me why?"

Leaving some of the details out, Megan simply reported that Bracken had taken her away from a difficult situation and she had not heard from her parents since.

Joyce nodded her wise head as she completely heard Megan out, and then asked, "Would you say that your mother is a prideful woman, dear?"

"Yes." Megan didn't even have to think.

"Then I should expect her if I were you. It's not every man and woman who draws Henry's attention as Bracken and you have. She would never wish the gossips to say that she showed a lack of interest in you."

Megan was extremely impressed with her logic. Such a thing had never occurred to her, but it was so true. Annora was not a hypocrite, but she did like to be seen making socially correct moves.

"I had resigned myself to not seeing them, something to which I'm rather accustomed," Megan admitted, "but I think you are correct. They will be here, possibly at the last moment and only until the ceremony is over, but they will come."

"Will you be glad if they come, Meg?" Louisa asked.

"Yes and no. You can see my quandary now more than ever, Louisa. It is easier to be away from them, but if I never see them, then I will have no opportunity to share Christ."

"Oh, Meg," Louisa said. "You have been such an example to me."

"I have also been a dreadful stumbling block as I struggled with some horrible sins. I'm only glad that God can save His chosen ones despite all I do to destroy His work."

"You are too hard on yourself, Megan," Joyce told her. "We all sin, but you show a clear pattern of trying to change, and those are the children God can work through no matter what."

Megan smiled at her, and they talked on. It was so wonderful to have the time. Bracken had been good at his word, and many of Megan's duties had been delegated until after the wedding. Her dress was done, and she was feeling more rested each day.

"I was hoping I'd find you together," a voice spoke from the doorway. All the ladies turned to see Richard and Derek enter and close the door.

"You're welcome to join us," their aunt told them, "but we must warn you — it's women's talk."

Both men smiled at Joyce.

"In truth," Derek's voice was low, "we just need your momentary attention."

"Sounds intriguing," Louisa said in a false whisper and found out very soon that she had guessed correctly. The men were seated, and the women listened in rapt silence for several minutes. After a time Megan asked but one question.

"When do you want this done?"

Richard answered. "The wedding is in four days' time, so I think sometime tomorrow will be perfect."

Megan's smile was huge. They spoke of the plan for several more minutes, and then the men went on their way. Megan, no longer diverted by Richard's plan, also took her leave. She had become resigned to not seeing her parents; now she needed time to prepare her heart.

"Why, Marigold," Annora spoke with pleasure to her oldest daughter as she entered the younger woman's bedchamber, "I love that dress. Is that what you will wear to Megan's wedding?"

"No, Mother." Marigold's voice was bored. "I've decided to go to London."

Annora was taken off guard.

"But you can't, dear. Megan is to be wed."

"I realize that." Marigold sounded testy, which was unusual where her mother was concerned. "I just won't be able to make it."

"But of course you can. We leave tomorrow. The wedding is but four days off."

"That's enough, Mother," Marigold

snapped at her. "I tell you, I *won't* be going."

Annora didn't know when she'd been so hurt. She believed that Marigold was acting completely out of character, when in fact the two of them had simply never been at cross purposes before. Never had Annora made plans for Marigold and really cared one way or the other if she fit herself into them. But Megan's wedding was quite another matter. She tried again.

"I think maybe you're not feeling well, dear. Why don't we sleep on it? You'll see reason in the morning."

Marigold glared at her mother. Annora was so taken aback that she didn't know what to say or do. Marigold saw the look on her mother's face and grew furious. She *hated* to have her plans thwarted.

"Honestly, Mother!" Marigold snapped. "Megan and I are not even close."

"But you haven't seen her in years."

"Yes, I have! I saw her in the village at Hawkings Crest just weeks ago." The words were out before she could stop them, and Marigold turned her back on her mother's look of absolute shock. Marigold was furious with herself for blurting out such news and worked desperately to control her voice and features.

"You saw Megan?" Annora asked when she recovered her voice.

"Yes," Marigold spoke slowly, still keeping her back to her mother. "We didn't have a chance to speak, but she looked fine."

"But why were you at the village there?"

Marigold's lip curled with hatred, but she actually maintained her voice.

"I was simply meeting Roland Kirkpatrick. You know, Lord Kirkpatrick's son." Marigold made it all sound so innocent that Annora immediately took the bait. After all, Lord Kirkpatrick was a duke. However, Annora momentarily forgot that Roland was not the oldest son.

"Is he interested in you?"

"I think so." Marigold was now able to turn with a smile that covered the lies in her heart.

"Oh, Marigold, my darling, that would be wonderful."

Marigold falsely agreed with her and was able to keep her mother happy until Annora remembered a task that needed attention elsewhere.

Once outside the room, Annora realized that they had not finished speaking of the trip. She shrugged, however, sure that Marigold would make the proper choice and attend her sister's wedding.

She wouldn't have gone away with such confidence had she read Marigold's real thoughts. That selfish young woman planned to be far away from Stone Lake even before the sun set that night.

Twenty-Five

"Bracken?" Louisa's voice wobbled slightly as she approached Bracken in the hall the very next day.

"Louisa, what is it?" Bracken stood in concern.

"Megan is gone." Louisa bit her lip, and Bracken's face clouded.

"What do you mean? She can't be gone."

"She told Helga that you quarreled last night."

An audience of family members was gathering now, each one looking tense as he watched the thundercloud covering Bracken's face.

"It's true that we did have words, but I was certain she was beyond this."

"Beyond what?"

"This childish habit of running away." Bracken's angry eyes stared off into the distance until all watched his expression turn to cold acceptance.

"I am glad it happened now," he spoke with regret.

"What do you mean, Bracken?" This

came from Stephen, whose strained features matched Bracken's.

"I can see it was too great to hope that she was ready for such a union. I see now that she is little more than a child."

"Oh, Bracken." His mother's voice held tears.

"I am sorry you have come all this way," Bracken turned to face his family, his features a study in anguish. "It would seem the wedding is off."

"No, Bracken," Brice said. "I'm sure if you will but find her, you can work this out."

Bracken slowly shook his head. "I won't be looking. She clearly does not want me, and I can see now that's best. It is also best for me to let her go."

Bracken strode from the main hall. His family stood in desolation. Even Joyce looked like a statue, her youngest daughter, Kristine, clutching her mother's hand.

"I've got to make him see reason," Stephen spoke as he started after him. The others did not move. They had seen that look in Bracken's eyes before and knew that this time his mind was made up.

All of Hawkings Crest fell into a depression as the day moved on. Chores were done and some work was accomplished, but no one was even hungry. Stephen had gone to Bracken, but as the others in the family had predicted, it did no good. After growing angry with Stephen for again taking Megan's side, Bracken took himself off on a ride. He was gone for hours, and Stephen and Brice had never been so upset.

They tried to talk with their mother, but it seemed to pain her all the more, so they made their plans quietly. They would go after Megan themselves. They even enlisted Richard's and Derek's help, and the men geared up and sent for their horses.

They were in the courtyard, Stephen already mounted, when Bracken rode through the gates with Megan sitting comfortably across the front of his saddle. They drew up, just as precisely planned, and Bracken captured the back of Megan's head in one great hand and gave her a hard kiss on the mouth.

Stephen was still staring at them in utter stupefaction when Richard put a hand to his chest and said in a high, dramatic voice, "She's very sweet, but her hair is the color of fresh carrots and frizzy like a bird's nest. Bracken has resigned himself to her looks. He's doing this for the king."

Stephen's face was more than they could have hoped for.

"It was all planned," he said in wonder as he took in each expression. "You all knew," he went on, continuing to stare at each of them.

Brice, Richard, his mother — everyone had been involved. The full import was slow in coming, and when it hit, Stephen threw back his head with a shout of relief. He swung from his horse and nearly ran to Bracken's mount. In the blink of an eye he had taken Megan down and hugged her, laughing all the while.

Bracken now joined them, claimed Megan, and moved toward the laughing group.

"You should have seen your face."

"That will teach you, Stephen."

"It's not often we catch you out."

"I wish I could see it again."

"You certainly deserved it."

Stephen laughed in good humor, but his eyes finally narrowed on his cousins.

"I hope you know that I might not be done with you."

Richard, who was an inch taller,

approached him, his manner playfully threatening.

"You had better be, Stephen. I stared like a fool at our lovely Megan, so hear me well, dear cousin, you had better be done."

Stephen's hands went in the air. "I concede, I concede."

"Come now," Louisa called to all. "We have all played our parts well to the point that some of us are starving. I have had Kimay sneaking food to me from the kitchen all day." The group laughed at this admission. "Let us all go in and eat."

Cheers went up for that good news, and as Bracken draped his arm around Megan once again, her heart swelled with joy. What a precious family she was marrying! Megan had never known such contentment among so many.

There was just one question that persisted. If Joyce had made a decision for Christ, what of her children? How was it that they did not seem to share her belief? Megan thought she could figure Bracken, since he would have already been lord of Hawkings Crest and away from the family, but what of the others? Megan could see that they all had strong convictions, but she doubted that each could claim to be a true follower of Jesus Christ.

Megan determined then and there to have some answers. She was to be wed in just two and a half days' time, but before then, she must strive to learn the background of her husband's relationship, or lack thereof, with God.

"Oh, Megan," Joyce spoke in pleasant surprise the next morning as the petite redhead came from the kitchens. "I have something for you, a wedding gift of sorts. Would you have time now to come to my room?"

"Of course." Wondering if this might not be her chance to speak privately before the wedding, Megan followed her.

"It's a gift that belonged to my husband's mother," Joyce continued as they walked. "She gave it to me just before I wed Greville, and now I want you to have it."

Megan was intrigued. Joyce's rooms were in the tower, and it was a few minutes before they entered.

"Sit here, Megan." Joyce indicated a chair. Megan took a seat and watched as Joyce moved to a small trunk at the foot of her bed. She returned with something dangling from her hands.

"It's a jeweled belt," Joyce explained.

"It's been in Greville's family for years. I want you to have it."

Megan's hands came out in wonder. The ornamented belt was exquisite. Stones of every conceivable color were set in fine chain-style gold. Megan stood to slip it around her. It was a perfect fit. She beamed at Joyce and then gave her a tender hug.

"I will treasure it always."

"Mayhap," Joyce spoke when they were seated once again, "you will have the opportunity to give it to *your* future daughter-in-law."

"Mayhap," Megan agreed before they both fell silent.

"There is something on your mind, isn't there, Megan?"

Megan nodded. "My father wanted me to live here at Hawkings Crest before the wedding so that I would know Bracken when we wed. It has worked better than I ever expected, but there are some things of which we have never talked. One of them is God.

"I am almost ashamed to admit this to you, but I have not spoken to him about that which means so much to me. We did not start well, and because I was raised at the abbey, I feared he would think me a religious zealot. I was not controlling my anger at that time, and I thought somehow that if he knew the stand I took in Christ, the seeming contradiction would cause him to shun all I believe."

Joyce smiled at her in true compassion and said, "Thank you for being so honest with me, Megan, but I must tell you, Bracken's lack of faith in Christ has little to do with you. You see, he has never hungered."

Megan stared at her.

"Think back, Megan. Think back to when you knew you wanted Christ as your own."

Megan was reflecting now.

"There had to be a hunger, Megan," Joyce went on, "or you never would have reached out."

A minute or two of silence passed before Megan recalled in a voice of wonder.

"I was desperate. My family did not know what to do with me, and there were days when I knew the nuns were ready to lock me away forever. There was such a void inside of me that I felt hollow all the time."

Joyce nodded and continued softly, "This is what I speak of, Megan. Bracken has experienced no such need. Not even when his father died did his heart feel the need. He is a devout man in many ways, but a personal relationship with God's Son does not seem to fit into the plans he's made for his life.

"I have such hope, Megan, that your marriage to him will make a difference. I am not telling you that your sins do not matter, but do not be afraid to be yourself with Bracken. He is a most compassionate man, and we have talked at length about what I believe. Your own story would be new to him, but I have told him what Scriptures say concerning Christ."

Megan drew a great breath. "And what of your other children, Joyce? Where do they stand?"

Joyce smiled. "You know Stephen and Brice well enough, I think, to see that they believe as Bracken. The girls know Christ, both Kristine and Danella, but of my sons, only Giles."

"I am sorry he will not make the wedding."

"So is he. But his term as squire is most important for his upbringing. It is what his father would want."

They were quiet for a time.

"Has it been very hard?" Megan asked, referring to Greville's death.

"At times," Joyce admitted. "When

Danella was wed and then had the baby, I missed him so much. When I came to Christ, I wondered if he'd ever made that choice. And now, I know he would have been so proud of Bracken and would have adored you as I do."

Both women stood and hugged. Megan praised God for Joyce's words. She was so wise and caring, and Megan thought of the different women of the Bible that she had admired over the years — Sarah, Ruth, and Priscilla. She shared her thoughts with Joyce, and the older woman only smiled in humility.

The conversation then turned to Derek, and both women wept over his newfound knowledge.

"He told me a man in London spoke with him," Megan said. "And it was just as you've said, he felt an emptiness deep within, and he cried out to God to fill that void."

"Louisa told me that she was shocked speechless when he shared."

"Yes," Megan agreed. "She was most upset, but I believe God used Derek's conversion to reach her."

"It's just a matter of time, Megan, until they all know. I believe this with all my heart."

Megan sat quietly, because in truth she did not feel quite so sure. She prayed then that God would increase her faith.

When they exited the room, they walked together to the great hall for the midday meal. Both knew God's peace in the way His hand had moved in their lives, and both prayed that their lives would continue to touch those around them in a positive way for God.

Twenty-Six

Vincent, Annora, and company arrived late that very evening. Darkness was swiftly falling as they rode through the gates. Megan, whose day had stretched on without end, swiftly changed her plans of retiring and made her way to the great hall.

Not many people were up and about, which suited Megan. The greeting she shared with her parents was subdued. Megan felt helpless as to how to make it easier, but when she suddenly noticed the fatigue in her mother's face, she knew she could at least offer hospitality.

"You've come far," Megan spoke softly while under Bracken's watchful eye. "Would you like some refreshment, or would you rather be shown to your room?"

"I will retire," Annora replied stiffly, and Megan, after a hushed word from Bracken, led the way, leaving her father in her betrothed's hands.

Megan had chosen a resplendent group of rooms for her parents that included two large bedchambers and a small salon.

Megan hoped that such an act would please her parents and make them feel welcome at Hawkings Crest. Indeed, Annora prowled the premises for just a moment, and Megan held her breath.

"Everything looks well, Megan."

"Thank you, Mother," Megan returned softly, trying not to betray the rush of emotions within. She continued to watch her mother. She knew Bracken wanted her right back downstairs, but something in Annora's demeanor caused her to linger. Megan knew she'd chosen wisely when Annora suddenly stopped and faced her nervously.

"I feel I must apologize to you, Megan."

The young woman's heart leapt. Could her mother actually be sorry for what she had done?

"As I'm sure you have noticed, Marigold is not with us," Annora went on, and Megan knew keen disappointment. "I am sure she is not feeling well right now; she is not acting herself." Annora's voice now grew very agitated.

"We had words, the first ever, and then she said she wasn't coming to your wedding. I'm sure she'll be very sorry later, and I do hope she will have a change of heart and arrive before the ceremony."

Megan stood mute for a full minute. In truth, she hadn't even missed Marigold. She realized now that she would have been surprised if the older girl had walked in, but this was the last thing Megan could say to her mother. Megan felt pity of sorts for Annora's belief that Marigold was acting out of character. Megan thought her sister's actions were completely in keeping with her personality. The small redhead now wildly searched her mind for some suitable comment.

" 'Tis all right, Mother," she finally replied. "I am just pleased that you and Father have come."

"Are you?" Annora's brow arched.

"Yes."

She *was* pleased that they had arrived. She was going to say more to reassure her mother and try to remove the frown from her face, but there was a great pounding on the door.

"I wish to be alone!" Annora's voice rang out to the intruder.

"Is Megan in there?" Bracken's voice thundered from without.

"It's Bracken," Megan said, and moved immediately to the door. He came in uninvited, his gaze fierce as his look encompassed both mother and daughter.

"We are trying to have a private conversation."

"I can believe that," Bracken said ruthlessly. "In here . . . where no one can stop you."

Annora's gasp echoed in the room, and Megan reached for Bracken's arm.

"Please, Bracken —" she began, but he cut her off.

"No, Megan, I will not leave. You still bear the scar from her last attack. I will not leave you alone with this woman any longer."

There was nothing else Megan could say. She turned to see that all color had drained from her mother's face.

"Is it true, Megan?" Her voice was a hoarse whisper. "Have I scarred you?"

Megan's hands moved helplessly in front of her. "It's very slight, Mother. I think it will fade."

Annora plucked a torch from its wall sconce and approached. She moved to Megan's side, and her free hand balled into a fist as she took in the tiny white line on Megan's otherwise flawless cheek.

Her hand then reached for Megan's arm. It was the first time Megan could ever remember her mother touching her in gentleness.

"Forgive me, Megan."

"I do, Mother." Moved by her mother's first apology, Megan could not take her look of anguish. "We shall put it behind us. Why don't you rest now."

Annora nodded, and Bracken reached for Megan's arm. They both bid Annora a good rest and left, closing the door behind them. It was a very silent couple that walked toward Megan's chamber. Neither spoke until they stood just outside the portal.

"Are you all right?"

"Why shouldn't I be all right?" Bracken wished to know.

Megan shrugged. "You seemed terribly upset."

Bracken took Megan gently by the shoulders. "I was the one who saw your cut, swollen face, Megan. I was the one who witnessed your tears in the chapel. Your mother may have many fine qualities, but she has a violent temper, and for that reason alone I do not trust her."

Megan could only nod. It was true.

"How is my father?"

"I think he wished you to stay and speak with him."

"I'll plan to see him tomorrow. In many ways," Megan continued, "you have ruined him for me."

"What do you mean?"

"I mean that I always thought his care of me was the best, but in truth he never did what needed to be done. He removed me from Stone Lake because he had no control over my mother, but my father should have done everything to keep us together as a family."

Bracken was very pleased by her words. He'd believed for many weeks now that her home had been nothing short of chaos, and it was good to see that she was now realizing how unhealthy it had been. Bracken believed their own home would be as it should, one of warmth and caring.

"What will you say to him?" Bracken finally asked.

"I don't know, but just as I said to my mother, I wish to put it in the past and go on. Bitterness will do no good."

"He deserves your bitterness." Bracken's voice was uncompromising.

"Oh, no, Bracken." Megan caught hold of his sleeve. "Bitterness only destroys the vessel that contains it. Bitterness accomplishes nothing."

"You sound like my mother."

Megan removed her hand. "We have much in common."

Bracken nodded, his black hair gleaming

in the light of the torch on the wall. "You share the same beliefs."

"Yes. I'm sorry I didn't tell you before."

Bracken only stared, thinking it made no difference.

"Do you think you can sleep?"

"Yes," Megan answered, but wished he hadn't changed the subject. She debated what to say next but waited too long.

Thinking she was tired, Bracken said, "Goodnight, Megan. I'll see you tomorrow."

"Goodnight, Bracken."

They parted, Bracken with his thoughts and Megan with hers. Bracken truly did not see that Megan's faith would be a hindrance to him, although he could not see the need for himself. He felt he was man enough to let Megan worship as she wished.

Megan's thoughts were entirely different. She prayed that Bracken's present belief in God would grow and that he would hunger for something much larger, something so huge that it would swallow him whole and at the same time make him more of a man than he ever dreamed.

"Did you sleep well?"

"Yes, Father, and you?"

"Fine."

For all Megan's good intentions of putting the past behind, the morning had not started well. Annora had slept in and broke the fast in her own room, but Vincent, having met Bracken's family, asked Megan if he could see her alone.

They decided on a walk outside the castle walls. Even though her father would be with her, Megan told several people where she would be. As had become the norm, Arik was close by.

They had walked along with few words. Vincent did not know what to say to this daughter who had changed so much, and Megan had told herself she was not going to apologize. She had done nothing wrong, nor was she bitter, but Megan also knew that if Vincent's conscience was bothering him, it would be no help to pretend that nothing had happened.

"I spoke briefly with your mother last night."

Megan nodded.

"She did not realize she'd struck you so hard."

Megan did not nod this time, but still said nothing.

"Megan, what has happened to us?"

Megan stopped and faced him. It was an honest question and deserved an answer, but the words were not there. Megan's hands moved helplessly before she said, "I do not know how to explain, Father, but I do know the changes are good. I do not wish to be as we were," she admitted.

"It's Bracken, isn't it?" Vincent burst out with such vehemence that Megan's eyes widened. "You can't believe the things he said to me. If you were not to marry him, Megan, I would make life miserable for him." He raked a frustrated hand through his graying hair. "If there were only some way that I could get you out of this."

At one time Megan would have thrilled to his words, but no longer. She had never seen him like this.

"Father, what did he say to you last night?"

"Not last night!" Vincent was still very agitated. "Before you left Stone Lake he told me I didn't care for you, and that I couldn't control my wife!"

Megan only stared at him. Vincent froze.

"Megan," he whispered, his voice raw. "Do you share his feelings?"

Tears filled her eyes. "I do not know how I could think otherwise. You never tried to stop Mother; you just always sent me out of her reach."

Vincent's heart literally pained him over

Megan's words. He could hardly breathe with the intensity of it. It was all so true. He had a wonderful relationship with his daughter as long as his wife wasn't near. And he had a tolerable relationship with his wife as long as he did what she asked and kept Megan clear of her. He had never cared enough about Megan to fight Annora. He thought about his daughter often while she lived at the abbey, but only visited her when he had other business in town. Weeks earlier, when he'd come to Hawkings Crest to check on her, it was the first time he had gone out of his way on her behalf.

What kind of man was he? There were names for his sort, Vincent realized, and years ago he'd nearly beaten a man for calling him such. He saw now that he should have listened. Much would have been different.

"I hate this strain between us, Father," Megan now said. "But I do not want to be the recipient of Mother's cruelty any longer. I have tasted otherwise, and I do not want to return to my old way of life. I don't know if you can still care for me, but I am afraid that things will have to be on our terms — Bracken's and mine."

Megan didn't know where she found the courage to speak so, but God blessed her honesty. Vincent's arms came out, and he enfolded Megan gently against him.

"I am so sorry, Meg, so sorry to have let you down."

Megan did not tell him it was all right, but she hugged him back tightly and prayed silently.

"Your mother has long been in control," Vincent admitted when they stepped apart. "Now Marigold has hurt her, and I wonder if she'll be ready to listen to reason."

"She is so blind to Marigold's true nature."

Vincent nodded sadly. How many times as a child had Megan suffered at her older sister's hands? Marigold would commit some crime and then see to it that Megan took the blame and was beaten by Annora. And all her father ever did was send her away. Vincent's eyes closed.

"Are you all right, Father?"

"I am not sure. I think I will stay here for a time and then try to talk with your mother."

Megan nodded. "I do not have high expectations for her, Father," she admitted. "But things do not have to be strained between us. You can come here as often as you like, with or without Mother. I know Bracken does not trust her, but as long as we're at Hawkings Crest, I think he will agree."

Vincent saw then that a miracle had taken place in his daughter's heart. She was talking submissively about Bracken. He was still choking on the words the young lord had shot at him, but if he put his pride aside, he could see that Bracken was quite possibly the best thing to ever happen to Megan.

Megan did leave him then, but she was not heavy of heart. He needed time alone, and Megan wanted the quiet of her room to pray. Arik escorted her back, and when Bracken spotted them returning he immediately approached.

"Are you well?"

"Yes," Megan told him.

"And your father?"

"He wanted some time alone. I told him that he and my mother would be welcome at Hawkings Crest, but it would have to be on our terms."

Bracken smiled. He liked the word "our" on her lips. While he stood quietly, simply watching her, Megan suddenly reached out and smoothed her fingers across his eyebrows.

"What was that for?"

Megan blushed, regretting the action.

"They were a mess. Don't you ever brush them smooth when you see to your hair and beard?"

Bracken's smile grew, and Megan, wishing to hide her embarrassment, tilted her chin and flounced away. Bracken watched her go. This was going to be some marriage, and with the wedding the following afternoon, he could hardly wait to begin.

Twenty-Seven

The wedding was set for 3:00 on the afternoon of September 20, 1531. The entire castle was aflutter, but the bride, dressed in a gown of exquisite styling and fabric, was remarkably calm.

Louisa had made the garment using her purchases from the village. Slashing the skirt front and sleeves, she had taken the cream satin and lined it with a deep green satin before lacing it with gold braid. The neckline was fashionably square and trimmed with the same gold braid. Stiffened with flour, Megan's small headpiece was made from the cream satin as well, and set perfectly atop her head of rich red curls.

Megan was ready by 2:00 and had enjoyed visits from Richard; Derek and Stephen; Louisa, Joyce, and Kristine; her father; and finally Brice. Megan knew her mother would be coming as well, and if anyone could make her nervous, it was Annora.

There was a sudden knock at the door,

and Megan held her breath as Helga answered. Annora swept inside, and just as Megan had believed, a dress of light blue velvet hung from her lovely, slim form. Annora stopped cold upon spotting Megan's dress, and she tried to dismiss Helga with a jerk of her head. That faithful servant looked to Megan, who nodded but asked her to return shortly.

"How dare she," Annora began, but Megan cut in respectfully.

"This is my home, Mother, and these are my servants. How dare you." It was all said so softly and without a trace of anger that it totally disarmed Annora.

She stared at Megan for several seconds and then quietly asked, "Where did you find the material?"

"From a woman in the village. She said she bought it from Elias the peddler."

Annora had nothing to say, and Megan voiced a question that in her mind had to be answered.

"Did you hate me so much, Mother, that you would sell my dress fabric?"

"Oh, Megan." Annora's voice sounded desperate. "I did it in a burst of anger. I don't hate you; I just don't know how to be a mother to you."

Megan's heart was sad, believing Annora

hadn't even tried. Annora would have done anything for Marigold and certainly must have thought she'd been a good mother to her eldest daughter.

"And now it seems," Annora admitted softly, "that I have not known how to be a mother to Marigold either."

"What do you mean?"

"Your father and I talked at length yesterday. He told me that from now on things would be different When I fought him, he told me that some of Marigold's activities have been reported to him. Do you know of what I speak?"

"No," Megan told her honestly.

"Well, the details do not matter." The older woman was obviously embarrassed to repeat them. "It seems she is going through a phase of," Annora searched for the word, "rebellion."

Megan stayed quiet for only a moment. " 'Tis no stage."

"Why do you say this?" Annora asked, her eyes begging her younger daughter not to destroy Marigold further.

"I know not of what father speaks, but many was the time I was punished for Marigold's deeds. She has never cared about anyone but herself. You are the only person she has not fought with for the whole of her life."

"How can you say this? Marigold is as sweet a girl as God ever created. You are but jealous." Annora's eyes begged Megan to admit it this time.

Megan smiled sadly. "I was at one time, but no longer. Now I pity her."

Annora looked positively crushed, and Megan marveled that she had not grown angry. Megan hated to have these words on her wedding day, but she somehow believed that when her parents left in the morning, she would never see her mother again. She was nearly certain of it when Annora turned away, defeat enveloping her. However, she surprised Megan when she stopped at the door.

"It was wrong of me to sell the fabric, but I am glad you found it." Annora finally looked at her. "It's beautiful on you, Megan."

She left before Megan could frame a reply. When Bracken and Helga entered the room a minute later, Megan was still standing like a statue.

"Are you all right?" Bracken demanded as he stopped just inches before her.

Megan looked into his eyes. "My mother said I looked beautiful." Her voice was that of a child's, breathless with wonder.

Bracken smiled tenderly. How long his little Megan had waited for such approval. He had known it all along.

"She is but learning what I have known for many months."

Now it was time for Megan to smile. Bracken offered his arm.

"Come, my dove. Come below and marry me."

Megan didn't need to be asked twice. Placing her hand on his arm and holding her head high, she walked beside him down the great stone staircase to the crowded hall below. All whom she loved were gathered there, and just minutes later she and Bracken were joined as husband and wife before God and England.

The festivities that followed were of the richest kind. A banquet was laid out and music played. There was laughter and dancing, and Megan noticed at one point that Joyce and Louisa had even managed to wring a smile from her mother.

The hours flew. Megan and Bracken were together at times, but often as not they were separated by the crowd. Megan had just finished a dance with Kendrick when Louisa captured her.

"You must be growing tired. Come upstairs and freshen up."

It was just the rescue Megan needed. Her feet were beginning to ache, and the noise was giving her the start of a headache. Louisa chattered as they climbed the stairs, and Megan took almost no notice of where they were going. Not until Louisa stopped outside a strange door did Megan balk, but by then Louisa had hold of her hand and nearly dragged her over the threshold.

Megan stood in shock. It was her room, but it wasn't her room. She had never been in this chamber, but all of her things were beautifully displayed and laid out — the tapestries, bed hangings, everything. Megan stared at the bed. It was a suspended canopy bed, draped in a soft yellow cloth. Her own rich counterpane lay smooth on the mattress. Megan didn't know when she'd seen anything so wonderful.

She would have stood for some time, simply taking in the wonder of it all, but something or someone pounded at the door. Megan started.

"What was that?"

"Only some of the servants securing the door."

Megan looked at her in confusion, and then her face cleared.

"I forgot about Bracken's plan for my sleepwalking, but where do I get out?"

Louisa pointed to a closed door, and Megan laughed to see Joyce standing nearby.

"I didn't even see you."

"I know." Joyce came forward with a huge smile. "That door is to Bracken's room and his dressing area. Then behind you," Joyce let her turn, "is the doorway to your salon. The only door into the passageway is through Bracken's dressing area, which means if you start to prowl you'll have to go past Bracken, then Lyndon, and quite possibly Arik."

Megan laughed and commented that she would have to look around, whereupon both women laughed.

"Later, Meg," Louisa said. "Bracken awaits you."

"Oh." She had been completely unaware of the time and only just now did she understand the purpose of Louisa's spiriting her away.

The older women helped Megan from her gown and saw her into a lovely night garment, also tenderly sewn by Louisa's capable hands. Joyce brushed her hair, and then both women hugged her and took their leave through Bracken's room, leaving the door open behind them.

Megan stood still for only a moment before her curiosity got the best of her. She approached the door and peeked inside. Leaning against the bedpost, Bracken stood and simply watched her. His beautiful, dark wedding coat was gone and he wore only shirt, trunks, and hose.

"Are you going to join me?" He sounded so amused that Megan came forward. The room was shadowy, so she could make little out.

"Louisa said we were coming upstairs to freshen up," Megan began when she stopped a few feet in front of Bracken.

"Do you feel refreshed?"

"Yes, but neither your aunt nor your mother mentioned that this was all a plan for my husband to steal me away."

Bracken's beard split with a grin. "Forgive me?"

"Yes," Megan told him and smiled in return.

"We are both strong-willed, Megan," Bracken surprised her by saying. "We both like to have our way."

Listening keenly to his serious tone as well as his words, Megan nodded.

"We have quarreled and we will quarrel again, but I want our differences to be put aside in this room. When we come to this room, I want our troubles and disputes to be left at the door."

"Yes, Bracken," Megan told him, thinking they were wise words.

Not knowing how she would respond, Bracken was warmed tremendously by her agreement, and he stood staring at her for just a moment, his heart swelling with love as well as pride that she was finally his. A second later he reached for her, and Megan came gently into his arms.

The following day was busy. It began with a huge meal to break the fast, and then came Vincent and Annora's departure. Megan was not certain how they would part, but it was better than she had hoped. Her father hugged her and thanked her warmly, and her mother, although reserved, did thank her for Hawkings Crest's fine hospitality. Annora was not a woman easily pleased, so Megan took this as high praise.

Midmorning saw everyone in various pursuits and pastimes. Megan and Kristine were playing a game, and most of the men were at the archery butts. Bracken and his mother found themselves alone in her salon in the tower.

"It was a wonderful celebration, Bracken."

"Yes, it was," he agreed. "I'd like to repeat it, only I wouldn't want to go through the waiting again."

Joyce smiled contentedly. "Just remember to court her, Bracken."

"Court her?" Bracken frowned. "What are you talking about?"

"I'm talking about wooing your wife."

"Why would I do that?"

Joyce sighed very gently. He really didn't know. He had spent so much time running Hawkings Crest that he had taken very little notice of the ways between men and women. Joyce was proud of the fact that her sons were not rakes or libertines, but Bracken was so unknowledgeable that it concerned Joyce. At a time when Bracken should have been observing his own parents' love, he was a fatherless young man running a huge keep. Joyce prayed and answered him gently.

"Bracken, I am only suggesting that you continue to do things that let Megan know you care. I know that Megan would never be unfaithful to you, but you can make her much happier in your marriage if you let her know she is loved and desired."

Bracken still frowned at her, and Joyce knew she would have to let the matter drop. Megan's face from that morning swam before her eyes. The younger woman's smile was bright, and her eyes were at peace, but her cheeks had been so pale. Maybe in time, her words to Bracken would take on more meaning.

WINDSOR CASTLE

"You say Marigold is here?" Henry asked of James Nayland.

"Yes, my king. She arrived yesterday."

"Yesterday? Was that not Bracken and Megan's day to be wed?"

"Yes, your grace, it was."

Henry frowned, and James waited for the storm, but the king remained calm.

"The wedding did take place, did it not?"

"Yes, my lord, just as scheduled, and in less time, I might add, than the six months you allotted."

Henry was silent for several moments. "Are the rumors still coming in concerning Marigold's association with young Kirkpatrick?"

"Yes. She has been careful, but a few have seen her."

"I must tread with caution where Lord

Kirkpatrick is concerned; I want to do everything possible to keep his alliance."

"Because of his wife's connections with Spain?"

"Yes. See to it that Marigold is at my table tonight," Henry now told the loyal counselor. "She hasn't graced our courts with her fair countenance in several months, and I wish to visit with her."

Hours later Henry had his wish, as Marigold, a vision in black, sat beside him at the head table. They had talked of many things over the course of the meal, but Henry now mentioned the wedding.

"Why didn't you attend your sister's wedding?"

"I will." Marigold didn't even hesitate. "It's next week."

"No, Marigold, it was yesterday."

She really could do the most amazing things with her eyes, but Henry was not fooled.

"Yesterday? Surely you jest, my lord. I am certain my mother said next week."

"No," Henry said with a shake of his head while pretending to be absorbed with his food.

"I'll have to send word of my regrets." Marigold's voice was a study of contrition.

"Why didn't you want the man yourself?" Henry asked, knowing that James Nayland, from a nearby seat, was hearing all and watching very carefully.

"My sister's heart was set on him." Again her voice was regretful.

"Well, she's a lucky girl. I have great plans for Bracken of Hawkings Crest."

"Oh?" Marigold tried for casual interest, but couldn't quite pull it off. Henry had to fight a self-satisfied smile.

"Yes. He's an earl now, but I have better for him."

So as not to turn his head, Henry only glanced down out of the corner of his eye. He could not see the beautiful blonde's face, but the hand, tightening to white around her goblet, told him all he needed to know.

Twenty-Eight

It was very hard for Megan to see Bracken's family leave, but the time had come. Unbeknownst to her, the family had discussed leaving in stages, but when all was said and done, it was decided that a mass exodus was best.

Megan knew she would miss them all, but Louisa's absence was especially going to pain her. She had been with them at Hawkings Crest for so long that Megan found herself asking just how she was going to handle her departure. If the tears clogging her throat were any indication, she was not going to enjoy it at all.

She was in deep conversation with that very woman as Bracken, just yards away in the courtyard, spoke with his mother and brothers.

"Plan to come again in the spring."

"Megan's birthday," Joyce guessed correctly.

"Yes," Bracken went on. "We will have a tourney and celebrate my wife's eighteenth year in a style befitting her."

No one could stop the smiles over the way Bracken had said *my wife*. It was a delight to watch his love of her blossom. They talked on for some minutes while Louisa and Megan had their own time.

"You'll come again soon?"

Louisa hugged her. "Of course I will. You could come to see me as well."

Megan's eyes widened, and Louisa laughed. It was clear that the younger girl had never considered this.

"Oh, Megan," Louisa now turned earnest, "I can't begin to express what you have done for me."

Megan smiled. "Not I, Louisa; God alone."

"Yes," the new believer agreed. "God alone. I like that, Megan. I will remember to walk with God alone."

Megan had to hug her again.

"I still have so many questions," she told Megan after a moment.

"And you will find the answers, Louisa. Of that I'm sure. And don't forget Derek. He will be searching as well."

As if he'd heard his name, that young man joined them.

"I can see that Mother is going to cry halfway to London." Derek's voice was light, and Louisa teased him right back.

"Oh, I don't know; I might cry all the way."

Derek gave her a comical look of horror and then thanked Megan solemnly.

"I hope you will visit often," she told him. "And bring your mother."

"I will plan on it," he said and bent to kiss her cheek.

The others gathered now, and soon all were exchanging last-minute hugs before riding on their way.

The courtyard seemed empty without them, and Megan's heart was heavy. In truth, she wished she could go to her room and have a good cry.

The idea was tempting, but Megan suddenly remembered that she had lost some of her privacy upon her marriage. Having to enter through Bracken's room was at times something of a hindrance.

"Will you be all right?" Bracken asked of her when the dust of the inner keep had begun to settle.

"I am not sure," she answered honestly.

Bracken put a gentle arm around her shoulders, but when she stiffened he immediately withdrew. It was clear that she wanted to mourn their leaving on her own. Still, he cared and wanted her to know this.

"I shall be at training fields if you need me."

"Thank you, Bracken," Megan told him, and watched as he turned and walked away in the morning sun.

The first day of November was upon them when a missive came from London. The king wished to see both Bracken of Hawkings Crest and his bride of six weeks. Megan nearly panicked.

"Why would he wish to see us? We have done as he asked."

"Megan," Bracken tried to reassure her. "There is nothing to fear. As you stated, we have done as he asked; he merely wants to see us."

"But Bracken, he's the *king*."

"He is but a man, Megan, and no one to be feared."

She tried to calm the frantic beating of her heart, but it was with an effort. The missive asked that Bracken present himself in one week, which left Megan little time if she had nothing appropriate to wear. Megan turned suddenly from her husband and started away.

"Where are you going?"

"To check on my clothing." *And yours!* Megan suddenly thought. She turned back. "Have you something to wear, Bracken?"

He hid a smile. "I'm sure I have several suitable choices."

Megan nodded absently and continued on her way. Bracken said something, but she didn't attend. It was all too sudden.

However, as Megan climbed the stairs a bright spot appeared on the horizon. Louisa lived in London, and Bracken was sure to plan a visit.

Megan had been to London many years ago and had enjoyed it immensely. She thought she might enjoy it once again, but her nerves were so rattled that she saw little as they rode toward the king's residence after a long day on the road.

Megan had never known such disappointment as to find out that they were expected to stay at Windsor Castle. Bracken promised her a visit to Louisa's before they returned to Hawkings Crest, but Megan, wishing she could see a familiar face, felt very let down that it could not be sooner.

The castle was grand, but Megan felt little elation as they entered. She was tired and dirty, and more than anything desired a bath and bed. She knew that her servants felt the same way, and if it had been possible to give a magical blink and be back at Hawkings Crest, Megan would have done so.

"Good evening, my lord. Good evening, my lady," a guard intoned as he met them in the vast foyer. "I will show you to your rooms. The king dines in an hour and requests your presence."

Bracken nodded, having clearly expected this, but Megan could have wept. With the late hour, it was inconceivable to her that the king had still not eaten. She and Bracken had not taken refreshment either, but Megan was too tired to care.

Gaining their rooms took some time as they walked down one massive hallway after another, but they were finally in their own suite. Helga was unpacking for Megan, but Bracken soon joined them and dismissed Megan's faithful lady with a nod.

"Will you be all right?" It seemed this was all Bracken asked her of late.

"It seems that I have little choice to be anything else."

"On the contrary, if you are not doing well, I will make your regrets to Henry."

"You can't do that!" Megan was horrified, and Bracken actually laughed.

"Megan, he is no monster. Indeed, he is

a man who likes to have his way, but if you are tired he will understand."

Megan stood and tried to reckon with all that had occurred. She drew a huge breath and let it out slowly.

"I will join you. I am tired, but not overly so, and I do not think I will sleep at all if I must wait until morning to meet the king."

Bracken smiled at her pluck but wasn't at all surprised. The Megan he knew rose to every occasion. "I'll call for you shortly."

"I'll be ready."

Thirty minutes later Megan was as good as her word. Her wimple in place, she was a vision in navy blue and gold when Bracken came for her. Since she'd taken some time to pray, her face was serene. She took Bracken's offered arm, and fortunately for Megan, he began a conversation meant to soothe.

"I really preferred it when you wore your hair down."

"You did? You never told me that before."

"I'm telling you now."

"Well, I'm a married woman now. It's not proper for my hair to hang long."

"Says who?"

"Well," Megan faltered. "Everyone."

"Umm." Bracken sounded clearly skeptical. "I guess I'll go along with it while we are here, but I am the final say at Hawkings Crest, and when we get home, you can do away with your wimples."

"Why, Bracken, that's outrageous! It's not proper, I tell you."

"And who says we need to be proper all of the time? It's probably 'everyone' again."

Megan smiled at his teasing, not realizing that he was quite serious about wanting her hair down. Indeed, it was a good thing she did not know. It would have left them arguing when they reached King Henry's massive dining hall.

"The Earl and Countess of Hawkesbury," the footman announced in a thundering voice as Bracken and Megan stood on the threshold.

As they stepped forward, Bracken felt Megan's hand tighten on his arm, and he spoke to her in a soft, reassuring voice.

"You will do me proud, Megan. You have nothing to worry about."

"What if I say the wrong thing?"

"You won't."

He sounded so confident that Megan felt reassured. Her chin rose slightly as they walked across the huge tile floor, and when she saw a group of women watching her handsome husband with appreciative eyes, she smiled with great pride.

Henry was in a group against one wall, and Bracken moved slowly in that direction. It had been years since they'd seen one another, but Henry recognized him. Bracken knew some pride of his own when Henry broke away and came toward them. Megan curtsied low, and Bracken bowed when the king stopped a few feet before them.

"Welcome, Bracken," Henry spoke, his voice deep and resonate.

"Thank you, my lord. If it please your highness, may I present my wife, Lady Megan, late of Stone Lake."

"Hello, Megan. Welcome to Windsor Castle."

"Thank you, your grace. I am honored at your hospitality."

The king smiled. He had heard that Marigold's younger sister could not hold a candle to that blonde beauty, but Henry found her lovely and very charming. It passed through his mind that she might also be as deceitful as Marigold, but then he warned himself not to judge too swiftly.

"I would like to meet with you

tomorrow, Bracken."

"Yes, my lord."

"Afternoon. Two o'clock."

"Certainly."

With that, the older man moved off. Megan stood in shock.

"That's all there is to it?"

Bracken's grin was lopsided. "Well, that's all there is for you. I must still meet with Henry tomorrow."

"Are you nervous?"

"No. Curious, but not afraid."

Megan was amazed at his calm. She did not know what she would have done without him.

They circulated some, and Megan met other lords and ladies, but it wasn't long before they were seated separately for dinner. Megan found herself seated among men and women she did not know, but who had obviously been to court before.

Megan did a lot of smiling and nodding, but because she was not comfortable with the way they mentioned different people who were not in attendance and systematically tore them apart, she didn't have much to say. It was one of the longest meals of her life. An hour after the meal ended, she had still not seen Bracken.

But God was taking care of her. Two

older women had come to speak with her. They were not among the women she had dined with, and Megan found real companionship with them. One was Lady Noella, who was Viscountess Dinsmore, and the other was Lady Evadne, wife of the Duke of Ellsworth.

They seemed genuinely interested in her, and within moments Megan was confidently sharing with them. She soon learned that both were old enough to be her mother, but it didn't seem to matter. They chatted freely and without restraint, and Megan detected no malicious intent in either woman.

Some 20 minutes later the threesome, who had been speaking near one of the hearths, moved from the heat. That was when Megan heard the voice. Her footsteps lagged, and she finally came to a halt.

"Megan?" Lady Noella spoke. "What is it?"

"That voice," Megan said.

Both women stared at her. The room was so noisy that it was barely possible to make out any one voice, but Megan looked certain.

"What voice?" Lady Evadne asked.

Megan's head turned slowly until she spotted a tall, well-built, dark-haired man just a few feet away. Megan stared at him, listening to his every word as though mesmerized. She was suddenly back in the forest on that awful night she had been ambushed.

We lost men tonight over a trunk full of homespun rags! There's nothing here but some good horseflesh. Let's ride.

"That's him," Megan said, her voice still soft.

"Who, Megan?"

"He's the one." Megan's voice was louder now. "The man who helped kill my father's men and steal my father's horses."

Everyone within ten feet of Megan stopped and stared. Megan took no notice. She was still watching the young lord when he turned cold eyes in her direction and stared at her. A shudder ran all over Megan. She wanted to cry Bracken's name, but she was too frightened to move or speak.

The crowd that had grown so silent all began to speak at once. The noise was so overwhelming that Megan began to tremble from head to foot. A moment passed, or maybe an hour, Megan couldn't tell. She felt a hand on her arm and someone calling her name, but everything was receding.

Megan slid into unconsciousness long before she realized that the hand holding her, and the voice calling her name belonged to the one she had wanted to call for just moments before.

Twenty-Nine

Megan moved her head to the side to avoid the smell that burned her nose, but still it persisted. She gasped and tried to speak, and suddenly the air cleared. With her head pounding, she attempted to open her eyes. They drifted open very slowly, and she took a moment to focus. When she did, she found Bracken leaning over her, his face harsh with concern.

"Bracken!" Megan gasped weakly, her small hands fisted into the front of his shirt. "He's here! The man who attacked us in the forest. He's in the dining hall."

"Hush, Megan," his voice soothed. "You've had a long day."

"No, Bracken, no." Megan's voice was turning desperate. "I swear to you, it's him. He's here."

"Megan, Megan." Bracken's voice was pained. "You're overly tired. Now try to rest; try to calm yourself."

He didn't believe her . . . wouldn't even listen to her. Megan began to cry, and Bracken, feeling very helpless, gathered her against him and let her sob. Megan continued to try to reason with Bracken but didn't realize that she was speaking only in her mind. He didn't answer her because he couldn't hear her, and Megan was growing weaker and more lethargic by the minute.

She was nearly asleep when she heard Bracken talking to Lyndon.

"What is it?"

"Henry wishes to see you."

"Now?"

"Yes."

Bracken placed Megan gently against the pillows and began to rise, but she suddenly gripped him with a strength he didn't know she possessed.

"Don't leave me, Bracken. Please, don't leave me. That man is here, and I beg you not to leave me."

Bracken hesitated. He'd never seen her like this and was seriously considering refusing Henry.

"I'll stay with her, Bracken." Lyndon's voice came low to his ears, and Bracken knew he could trust none better.

"I must go, Megan, but Lyndon will be with you all the time."

"Bracken."

"Shh," he hushed her again. "I will

return as soon as I am able and come directly to you."

Miraculously, Megan calmed. She knew in her panic she had not been trusting God, but now it was time. Megan wished Bracken did not have to leave, but she would accept the situation.

Bracken saw the acquiescence on her face and rose. Megan sat up, and although still shaking, walked with him to the door. They did not exchange words before he left, but Bracken looked deeply into her eyes before opening the door and stepping without.

"Tell me about the incident of which your wife speaks."

Bracken answered his king quietly, telling him in detail of the attack in the forest, as well as the report that the same attackers had been seen near the home of Black Francesca.

James Nayland was nearby, taking in every word as well, but neither he nor Henry gave a flicker of recognition. They had been given secondhand news of all these events, and some that Bracken was not aware of, but neither man let on.

"Young Kirkpatrick denied ever seeing your wife and has now left. He was very insulted," Henry said at last.

"Yes, my lord."

"Can you control your wife or not, Bracken of Hawkings Crest?"

"Yes, your grace, I can. I am most sorry for the incident."

Henry stared at him, his expression giving nothing away.

"We will not meet later today as planned." They stood now in the wee hours of the morning. "Come to my chambers tomorrow morning. Ten o'clock."

"Yes, my lord."

Bracken was shown out, but neither Henry nor James Nayland made a move to retire.

"He tells the truth," Henry stated.

"I believe you are right, my lord."

"The girl, Megan. Is she all right?"

"She is resting but very upset."

Henry nodded. "For a time I thought she might be of her sister's ilk, but I think not."

"I quite agree with you, my king. I believe Megan sincere in her outburst."

"I hate to do it, but if there is one more charge against young Kirkpatrick, I'll give him the boot, his father's connections or no."

James nodded. "I can't see as you have any choice."

"I thought you would see it that way. Go to bed, James. I'll see you at noon."

"Goodnight, Henry. Sleep well."

The faithful servant and friend left on silent feet, but even if he'd stomped away, Henry would not have heard. He was deep in thought with the task of weighing two men in the balance, and it was nearly an hour later before Henry made his choice and sought his own bed.

"I wish to try to explain to you."

"There is no need," Bracken told Megan the next day as they sat together for their noon meal in the private salon in their suite.

"Yes, Bracken, there is. I am calm now, but I don't think you understood."

"Megan," Bracken jumped in, "I understood everything. You saw the man that attacked you in the forest and stole your father's horses."

Megan could only stare at him. "If you understood, then why didn't —"

"Because you were my only concern at the moment. You were hysterical. There was nothing I could do about Roland Kirkpatrick, so I just —"

"Is that his name?"

"Yes, but as I stated, you were my

concern. I also knew it was only a matter of time before Henry would wish to see me."

"What did he say?" Megan looked uncertain for the first time.

"He wanted to know what you were talking about and then asked me if I could indeed control my wife."

Megan's eyes dropped, and she blushed to the roots of her hair. Bracken didn't try to lessen her embarrassment but let the full import of her actions sink in.

"Kirkpatrick was highly insulted, and Henry did not seem overly pleased with the whole incident," Bracken told her softly. "I understand you're upset, Megan, but it seems nearly everyone in the room heard you accuse the man."

"But he did it." Megan thought this explained all.

"Be that as it may, you insulted the man. I believe you, and somehow I think Henry does as well, but what if you'd been wrong? Think of the shame. We've drawn enough attention to ourselves as it is."

Bracken's last words were voiced in irritation, and Megan became a bit testy herself. They continued to eat, but now there was a strained silence between them. After a time, Megan spoke up, telling Bracken in very few words that she wanted to be alone.

"You'd best ready yourself for your meeting with Henry."

"That meeting is canceled. I am to see him tomorrow morning."

Megan looked as frustrated as she felt. "What are we to do around here until tomorrow?"

Feeling put out with his wife, Bracken stood. "I don't know about you, but I am going to the archery butts. Windsor's targets are some of the finest in the land."

"And what of me?"

Bracken speared her with a glance, knowing he was being ruthless. "We are delayed here, Megan, because of your outburst. Do not vent your wrath on me for something you have done."

Megan knew he was right, but her pride rushed to the fore.

"Very well, I shall take a walk on my own."

"I shouldn't do that if I were you."

"Why? Is Lord Kirkpatrick still here?" Megan's face had become fearful, but Bracken hardened his heart against all compassion.

"No, but the entire castle is talking of you, and I should think you would want to lie low, as it were."

Knowing he was being unfair but feeling very frustrated in the whole ordeal, Bracken turned away. It was amazing how easy it was to take things out on his wife. Had he been home, he would have pursued Roland Kirkpatrick to the ends of the earth seeking answers, but this was Henry's domain, and he was not at liberty to take the law into his hands or even to begin an investigation.

Of course, one could learn many things just by walking the hallways and grounds of Windsor Castle. Bracken had spoken the truth to Megan about visiting the archery fields, but he did not intend to take a direct path there.

Megan retired to her room and spent the next hour in prayer. Bracken's words had been right, but his delivery of the message was one of the harshest she had ever received. Megan was wrapped in pity for some time.

Many minutes passed before Megan realized the embarrassment she had caused her spouse. They had been invited as guests of the king, and Megan had spouted off after dinner like a servant girl.

Hot tears filled her eyes as she confessed

her sins to God and made an effort to give the whole ordeal over to His care. Megan longed for her copy of the Psalms and Proverbs, but she had feared bringing it from her room at Hawkings Crest. Instead, she stopped and dwelt on a few of the many verses she had already taken into her heart. She found the most comfort in the first few verses of Psalm 27.

"The Lord is my light and my salvation; whom shall I fear? The Lord is the strength of my life; of whom shall I be afraid? When the wicked, even mine enemies and my foes, came upon me to eat up my flesh, they stumbled and fell. Though an host should encamp against me, my heart shall not fear; though war should rise against me, in this will I be confident . . . For in the time of trouble he shall hide me in his pavilion; in the secret of his tabernacle shall he hide me; he shall set me up upon a rock."

Megan asked God to score these verses into her heart so that her words and actions would be changed forever. She so wanted to leave a godly impression with those watching her in this place, and even though she knew they thought her a hysterical young female, she determined to leave a better last impression than she had a first.

Megan had just come to this resolve when Helga asked if she would see Lady Evadne, the Duchess of Ellsworth.

"Of course, Helga. Please show her into the salon."

Megan took a moment to check her appearance and then worked at not showing her embarrassment as she joined the duchess.

"How are you, Megan?"

"I am doing well, my lady; thank you for asking." Megan's cheeks were slightly pink, but the other woman didn't seem to notice.

The duchess laughed softly. "Please call me Evadne. I tell you, Megan, sometimes I am very dull."

The younger girl stared at her.

"I just figured out that you are Megan — Louisa's Megan!"

"You know Aunt Louisa?"

"We've been friends for years. She could hardly wait to tell me of her conversion. Had I realized it last night, I'd have told Noella. She would have been thrilled as well."

Again, Megan could only stare. They had both been so kind last night, but it had never once occurred to Megan that they shared a faith in Christ.

"I didn't realize," Megan finally said. "I'm sorry to say that Louisa never mentioned you."

Evadne smiled. "She never said anything about Elly?"

"Why, yes, she did."

"That's me. She's never called me Evadne. We met shortly after I became the Duchess of Ellsworth, and the name Elly started as a joke. Now it's all she ever calls me."

"You're Elly?"

"Yes."

Megan couldn't stop her smile. "She's talked of you repeatedly, telling me how thrilled you were going to be when she told you of both her and Derek."

"And I *was* thrilled, as you can well imagine, but right now, my feet hurt."

Megan gawked at her.

"Oh!" the younger woman finally cried. "Where are my manners? Please sit down."

They both landed on the settee in a gale of laughter and talked for the next two hours. Megan had never met such a woman. She reminded her greatly of her mother-in-law, and Megan was like a sponge whenever the older woman talked. At one point Evadne questioned her about the night before, and Megan felt free to explain. Evadne promised to pray that God's will would be done.

The time was growing late when Evadne asked Megan how she enjoyed marriage. Megan did not take offense; she was glad to share with someone.

"We had words this morning over the incident last night, but most often Bracken and I get on very well. We have our times of trouble, but in truth I love being married to Bracken. He is beyond kindness to me."

The duchess studied her face. Uncertainty appeared momentarily in Megan's eyes.

"There is something you don't like, isn't there, Megan?"

Megan's face flamed, and her eyes dropped. "I can't speak of it, Evadne. It's a sin for me not to be content with my lot."

Silent for some moments, the older woman placed her long, tapered fingers beneath Megan's chin and raised the girl's eyes to her own.

"I will not press you to explain, Megan, but if it's what I'm thinking of, you're wrong. There's no sin in such pleasure. Do not settle for endurance. 'Tis something to be enjoyed."

Megan's blush only deepened, and Evadne could tell that her words had not been taken to heart. The older woman determined to pray.

"I really must be going."

They both stood.

"I can't wait to see Louisa and tell her of your visit. I am sure Bracken plans for us to go there."

"Oh, Megan." Evadne's voice held regret. "Louisa and Derek left just last week for Joyce's home in the north. I know she planned to stay for a time."

Megan surprised her with a smile. "Then I am especially glad that God gave me this time with you. It was just what I needed."

The two embraced.

"Take care, Megan, and go with God."

"Thank you, Evadne. You will never know how you have blessed my heart."

They parted then, and when Bracken returned an hour later Megan was still on a cloud. She told him of their meeting, and Bracken was truly pleased for his wife. Still, he knew that the news he must share would remove some of the sparkle from her eye.

Just before he'd returned to their room, a missive had been delivered to him from

James Nayland. It seemed that Megan was expected to attend Bracken's meeting with the king as well.

Thirty

Megan could eat nothing the following morning, but she felt no hunger, only fear, when she eventually stood outside Henry's chambers. When they had left their rooms, Megan found dozens of speculative eyes resting on them. It was almost more than the young countess could take.

She had tried to give herself and the situation to God, but still her stomach clenched. The apprehension was not just for herself, but Bracken. He had proven himself a loyal lord, and now Megan, in a moment's time, had evidently ruined his reputation. She felt more grief for that than anything else she'd ever done.

Bracken had not laid such a claim at her door, but it was the truth. He had been very kind to her when he'd returned yesterday, and they had spent a pleasant evening in their own rooms, but Megan knew well what she had done.

"His royal highness, King Henry, will see you now."

The footman seemed pompous enough

400

to be a king himself but Megan took little notice. Bracken stepped back to let her precede him and within seconds they stood before England's king.

"Come forward."

The two approached, and Megan found herself under Henry's close-eyed scrutiny.

"I hope you will grace my court often, Lady Megan, but it is to be hoped that you will learn to control your tongue."

"I am sorry, your grace. It was very foolish of me."

Henry nodded and felt solid confirmation that Megan was nothing like Marigold. That blonde creature would never have admitted to a wrong. An instant later he transferred his attention to Bracken. Megan was forgotten.

"I have some lands for you, Bracken of Hawkings Crest. Are you up to the added responsibility?"

"Yes, my liege. I accept them with humble gratitude and the hope of serving you better."

"Very good. I also have a new title for you and anticipate that you will continue to serve me well as the Duke of Briscoe."

Bracken's head bowed. "This humble duke thanks you, my king, and offers his sword to defend your crown as you rule

England, the greatest country in all the world."

"It is good," Henry's voice rang out. "Journey home safely now. I will like as not send for you soon."

Bracken and Megan bowed their way from the room, and a moment later the footman announced their presence into the hall.

"The Duke and Duchess of Briscoe."

Megan's hand rested calmly on Bracken's arm, but she could not for the life of her understand why. Bracken had been made a duke! It was all too fantastic to be real, but the fact that he had not been rebuked caused her no end of relief.

Megan realized then how proud she was of her husband. She had never heard him talk as he had to King Henry. Where had he learned to say all the right things?

The same eyes studied them as before, but this time Megan took little notice. She was too busy working through all that had just occurred. They were back at the rooms before Megan even felt her feet on the floor, and once inside Megan could only turn and stare at her husband. Bracken stared right back, his face solemn.

"Were you surprised?"

"Yes," he admitted. Indeed, his voice

sounded like he was trying to take it in as well.

"I am very pleased for you, Bracken. I thought Henry might banish you from court because of me."

"Oh, Megan, why did you not tell me of your fear?"

She shrugged. "I thought you would only say 'twas my fault, and that would be true."

Bracken shook his head. "It was unfortunate, but not that severe. And also keep in mind — Henry does not do things impetuously, Megan. His plans for me were most likely settled long before now. Do not forget that I rode into battle for him over a year ago. He does not forget such things."

Megan nodded. "Nevertheless, I am pleased for you, Bracken. You will serve well the title of duke."

"What of yourself, Megan? You are now a duchess."

Megan shrugged. "It was you I cared about."

Bracken was very moved by her words. He would have shown what was in his heart, but the situation was not private enough; they could be disturbed at any moment. Unfortunately for Megan, it never occurred to Bracken to just reach out and touch her hand or gently kiss her lips. And just as unfortunately, it would take some time for Bracken to understand that this was the very reason she stiffened at his touch.

Megan spent her first Christmas at Hawkings Crest alone. Bracken had been called to Henry in the middle of December. The king, weary to death of losing men, money, and time, sent Bracken and several other lords north. As emissaries of peace, they rode out with a full battalion of men to the Scottish border.

Still just a bride, Megan stayed at home in the country. Many young women in her situation would have gone to their parents' home, but even though Megan had heard from both her father and mother, she did not feel welcome at Stone Lake Castle for a prolonged stay. Also, the fact that she didn't know when Bracken would arrive home caused her to stay put.

This did not bother her. She had many things she wished to do in Bracken's absence, and the castle spent one of its busiest winters with Megan at the helm. Louisa came for a visit, staying for almost a month. While she was there, a group of knights stopped in long enough to deliver a letter to Megan. They had seen Bracken, and although he didn't know when he would be able to come home, he had wanted them to bring word to Hawkings Crest.

Megan waited until she could find time to go to her room and be alone to read her letter. It was very short, and Megan could see that he'd ordered a scribe to write it, but it nevertheless touched her heart.

Megan,
I am well. Thinking of you. If you are with child, please take care. Will be home soon. Act in wisdom.
Bracken

Although it was short, the letter meant a great deal to her. She was not with child, and for the first time Megan wondered just how disappointing that might be to her husband. Every man wants sons to continue the line, but not every man receives his wish. Her father was a fine example of that. Vincent's only brother was dead. Megan assumed some distant cousin would take Stone Lake Castle on her father's death.

Who would inherit Hawkings Crest if there were never a male heir? One of

Bracken's brothers most likely. Megan would like to present Bracken with a child; indeed, she was sure it would make him quite glad. If only it didn't require . . . Megan refused to finish the thought.

You are positively wicked, Megan, she told herself. *How can you expect Bracken to see you as a godly woman if you act like that? If you can think of nothing better to dwell on, you had best get back to work.*

Bracken's back ached some, but the castle was in sight, and that was all that mattered. A night here at Wyndmere, as a guest of Lord Trygve Osborn, and then tomorrow he could ride for home.

The men had never met before Henry's call, but they had been together in the north country for over 12 weeks, and there was little they hadn't shared. Bracken found Tryg, who was ten years older, to be a man of his word, a mighty warrior, and a lover of all that was right. Bracken had come to admire him greatly.

Being to the south now, since they had just reported to Henry in London, and being just a day's ride from Hawkings Crest, made it difficult to stop over, but Tryg pressed him and Bracken agreed. It would be good to sleep in a bed and sup from a table and trencher.

They rode side by side through the massive gates, their men stretched out behind them. All the keep seemed to cheer over their lord's arrival. Trygve was the Marquess of Overton, and he had shared with Bracken many times about the loyalty of his servants.

Trygve had also shared about Ann. The men were dismounting in the inner bailey when a woman came running, and Bracken knew it was she. She was tall, slim, and blonde, and in a moment she had thrown her arms around her husband. Trygve swung her around with a great laugh, and when they stopped, he looked down only at her. Bracken watched unashamedly as Ann's hands tenderly cupped her husband's face and she reached up on tiptoe to kiss him.

"I missed you so," she said.

"And I you."

"I love you, Tryg," she said, and kissed him again.

Bracken turned away then and did not hear his friend's reply. He didn't have to take his imagination far to know that his reception from Megan would be vastly different. She ran Hawkings Crest to perfection, and he knew she would do anything he asked, but she was not an affectionate woman. Indeed, he was finding, quite the opposite.

"Bracken," Trygve now called to him, his arm still around his wife. "Come, meet my Ann."

Bracken came forward and was rewarded with her warm smile.

"You have ridden far, Bracken, and I am glad you have taken time to stop before going home."

"My men and I appreciate your hospitality."

Ann smiled again. "I will go now and see to your needs." She smiled at Bracken and then said to her husband, "The children are anxious to see you."

"We will be right along." He watched her go and turned back to Bracken with a huge smile. He threw an arm around the younger man's shoulders and urged him to the house.

"Come, Bracken, come and eat. Before you know it the morning will be upon you, and you can go home to Megan." Out of pure contentment, Trygve gave a great shout of laughter. "Then it will be your turn to be greeted as I have been."

Trygve happened to glance at Bracken's face then, and what he saw stopped him short. It was gone now, but he had very definitely seen a hardness in Bracken's eyes.

"Did you fight with Megan before you left?"

"No." Bracken faced him, but his body was a bit stiff.

"What is it then?"

"I don't know what you mean."

"Yes, you do. I said you would be greeted as I was, but that's not so, is it?"

"You overstep yourself, Tryg," Bracken warned.

"Nay, Bracken, I do not." The older man was not easily intimidated. "We have shared nearly all and learned much from each other in these last weeks, but each time we spoke of our families I sensed an emptiness in you. Do you love your wife?"

"Yes," Bracken answered without hesitation.

"Have you told her?"

Bracken frowned. "I protect her and provide for her. I tell her in a thousand ways every day."

Trygve shook his head. " 'Tis not the same, Bracken. A woman needs to hear."

"That's ridiculous!" Bracken disdained. "She is not an affectionate woman; it would change nothing."

"Bracken, you are wrong. Do you court her? Do you romance her?"

This was the second time someone had advised him to do such. His mother's words seemed so long ago that he had completely forgotten about them. Still . . .

"You do not know her —" Bracken began, but Trygve lay hold of his broad shoulders.

"I do not need to know her to know *about* her. Ann and I knew each other two hours when we became husband and wife. I found her beautiful, so 'twas no difficult thing. I learned later that it was torture for her. For months she froze at my touch.

"Then she began to grow thin and depressed. It took some time, but I finally understood that it's different for a woman. I began to bring her flowers, hold her hand, and even kiss her without expectations.

"She began to return my embraces, and even conceived, and now, Bracken, I am greeted as you saw. We have been married ten years, yet I still court and romance her. In return, she longs for my presence."

Bracken stared at the older man. It had never once occurred to him that Megan was responding to his treatment of her. He thought now about the way she hugged his family and even the children who lived at Hawkings Crest. She was certainly affectionate with them. He was doing something wrong — quite possibly everything.

"I do not wish to pry into the most private part of your life, Bracken, but what I have told you is true."

Bracken finally nodded but didn't speak. A part of him still wanted to deny all of this and lay the blame at Megan's feet.

"Come along," the older man continued. "We will wash and eat, and you can think on what I've said. 'Twill be no embarrassment for me should you want to discuss this again."

Bracken thanked him sincerely, and the men walked toward the high, stone edifice. Wyndmere was a fine home, a showplace, but Bracken took little notice. His heart was completely centered on the little redhead awaiting him at Hawkings Crest.

STONE LAKE

"Why, Marigold." Annora's voice held surprise at the sight of her oldest daughter but no particular pleasure. She hadn't been home for months, and even though Annora had worried for her, she had also enjoyed a better relationship with Vincent than she'd ever had in her life.

"Hello, Mother." Marigold's voice was very sweet, but for the first time Annora did not respond in kind.

"Where have you been?" Annora wished to know.

Marigold hesitated. Her mother was not happy with her, and this was something new. In truth, she was only home because she needed money, but that wasn't going to work if Annora was vexed with her. A new tactic was needed.

"Why, Mother, did you not receive my letter?"

"No." Annora's voice was cold.

Marigold's sigh was deep. "No one is dependable these days. I wrote telling you I was spending the winter in France. I hope you weren't worried."

"Not overly," Annora said, suddenly realizing it was the truth. Again this perplexed Marigold.

"Oh, Mother," she remarked, as though she just had a thought. "You're not still upset about my missing Megan's wedding, are you?"

"No, Marigold, I'm not." This, too, was the truth. "Megan has done well for herself. I am quite proud of her."

Marigold nearly panicked. Her mother had never in her life had a good word for her younger sister. What in the world had gone on? For the first time Marigold saw that she'd been away too long.

"Whatever do you mean?" she asked, just managing to keep her voice light.

"Oh, hadn't you heard?" Annora's voice was triumphant with genuine pleasure. "Bracken's been made a duke. Your sister is the Duchess of Briscoe."

Under the guise of adjusting the hem of her gown, Marigold managed to duck her head and turn away. Her face was a mask of rage. She didn't speak until she had her voice under control.

"Well, now, isn't that grand! Maybe I should go and visit to extend my apologies and then my congratulations."

Marigold turned with a smile, and Annora, still wanting to think the best of this selfish child, was swiftly taken in.

"Oh, Marigold, that's a wonderful idea. I know they would love to have you."

Marigold nodded serenely before the conversation went to general topics. Annora's heart was filled with well-being over Marigold's benevolent attitude. Marigold's heart was filled with hatred, first for Henry, the man who had increased

Bracken's title, and then for her sister, that redheaded cow who had been lucky enough to land on her feet.

Thirty-One

Bracken did not leave Wyndmere as early as he had expected, so he and his men did not gain Hawkings Crest until sometime after midnight. Bracken bathed and called for Megan in the night, but they did little more than greet each other. Megan wished they could have visited, talked of his trip, and discussed whether he was home for a time, but Bracken fell asleep very swiftly and she returned to her bed.

The hour was late before Megan rose the next morning, but even when she moved silently through Bracken's chamber she found him fast asleep. Indeed, the day was long spent before he rose, and by that time Megan was out in the keep, going about her chores for the day.

Bracken, a little embarrassed to have to hunt for his wife on his first day back, attempted to find her by casually searching on his own. In truth, this was no difficult task. He loved Hawkings Crest, and a stroll through first the castle and then the keep was a pleasure.

Bracken had not been out ten minutes when he saw that Megan had been busy in his absence. There was a freshness in nearly every room of the castle. The rooms were not only clean, but Bracken spotted new wall hangings and rugs everywhere. He smiled when he thought about what she might have spent, but it did not concern him.

From what he could tell, Megan was nowhere in the castle, so Bracken took himself outside. Here, too, things looked changed for the better. Always neat, there was a new cleanliness to every corner of the inner bailey. But something wasn't right. Bracken was walking around in an attempt to put his finger on what was different when he saw that the byre was missing.

He shook his head slightly, but his eyes were not playing tricks on him. Bracken was walking slowly toward the location of the old byre when he spotted the new one. Duke and duchess had talked of the need for a new byre, but he never dreamed Megan would have one built on her own. It was a fine structure, both in design and function, but anger was swiftly filling Bracken and dampening his appreciation for the improvements.

Without caring what people thought, Bracken began asking everyone within sight where Lady Megan had gone. Even at that, it took some time, but he eventually found the way.

"Here, Noleen," Megan instructed from her place outside the castle walls. "Return to the castle with this basket."

"Yes, my lady," the servant girl replied. "Do you need more?"

"No, I think this will do."

Megan smiled at her, and Noleen moved away. The duchess went back to gathering herbs, leaves, and bark, but a moment later she heard Bracken speak to Arik and turned with a smile. The smile swiftly died as her husband neared; she saw that he was coldly furious.

"I could not find you," he began. Megan stared at him a moment. He was livid. Megan frowned. She thought they were far beyond this point in their relationship. Nevertheless, her voice was very repentant.

"I'm sorry, Bracken. I told several people where I was, but I see now that I should have stayed until you were awake."

"It seems that you have been very busy."

Normally Megan would have smiled at

this, but it seemed he was not pleased by her efforts.

"It was a long winter, and I took advantage of your absence to see to some things."

" 'Took advantage.' " His anger seemed to be growing. "You have stated that accurately. You wait until I am gone and then order the building of a new byre."

Thinking he was still tired from his trip, Megan blinked at him and said slowly, "We discussed all of this, Bracken, and made plans to build it just after the new year."

"I did not want the byre where you placed it." He was not even trying to be reasonable.

Megan was becoming angry herself. "It's in the very place we discussed."

"While I was away I decided it was best to build the new one in the original location."

"While you were away? Why did you not send word?" Megan demanded.

"Because I didn't think my *wife* would go behind my back."

Megan had never been so hurt in all of her life. He had said the word "wife" in a way that made Megan feel as if she were repulsive to him. And what in the world was this really all about? It was inconceivable to her that he would really be so angry about the byre, but she could think of nothing else.

Husband and wife were still glaring at each other when Clive appeared in the clearing. Bracken, not knowing if an emergency was afoot, diverted his attention.

"What is it?" Bracken demanded.

The boy answered timidly. "I'm sorry to disturb you, my lord, but Lady Marigold is here."

"My sister?" Megan's mouth nearly dropped open.

"Yes, my lady."

Megan was so surprised that for a moment she didn't know what to say. In truth, her sister terrified her. Bracken had said a long time ago that he would never let her be hurt, but one look at his still furious face told her she would gain no support there. Megan knew she would have to face Marigold alone. She squared her shoulders and turned to Clive.

"Please see that Lady Marigold is made comfortable and tell her I'll be along shortly."

Bracken had not said anything during any of this, and now Megan was too upset to even look at him. She gathered the piles she had been sorting into the basket and lifted it by the handle. Without a backward glance, she moved toward the castle, Arik falling in behind her.

"Megan!" Marigold exclaimed with every semblance of delight as soon as the young duchess joined her in the great hall.

"Hello, Marigold."

"That is all? Hello, Marigold?" In a cloud of scent, the older girl then moved forward to give Megan a hug, and although Megan returned the embrace, she was not at all easy.

"My goodness, Megan," Marigold exclaimed after she'd stepped back to inspect her. "Being a duchess must agree with you. You're nowhere near as fat as you used to be."

Megan barely managed a smile. It had always been this way. Marigold complimented her constantly, but in such a backhanded way that Megan always felt as if she'd been slapped.

"Mother wrote that you had not been home lately." Megan was desperate to change the subject.

"No. I wintered in France. I wrote Mother, but you know how forgetful she is; she probably mislaid the letter."

Megan didn't know any such thing; her

mother was very organized. But the women had now taken seats near one of the hearths and Megan remained quiet, her mind wandering to the long afternoon that certainly lay ahead.

"I'm sorry to have missed your wedding, Megan. Did Mother explain how ill I was?"

"No. She led me to believe that you simply chose not to come." Megan's voice was calm, but she always grew very tired of Marigold's lying ways and was not going to allow them.

Marigold looked at Megan in surprise. "It would seem that the kitten has grown claws."

"No, Marigold, I am not being catty," Megan said gently. "I just wanted you to know that I know you're lying."

Marigold threw herself back against the seat.

"Oh, come on, Megan," she said in disgust, all sweetness gone. "You sound like an old woman."

"I do not enjoy lies, Marigold, and I'm not going to pretend otherwise."

The older sister eyed her disdainfully. This wasn't going to be any fun if Megan insisted on being so forthright. As usual, Marigold had another tactic up her sleeve.

"Well, enough talk about us. Where is that delicious duke of yours?"

"Bracken is in the keep. I imagine he will be along shortly, but I fear he's not in a good humor."

"Lovers' quarrel?" Marigold's eyes were huge, her voice sweet as honey. Megan was not fooled.

"No," she told her shortly, and then asked if Marigold would like a tour.

That took the next two hours. By the time they were finished, Megan felt like a limp rag. Marigold had been ready with a compliment for nearly everything she saw, but each one held an underlying criticism. By the time they parted in order to ready themselves for the evening meal, Megan was shaking all over.

Relaxing some while Helga was doing her hair, Megan tensed all over again when she heard Bracken enter his own room. She need not have worried. He was there for quite some time but did not seek her out. Megan could have wept. What a terrible homecoming. She had missed him so much and worked so hard to please him, and all it had gotten her was his wrath. Now Marigold had come to Hawkings Crest, and Megan felt utterly defeated.

She and Bracken hadn't even talked! It

could be that he would be leaving again soon. If Marigold tarried, they would have no time together at all. On the way downstairs, Megan determined to put her own hurt aside and do what she could to repair the damage. However, one look at Bracken's stony features told Megan that Bracken was not ready to forgive.

This was proven when the evening meal followed the day's pattern of being long and difficult. Bracken did not say five words, and Marigold chattered away until Megan had a headache, something Marigold was aware of and enjoyed immensely. Marigold had seen few keeps as grand as Hawkings Crest, and her fury over her sister's good fortune knew no bounds. She could see that Bracken's men were all captivated with her, and whenever that happened Marigold was in her element. The only problem was Bracken himself.

Why had she not noticed when Bracken was at Stone Lake Castle that he had grown into a man of tremendous size and fine appearance? Marigold found him very handsome and desirable. Some of his men were as well, but if she was really going to score a conquest here and hurt Megan in the process, it would have to be the lord himself. However, every time she looked at

Bracken, Bracken was looking at Megan, who was not even aware of his scrutiny.

That things were not well between them right now was obvious, but Bracken still had no interest in Marigold. It galled that slim blonde to no end to sit with a man who found her fat sister more interesting. She would have to think of something.

She had entertained thoughts of being the duchess herself, but it didn't look as though Bracken would actually send Megan away. This meant that her stay at Hawkings Crest would have to be cut short. Maybe she could think of another way to disrupt things. Then when she left, she would at least know there was disaster in her wake.

For the next two nights, Megan walked in her sleep. She did not get even as far as the passageway. Lyndon woke her the first night, and Bracken the next. It was the only time her husband had spoken to her. Megan was beginning to grow frantic. It would seem that Marigold's visit was going to stretch on indefinitely, and Megan knew that until she left, things would not be resolved with Bracken.

She began to ask herself questions. What had Bracken seen and experienced while he'd been away to make such a radical change in him? He said the byre angered him, but Megan had the distinct feeling that there was something more. She continued to pray and try to reach out to him, but by Marigold's fourth night at Hawkings Crest, Megan was exhausted and completely defeated. She knew she was being a poor hostess and, indeed, Bracken frowned at her quite fiercely; nevertheless, she went to bed early and slept through the night without waking or walking.

The next morning Bracken was up early, but not out of his room. He sat for many minutes and thought about his actions of the last days. He could honestly say that right now he hated himself. Why was he treating Megan as though she were a disobedient child? Why had he not taken Trygve's words to heart and come home to woo and court her? Bracken shook his head in disgust. Why had he reacted as he did?

Bracken suddenly stood. He didn't know if it would ever happen again, but he must go now and try to make repairs. He would start by apologizing for the way he had behaved. Megan was not in her room, so Bracken continued on to her salon. She was there, still in her dressing gown, the Psalms open before her.

"Good morning, Megan," he said civilly.

"Good morning, Bracken," Megan replied, trying not to overreact. It was the first time in months that she had heard the normal sound of his voice.

"I have come about last night. I am sorry."

Megan smiled sweetly. " 'Tis all right Bracken. I'm sorry I turned in early, but in truth I was so weary."

Bracken frowned. "No, Megan. I'm talking about in the night, when you came to me."

Now it was Megan's turn to frown. "I did not come to you in the night."

"Of course you did."

Megan stiffened and shook her head. "What game is this you play?"

"No game." Bracken frowned in return. "You came to me in the night. In my anger I sent you away."

Megan's eyes could have swallowed her face.

"I would do no such thing."

Bracken hesitated. This was quite true. He had been very surprised. "Could you have been asleep?"

"You know me well enough to know I

426

would not — awake or asleep."

Bracken stared at her. "But your voice. I heard you."

Megan froze and then said flatly, "My sister."

Bracken shook his head. "The voice, it was yours."

"Think, Bracken." Megan sounded impatient. "You have commented yourself on how much we sound alike."

"But I was so certain 'twas you."

"Oh, come now, Bracken!" The last fragment of Megan's tolerance was gone, and she was now in high fury. "Do you mean to tell me you do not know my generous curves from those of my slim sister?"

"I did not touch the woman in my bed!" he thundered. "And how would she get in?"

"I wouldn't know." Megan's voice was cold.

Bracken looked desperate. "We shall ask Lyndon. Come with me so you can hear his reply."

Megan dutifully followed, her body stiff with outrage.

"Lyndon," Bracken called to him when they reached the antechamber, but the young knight did not stir. Bracken shook his shoulder.

"Lyndon."

Still nothing. Bracken placed his torch in the sconce on the wall and carefully turned Lyndon's head. He lifted his one eyelid and stared for a moment. Lyndon never stirred.

"He's been drugged."

Megan's hand went to her mouth. "Will he be all right?"

"I don't know. Return to your room whilst I find Arik."

The next hour was nightmarish for Megan as she sat in her room. Could Marigold really have gone this far? Each time Megan asked the question, her mind gave her an unqualified yes. She made herself dress and ready for the day, and a short time afterward Bracken came for her. Lyndon was sitting up on the edge of his bed.

"Lyndon, are you all right?" Megan asked, her voice tearful.

"Yes, my lady. I'm sorry I let you down."

"No, Lyndon, it was not your fault."

"She asked me to have a drink with her."

"Who?" Bracken wished to know.

"Lady Marigold. I sat with her, but then felt very tired. I dreamt she came to my room but wouldn't let me kiss her."

Lyndon realized to whom he'd spoken just then and blushed. He turned tortured eyes to Bracken.

"I'm sorry."

"It's all right, Lyndon." Bracken's voice was compassionate. "Sleep some more. I will wake you later."

Arik remained with Lyndon while Bracken and Megan went back to Megan's room. They stood quietly for some time before Megan spoke.

"She must leave," she said, and then held her breath. She did not know what she would do if Bracken argued otherwise.

"Yes," Bracken agreed. "Will you tell her, or shall I?"

Megan's chin raised with determination. "She is my sister; I will do the task."

Thirty-Two

Megan found her sister in bed. For the sake of privacy, she had given her an elegant suite of rooms in the tower, but she now felt not the slightest compunction about walking in uninvited.

When Bracken had questioned her about talking with Marigold, she had not understood that he would not accompany her. Nevertheless, she now stood over her sister like an enraged warrior, waited for her to awaken, and then spoke with calm force.

"You will leave here today, Marigold. Your lies will not work here, nor will your deceit. Bracken is well aware of who came to him in the night, and you will leave Hawkings Crest now."

Marigold only smiled and stretched like a spoiled cat. "Did Bracken tell you how much he enjoyed himself?"

Megan didn't so much as blink. "Get out, Marigold. You have one hour."

With that she walked away. Arik was waiting for her, something Megan was very pleased about as she was shaking so violently that once on the tower stairs she tripped. Arik's great arm alone kept her from going headfirst down the full length.

She continued on to the great hall and ordered food for her sister's entourage. She would never send them away hungry, but this way she would not have to share one more meal in her sister's company. It was more than an hour before Marigold made her appearance, and Megan could see that she was not ready for travel. Bracken was still nowhere to be seen. Megan once again had to handle the situation on her own.

"Is there something wrong with your hearing, Marigold? I told you to leave."

The older girl's look was wounded. "But I didn't think you really meant it. Why, Megan, we have barely had time to get reacquainted."

"I will not have you living here trying to seduce my husband. Now leave."

The hall had strangely emptied, save Arik who stood behind Marigold. Neither girl really took notice of him. Marigold continued her sweet act for several more minutes before the real woman came to the surface. She snarled at Megan in a way that made her feel frightened, but the younger sister held her ground.

"I can see that I will have to order your

things packed and have you removed bodily."

"You wouldn't dare," Marigold retorted, her lip curling.

"Just watch me," Megan told her.

Marigold's small bosom heaved. "You little fool," she spat. "He asked me to come to him and expects me again tonight. He told me that I'm the most beautiful woman he's ever seen and that you repulse him."

Megan sadly shook her head. "You've told so many lies, Marigold, that you have begun to believe them yourself. I find I am not angry with you — I pity you too much for that."

Marigold's open hand struck Megan's cheek. It was not a hard blow, but Megan hadn't seen it coming. Her head was tossed to the side. The younger woman was just reaching for her cheek when Marigold let out a bellow that brought Megan's head around fast. Bracken, as well as much of the castle, came running to see that Arik had come forward and quite literally lifted Marigold by her upper arm. Marigold screamed in agony until the huge man shook her like a rat. When at last she hung limp and silent from his huge fist, he spoke to Megan in that rusty voice.

"Go to your room. I'll see to this."

Megan didn't hesitate. She heard Bracken's voice somewhere behind her, but she nearly ran from the hall without looking at anyone.

Megan would have given anything not to have it come to this point, but she hadn't known what else to do. She told herself she was not going to cry; but the effort caused her to stand trembling alone in her room for an hour.

It was at that time that Bracken came. Megan turned from the window to watch him approach, but when he tried to take her into his arms, Megan stumbled away.

"Don't touch me, Bracken." The tears would hold no longer. "I can't stand for you to touch me until I understand what has happened between us."

"Megan." Bracken's voice was pained and he tried again, but still she resisted him.

"No, Bracken, I mean it," she cried. "You said you would never let me be hurt again, but now something has made you hate me, and until I understand I don't want you to —"

She stopped when he pursued her into the salon. Megan tried to evade him, but Bracken caught her in his arms in just seconds. Megan cried and shoved against his chest, but to no avail. Bracken lifted her high in his arms, sat in a large chair by the fire and placed Megan in his lap. Megan worked with all of her might to get away from him, but he would have none of it.

She eventually cried against his chest until she lay spent and silent. The past days, the morning's ordeal with Lyndon and then Marigold, and the torrent of tears, had all worked their way. Megan could not have moved if she tried. Bracken dipped his head to see if she slept, but only found her staring vacantly across the room.

"Your sister is gone," he began softly, his heart beating under Megan's ear. "I sent Arik with you and did not accompany you myself because I feared I would strike Marigold. Now I wish that I had. Arik is at this time berating himself for not seeing her intent. He blames himself that you were hurt."

Bracken dipped his head again. Although Megan had not moved, there was now a tiny spark of life in her eyes.

"I have much to tell you, Megan, but not now, not while you are worn and upset. I want you to go to bed. When you awaken, we'll talk."

Bracken dipped his head one last time,

and this time Megan looked at him. Bracken held her eyes for the space of several heartbeats before leaning forward and pressing a kiss to her forehead. He lifted her then, walked into her bedchamber, placed her on the bed, and bent over her.

"I'll send Helga to you. When you have rested and feel better — maybe after you have had a hot bath — then send for me. I wish to speak with you."

Megan managed a small nod, and Bracken stood a moment longer.

"As for the charge that I hate you, Megan, nothing could be further from the truth."

With that he was gone, and moments later Helga appeared. She helped a silent Megan from her gown and settled her comfortably back in bed. Even after her mistress slept, Helga sat nearby sewing and keeping watch over her charge.

Megan awakened feeling much better and was greatly refreshed after her bath. She did not send for Bracken as he'd directed but sought him out herself. He was at the new byre. When Megan learned of this, she was tempted to return to the castle but made herself carry on. She found Bracken walking through the byre inspecting every square inch. Megan stood for a time and watched him, but as soon as he noticed her, he stopped what he was doing and approached.

Dark eyes searched her face for signs of fatigue or pain, but he must have been satisfied with what he saw for he nodded slowly and said, "Will you walk with me?"

"Certainly."

They were quiet until some distance outside the walls, and then Megan said softly, "I am sorry about the byre, Bracken. 'Twas never my intent to deceive you."

"I realize that, Megan. I completely overreacted."

"So, you're not angry?"

"No. I did think it would be best to leave it where it was, but I can see now that our first location is a fine one."

Megan was so relieved that for a time she fell silent.

"When do you go again?"

"Go again?"

Megan looked at him. "Yes. I was under the impression that you would only be home for a short time."

Bracken shook his head. "I know of no such plan. I will be here."

Megan nodded.

"Does that disappoint you?" Bracken

tried to hide his dread of her answer.

"Oh, no, Bracken." Her eyes were wide. "I missed you."

"I missed you also."

Again they fell silent. To be parted from a new spouse for weeks was no easy thing, but to return as they had, under such stress and strife, was very difficult indeed.

"I'm sorry about your sister."

"Thank you, Bracken. I fear she will never change."

"She is a vile woman."

Megan had no choice but to agree.

"I am glad you are nothing like her."

"She told me that you asked her to come to your room."

Bracken turned and gripped her shoulders. "Did you believe her?"

"No," Megan said softly. "She has always been full of lies, and I know you would not do such a thing."

Bracken nodded and dropped his hands. Her words relieved him greatly.

"Was it difficult, your being away?" Megan asked.

Bracken began to share, his voice a bit quiet because he just realized how little they had talked, but he did tell Megan where he had been and the way they had lived. Bracken told how he had managed to visit his mother. He'd even seen Danella and her family for the first time in more than a year. Megan listened in silence to every detail.

"I met a man," Bracken finished by saying. "His name is Trygve Osborn, Marquess of Overton. We worked and lived together all the time I was away, and I have come to greatly admire him. We spoke much of our families, and he said I was not treating you well."

They had seated themselves under a tree now, and Megan's eyes rounded. "But, Bracken, I do not know such a man."

"I know, but he says he does not need to know you to know that I have treated you poorly." Bracken hoped she would understand his meaning from these few words, but her look was as innocent as a child's.

Bracken cleared his throat. "He and his wife, Ann, have been married for over ten years, but he also said that for months after the vows were spoken Ann would freeze at his touch."

Bracken watched Megan's eyes drop and her face flame. He opened his mouth to tell her he would try to be more understanding in the future, but she rushed in.

"I'm sorry Bracken. Before we were married, I just didn't know anything about the ways between a husband and wife, and ofttimes I am still not sure."

Bracken's pledge was momentarily forgotten. He stared at her bent head.

"Megan, what do you mean, you didn't know anything?"

"I just didn't. I think most girls talk to their mothers, but I was not with my mother, and the nuns never taught us. I am sorry I did not know and that I am still so ignorant."

Bracken felt pain wash over him. She had been so innocent. In truth, he was no more experienced than she, but he had had some idea of what marriage would bring.

"Oh, Megan," Bracken said and reached for her hand. He felt her stiffen and watched as her eyes flew to his. He knew in that instant he was going to have to show and not tell her that he was ready to change. He could give her a promise right then, but without proof of his actions, she would never believe.

Bracken continued to hold her small hand as they talked, but Megan never did relax. Still, Bracken ignored her tension and kept his touch very light and tender. He wasn't a man given to praying, but this was enough to make him want to drop to his knees and beg God to help him show Megan what was in his heart.

Thirty-Three

Bracken was beginning to feel like a spy. Since he had talked with Megan more than two weeks ago, he had worked at understanding women in general in order to gain a clearer picture of his wife. He had never studied the creatures before, and he was finding them fascinating. His greatest discovery was that they were so emotional. Bracken was a man of deep emotions, but he did not, as a rule, allow them to control him.

A few days past he'd watched a servant in the keep scolding a female underling concerning her shoddy work. What the servant said was true, but Bracken watched in amazement as great tears filled the young woman's eyes and she went back to her task sniffing and blowing.

Bracken could only shake his head. It caused him to think about his own sisters and how remarkably different their interests had been from his own as they were growing up. Some of it had to do with age, but most of it was because of their gender.

Bracken found himself asking why God hadn't created women to be a little more like men.

It was at the moment that Megan sought him out, and Bracken found himself very thankful that they were so different. She had a question for Bracken, but he was so preoccupied with the woman herself that he could barely answer. Even without touching her, he knew her skin was like warm satin. The green velvet of her dress made her eyes the color of the forest on a spring day. Her sweetness and the very sound of her voice were like a web around him. He had managed to reply, but Megan had stared at him rather strangely.

Even though he desired to do so, Bracken had still not begun to show Megan his affection during the course of the day when she needed it most. Still, he was learning plenty. Fortunately, for Bracken, spring was around the corner, and love was in the air. It was affecting the whole castle.

Right now he was watching Stafford and Pen. The two had been married for six months, and Pen still eagerly ran to embrace the young warrior every time she saw him.

He witnessed as Stafford placed an arm

around Pen's waist and with his free hand tenderly stroked her cheek. Even from a distance he could see her eyes soften before she placed a hand on the back of Stafford's neck and brought his lips down to hers. They kissed briefly, and when Pen turned away, Stafford gave her a playful smack on the seat. From where Bracken stood he could hear the girl's laugh. Bracken then turned to find Lyndon watching him as he studied Stafford.

"What is it, Lyndon?" Bracken's voice was curt, but Lyndon couldn't stop his smile.

"Bracken, what are you about?" he asked good-naturedly.

The duke hesitated. Lyndon had recently become betrothed; maybe he could help. He also knew Lyndon would never gossip the matter over the entire keep.

"What do you do to make Gabriella know that you love her?"

Lyndon, seeing his sincerity, thought a moment.

"Sometimes I take her flowers from the meadow."

Bracken snapped his fingers together. "That's it! Tryg said something about flowers. I'll do it!"

Bracken walked away then, looking more like a boy in love than a seasoned knight. Had he looked back, he would not have found Lyndon laughing, but instead would have seen that his friend's eyes were filled with fondness and admiration.

Megan was in the kitchen working over some of her herbs when Bracken found her. She was measuring, pouring, and working so intently that it was a moment before she noticed him.

"Oh, Bracken," Megan smiled. "I didn't see you."

"These are for you."

Megan stared at the bundle of purple flowers in his hands. Some were a bit smashed and the stems on others were broken, but they were pretty nonetheless.

"Thank you, Bracken." Megan's voice spoke of her confusion. "I don't recognize what herb they are. Were they for something special?"

"Nay," he shook his head. "Just for you. For your bedchamber or salon."

Megan looked at the flowers and then back at her husband, her brow still knit with bewilderment.

"Bracken," Megan began. "I still do not —"

He cut her off. "I was only thinking of you and wished for you to know it."

Bracken watched as understanding dawned. The transformation was amazing.

"These are for me?" Megan's eyes began to glow. "You gathered these for me?"

Bracken cleared his throat, now wishing they were alone.

"Yes."

"Oh, Bracken," was all Megan could say as she smiled up at him with shining eyes. "They are splendid flowers. Indeed, they are most wondrous. I'll go right now and put them in water." Megan turned away but came right back.

"Your brows are mussed," she explained seriously as her soft fingers smoothed over his brow. As she turned away, Bracken pulled the wimple from her hair. He did this often, and normally Megan would have complained, but so taken was she with the flowers she didn't even turn. All those in the kitchen who had witnessed the scene smiled as Bracken then made his way outside, a huge grin parting his beard.

By evening, the flowers seemed to be the talk of the entire castle. Megan heard little whispers here and there, but it was some time before she understood it was the flowers from Bracken about which they were speaking.

"You should've seen 'im a grinnin' after 'e 'anded 'em to 'er," Megan heard a woman say who was setting up for the evening meal. "It's spring all right. I tells ya, 'e's in love."

Megan did not let on that she'd heard — it was all too fascinating to stop. The other women all agreed and Megan listened for a few minutes more before moving on in great thought.

Bracken was acting oddly, but Megan didn't really think that spring was involved. In fact, when Megan stopped to think on it, Bracken was coming for her less and less. With the thought came regret that she'd shared her true feelings with Bracken a few weeks back. She must have said something to make him think he was upsetting her.

In truth, the physical side of marriage was not something Megan enjoyed, but that was life; some things were pleasure and some were duty. Megan wasn't certain, but it seemed to her that only women of loose morals found pleasure in such union. However, Evadne's words at Windsor Castle still came to mind: "Do not settle for endurance. 'Tis something to be enjoyed."

Megan resolved to talk with Bracken. She never wanted him to think she was angry with him, and she did so want a child. The thought of bringing this up to Bracken caused her face to heat on the spot, but she knew it must be done. Megan could have used some time to calm herself, but Bracken suddenly appeared at her side. She watched his mouth open and shut as he changed his mind about whatever he was going to say. Megan stood quietly as he then took in her pink face.

"You're blushing."

Megan shrugged uncomfortably. " 'Tis nothing."

Bracken looked unconvinced, and Megan cleared her throat.

"May I speak with you after the meal, Bracken?"

"Certainly." He watched her a moment. "Are you sure you don't wish to speak now?"

"It can wait."

"All right. In my chamber then?"

Megan shook her head. "You do not want us to quarrel there."

Bracken's brows winged upward. "You're planning an argument?"

Megan looked helpless and finally admitted, "In truth, Bracken, I am not sure."

Bracken weighed her words a moment before nodding and wisely let the subject drop. She was becoming quite anxious, and he needed to show her that he was more than willing to abide by her wishes.

The meal was plentiful that night and enjoyed by all, but both duke and duchess were preoccupied; Megan, with regret for setting up an audience with her husband, and Bracken, with speculation as to what she might say. Indeed, he didn't intend to wait long. As soon as Megan was through, he asked her to join him in the war room.

Megan agreed readily enough, but it took a moment for her to get started. She paced the room some and then started to sit on a chair. Bracken motioned to her, however, bidding her to join him on the long settee. Megan did so, but she was clearly not relaxed. In fact, when she began to speak, it was with her eyes on a distant spot across the room.

"Have I angered you, Bracken?"

"No," he answered as he studied her profile. "Do I seem angry?"

"Not exactly," Megan said softly. "Just different."

Bracken had hoped she would notice, but it was supposed to bring pleasure, not confusion.

"This is a problem?"

Megan knew then that she was not explaining herself well. She made herself shift so that she could face Bracken and look into his eyes.

"Since we talked outside the walls, Bracken, you do not touch me as much."

Bracken leaned forward so his face was on her level. He whispered, "You could touch me."

Megan looked horrified and would have moved from the settee, but Bracken gently captured her hands.

"Nay, Bracken, I could not!" Megan's voice was breathless as she pulled to free her hands. " 'Twould be a sin."

Bracken's smile was very tender, but he did not release her. "Oh, my little Megan, no, 'tis not a sin. My mother is a woman of God, like yourself, and I know she delighted in my father's touch."

"But, Bracken," Megan knew she might hurt him, but it had to be said, "with her commitment to Christ, she is different now. I do not think she would feel the same way."

Bracken only smiled. "I know all about my mother's belief, Megan, but it was her who told me to court you."

"Court me?"

"Yes. She said to woo my wife gently. I did not fully understand her at the time, but now I see that this way you will know what is in my heart, and our union will bring happiness to you."

Megan was more confused than ever. She so admired Joyce and would have loved to talk with her. Could Bracken really be right? Is this what God had for her? Megan felt something stir within her. Bracken had been unspeakably tender with her in the last two weeks, and it seemed she cared for him more every day.

Megan was still thinking on all of this when Bracken pulled her close. Megan held herself still as he put his arm around her, but there was nothing to fear. Bracken began a gentle dialogue, meant to soothe and make Megan feel cherished.

"I'm planning a tourney."

"You are?" Megan's voice was slightly breathless with her anxiety.

"Um hmm. Next month. In honor of my wife's eighteenth birthday."

Megan turned her head to look up into his face, her apprehension forgotten. He was serious!

"Bracken, why did you not tell me?"

"I just did. All of my family is coming; yours, too, I hope."

"Oh, Bracken," Megan's joy was so complete that she laid a hand spontaneously on his chest. "You are too good to me."

"You are my wife, Megan," he replied, staring down lovingly into her eyes. "How else am I to treat you?"

Megan could only smile in absolute serenity. After kissing her gently, Bracken pressed her head onto his chest. Megan was uncomfortable at first, but soon the beat of Bracken's heart came to her ear. Suddenly she was back atop his horse, Warrior, safe in his arms as they returned from the Stone Lake abbey. It wasn't long before she had relaxed completely. They talked for another hour, and when they finally rose to take the stairs, both were bathed in tenderness and contentment.

Thirty-Four

Bracken's treatment of Megan over the next week was unlike anything she'd ever experienced. Something wonderful was happening between them, and Megan had never known such joy or peace.

"Come to me, Megan," Bracken had bid one night early that week. The day had been long and Megan was tired, but she complied. When she had joined him, however, he had simply put his arms around her and pulled her close. After a moment, Megan had said, "Bracken, are you angry with me?"

"No."

Still he did not move beyond settling her a little more securely beside him.

"Are you certain?"

"Yes, I'm certain. Go to sleep, Megan."

"In here?"

"Yes, Megan," Bracken had answered, and she did not miss the laughter in his voice. It had done nothing to help her relax, but she tried to do as she was told. It had been a busy day, and after a moment

Bracken's heartbeat came to her ear. Megan sighed hugely when she heard that sound, and although Bracken had never let on, he felt her relax against him. Within ten minutes she had gone to sleep.

Bracken then relaxed as well and thought about his relationship with his wife.

At one time all I did was take from Megan. I never knew how remarkable it would be to give to my wife.

On this contented thought, Bracken had joined Megan in sleep until morning.

Now some four weeks later, things were still going well. Megan's birthday was upon them, and she had the entire castle cleaned and ready for their expected guests. Bracken's family had sent word of their arrival, and the day had finally arrived. Megan was so excited that she could hardly remain still.

"By the time they arrive, you're going to be dead on your feet," Bracken warned her, pulling her close for an instant. Warmly accepting Bracken's embrace, Megan only smiled, smoothed his eyebrows, and sailed on her way.

Joyce, Brice, Kristine, and Giles arrived together, and within the hour, Stephen had come with Louisa and Derek. Megan's head felt as if it were spinning. She was in conversation with Kristine and Giles, whom she had just met, when Joyce grabbed her eldest son's arm and pulled him from the group.

"You did it, Bracken. I can tell by the way Megan looks at you that you did it. You're courting her."

Bracken only smiled. "I want to laugh when I think of how confused I was by your words, but then I met Tryg." Bracken went on to explain to his mother, and her eyes were shining with tears of happiness when he finished.

"It's a miracle, Bracken. I have prayed so long and so hard."

Having heard these words from his mother many times, Bracken simply hugged her, and Joyce was pleased that he did not question her. In truth, she had been very worried over their marriage.

Not many months past, Louisa and Derek had come for a visit. It was at that time that Derek shared with his aunt and mother that the Scriptures said a believer was not to marry an unbeliever. Joyce had felt as if the very ground had been snatched from under her. She saw herself sitting with Megan in her room at Hawkings Crest and

454

telling her how excited she was that Megan was marrying Bracken. Joyce had been so sure at the time that this would be Bracken's turnaround, and then Joyce learned that the union had not even been God's will.

This news drove Joyce to her knees as nothing had ever done before. She prayed for days. Her heart was so burdened for her son and Megan that she could hardly function, but then the Holy Ghost moved in her heart. Joyce finally came from her knees to see that God's hand had still been there. He had not lost control of the situation.

She began to pray for Bracken in a new way. She asked God to show her son how to treat his bride. She knew without the indwelling of God, his change would not be like her own, but she did believe with all of her heart that God could work in the heart of any man.

She also prayed for Megan. Joyce was certain of one thing — had Megan known that it was against God's Word to marry an unbeliever, nothing whatsoever could have induced her to do so. Joyce prayed that God would show Megan how to respond to a sin committed in ignorance. She also prayed that as Bracken became more tender, Megan would be more receptive. From what she had seen in the first few minutes of her arrival at Hawkings Crest, God had answered her prayers with a resounding *yes.*

The only thing left to see to was choosing the correct time to tell Megan. Joyce felt that to leave someone in ignorance was a sin as well. Telling her would not change Megan and Bracken's situation, but it might that of the next generation. Joyce felt this was of the utmost importance. She was still praying about the matter when the group headed en masse for the castle to refresh themselves and partake of the noon meal.

"Is something wrong, Megan?" Bracken asked his wife the next evening.

Megan stared at him. It was nearly inconceivable that she should not have married this man, but Megan wanted above all else to be a godly woman, so she had taken Joyce's news as best as she was able. She could see, however, that it must be affecting her, or Bracken would not have noticed. Now, how would she tell him what was on her heart?

"I try to study in the Holy Scriptures every day," she began. "And I love my quiet times spent with God."

Bracken nodded. He had seen her reading often.

"But not everything I read or learn of is easy to take. Ofttimes I am convicted of sins that I was not aware of." Megan hesitated, praying that she would not have to tell him that their union had been wrong. As it was, Bracken's mind was elsewhere, and his question rescued her.

"If you want to do something, Megan, then do it. Your faith is your choice."

Megan gently shook her head. "I must take the Scriptures in their entirety, Bracken, and not pick and choose what I wish or what suits me."

Weighing her words, Bracken stared at her, his eyes narrowing.

"I thought God wanted us to be happy."

"He does," Megan said. "And happiness is mine — so are joy and peace — as soon as I obey."

Bracken shook his head, and Megan said, "So you mean to tell me that your father only enforced half of his words?"

"What do you mean?"

"I mean that if your father instructed you to go hunting in the forest and then to take your catch to the kitchens, it would be acceptable and obedient to hunt and then leave your game with the guard at the gate?"

"Of course not," Bracken told her.

"So it is with God, Bracken. He wants all of His instructions obeyed. If we only obey half of His Word, we sin."

This was new to Bracken, and again his eyes narrowed as he thought. Finally, he said, "But I am no child in need of a father's training, and neither are you."

Megan smiled at him with understanding, his point well taken, but still she said, "I will always be in need of my heavenly Father's care and teaching. And I think if you will search your heart, you will see that if your own father were still alive, you would consult with him on many things. It is the same with me and God."

Bracken's face showed understanding for the first time. No one had ever compared God the Father to his earthly father, a man Bracken missed very much indeed. It made perfect sense.

But suddenly Bracken had more spiritual matters to think about than he was comfortable with. For years he had tried to tell himself that there was no difference between his mother's faith in Christ and his own belief in God. However, when he was being very honest with himself, he had to admit that the changes in his mother, the lack of fear and overriding sense of peace he witnessed each time they were together, had little to do with the passing of years and steps toward maturity.

Likewise, both Louisa and Derek had changed, and in his heart Bracken knew why. He had never known Megan before her conversion, but Bracken understood that the reason she gave of herself so freely to him was because of God's work in her life. Still, Bracken was not convinced that he needed to make this step.

Wasn't his keep in fine shape? Didn't he treat his wife and servants with respect and caring? Didn't he have the king's approval and land and wealth to last him out and hand down to his seed? Why did he need to become religious? It still did not make sense. Rather than work it out, Bracken sought to change the subject.

In her wisdom, Megan let the matter drop, but she praised God that they had talked of spiritual matters as they never had before. She truly saw it as a step on the path to a new life in Christ for her spouse.

Vincent and Annora arrived the next day. Annora did not go so far as to embrace Megan, but this meeting was vastly different from the one before the wedding or the departure thereafter. Vincent did give his daughter a mighty hug, and as most of the guests were outside preparing for the tourney and the great hall was rather empty, Megan sat by the hearth with her parents for a visit.

Vincent opened the conversation with a painful subject.

"Has Marigold been back?"

"No," Megan spoke with relief. "And after the incident with Arik, I do not expect to hear from her."

Vincent was silent for a moment.

"What is it, Father?"

Annora spoke up. "Marigold was at Stone Lake just days ago. She was asking for money. When your father refused, she became enraged. When she learned we were coming here for your birthday, she began making threats against you. Your father told her to leave and not return. We came as soon as possible."

Megan stared at them, not at all surprised. Marigold was certainly capable of all they had related and more.

"I'm sorry, Mother," Megan told her softly.

" 'Tis not your doing, Megan. I can see

now that your sister has played your father and me against one another for many years."

"I did not want to send her away, but I cannot trust her at Stone Lake any longer." Annora nodded in agreement with her husband.

There was something urgent in both their manners, and both looked a little shaken. From what they had said, Megan was still not certain that it was all that great a problem; it sounded like idle talk from an angry woman.

On the other hand, she did wonder if maybe she should inform Bracken. As though her thoughts were a plea, Bracken entered the hall and came across to them. He sat with them, and Megan quietly explained what Vincent had said.

Bracken's eyes studied her before he said, "You are not afraid?"

"No, Bracken, in truth, I'm not. I know she is capable of nearly anything, but I am so protected here."

Bracken nodded and reached for her hand. He then turned to Vincent and Annora.

"We thank you for coming, not only for this news, but for the celebration as well. I will inform my people of these threats, and special care will be taken during the tournament."

"My men know as well," Vincent put in quietly.

"Mother," Megan said then, "you must wish to freshen up. May I show you upstairs?"

When the women had gone, Bracken also seemed ready to leave, but Vincent detained him.

"I do not wish to upset Megan on her birthday, but there is more."

Bracken sat and regarded the older man with interest.

"I have never seen such a look of madness in a woman's eyes."

"Marigold?"

"Yes. She said that Megan was nothing but a cow and didn't deserve you. She said she would be the Duchess of Briscoe and would see to it that Megan suffered well before she died." Vincent leaned forward now, his face fearful. "I urge you, Bracken, do not let Megan out of your sight."

The words were still ringing in Bracken's ears some 20 minutes later when he went looking for Megan. She was just coming from her mother's room, and they met in the wide passageway.

"Is your mother settled?"

"Yes, but she kept looking at me oddly. In truth, Bracken, I feel sad for my parents that it has taken them so long to see Marigold's true nature."

Bracken only stared at her.

"Bracken, what is it?"

It was only right that she should know so that she could move with caution, but as with Vincent, Bracken had no desire to frighten her. He sighed very gently and reached to smooth her cheek with the backs of his fingers.

"Your father feels that Marigold is going mad and truly fears for you because of this."

Megan stepped a little closer to her husband, and Bracken put his arms around her. Megan spoke with her cheek laid against his hard chest.

"You won't let her hurt me, Bracken." It was a statement.

"No, I won't, but you need to walk with caution."

"During the tourney?"

"Yes. I believe your father thinks she might try something."

Megan tipped her head back. "I'll make sure you or Arik are close by at all times." Megan put her cheek back to Bracken's broad chest, and a moment later felt him pulling off her wimple.

"Bracken!" she scolded and reached for his hand, but it was too late — her hair hung in a red mass down her back.

"I've told you many times," Bracken said without apology as he held the wimple behind his back, "I want to see your hair."

"But my mother is here," Megan complained while attempting to smooth her unruly curls. "What will she say?"

"It matters not." He was unperturbed. "Just remind her that she is at Hawkings Crest and can go without her wimple as well."

Thirty-Five

Megan had not attended a tournament since she was a young girl, so the following days held a great many surprises for her. Competitions at the archery range and all swordplay would take place on the actual day of Megan's birthday, and the following day would mark the wrestling matches and the javelin throw. The last day would end with a jousting competition.

The opening of the tourney started with a parade of the knights whose castles had answered the invitation. The men were in full pageantry dress as they paraded proudly onto the jousting field. The colors from six other keeps joined those of Hawkings Crest, Stone Lake, and White Hall, Joyce's family home.

Megan was in the stands with all the other ladies. She watched proudly as Bracken, sitting atop Warrior and as the host of the games, rode proudly in front. Lyndon and Kendrick were just behind him. Megan's pride grew as they circled the practice field that had been splendidly laid out for this occasion, and it tripled when she heard two older women talking behind her.

"My room is so comfortable and clean."

"As is mine. So roomy."

"Marcus and I had to share a room with four other couples at the last tourney we attended, and we did *not* get the bed."

"Dreadful."

"That isn't the worst of it. The men in the room snored so loudly I hardly slept all night; Marcus was the worst."

Megan heard both women laugh softly, but she did not turn around. A swift shift of her eyes told her that her mother-in-law had heard as well. Joyce reached for Megan's hand and squeezed gently. Megan had all she could do not to laugh.

By the final day of the tournament, the knights of Hawkings Crest had more than proven their worth to all present. They had won the archery competition hands down, and Arik had taken on all comers, sometimes two at a time, in the wrestling. There was only one knight, a huge, bald-headed man, who caused Megan worry.

His name was Sir Rodney of Helt, and he'd beaten Bracken when they wrestled and nearly outthrown him in the javelin.

Today it was time for the joust, a sport where a man could be accidentally killed, and Megan knew some very real fear as the men paraded in once again.

She managed a smile as the knights from Hawkings Crest were once again the first in line, but her heart was beating with trepidation. She calmed some when she saw Bracken headed her way. Horse and rider were in full armor, and Warrior pranced with anticipation. Bracken reined him in with a sharp word, and within moments he stood before the grandstands as though made of stone.

Megan stood and Bracken held out his halberd. She pulled the scarf free that hung from her waist and sported the Hawkings Crest colors, and then tied it onto the end of his lance. His head dipped in her direction, and his eyes twinkled. Megan beamed at him and thought her heart would explode with love.

She sat back down and tried to calm herself, but it was all moving so fast that Bracken and Sir Rodney faced one another before she felt ready. Oddly enough, it was her mother who noticed the strain on her face, and in a gentle voice was able to calm her daughter's fears.

"Your father says he's not seen many

knights with Bracken's strength or power. Fear not, Megan."

"Thank you, Mother," Megan told her and was sharply reminded of a conversation with Bracken just the night before.

"I'll pray for you during the joust, Bracken," she had told him.

"I have my armor and a strong horse, Megan," he reassured her. "There is no need to pray."

"I will pray anyway," she had said. "The Scriptures say, 'There is no king saved by the multitude of an host; a mighty man is not delivered by much strength. A horse is a vain thing for safety; neither shall he deliver any by his great strength. Behold, the eye of the Lord is upon them that fear him, upon them that hope in His mercy.' "

Bracken had looked at her in shock for many minutes before finally saying, "This is in the Holy Bible?"

"Yes, Bracken, in Psalm 33. I can show you."

He shook his head. "There is no need. I believe you and beg your forgiveness for my arrogance. I would indeed desire your prayers."

Calmness now covered Megan as she prayed for Bracken and each man participating. She knew that he might not come away whole, but the tourney was in God's hands and Megan knew she would not find peace in any other place.

Megan paced the rug at the side of her bed and stopped every few seconds to stare in the direction of Bracken's room. The light from the torch on the wall cast shadows on the floor, but Megan took little notice.

You could touch me, had been Bracken's words to her many days past, but Megan had not as yet made a move to do so. However, she was so proud of the way he'd beaten Sir Rodney of Helt that the desire to be with him was overwhelming her. Her only hesitation now was that he might already be asleep. A sudden thought came to mind, and Megan moved to light a candle. Once lit, she shielded the flame carefully with her hand and walked quietly into Bracken's room.

As Megan hoped, he lay on his stomach. She also took note of the fact that his head was turned away from her. Because he was a light sleeper, she knew Bracken was aware of her presence, but he didn't speak even when she set the candle down on the small table by the bed and climbed up to kneel beside him on the soft mattress.

Bracken's heart was pounding in his chest as he felt Megan settle on the bed. He had known it would only be a matter of time before she came to him, but right now it felt like years since Bracken had begun his tender assault on her. The desire to roll over and sweep her into his arms was almost overpowering. He forced himself to exhale very slowly as her small hands reached to rub his bare back. He wanted desperately to respond in such a way that Megan would not be fearful, but would instead know just how welcome she was.

After a moment he simply said, "That's nice."

"I thought you might be sore." Megan's voice was a little breathless, and for the world Bracken would not have told her that his vassal had given him a complete rubdown.

"It's kind of you, Megan."

They were silent for a moment, and then Megan spoke quietly, her hands having no real effect on his muscles but tremendous results on his heart.

"I was proud of you today, Bracken. You fought so well that I had to confess my pride that you belonged to me." She heard him chuckle and smiled as she continued to rub.

"Does one area of your back hurt more than another?" she asked solicitously.

"You're doing fine," Bracken told her, a smile in his voice.

They fell silent for a time; indeed, Bracken was nearly asleep when Megan spoke.

"I have news for you, Bracken."

"Hmm?" Bracken murmured, thinking she could tell him the castle was under attack and he still wouldn't be able to move.

"I am with child, Bracken."

One second Megan was rubbing his back, and seemingly an instant later her head was on his pillow with Bracken bending over her, the candle held high so he could see her face.

"Is it true, Megan?" He felt as if he'd run for miles.

"Yes," Megan said as she tried to see his face. "I waited to tell you because I felt a need to speak with Louisa. She confirmed my suspicions."

"How long?"

"Just a month now. The baby won't be born until December."

Bracken's huge hand sought her stomach and spread over the fabric of her gown. Her abdomen was still flat, but it wasn't hard to envision her swollen with his son. His eyes sought hers.

"Oh, Megan," Bracken breathed. "Are you all right? Do you feel ill?"

Megan shook her head no and smiled. "I am a bit tender, but all else is well."

Bracken's look became almost fierce. "We will not lie together until after the child is born."

Megan chuckled softly and her fingers stroked his beard. "Oh, yes, we will, Bracken. You are overreacting."

Bracken captured the hand at his face and pressed a kiss to the palm. "We will turn your duties over to others," he stated emphatically. "In fact, Louisa is already here, and we will simply ask her to stay until the child has come."

Megan shook her head, and Bracken frowned. "That is out of the question, Bracken. A woman needs great strength to have a child. If I lie about until my pains begin, I will not have the endurance."

Bracken sighed deeply. He wanted to coddle this woman, and she would have none of it. Indeed, she very logically destroyed all of his arguments. However, he was going to lay down the law on some things.

"Megan," Bracken began, but the diminutive redhead cut him off.

"We can't argue in this room, Bracken," she took great delight in telling him.

"We're not going to argue," Bracken informed her. "I'm going to tell you a few facts, and you are going to listen and obey."

"I'll argue with everything you say," she promised.

"Then we'll go into your salon for this discussion."

Megan feigned a huge yawn. "I'm much too tired to move," she told him with a dramatic sigh.

Bracken tried to hide his smile but failed miserably. Megan grinned unrepentantly and spoke invitingly.

"Come, Bracken, lie down and put your arms around me. I am weary, as are you. The entire castle will surely know of this news tomorrow, and we will both need our rest."

Bracken could find no argument for that and did as Megan asked. Megan was asleep in less than a minute, but Bracken took some time. He was calmly going over in his mind all the changes he would lay out for Megan in the morning.

Bracken had searched for 20 minutes the

next day before finding Megan in the creamery. She and Eddie were in close conversation, and he waited with barely concealed impatience for their conference to end. That Megan was very aware of his anxiety was quite apparent when she finally approached him and stood smiling up at him.

"Did you need something, Bracken?" she asked sweetly.

"We will talk, Megan," he said, telling himself to stand firm.

"Of course, Bracken. I must go to the byre and then —"

"The war room. Now."

"As I was saying," Megan said swiftly, "the byre can wait."

She sailed ahead of him, and the castle folk, who had heard the news just as Megan predicted, smiled as they watched them depart.

An hour later Bracken was finishing.

"Half of your duties will be delegated. It is still my desire that Louisa stay, but if you will not have that, then you will do as I ask."

"But, Bracken, there is no purpose," she tried one last time. "I am perfectly able to continue in *all* of my duties."

"My mind is made up," Bracken said,

pinning her to the settee with his eyes. Megan sighed but did not comment.

"What goes on in that head of yours, Megan?"

The beautiful green eyes narrowed. "I was thinking that mayhap it's time for Henry to call for you again."

Bracken's own gaze narrowed in order to cover the laughter lurking in the depths of his eyes. He slowly shook his head.

"I do not plan to let you out of my sight."

Megan smiled then. She knew he had spoken out of concern for her, and, indeed, he was acting so adorably that she could hardly fault him.

A month later, Megan's thoughts were not so benevolent. Bracken seemed to dog her every move, and there were days when Megan wanted to run and hide. When she thought she could stand it no longer, he seemed to ease up. Maybe it had taken that long for him to see that she was going to be fine. Whatever the reason, the duchess was thankful.

Megan would have been surprised to know that much of Bracken's attention, and then the lack thereof, stemmed from the fact that he had just received word that Marigold was now back in France.

"Helga, what did that woman say to you?"

The faithful servant bit her lip, but she knew it was no use. When the Lady Megan used that tone, she could never deny her. The women were coming from the archery butts, where they'd been watching the men practice. Megan had noticed several women coming to speak with her personal maid. Helga seemed to grow more agitated with every step, and Megan had to question her.

"Helga?"

The older woman wrung her hands. "It's just more of the same, my lady."

Megan nodded and did not comment. For over a week now there had been news in both the keep and the village that Roland Kirkpatrick was back in the area. Word was out that he was still angry with Bracken over what had happened at King Henry's court.

Megan had spoken with Bracken each time she became worried about the situation, and each time he had reassured her. But now her fears were returning. Telling herself she must try to reason with Bracken once more, Megan dismissed Helga and made her way toward the castle.

"Bracken," Megan said to him as soon as she had found him in the war room. "There is more word from the village."

"Megan," Bracken replied patiently. He had been out earlier and heard the news as well. "Are you thinking about Roland Kirkpatrick again?"

"Yes, Bracken. Your lack of concern —"

"I am concerned," Bracken cut her off, "but I'm not frightened as you seem to be. I will protect you. When I come face-to-face with the man, I will confront him."

"It's not me I'm worried about."

"Megan," Bracken stressed the words again. "Henry has given me leave to handle this as I see fit. I do not fear Roland or the situation."

"What if he seeks you out first?"

"So be it. He's not going to take me by surprise, Megan. I am able to deal with this." There was amusement on his face as he spoke these last words, and Megan knew more frustration than ever.

His lack of concern was maddening to her. She wanted to stay with him in the war room until she had talked him into taking immediate action, but knew it was of little use.

"I think it's time I make a visit to the village," Megan said to Helga once she had gained her chamber.

Helga knew that tone and said in a voice breathless with fright, "Oh, my lady."

"Not today," Megan told her as if this would calm all of the servant's fears. "Tomorrow, Helga, and I shall need my cloak."

"What was Lady Megan about today?"

Bracken shook his head over Lyndon's question. "I was not able to speak with her. I left word of our going with Clive."

Lyndon could see how this would be true. Bracken's decision to go to the village had been rather sudden, and he had only planned to be gone for a portion of the day. Indeed, it was good to see Bracken relaxing again. Many in the keep had chuckled over his hennish care of Megan, but Lyndon knew that when God willed and his own Gabriella carried his child, he would be just the same.

Bracken, Lyndon, Arik, and Kendrick, along with several other knights, arrived in the village just before noon. They made their way to the pub, and after being served a noon meal of pork, coarse bread, and ale, began to listen and observe. It wasn't long before they learned that Roland was out of the area that day.

Bracken felt their trip had been a waste of time.

They were just leaving when Lyndon heard of a small fair going on at the other end of town. For amusement's sake, they made their way in that direction. The first cart, filled with apples, was run by an old woman with a humpback and a filthy face. The men, all but Arik, sauntered past her without a second glance. Bracken noticed the way the huge man stopped, but thinking he was in a mood merely left him and traveled on.

He learned little else about Roland that was new at the fair, but he was no longer sorry they had come. Bracken was well respected in the village, and this was proved to him by how many merchants approached and told what they knew. Some, he was sure, also did this for Kirkpatrick, but for the most part they were a loyal group.

The men made their way back out of the fair and met Arik at the edge. He was just as they'd left him, parked at the old woman's stall, his arms folded across his broad chest.

"What troubles you, Arik?"

The giant did not answer or even look at him.

Bracken glanced around in frustration and then scowled at the old woman who let out a coarse bark of laughter over absolutely nothing. She didn't seem to notice the look but pottered around in her shuffling gait, adjusting her fruit for better display.

"Arik," Bracken went on patiently, "if you've news, tell me. If not, let us return to Hawkings Crest."

Arik looked at him this time, staring down into his eyes silently before slowly shifting his gaze to the old woman.

Bracken was swift on the uptake, and he moved casually over to inspect her stand. She had little, but he wasn't really concerned. He stood in front of her cart, and she stood at the rear. With his eyes on the fruit, he spoke softly.

"I've coin for more than fruit, if you have it."

When the old woman didn't answer, Bracken shifted his eyes without moving his head in order to look at her. His eyes grew in utter disbelief when blackened teeth peeked out at him through a crooked grin and one lid dropped over the most beautiful green eyes in all of England.

The desire to grab the Duchess of Briscoe and run with her on the spot nearly got the best of him. Bracken started toward her, but stopped when she dropped her gaze and began to sing in a hoarse voice and putter with her fruit. A swift look around told Bracken that the fair had suddenly become crowded. To take her now would cause an incredible scene.

Bracken turned back to Arik, his body stiff with rage.

"I will see you back at Hawkings Crest," he spoke through clenched teeth. "Come to me the moment she is safe."

Arik nodded calmly, and Bracken forced himself to walk away without a backward glance.

Thirty-Six

Megan paced the confines of her salon and tried to be calm. She had confessed her foolhardiness to God the Father, but she had yet to speak with her husband. She knew he was aware of her presence because she had seen Arik talking to him, but he had not yet chosen to make an appearance.

When she finally heard his door, she froze in her place and waited for him to appear. Megan's heart sank at the sight of him. She had been home and cleaned up for over two hours, but he was still furious.

"I'm sorry, Bracken," Megan said softly when he stopped in the doorway, but he did little more than glare at her.

"It was unwise of me," she continued. "I was worried for you, and I simply did not think. I have dressed that way many times before, and I knew there was no better way to gain information."

It was the worst thing she could have said. Bracken was suddenly swept backward to the agonizing time he had rushed to find her before the marriage. On the way to Stone Lake they had talked with Elias the peddler, only to be told that they'd given an old beggar woman a ride and had certainly not seen Lady Megan. To think that she had dressed that way twice made Bracken more angry than ever.

"How you could do such a thing in your condition is beyond me," he said between gritted teeth. "I am so angry right now that I can't even bear to look at you."

Bracken turned away before Megan could make a sound. She didn't know when she'd been so crushed. Tears filled her eyes and spilled down her face. She knew well that she had done wrong, but if he could just find it in his heart to forgive her, Megan would press on to do better. As it was, Megan didn't want to press on at all. She sank into the nearest chair and sobbed, her heart feeling like it was going to break in two.

Two days later Bracken had still not spoken a word to her. He took his meals in the war room and avoided Megan at all costs. Her hurt and humiliation were beyond description, but she didn't know what to do. At one time Bracken had told her to grow up. If Megan had thought it would do any good, she would have searched him out and said those exact words to him.

He was acting like a child in a tantrum, but telling him such a thing was impossible for more than one reason. He seemed determined not to let her near him. He ate alone and was always gone from his bed long before Megan rose. If Megan started toward him in the keep, he would turn away. It shamed Megan to be ignored, so she stopped trying. His men seemed just as vexed with her as he, and Megan was beginning to feel desperate. She finally approached Arik, her heart in her eyes.

"Arik, I feel a need to see the meadow. Will you go with me?"

He nodded without hesitation, and the odd couple made their way out the gate. Arik was very soothing company. He said nothing, and Megan was left alone with her thoughts as she walked among the beautiful wildflowers.

"For a man so concerned about his baby," she said to God, "he seems to have completely forgotten I am even with child. I have told him I am sorry, Lord, and now I know not what else to do. It was wrong of me, and I know that sin has its consequences, but this is too much. It is his anger and pride that stand in the way of our reconciliation.

"His anger makes me feel lonely and cold inside. If this continues, I feel I would do better at Stone Lake, but I don't wish to leave. What will I do if he never forgives me?"

The thought made tears pour down Megan's face. With her back to her protector, she cried for several minutes. She was still deep in her misery when Arik's voice surprised her.

"Rise, Lady Megan."

Megan started violently and then followed Arik's gaze to see men approaching. She did not know them, and they were dressed in rags, so she swiftly did as Arik bid. Megan dashed the back of her hand across her eyes and spoke with only a slight sniffle in her voice.

"We have no coin to give you. If you have something to sell, you'll have to go up to the castle."

They didn't seem to hear her. They came in closer . . . not speaking, and acting oddly. Arik stepped partially in front of Megan, and the young duchess' brow rose when the men were not deterred. Most men were petrified of Arik. It was at that instant that Megan noticed others coming in from behind them.

"Arik?" she said fearfully. The big man drew his knife. Upon seeing it, Megan's heart suddenly rocketed with panic. She was too terrified to even scream, but Arik grabbed her arm and moved Megan so none could advance from the rear. The men came in closer, and Megan saw that more approached from the woods, seemingly dozens of them.

Had Arik been alone, he would have stood and fought, but his only concern was Megan. He turned and began to run, nearly dragging her with him, but the men were soon on top of him. He sent Megan on with a hoarse shout to run and a shove that nearly sent her to the ground. But Megan had gained only 50 yards when some of the men caught her. She fought as well, but there were too many.

Seeing Megan with men surrounding her gave Arik renewed strength, and the dozen men attacking him with clubs flew everywhere as he dislodged their relatively small bodies in order to get to her. Megan was still struggling herself, and just as Arik gained his freedom, she watched a tall man come up behind him with a huge cudgel.

Megan found her voice now in a full scream as the club hit Arik alongside the head, not once but twice. Watching in horror as the big man's legs buckled, Megan screamed again. A hand was clamped over her mouth, and an angry countenance suddenly appeared in her face. Megan stared in terror at Roland Kirkpatrick's furious eyes just before a cloak was thrown over her head.

The horseback ride was the longest of Megan's life. The cloak had been removed, but a cloth had been tied tightly across her eyes, completely blinding her. Her hands were bound in front of her, and she had long since lost the feeling in her fingers.

Just when Megan had lost all track of time and direction, her horse stumbled and she fell. Her numb hands grabbed desperately for some hold, but found none. Megan fell hard onto her shoulder, much as she had months before while riding in the processional from Stone Lake. However, this time Bracken was not there to take her atop Warrior.

Rough hands lifted her and tossed her back onto her horse, but they let go before she had her balance. Blinded, and with numbed fingers, Megan could find no hold, and she was knocked unconscious when she fell off the other side and landed on her head. She awoke, feeling quite ill, to the sound of angry voices.

"She's no use to us dead!"

"What do you want me to do?"

"Be more careful, you fool!"

Megan recognized Roland Kirkpatrick's voice, but for all the anger, Megan was lifted gently.

"Now hand her to me," Roland ordered, and Megan felt the jostle of arms as she was settled across his saddle. The horse had no more moved when Megan felt a hot rush that made her heart sink with dread. The need to relieve herself was almost unbearable, but it was not the same. Megan knew she was losing her baby.

"Oh, Father, please, no," Megan whispered tearfully.

Roland naturally misunderstood her. "If you do as you're told, you have nothing to fear. Just sit quiet now; we'll be there soon."

Megan tried to stem her tears, but they seeped out anyway. It was all her fault. She had gone to the village and caused Bracken's anger, which had put her in the meadow. It was too late for regrets, but Megan felt them nonetheless.

"It's not time yet," Roland tried to reason with her.

"I want her dead, do you hear me, Roland! Dead! If you won't do it, I'll see to it myself!"

Megan listened with dread to the sound of her sister's voice. It never once occurred to her that Marigold was behind all of this, but when she could make her mind concentrate, it made perfect sense.

How foolish she had been. She had heard Roland's men talking. All the intrigue surrounding Bracken and Roland was really over her. Had Bracken known this? Is that why he'd been so furious? Megan pushed regret aside. She had apologized to Bracken, but he had rejected her. She had tried to bridge the gap between them, but he had been unwilling. At some point she had to stop thrashing herself for the sins of the past.

It looks as if they plan my death. Perhaps this is what it's going to take, she prayed in her heart. *Bracken will surely be in pain over my loss, and perhaps this will bring him to You, Father God.*

Megan was warmed by the thought. It helped, since she felt with a certainty that her baby was gone. It also helped to lay still. In the six days she'd been in this run-down castle, there had been much blood and no one to help her in any way.

Marigold and Roland's voices were fading now. Megan wasn't certain if they were moving away from her door or if she was falling back to sleep. They had fed her and given her water, but she was still so weak. Megan was still wondering why that would be when she drifted off once again.

"A week, Lyndon. My wife has been gone a week, and I am no closer to finding her."

This was very true. With Lyndon always at his side, Bracken had followed the trail of Megan's abductor, but it had led nowhere. From there they had searched and questioned everyone within miles. There were still no leads. Now the two men stood in the war room. Lyndon, nearly as torn up over Megan's loss as Bracken, said, "We will find her, Bracken. I know this. I feel it."

The duke turned tortured eyes to his friend. "What have they done to her?"

"Don't think about it, Bracken; it will distract you. Just concentrate on finding a way."

Bracken nodded. They were words he needed to hear. If he thought overly long on Megan or the baby, panic would set in and then he would be of no use to anyone.

In order to keep the anxiety at bay, Bracken found himself trying to pray.

I will make amends, God, if you will but spare Megan. I have wronged her, and I will make repairs if You will but give her back to me. The thoughts had no more formed when Kendrick came to the door.

"Lord Vincent has arrived." The loyal knight was breathless with excitement. "He brings word."

"You should have kidnapped a maid as well, Roland," Marigold said bitingly. "Megan looks worse than ever."

Roland looked at the madness in Marigold's eyes and then at her pathetic sister and asked himself how love could drive a man to such an act. The stories Marigold had told him concerning her evil sister, Megan, had made him hate the girl, but then he watched the small redhead fall from her horse twice and never utter a sound. To protect his investment, he had taken her atop his horse, but then he had told her not to cry and she had quieted swiftly.

Not until they arrived at the castle did he realize how tightly her hands had been tied. He released her and then watched as she shook all over with pain when the blood rushed back to her fingertips. Still, she did not utter a word. And then, when he'd finally removed her blindfold, she'd blinked, focused on him, and spoken only four words.

"Please, let me go."

Roland had actually considered it. He was a man who had little care for his own life, so Bracken's wrath did not disturb him, but he knew if this woman was his own and someone had taken her, he would be crazy with grief.

He made himself leave the room before he could relent. At the time Marigold had not yet joined him, but he knew that to let Megan go would send Marigold into a frenzy. After she arrived, Roland wondered if it really would have mattered. She was more agitated than ever.

It wasn't enough to have Megan kidnapped with a plan to ransom her, Marigold had wanted the younger girl humiliated. She had demanded that Megan be paraded naked through the castle before all his men. Roland's stomach rolled when he thought of how close he'd come to agreeing.

He'd gone to Megan's chamber, and holding a sword at her chest, told her to rise and undress. In order to go through with it, he had forced himself to ignore her white face and violent trembling, but when he'd seen the dark spotting on her shift, he relented, telling her to dress again. Turning, he swiftly exited the room, thinking as he did that he would rather face Marigold than force this on Megan.

He didn't see Marigold for more than an hour, but he needn't have worried. By the time he came face-to-face with her, she had completely forgotten her orders.

Now it was the following evening. After bringing Megan into the great hall for dinner, Roland thought she looked paler than ever. Something deep inside of him told him he was not seeing a woman in her monthly flow, but something much more significant. He had to remove Marigold from the room and find out.

"Why aren't you eating?" Marigold asked Megan, her voice now as sweet as a child's.

"I'm not very hungry," Megan told her sister kindly, and Roland knew then that Megan recognized her sister's madness.

"Why not?" The older woman frowned, and her voice changed, causing Megan to pick up her fork. Roland watched her hand shake.

"Well, I guess I'll try a little."

Marigold smiled as if all was well in the world and then began telling Megan and Roland about the different men who had loved her.

"Of course, Bracken does too, Meg. I'm sure it will take some time to get used to the idea, but then it really doesn't matter since you'll be dead." Her voice was as sweet as that of a young girl in love for the first time.

The sound of it chilled Megan to the bone. She watched as Marigold went on eating, but she felt so ill that she had to lay her fork down. She felt Roland's eyes on her and glanced at him before swiftly reaching for the utensil to spear a small carrot slice. Roland hated the fear he saw in her face but knew he deserved it. It was impossible for her to know that he himself had never killed anyone in his life.

"I want something sweet," Marigold suddenly demanded like a spoiled tyke.

"Very well," Roland said smoothly, now seeing a way. "Let me return Megan to her room, and you and I shall retire to the fire with tea and dessert."

"Why are you taking her up?" Marigold's harsh voice was back. "You have men for that."

"I wish to see to it myself. After all our

hard work I do not want our prisoner to escape."

Marigold's laugh was hard. "She's not bright enough for that, but suit yourself. I shall be waiting."

Roland took Megan's arm and led her from the table. He had no reason to be harsh with her, but he rushed her along until they were out of the great hall. He didn't speak until they were back at Megan's room. Roland opened the door and allowed her to precede him. Megan, thinking he would shut her in and leave, turned in fear when he stepped in behind her.

"Are you with child?"

Megan was so stunned by the question that she did not at first respond.

"I must get below. Answer me at once. Are you with child?"

Megan turned her face away and spoke just above a whisper. "There is no need to concern yourself. What's done is done."

Had Megan been looking, she would have seen the way Roland's hands balled into fists of anger and regret. He didn't speak but stood still a moment before turning to join Marigold below.

Thirty-Seven

"How did you learn of this place?" Bracken whispered to Vincent as they stood outside the rundown keep that sat halfway between Stone Lake and Hawkings Crest. Vincent had come to Hawkings Crest with news that he knew of Megan's whereabouts. It was late at night, but they had ridden out so swiftly that the men had not even had time to speak.

"Marigold was reported seen here."

Panic clawed at Bracken's throat as he grasped the older man's arm with incredible strength.

"Marigold is behind this?"

"I fear so." Vincent winced at the younger man's hold, but understood. "For a time she covered herself well, and her mother and I relaxed, but the lies about France have now come to my attention. We will recover Megan," Vincent added and watched as a look of steel entered Bracken's eyes.

Within moments they had the castle surrounded and all moved in for an attack.

496

The castle defense was feeble at best, as Roland had not done a good job of arming the keep. He had less than a dozen guards, and they seemed totally unprepared for an attack. Few lives were lost as Bracken's men broke through the door. In less than 20 minutes Bracken stood in the great hall, his sword and shield making him appear larger than ever.

He didn't move a muscle when he saw Roland and Marigold by the hearth. It looked as if they'd both been up all night. They stood at the same time, and still Bracken did not move, not even when that lying wench ran across the room and threw herself at Bracken's chest.

"Oh, Bracken!" she cried dramatically. "You've come for us. Roland kidnapped us both and has already forced himself on Megan. It was my turn tonight, but you have spared me."

Bracken did not even look at her. His eyes remained on Roland, who seemed amazingly calm. Bracken knew by just studying the man that Marigold's words were all lies. Roland had not touched Megan, and Marigold was up to her usual deceitful tricks. Bracken moved her aside with one arm. Marigold put on a lovely display of hurt and rejection.

"Bracken?" Her voice was pained. Then her father entered behind him.

"Father!" Marigold screamed in outrage and began to back away.

"Halt," Vincent shouted as he came toward her, but Marigold turned and ran. The older man pursued his daughter, but Bracken turned back to Roland.

"Where is she?"

Lyndon and Kendrick had flanked and grabbed Roland, but he still managed to motion with his head to the upstairs.

"If she has been harmed, you'll die."

Thinking of the lost child, Roland wanted to say, "Kill me now," but refrained.

Bracken swung away, and in minutes stood outside Megan's door. He smashed the lock and moved slowly inside. The room was dim with only one torch burning. Bracken found Megan sitting on the side of the bed. She looked pale but unharmed, and Bracken was so relieved that for a moment he could not move. Even when she smiled and spoke, he could not propel his feet forward.

"You came," she said softly, her voice so full of wonder that Bracken's joy deserted him.

"You doubted?" he frowned.

Megan gestured helplessly with her hands. "You were so angry, Bracken, and although I knew they planned to ransom me, I wasn't certain if you would —"

"Of course I came," Bracken cut her off, feeling very hurt and wanting to lash out in return. "You carry my son."

The change in Megan was frightening. The light left her eyes so rapidly that Bracken blinked. He watched as she turned her face to the wall.

"Then you have wasted your time." Her voice was flat, and Bracken felt a fear so great that it robbed him of breath. "I fell from my horse. There has been much blood."

Bracken discarded his sword and shield to cover the distance between them in only a few strides. He went down on one knee before Megan, and although still feeling breathless, spoke earnestly.

"I did not mean that, Megan. It's you I've come for. I am sorry about the babe, but truly, it's you I want."

Megan turned dull eyes to his, her voice utterly emotionless. "It's all my fault. I have lost our child. The blame surely lies at my door."

"No, Megan," Bracken began and touched her for the first time. Her skin was so hot and dry that alarm slammed through him all over again. He could feel his emotions spinning out of control and shook himself in order to keep his head. He could tell her the way he had yearned for her every moment she was gone; indeed, he'd nearly been out of his head. But Megan was ill, and right now she needed his cool logic.

"Come, Megan, we're going home now."

Megan didn't even look at him as he rose and lifted her, nor did she speak. Her lack of response concerned him more than anything. What had she been through in the last week?

By the time they gained the great hall, Vincent had Roland bound. He was still being held, but when Bracken stopped with Megan in his arms, he was allowed to approach. Roland stared at the duchess, and Megan sighed gently.

"I am sorry for the loss of your child."

"You do not hate me, Roland; I know this to be true. Why then, why have you done this terrible thing?"

Roland turned his face away in shame. "There are times when love drives a man to foolishness. I am just such a fool."

"Marigold," Megan stated, and Roland turned back to see her shudder.

"She will bother you no longer."

Megan took in the grief in his face, and her heart sank. She was terrified of her sister, but she did not hate her or wish to see her dead. However, the look in Roland's eyes told her she was not going to gain her wish.

Bracken, seeing the alarm on his wife's face, lifted her a little closer to his chest and moved to the door. Megan spotted her father in passing, and although he gave her a tender look, she also read the mourning in his eyes.

"Bracken?"

"Hush, Megan," he told her. "Until you are home and safe, I refuse to discuss it."

Megan had little choice but to comply, but the sky was swiftly growing light, and there was no missing the covered form at the bottom of the great stone stairway that led to the keep. Megan's hands fisted in Bracken's coat as she saw the wisps of blonde hair at the edge. Bracken turned her away as soon as he was able, but Megan had already begun to tremble all over.

"How is Arik?" Megan asked some 30 minutes into their journey.

"He will be fine. He wanted to join us,

but for once I had my way."

Megan didn't comment, but Bracken could see that she was well pleased.

"We are moving very slowly," Megan then said.

"Yes."

It was fully daylight now, and although Megan felt bruised, cold, and achy, she was anxious to be home.

"Why?"

"Because you are not well."

Megan did not answer for a time. "It's very cold for June."

"It is not cold at all; Megan, you are ill."

Megan stared up at him in surprise, and for the first time noticed the perspiration beaded on his forehead.

"Why don't you remove your coat?"

Bracken finally looked tenderly down at her where she lay wrapped in his arms and coat, but didn't answer. Megan suddenly realized she was shivering against him and felt foolish.

"Try to sleep," Bracken told her softly, his look loving.

"I am not sleepy."

"All right." Bracken's manner was indescribably congenial. "Then tell me how often you dress as an old woman and go a wandering."

Megan heard the laughter in his voice but was afraid to believe her ears. She lay staring up at him in wonder until he glanced down. Megan watched one lid drop as he winked at her and still felt amazed. She lay contemplating the change in him until she remembered her child.

"I am sorry, Bracken, that I lost our baby."

"There will be other children, but there is only one Megan."

Megan's mouth opened in surprise at his compassionate tone as well as his words, and when he looked down and smiled at her in complete tenderness, Megan came undone.

She turned her face into Bracken's chest and sobbed. He did not try to hush or calm her but left her to her grief. Less than an hour later, she fell fast asleep.

Bracken, so certain that arriving home would fix everything, knew deep pain when Megan remained unwell. Her body burned with fever, and although Bracken had expected delirium, he was disappointed. Disappointed because anything would have been better than her stillness. She was sleeping round the clock, and there were times when her breathing was so quiet that

Bracken was certain he had lost her.

He was rarely gone from her side. When he did leave, the only one he trusted in his absence was Helga. He'd never seen a woman so upset, yet able to cope, as Helga was. She had come to love her mistress unreservedly, and Bracken trusted her above all other servants.

The physician had come several times, and although he'd been very solemn, each time he seemed content. However, not until the third day, when Louisa unexpectedly arrived, did Bracken begin to feel hope. There was a slight stir at the door and suddenly Lyndon was there beckoning to him with an anxious hand. Bracken moved into the passageway and immediately took his aunt into his arms.

"How did you hear?"

"I didn't —" Louisa admitted, "not until I arrived. But for some reason I felt compelled to come. May I see her?"

"Certainly, Louisa, and then I must speak with you."

The woman studied his haggard face for a moment and then nodded. A minute later they stood by Megan's bed.

"Megan." Bracken's voice was a caress. "Aunt Louisa is here to see you. Please wake up."

Megan's hand moved slightly on the counterpane, but she did not waken.

"Megan," Louisa tried.

Still nothing. The two stood by her side a moment longer, and then Bracken led his aunt from Megan's room to her small salon.

Louisa studied him as he closed the door, understanding his need to be near Megan without disturbing her, but when the job was done he did not speak. Louisa continued to watch as Bracken paced the room like a caged animal. It took some time for him to speak, and when he did, Louisa had to hide her astonishment.

"I need God, Lou. I need Him now."

"What do you mean, Bracken?"

"I mean, I need His help, and I don't know how to ask."

Louisa took a deep breath and then slowly made her way to a chair. She took a minute to think and pray before asking Bracken to join her. He sat across from her, his desperate eyes pinned to her face.

"If you want God right now because you want Him to do something for you, then I am afraid I can't help you."

Bracken's shoulders slumped. "Then you don't think He can heal Megan?"

"Oh, Bracken," Louisa spoke with a

surety. "I *know* He can heal Megan, but it may not be His will to do so."

Bracken frowned at her.

"Dear," Louisa continued patiently, "God is not like some magical stone we can pull out of our pocket to use when we have a want or need. You can call out to God right now, and He will save you, but that does not guarantee that Megan will live."

The large man's hands clenched in pain. His eyes closed for an instant. When he spoke, Louisa heard the desperation.

"The thought of her dying destroys me, Louisa, but even if she lives, I don't think it will fill this emptiness I feel inside. I want to be changed — I want to be a better man — but I continue to make the same mistakes over and over."

Louisa smiled gently. "The changes God makes are very real, my dear nephew, but you will still sin again and again. However, the hopelessness will be gone. For every sin there is forgiveness, and fellowship so sweet that I cannot find the words to describe it to you."

"But, Bracken," Louisa warned him again. "I mean it when I say there are no guarantees. You must come to God His way, through His Son, Jesus Christ. You cannot come with the intention of bargaining on your own terms."

Louisa had never seen Bracken's eyes so impassioned as he looked at her, his upper cheeks were flushed with the intensity of it. She had prayed for just this time every day since she'd understood her own need, but never did she dream that she herself would be involved.

"Show me the way," Bracken pleaded with a low voice. Louisa did so with joy. She explained the way of salvation to her nephew and then asked if he wanted to be alone. To her surprise, he wanted her there and he wanted to pray out loud.

Tears poured down Louisa's face as she listened to Bracken's confession. The words were humble, but she heard the confidence in his voice as he prayed, knowing he was being heard. When he raised his head, he did not smile, but his broad chest lifted in a great sigh of relief. Neither one could speak, and for just a short time they sat in silence.

"I'd best return to Megan," Bracken said at last.

"Yes."

He stood to go, but paused. "Louisa, is it wrong to ask God to heal Megan?"

"No, Bracken, as long as you are ready

for His answer, yes or no."

Bracken nodded. He started away again, but paused once more. This time he returned and pulled Louisa from her chair. He gave her a hug so tender that her tears began again.

"As I sat by Megan's bed I literally begged God to spare Megan so she could tell me of Him. Then He sent you. I do not know if this is a sign that I shall lose my wife, but you are here and for that I thank you, Louisa."

Bracken did leave then, but his aunt couldn't follow. She sank back down in her chair and had a long cry. She cried with joy over Bracken's conversion and also petitioned God on Megan's behalf.

Thirty-Eight

Another week passed before Megan opened her eyes, but by that time the entire castle was aware of the change in Bracken. He had never been a cruel lord, but the serenity that now surrounded him was unmistakable to all who had contact with him.

Bracken had known the most amazing peace since his conversion. He had not even entreated God concerning Megan's recovery, but prayed, "Thy will be done; Thy will be done," each and every time he knew anxiety over her condition.

Just minutes before Megan awoke and called his name, the physician had finished checking her. He had been most thorough in his examination, and upon leaving he'd given Bracken a very hopeful report. The young duke's heart was near to bursting as he sat back beside the bed and watched Megan stir.

"Bracken?"

"Yes, Megan." He tried to keep his voice quiet, but hearing the sound of hers made this a chore.

"Is Marigold really dead, Bracken, or did I merely dream it?"

"She is dead, Megan; I am sorry."

Megan nodded weakly. "I feared so. I have long prayed for her, but Marigold never had love for anyone other than herself. How are my parents?"

"I believe they are doing well. They were here to see you."

This news caused Megan to try to lift her head. "They were here? Who saw to their comfort?"

"Louisa."

"Louisa was here?"

"She is still here and longs to see you."

Megan managed a weak smile, and Bracken beamed at her.

"There is something different about you, Bracken, or do my eyes deceive me?"

"No, Megan," he told her warmly. "There has been a change."

"Then you have forgiven me about the baby?"

"There is nothing to forgive."

Megan now stared at the canopy above her, her eyes sad. "I dreamt of the baby often, Bracken. I heard you speak to me, and I wanted to wake and talk with you, but I knew as soon as I left my dreams that my baby would be gone."

"No, Megan, the babe is not gone. He lives strong within you."

Megan turned to look at him, hurt etching her every feature. "Oh, Bracken, do not tease me so. My heart can't take it."

Bracken bent over her, his face now so close that she could feel his breath on her cheek. He had not planned to tell her this just yet, but her dreams had left him little choice.

"I would never be so cruel, Megan. I tell you true. You have lost some blood, but our babe is made of sterner stuff." Tears filled Bracken's eyes before he finished. "You will still be a mother before Christmas."

Megan could only stare at him, her mouth opening and closing with no sounds issuing forth.

"I didn't want to tell you because I feared it would overly excite you."

"Oh, Bracken, are you certain?"

"Yes, my love." With that he drew the covers back. When Megan's torso was uncovered, Bracken smoothed the fabric of her nightgown and took both of Megan's small hands and gently laid them on her stomach.

"In time, Megan, you will know for your-self. The babe moves strong within you even now, but he's too tiny to make his presence known. I feared I would lose you, but God has other plans. He has given me both my wife and my son."

"Oh, Bracken." Megan searched his eyes and saw the truth within the peaceful depths. "Please hold me."

Bracken moved to do so but murmured, "I don't want to hurt you."

"You won't. I just need to touch you."

She felt bruised as Bracken's arms surrounded her and lifted her to his chest, but Megan had never known anything so sweet. She managed to put her arms around his neck and lay content for several minutes.

"I am so tired," she admitted at last. Bracken placed her back against the pillows.

"Mayhap you should sleep for a time."

"I don't think I have much choice," Megan murmured sleepily and her lids grew heavy.

"Bracken," she managed before slipping away. "Does my mother know of the baby?"

"No. No one save the doctor."

"Send word to her, Bracken. She has lost Marigold. Maybe knowing of this child will help the pain."

She couldn't say more, but Bracken sat beside her for a long time after she slept. Barely able to talk, but still thinking of others — this was his godly wife. This was a woman in whom God had worked. For the second time that day, Bracken cried. He had cried when he told Megan she was going to be a mother and again as he thought about what that meant for him. His father was dead many years now, but he finally had a heavenly Father to show him how to get the job done.

"I brought you some fabric, Megan," Annora told her daughter. "You'll need some new gowns once you start increasing."

"Thank you, Mother. Was the trip very hot?"

"Dreadfully, but this news of your baby is more important."

Another week had passed. Megan was sitting up in bed, waiting patiently while Annora displayed the cloth. She beamed at her mother when she saw that all the colors were perfectly suited to her. Her mother, however, was wearing black these days, and Megan hurt with the reminder.

When Annora declared that her daughter had had enough company and began to gather the fabric in order to leave, Megan asked the question that had been on her heart since her parents had arrived.

"How are you, Mother?"

To Megan's surprise, Annora sat back down and stared at her.

"I see her everywhere. I hear her voice in yours, and each time I think of her the memory mocks me. She was a fake, but I saw only what I wanted."

"Oh, Mother." Megan's voice was compassionate. "Don't torture yourself. It's over."

The older woman turned her face away. "When I think of the plans she had for you, I feel I almost hate her. You must feel the same way."

"No, Mother, I don't."

Annora stared at her incredulously. "Megan, how can that be so? How can you be feeling anything but hatred toward your sister?"

"Because I always saw her for who she was. What she did was reprehensible, but Marigold had always treated me badly."

"It was not the same for me." Annora's voice was sad.

Megan nodded, well aware of the blow her mother's pride had taken concerning her oldest child. As Megan watched her, she saw Annora's chin rise as though ready to do battle. Megan tensed, but it was not for her.

"I shall never forgive her," the older woman stated, her voice now strong. "Dead or not, her evil acts will always live in my heart. I think in time you will feel the same."

"No, Mother," Megan told her gently. "It's over for me and will remain so. I have forgiven Marigold just as God forgives me when I sin."

Again Annora stared at her. "How can you even compare the two?" she asked. "What is it that causes you to treat the situation with such compassion?"

Megan tried to explain, but as soon as her voice became fervent in mentioning Christ's saving blood and the fact that all people sin, her mother cut her off.

"I am upsetting you, Meg. I shall check on you later."

"Don't go, Mother," Megan entreated her, but the other woman was now standing.

"Yes, Meg, it is time." The older woman's movements had become very agitated.

"All right." Megan's hands were tied. "If you should decide you would like to discuss it, I will be here."

Annora paused in her flight, her movements almost awkward. She came swiftly toward Megan and bent to kiss her temple. The older woman then left before Megan could say any more.

"She did not wish to speak of forgiveness, Bracken," Megan spoke from her place in the courtyard as her parents rode away. "I tried several times, but she was closed to the subject." Megan turned to look at her husband. "She will find no peace as long as she hates Marigold. I know this for a fact."

Bracken's arm went around her, and he navigated her back to the castle. "We will continue to pray. God willing, you will gain another chance to speak to her before her heart grows overly hard."

"I could write to her. Maybe I should do that now."

"I'd rather you rested now. Write your letter this afternoon."

"Bracken?" Megan asked conversationally. "Do you plan to treat me as a child until the baby is born?"

"Am I treating you as a child?"

"Did you know, Bracken, 'tis rude to answer a question with a question?"

"Did I do that?"

Megan had to laugh, but she still agreed to go to her room and put her feet up for a time. Having been up and around for only a week, she was tired enough to fall asleep, but just as she was dropping off, the baby moved for the first time. Megan didn't call for anyone or move from her bed, but thoughts of sleep were miles from her mind.

Autumn was upon them when Bracken watched an old woman shuffle across the inner bailey. Her head was uncovered, showing her very gray and wispy hair, but within seconds Bracken was back at the village standing at the old woman's apple cart. He told himself it couldn't be his wife, but he began to look for Megan anyway.

This wasn't hard to do because someone, usually Arik, watched her constantly since the kidnapping, but Bracken heaved a great sigh of relief when he spotted her waddling her way from the kitchens. It was beginning to look as though she was going to be as wide as she was high. Bracken had not known many expectant women, but he was quite certain that Megan's middle could win a prize.

The dresses Megan and Louisa had sewn just two months before were now being taxed to the limit, and the baby was not due for two months. Bracken felt pained when he thought of how far she had to go.

"Have you eaten something that disagreed with you, Bracken?" Megan wished to know as she neared.

"No," he said honestly. "I was contemplating how much larger the baby would grow before December."

Megan sighed, rubbed her stomach, and pulled a face. "I look horrible."

"I didn't say that, but you do look uncomfortable and your time is not yet near."

"Which," Megan stated emphatically, "is a kind way of saying I look awful."

Her face was so humorous and adorable that Bracken laughed.

"Ah, Megan," he said on a sigh. "I do love you so."

Megan froze in her place. She stared at Bracken as though seeing him for the first time.

"Are you in pain?" he asked anxiously. "Should I send for Helga?"

"You told me you love me," Megan said in a voice of wonder.

"Of course," Bracken shrugged. "I say it often."

"Nay, Bracken, you do not. This is the first."

"I do say it, Megan; in a hundred different ways I say it. Every day I provide for your needs and see to your comfort. You have clothing, food, and loyal servants. I touch you with tenderness and respect, and when you cry my arms are waiting to hold you.

"I do say it, Megan," he concluded. "You have not been listening."

Megan stared at him. "I find no fault in your care of me, but a woman likes to hear the words."

"It cannot make that much difference," Bracken replied, trying to dismiss the subject, but her eyes were so full of yearning and hope that he had a hard time looking away from her.

"I am not good with words," he tried to explain, but Megan gave him no quarter.

"I need to hear only three."

Bracken glanced around swiftly and suddenly grabbed Megan's arm and pulled her into a dim corner of the passageway. He took her face between his hands and looked into her eyes.

"I love you, Megan."

The round redhead sighed with unbelievable pleasure. "And I love you, Bracken of Hawkings Crest," she whispered.

He bent and kissed her, and Megan's eyes closed in bliss. He was right, he did "tell" her everyday that his love was constant, but there was something very special in hearing the words.

The baby suddenly kicked between them, and Bracken's hands immediately dropped to Megan's stomach. He had felt the movements often, but the look of delight in his eyes never waned.

"Perhaps it will be sooner than we think," Megan whispered. "I am so large that maybe my dates have been wrong."

"Perhaps. We will pray for God's timing and be patient."

Megan loved it when Bracken spoke of God with such submission. When his arms came around her, she lay her head on his chest and sighed with contentment.

You have given me so much, heavenly Father — more than I ever dreamed. Please bless this child in my womb. Help us to show You to him.

Bracken's thoughts were much the same, and for a time the world ceased to exist. Duke and duchess would have stood holding one another for quite some time, but there was a sudden commotion coming from the great hall. Several servants passed, and someone said the names Lady Joyce and Lord Stephen.

"Oh, Bracken." Megan grabbed his arm in excitement.

The duke needed no other encouragement. He took Megan's small hand in his, and they made their way out to the great hall to greet his family.

Thirty-Nine

"I was upstairs with Megan when Vincent pursued Marigold. She ran through the castle and then out to the front steps. He never laid a hand on her. She fell down those high, stone steps and broke her neck."

"She was so evil," Giles commented softly, a frown knitting his young brow.

"Yes," Joyce agreed, her heart going out to Bracken and Megan.

"What has happened to Roland Kirkpatrick?" Stephen wished to know.

"He is in the Tower awaiting his sentence. I do not believe things will go well for him."

The family was gathered around the hearth in the war room, and for a moment they were silent. Bracken had been relaying the events of the past months. Megan had written concerning some of them, but Joyce was naturally interested in the details.

"Tell us the rest, Bracken," she entreated after a time.

"We took the journey home very slowly.

When we arrived, I felt certain that all would be well. This was not the case. Megan lay sleeping for days, and at times she grew so still that I feared I would lose her."

Bracken reached for Megan's hand, and continued with his eyes on his mother.

"I have never known such fear. In the past I have made vows to God, but always on my terms. This time I only asked God to spare Megan because I knew she could tell me how to find Him. The hole in my heart went on without end. I have never known such desperation. I wanted for the first time to have a relationship with God's Son, and I had no idea how to go about it."

"And then Louisa came," Joyce filled in, her heart in her eyes. Bracken smiled as well at the remembrance.

"Yes. I asked how she had heard of Megan's illness, but of course she hadn't. I know now that God sent her when I needed her most."

"And what did she tell you?" Stephen asked. He still believed as Bracken once had, that God had no real place in his life. Keeping this in mind, Bracken answered gently.

"She was not easy with me. She told me that there would be no bargains, no guarantees. Louisa said my submitting to God would not spare Megan. God could still decide that her time on this earth was over."

"And yet you still believed?" Stephen seemed fascinated.

"Yes. It sounds cold, but I knew that not even Megan's spared life would fill the emptiness I felt within. I had run from God for years. It's a wonder He did not give up. I knew that it was long past time for me to surrender."

Bracken turned then and looked at Megan, his hand still holding hers. "God has given me my wife and my child, but of more importance is what He did for my spirit."

Megan smiled tenderly into his eyes. She had longed and prayed for this without really thinking how precious it would be. The change in him was so dramatic. Their life was not perfect, but when God spoke through the Holy Scriptures about new life, Megan had only to look at her husband to know just what He meant.

The warm fellowship of the group was interrupted when Stephen suddenly stood. Megan had been so intent on Bracken that she had not noticed his discomfort. Without looking at anyone, Stephen wordlessly walked from the room. No one spoke for a time, but then Bracken broke the silence.

"He will come," the older brother spoke with confidence.

"Yes," Giles agreed, a smile on his face. "He fights as you did, Bracken, but as with you, it is just a matter of time."

Bracken reached and clapped Giles on the shoulder. "It's good to have you here, Giles. Maybe Mother would agree to your staying for a time."

The younger man's eyes lit up, and he turned to Joyce.

"Mother?"

"I don't see why not." She smiled at him. "It will be quiet with Kristine at Danella's — she is expecting again — but I shall survive."

"It's settled then," Bracken announced and stood. "Let us go and see how you're doing with your archery."

Bracken's hand dropped for a moment onto Megan's shoulder, and then the women watched them move away. The conversation waned after that, but neither woman cared. Feeling tired of a sudden, Megan was content to doze. Joyce, after her long journey, wanted to sit quietly and pray.

Megan's first pain hit her in the kitchens.

A month had passed. Stephen had moved on, but Joyce was still at Hawkings Crest, and Giles was also in attendance. No one noticed the duchess' sudden look of shock or the way she held onto the edge of the table with a white-fingered grip. After a time, she stood erect and rubbed the dampness from her upper lip.

The next contraction was over 20 minutes later, but it lasted much longer, and Megan was thankful that she'd taken herself off to be alone in her parlor. She panted for a time afterward and debated calling for someone. The thought of lying in bed, as she was sure everyone would insist she do, was not to be tolerated.

Feeling fairly well, Megan forced herself to rise and go about her business. In no time at all, she grew fairly adept at turning away from the people around her or sitting down when she felt a pain coming on. She was not one given to moaning or crying out, but some cramps taxed her to the limit of her self-control.

Hours had passed when Bracken sought her out. He was slightly preoccupied, so although Megan had just had a contraction that flushed her face and beaded her brow with moisture, he didn't notice anything amiss.

"I am going hunting. The hour is not early, but with the light snow from this morning, the timing is good."

"I'd rather you didn't, Bracken," Megan said unexpectedly.

The duke blinked at her. "What did you say?" His voice told of his incredulity.

Megan sighed. "I'm sorry, Bracken; I just wish you could be home right now."

He studied her intently for a moment, first her eyes and then her swollen stomach.

"Your pains have started," he stated seriously, his voice low.

"Yes," Megan admitted.

" 'Tis too soon," he said, as if to reason with her would make them go away.

"They have come," Megan told him logically.

"When?"

"Hours ago."

Bracken bent promptly and lifted her in his arms. Megan protested and tried to gain his attention, but they were at the bottom of the stairs before he listened to her.

"Please, Bracken."

"Please what?" He stopped and stared down at the round bundle in his arms.

"I do not wish to go to bed. The pains

started around 20 minutes apart. Now, hours have passed, and they are still some ten minutes apart. I cannot lie in bed for hours, Bracken, or I will lose my sanity."

The indecision was clear in his eyes. Good sense told him to take her right to bed, but eyes humbly entreated him and told him to listen to her words. He stood for long minutes and then slowly lowered Megan so she could stand.

"I will abide by your wishes —" he began just as a pain hit her. Bracken forced himself to stand helplessly by as Megan held onto his arm with strength that only severe pain can bring. She panted as it subsided, and Bracken felt breathless himself when he spoke.

"Please let me take you up, Megan."

The small woman emphatically shook her head. "I tell you true, Bracken, it will be hours yet. Let me stay active."

His great chest rose in a heartfelt sigh. "As you wish. I will be at your side at all times, and I will have Helga ready our room, but for the time I will do as you ask."

More hours passed, and still Megan felt no real urgency. To Bracken's chagrin, his mother agreed with Megan's handling of the situation. Joyce stayed close herself, but she did not urge Megan to alter her plans.

The evening was growing long when Megan's demeanor changed. She sat quietly through two more very close contractions before speaking to her husband.

"I wish to go upstairs now, Bracken."

The young duke heard her, but for a moment he could not react. He had watched the intense pain these last spasms had brought, and for a moment he was paralyzed with anguish for her. She had shown the qualities of a knight the way she suffered without complaint, but watching her, there was no disguising the misery.

"Bracken," Giles said, shaking his brother's arm. "Help her."

Still the older man did not move.

"Bracken," Joyce now tried. "Megan is ready to go upstairs."

Joyce and Giles shared a look and then glanced at Megan. They found her looking oddly at her husband. She stared at him for the space of several minutes and then spoke gently.

"I need your help, Bracken. I know that the day has been long, but if you could only get me to our bedchamber, I will give you your son."

The word *son* seemed to snap Bracken out of his trance. He moved swiftly then, but with extreme gentleness. He lifted Megan as if she herself were the child and bore his precious bundle carefully to her bed. He bent over her once she was settled but had to wait while she gripped his hand for another pain. When it subsided, he whispered, "I'm sorry."

"It's all right," Megan smiled at him in love. "I understand." Megan stroked his beard until another paroxysm gripped her, and Bracken moved to allow his mother and Helga access.

The remaining time was not long, but to Bracken it felt like hours. It was just before midnight when from his place in his wife's salon he heard a baby cry. He had been trying to read Megan's copy of the Psalms and Proverbs. He now set that aside and stood but could move no further. The door was open, and he heard his mother praise God in a loud voice, but he couldn't make himself walk in.

I have a son, his heart kept repeating. *I have a son.* It never occurred to him that Megan might not be safe, but not until Joyce called to him could he propel his body forward.

He walked into the room on shaky legs and found little light and even less activity. Megan lay still, her eyes on his as he entered. Joyce sat on a chair near the bed, a small parcel wrapped in her arms. Helga stood on the opposite side of the room, her eyes suspiciously moist.

"How are you?" Bracken asked when he stood by the bed.

"I am well. What do you think of our baby?"

Bracken turned to bend over his mother. He smiled.

"He's not very big, is he?"

"*She*, Bracken," Joyce told him, and watched his look of astonishment.

"She?" Bracken turned just his head to ask his wife. Megan nodded with a sleepy smile.

"I know 'tis not what you planned, but she is all ours."

"She?" Bracken now asked of his mother. Joyce chuckled.

"Take her, Bracken; hold her," Joyce urged. "You will not yearn for a boy."

It was the best thing Joyce could have suggested. Bracken took the baby in his hands, awkwardly at first, and then moved her with confidence into the light. Her face was bunching up to cry, and Bracken chuckled low in his throat.

"Not only have you given me a daughter," he lovingly accused Megan, "but I find the first time I hold her that she is a termagant."

Megan laughed as well. "Is she not beautiful? I think she has your chin."

The baby let out a wail then, but her parents ignored her.

"My chin? You've never seen my chin." Bracken's bearded face was still turned to Megan.

"But I can tell," she stated with complete confidence. "Will you bring her here?"

Joyce and Helga exited quietly when Bracken put their daughter in the crook of Megan's arm and sat on the bed beside her. They looked at her for long minutes and then at one another.

"What shall we call her?"

"I don't know, Bracken. I had only a boy in mind."

Bracken troubled his lower lip.

"Gwen is a pretty name."

"She doesn't look like a Gwen," Megan told him, her eyes on the baby. "How about Ursula?"

Bracken's nose wrinkled. "I knew an Ursula once. She was an old hag."

And on the search went. It was a ridiculous time of night to be discussing names, but more than an hour passed before it occurred to them that a name did not need to be decided upon immediately. Bracken sought his bed with the intention of sleeping through the night. He might not have bothered had he known that the matter would still be decided before morning.

Somewhere around 3:00 A.M. he woke to the sound of the baby crying. When he got to Megan's room he found the baby lying comfortably at her breast. Bracken stretched out carefully on the bed to watch. Megan's eyes were closed when it came to him.

"Meredith."

"What?" she blinked, and then frowned at him.

"Meredith. Do you like the name Meredith?"

Again Megan blinked. "I do," she said with some surprise. "Indeed, it's a wonderful name."

Bracken nodded, well satisfied. "It will be so. Meredith of Hawkings Crest."

"Do you think she'll be Mary or Edith?"

"Meredith," Bracken stated firmly, and Megan agreed. A moment later she looked down to see the baby staring right at her.

"Did you hear that, my darling? You're our little Meredith. Isn't that a wonderful name?" Megan pressed a soft kiss to her daughter's brow and glanced up to find

Bracken's eyes on her. She thought he would have been watching the baby, but in the dim light she could see that he studied her intently.

"I love you," he said with sudden tenderness, causing tears to rush to Megan's eyes. "And I have loved you since I stood in the Reverend Mother's office and knew that I would storm the abbey if that is what it took to get you back."

"Oh, Bracken," Megan whispered. "I never knew."

" 'Tis my fault. For far too long I was afraid to let you know you were in my heart."

"It's good to know now."

Bracken leaned to kiss her, and when he moved they both saw that the baby was asleep again. Bracken tenderly lifted little Meredith, and when he was on his feet, called for Helga. When both infant and servant were gone, Bracken went back to the bed.

"Will it disturb you if I join you?"

"No," Megan assured him. "It's lonely in here."

"It was in my room as well."

Megan moved very carefully as she was still quite tender, but a few minutes later, her head was pillowed on her husband's chest, his arm wrapped securely around her. She lay very still as the beating of his heart came steadily to her ear. Megan had worked at not holding onto Bracken's life too tightly, reminding herself always that he belonged to God, but at that moment, she found herself praying that she would hear his heartbeat for years to come.

Meredith needs us both, Father God, she prayed silently. *If it be Thy will, may we raise her together and show Your love to her and to all who may follow.*

Megan then smiled at her own prayer. Meredith was just hours old, and here she was praying for more. What must she be thinking? Megan found it was not a hard question to answer. She was thinking of how much God had already given them. He was sure to have much more in mind, much more indeed.

Epilogue

Word of Bracken's arrival came to Megan, and she swiftly passed baby Gwen into Helga's waiting arms. She spoke a word to the other children, who obediently remained upstairs, their beautiful dark eyes watching their mother exit.

Megan ran downstairs to the great room, but Bracken was not fast enough and Megan met him in the keep. He put an arm around her and swept her into the newly built chapel. When he found it empty, he pulled her up against him and found her lips with his own.

"I missed you," he said when at last they could speak.

"And I you. Bracken," Megan could wait no longer, "is it true?"

Bracken's eyes closed in agony. " 'Tis true. Henry has found Catherine Howard

536

guilty of misconduct and had her executed."

Megan let her head fall forward against his chest. "This is the fifth wife, Bracken; how much more will our king demand?"

"He is obsessed. There is already talk of Catherine's replacement."

Megan moved to look at him. Her eyes were sad. Bracken reached to touch her cheek.

"How are you and the children?"

"We are well."

"How about young Stephen's touch of flu?"

"He is also well. If activity means anything, he's a specimen of health."

"I saw my brother Stephen in London. He talked of coming here to visit."

Megan shook her head. "He's not been, and I can't say as I'm sorry." Her tone was teasing. "He spoils the children terribly when he's here, especially young Stephen when the other children are not looking."

"Now I wonder why that is." Bracken drew the words out, and duke and duchess smiled at one another.

They both loved remembering the birth of young Stephen, now eight, and the rebirth of the older Stephen. Megan had been far along in the pregnancy when they'd made a trip to Stone Lake Castle.

Stephen had accompanied them.

It was not the best time to go, but Megan's mother had just given birth to a baby daughter. Because Annora was doing so well, Vincent had begged them to come and meet Megan's baby sister, Mercy. Vincent and Annora had named her such because of the mercy God had shown them in the way He worked in their lives and marriage. It was on the way home from Stone Lake that Megan's pains began. Stephen had never been so frightened in all of his life as Bracken and Helga prepared Megan to give birth in the forest.

Bracken and Megan were confident, calm even, but Stephen nearly came undone. Megan did not understand what was so frightening, but when Bracken left them for a time, Stephen began to talk.

"What if you die?" There were tears in the young man's voice. Finally Megan understood.

"Then I'll live forever with God," she told him serenely.

"Oh, Megan." Stephen's tone was tortured. "To have such assurance must be a wondrous thing."

"You can have it as well, Stephen."

"Nay, Meg, not I." His look was heartrending.

"Yes, Stephen, you. Trust me. I would never lie to you."

The words were a turning point for Stephen. He respected Megan as he did few people. He was ready to listen for the first time, and by the time Megan's baby was born, Stephen was a new creature. It was simply a normal course of events to name the child after Bracken's brother.

"And what of little Arik and Gwen?"

Megan pulled a wry face.

"Arik has it in his head that he must have a sword for his fourth birthday next month, and he can talk of little else. Of course, big Arik is encouraging him in this pursuit. Meredith has experienced a growth period and is almost as tall as I am. Gwen has a tooth in her mouth and is still spitting up all over me on a regular basis."

Megan was smiling and Bracken laughed at his wife's description of their brood. He had been away for only a month, but so much had occurred. Indeed, not just in his family. England itself was changing before their very eyes.

"Come, Bracken," Megan now urged. "The children are most anxious."

He did not need to be asked twice. Within minutes Bracken's children were swarming him, and he held and kissed each one in turn. He couldn't stop staring at them. They *all* seemed so much taller and more grown up. He had two hours with them before the time grew late and they were ushered off to bed with promises of a special outing in the morning.

Bracken then ate a hasty meal and rushed to be alone with Megan as soon as they were able. They sat before the fire in the bedchamber for many minutes, not speaking but getting silently reacquainted.

Finally Megan said, "What is to become of us, Bracken? In truth, I am frightened."

"There is no need. God makes kings, Megan, and He is still in control of England. The monasteries have been dissolved, and Henry's push to restore what he calls the true church of England is crushing many innocent people beneath his political heels, but our God is the king of the universe."

"Then you are never afraid, Bracken," she stated, her face turned up to see him.

"I would be a fool not to be alert, my love, but I fear not for tomorrow. Has God not proven to us repeatedly that He will see to our every need? Has God not proven His love over and over?"

"Yes, Bracken, He has. I am not

trusting."

"Then I will pray that your trust increases."

Megan smiled at him again and put her head back against his arm. He never made light of her shortcomings or rebuked her harshly, but with love and tenderness led the way by word and example.

"You've grown rather quiet," Bracken commented.

"I was confessing my sin of faithlessness and then thinking about the future."

"Worrying?"

"No, not this time. This time I must leave it with God. This time I must trust completely."

Bracken turned her so she was in his arms and he could look down into her face. "In the Holy Scripture a dove is at times the symbol of peace. You're my dove; did you know that, Megan?"

"Oh, Bracken." Her eyes sparkled at his praise. "I love you so."

His head lowered to better place a gentle kiss upon her lips, but he stopped to say one more thing.

"There are no guarantees concerning tomorrow, Megan, but believe as I do, my dove. God alone holds England in the palm of His hand, and as long as He gives me breath I shall be here for you."

"Thank you, Bracken."

"For what?"

Megan smiled, thinking that God had outdone Himself the day He had created her knight, but she didn't answer and Bracken knew that enough had been said. The duke's head lowered once again and this time he kissed his precious wife so tenderly that words were no longer necessary.

The employees of Thorndike Press hope you have enjoyed this Large Print book. All our Large Print titles are designed for easy reading, and all our books are made to last. Other Thorndike Press Large Print books are available at your library, through selected bookstores, or directly from the publisher.

For more information about titles, please call:

(800) 223-1244
(800) 223-6121

To share your comments, please write:

Publisher
Thorndike Press
P.O. Box 159
Thorndike, Maine 04986